Tender

Also by Mark Childress

A WORLD MADE OF FIRE

V FOR VICTOR

Tender

A NOVEL

MARK CHILDRESS

harmony books *new york*

Grateful acknowledgment is made to Peer International Corporation for permission to reprint an excerpt from "Blue Moon of Kentucky" by Bill Monroe. Copyright 1947, 1954 by Peer International Corporation. Copyright renewed. International copyright secured. All rights reserved. Used by permission.

Published by Harmony Books, 201 East 50th Street, New York, New York 10022. Member of the Crown Publishing Group.

HARMONY and colophon are trademarks of Crown Publishers, Inc.

Manufactured in the United States of America

Library of Congress Cataloging-in-Publication Data
Childress, Mark.
    Tender: a novel. / Mark Childress.—1st ed.
      p.   cm.
    I. Title.
PS3553.H486T46   1990
813'.54—dc20   90-4298
                                                           CIP

ISBN 0-517-57603-1

10 9 8 7 6 5 4 3 2 1

FIRST EDITION

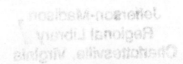

For my mother and father

Baton Rouge

*T*he lights go out all at once. Twenty thousand girls leap to their feet, screaming. Leroy stands just out of sight in the darkness, fingering the velvet edge of the curtain. He is lightning, getting ready to strike. He is Leroy Kirby, and all those girls are screaming for him.

Three drummers make thunder on their drums. The horn players stand up to blast a fanfare. All the spotlights switch on at the same instant—fifty thousand watts blazing down on the white stage—but still Leroy does not appear.

Make them wait. Make them beg for it. Leroy knows how to do this. He has done it hundreds of times. Get them all hot and bothered. Stretch it out until they cannot stand it another second. Then stretch it some more, and watch their frustration melt into pure desire.

He pushes a shock of hair from his eyes, hikes his jewel-studded belt, and trots out into the light.

The Louisiana Coliseum erupts in a frenzy of screaming girls and flashing flashcubes, thousands of Kodaks freezing the moment when Leroy storms the stage and grabs the microphone.

The girls love him. They love him. They forget themselves and rush toward the light. They cry out, shoving and wiggling against one another, a sea of hands waving in the air.

The trumpets scream high notes. Leroy strides the stage from side to side, sweeping his satin cape around in flashy circles. His new costume weighs forty-three pounds and cost fourteen thousand dollars: a hand-embroidered jumpsuit of stretchy fake satin, with a ferocious Bengal tiger springing around from the back to the chest, appliquéd from gold thread and rhinestones, fake emeralds and sapphires.

He pops the quick-release snaps down his arms, twirls the cape over his head, and flings it back to the bandleader's feet. A stagehand scurries out to retrieve it.

The girls scream for the glittering tiger. Leroy makes a full turn with his arms up so they can admire it all the way around.

Sweeping the forelock back with his fingers, he grins his famous crooked grin—half threat, half invitation. Any girl with hormones knows exactly what he means when he snarls up his lip that way, a picture of indifference to all their commotion. You can look all you want, girls, but nuh-uh, don't touch. You like that leg? You like that? Here's some more of it. Look at this here. This is lightning up here in a tiger suit, ladies. This is the rocking man driving you wild.

He strikes the famous pose with his leg cocked to one side and his blue Fender Stratocaster laid across his hip like a tommy gun, ready to blast anybody who comes too close.

He leans to the microphone. "Well, good evenin'."

That sets off a whole new uproar, which continues until Leroy waves the band to start playing. He swaggers with the mike stand to the lip of the stage, just out of the girls' eager reach.

4

The lead drummer fires a rim shot, and Leroy begins to sing:

Well there's nothing wrong with dying
A lot of people do
I know there's no more heartache in the place they take you to

The girls know this old song by heart. They shriek from the very first line. For a minute it seems they might jump up on stage and try to tear off Leroy's clothes, the way they used to do.

Leroy has brought this on himself. The girls need him. He makes them scream. In their own lives they are not allowed to scream. Only when Leroy is onstage, bumping his hip out, beating on his guitar, shouting "You're Breaking My Heart" or "Rockin' Saturday Night" or some other song they know so well that the very first thumpety-thump of the bass line gets their girl blossoms opening out, their native chemicals to mixing and bubbling—only when Leroy is pressing their thrill buttons, A, B, and C in the ritual order—only then will the girls abandon all reason and give in to sweet, heedless insanity.

They jump up and down, screaming, growing moist and warm in their secret places.

Leroy grins. He is alive with light.

Like a striptease artist, he draws one of the carefully folded scarves from his secret pocket, an inch at a time. He flirts it in the air, then releases it out over the heads of the girls—they struggle and claw for it.

Leroy follows it down with his eyes. One girl gets her hand on it. She waves it over her head, turning on the others with a triumphant glare.

She is not a girl.

She is a heavyset peroxide-blond woman, past fifty. Older than Leroy's mother was when she died.

And now he cannot fail to see that the audience is mostly middle-aged women, curled and sprayed and done up in their best Sunday dresses. Didn't they scream like girls? They are out of their seats streaming down for the stage, snapping away with their cameras, begging Leroy for one of his scarves.

The illusion is shattered, but they don't know it.

He draws out another scarf, releases it. He wiggles his leg. He drops to one knee. The women scream.

5

He sings the songs they expect to hear, one after another.

He glances up to the ceiling of the arena. He can see past the banks of floodlights, through the steel girders and the roof, all the way to heaven. He sees the stars in their places, clouds floating through the blue starry sky. He sees his mother smiling, waiting for him.

The concert is over. Leroy lopes into the wing.

The light drains out of him, all at once.

Bubba Hayes places the cape around his shoulders. "Good show, boss." Four security men trot out ahead, playing their flashlight beams at Leroy's feet as he strides the darkened tunnel. Cheers and screaming echo behind him, and the announcer's voice: "Ladies and gentlemen, Leroy is now leaving the auditorium . . ."

The limousine waits, motor running, in the underground garage. Leroy pulls on his wraparound mirror shades and slides in back.

Bubba jumps in behind him. "Go!"

The driver takes off with a four-tire screech. The limousine shoots up the ramp, through two lines of police cars, and onto the interstate before the women in the auditorium have a chance to stop screaming.

Leroy slumps in the seat. He has given too much of himself. He is empty inside.

Bubba stretches his massive legs on the floorboard. "You were hot tonight, boss."

"Don't talk to me, Bubba." He will get to the plane and get in his pajamas and have a little visit with the Doc, and then off into the night sky. He will be all right. He has lived through it, one more time.

He rides to the airport hearing the sirens of the police escort.

The motorcade steers past the terminal and onto the taxiway, gliding up beside Leroy's private Boeing 707.

He wills himself out of the limo, up the portable stairway, and into his cabin. Bubba slams the hatch behind him.

Leroy shucks off the cape and begins yanking at zippers and clasps, freeing himself from the costume. He unlaces the girdle—sweet relief when he gets his belly out and takes his first deep breath in hours. "Go on up, Bubba," he says, snapping the elastic on his underpants. "Tell the Doc to come back."

"Whatever you say." Bubba stares at him a minute, then disappears. Bubba doesn't approve of the Doc.

Leroy pulls on his blue silk pajamas and settles on the bed to wait. He takes comfort from his luxurious airplane: the nubby blue carpet, oak paneling, the midnight blue velvet bedspread on the mahogany bed. He has gone above his raising, as his mother might say.

The plane rolls away from the terminal.

Leroy feels the floor shaking under Bubba's approach. You would think you pay three point two million dollars for an airplane, they could provide you with a floor that doesn't shake like some cheapass trailer home in Tupelo, Mississippi, but that's the breaks and Bubba Hayes is filling the door, bigger than he ever was stalking the defensive line for Humes High School. "The Doc says not yet. He says to wait until we take off, then he'll come back."

"Well goddamn," says Leroy. "Who does he think he works for, you or me?"

"I don't know," Bubba says. "You can ask him. And Bob says fasten your seat belt."

"Okay, okay." Leroy stretches on the bed. He snaps the eighteen-karat gold buckle of the bed-size seat belt he has installed at the insistence of the Federal Aviation Administration. "You go tell Doc to bring his ass back here the minute we're up and away."

"Sure thing." Bubba retreats up front.

The plane screams down the runway and lifts off.

Leroy stretches out, remembering the looks on the faces in the first rows. Those are the women who fight hardest, stand in line the longest, to be closest to him. Leroy focuses on individual faces among them; he gives each one a little wink, a little sneer, something to last her the rest of her life.

Sometimes, like tonight, the years fall away. He is a perfect boy again, the last boy in the world, the only boy they will ever have to love.

Tonight they loved him. He was good. They didn't expect him to be good. Probably they came out to see what was left of him after all the bad press, the hospitalizations and cancellations.

It's not easy to be good, but lately Leroy has discovered how much harder it is to be bad, night after night. It takes three times the effort to stand up there struggling and pretending.

It takes plenty of medication to make up for that.

Now the good Doc appears with his bag. His eyes hold a kindness that is its own prescription: I know what's up; I know what you need; you'll be fine when you get it. "Good show tonight?"

"The best," Leroy says. "Now listen, I don't want to go to sleep, but I can't set still. I'm flying."

The Doc opens his bag of marvels. "Don't worry, we'll bring you right in for a landing."

It isn't really addict time as long as you're intramuscular, according to the Doc. It isn't time to get worried until you get a hankering to take it direct to the vein—and not to worry, we'll taper you off long before you ever get there. We'll keep you steady.

"I don't know, Doc." Leroy rolls up his sleeve. "I'm real tired all the time, but I'm jumpy, you know?"

"You need some time off," says the Doc, swabbing Leroy's arm. The Doc gives the world's best injection. He takes a strong grip on the arm and starts tapping the flesh, tap-tap-tap, to deaden it; then the one hand keeps tapping while the other steals down to fetch the needle and pop! you kapow! in the arm so fast you don't even know you've been stuck.

But you know the Doc has gotten the formula right when the calm eases down through your bones the very next minute, smoothing out all the tight parts of you.

"Nothing to it." The Doc closes his bag and departs quietly.

Leroy drifts off on the melting surge of the sedative. He made all those women delirious tonight. Now it is his turn to feel good.

They lunge across the footlights crying, "Leroy! Leroy!" as if he is deaf or too stupid to know his own name. They wail and tear their hair, twisting Kleenex into knots, licking their lips trying to get at him, get at him, just lay the tip of one finger on the actual flesh of him, so that one day they can draw their grandbabies up on their laps and point to the immortal Leroy Kirby on television and say, "See? Do you see him? I touched that man once."

He floats, smiling to himself.

After a long time in a dim, comfortable place, he is seized with a sharp urge to pee. He moves to unfasten the seat belt and discovers that the buckle has frozen shut.

He fiddles with it. He pries at the gold lip with his thumb. No good.

His belly is too big to squeeze out under the belt. His head is too near the headboard to get out that way.

He is trapped. Trapped in his own bed on his own airplane at thirty thousand feet.

He reaches for the receiver of the pink Princess telephone. His hand misses the phone, then finds it.

In the forward cabin, Bubba picks up. "Yeah, boss."

Leroy says, "Bubbacomegetmeout."

"Say what? I didn't catch that, boss."

Leroy licks his lips. What is wrong with his tongue? His tongue and the seat belt are conspiring to keep him here forever, trapped on his back like an upended june bug. He manages to get out one word that sounds like "stuck."

"Aw come on now, Leroy, come on, now, don't gimme this," Bubba complains. "We're trying to play cards, now, okay?"

Leroy says "shit" and hurls the phone against the wall. Then he tries to pick it up, but he cannot reach it; he is trapped. He can hear Bubba squawking, "Boss? Boss?" then he feels the heavy tread through the floor of the plane.

Bubba stares down from the doorway.

Leroy groans, plucking feebly at the buckle. "It's—it's busted. Gemme out."

Bubba leans over and snaps the thing open, click-snap. "There." He stands back, folds his arms.

Leroy can't bear the look of sympathy in Bubba's eyes. The seat belt has made him a fool in front of his oldest friend.

He tries to ease up from the mattress. He cannot find the right way to do it. He is so used to having things done for him that his body has forgotten how.

"Bubba," he says heavily, "I need help."

Bubba comes to the side of the bed. "I wish you could get a good look at yourself," he mutters. "Jesus."

Leroy stares up at his friend like a man peering from death into life, from darkness into a bright room. "I don't know, Bubba," he says. "It wasn't always like this."

Tupelo

1935-1948

1

*A*gnes Kirby and her
mother sat near the window, communicating with the spirit world.
They balanced the Ouija board between them on their knees, their
fingertips poised on the rim of the heart-shaped planchette. The needle
in its glassine circle skimmed across the board, glancing off *yes* or *no*,
hovering over the Mystifying Oracle, a silhouette man in a turban,
caressing a black crystal ball in midair.

"Sure is jumpy today," said Doll. Perched on the chair, her feet
tickling the floor, she looked like a small, old gray doll. "You're making
it move."

"I'm not," said her daughter. "I'm barely touching it."

"Take your hands away and let's see."

Agnes folded her hands on her great swollen stomach. She was pregnant to the ends of her toes.

Agnes had always been partial to visions and omens and portents. The new life growing inside her made the voices more distinct.

Agnes knew things other people were denied. She could see a sign from heaven in the sparkle of a broken mirror in the yard. She could make out spiral castles and snakes at the bottom of her teacup. Sometimes she could make the Ouija board speak in plain English.

Under Doll's hands, the planchette went nowhere. "See? When I do it myself, it just sets there."

"It takes two to get a clear connection. Says so in the lid of the box." Agnes wiped the board with her handkerchief to improve the glide, then consulted the paper on which she had recorded the spirit's message so far:

GET A DEAD IF ANYONE GOD IS BOY BLESS NO NO NO
LARRY A REAL LIFE IF YOU GET ME ALIVE

"It doesn't make much sense," Agnes said. "Wonder who it is? I don't think it's Papa. It might be Cousin Larry."

"Larry's not dead," said Doll, "he's just peculiar."

Agnes said, "If you're as peculiar as Larry, I bet you don't have to be dead to talk on this thing."

Doll coughed, lighting a Chesterfield. "Let it rest a minute."

Agnes shivered at the breath of cold air off the window. In this stretch of lonely Mississippi, this winter seemed colder than anywhere on earth. The sky froze up white; the woods faded to gray. Freezing rain slanted in sideways. The north wind howled down the pine flats, icing the branches and fences of East Tupelo, whistling through cracks in the floor.

When Agnes moved the Ouija pointer to the center of the board, she felt a sharp jab inside, a tiny toe aimed at her softest spot. "Mama," she said, "if you ever die, do you think you'll be able to talk to me on this thing?"

"I can't imagine," said Doll. "There'd have to be some better way. I'd call you on the telephone."

14

"Ha. That's a joke," Agnes said. "We can't hardly pay the electric."

"Things are bound to get better," said her mother as her fingers crept back into place. "Maybe we should ask it a question. What the New Year will bring."

Agnes wiggled forward on the chair. "I know. Let's find out about the baby."

"Is it kicking?"

"Like murder."

"You have had it rough," said Doll. "That's always the way with the first."

"Easy for you to say. It's not you getting kicked." Agnes popped a chocolate-covered cherry in her mouth. The sweet syrup was a guilty pleasure. She couldn't remember the last time she'd looked in the mirror and seen her pretty face, before she fattened out and the red blotches came up in her nice olive skin. Her whole body was inflated.

She let her mind turn all blue inside. She listened to the moan of the wind, the voices of spirits.

The planchette floated to the corner of the board and awaited her question.

"All right now, Ouijee," she said. "Will it be a boy?"

The pointer executed a little circle, and moved over the number 2.

"Yes or no, Ouijee. Come on and tell. Is it a boy?"

The pointer darted to the word YES, out in an impatient circle, back to YES.

Doll stubbed out her cigarette. "Well he sounds pretty sure about that."

"I knew it," said Agnes. "We got our connection now. Tell me how long I have to wait, Ouijee. Tell me how many days."

The planchette went straight to the number 5.

"Five days? Thank you Lord. That's good news. What day is that, Mama?"

"Friday."

The needle circled the number 2 as if to drive home a point.

Doll said, "You swear you not making it move."

"I think it's you," Agnes said. "Come on, Mr. Ouijee, tell us something we can use. Tell us what he's like. Will he be a good boy?"

The pointer struck out at a strenuous angle to the word NO, then NO again, NO NO NO. It moved off around the board, faster and faster, flying under their fingers. The wooden heart made a little skip and dropped one velvet foot off the edge of the board.

"Looks like we don't have to worry about him being too good," said Doll.

Agnes replaced the heart firmly on the board. Doll touched it gingerly, as if it might shock her. The planchette skated out in a figure eight, settled on the letter *L*, then *O*, around and back to *O, K.*

" 'Look'?" Agnes glanced up. "What does it mean, 'look'?"

She glanced out the window.

A flutter in her chest, like a bird unfolding wings. She saw a wonderful vision: a blue sky, a delicate curl of white clouds, and two boys, identical boys, blond and perfect as angels, holding hands, floating in the blue.

She came out of her chair. The Ouija board slid to the floor. This was her vision. These were her boys. Doll could not see them.

They were saying something—trying to tell her their names—but the glass blocked the sound. She felt proud of the way they could hover without wings. They were flying through the sky, laughing, pulling each other's ears.

Sleet drove against the window. The trees drooped under their coat of ice.

Doll stared at the rapture in Agnes's face.

"Oh, Mama, I saw 'em. It's twins. Twin boys. I saw 'em both, clear as day."

"You never did."

"I've never seen anything so plain in my life! I just looked out the window, and there they were. Two boys. Just alike. That's why I—oh, heaven, that's why I'm so big! Dr. Hunt never said there was two! We can't afford two!"

"Now hold on, honey." Doll reached for her hand. "Don't go make yourself sick over some wild idea in your head. You haven't felt two of 'em kicking, have you?"

"No . . ." Agnes rubbed her stomach, trying to remember. "I'm not sure. But I saw it. It's true. I know it's true."

"This game has gone to your head." Doll helped her into the chair.

"Two boys." Agnes's voice was dreamy. "And they're going to be famous. Like the Lindbergh baby."

16

"Bite your tongue," Doll said. "That poor woman. God forbid that should happen to you."

"Well you know what I mean," Agnes said. "They're not going to grow up to be worthless."

Doll studied her daughter awhile, then went to dip water for the teakettle. "You *are* mighty big," she said. "But it ain't good to be so psychy. It gives me goose bumps."

"Twins are good luck," Agnes said, gazing through the window. The ice was beautiful, breaking the backs of the trees.

2

Ray was sprawled across two chairs by the wood stove, having the sleep of his life, when Doll shook his shoulder and said, "Ray, it's time."

He squeezed his eyes shut. He was in the middle of a dream that was almost exactly like real life, except people were treating him nice and giving him everything he wanted.

But now he was awake. That was his wife in the back room howling. And this was the middle of Ray Kirby's own night.

He found his boots, squeezed his feet in. Then he remembered his pants.

He pulled off the boots and started over. The whimper from the bedroom rose to a terrible cry.

"I'm up, I'm on my way," Ray hollered, dancing across the floor on one leg.

He snatched the first coat on the rack but couldn't get his other arm into it. It was Agnes's coat. Slow down, Ray. Take your time and don't screw this up.

He stuck his head through the curtain. His wife, in the bed, was immense. She lay flat on her back with her knees in the air. Her eyes were terrified.

"You better hurry," said Doll, winding a towel between her hands. "She broke her waters and she's coming on strong."

Ray ran out the door. Agnes's tortured face stayed with him all the way up the hill to his daddy's house. He banged up the steps through the door and charged around the kitchen, yelling for his daddy and the key to the truck.

Jessie wandered in, red-eyed, scratching his arm.

"The truck, Pop, it's time! I got to go for the doctor!"

"The key's in it, fool," Jessie said. "What's the matter, somebody sick?"

"Agnes is having her baby!" Ray brushed past his father. "Go back to bed."

Jessie tottered after him to the door. "Cold night for a baby . . ."

Ray ran, praying the old Ford would start.

He climbed in, stomped the gas pedal, and laid into the starter. The motor flopped and chugged and would not turn over.

Ray rested his face against the wheel. This was the coldest dark night of all time. He was nineteen years old, and the whole world was set to crash down on his head. He loved Agnes, but suddenly she looked like some kind of monster. His wife . . . how had he come by a wife? He had never even had a girlfriend. The ugly part of him wanted to put the truck in low gear and slide down the hill to Aurelia's dance parlor, pick a fight, find some little skinny girl to sit on his lap. Or better still, take to the highway and drive someplace where nobody knew him at all.

But that was trash thinking. Everything he had was in that little house: his wife, his shotgun, his toolbox. His duty. That's what it was. The damn duty. The part where he swore to be faithful no matter what.

Every part of him begged the engine to start, and he tried again, and it started.

He felt for the gear and took off. Fine sleet was slicking the Saltillo Road. The pickup's rear wheels skidded out crazily around the first bend.

Ray wrestled the wheel. The truck slithered downhill and onto the Birmingham highway. Mailboxes ticked by.

He drove off the road into the doctor's yard, laying down on the horn all the way to the front steps.

Dr. Hunt came out in his robe, half asleep and disgruntled at the sight of tire tracks through his rosebushes. But he went to fetch his bag without ever asking Ray how he intended to pay.

Ray walked the front porch, back and forth. He had nailed every one of these boards in place with his own hands, but until this night he had never truly known his porch. In the glare of the light bulb he counted the planks and squatted to examine knots and wormholes, the worn lip of the step where feet had come down. Agnes screamed. Ray ran his hand down the railing. He should get a piece of sandpaper and work on that before somebody took a splinter. He'd been in such a hurry to get the roof up that he'd let all the little things go. Agnes screamed. . . . If Wilbur Dees had a good year and Ray got more customers on the milk route, maybe he could buy a couple gallons of paint and make the place look less like a shack. At least the roof didn't leak, and it was a place of their own. . . .

Agnes screamed as if she might die.

Ray went down the steps and out into the yard. He was sorry for her pain, but he could not let himself think about it. Doll had told him to get out of the way, and Ray had obeyed gladly. He would sooner freeze to death than go back in before it was over. He knew he was a big yellow coward; that was all anybody seemed to expect of him.

He stood in the yard, breathing the cracking cold air through his nose, crunching frozen grass underfoot. The sky all around was dark as blindness.

He pictured himself drinking a beer at Aurelia's, his feet propped on a chair. In this daydream someone cranked the Victrola and a quavery

20

voice came out, a girl singing about the zing of strings in her heart. . . .

The door squealed. The doctor came onto the porch. He had the cool, unreadable eyes of a man accustomed to bringing bad news. "She delivered fine," he said, "but the baby was stillborn."

Ray opened his mouth. Nothing came out.

From inside, a ghastly wail. The doctor blinked. "I better go to her. You all right out here? I'll come get you."

Ray's heart crumpled. "Was it—"

"It was a boy," said the doctor. He went back in the house.

~~~~~

Her cries died away for a while, then started up again in that eerie rhythm that reminded Ray of passion. That's what got them into this. He knew which time, exactly. It was a warm April Sunday, in the afternoon, after a fish fry at church. They came home full and happy, stretched out for a nap, and the ticklish breeze through the windows gave Ray a randy idea. He set to work on it. He got her making long agonized shouts. At the moment when everything happened, the inside of his brain went dark and he forgot where he was. He woke up spraddled out sideways, with Agnes patting his face, saying, "Ray? Ray?"

He knew there was something different about that time.

~~~~~

He stood at the door, trying to make himself go in. He should open the door and go to his wife, take the dead baby out of the room so she would stop screaming.

When he reached for the knob, a spark nipped his finger. He took that as a sign and drew back.

Doll came to the door, her eyes wide. "She's going again."

"She's—"

"Doctor thought she was through, he was washing the . . . child, and she said it was hurting again, the same pain. She's having another one. Just like she said."

"God almighty." Ray pushed past her, through the door. Inside, in the flood of warmth, his teeth started chattering.

In the other room Agnes cried, "Oh! Stop it!"

21

Doll took Ray by the arm. "Don't go in there."

He yanked the curtain aside. The sight of the doctor on his knees in front of Agnes's open legs shocked him more than anything. She was all there for anyone to see.

Her eyes were fixed on the ceiling. Her nostrils flared. White hands gripped the sheet. She was beautiful, now, in her pain—not a monster at all, but a frightened animal, fighting, wild and alive. Ray had never noticed the strength in her face. Her lip was bleeding where she had bit it.

The doctor knelt before her, murmuring: "That's good, that's good now, come on now and push, he's coming. . . ." A soothing drone, his hands moving, glasses shoved back on his head. His instruments gleamed on the night table.

Ray said, "I'm right here, honey." His throat tightened.

On the dresser was a little mound covered by a white pillowcase. Ray lifted the corner. His firstborn son lay curled on his side, on a white washcloth. He was blue. His eyes were closed, impossibly tiny fists pressed to his chin. The cord tailed off between his legs. His foot was no bigger than Ray's thumb.

"Our baby's beautiful, honey," he said. "Come on and be brave."

"Ow! Jesus! Ohh!"

"It's coming!" Doll cried.

"Be brave. . . ." From the corner of his eye Ray saw the flash of the doctor's knife.

Agnes was weeping. The doctor wrapped his fist around a pair of greasy tiny ankles and lofted the infant into the air. He gave one good swack with his flat-open hand. A cough, the tiniest sputter; then a bleat grew into a cry.

The doctor cradled him in his hand, grinning and touching his puny nub with a finger. "Look! A boy."

And he was: pink and ugly, a crown of black hair slicked to his head, his features smashed together by the pressure of his journey. The doctor stuck a finger in his mouth, ran it over his gums, shook a string of mucus to the floor. The child took a deep breath and filled the room with his howl.

"Oh God," Ray said, "it's a boy, he's just fine." Then he fell on his knees and wept.

The doctor steered Ray to the porch. "You look after her. She'll have a hard time at first. But she's got a good healthy boy there, take her mind off it. You all right?"

"Sure." Ray's voice sounded old. "Kinda shaky, I guess."

"Mr. Dancey has some caskets that size," said the doctor. "I'll get him to send you one over on credit. My advice to you is bury that child and go on. Don't let her dwell on it too much." He went down into the yard. "I've got to look in on some folks in Shakerag on Monday. I'll stop by on my way."

"Doc, we sure do thank you."

"My pleasure. Take care now." The doctor climbed into his Dodge and drove off.

Ray snapped off the porch light. The sky was a most amazing deep jewel blue, heavy with stars.

Maybe this was like one of Agnes's visions—the sky glowing this unnatural blue to announce Ray's sons.

One son had gone straight to heaven without stopping. The other was inside, and alive.

Ray felt the young part of his life rushing away from him. He put out his hand to stop it, but it was gone. He couldn't cry or run away now. He was a daddy. He had to learn to act like a man.

3

*T*he undertaker's boy brought a casket no larger than a shoebox, a perfect replica of a full-size coffin—carved braid on the sides, a cherub medallion in the lid, tufted blue sateen lining. Ray clothed the dead child in a cotton dress and placed him inside.

Doll rocked in the corner, crooning to the bundle in her arms. Peace rose like smoke from the chimney. Ray nodded off in a chair.

In the afternoon the aunts and cousins and ladies of the church arrived with platters of fried chicken and glazed ham, potato salad, three colors of Jell-O, sweet potato pudding, ham biscuits, chess pie. . . .

Doll managed the ladies in and out. She let them stand awhile wring-ing their hands over the tiny coffin, then ushered them through the back room for a glimpse of Agnes and the surviving child.

Ray sat in a chair in the corner. His daddy, Jessie, and his mother, Minnie Mae, did most of his greeting for him. The procession went on after dark. Preacher Bayley came by and stayed a long time in the other room with Agnes. When he came out, he fixed himself a big plate and eased down beside Ray. "She's a strong little lady," he said, "strong in the Lord," then he went on to say some more Bible things. They prayed awhile and talked about what kind of service.

Ray was faithful enough at church, but it made him uncomfortable to have the preacher in his house, sniffing the air. God knows Ray had committed every important sin except sloth, and probably that one, too, without knowing what it was. His heart lightened when the preacher finished his coffee and left.

Doll herded the last visitor out, then took off her apron and said, "Rayford, I got a house of my own that is going to ruin. I'll be back later on. You go set with her." She pulled on her coat. "Talk her out of this idea she's going to Priceville tomorrow."

"Yes'm." He stretched his arms. "You must be wore out, Doll. You been right in there pitching."

"Poor Agnes . . ." Doll stopped at the mirror to adjust her hat. "At least she's got that fine boy."

"That's what folks have been saying all day." Ray helped with her coat. "Want me to whistle Johnny to bring down the truck?"

"No," she said, "I think I could do with a walk in the air."

He leaned out the door after her, blowing smoke. "It's so cold."

"I'll be back in the morning," she said. "You go see after her."

Ray watched out the window until she was gone.

All day, through the comings and goings, the hugs and murmured sympathies, he had stayed within an arm's length of the coffin, watching over it, longing for a quiet moment.

Now he stole a glance around the room, leaned down, and kissed the lid of the box.

He hiked his trousers and went through the curtain. The bedroom smelled of rubbing alcohol and talc. The night-light spread a warm glow. Agnes was propped up on pillows, her auburn hair streaming over her shoulders—the way she'd worn it when they were first courting. She smiled, and Ray's whole life lit up for a moment. He let out a long, easy sigh—that was air he'd been holding in since sometime the night before. "You look good," he said.

"Come here." She patted the covers.

"Everybody's gone." He eased down to the edge of the bed. "How do you feel?"

"Wonderful," she said, blinking drowsily. "I swallowed half that bottle of stuff."

"Does it hurt?"

She laughed, a soft musical sound. "You bet it does. Like they tore me in two."

"You did a good job," he said. "I was proud." Her hand was warm, under his. He followed her eyes to the old pine crib by the fireplace. "I hadn't even got to hold him yet."

"Bring him here," she said.

Ray unfolded himself and crossed the room. In the half-light the new boy was a picture of peace: asleep on his back, a thumb in his mouth. "I'm afraid to touch him. He's so little."

"He won't break," said Agnes. "Just hold underneath his head."

Ray gathered his son in the crook of his arm and crept to the bed. "Here, you take him."

"Isn't he pretty?" Agnes spread him on her lap. "Aunt Elna says he's got my mouth, but everybody else thinks he looks like you."

"Doesn't look like much of anybody yet," said Ray.

The baby scrunched his face into a pink yawn. Agnes tickled his chin. "Hello, there. Hello, big man. Come on. Wake up and look at your daddy."

"Hello," Ray said in a squeaky, high voice, as people do around babies. "Hey there! Hey! What's your name?" He put his pinkie finger in the little palm. "Damn, would you look! Look honey, he's got a real grip!"

"His name is John Leroy Kirby, don't you think that has a fine ring?" Agnes said. "We'll call him Leroy. Doll told me it means 'the king.' How about that?" The infant made a pewling sound. "What's the matter, big man, you hungry?" Agnes slipped the shoulder of her night-gown; her white left breast plumped out.

The baby sucked at the air until his mouth found the nipple, latched on, and set to vigorous sucking.

Ray stared, amazed. He had spent time at that nipple himself, but suddenly there was somebody there who knew how to get milk.

A lazy smile spread on Agnes's face. "Look at you. Hadn't you ever seen anybody nurse?"

"Yeah. But not you." He ran his finger over the soft hair on her forearm, the flush of her skin. He touched her breast and felt the pulse of the milk flowing out.

"Doll and I worked out their names so they match," she said. "This one is John Leroy. His brother is Jessie Leray, after your daddy and you. Leroy and Jessie. You like that?"

"It's okay," said Ray. "Whatever you want."

"They're your babies, too," she said.

He pressed a finger into her breast, then lifted it to watch the white spot disappear.

Agnes's eyes were locked in an embrace with the child. "Mama said you were in there looking after Jessie."

He shrugged. "Everybody acted like I wasn't even there."

"Go bring him here," she said.

Ray lay very still, touching her arm.

"Go on and get him, sweetie. He's cold in there all by himself."

Ray coughed. "He's all right."

"He's so quiet," Agnes said with a little secret smile. "I want to see him. Go get him."

Ray looked at her awhile. "Doll said you were thinking to go to Priceville with us tomorrow."

Agnes held on to her smile. "She said you're taking Jessie up there. I got to go with him."

Ray took care to sound gentle. "Doctor says you should stay in bed a week at least. I'll watch out for him."

"I don't know why everybody's got all these ideas about my baby," she said, and Ray heard the razor's edge in her voice, behind the dreamy fog of the sedative. "I can go. I'm not a cripple. You won't have to lift a finger for me."

"But honey, that's why I'm here," he tried. "Ol' Stepin Fetchit. Anything you want, I'll get it for you."

Her voice tightened. "Well then get up and go get my baby and bring him to me."

"He sure turned into *your* baby all of a sudden," Ray said.

"He *is* my baby! Everybody acts like I've got no right to see him! Go get him, now, Ray, or I'll get up and get him myself!" Her face flushed.

"Hold on, hold on—" Ray held up his hands. "Look there. You lost a customer." The little mouth had pulled free of the nipple and was busily sucking on air.

While Agnes was tending to that, Ray fled the room. His anger made him ashamed. He remembered the doctor saying how hard this would be for her. And Agnes was partial to moods and crying fits and odd bursts of emotion anyway. Once or twice a week she said something that made Ray wonder whether one of her bolts had come loose. She would awaken Ray at three in the morning to announce she had dreamed about Franklin D. Roosevelt flying a red kite. Some people might think she was crazy, except they didn't love her the way Ray did and they didn't know the strange way her premonitions had of coming true. Within the week the *Commercial Appeal* might print a picture of FDR with a little boy and a kite.... Or one baby would turn out to be twins....

Ray opened the lid and lifted the dead child. He looked just like the one who had lived, except he was blue. Ray carried him on his arm.

Agnes had settled down among the pillows, cradling Leroy against her side. She glanced up—that radiant smile. "Oh, look ..."

She took Jessie and nestled him against her other side, smoothing his hair. "Oh, I told you he was cold. Look how sweet he is. Look, Leroy, look—here's your brother."

Ray leaned on the dresser. He couldn't think what to say.

"Why do they want to bury him?" she murmured. "He's not even a day old. I don't think we should let them."

"Honey, we can't keep him here."

"Why not?"

"Well, we can't, Agnes, what's wrong with you? The baby—the baby's dead."

"No he's not." She stroked the little white throat with her thumb. "He was just cold."

"I think you took too much of that stuff," said Ray.

She touched his hand. "Come here and get under the covers with us. Say, 'Come on, Daddy, come here where it's warm.' "

"Agnes. Let me put him back."

"No." She drew the quilt to her chin.

Ray stood looking down at her. Her woozy smile made him want to give in. He could hear himself making excuses for her. Hadn't he bent to kiss the coffin when he thought no one could see? How was this any different?

He eased down to the bed. It was only for one night. At least they could have one night all together.

He snapped off the lamp and burrowed in where it was warm.

4

*E*ast Tupelo was a sprin-
kling of poor houses at the scratched-out back edge of Mississippi.
Across the tracks and the Memphis highway lay the big town, Tupelo,
with its shirt factory and sawmill, cannery and cotton gin, the Paramount Theater, a traffic light at the main intersection. The stores around
the courthouse square were run by old men, and energetic young ladies
who did all the actual work. Everybody went to the square and to
church and the picture show for something to do. The men in town
went to Aurelia's dance parlor for something else to do.

There were spells of fine weather from time to time, but mostly this country was hard. The summers were too hot, the winters too blustery cold. The streets were dust or mud, depending on the season. Tornadoes roared down from the sky without warning. Fire ants gathered in swarms large enough to kill a man.

Four rich white men owned most of Lee County. Everyone else was poor. There was no one in between. People lived here because they always had.

Out from town, in a sandy graveyard beside the Priceville Assembly of God, seven mourners gathered around a narrow hole. Two of the men lowered a tiny coffin and drew the ropes up. The preacher read the Twenty-third Psalm.

A shadow swept over the grave.

Ray Kirby cradled his howling son. Agnes stared at the mound of red clay.

Ray took her home. She turned all her sorrow on Leroy. She knitted booties and caps for him. She bathed and nursed and powdered him and sat by his crib while he slept for hours, for days. She played with his toes, sang him songs about monkeys and the circus. He was smart, for a tiny red thing that could not even focus his eyes. He turned his head to follow her finger trailing in the air.

After months of being ignored, Ray wandered off to Aurelia's dance parlor. He sat drinking beer in red light, troubling over the way his wife clung to her grief, to the air around the child. It was unhealthy.

But Ray discovered that four or five beers and a shot of whiskey were all it took to make him stop thinking about it.

He owed Wilbur Dees more than two hundred dollars, but a second shot of whiskey could wipe even that information out of his head. He could lean on the bar, stare at faces looming in and out of focus, and think about nothing at all until it was time to fall down somewhere and get up before dawn to drag milk cans onto the back of a truck.

One morning Ray didn't make it in until seven-fifteen.

Wilbur Dees was waiting for him, with a tight little smile and a check for four dollars. "Kirby, here's what I owe you," he said. "You know milk goes bad in the heat of the day. There's fifty men standing in line for your job. Take a walk."

"Wilbur," Ray protested, "how am I gonna pay the house note if you won't let me work?"

"You find a way or I'll take the house," Wilbur said. "We don't need any deadbeats around here."

Ray stared at the check. He carried it down the road to Aurelia's dance parlor and showed it to Lether Gable and Agnes's brother Travis. They had just gotten off the night shift at the shirt factory and were drunk already. When they grasped what had happened, they shouted and cursed and said Wilbur Dees was the most worthless son of a bitch in Mississippi, to take a job from a family man. They called for whiskey and drank a toast to his painful demise. Aurelia told them to quiet down.

Agnes's brother Travis peered at the check. "Four dollars," he sneered. "You been there before sunup every day, as long as I—hell, Ray, how long you been there?"

"Two years and some."

"Two years. You could get struck by lightning tomorrow, and think what you would have spent the last two years of your life doing. Busting your ass for Wilbur Dees." Travis waved the check in the air. "We oughta make him eat it."

"Let me see that." Lether Gable snatched it, smoothed it flat on the table. "I think we can do better than that."

Lether had dark, hooded eyes and three gold teeth; he was always around when somebody got cut, but no one ever saw him with a knife. He glanced to the bar. "Aurelia. You got a pen with blue ink?"

Travis sat up. "Lether's up to something. Look at his eyes."

"What are you up to?" said Ray.

Aurelia waddled over with a pen. "Honey, I didn't know you could write."

Lether bent over the table. "There's not much difference between this check and a check for forty dollars." He made three strokes. "And I just took care of that."

"Wait a minute!" Ray grabbed it away. There was a new zero behind the 4. On the second line Wilbur's "Four" now read "Fourty." The ink matched, and the spidery hand. Lether Gable was a born forger.

Ray took a pull on the whiskey. The longer he sat there, the better the whole idea seemed to him. Wilbur hadn't even given him a chance to think up an excuse.

Before long Ray was marching down Main Street to the Bank of Tupelo with Lether and Travis at his elbows, urging him on. Mrs. Loomis in her bun and wool suit handed over four crisp new tens and asked after Agnes and little Leroy. Ray said, "They're fine, thank you ma'am."

He imagined her eyes drilling into him all the way to the door, but he got outside free and clear.

"We should have made it four hundred," said Lether. They shared a big laugh on Wilbur Dees all the way back to Aurelia's, where they drank up the money.

Ray stumbled home that night to find Agnes fussing over her mother, who had taken a cough. The next day Doll was gasping for breath.

Dr. Hunt pronounced tuberculosis and took her to a machine at the hospital in Tupelo. She withered away.

Three weeks later they gathered around another hole in the Priceville graveyard.

Ray blamed himself. He figured it was God paying him back for his crime. He swore to act right from now on.

Agnes tried to contact Doll through the Ouija board. Ray told her she was acting silly and it was bad medicine to mess with those spirity things. Agnes sat with her own two hands on the pointer, waiting for a connection.

On a bright April morning two sheriff's deputies came to the door. They had Lether and Travis in the back of their car. Politely they asked if Ray was home.

Agnes had an urge to hide something, anything. "What do you want with him?"

The tall one said, "Would you ask him to step out here, please."

"He's asleep," Agnes said. "Why don't you come back tomorrow?"

Ray came to the door. "It's all right, honey. I'll be back before you know it." He followed the deputies to the car.

Ray's daddy bailed Ray and Travis out of jail and left Lether Gable to rot.

Ray tried explaining how good Lether's idea seemed at the time. But all Agnes could say was "Ray. How could you be so stupid!" He hated the look on her face when she said it. He couldn't think of an answer.

The lawyer told Ray to plead guilty to forgery and tell how the other two put him up to it, but Ray refused. He was no rat, he said.

At the last minute he changed his mind and threw himself on the mercy of the judge, who turned out not to have any. Ray, Travis, and Lether each got three years' hard labor at Parchman State Prison.

The first Monday in June the sheriff put Ray with a bunch of colored men on the back of a truck and drove down from the hills onto the Delta, so flat and so far across that you could forget there was ever such a thing as a hill. Many times in those years Ray wished he had paid more attention to the scenery. That dusty afternoon in the truck was his last as an innocent man. Once you got to Parchman you were guilty forever.

At first Ray wouldn't mix with the Negroes in the cotton fields, but one summer under the same broiling sun put an end to the distinction. Biting flies and the guards and the sun were the common enemies—and the clock, ticking slower every day.

Ray was a model prisoner. After one year he was allowed to write a letter home.

> *Dear Agnes,*
>
> After what I did I would not be surprised to never hear from you again. If you still care that is enough for me.
>
> I could write a million times how sorry I am but that wouldn't help you out of what I have got you in to. Besides you already know how sorry I am, ha ha. How are you. I am fine. It is late at night here and too hot (Aug!) They work you hard at this place but if you do like they say they leave you alone.
>
> I bet the boy is growing fast. Dont fret I never see L. but I did see Travis last week hes on a crew in the next farm. He look fine and helthy. Dont work too hard I'm coming home before you know it and I dont want those pretty hands all scared up from a sewing machine. (Just kidding)
>
> Well anyway I guess that's all for now.
>
> > *Your loving husband,*
> > *Ray Kirby*

Agnes carried a torch for Ray the whole time. She wasn't ashamed. If anyone asked, she said her husband was down at Parchman doing time for something he didn't mean to do.

On a gray day in March Agnes went down to Parchman on a bus. The prison matron took away the can of butter cookies she'd baked for Ray and put her to wait in a little glass booth. Ray appeared on the other side in his white prison suit. They pressed their hands to the glass and spoke into telephones.

"Come home soon, Ray," she said. "I miss you bad."

"Soon as I can, honey. They've got it in front of the prison board now. I'm bound to get something for good behavior."

From the look in his eyes, Agnes could tell that two years at Parchman had worn him down. The wild spark was gone from his eyes.

A guard came to take him away.

Agnes stepped out of the booth. The matron smiled and said the cookies had been seized as contraband. She had not even bothered to brush the crumbs from the lapel of her uniform.

That was the worst moment of all, when Agnes spotted those crumbs.

On the bus home she wrote a long letter begging Ray to escape or do anything, just get out of that terrible place. She carried the letter for three days in her purse, then threw it away. Didn't he have enough pain?

She slid down into her crowded life, the little room at the back of Ray's parents' house, where she had lived with her baby since Wilbur Dees had her evicted. Jessie Kirby was nice to her; Minnie Mae mostly stayed in her room, working jigsaw puzzles.

At six each morning Agnes went to the shirt factory to run a big black Singer machine next to a girl named Dot Simmons, who kept her entertained with a bottomless stream of inside dirt on the Hollywood stars.

"Did you know that Vivien Leigh had to go to bed with David O. Selznick before he would let her play Scarlett?" Dot shouted one day near the end of the shift. Dozens of Singers made a thunder in the vast sewing room.

Agnes set a sleeve against the steel needle. "Depends what the man looked like," she said. "I probably would have done it if they'd let me play Scarlett."

Dot burst out laughing. "You are a distraction!" The whistle sang. The last sleeve worked its way around the arm of the machine and dropped into the basket.

The roar of the machines faded like a headache. Agnes snipped the thread. "I used to have perfect skin like Vivien Leigh," she said.

Dot packed the lunch remains into her canvas bag. "Let's go see it again. Tonight."

Agnes stretched up from her chair. "Lord, wouldn't that be nice. You know I can't."

"Oh why not? Your sister can spell you a night off for once. We can sit in the second row and let 'em burn Atlanta in our laps."

"Don't tempt me." Agnes pushed her heavy wheeled basket down the ranks of machines. The wide door glowed in the afternoon sun.

She stepped outside, blinking. The smell of machine oil vanished in the breeze.

The factory stood at the edge of the woods in a place called Mill Town. The trees were still bare, but a thrill of green ran along the branches. The dogwoods had burst the Sunday before; their smoke floated among the trees.

Dot said, "That's the first honest smile I've seen on your face in a long time."

"It's the day." Agnes held out her arms, drinking the warm light into her skin. "I thought we'd never have another day like this."

Dot smiled and wandered off with a crowd of girls from the cutting room.

Today, for the first time since the shadow fell, Agnes felt human again. All of one piece. She wandered down the railroad tracks, taking her sweet time. She was not done with grieving for Doll or little Jessie, or pining for Ray, or wondering whether her precious boy would quit breathing in his sleep or get hit by a train. But she was able to give these fears some air on a day this fine. Her grief tasted old.

Gravel crunched under her feet. Crickets hopped through the new grass. One day soon Ray would be free, and then their lives could start up again. They would make love in the early morning and raise a fine boy who would grow up to take care of them in their old age.

She stooped to pick a dandelion, and here he came through the bushes, a blue-shirted four-year-old strike of lightning aimed at her legs—

"Pow!"

"Oh, you got me," she cried, clutching her side, fluttering down to the grass. She draped a hand over her eyes and played dead.

Leroy shrieked, "Get up, Mama, get up and do it again!"

Agnes let out a dramatic groan.

"Satnin fell down on the graaa-ass," he sang, throwing his arms around her.

"Oh, poor me," she wailed. "Look what you done to your mama." She grabbed his wrist and hauled him in to hug the life out of him. "You sweetie." He giggled and tried to pull free, but she said, "Aha! Now I've got you!" in a Wicked Witch voice while she pinned him to her knees and kissed him to her heart's content.

"Satnin, quit," he whined. "Satnin" was the way Leroy tried to pronounce "Agnes" as a baby, and the name had stuck. (His baby name for Minnie Mae was "Dodger," for some reason no one could quite figure out.)

"Be still, boy." Agnes licked her finger and dabbed at a small crusty scar near his ear. She didn't even have a decent picture of him. Every time the Olan Mills man came through town, Leroy had a cut on his face from jumping headfirst into a pile of leaves or some other rambunctiousness. Agnes was afraid people might see the picture and think she beat him—she who wouldn't even touch his hair with a scissors.

"Were you nice for Aunt Irene today?"

"Uh-huh."

He was the most beautiful boy: soft blond hair like his father's, but softer; a sweet oval face and Agnes's olive skin; great big brown puppy eyes, a pouting mouth; a secretive, wise kind of face. He was rough-natured but a little solemn—old Jessie said he looked like Winston Churchill—and he cried a lot for a boy.

He started talking before his first birthday. He carried on long conversations with himself. He loved to wear hats and build highways in the sand, to fling himself across a chair, to stare cross-eyed at an insect. He laughed and clapped hands at the sound of a train going by. He listened thunderstruck whenever his uncle Johnny tuned up his guitar.

Agnes said, "Did you miss me today?"

"Uh-huh."

"I missed you, too." She pulled the mashed dandelion from her waist pocket and gave it to him. "Did you eat your lunch?"

A shadow came over his face. He settled on the grass and pulled the head off the flower.

"What'd you have?" she said.

"I don't know."

She ruffled his hair, felt his forehead. "What's wrong with you? Are you sick?" He looked fine, except for his mournful expression.

Suddenly his eyes clouded over. "I want my daddy," he said.

"Leroy, don't, honey. Come here to me." She wrapped him in her arms. "Did Aunt Irene say something about your daddy?"

"Uh-huh." His voice shivered.

"Tell Satnin what she said."

"She said if I was bad, and, and—if I was bad, he won't come home."

"Listen to me. Daddy loves you. He's coming home as soon as he can. He'll be here before you know it. Aunt Irene was bad to tell you that." Agnes tightened her jaw. "Daddy talks about you all the time in his letters, didn't I read that to you?"

"I don't know," said Leroy.

"Well he does. He sent you a brand-new ball, remember? He loves you, honey. He can't wait to come home and see you."

Leroy blinked. His eyes drifted to something rustling in the tall grass. He wiggled free and took off to see what it was.

Agnes ran up the hill after him. This boy was her life. She never wanted him out of her sight.

5

*L*eroy loved Sunday. The sun came up slower. Everybody stayed longer in bed. The whole house was his to explore. He stole to the front porch to say good morning to Granddaddy's dogs, through the chilly yard to the outhouse (a faraway tinkle, way down in the darkness), to the kitchen for a crust of cornbread.

A noise came from the back of the house—a grinding cough like a car starting. Leroy's granddaddy shuffled into the kitchen. Jets of white hair stood up on his head. The air around him smelled old. His hand quaked reaching for the coffeepot.

"Hey, Granddaddy!"

The old man jumped and muttered something, but without his teeth you couldn't tell what. He bent to poke in the stove.

Leroy ran out to gather the three biggest sticks he could find. Granddaddy always acted grumpy on Sunday morning. It had something to do with the way he acted on Saturday night, when he sat around the kitchen with his friends and drank from a bottle of whiskey. He sang and laughed extra-loud. By Sunday all the fun inside him was used up.

When Leroy came through the door with the firewood, Granddaddy made a shushing motion with his hand as if the tiniest noise might break him into pieces.

Leroy set the sticks down as softly as he could and retreated to the room where his mother was sleeping. Her smell was sweeter, like roses. Her head was buried under pillows, one foot dangling off the edge of the bed. He grabbed the big toe.

The second toe pinched his finger like a crab. He yelped and jumped back, giggling.

The pillow stirred. "Who's grabbin' my toe?"

"Hey, Satnin. It's Sunday. Get up." He tickled the soft of her foot until she was obliged to haul him up into bed with her.

"Come *on*," he said. "Granddaddy's up."

"I bet he looks purty, after all that caterwauling last night," she said.

Leroy grinned. "He looks like—he looks like a *monster*."

"Oh, hush, you meanie. . . ." She had to smile.

A round of new noises came in: the chug of the coffeepot, Uncle Hardy's door dragging open, Aunt Irene yak-yakking, the dogs barking in the yard.

"Let's just lay here a minute and let Irene get the biscuits started." Agnes stretched out. "I was right in the middle of the nicest dream." Leroy snuggled in the bend of her arm. She combed his hair with her fingers. "I heard you talking again last night," she said. "Who were you talking to?"

"My friend," Leroy said.

"What's his name?"

"I don't know."

"What does he look like?"

"Like me," Leroy said.

40

Her fingers stopped.

A frying pan scraped on the stove.

She went on softly stroking his hair. "You and your friend have been talking a lot, haven't you?"

"Uh-huh."

"Are you lonesome, sweetie? You're a big boy now. Big boys can make real friends. They don't have to pretend."

Leroy didn't say anything. He felt embarrassed. His friend in the mirror was a secret.

His mother pulled on her red-dotted dress. Leroy helped with the zipper. She tilted her head, brushed her hair with long, vigorous strokes.

"Put on those black pants with the crease," she said. "And that white shirt. No, honey. The clean one. Look where I'm pointing."

Leroy wrestled into the pants. He loved when his mother fixed herself up all pretty. He thought every boy in the world must wish for a mother as pretty as that.

"About to come out of those trousers," she said. "You're growing too fast." She buttoned the shirt, hooked the suspenders so the trousers rode up his chest. "Now. Go to the table. I'll be right there."

Leroy went like a shot. The grown-ups were roaming the kitchen, pouring coffee. Granddaddy had found his teeth and was using them on his breakfast.

Uncle Hardy said, "Howdy, Leroy."

Leroy said howdy and slipped into a chair.

Aunt Irene slid a fried egg onto his plate. "Where's your mama?"

"She's coming."

"This is her eggs getting cold," said Irene. "I'm not standing over this stove all morning. Other people have to get dressed, too."

"Be quiet, Irene," said Hardy.

Agnes opened the door just then, as if she'd been listening behind it. "Morning, all."

They said "morning" and settled back to their plates.

Old Jessie looked like a different man—combed, powdered, clean-shaven, and wearing his brown pin-striped tailor-made suit with pearl buttons. He always said people hold a high opinion of a man in a tailor-made suit.

"Sister, the biscuits smell good," Agnes said.

Irene touched the bags under her eyes. It always took Irene a long time from when she woke up until she looked like herself again. "I hope the eggs are still fit to eat," she said.

Hardy scrutinized the sports page of the *Commercial Appeal.*

"You lookin' mighty picturesque this morning, Agnes," said Granddaddy. "Like the first day of spring."

"Lord, I wish it was. It's a long way off yet." Agnes shook out her napkin. "But thank you, Mr. Jessie, that's sweet of you to say."

Irene held up the pan. "You want some grits?"

Agnes smiled her prettiest, most springlike smile and said no, thanks. She appeared to be winning some kind of contest with Irene.

Irene struck the pot with a spoon. "Fine. I'll pitch 'em to the dogs." She went to the door. The dogs were noisily grateful.

"Waste of food," said Granddaddy. "You can burn in hell for that."

"Not if a dog eats it," Hardy said behind his newspaper. "That's only if you throw it in the fire. You're okay as long as it gets eaten."

"We'll ask Preacher Bayley about that," Granddaddy replied.

Irene made a face. "Thank you for defending me, Hardy." She clanked the dishes into the washtub and marched to her room.

Hardy folded the paper and went after her.

That left Granddaddy with Leroy and Agnes, and the dogs snuffling at the door for more grits.

Granddaddy cleaned his plate with the edge of his biscuit. "That Irene gets on my nerves," he said. "I told those boys not to marry sisters. Ray got the better end of the stick, if you ask me."

"Oh, hush, Mr. Jessie, she'll hear you." Agnes hid a little smile. "You shouldn't pick on her so."

Granddaddy made a scornful sound, between a cough and a laugh.

"Five minutes," Hardy shouted up front.

"I've made Dodger's tea," Agnes said. "How's she feeling this morning?"

Granddaddy said he didn't know. He had slept in the same bed with Dodger since the beginning of time, but they didn't pay much attention to each other. Dodger spent all her time with her puzzles, sorting out millions of pieces into pictures of the English coast or German fairy-tale castles.

A stir ran through the house—doors slamming, quick steps, the grown-ups all swirling into the kitchen at the same time, ready to go.

Hardy and Irene and Granddaddy squeezed in the front of the truck with Uncle Johnny; Leroy scrambled over the tailgate and settled against the cab, beside his mother. The truck bounced down the yard, raising a cloud of pink dust. Agnes gathered her hair in one hand.

Leroy watched the world slide by backward, the road unrolling like a carpet of red dirt. A family of deer bounded off across a bean field. The truck passed through ribbons of sunlight and shade.

Leroy put his hand out into the wind and made a jumping fish.

"You'll lose your hand that way," his mother said, but she must not really have thought so; she didn't make him stop.

Pickups and cars were parked all over the yard of the Priceville Assembly of God. Leroy hopped down and took off running for the graveyard. Agnes let him run. On Sundays she let him go off with other children since the church sat well back from the road and there were plenty of grown-ups to keep an eye on him.

A pack of older boys huddled near the crumbling gray monument to a Confederate soldier named Augustus P. L. Brantley. This stone was held in awe by the boys. Any Confederate with a name that grand must have been buried with a Rebel flag or rifle or some other treasure that needed digging up. They were discussing plans for this when Leroy wandered into their circle.

"The coffin just rots away," said big redheaded Ronnie Bass. "When you dig down with your shovel, it's like cutting into a layer cake."

Some of the boys laughed at that; others made gagging sounds. They made a point of ignoring Leroy since he was younger.

He held on to the tree and listened to their talk.

"You don't know that, Ronnie Bass," said one. "You just making that up."

"I swear to break my mother's back," Ronnie Bass said, and nobody doubted for a moment that he was the kind of boy who could do such a thing. "Jack Fox and me tried to dig up his great-grandmama. Nothing left but stripes in the dirt."

The boys shivered. The church bell rang, and they darted off among the stones.

Leroy ran to his mother.

They went in to darkness and three small high windows, pine

benches, a pulpit, a piano, the smell of old hymnals and dust. Kirbys took up half the church, and Agnes's kinfolks, the Smiths, took up most of the rest, so anywhere you sat you were next to family. Granddaddy had saved a spot in the second pew.

The preacher was late, Brother Wilson announced. "Please turn to a hundred and twelve, 'Blessed Assurance,' if you don't know it already."

Almost everyone did, and when Sister Wilson sounded the first chord, they set in to sing. A deep masculine undertone supported the trembly sopranos of women and children.

Leroy sang with his mouth wide open, trying to hear his own voice apart from the others.

Preacher Bayley came down the aisle, brushing dust from his coat. He stood with hands folded as Sister Wilson rounded the final amen. Then he stepped to the pulpit. "Sorry I'm late," he said, "but your pastor got stood up by an A model Ford this morning and had to resort to a mule."

Laughter flickered in the pews. Leroy curled up with his head in his mother's lap.

Today the reading came from the Book of Genesis: Thus the Lord sayeth something, and somebody was affrighted, and did not cling to his figment, or something.

Leroy drifted off on Preacher Bayley's steady drone. It was wonderful to lie in the softness of his mother and gaze at the red bumps and hairs on the necks of the people in the row ahead. He lifted out of the pew and hovered in the air, looking down at himself.

Sister Wilson startled everyone back to life with a vigorous pounding of "Take the Name of Jesus with You." The collection plate set off on its journey, picking up nickels and quarters and the occasional crimped dollar bill. Agnes gave Leroy a dime to put in.

After a last prayer the preacher released them and went to the door to shake hands.

Agnes stood talking to her older sister Inez as if they hadn't seen each other in years. Uncle Leroy and Hardy and Inez's husband, Jake, stood smoking cigarettes with the other men. Granddaddy stood in the sanctuary door with his hand on the shoulder of the preacher, who was nodding his head.

Agnes called Leroy over, brushed the seat of his pants. "Look how big he's getting, Inez."

44

Aunt Inez squeezed his arm. "I heard you singing behind me, Leroy," she said. "You sing real sweet."

"He does, doesn't he," Agnes said. "Like an angel."

Leroy turned red, but he knew it was true, and it felt good to hear them say it.

"I better go, Jake's about to have a fit," said Inez. "I made potato salad. We'll see you there."

Uncle Johnny started the truck, and they all climbed in. The sun was hiding in a cloud; Agnes shivered and put her arm around Leroy as the truck bumped onto the highway.

Leroy waved at a colored family walking by the road—the daddy first, then the mama and a whole string of children in white Sunday clothes.

"Satnin, where do they go to church?"

"They've got their own church in Mount Zion."

The truck turned onto the Saltillo Road. Agnes held out her hand, palm up. "Mr. Jessie was right. It's starting to rain."

The droplets fell faster. Everybody piled out of the truck and hurried inside.

Leroy went to the little room off the kitchen, struggling with his shirt. The cuffs got hung up on his wrists. He stood with his hands pinned behind him until he figured out how to put one foot on his shirttail and set himself free.

Rain drummed on the roof. Leroy pulled on dungarees and an easy blue shirt and wandered up the hall. Through the front door he saw just the edge of his mother outside on the porch. He opened the door. He saw his mother in the arms of a tall man who was bending her over, kissing her on the mouth.

Leroy froze.

They were so wrapped up together that they did not hear him. Rain poured from the roof.

He watched with wide eyes. Strange bolts of lightning shot through him. He should fly at the man and knock him away from his mother—

He must have made a noise. Agnes stopped kissing and turned around. She winced, forced a smile onto her face. "Leroy. Remember your daddy?"

The man hiked his trousers. He was tall and thin, like his picture, with big ears and a strong, handsome jaw. He wore a dripping black overcoat, an uncertain smile. "Hello, son. You sure have got big." He held out his hands.

Leroy stayed where he was.

"Give him a minute," said his mother. "Sweetie, we shouldn't have startled you that way. It's all right. You'll get used to each other real fast."

Leroy moved over behind her. His mind whirled. This was the man in the picture. The man in the letters.

"You don't remember me, boy? I reckon you don't." The eyes were sad, and kind, but something held Leroy back.

His father said, "Well. What say we go take a look at the folks. Damn, I'm *home*!" He slammed his hand on the door.

Agnes laughed, hugging him from behind. "Yes you are. I don't believe it. You're really home."

They went in, laughing, shouting to the others. Leroy stayed on the porch, watching the rain.

He had dreamed of his daddy, cried and pined for his daddy, and now here was this tall strange man. Leroy was afraid. How long would the man stay? What gave him the right to kiss Leroy's mother like that?

He opened the door. Everyone was shouting and laughing and slapping the man on the back, hugging, calling for Dodger to come, Hardy, look, it's Ray, he's home, praise the Lord!

The man hugged everybody.

Leroy edged inside, around the excitement.

His father spotted him, laughed, and reached out with strong hands. "Look at this boy, would you, folks? Have I got the finest boy in Mississippi?" He swung Leroy up in the air, onto his hip.

Leroy adjusted himself, breathing his father's air of sweat and cigarette smoke. His mother looked so happy, but then why was she crying? Leroy buried his face in his father's shirt and started crying, too.

For some reason, that made everyone laugh.

6

$\mathcal{T}$he other boy came in on a moonbeam. He spoke in a silvery voice that sat Leroy straight up on his cot.

Go look in the mirror.

Leroy eased his bare feet to the floor. His mama and daddy wheezed and whistled in the four-poster bed.

Leroy stole up the hall to the parlor. A shaft of moonlight fell through the window and glanced off the oval mirror, spreading pale light in the room.

Leroy stared at his skinny legs poking out of the nightshirt, the wild tangle of hair.

He pressed his hand to the cool silvered glass. The other boy's hand came to meet it.

Leroy smiled. The other boy smiled.

The other boy was exactly like Leroy, except for the strange things he whispered in Leroy's ear.

You have to sleep by yourself now.

Leroy said, "I'm a big boy."

It's not fair. There's plenty of room in the bed for everybody. You could scrunch way over in the corner so you wouldn't take up hardly any room.

"They won't let me," said Leroy.

It's cold over there by yourself. What if you had a bad dream?

The voice was faint, but Leroy could hear its echo in the stillness of the parlor. He knew it must be coming from inside his head, but it was not his own voice. It said things he would never dare to say. It told him things he didn't know.

He hugged himself and yawned.

Things were better when it was just you and Mama and me. She loved you all the time.

"I'm sleepy," said Leroy.

You can get in there with them. They won't even know. You can squeeze over in one little corner of the bed.

Leroy thought about it. His father might say go back to the cot, but then he would just go back to the cot.

He crept down the hall to their room, the side of their bed. He lifted the edge of the blanket just enough to make a hole to crawl into.

He curled into the crook of his mother's leg. Her warmth soaked into the mattress and toasted the sheets. She sighed and reached down with her hand. Her fingers went to sleep in his hair.

48

7
~~~~~~~~~~~~~~~~

*I*t took everyone a long time to get used to Ray. Once he came in the door he was *there*. For nine months he played solitaire in his bathrobe and smoked cigarettes and did odd jobs for Mr. Bobo at the hardware store. In his spare time he taught Leroy how to catch a baseball and told him stories he'd heard in prison. "Son, don't you ever go there," he would say, shaking his head. "It's too damn hard to get out."

Agnes worked six days a week at the shirt factory. She was so glad to have Ray home again that she tried not to nag him about a job or a place of their own.

Leroy and his mama and daddy were like any family now. They loved each other. They sang together in church. With some coaching from Ray, Leroy started to pick out words from the hymnal. By the end of the summer he was reading the shredded wheat box and "Dick Tracy" in the newspaper.

Leroy watched his daddy shaving and sleeping; he studied the way his hands moved and the boom! that exploded when he laughed. He watched his daddy's eyes following his mother around the room.

One morning he caught his first glimpse of his daddy without any clothes. He was horrified by the sight of that knobby pink snake hanging down among all that hair. For a while he imagined it was the sign of some terrible deformity.

～～～

Come September Leroy headed off to school for the first time. His mother took him as far as the door. Leroy smelled clean clothes, new crayons, unsharpened pencils. A nice lady in a red dress pinned a name tag to his shirt and sent him to stand in a line of frightened boys and girls.

The lady said, "Come this way, class," and led them to a room with big windows and rows of chairs hooked to little tables. She gave them a sermon about Manners, got out some wooden animals for them to play with. After a while she made them all lie down on a canvas rug and take a nap. Nobody slept.

Leroy liked school. It was fun having real kids to play with all day. He didn't always listen to the teacher, but he liked the singing and the games—especially red rover, since he had discovered he could always bust the line by aiming between two girls.

For Christmas that year he asked Santa Claus for a baby sister. Instead he got a box of sparklers and a shiny paper windmill on a stick.

The next day his father put on good clothes and packed his suitcase and announced he was going to Memphis to find a job. "There's no chance for me here," he said. "Wilbur Dees has poisoned the well."

Agnes's eyes brightened with tears. "You just got back, Ray. You can't go off and leave us again."

"Honey, everybody knows me down here," he said. "I'm a felon, all right? I can't join the army. But they're taking anybody at the war plants in Memphis. I know I can get something."

After a long time Agnes said, "Maybe you're right. I guess it's better than prison."

"They pay good money up there. I'll get us out of here, Agnes. You wait and see."

Leroy hung back in the doorway. He was not sorry his daddy was leaving. He liked having his mother all to himself.

Ray patted his head and kissed Agnes. "Take care." He buttoned his coat, walked to the highway, put out his thumb.

Leroy and Agnes watched from the backyard until a big black Dodge slowed to a stop. Ray waved good-bye and climbed in.

That night the mirror told Leroy that his bad thoughts had pushed his daddy out of the house. Leroy ran to his room and cried with his face in the pillow, choking back the sound until his throat hurt.

He talked more to his secret friend after that. The silvery voice told him things to do—wicked things like putting salt in the sugar bowl or banging the wall of the chicken shed just as the hens dropped off to sleep. Whenever Leroy took one of these dares, he got caught and wound up having to sit in a chair in the corner.

The mirror said it was only a matter of time before Leroy was grown up, and nobody could stop him from anything.

Ray landed a job sweeping floors in an airplane factory in West Memphis. He came home most Friday nights, worn out but bearing new money, a sack of peppermint sticks, stories of his life in Memphis: the crazy characters in his rooming house, the old bluesmen who sang on the curbs of Beale Street, the big river rolling. The bustling town.

Agnes always looked happiest on those nights, after Ray had his bath and they sat around the table eating supper. One Friday she told them about a dream she'd had: They lived in their own little house, with green shutters and flowers in the yard.

Three weeks later Ray got a raise and they moved to Kelly Street, two blocks away. The house didn't have shutters, but Agnes said it was the house in her dream. There were four neat rooms and yellow flowers in the yard and a falling-down shed that was Leroy's playhouse, a place for his friend to hide.

A summer went by, and another.

Agnes had a vision that they won a radio in a sweepstakes contest, but they didn't.

Ray lost his job at the war plant, came home, found a job at the sawmill. There was never any money.

The year Leroy turned nine, he cut his lip sliding into Elmer Russell's thumb at third base on the school playground. The Germans surrendered. The President died. The new President dropped a big bomb on Japan. The Japs gave up. Every week there was a parade in Tupelo for a returning hero. Ray lost his job at the sawmill.

～～～

Late at night Leroy heard an urgent stir of voices in the kitchen. He sneaked to the door. It was open an inch. Ray rested his chin in his hands.

Agnes sat facing the other way. "You've got to do something," she said. "I can't make all the decisions. You've got to find work. They've cut me to half time. We can't pay the rent."

Ray sighed. "We just can't get ahead."

"Not as long as you lay around here all day playing catch with Leroy," said Agnes, "instead of setting some kind of example."

"Oh, get off my back," he said.

"You better be glad I'm on it"—she was really steaming now—"because if we don't come up with sixty-two dollars by Friday, I'm the only thing you'll have left in this world. We'll be out in the street."

Ray lifted his eyes. "I'll find us a cheaper place."

He found a house on Berry Street for twenty dollars a month, fifteen dollars more than it was worth. Leroy and his mother stared from the yard. The windows were broken; the porch roof caved in. The trees had been cut by the previous tenant for firewood.

Ray ignored the look on their faces. "We'll fix it up," he said, sweeping open the door to demonstrate how well it worked.

They moved their possessions in Johnny's pickup. Agnes tacked newspapers over the windows and scrubbed the floors and fogged the air with Flit and tried to act cheerful for Leroy's sake.

Leroy wrinkled his nose. "It stinks in here."

"It's the bug spray," she said.

"Why do we have to live here?" He knew why, but some meanness inside made him ask.

"What do you think? We're poor. Put these pillows over there."

52

He picked his way through the confusion of boxes. "Nobody's as poor as us, huh, Mama."

"We've got a roof over our heads, at least." Agnes inspected a hole in the ceiling. "You can go down by the railroad tracks any night and see people who are worse off than us."

Agnes always told Leroy he could be anything he wanted. She said he'd been given the luck of two boys—his twin brother's talent and fate and good fortune along with his own.

"Sometimes I think you got all your daddy's luck, too," she said after Ray lost his job at Wilson's dry cleaner's. "The poor man has never had any."

Leroy had a dream so real it woke him up sweating: his father rushing in and out of a burning house, trying to save the furniture.

He kept his bad dreams to himself. He was aware that he was growing up different from other boys. His features were almost too pretty: his delicate mouth, his long eyelashes like a girl. He spent hours inspecting himself in the mirror.

He was Agnes's boy, as he had been since his first moment on earth. She told him when to get up, what to wear, how to eat, how to act, what to say when a grown-up spoke to him, and all the other things in a day.

He loved the little flecks of gold in her gray-green eyes; her eyes were always smiling at him, even when her mouth was not. She had a habit of resting her face in one hand, looking sideways at the world. She had soft, straight hair the color of a new copper penny, gathered in a ponytail with a white satin ribbon. She carried herself with her shoulders squared, chin up, swinging that ponytail, looking left and right for the first sign of somebody who might bring harm to Leroy.

One day a big boy came into the yard where Leroy had spent a whole morning with his dump truck and Dodger's trowel, carving out a network of play highways in the sand. The boy had mean eyes and a dirty shirt and snot running from his nose. For no reason at all he took Leroy's dump truck away and kicked holes in his highways. Leroy sat down in the sand and began to cry. The boy yelled "crybaby" and used his feet to churn Leroy's fantasy city into a big mess of ruined sand.

About that time Agnes burst through the door, screaming, "Come here to me, you big bully!" Before the boy could get himself cocked to take off, she crossed the yard and seized him by one ear, bent him over, whaling away at his backside with her free hand, smacking him all the way to the street. "And don't you *never* let me catch you in *my* yard *again*!" The boy ran spraddle-legged getting away from her. He never looked back.

Leroy knew other boys weren't so close to their mothers, but the mirror told him they weren't lucky enough to have a mother who worried and fretted over them every minute of the day. When he told the boys he wasn't allowed to go off swimming in the creek, they called him a mama's boy. He turned hot in the face and ran home, ranting to himself.

He didn't need them. His mother was the only one he needed—no one else, not even his daddy. His daddy loved Leroy when he was home, but that wasn't even most of the time.

Agnes strained her back and lost four weeks at work. Leroy saw the pile of unopened bills growing on the chest of drawers and knew what it meant.

When someone knocked at the door, Agnes and Leroy hid behind the curtains until whoever it was got back in his car and drove off.

Through the week they ate hoecake and greens. Every Sunday at Granddaddy's Leroy ate meat loaf and yeast rolls enough to last him until the next week. Aunt Irene always remarked on his appetite.

In April he busted the seat out of his school pants. Agnes had to mend them with some bright yellow fabric that didn't even begin to match. Leroy spent the last weeks of fourth grade creeping around with his back to the wall.

~~~~~

On a summer night he lay near the window, listening to the way his folks talked when they thought he was asleep. Their voices were softer. They didn't pick at each other so much. Ray told stories of his time in Memphis. Agnes listened and laughed and made a fuss over him.

They seemed like different people. Leroy mulled it over as he drifted to sleep.

A nice dream was broken by his father's voice: "Get up, son, we've got to get moving."

Leroy shook himself awake.

It was the deepest part of night. Ray wore blue dungarees, no shirt, his ratty blue bathrobe. A shock of hair hung in his eyes. "I hadn't got time to explain. Just get dressed. Then run help your mother." He stumbled through the room, gathering things in a box.

Leroy went through the door and found his mother weeping. The sight sent a chill through him. "Satnin, what's wrong?"

"Nothing." She covered her eyes.

"Where we going?"

She blotted her nose on a corner of the sheet. "Go put on your clothes. We can't stay here tonight."

He shivered in his underpants. "Don't cry," he said.

Ray stuck his head in the door. "Come on now, honey."

"I'm moving as fast as I can!" Agnes threw him a terrible look.

Leroy went to pull on his pants and shirt.

His father came in with the box and a paper sack. "Put all the clothes from your drawer into this."

"Why is Mama crying?"

Ray eased down to the edge of the bed. "Well, I'll tell you, son. She didn't expect we'd have to move at this time of night. Neither did I."

"Why are we moving?"

"Mr. Tyrell Banks wants his rent money, and I don't have any to give him. Now be a good sport for your old dad, okay?"

"Okay." Leroy rubbed his eyes.

Ray got up, wandered into the kitchen.

Leroy gathered his shirts and socks, arrowheads, baseball and glove, Sunday shoes, the silver dollar his granddaddy had given him for his ninth birthday. The old man had told him if he always held on to that dollar—never gave in to the temptation to spend it—he'd never be all the way broke.

Leroy knew he should give the dollar to his daddy to give Mr. Tyrell Banks, but he didn't want to give his last money to the man who made his mama cry.

His mother's reflection came into the mirror beside his. "Come on, honey," she said, "Daddy's gone to start the car."

"I want to stay here." Leroy turned. "I like this house."

Agnes lifted her gaze to the ceiling. "Give me strength." She sighed. "Sweetie, the sooner we get out of here, the better. Now come on."

Loaded with boxes and paper sacks, they struggled down the steps to the open trunk of the Plymouth. The stars were hidden by clouds. The air held a damp chill.

Ray sat at the wheel, racing the engine.

"Oh, keep your pants on," Agnes shouted. She stuffed in the sacks, slammed the trunk, and marched Leroy to the passenger side. "Get in the back."

Leroy loved to ride up front, but he knew better than to cross his mother when her voice had that acid tone. He wiggled down in back and hoped his father knew better, too.

"Good-bye and good riddance." Ray sounded nearly cheerful. "I'm with you, Agnes. We've lived in some awful holes, but this was the worst. We're better off anyplace else. Even if we have to move back in with the folks."

She slammed her door. "We can't go busting in there in the middle of the night."

"You're right." Ray yawned, juicing the pedal with his foot.

"Stop making all that noise. You'll wake up the neighbors."

"They ain't our neighbors anymore," Ray said.

Agnes stared at him a long moment, then broke out laughing. Ray joined in.

Leroy knew they had both lost their minds.

The Plymouth scratched down the hill. At the foot of the drive a pickup truck sat idling, its lights on, a beefy arm propped in the driver's window.

"There he is," Ray breathed.

As they glided past, Agnes stuck her head out the window and cried, "Tyrell Banks, you son of a bitch!"

Leroy shrank down, thunderstruck. He had never imagined such words from his mother's lips.

She was shouting with laughter, and Ray laughed, too.

How could they laugh? Weren't they ashamed to be poor?

Leroy was ashamed and scared. Where would they go? How could they buy breakfast, or dinner? Where would they sleep? Where would Leroy go to school?

"You're gonna wake everybody *up*," he shouted.

Agnes quit laughing. She turned around in her seat to look at him. "We're gonna wake everybody up," she said to Ray.

56

"Hell, we might as well!" Ray hollered out the window, "Wake up! Wake up! Whoo-ee! The Kirbys are hittin' the road!" and leaned on the horn. "Cheer up, son. Things could be worse."

"He's right, Leroy," his mother said. "We're all together, and we've got our car...."

"We don't even have a roof over our heads." Leroy wasn't ready to be happy, no matter how hard they tried. It was all too confusing, this cheerful act they were putting on to fool him.

They drove the empty streets of Tupelo. The only light came from the marquee of the Paramount Theater.

Agnes studied Leroy over the seat. "You know," she said, "your grandmother Doll always said it's better to laugh than to cry. Sometimes it's almost the same feeling."

"A roof over our heads," Ray repeated. "That's you talking, Agnes."

"He's just scared," she said. "Leroy. Listen to me. You don't have to worry. We'll find a new place."

Ray said, "There's always the Whispering Pines."

"You're not taking this child out there."

"Aw honey, why not? It's cheap."

"And so is anybody who goes there," she said.

"Look at it this way. We'll probably be the first married folks they've ever seen. They may *give* us a room."

He turned right on the old Oxford highway.

The sign of the Whispering Pines Tourist Court was a blue neon man in the moon, winking his eye. The rooms were arranged so that guests could park right at their doors. Nearly every door had a car in front of it.

"It's rocking tonight," Ray said, switching off the motor. "Stay here. Keep an eye out. No telling who you might see." He got out and went to jingle the bell on the door marked OFFICE. Presently a light appeared inside, and a man in a Hawaiian shirt.

"Leroy, sit up so he can see you," said Agnes.

Ray chatted and waved his hand at the car. The man leaned around the door for a better look.

In a moment Ray was back with a key. "Hot dog, there's room at the inn," he announced, starting the car. "Three bucks. He gave us half price."

Leroy trailed his father into Room 8. It was no bigger than their old room off Granddaddy's kitchen, the ceilings and walls of shiny yellow pine, pocked with dark knots and swirls. There was one double bed, a chair, an ivory-colored radio on the dresser.

Agnes came to the door. "Oh, Ray, it's even the same room," she breathed.

"I don't know how you remember. That's been a long time." Ray flicked on the light in the bathroom. "They all look alike."

Leroy went to inspect the lamp, a plaster cowboy on a bucking bronco. "Did we stay here before?"

"Your daddy and I did, one time," his mother said with a little secretive smile. "You weren't even born."

Leroy switched on the radio. Static. He turned the dial. The first clear signal was a plinking guitar, an old man's doleful voice.

"Turn it louder," said Agnes, closing the door. "That's Red Fairlie."

A quartet of male singers swelled in the background. Red Fairlie sang as though he wanted to cry.

> *When I was no more than a towheaded boy*
> *I found an old hound dog named Blue*
> *He followed me home from the churchhouse one day*
> *His eyes said, "I'm the dog for you"*

Agnes turned away to slip the white cotton nightgown over her head.

Leroy sank cross-legged to the floor. Red Fairlie sang in a thin, reedy voice; Leroy imagined him rawboned and shaggy, something like Uncle Johnny, with sorrowful eyes and a split between his front teeth.

> *We played in the fields and we swam in the streams*
> *We did the things boys and dogs do*
> *If ever a lad had a friend in the world*
> *Let me tell you, son, I had Old Blue*

Red told his sorrowful tale with simple words anybody could understand. All the radio songs Leroy ever heard had lovey-dovey words, stuff he didn't care about, but this was a story that might be happening to him.

The end of a day, we were running for home
That snake meant to strike out at me
I just didn't see it, it happened so fast
Old Blue laid his head on my knee

Leroy pictured a red, long-eared dog peering up at his master with bottomless, quizzical eyes. To his surprise, he felt a lump of sadness forming in his throat.

The tragedy rolled on. The quartet swelled oo-EEE-ooo between the verses. The guitarist plucked out a little melody to give the words time to sink in.

Leroy felt sadder and sadder. Old Blue was Joe's best friend. His time had come. And Joe had to do the awful deed himself.

Ray rolled his eyes as he wandered to the bathroom. Leroy didn't care. Let him make fun. He didn't know how it felt to be sad. He couldn't hear Leroy's heart pounding with the thrill of this song, the sweetness of his melancholy. Leroy wiggled into the rug. He thought his own life was hard ... nobody was making him shoot his dog.

Leroy listened with his whole body, as if new ears were opening up all over him. The words, the sad wail, the plaintive guitar: Everything blended into one gloomy, delicious feeling.

Well the rest of my life has been hard, in a way
I'm weary, the river is wide
But I know I'll be happy in heaven one day
When I have Old Blue by my side

Leroy sat with his mouth open. He'd never heard such a song in his life. It told its whole sad story in a couple of minutes and then it was over, twang-twang, good-bye Blue. Oh, he wanted to cry. He wanted to hear it again.

He stared at the radio. How could a radio make him feel this way?

Poor Joe didn't have a dog. Leroy didn't have a roof over his head. The world is so hard on boys who try to be good.

His mother stretched out on the bed. "You like that song, honey?"

Leroy nodded. He was afraid to speak because he might bust out crying, and he was too big for that.

"I like it, too. You take those pillows and make you a pallet right there."

Ray came in from the bathroom, shedding his pants. He stooped to help Leroy arrange blankets on the floor. "This rug ought to be soft enough, son," he said, reaching to pat Leroy's hair.

Leroy shrank away. He didn't want his father to touch him. He lay down on the floor and pulled the pillow over his head.

Ray flopped on the bed. "Everything will look brighter in the morning," he said, switching off the light.

The bed made squeaky settling-in noises. Outside, car doors slammed. A bunch of laughing people took a long time going into their room.

"Doll would die if she could see us out here," Agnes said in the dark.

"That's what you said the last time," said Ray.

Leroy turned over. He lay with his hands behind his head, watching the play of shadows through the venetian blinds. He mourned for Old Blue, and for the boy who loved him.

8

*B*efore dawn the cars started one by one and drove away from the Whispering Pines. Leroy sat on the floor by the window, watching them go. He had slept only an hour or two before hunger and the strangeness of the place woke him up.

The floor was hard. The rug smelled funny. Leroy's stomach was an empty cave. He pulled down one slat of the blind with his finger. The blue neon moon-man winked and smiled a big, leering smile that made him uncomfortable.

He tried crawling in between his mama and daddy, but they were already hanging off the edges of the bed. Ray grunted and pushed him away.

Leroy went to the bathroom, flipped the light switch. The dazzling white tiles blinded him. He stood with his eyes closed until they began to adjust to the glare.

Over the sink was a cracked mirror.

Leroy climbed to the edge of the tub, squinting at himself.

"Are you here?" he whispered.

Wherever you go.

"We got thrown out of our house. I have to sleep on the floor."

Mama didn't want to come here. She's smarter than Daddy. You know that now.

"He doesn't have any luck," Leroy said. That was his mother's favorite explanation.

Was he even ashamed? No. He made jokes about it.

"He was trying to cheer us up."

You should show him a thing or two. You're not far from Grand-daddy's. Down the highway and across the railroad tracks. You could go there for something to eat. Peanut butter and crackers. That's not running away. When they wake up, they'll be sorry, what they did to you.

"They'll be mad." Leroy stuck two fingers in his mouth and pulled his cheeks apart, in an awful imitation of how mad they'd be.

You wouldn't be running away from home. You don't have a home.

"I don't know. . . ."

They might be happy without your mouth to feed.

"No, they wouldn't."

One way to find out.

Leroy climbed down from the sink.

The idea made him tingle all over. He had never done anything so rebellious or dangerous. He could show them he was not just a dog they could drag along with them in the dead of night, and put down to sleep on the floor.

Sometimes he did what the mirror told him to do when he *knew* it was wrong. A raw scratch of excitement at the back of his throat told him this was going to be one of those times.

He snapped out the light, crept into the room where his parents were sleeping, and silently dressed himself. He was going. Not far—just to Granddaddy's—but he was going.

He coaxed the door open. A stretch of light advanced over his parents' bed. They did not stir.

He eased the door shut. Ray's Plymouth was the only car left in the parking lot. A mockingbird laughed in a flowering tree. Dawn was turning everything gray except the electric blue man in the moon.

Leroy waded through a weedy strip to the road.

He imagined his mother waking up in there, finding him gone. She would run all the way to the road in her nightgown, searching for him.

If he sneaked back in now and lay down on his pallet, she would never know.

Mama's boy.

He squared his shoulders and walked fast until he was well out of sight of the Whispering Pines.

The whine of trucks on the highway was farther away than he had supposed. Jaybirds jabbered, dashing down through the trees. Leroy walked and walked, muttering over his injuries.

The sun climbed the sky and warmed the cuts in the roadside to pink.

At last he reached the tall grass at the shoulder of the Birmingham highway. He looked for some landmark that would tell him which way to go. The only sign was a vine-covered man in the moon looking back toward the Whispering Pines. The woods and the black ribbon of highway appeared to stretch forever in either direction.

Three cars whizzed by, heading off toward the rising sun. Leroy followed them.

For a while he kept to the edge of the road, but the traffic zoomed by so close and so fast that he moved down into the ditch and struggled ahead. Then the ditch turned into a swamp, and he had to take his chances again on the shoulder.

A dump truck roared by, whipping up a cloud of gravel and dust.

Leroy lost his footing and stumbled down the slope into ankle-deep watery muck.

This plan was not working.

He clambered up the opposite bank, to the railroad tracks. His feet squished in his shoes.

He set out down the tracks, humming the tune to "Old Blue" as he hopped from tie to tie. He made fairly good time once he got the hang of skipping two ties in one leap. He was really bounding along by the time the blast of a train horn sent him leaping straight up in the air.

He came down on one knee. He looked back into the bright burning eye of a train.

He scrambled off the tracks, down the ditch, to the opposite bank.

The train thundered past, shaking the earth, blasting the air with its horn, big and heavy and screaming fast enough to obliterate anything that might wander under its wheels.

Leroy waited a long time for the earth to quit shaking. He yanked himself free from a blackberry bramble and set off again down the highway, in a daze.

The road shimmered into the distance. A flock of crows undulated around a bean field like a bad omen.

Leroy decided to pray. That's what they said in Sunday school: Pray for help in your time of trouble. He closed his eyes. It took nerve to pray for rescue from trouble he had brought on himself, but he did.

He imagined God would tell him just to walk back to the Whispering Pines and give up this foolishness.

The rattle of a big truck approached, squealing brakes.

Leroy opened his eyes. Not a truck, a blue rattletrap bus, with a legend on the side:

GREATER MOUNT ZION AFRICAN METHODIST
EPISCOPAL BUS
(Praise the Lord)

The bus drew to a halt. The door slapped open. A big Negro man in a white choir robe looked down from behind the steering wheel. "Boy, what you doing out here?"

"Walking home," said Leroy.

"I reckon you are. Want a ride?"

Twenty Negro people jammed up to the windows to peer down at Leroy. From the hood came a clamor, atta *pow*! atta *pow*! as if the bus couldn't wait to get rolling again.

The driver said, "Come on now, we running late."

"I'm not sure which way I'm going."

The big man reached for the door lever. "Either get in or stay off."

"Okay. I mean, yessir, please, I'll get in." Leroy stepped up into close, crowded air, the smell of gardenias and Wildroot hair oil. All the eyes came away from the windows to fix on him.

The people were very black, dressed in white and bright pink and bright yellow and blue. The little girls were decorated with hair ribbons, the ladies with fruit on their hats.

Leroy took a seat. He felt everyone around him letting out a breath, but no one said a word. The bus lurched ahead. They'd probably been singing or talking until he got in. His ears burned.

He inspected the gold ring in the driver's right ear, the folds in the flesh of his neck.

The man spoke to his rearview mirror: "You got a name?"

"Leroy. Leroy Kirby."

"Well, Mr. Wandering Kirby, I'm Brother Love. Love's my name and my game. Where you stay at?"

"East Tupelo."

This information ran back through the bus.

"That's five miles from here. How you get all the way out here by yourself?"

The truth seemed too complicated to explain. Leroy said, "I got lost."

"I say you did," Brother Love said. "I can ride you there, but first got to get these folkses to church. Can't keep the Lord waiting."

The younger children stared at Leroy with big eyes.

He settled back and looked out the window, wishing he could melt into his seat.

The bus turned off on a sand rut and bumped over the railroad tracks, across a wide cornfield, to a stand of large oaks.

Leroy kept his seat as the people collected their Bibles and hats and filed past him down the steps, into the yard.

The Greater Mount Zion African Methodist Episcopal Church was a tottering old farmhouse covered with brick-patterned tar paper. Everyone was gathered under the trees, chatting and watching the children play, just the way they did at the Priceville Assembly of God.

"I guess I'll just walk out to the highway and get on home," Leroy said.

"You can't walk all that way." Brother Love struggled to reach his shoelace. "I'll ride you as soon as we're done. Won't be more than an hour. Folks can't go much longer than that."

Someone rang a handbell.

Leroy said, "Are you the preacher?"

"No, I'm just a brother, but I got all the words to the songs right here." He tapped the side of his head with a finger. "Come on inside and hear some real singing."

"I can't go in there."

"Why not? You scared you'll turn black?" Brother Love laughed, a big rumble, and hoisted himself from his seat. "The colored folk don't keep nobody out of our church, honey. That's just you white folk."

Leroy's heart was still hammering from his encounter with the train. He knew he should go home, but the Brother was right: He couldn't walk five miles.

He followed the big man down from the bus. A crowd of children surrounded them and tugged Brother Love by the hands toward the farmhouse. His presence stirred the crowd to gather and go inside.

Leroy was carried along in their flow. He felt whiter than anyone on earth, but once everybody had a good look at him, they turned their attention to the business of church.

The walls of the farmhouse had been knocked to the posts to make room for the congregation. An assortment of folding chairs stood in neat rows; the pulpit was a pine plank nailed to upright two-by-fours. The people chattered and hugged each other, scraping chairs and their uncomfortable Sunday shoes on the floor. On the wall was a big tinted picture of Jesus—a movie-handsome Jesus, with wavy brown hair and a pointy beard like Errol Flynn's.

Brother Love motioned for Leroy to stand with the children in back.

He found an inconspicuous spot against the wall, between a tall, bowlegged boy and a skinny girl with high heels and three pigtails.

The Brother held up his arms and made his way down the aisle, shushing the chatter with his hands. He was in no hurry. He smiled and greeted the people, tuning up his voice—"Hmm, yeah, oh, whoa yea-ah, praise his-uh—naaaaame. . . ."

A light-colored baby-faced man in a formal black suit stepped to the pulpit. "Jump up, you sinners!" he cried. "Jump up and run out! We don't neeeed you in here!"

66

A charge of excitement ran through the crowd. "Amen!" cried two women down front.

"All you demons and devils, all who refuse to live by the word of the Lord—you get up now and run, don't you walk, now, you *run* out the door of this house. We don't neeeed you in here!"

"Praise the Lord!"

Leroy grinned. The man looked so mild and youthful and amiable, and then those words came shooting out of his mouth like hot bullets.

"All scoundrels and heathen, blasphemers and rabble, all you unholy unrighteous ungodly worshipers of Mammon and Satan, I give you fair warning! You won't find a friend in this house!"

"No sir!"

"No!"

"We don't neeeeed you in here!" He waved his arms. "We *all* love the Lord."

"Yay!"

Leroy loved how the listeners jumped right into the preacher's sermon with their shouts, syncopating the breaks in his rhythm. It fitted together like music.

The preacher held up his hands. "I feel a need for a song," he said. "Brother Love, will you come forward?"

"I will," said the Brother.

"Chase the devils away with your song!" The preacher threw his arms in the air and stalked to the corner of the room.

Brother Love held out his hands.

Well chillun let me tell you I done travel glo-ry's rooooad before—

"Tell us, Brother!"

I been up that hill, and down that hill, and roll that stone away from the hooooole, chillun—

"Ow! Yea!"

Yes I beennnnn. Huh. Lookin' for my Lord.

"Yea!"

But he gone—
Yeah! Hey! That Jesus been gone—
Yeah! Hey!
And he never
Nev-er
Gon-na
Come here no mo

"Oh, yeah!"

Leroy stood with his mouth open. The soft-spoken Brother possessed a great deep rolling barrel of a voice. He appeared to be making the song up as he went along.

He say bring *me down some wine,*
Mary mama—done stuck *me in my side,*
*Mary mama—hep me—*hep *me girl—*

He stopped. Everyone in the room took a breath.

Leroy pressed against the wall, dizzy with pleasure.

Then Brother Love lit into a rollicking spiritual, a chorus everybody could sing, and everyone did.

Tell . . . me tell me Jesus,
When you comin' home?

Oh, they knew how to sing. They made the windows tremble with the joyful abundance of their noise. Wasn't this just the kind of song Jesus would want to hear on a Sunday morning? They sang with all their lungs. They sang to knock down the roof, to silence the birds, to put an end to all other kinds of singing.

The pitiful congregation at Priceville would drown in the wave of their very first note.

Brother Love called the lines a half beat ahead. "And if he tell you . . ." The crowd pitched it back to him: *"tell you, tell you"*—"where he gone"—*"wheeeeere he gone."*

The hairs prickled up on the back of Leroy's neck—a physical thrill even stronger than the wave of sadness that had rushed over him when he heard about Old Blue last night. The old farmhouse rolled under his feet. He had never imagined music could stir up such violence inside him—these lightning storms popping and cracking in his chest.

He forgot who he was and began clapping his hands, singing along, *"Telll you tell you...."* The people around him jumped and hollered and danced, all carried away.

The pigtailed girl hopped up and down, squealing.

Her sharp heel came down on Leroy's right foot so hard he thought he would faint.

He staggered to the door. White spots danced in his eyes. He fell onto the railing, groped down the steps to the yard, and collapsed in the sand. He clutched his poor, howling foot.

The spiritual churned on behind him, rising and rising; how much higher could they go?

"You all right?"

He looked up. The girl who had stepped on him peered through the door, that extra pigtail poking up atop her head. Her eyes shone at the spectacle of Leroy sprawled in the yard.

"I'm all right," he said, pulling off his shoe.

She said, "sorry," and disappeared inside.

She hadn't done it on purpose, but Leroy took it as a sign. He didn't belong here. He had stumbled up under her foot. He wasn't one of them, no matter how their music swept him up and filled him.

He rubbed his throbbing foot with his thumb.

He was astounded that Negroes were *better* at something than white people. He had never considered it. He had heard just the opposite all his life. His mama and daddy and kinfolks turned up their noses if a colored man looked at them sideways; they'd probably die if they'd seen Leroy carrying on that way, singing and clapping, in a church full of them.

It stirred him to think he might be right about something as important as the Negroes, and his mama and daddy might be wrong.

But they hadn't heard the singing! Music didn't work these powerful changes on them! They heard Red Fairlie singing about Old Blue, and to them it was just a sad song; it didn't leave them with the kind of terrible emptiness that got Leroy up from his sleep and put him out wandering the road at dawn.

Gradually the spiritual thinned out and was overtaken by a sermon, punctuated by shouts and flights of leftover melody.

Brother Love appeared at the door. "There you are," he said. "What you doin' out here? Don't care for our singing?"

"No!" Leroy said. "It's . . . I never heard anything like it. I mean it. It's just—I've got to go home. They'll be worried about me."

"If you stay awhile, you get fed," said Brother Love. "We feed the hungry and give rides to the sore of the feet."

Leroy pulled on his shoe. "I can't. I'll be in trouble."

"Don't want that." The Brother picked his way to the bus. "He'll be preachin' another half hour at least. I reckon I can ride you and make it back before they commence to eating."

For a big man, Brother Love moved fast.

Leroy limped along after him. "Y'all sing so *strong*," he said. "I never heard anybody sing like that."

"You like to sing, Master Kirby?"

"Sure," Leroy said, flushing red. Brother Love had placed his finger on the nerve that was making him jump.

"I saw you having a big time back there." The Brother started the engine—atta *pow*! "You come down anytime and sing with us. Just come on when you get ready."

"I don't know if my folks'll let me," said Leroy.

"Just ask 'em. They might."

The bus bounced across the ruts in the field and onto the highway. Leroy settled in the front seat.

He pictured the Sunday table at Granddaddy's: roast chicken, fried potatoes and okra and squash, butter beans and corn sticks and Aunt Irene's cheese-onion pie. Smoky iced tea over rough chunks of ice. *Dewberry cobbler.*

Fat chance they'd give him much dinner, though, after what he'd done. Probably a slice of light bread and a whipping.

He rode in gloomy silence, dreading his punishment.

"Kirby, what was you doing on the road by yourself?"

"Trying to get to my granddaddy's."

Brother Love's earring flashed as he turned. "Man, you got trouble all over your face," he said. "You by any chance running away?"

"No," Leroy said. "Me and my folks—we don't really have a place to live right now." He peered through the windshield. "See up here, by the big tree? You can let me off there."

Brother Love pulled the bus to the shoulder. "Nothing here but a barn."

"It's right up that hill," Leroy said. "Listen, I sure am grateful you gave me a ride."

"Always hep a man who likes music," said Brother Love. "You do like I say. Come on down anytime."

"I'll try," Leroy said. "I never heard anything like that before."

"Happens every Sunday morning." The Brother grinned.

Leroy stepped down.

Brother Love maneuvered the bus in an impossible circle, way almost into the ditch; he kept driving and mowing down weeds and somehow got it back on the road, headed the other direction. He squeezed his arm through the window to wave good-bye.

Leroy waved back. The music still buzzed in the bones of his arms. He wished the ride had taken longer so he wouldn't be standing here now, staring up the weed-eaten rise at Granddaddy's chimney.

His feet weighed two thousand pounds apiece. He dragged the left one ahead, then the right, making his way up the slope, stopping here and there to kick open an anthill or examine a scurrying thing. He had a fleeting impression of a long-ago day in this spot—running to his mother, her arms out. She was so glad to see him.

Now she must hate him. He was cruel to run off and make her worry. The fire of his rebellion had already begun to flicker; when he reached the back fence, it sputtered and died.

They were here. The Plymouth under a tree. Granddaddy's pickup truck waiting with its tailgate down. Chickens pecking, muttering in the chicken yard.

The little crooked house where Leroy was born stood off down the hill toward the Saltillo Road. It was empty, the front door hanging by one hinge. In a way, Leroy thought, that house belonged to him. He was the only one born there.

His mama said they might live there still, in their own little house down from Granddaddy and Dodger, if it weren't for a man named Wilbur Dees. She said it was like the Bible story of the dog with the mange.

Leroy could hide out down there awhile and figure out what to do.

Or he could plunge right on in the big house and take what was coming to him.

It would only get worse if he waited. Like ripping a bandage off a sore. Get the hurt over quick.

He slipped between two strands of barbed wire. The chickens ignored him. He walked in a straight line past the woodshed, past the pump house and the fig tree, up the steps, through the screen door, and into the kitchen.

Granddaddy's dogs bounded up, barking, proclaiming. The kitchen was empty except for the dogs and the smell of Sunday dinner.

Leroy snatched up a corn muffin and ate it like that, three bites, swallowing so hard he nearly choked.

He went up through the house, trailed by the yelping dogs.

Everyone was on the porch: his mother and Granddaddy, Ray and Hardy and Irene leafing through the *Commercial Appeal*, Dodger snoozing in a rocking chair.

No use hiding now. Leroy took a deep breath and pushed through the screen.

Everyone but Dodger turned to look at him.

"Hey, Leroy," his mother said.

He waited for her to say something else. For an uncomfortable time she just smiled at him.

Granddaddy went back to the stick he was whittling, the others to their newspaper.

Finally Leroy had to say something. "I—I couldn't sleep in that place. I went for a walk."

"That's what we figured," Agnes said. "You hungry?"

"Uh-huh."

"Run on and wash up then. Dodger saved you a plate."

Leroy couldn't believe his ears or his eyes. His mother was *smiling* at him.

He floated into the house on a cushion of air. All that dread he'd worked up . . . they hardly glanced up from the paper. As if he'd been in the backyard all this time, playing with his toes. Not so much as a "where have you been?"

Halfway down the hall it hit him. He touched down on the ground.

72

It was worse than any of the awful consequences he had imagined for himself.

The mirror was right.

Nobody had worried about him. At all.

They didn't care. He could have stayed gone all day and they wouldn't have noticed. They hadn't even begun to wonder how he managed to travel ten miles on his own.

But that couldn't be his mother out there, his own mother who never ever let him out of her sight—

Leroy turned.

They were all up out of their chairs, watching him through the window.

His mother was not smiling now.

Her smile had been his punishment. Her casual how do you do was an act. She had worked it out with the others to let Leroy think, for one terrible moment, that she cared that little for him.

It was worse than his crime. Leroy ran back through the house and threw himself across his granddaddy's bed.

9

*H*e carried forever the memory of the time his mother was cruel to him. He tucked it away and pricked himself with it whenever he got to feeling too safe.

He loved her so much his heart hurt. Sometimes he would lie in bed imagining she had died, wallowing in the grief he would feel. He had a dim notion that maybe when he grew up, he could figure out some way to keep her from dying.

He couldn't imagine living in the world without her. He might have to kill himself.

Life was sweet, but already he could sense the dark tragedy lurking behind all that sweetness—when people start dying out from under you, when the walls of your life begin to crumble away.

He knew he should tear himself loose from such awful speculations. His mother told him all the time how powerful your thoughts can be, how you send only good thoughts to the people you love—as if she could hear the motor running in his head.

But somehow Leroy's grudge and the thought of losing her got mixed up together. He began to imagine that Agnes would die, and it would be his fault because he'd been angry at her.

She never said a word about the Whispering Pines or asked him why he ran away, where he went. He never mentioned Brother Love or the new kind of singing he'd heard.

He kept planning to sneak out and hike to Mount Zion and hear some more of it, but the distance between here and there stretched out in his mind until it was endless long miles.

There was sadness and strange weather and no money, all that summer.

Leroy was catching on to the ways of grown-ups. They meant about half of what they said. They could say yes at the exact moment they were thinking no. They could smile and say, "Oh, Sister Wilson, what a pretty dress!" and then turn right around and make fun of her orthopedic shoes.

When grown-ups wouldn't look straight in your eye, they were lying. When they got tired of you and ordered you off to bed an hour early with a sermon about how it was for your own good, you knew they were lying.

And when Leroy's fifth-grade teacher, Mrs. Dempsey, called him over after morning assembly to say she'd never heard anyone sing "God Bless America" so sweetly, Leroy said, "Thank you ma'am," and went on his way thinking: Oh, she's lying.

Later that day, though, walking home with his mother, he realized there was no good reason Mrs. Dumpsey would have gone to the trouble to call him over, just to tell him a lie. She must have meant *some* of what she said. . . .

He flushed all over with pleasure. His mother felt his head to see if he was taking a fever.

The next morning Mrs. Dempsey lined everyone up on the basketball court for citizenship class and told Leroy to step out of line. "We're going to see Mr. Potts," she said, leading him down the line of kids to the hallway.

Leroy followed, burning with shame. The others stared as he went by, glad it was him and not them. Only the worst kids were taken to see Mr. Potts.

Leroy couldn't imagine what he had done wrong. Could she have heard him thinking her nickname out loud?

She told him to sit in a chair by the Pepsi machine. Through a half-open door he caught a glimpse of the teachers' lounge, where the prim ladies went to smoke cigarettes, drink Coca-Colas, and laugh. The air was blue with their smoke. As Leroy watched, Mrs. Moore, the third-grade teacher, hiked her skirt up her thighs and tugged at her garter.

A flash of white underpants—he averted his eyes.

Mr. Potts's door swung open.

"Come in, Leroy," said Mrs. Dempsey.

He arose in a daze. Just please not a whipping. A lecture would be bad enough, but if word spread through school that the infamous paddle had come down off Mr. Potts's wall, Leroy would be one of the doomed boys who had to huddle at the corner of the schoolyard, taking pretend drags off blades of grass and playing tough to hide the fact that none of the nice kids would have anything to do with them.

Mr. Potts sat with his feet on his desk, hands behind his head, skinny elbows sticking out to the sides like wings. He was long and thin, with a shiny bald head and shiny horn-rimmed glasses. Besides being the principal, Mr. Potts was the gym teacher; his fearsome reputation was cinched the day he yelled at Elmer Russell to quit throwing the dodgeball like a sissy, and Elmer threw it so hard it broke Emma Davis Foster's legbone right out through the skin.

Mr. Potts cleared his throat but kept his feet on the desk. "Miz Dempsey tells me she's found us a regular Gene Autry," he said.

Mrs. Dempsey came up behind him. "Leroy, I told Mr. Potts about your singing. He wants to hear you."

Leroy swallowed. He had no idea what she was talking about. Had he been singing in class without realizing it?

"Sing," said Mr. Potts.

"You mean, here?" Leroy had the feeling they were taking a long way around to humiliate him.

"I'm sorry, Mr. Potts," said Mrs. Dempsey. "I should have explained to the child before I brought him in. Leroy, our school has been asked to put up one student for the talent show out at the fair next month. I told Mr. Potts how nicely you sing, and if he agrees with me, you're going to represent the whole school." She beamed down at him. "Isn't that wonderful? Now, I want you to sing 'God Bless America,' just the way you did in assembly."

Leroy was first embarrassed, then relieved, and then a big goofy grin spread over his face. "You want me to sing at the fair?"

"Miz Dempsey, I got real work to do," said Mr. Potts.

"Okay, Leroy, here we go," she said, leading off in her own thin soprano: *"God . . . bless A-merica . . ."*

". . . land that I love." Softly Leroy picked up the verse. *"Stand beside her, and guide her . . ."*

Closing his eyes, he somehow sang his way through the first verse and into the second, and got louder going into the third, and sang straight to the end of the song. He had never sung it all the way through by himself. It was different singing by himself—lonelier, more exciting. Until the day he died he would wonder how he ever managed to remember all those words.

He sang with his eyes closed. He saw a blurry white light out in front of him, the place where the song was. He was looking inside himself, at his own burning light.

He opened his eyes to find Mr. Potts smiling, the teacher wriggling with pride. "Didn't I tell you, Mr. Potts?"

The principal swung his feet to the floor. "I tell you what. If he keeps his nose clean between now and then, you take him on out there. I think we might have a shot."

Leroy jumped up and down in his skin. Mr. Potts liked his singing! They wanted him to sing in front of people he'd never even seen! He wanted to grab the paddle and smash out the window and shout *Happy New Year!*

"Don't worry," Mrs. Dempsey was saying, "he's a good boy. Now sometimes he doesn't pay attention . . ."

"Oh, and get him another song," said Mr. Potts. "Get him a song that'll win us a prize."

"We will," Mrs. Dempsey said, bustling to the door. "Come on, Leroy, let's leave Mr. Potts alone now. Tell him thank you."

"Thank you," said Leroy.

"You bring us back a blue ribbon," said Mr. Potts.

Some of the teachers were craning around the door to see who that was singing. One or two clapped when Leroy came out.

He made a little bow.

They laughed. The door drifted shut. Leroy trailed his teacher down the hall. "I know a song I can sing," he said.

"Oh, I'm sure you'll do fine. Have your mother call me and I'll give her the details."

Leroy stopped. His mother couldn't call. Granddaddy wouldn't have allowed a telephone even if they could afford one.

"Listen . . ." Leroy hurried to catch up. "She comes to get me after school. Maybe you could tell her then."

Mrs. Dempsey said that would be fine. Leroy drifted on his own soaring spirits back to the gymnasium, where the others were staring at a big colored map of Mississippi. He passed among them to his seat, trying to swallow his grin. He felt a hush in the air as everyone tried to figure out why he looked so happy.

10

*L*eroy combed his hair for the fourth time. He did not want to start a conversation with the mirror, so he used the reflection in the glass of Granddaddy's clock. The brass pendulum swung back and forth. It was ten past eleven. The talent show would not begin until three-thirty. Between now and then, Leroy believed, he might die of waiting.

Granddaddy had gone off early to the fairgrounds to sell his chickens. Hardy and Irene went along to make sure he got a good price this year and didn't just give them away to his friends. They left the baby at Aunt

Inez's for the day. Leroy imagined it must be getting some good sleeping done over there since all it ever did in this house was cry, cry, cry.

Leroy had waited a long time before he let himself put on his costume. Now he was afraid to go outside or do anything. His mother had made him a peanut-butter-and-banana sandwich, but he was afraid to eat it; if he got peanut butter on his starched white shirt, it was all over. Agnes would never let him onstage.

He had borrowed a black cowboy hat and a leather holster belt from his uncle Johnny; to make them fit, he had pinned up the belt and stuffed paper in the hat. He looked rough, tough, and ready, a slicked-up gunslinger.

As Agnes left for work, she had warned him not to show up at the shirt factory before twelve o'clock. "I know how anxious you'll be," she'd said, "but Mrs. Crawley doesn't like children hanging around the doors."

Leroy wished he could push the clock's hands ahead and make time run as fast as it should.

Today was Wednesday, Children's Day at the Mississippi-Alabama Dairy Fair, the biggest event for ten counties around.

On Monday Leroy's daddy had set out for Lafayette County, trailing the rumor of a highway crew that needed extra hands. "Sorry to miss your big day, son," he said as he left. "You go knock 'em out."

Leroy kept picturing himself on a stage while his mother and a million other people listened to him sing. He had to find something to do while time dragged itself by. All this nothing was starting to make him sweat.

He wandered to Dodger's room. As always, no matter the weather, she was wrapped in her crocheted shawl, bent over her jigsaw puzzle. She had been at work on this particular scene since August: a forbidding foreign coastline, rugged mountains plunging into the sea. So far it stretched over most of two card tables. When it was finished, it would be as big as Dodger's bed.

There were gaps and ragged edges in the waves, the trees lining the top of the cliffs, the milky sky. The lighthouse on the promontory was missing its top—three or four pieces hiding somewhere in Dodger's careful groupings of white pieces and blue pieces and white-pieces-with-blue-edges. She'd probably been looking for those pieces for days.

80

"Hey, you finished the cliff," Leroy said. "That looks good."

Dodger straightened the shawl, studying the terrain near her elbow. "If you want to help, stay quiet and look for tree trunks."

Helping Dodger work her puzzle was supposed to be fun, but if you didn't keep still and pay attention every minute, she would run you out of the room. She vibrated impatience, watching Leroy. She used to be sweet, but not lately. She always complained she was cold. Although she couldn't have been more than fifty or sixty years old, she acted eighty.

Leroy noticed three odd-shaped whitish pieces at the edge of the ocean. They didn't quite fit where Dodger had placed them, but she had pressed down with her thumb to squeeze them in.

When she wasn't looking, Leroy plucked them out and dropped them into the spaces atop the lighthouse. They fit exactly.

Dodger's eyes traveled along the puzzle's borders, fixing on the spot where the pieces were missing. Then she saw the lighthouse.

"Hm." She took a little sip of her tea. "Where'd you find those?"

"On the floor," Leroy said, "under the edge of the rug." He knew his lie was useless, but he had to try it.

"I guess you win a prize," she said, sounding not at all pleased.

The word *prize* set off a chime inside Leroy. He pushed away from the table and ran up the hall to the clock. Nearly half past eleven—time to go!

He grabbed his hat and belt and cap pistols, stuffed the cowboy necktie in his pocket, ran down the hall, yelling, "Bye, Dodger!" and banged out of the house.

He ran almost to the road before he caught himself—slow down! Don't sweat up your shirt! Don't fall down and tear a big hole in your face!

Don't forget all the words to your song and stand there like an idiot until they have to drag you off the stage!

Oh, that would be worse than dying.

If that happened, Leroy could always sing "God Bless America." But there was no way it could happen. He knew the song so well *the things boys and dogs do* the words ran through his head *laid his head on my knee* until it seemed he might *alone with Old Blue* go crazy trying to think of anything else *I'll be happy in heaven one day.*

He'd practiced it loud, long, all over the place now for weeks, until everybody in the house was walking around singing it under their breath.

He set off along the tracks toward Mill Town. An infection of old tires and furniture and metal junk spread up both embankments.

Leroy never walked on a train track now without looking behind him every five steps or so. He took a deep breath and sprinted across the high trestle. Now he had to find his mother among all the people spilling from the Tupelo Garment Factory.

It was the biggest building in Tupelo: whitewashed sheet metal, five stories high, eyeless, unadorned. On most days the thunder of sewing machines poured from its open mouth, but now workers poured out instead, laughing and talking. The bosses had shut down the factory for half a shift so the workers could take their children to the fair.

Leroy spotted his mother with a group of ladies who had gathered under a mimosa tree to brush the lint from each other's dresses. She was the prettiest one of them—that reddish chestnut ponytail swinging, her big broken-open eyes like a kitten's. Leroy waded through a circle of younger kids on bikes (*everyone* had a bike except Leroy) and took off running for the tree.

When she saw him, her smile brightened out. "Look here, Dot, look at my boy," she said, waving her finger at him.

A little gnarled bird of a woman left off picking bits of thread from Agnes's dress and looked straight into Leroy's eyes. "Aren't you the pretty one," she said. "Hey there. I'm Dot. Miz Simmons. Remember me? I'm your mama's best friend."

Leroy thought: No, you're not, I am, but his mother was watching, so he smiled and said hello.

Agnes said, "Leroy, where is your tie?"

He pulled it from his pocket.

"Let me see it. I ironed that tie. Here, I'll keep it for you." She folded it away in her pocketbook.

The factory ladies beamed down.

"Oh he's adorable, Agnes," said one. "Make him put on his hat! How old is he?"

Leroy held the hat in his hand. "I'm ten," he said.

Dot Simmons said, "Darling isn't the word. Would you look at those eyes. Those are Valentino's eyes."

"Who's Valentino?" said Leroy. They laughed as if he'd made a joke.

"He was a movie star," his mother told him.

"A movie star with bedroom eyes," said the little woman. "I'm telling you, Agnes, give this child seven years, and he can have any woman in Tupelo."

The ladies erupted in giggles and embarrassed whoops.

Leroy liked all the attention, but his mother was turning red. "Dot! Hush! I'm not going to let him come down here, you talking that way."

"I'm sorry, Leroy," said Dot. "Don't pay any attention to me. I hear you're going to sing a song at the fair."

"Yes ma'am."

"We'll all be out there rooting for you," she said. "Agnes, y'all going ahead?"

"Yes we are, Miss Trash Mouth." Agnes hefted her purse. "Come on, Leroy, let's get away from these awful girls."

"Bye, Leroy," they called. He did a little bow. They laughed.

His mother said, "Come on and quit showing off."

They set off down Oak Street. The homes of the people who owned the shirt factory were set back on wide, tended lawns.

"Did you practice your song?" Agnes said.

"Yeah."

"Brush your teeth?"

"Yes ma'am," he said.

"You nervous?"

"Not really," said Leroy. "You don't think there'll be too many people?"

"I don't know." Agnes smiled. "They let the whole factory go. And it's Children's Day at the fair. I bet there's a crowd."

"That's okay," Leroy said, trying to ignore the watery sensation in his knees. "I don't know. Do you think maybe I ought to sing a different song, or something?"

"Why? That's a wonderful song. Anybody that doesn't like that song is crazy."

Leroy scuffed his toe. "I wish Daddy was gonna be there."

"Well he can't." She squeezed his arm. "You understand, don't you?"

"Yes ma'am."

"What's wrong with you? Cheer up! This is your big day! When you get up on that stage, just look straight at me and pretend all those people aren't there. Sing it like you did last night. You'll do fine. I'm going to be so proud of you."

Leroy felt the words and her touch as a kind of balm. She believed in him. As long as he kept his mind on the song and took the big chance, he could do it. He sounded good when he sang. Everybody said so. His mother said so.

They passed along the edge of downtown, through a poorer district of faded white houses. Scruffy dogs barked at everything. More people were in the streets now, converging in one direction.

There it was—over the trees! The fair! It came once a year, and each year it was better. The Ferris wheel lifted its rocking gondolas up to the sky. Pennants danced from the summits of tents. The air carried the smells of manure and fresh hay, cotton candy and corn dogs, the bellow of cows and loopy calliope music.

There was no way to get to the fair without picking a path through tents and tent lines and sudden dead ends, but the reward for all that trouble was a dazzling view. Streamers flapped in the breeze. The midway boulevard seemed to stretch forever from the spangly arch at the near end. Even at noon all the lights were turned on:

ROYAL   *   DIXIANA   *   SHOWS

The twinkling arch led the way to Amusement: the World's Smallest Man, the Indian Giant, the Zipper, the Twister, the Cyclone, the Dodgems, the Tilt-a-Whirl, the Guess Your Weight girl, the Test Your Strength man, shills, barkers, carnies and floozies, children and stuffed animals of all ages. The old standbys were there near the front: the carousel, the Ferris wheel. Little children craned up fearfully to see what they'd gotten themselves in line for. Hoboes poked in the trash for corn dogs. Screaming laughter cascaded down from the rides.

Leroy gripped his mother's hand, memorizing the sights all over again.

"The fair's bigger this year," Agnes said. "It's almost too much to take in."

"I want to ride."

"Wait till after you sing. If you ride now, you'll get sick to your stomach."

"Oh come on, Mama. Just one."

"No, I said." She steered him past the arch. "The midway will be here all day. You just come on along."

A sudden aroma from a snack wagon sent Leroy straying wide to the right. Cotton candy. He put on his most hopeful smile.

"And watch you get it all over yourself? No sir. I made you a sandwich. Didn't you eat it?"

Leroy shrugged. "I wasn't hungry then."

"Let's go back here." She headed for the first exhibit hall.

For the next hour Leroy wandered the vast sheds, a few steps behind his mother. The only exhibit Leroy wanted to see didn't come until the very end. Agnes stopped at every quilt display and persimmon jam demonstration and sweepstakes booth in the place. She picked up leaflets and booklets and handed them over to Leroy while she stopped to chat with Sister Wilson, to chuck Annie Selwin's new baby under the chin.

Leroy deposited the leaflets on the tables as he passed. He dawdled and waited and practiced his song in his head.

At last he spotted it, looming over all the exhibits at the far end of the last exhibit hall: the famous giant cow from the Seale-Lilly Dairy of Jackson.

"I'm going to the cow," he said, tearing off before Agnes could say a word.

This last hall was reserved for the giant cow and the truly boring exhibits: the power cooperative, the insurance companies, the washers and stoves, the permanent wave machines and automatic milkers and hay balers and pea shellers and backyard mink ranches. Every bit of fun in this building was concentrated in the cow.

It returned to Lee County every year to stand on its flatbed trailer and watch over everything with its painted white eye. It was huge and red, molded of shiny papier-mâché, with the words SEALE-LILLY branded on its side. Leroy was glad to see the top of its head still grazed the rafters; it had not shrunk too much this year.

Its keeper, a pretty blond-haired woman, stood at a table near the huge right front leg, handing out free samples of milk. There were not many takers. Leroy supposed that most everybody had tasted milk before, and nobody much wanted it at the fair. If she'd been giving away free Coca-Cola, they'd be lined out the door. Most people ignored her and gawked at the cow.

"Your job to milk that big cow, sweetie?" a rough-faced man called to her.

"No, sir," she said, with a grim smile.

The man haw-hawed and went on.

The milk lady was gazing into the middle distance when Leroy came up. She might have been twenty-five years old, or forty; blond hair was swept up on top of her head in a lacquered column, like the women in *Life* magazine. She didn't appear to be enjoying her job.

Leroy gazed up at the cow's shiny chest. "How big is that thing?"

"Thirty-five feet, including the trailer," she said.

He said, "That's big."

The woman touched her hair as if it were a bandage coming loose. She noticed Leroy's costume for the first time. "You want some milk?"

"Sure." He felt sorry for her.

She poured from a sweating chrome pitcher into a Dixie cup with a picture of the cow on the side and the legend MILK FROM THE WORLD'S LARGEST COW.

It was cold and foamy and tasted like all other milk.

"You're sure dressed up for the fair," she said.

"I'm in the talent show."

"Really? What's your talent? You a cowboy?"

"I'm a singer," said Leroy, and the realization that he was—that he would be, this afternoon—sent an electric prickle through his scalp.

"What time do you sing?" she said. "I'll try to come hear you."

"Three-thirty, I think."

"Okay. You sing good, now."

Leroy tried to return the paper cup; she said he could keep it. Just then his mother came up. "Mama, want some free milk?"

"No, thank you," Agnes said, with a distracted smile for the milk lady. "You-all aren't running a contest, are you?"

"No, ma'am."

Agnes led Leroy by the arm along the flank of the cow. "I've entered every contest in the place," she reported. "I've got one of my feelings. We're bound to win something. We're bound to. They're giving away a free trip to New Orleans. I hope we win that."

"Will you take me?"

"It said a trip for two. But maybe we could drive down, so we could all go. I've got a feeling we're going to win." Her face shone as if they'd already called out her winning number. "Maybe it means you're going to win the talent show."

His heart kicked at the idea. He hadn't let himself hope for such a thing. "I don't know, Mama. I'll try."

"I know you will. And that's all you can do."

A dim passageway led to the poultry barn, where long avenues of wire-mesh cages were occupied by cooing, clucking, feather-ruffling fancy birds of every kind. The really outrageous varieties—pigeons that looked like hamsters, roosters with way too much tail for their bodies— had an avenue all to themselves.

Leroy spotted his granddaddy perched on a chair, surrounded by his cages of plain white Dominicker chickens. He didn't seem to have sold a single one.

He held his hands up. "Whoa, watch out."

Leroy stopped short. "Did you sell any chickens?"

"They've gone and changed the damn rules on me."

"Afternoon, Mr. Jessie," said Agnes, with a squeeze for his shoulder. She took off her hat. "Where's Hardy and Irene?"

"Soon as we got here, she went to worrying about that young un, and nothin' would do till Hardy took her back to it."

"She worries too much," said Agnes. "What did you say about the rules?"

"That young Samples came over, the fair board, you know, while I'm settin' up my cages," said Jessie. "Says, 'Hey, good morning, Mr. Kirby, howdy howdy,' then he says the fair board passed a new rule this year. Not gonna be any selling of livestock at the fair. Just birds for show from now on. Birds for show. Twenty-eight years I been selling my chickens at this fair, and I told him about it, too. I sure did."

"That's too bad," Agnes said.

"You damn right it's too bad, scuse my language," he said, touching the brim of his hat. "Who does he think he is? I said, 'Edwin Samples, I remember the time you wet your britches on that merry-go-round, so don't go giving me your lip.'"

Agnes winced, and laughed.

Jessie was still angry. "I said, 'You don't want no eating chickens sold at your fair. What you want is these two-legged hats.'" He fanned his face with his hand.

Agnes looked down at her hat, and smiled.

Leroy's stomach turned over—an announcement from his nerves. "Mama, I think it's almost time."

"Mr. Jessie, come go with us and hear Leroy sing."

"Got to wait here till Hardy comes back with my truck. Unless you want me to carry these chickens back home."

"Aw, come on, Granddaddy," Leroy said, pulling at his elbow.

"Yes," Agnes said, "take your mind off things."

He shook his head. "I can't leave this spot. If folks can't buy these chickens, they're liable to steal 'em. Folks want a chicken they can *eat*."

Agnes said, "We'll see you back at the house."

"Hey, boy, come here." Jessie stuck out his hand. "Give a wink to the girlies in the crowd now. That's how you win. And good luck to you."

He patted Leroy's shoulder. Leroy took off after his mother. They came out of the barn into fresh air.

Agnes stooped down, buttoned his neck button, turned up his collar, unfolded his tie. "Stand still. I can't tie it with you squirming."

"It hurts. It's too tight."

"You're too big, is the problem." She moved behind him to fashion the knot. "I just bought you this shirt."

Leroy protested in a frog voice: "I can't sing if I'm choking to death!"

"You'll look nice anyway." She cinched the knot and turned him by the shoulders. "You've kept this shirt nice and clean. I'm proud of you."

He tugged at the collar.

"Don't you pop that button. . . ."

They passed through the distinctive airs of the Swine Barn, the Dairy Barn, and the Hooved Animals exhibit on their way to the arena where Leroy would sing. This was a great circle of cinders with a grassy infield, wooden bleachers set around a show ring for horses. On the far side was the covered grandstand, and standing before it, the stage.

The stands overflowed with people. The crowd spilled into the bleachers on both sides. There were more people standing along the fence.

There were hundreds and hundreds of people in the grandstand, more than Leroy would have imagined at the whole fair. He felt a completely new fear spreading down through him, freezing his blood. Sweat sprang out on his forehead in cold little beads.

"Oh, look," said his mother, "how sweet! The baby show."

Leroy put his hands in his pockets and stared. The stage teemed with babies.

Every baby in Lee County appeared to have been gussied up and brought to the fair for display, like the pickles and jellies and hogs. They were stitched and ironed in blue velveteen and white cotton and pink taffeta and hair bows and hair oil and shoe polish. Each one had a number pinned somewhere on his clothes. The crowd in the bleachers was made up of their families, beaming and waving and seeing only one child onstage.

In the first row five middle-aged women judges were making marks on notepads in their laps. Someone had put on a record of nursery music, and the babies were supposed to be dancing to that. They stumbled and tottered; some of them cried. Some grinned and waved at their mommies. The judges made notes.

Then the crying took hold and swept across the stage like wildfire. Even the children who were grinning stopped grinning and looked at the ones crying, to see if they were missing out on something.

The grown-ups onstage looked stricken.

The record stopped with a grinding scratch. A teacher-looking woman stepped to the microphone. "Ladies and gentlemen, I believe that's the end of our baby show. Please come claim your children. We'll have the judges' decisions in a moment."

"Did you see that number one-oh-five?" Agnes said. "Oh, she's a little doll. She's going to win."

"I don't know how you can tell one from the other," said Leroy.

Parents came down from the bleachers to retrieve the crying and confused contestants. The head judge walked to the microphone and began reciting a long list of winners. Each name brought cheers from this little pocket or that, but waves of disappointment passed through the crowd as the list grew longer and names were not called.

Then the grand prize announcement: "Congratulations to contestant number one-oh-five, Debbie Sue Bradley, our new Little Miss Tupelo. Debbie Sue is four years old, the daughter of Mr. and Mrs. Donald Bradley of Tupelo."

"Mama! One-oh-five!"

"I told you," said Agnes.

The thrilled parents brought their little champion back to the stage for a bouquet of flowers, a satin sash, a sparkly tiara. Everything fit her just right, which made Leroy suspicious. She accepted her honors with a twinkly, superior smile and a show-off curtsy.

"Isn't she pretty," said Agnes, as if she were looking at some rare flower.

"They just taught her a bunch of tricks," Leroy said. "Big deal."

"Why Leroy, she's precious. Listen at you. You make her sound like some kind of little monster."

"I bet she is."

"You're awful. She's lovely. She has beautiful hair, and you can bet her mama doesn't have to hold her down to get her to wash it."

Leroy said, "The ones who lost are just as good."

"Everybody can't win. You remember that."

The fray onstage smoothed out. Older students bustled around collecting rattles and pacifiers.

A group of men and women came into the first row of seats. These must be the talent show judges. They looked sterner and less easily impressed than the baby show judges.

Many of the babies' parents had settled in for the talent show, and now the talented kids were coming in with their families, along with people whose feet needed a rest from the midway.

Agnes touched Leroy's shoulder. "Be ready in case you have to go first."

"They can't make me do that," he said. But he slung the gun belt around his waist and fastened the buckle, just in case.

He was overwhelmed by the size of the arena, all those faces. He'd been here plenty of times, and this place had never seemed enormous before. How could he sing in broad daylight with everybody in Tupelo watching?

"Could I have your attention?" a voice boomed, accompanied by an electrical squeal that sent a wince through the grandstand. The terrible sound had come from a small, square woman in spectacles. She stepped back as if the microphone might electrocute her. She moved her lips, but no sound came out; then it came out howling and went silent again.

"Wait! Wait!" cried a man to one side of the stage. "They're fixing it."

The squared-off teacher folded her hands before her and smiled patiently, setting a good example. When she got a signal from the wing, she proceeded. "Good afternoon, ladies and gentlemen, boys and girls, I'm Bertie Claire. On behalf of the Lee County Board of Education, welcome to the thirteenth annual Dairy Fair talent show. This year's theme was supposed to be 'Peacetime Under the Stars,' but since the demolition derby was moved to this evening, we're holding our contest in the afternoon."

She went on through scattered laughter. "The judges will evaluate merit, appearance, comportment, and special appeal. There will be three prizes. Now we need our contestants in the roped-off area behind the stage. The show will begin in a moment. Thank you very much." She bowed and stepped off. A few people clapped.

"Leroy, it's time." His mother bent down. "I'll watch you from here. Just go back there and practice your song in your head. You'll do fine, sweetie. Mama's right here." She kissed him and shooed him away.

He joined up with a string of nervous-looking kids gathering behind a velvet rope. He picked a spot with a clear view of center stage.

Mrs. Claire announced that Pamela Foster would go first. A brown-haired girl to one side gave a shriek as if she'd been stabbed.

Doris Ann Mason would go second, Mrs. Claire said. A homely girl with braces shrank away to the rope, biting her lip.

Leroy felt better seeing the looks on their faces; they looked more foolish and trapped than he did.

He took a deep breath and stood back by himself, working up his confidence. He was on his own now. One boy and a microphone. He could make a mess of the thing, or he could go out there and sing his song. It was a good song. Anybody ought to like it.

Mrs. Claire read down the names. Leroy was almost sure they'd left him out when she said, "Leroy Kirby, fourteenth, and fifteenth and last will be Mary Lynn Bradley. Any questions?"

No one said a word.

Leroy considered: Next to last was a good place. Let everybody else get it over with first.

"If you go over four minutes, I'll have to stop you." Mrs. Claire rang a brass dinner bell. "Now. There's a mirror over here for you girls to check your hair. Good luck to you all."

Pamela Foster turned out to be a tap dancer, as did Doris Ann Mason and several others. The entire enrollment of Miss Irma's School of the Dance had been entered in the contest. Leroy saw Miss Irma with her skull-tight black hair and painted eyes, fussing over the girls' costumes. He hoped the dancers would cancel each other out and give him a chance.

He looked out at the crowd. He ran over the words to his song. He never really saw any of the other performers; they were doing things out at the sides of his eyes. He ignored them except when they made mistakes. Then little pulses of pleasure ran through him.

He had to avoid singing too loud, like a boy named Pigeon Stevens from Oxford who busted everyone's ears with the squeal from the microphone. Wanda Darnell of Taylor had precisely the opposite problem: Her song disappeared on its way from her lips to the mike; she seemed to be mouthing the words to a record someone had forgotten to put on.

Leroy spotted his mother in the fourth row, and the milk lady perched right down in front. He sneaked a look in the mirror. The necktie was about to strangle him. Now that he noticed, the tie with the sleek, oversize black hat made him look a little ridiculous, like a desperado dressed for Sunday school.

He undid the knot.

If he took the tie off altogether, Agnes would kill him. Instead, he looped it loosely around his neck and tied it at the side so the two ends hung down like a skinny bandanna.

He heard the mirror's silvery voice: Good luck. . . .

The waiting was almost over. The twelfth act, a little redheaded tap dancer, suffered the humiliation of Mrs. Claire's dinner bell. She quit tapping and slunk off in shame.

Lucky thirteen was a pimply fat boy from Pine Flat, a sixth grader named Rocky Paul. With surprising grace he crossed to the spinet piano and sat on the bench and put his hands on the keys. His shirt bulged open at the buttons. The fat on his arms shook as his hands moved over the keys, and his hands quaked. Leroy could see them.

But Rocky could play. The piece was a stormy-sounding thing that started off way high and diddled around all spooky, then ran down to the bottom for thunder and lightning and noise. Then came an easy middle part, and as Leroy watched, the shaking in Rocky's hands grew more and more violent. And then smack in the quietest, easiest part, the boy's fingers froze up forever.

He sat looking down at his hands in the silence.

Everyone knew the piece was not finished. Someone coughed. No one applauded. It would have been cruel to applaud.

Mrs. Claire went out to lead him off to the wing, whispering in his ear. With her free hand she waved Leroy toward the stage.

Leroy, it's time.

He took a long, slow breath and released it. He walked to the microphone. On the way he remembered to smile. He tried not to imagine what his mother must think of his necktie-bandanna.

The air was thin here, at the middle of the stage. Late-afternoon light streamed down in golden shafts, like spotlights.

There were other lights, too, in the eyes of hundreds of strangers. They had clapped for every performer except Rocky Paul, and even that was a kindness. Leroy hoped they could work up a little kindness for him.

He leaned to the mike and felt an electric tingle in his lips. "Hello, uhm, my name is Leroy Kirby, and I'm in Miss Dempsey's class at East Tupelo Consolidated School. I'm gonna sing a song for you. It's called 'Old Blue.' "

Leroy had learned the song by imagining Red Fairlie's guitar kicking it off in his head. Now he stretched up until he was almost kissing the microphone and conjured the first twanging notes.

> *When I was no more than a towheaded boy*
> *I found an old hound dog named Blue*

His voice sounded huge, vaulted out into space through a miracle of electricity, his own clear, high notes bouncing back at him from the upper reaches of the grandstand.

> *We played in the fields and we swam in the streams*
> *We did the things boys and dogs do*
> *If ever a lad had a friend in the world*
> *Let me tell you, son, I had Old Blue*

The song fooled the audience. People smiled at first; they thought they knew a corny old song when they heard it. But as the story went on, and Leroy sang it as purely as he knew how, he saw their faces changing. He could feel every one of them wanting him to do it right. No one wants you to freeze up and stare at your hands! You take all the good wishes people are sending with their eyes, turn them around, send them back. Make them glad to hear you. Sing as if you want to be heard.

By the time he had sent poor Old Blue off to heaven to wait for Joe, Leroy saw real tears in the eyes of the Seale-Lilly milk lady, in the first row.

But I know I'll be happy in heaven one day
When I have Old Blue by my side

The end brought a big rolling drum of applause. To Leroy it sounded bigger than all the other applause put together. He bowed from the waist, bowed again, and ran off the stage. Mrs. Claire was smiling and clapping. "What a beautiful song!" she cried.

He wandered down the steps, flushed with pleasure, in a daze from the light as he'd seen it, hovering there, just in front of his eyes. It was a light from inside. It came on when he sang, and just now, when he sang for that big friendly crowd, it glittered and flashed. He wanted more of it. He felt hungry and satisfied, both.

He went to look in the mirror, to see if he looked any different. His eyes were bright. He was breathing too hard. His Stetson was on crooked.

He wanted to get right back up there and sing another song, "God Bless America," anything, something. Just feel more of that affection, rolling down in big waves.

He knew he had won.

And why not? He got the most applause. No one could argue with that. He *had* to have won.

He took a moment to glance over at the final contestant, Mary Lynn Bradley, age six, of Tupelo.

Bradley. Mary Lynn Bradley.

The little girl who won the baby show had the same glossy ringlets of hair, and her name was . . . Debbie Sue Bradley. This must be her sister

Mary Lynn twirling a baton, singing "Sentimental Journey," and tap dancing, all at the same time.

Leroy moved closer to watch.

Mary Lynn pirouetted around, never missing a word of her song in that big, brassy six-year-old voice. She touched a match to the ends of the baton and began twirling a circle of fire. She finished "Sentimental Journey" and started in on "God Bless America"—that was Leroy's song!—still, he had to admit she was really stomping and clackety-clacking and twirling those flames and shaking her glossy blond curls. He felt a sick change in his stomach.

She tossed the baton way up in a looping arc, spun around like an ice-skating acrobat, and caught the thing behind her back without igniting her hair. People stood in the aisles and cheered.

Just that fast—as fast as he'd won—Leroy knew he had lost.

Mary Lynn stayed to enjoy her ovation. Even Leroy was clapping by the time she came off. She ran by without turning her nose, straight into the arms of her beaming mother and father, Mr. and Mrs. Donald Bradley.

She was good. She thought she was better, probably, than she was. She brought down the house, as her parents had trained her to do.

The judges had no choice. They gave her first prize. Leroy won second—a red ribbon, a five-dollar bill, free admission to any ride on the midway for the whole night, and another sweet round of applause.

Rocky Paul came in third, an obvious sympathy choice, but he grinned and bowed as if he didn't realize that, and waved his dollar bill over his head, and got the biggest hand of anybody. His eyes were red.

Agnes squeezed through the crowd, crying, "Leroy!" and grabbed him, and hugged him against her. "You were wonderful. Wonderful! You scoundrel, give me that tie!"

The shirt factory ladies oohed and ahhed and said he should have won.

Mrs. Dempsey hugged him, too, brimming over with praise. "I know Mr. Potts is going to be just as proud as if you'd won first," she declared.

The milk lady flew up to wrap her arms around Leroy. "Oh, you made me cry!" she said. "Look, you've ruined my makeup! That was wonderful, child!"

Leroy just grinned and said, "Thank you." He was no longer hearing what anyone was saying; the surge of joy had washed him into a new world. Second place was just as good as first, when you knew you were better. When you had your first taste of the rare air at the center of the stage. It was better than singing in church—everyone watching him, liking him, paying attention to him.

His mother led him through the throng heading in for the demolition derby. Just as they came to the Royal Dixiana sign, the loudspeaker said, "Agnes Kirby, please come to the Main Exhibit Hall and claim your prize. Agnes Kirby."

Her hands flew to her face. "Oh, I won!"

"Mama!" Leroy jumped up and down. "Come on, let's go see!"

They hurried past all those unfortunate people whose names had not just been called on the loudspeaker.

They had to ask in five different places before they found the man holding Agnes's entry form in his hand. "Congratulations!" he said. "We drew your name."

Agnes clasped her hands together. "Oh, what did I win?"

"The Royal Princess bassinet," said the beaming man.

Her face changed. "The what?"

"The Royal Princess bassinet," he said. "It's Monkey Ward's deluxe model. You entered the baby show contest, didn't you?" He held up the slip with her name.

"I guess I did," Agnes said. A shadow came into her eyes. She turned away.

"Take this paper down to Ward's," the man said. "They'll deliver it right out to you."

"Thank you so much," Agnes said. "Leroy, stop looking at me and come on. Thank you, mister."

Leroy trailed her to the midway.

"Maybe we can sell it to somebody, or something," she said, stuffing the paper into her purse.

"But you won, Satnin, you sure did. You said you'd win something, and you did."

"I tell you what, sweetie," she said. "I'm worn out. I'll go home and tell everybody how good you sang. You made me so proud today. You stay here and ride your rides as long as you want."

"You mean it? Really?" Leroy couldn't believe it. "By myself?"

"Now, but you be careful. . . ."

Leroy spent that night spinning through space, upside down, whirled around, through a million rides. He rode every ride fifteen times. He spun out his brains. He didn't go home until they turned off the Tilt-a-Whirl. He was ten years old, and he had found something he knew how to do.

11

$\mathcal{T}$hat day at the fair was
the best moment the Kirbys ever had in Tupelo, and Ray missed it
because he was off chasing a highway crew that turned out not to exist.
He came home dog-tired and disgusted and found Agnes all in a stir
about Leroy's singing. "He's a natural-born singer," she said before she
offered him the first bite to eat. "It's one of those childhood prodigy
things, like Shirley Temple."

"What was Shirley Temple when she started, about three years old?"
Ray said with an indulgent smile. "Leroy is nearly eleven. He's over the
hill."

"Dot Simmons says Judy Garland makes a million dollars a picture, and she wasn't even born talented. It's true. Her mother took her to Hollywood and made her a star. We've got to do something like that for Leroy."

"Oh, that's great," Ray said. "Hollywood. Is there anything to eat in this house?"

"I'm telling you he should have won first place, and he would have, too, if those Bradley people hadn't fixed it with the judges."

"Where is he anyway?"

"In the barn, playing," she said.

"He's always off playing by himself."

"I know. . . . The other boys all have bicycles, and I don't have the heart to make him play with them."

"It's not good for him, Agnes. He spends too much time alone. I don't know why you fuss over him so much. He's liable to get more peculiar than he already is."

"Oh Ray, he's not peculiar. He's special. I've always told you how special he is. You should have heard him. There wasn't a dry eye in the place. Everybody's been talking about it. Do you know it went out over WELO? Inez heard it in the beauty shop. Amelia Self stopped me on the street."

Ray was grinning. "Of course he did good. He's got natural talent from his daddy's side of the family."

"Oh Ray, can't you see I'm serious?"

"Honey . . ." He kicked off his shoes. "Tell you what. You and Dot quit your jobs and take Leroy out to Hollywood to be a movie star. I'll stay here and eat my supper. How's that?"

"Your stomach is the only thing you care about," she said.

Ray turned suddenly weary, and older. "It kind of drowns out everything else, Agnes. I been eating tuna fish from a can for five days."

Agnes started to work up some sharp reply to that, but she saw how downtrodden he was and put her arm around his neck instead. "Poor Ray, I'm sorry," she said. "Why would that foreman send you out all that way and leave you high and dry?"

"I'm just lucky I guess," he said, and then, in a matter-of-fact voice: "I'll tell you something. I started not to come back."

Agnes stared at him. "What did you say?"

He stretched his arms. His elbows popped. "I was sitting at this gas station in Sardis, waiting for somebody to drive in so I could bum fifty cents to get enough gas to come home. And I thought: Boy, where in the miserable world are you headed? Back to tell her you've screwed up again? That's when it occurred to me, you know, that road goes in two directions."

"Oh, sweetie . . ." She tightened her hold on him. "Aren't you glad to be home?"

"It's not my home, it's Daddy's," he said, staring at his fingernails. "I can't keep us in a house of our own."

"Why does that eat at you so?" said Agnes. "You don't hear me complaining. Something will open up soon. Miz Crawley says they'll be needing new men on the loading dock after the first of the year."

"Well that's cash in my pocket right there, ain't it?" There was a new bitter note in his voice.

Agnes left off hugging him and moved away to the counter. "You're just hungry, that's all." She picked up a knife and sliced the crown off a tomato. "I've got some nice bacon from breakfast. I'll make you a sandwich. You just put up your feet and relax."

"Let's face it, Agnes. I'm no good for you." His eyes were dead calm. "Nothing's gone right for us. You'd have been better off marrying just about anybody else."

"You're right about that," she said, rattling in the mayonnaise jar with a knife. "Don't think I haven't thought about it. I could have married Eddie Spencer or Walter Andrews, and I'd be living in a fancy house with a colored maid." She cut the sandwich on the slant—as she would cut it for Leroy—and set it down before Ray. "Here. Eat this."

He took a long pull from his glass of beer and ate the sandwich in four bites. "Why didn't you?" he said, chewing. "Marry one of them, I mean."

"You know why," said Agnes. "We did what we had to do. Now we just got to live with it."

"You make it sound pretty grim."

"I'll tell you something, you want to talk about grim. If you ever run off and leave me like that"—she shook her finger—"I'll come after you, and I'll find you, and I'll make you sorry you ever were born."

Ray rolled his eyes. "I heard *that*."

100

A little smile came to her face. "Besides, honey, I love you, and that's something I have never been able to help."

He got up from his chair, still smacking pieces of bacon between his teeth, and put his arms around her. They stood like that, feeling the lines and curves of each other's body.

"You say he's outside?"

"In the barn," Agnes whispered. "He stays there for hours. I wonder sometimes what he does. I think he needs something to do."

"You don't think he'll come in?"

She shook her head. He kissed her.

"Mm, bacon," she said.

Ray went to hook the screen doors, just in case. "Where's the rest of 'em?"

"They went to the picture show," Agnes said.

He grinned. "I hope it's a double feature."

She reached around for her zipper. "Welcome home, Ray."

"Hell, it's good to be home," he said, laughing, diving for her.

12

*W*hat are they doing in there? Leroy wondered. It must be some fun, to judge from the way his mother was giggling, but it must hurt some, too, since every so often she let out a shriek that seemed real, and his daddy growled, and the two of them sounded like two dogs fighting.

The longer he listened, the more it seemed like fun they were having. His mother's laughter held an unmistakable note of delight.

On his own Leroy had picked up enough information to realize that something important was happening, and he was not supposed to be listening under the window.

When he was four years old, he had cornered his cousin Daisy in a stairwell and made her pull down her underpants and show him what was down there. Daisy obeyed, but there wasn't much to see—a little pink fold of skin like a smile, right where her thing was supposed to be.

For the longest time Leroy couldn't connect that and the way his mother looked when she undressed for her bath. It just wasn't the same. He puzzled it out. His daddy was hairy there, too. Maybe the hair comes in when a person gets taller.

He found out more from the Triplett boys, who had the run of their house on Dolores Street since their father worked all the time and their mother was dead. The Tripletts smelled funny, and they kept trying to get Leroy to do things he didn't want to do, like steal money from his mother's pocketbook. Still, he couldn't deny the strange thrill he got hearing them talk about dirty stuff.

The way they explained it, the man puts his thing inside the woman. Leroy couldn't quite figure out how—through the front or the back?—or whether the man pees the baby up in there or what, or why anyone would go to so much trouble. He was sure the Tripletts would make fun of him if he asked, so the image stayed fuzzy in his mind.

One afternoon Willis Triplett brought a little colored girl named Sally to the house on Dolores Street while Leroy was there. Willis announced that he'd promised Sally a box of chocolate-covered raisins if she would let the boys do it to her, and she had agreed. Of course, she didn't have any idea what they were going to do; neither did Leroy or the other boys who stood around the Tripletts' basement, scuffing their feet and checking out each other's reactions.

Willis Triplett said he figured somebody else ought to go first since he'd been the one to talk her into it.

Sally said she didn't see any candy; where was it?

Willis told her to get on out of there, then, and quit wasting their time. She stuck out her tongue and ran home.

When Leroy thought about this at night in his bed, he was amazed to find his thing standing up hard, like when he had to pee in the morning. It hurt in a funny way that wasn't so bad once he got used to it. As soon as his mind wandered off, though, it shrank down again.

Now, crouched among Dodger's blue hydrangeas under the window, he felt the swelling and decided it must be a powerful feeling, the way his mama was carrying on. She moaned and sighed.

103

Leroy looked around for some way to get an eye over that windowsill and see for himself. It drove him crazy. Everyone else seemed to know all about it.

He spotted an upended concrete block under the porch steps and went to drag it through the sand. The noise from inside would have drowned out a herd of dogs barking. "Ow!" she cried. "Ow! Ow!"

Leroy stood the block on one end, eased himself up.

Sunlight fell through the highest panes, falling in one broad stripe across the bed, his father's bare behind bouncing up and down, his mother's leg splayed to one side—where was her other leg?—they were stuck to each other, mounted to each other, locked together, rolling—

He straightened for a better look. The block toppled out from under him. He fell in slow motion to the dirt.

He scrambled away, across the yard to the barn, the shame of it burning a hole in front of his eyes.

A whole string of disconnected notions slid together in his mind. When a husband and wife make a baby, they lie down and make animal noises and bump against each other. Somehow this was hooked in with the thrill and the funny hardness in Leroy's pants, the teacher who showed him a flash of white underpants, Cousin Daisy, certain things the Triplett boys had said about girls. . . .

It made him ashamed. A lot of people must do it or there wouldn't be babies. Still, it made him ashamed of them. He had imagined something soft and sweet, like a nice ticklish backrub—never a sweating naked spectacle like that! If that's what they do, Leroy thought, if that's what *I'm* supposed to do—well then, they can keep it. Who needs babies? They cry and pee their pants, and they don't know a thing.

He huddled under the cedar bush, rubbing a branch between his fingers for the smell.

He could run in and tell them to Stop!

But he'd seen his father hook the screen door. That was what had brought him out of the barn and snooping under the window in the first place.

He crept across the yard, through the large open door, up the frail ladder to the hayloft.

His hiding place was concealed in the darkest corner of the loft, behind a jumble of cardboard cartons. Leroy moved the biggest box to the right, stepped into the secret entrance, and slid the box back in place. That was his last point of contact with the outside world.

He switched on the light bulb.

The forty-watt shine revealed every inch of his domain: X-Man and Space Man and Superman comic books, his red second-place ribbon from the fair, Aunt Irene's cast-off issues of *Confidential,* full of brassiere advertisements, and the Big Chief tablet containing Leroy's drawings and doodles and secret lists.

He drew the outlines of imaginary islands he planned to own one day. He sketched elaborate mansions with big trucks colliding in front of them. He made posters for his future singing engagements, complete with fancy borders and words he borrowed from the *Memphis Commercial Appeal.*

The One
The Only
The Astounding
L E R O Y K I R B Y
Sings The Songs You Love To Hear!!!
Live!
And In Person!
Two Shows Nitely!

He picked up his pencil, licked the tip, wrote his name on a clean sheet.

Leroy

That looked all right. But what about

* * * l e r o y * * *

Better still. He wrote his name fifteen times in different styles—some with big, blocky letters, some spider-thin.

His mind flashed to that stripe of light falling through the window, the rising white flesh. . . . He sketched the line of their bodies, the way his father's hip joined with her—

105

Oh. His own mother. He saw her. It made him excited. That was a terrible thing, but there it was. He wadded the paper and threw it in the corner.

He filled a whole blank white page with one word:

LEROY!

Through the walls of the barn came the screak of the back door, his mother's clear voice in the late afternoon: "Leroy? Come on in now, it's almost suppertime."

13

For Christmas that year Leroy got a note: "Dear Leroy, A little short this time, but soon I promise, the bicycle. Be a good boy Love Santa Clause."

His eleventh birthday slid by with a cake and a candle, no presents. He waited and waited for a baby to come, but his mother didn't get any bigger.

He sang all the time. He went to school and church and to the gangster pictures with his uncles Johnny and Hardy, who had convinced his mother he was old enough.

In the dark, blinking up at the screen, Leroy dreamed about having more money than anyone else in the world. He'd buy his mama a fur coat, like the slinky woman in the movie. For his daddy, a long, shiny black Cadillac. And one for himself. He was ashamed of his parents for being poor. He pretended his life was one big mistake. The truth was he had been born to glamorous wealthy people like the ones in the movies, and somehow he'd been switched with Ray and Agnes's baby at birth.

It was his duty to be as cheerful as he could until his real parents came to rescue him.

He munched popcorn so fast the little dribs went down his shirt. Johnny poked him and said, "Watch out for this guy, now, he's trouble," then Hardy shouted, "Get him! get him!" and the man in the double-breasted suit went down in a rainstorm of bullets.

The whole audience groaned, except Leroy. He was looking at the dead man's sharp clothes. If he were a movie star, he'd get to wear clothes like that—new creases, high collars, glossy shoes, crisp bullet hole in the breast pocket. Even dead, that man looked good.

After Leroy's big day at the fair his mother had loosened her grip just a little. She still walked him back and forth every day to school, but one Saturday morning she let him go to the Paramount Theater all by himself for the kiddie matinee.

He sat in the second row. A whole string of cartoons whizzed by, then the program changed to old-fashioned pictures, the kind with no talking. A man sat down at a piano in front of the screen and played music to go with the action.

First came a short movie about policemen who rode around on a truck and knocked each other in the head with nightsticks. Then the piano man swelled at his keyboard and thundered a grand-sounding theme.

Paramount Pictures Presents
"THE SHEIK"

—based upon the novel by—
Miss E. M. Hull

Leroy's eyes jumped when he saw the next title.

Starring
RUDOLPH VALENTINO
with
Agnes Ayres

He scrunched down in his seat. This was going to be good. Dot Simmons, that friend of his mother's—she said Leroy had Valentino's eyes.

The movie started out dull, the story of a prissy English lady who had somehow wound up alone in the desert. When the kids in the audience realized it wasn't funny, they started talking and running up the aisles and pelting each other with popcorn.

Then Valentino appeared, striding about in a tent with a carpeted floor. The camera moved in for its first good look, and sure enough, Valentino's eyes were magic—hot black jewel stones in his beautiful, fine-boned face.

He appeared to be nearsighted or staring at something far away. He wore makeup to bring out the dramatic curve of his eye bones.

Bedroom eyes, that's what she'd called them. Leroy wanted eyes like those, eyes people would talk about. He supposed you could learn that by practicing—looking straight into the middle of yourself in a mirror.

No one else was paying attention to the movie, but Leroy sat riveted. The sheik kidnapped the girl and kissed her in his tent. Leroy imagined how they would look doing that bent-backed thing, rolling around naked on the plush satin pillows.

After a lengthy interval during which the girl was terrified, they fell in love. Late in the story Valentino revealed he was not a sheik at all, but the Earl of Glengarryl in disguise. They kissed. The end.

But it wasn't the end. The movie left an unfinished spell. Leroy brooded about it all the next week. He was haunted by the way Valentino seemed to be watching him from the screen. He practiced his bedroom eyes in the mirror.

He went back to the Paramount the next Saturday and sat through the newsreel, the same endless cartoons.

The pianist sat down and started to play. The feature was *Tarzan and the City of Gold*. Valentino was nowhere around. Leroy went to the lobby and cornered the popcorn girl, but she didn't know anything.

Agnes said there weren't any more dimes for the picture show, didn't he know they were poor?

Yes, he knew.

One afternoon Ray drove in the yard honking his horn, a big, wide smile on his face. "Honey, I got a job," he hollered.

Agnes threw out her hands, ran down the steps, pulled him out of the car to hug him. Leroy came around and hugged him, too, but already he was thinking: What kind of job?

"Oh that's wonderful!" Agnes cried. "What kind of job?"

"Selling candy."

"Candy! Oh boy!" Leroy danced off across the yard and came back. Now there was a job you could brag about at school!

"Door to door?" Agnes was trying hard for her smile.

"No listen, it's better than that," he said, "it's a real job, I promise. I'm a route man, salary plus commission"—Agnes brightened at this—"with a new company out of Nashville. The R. R. Parker Company. They make Plink Planks and Howdy Hos and Sweet Tooth candy bars."

"I never heard of any of those," Leroy said.

"No, son, but you will. They're going to take over the candy business. And I'm getting in on the ground floor. We'll have some after supper, what say?" Ray lifted him and started to swing him around, but then he realized it would throw out his back. He set him down and patted his shoulder. "There you go, sport. Run play and let your mama and me talk."

Leroy scuffed out of the room. Grown-ups never wanted you around as long as you wanted to stay.

As soon as the supper dishes were done, Ray opened his brown candy satchel and passed out samples all around. Everyone commented on how nice the wrappers looked. Ray told them to go ahead and unwrap the candy and eat it.

Leroy tried the Plink Plank first. It was hard in the middle and sticky on the outside, with red jelly that squirted out both ends. It tasted like cherry cough syrup.

The Howdy Hos looked more promising; in fact, they looked like M & M's. But instead of chocolate on the inside, there was a lemon-flavored goo that puckered Leroy's mouth into a knot.

110

After the first bite no one else ate any. Dodger folded the wrapper back over the end of her Plink Plank.

Leroy unwrapped the last one, the Sweet Tooth bar.

It was caramel with some peanuts and gummy stuff, not a Snickers exactly, but sort of. "This one's not so bad," he said, "the Sweet Tooth."

"Oh, they're awful," said Agnes, staring at the wrapper in her hand. The red jelly of a Plink Plank had squirted all over her skirt. "Ray, who are these people? Did you taste this mess?"

"What's wrong, honey?" His eyes widened in alarm. "You know I don't care for candy...."

"Ah-oh." Hardy crumpled his wrapper and made a quick exit.

Agnes said, "How on earth could you take a job with these people unless you tasted it first?"

"Look, I've got orders from all over the place. The man gave me a week's salary in advance. Eighteen dollars. Look here." He unfolded his wallet and held it out.

"Ray. Honey. I love you," said Agnes. "I always will. I don't know who placed those orders, but I guarantee they hadn't had a bite of *this*."

Ray folded his wallet and stuck it away. "Okay, Agnes, I heard you," he said. "I got a paying job, that's all. I guess I expected a little congratulations."

"It's got nothing to do with you, sweetheart." She shook her head. "You couldn't sell this candy to a starving man. This is terrible, honey. I mean, it's bad." She waved the Plink Plank wrapper and dabbed at her skirt with a napkin, and laughed in spite of herself.

Ray laughed, too, just enough to start Leroy snickering, and they all broke out—even Granddaddy, even Aunt Irene, who'd hung around to witness a fight. They laughed until they were silly with tears.

On Monday morning Ray set out with his sample bag. He found every merchant in Lee County in a rage against him. Dozens of customers had demanded their money back. Two people claimed they had been poisoned. Clothing had been stained, teeth chipped. The grocers swore and waved candy wrappers in Ray's face.

He gave back all the money he'd collected. He apologized until his guts hurt. He told everyone it was a bad batch, the problem was being worked out at the factory, he'd get back in touch real soon.

The R. R. Parker man had checked out of the hotel where Ray met him. From the lobby Ray placed a trunk call to Nashville, but the company's telephone had been disconnected.

"At least you didn't lose any money," Agnes said when he got home that night. "You got a little embarrassed, but you can get over that."

"That's what you think," Ray said with a sick look. "I gave that man a hundred-dollar deposit on the candy."

"You—you *what?* I thought he paid *you!* Where on earth did you get that kind of money?"

"I borrowed it from Daddy," Ray said. "I tell you, honey, I don't think there ever was an R. R. Parker Company. Just that one man with a truckload of bad candy. He probably goes around pulling one over on suckers like me, at a hundred dollars a whack."

"You said it," said Agnes, "not me."

When old Jessie discovered his savings were gone and not coming back, he pitched a remarkable fit. He gave Ray one week to find a new place.

On the first day of March they moved to a white clapboard house on North Green Street. "I swear, this is the last chance for Tupelo," Ray said at the threshold. "If this doesn't work out . . ."

"Hush. Don't say that. You'll jinx it," said Agnes. "This is nice."

Leroy ran down the hall to look for mirrors. He found three, including a fine round one in the blue-painted room they said would be his. "It sounds so empty in here," he called, admiring the bounce of his voice.

"It'll sound different once we bring in our things," said his mother.

She was right. They moved in as if they were home, at last and forever. Someone had planted daffodils in the yard; Agnes said every one that opened was a gift from a stranger. She stayed late at work to run up curtains for the windows. Ray painted the porch. Leroy pulled weeds and cleaned out the woodshed.

The birds came out singing one morning, an April Friday, a beautiful day. Feathered clouds drifted through the sky.

Staring out the window during arithmetic, Leroy noticed the clouds moving faster.

By the time the last bell rang, and he stepped outside, the schoolyard was bathed in warm yellow light. The air had an odd radiance; every particle of dust seemed to shimmer.

A wall of ominous clouds was building to the west, shot through with

112

lightning veins. A roll of dry thunder. Dogs barked from here to the far side of town.

The kids took off running for home or the line of yellow buses behind the school.

Leroy waited for a flash and then counted: one one thousand, two one thousand. . . . If he didn't piddle around, he could make it home without getting rained on. He set off running down a red clay embankment, across the old county road.

He made his way through patches of bamboo, a meadow of black-berry thorns, the yard of creepy Mr. Brewster with his painted-over windows and boarded-up doors. The clouds piled up deep blue and wicked. The air was too still.

He reached the end of North Green Street just as the air began to move. Leaves skidded over the pavement. A cold splash of rain struck his cheek. He was out of breath, but he didn't slow down. He came around the house to find his mother chasing laundry all over the yard. Bed sheets tumbled across the grass. Ray's shirts danced on eddies of air as if ghosts were wearing them.

"Oh Leroy, help me, it's all blowing away!"

"I—I ran—all the way," he panted, snatching up socks and under-wear, chasing her nightgown into the Templetons' rosebushes.

"Look, that's Doll's embroidered pillowcase! Grab it!"

A minor whirlwind seized the thing and brought it within Leroy's reach. "Mama, we got to—go in the house!"

The wind blew a hard gust. Raindrops zipped by sideways.

Then came a sound from the lowest end of the register, down below the shudder of thunder—a hiss like radio static coming from one side of the sky and from everywhere, at once. The hissing was punctuated by sharp reports, snapping.

That was the sound of houses and trees being smashed to bits.

They abandoned the laundry. They ran in two directions.

"No, not the house, it's not safe!" Agnes cried. "Come on, run!"

Leroy ran after her down the street, through the Purvises' yard, up a slope, and into the woods. His heart hammered in his chest. The sky darkened and seemed to lower itself. A rain smell came in.

The hiss grew to a roar, like a train, like a runaway train heading straight for them.

Agnes ran through the briars to an opening in the earth—a mouth in the brow of the hill. She ran to it as if she had been born knowing where it was. It was just big enough to squeeze through on hands and knees.

Inside was a dark little cave, snaky and full of cobwebs, too dark to see.

"You all right?" Agnes whispered.

Leroy clenched his teeth and said, "Nn-hh," which meant yes.

She folded him in her arms.

Just outside the hole now a dull golden light, a whorl of fine dust, the crash of trees being snatched up by the roots and blasted to splinters.

"We're going to sing, now come on," Agnes commanded, and started the song off herself: *Ah-amaaazing Grace.*

Leroy heard something huge metal banging and crashing by the cave, but he opened his mouth and sang.

> *How sweet the sound*
> *That saved a wretch like me. . . .*

The wind reached such a pitch that it drowned out the song, but they kept singing.

Leroy's ears popped. A pouf! of dust burst in the mouth of the cave. The light outside turned green. Something large and dark seemed to be passing over.

'Twas blind, but now I see. . . . The world shook itself for a moment, uncoiled and flexed and rearranged itself, and then the clamor of the orchestra died *to sing God's praise,* and the darkness passed by.

They stopped singing. The wind moved away, a living creature—hesitating, turning to listen, resuming its progress.

"We're all right, we're all right," Agnes whispered, as a prayer.

Leroy clung to her. "Is—is it coming back?"

"I don't know. We'll stay here. We're safe here."

"Mama, I'm scared. . . ."

"Let's sing some more. Oh God, what can we sing. Let's sing 'Dixie.'" She started and Leroy joined in and the wind did not come back for them. The song kept them safe in the dark.

After a while the sound of usual wind resumed. Rain pattered down. Leroy recovered enough of his nerve to want to go out for a look.

Agnes said funnel clouds travel in packs, and he'd better not so much as stick his head out of that hole until she gave the word.

"Oh Lord, I hope your daddy's okay," she said, and then: "We need to take our mind off it. Let's talk about the fair. Tell me what it was like, standing up there in front of all of those folks. I could never do that in this world. . . ."

In the months since the fair Leroy and Agnes had relived it dozens of times—never too many for Leroy. He had been a hero for days at school, after Mrs. Dempsey had him perform "Old Blue" at assembly and nearly every kid applauded. His aunts and uncles had started asking him to sing at family gatherings. Sister Wilson had invited him to join the church choir. He said he had too much homework, but the truth was the Priceville choir seemed a pale thing to do, now that he was going to be a famous movie star like Valentino or Errol Flynn.

Leroy liked singing all by himself, with people watching. There was no bigger thrill. It was sweeter than the sweetest cake you ever tasted, having people look at you, approve you, tilt their heads, and smile at the sound of you. He wanted some more of it.

"I don't think I've ever seen a crowd pay attention to anybody that way," his mother said in the dark. "You just went up there and opened your mouth and sang it. You didn't mess around."

"They clapped a long time," Leroy said, "didn't they? It sure seemed like they did."

"They did. I bet they clapped a whole minute."

"Well, maybe half a minute, anyway."

Outside the wind blew, and the rain, but a thunderstorm had never sounded so mild.

Agnes relaxed her grip on him. "Sweetie, you know how bad it made your daddy and me feel when we couldn't do anything for Christmas, or your birthday. You know how bad we want to get you things. Now if everything we own hadn't blown away, I've been thinking we may be able to get you a little something."

"Oh, boy!" Leroy breathed a quick word of thanks to the tornado for this turn of events. "Oh that's *great,* Satnin, I been wanting that bike for so long! Can I get the red one? They got it at Mr. Bobo's hardware—"

"Wait a minute, honey, hold on," she said. "I looked at the bicycles.

The one you want costs sixty-three dollars. Do you know how much money that is?"

"Yes, ma'am." Leroy had only just gotten the bicycle, and here she was taking it away.

"That's three months' rent," she said. "That's just too much."

"But Mama, you promised. Everybody's got a bike. I'm the only one—"

"Just wait, and listen to me. I was down at Mr. Bobo's for those dish towels, and while I was standing there trying to decide, I looked up, and did you know he's got three or four different guitars up on his wall? Have you ever seen those?"

"No," Leroy said in a huff. It was always no, you can't have that, we're too poor, why don't you have this instead since it's cheap? "I don't want a guitar," he said.

"How do you know you don't? Think about it a minute. If you had a guitar, you could learn songs and practice your singing. I'd love to set out on the porch in the evening and listen to you."

"I tried playing Uncle Johnny's," said Leroy. "It hurts my fingers."

"Well honey, you don't just pick up a guitar and start in to play. You got to practice anything like that before you can do it."

Leroy flicked a crawly thing off his neck. "I don't care," he said. "I don't want it."

"We'll go down there and look at them and you'll change your mind."

Leroy said, "The only thing I want is a bicycle and if I can't have that I don't want nothing."

"Don't you give me your smart lip, young man," Agnes said, and even in a cave, hiding from tornadoes, that commanding tone made him wary. "You just said how much fun it was, singing in front of those folks. If you had a guitar, you could play and sing both. Now come on."

Leroy stopped pouting long enough to consider. Jimmie Rodgers had a guitar, and it didn't hurt him any. The same with Roy Acuff and, of course, Red Fairlie.

A guitar would give him something to do with his hands while he sang. He'd spent plenty of time strumming a stick and pretending. "I don't know," he said, "I guess maybe we could *look* at one."

When the rain slackened, Leroy begged to stick his head out for a peek.

"Oh, I don't know," Agnes said. "Maybe you're right. Your daddy'll be worried to death. You sit here. Let me go first." She crawled out, called him after.

Leroy wriggled through the hole. The woods outside looked the same as before, only darker.

"I could have sworn . . . maybe it just passed over," said Agnes. "Well, praise the Lord anyway, it's broken the drought. Let's go home."

They picked their way down the hill. Leroy felt vaguely sheepish about his big churning terror. Then he reached the end of the path and the Purvises' yard and saw what the wind had done.

The Purvises' house was a clean-swept foundation. Some fragments were strewn about, but most of the house had simply blown off somewhere else. The Purvises were gathered in the yard beside the slab. Roland, the boy from Leroy's class, was trying to console his mother.

The house next to the Purvises' was gone, and the house beyond that. The next three were missing their roofs. All the other houses on that street were gone.

A siren howled on the highway. Leroy followed his mother around the corner, to North Green Street.

Agnes said, "Oh, Lord, thank you, sir."

The front porch had been stripped from the white clapboard house, but otherwise it was safe. The funnel had picked up its tail and skipped every house on North Green before smashing down again on Holcomb Street, at the end of the block.

Ray screeched up in his delivery truck. He cried, "Jesus H. Christ!" and went to help dig people out.

Leroy and his mother gathered blankets and made cheese sandwiches and coffee, which they carried to the mute families standing in their yards.

Eight neighbors slept over at the Kirbys' that night. Agnes fixed a pot of bean soup. Everyone sat around remembering the moment the sky turned green. Everyone said how thankful they were that nobody died, and only twelve people were hurt—mostly Negroes from Shakerag, which of course was regrettable, but it could have been a lot worse. . . .

Leroy curled up in a blanket at the corner of the dining-room floor, drifting to sleep through their talk. He didn't want to dream about the tornado. He decided to think about something good, so his mind would switch to a nice dream as soon as he was asleep.

He pictured a guitar, a shiny guitar with bright strings and a real leather strap. He was strumming away, and the chords sounded sweet. People stood up and cheered for him.

14

Agnes told everyone
the tornado skipped over North Green Street because she and Leroy
were singing "Amazing Grace" when it struck. She felt guilty every
time she walked by those poor ruined houses.

The neighbors fanned out through the woods, picking up pieces. The
neighborhood rang with hammers and saws.

Agnes baked marshmallow brownies to carry to the displaced people.
On Monday she told Leroy she had too much to do to run down to Mr.
Bobo's store *this minute* to look at guitars. She said this again on Tues-
day, Wednesday, and Thursday.

On Friday she surrendered.

They walked past the Purvises' place on the way. The framing timbers of a new house were already up; Roland balanced next to his daddy, hammering on a roof beam.

"Hey, Roland," called Leroy.

Roland peered down. "Hey."

"You folks are coming right along there," said Agnes.

"Yes ma'am, we're trying." Mr. Purvis wiped sweat from his face. "The missus sure appreciated the brownies."

"Hey Roland, guess what," Leroy said. "I'm getting a guitar for my birthday."

"Leroy, you hush! We'll see you-all later." Agnes marched him down the street. "The idea! Them up there putting their house back together, and you down here bragging about your birthday present."

"I wasn't bragging," he said.

"You were. Sometimes you have no respect for other people's feelings."

"Good grief, Mama, all I did was tell him about it," Leroy protested. "Anyway, it's not like I'm getting a bicycle or something."

"If you don't hush you may not get anything."

He hushed.

The Tupelo Hardware was doing great business. Three men loaded lumber and boxes of shingles out the front door. Agnes ducked to avoid being knocked in the head with a board. "Let's come back when they can wait on us," she said.

"Aw come on." Leroy tugged her arm. "You *promised*."

"Yes, I know I did." Clutching her purse, she stepped around the tailgate of a pickup and into the store.

Mr. Bobo was ringing up nails and windowpanes and plaster and shingles at a lightning pace. His boys dashed around, calling out prices and carrying sheets of plywood.

Leroy turned a corner and found himself eye to eye with the object of his adoration: the red-lacquered, chrome-fendered, headlighted twenty-two-inch Murray Flyer.

The bike had lines like an airplane, a rocket, a future machine. It was so red Leroy could taste it. He ran his hand down the spokes. He inspected the colorful witch's hair dangling from the handgrips.

His mother came up behind him. "It's pretty," she said, "but you might as well not torture yourself."

"Oh, Mama . . ."

"Don't 'oh, Mama' me. I am not going to stand here and have this conversation again in front of all these people."

Just then Leroy spotted three guitars hanging from hooks above the sewing notions. The guitars didn't sparkle or gleam, and they wouldn't take him to ride the streets of Tupelo, but he liked how they looked hanging there. He stepped closer.

The guitar on the left sported some pearly-looking stuff on the neck. The one in the middle had an inlaid wreath around the sound hole. The third guitar was made of plain wood the color of peanut butter.

"Mr. Bobo, when you get a chance," Agnes said.

"George, come ring up these folks, would you?" The paunchy silver-haired storekeeper ambled down the counter. "Hey there, sonny boy, Miz Kirby, how can we help y'all today?"

"Those guitars there," she said, "how much do they cost?"

"You lookin' to play a little music, Miz Kirby?" he said, winking.

"It's for Leroy."

"Aha, I see," said Mr. Bobo. "Well in that case, we might cut you a deal. Now this baby here, this is the Jimmie Rodgers Custom, she'll run you eighteen and seventy-five. The one in the middle is the Classic String, and that's thirteen and seventy-five. The plain one, I forget what they call it, the name's on it somewhere. Eight seventy-five."

"I want the Jimmie Rodgers one," Leroy said.

Agnes touched a string. "What's the difference between 'em, Mr. Bobo? I never played one myself."

"Me neither, but don't waste your money. One sounds as good as the next. The only difference is where they make it look fancy or not. You want to see this one?"

"If we could," Agnes said.

He lifted the plain guitar off its nail and laid it in Leroy's hands.

Leroy cradled it on his knee, slipped the strap over his shoulder. It was bigger than it seemed on the wall. "What are all these knobs for?"

"That's where you tune it."

Under the silver pins the words *Sound Star* were inscribed in a fancy script.

Leroy Kirby, Sound Star.

The guitar was cool to the touch. It rested down on his hip. His cupped hand fit into the curve in its side.

He raked his fingernails over the strings. A sound came out that had nothing to do with music.

"Is it supposed to hang that low on him?" his mother asked, as if Leroy were trying on clothes.

"You can adjust the strap," the storekeeper assured her.

"If we got it today, would you let us have it on time?"

"Satnin, can't we just *look* at the other one?"

"How 'bout a dollar a week till it's paid," said Mr. Bobo. "George'll ring you up."

"We sure thank you. Leroy, thank the man."

"Thanks ..."

"You go practice that thing, sonny boy," said Mr. Bobo. "Maybe you'll get famous."

Didn't he know? Leroy was already famous. The whole world knew about the boy with the killer guitar.

He wore it to the front of the store, waving the neck in the air.

"Don't break it until I pay for it," Agnes called.

He went out to the sidewalk. The guitar felt just right, slung low on his leg. He pointed it like a tommy gun and mowed down ten strangers in the street.

Uncle Johnny showed him how to hold the pick.

Leroy strummed. The guitar made a sound like a bunch of wires flopped against a hatbox.

Johnny took it away from him. "You been playing with the tuning pins? These strings are loose as a goose."

"When they're tight it hurts my fingers," said Leroy.

"Your fingers have just gotta hurt if you want it to sound like anything. Here, give me your hand. See these whelps? You're too tender. Look at mine. If you play enough, you'll get these calluses. You won't feel a thing."

"You promise?"

"Sure." Johnny twisted the pin, adding tension to the string. They sat on his shady front porch with Johnny's guitar-playing accessories arranged on the rail at his elbow: a sweating bottle of Pabst Blue Ribbon, a pack of Camel Kings and his army Zippo, a pie plate to catch his ashes.

Johnny was Agnes's bachelor brother, a long, soft-spoken man with a cowlick that stood up from his crew cut like a feather. He kept to himself in his house up the hill from old Jessie. Johnny didn't have much need for anything but his truck and his beer and his guitar; he'd never paid much attention to Leroy until he came over that afternoon with the Sound Star.

"Give me the E string off mine," he said, nodding to his Gibson.

Leroy picked it up gingerly. Johnny's guitar was a fine instrument, wildly expensive, with a pearly neck and an inlaid wreath, both. The finish was scratched away under the sound hole where his pick had come down all those times.

"Which one is the E string?"

"The big one on top," Johnny said.

Leroy thumbed it. A clear, round note came out.

Johnny turned the knob. "Again."

Leroy plucked and kept plucking until Johnny found a note in Leroy's guitar that seemed to match.

"Now the A."

They went through the strings one by one. The notes weren't arranged in any reasonable order: E, then A, then D, then G, then B, then E again; Leroy became confused.

"Don't worry about it right now," said his uncle with a comfortable smile. "Let's play a song." He parked his lit cigarette between the E and A strings of his Gibson. "You know this one?" he said, leading off a sweet, plaintive melody from out of the hills.

The fingers of his left hand pressed the frets so that the blood went out of the fingernails. The pick was an extension of his other hand; it seemed to choose among the strings by instinct. The song twined around itself, winding up through some delicate miracle in the place where it started.

"That's pretty," said Leroy. "What's it called?"

" 'Wildwood Flower.' " Johnny took a drag of his smoke.

"I'll never be able to play like that."

"You got to keep after it," he said. "Want me to show you some chords?"

For an hour Johnny strummed over Leroy's shoulder and pried his fingers into the right positions. He taught him three chords, had him practice them fifty million times, then showed how they fit together into a song: "Can the Circle Be Unbroken."

Leroy had to stop while he figured out where to put his fingers for each chord. By the fourth time through the song he was managing most of the changes and even half singing along.

Johnny slapped his shoulder and said, "Thataboy!"

"I don't know." Leroy frowned. "It sure is a lot to remember." His fingertips felt as if he'd been rubbing them on sandpaper.

"After a while you'll get where you don't have to think," Johnny said. "If you take those chords and mix 'em up, you can play a whole lot of songs. Like this one." Bracing his knee on the chair, he whanged at the strings and broke out in a shout: *Weeeeell, Lawdy Lawdy Lawdy, Miss Clawdy . . .*

Leroy grinned. The chords sure sounded dirty when Johnny played them that way. His voice was as cracked and calloused as his hands. He banged out the time on the box and sang about how he'd given Clawdy all his money, and still she stayed out all night with other men. Nothing left for a man to do but hit the road, bye-bye, baby.

He flailed away at the last chord and broke out in a grin. "Now don't go telling your mama I sang you that song," he said.

Leroy shook his head. "That's wild. Where'd you hear that?"

"In a colored joint up in Memphis. You know me and Travis are headed up there for good."

"Mama told me."

Johnny stretched his arms. "I'm just about done with this town." He sat up in his chair, peered off down the hill.

Leroy followed his gaze. He spotted Ray and another man walking up the rise toward Johnny's house.

Johnny said, "I believe that's Lether Gable."

"Who?"

"Never mind, just hang on to your billfold."

"Howdy, Johnny," Ray called.

Johnny kept his seat. "Hey, Ray."

Lether Gable was a runty bowlegged man with glittery eyes, a silver belt buckle, and pointed cowboy boots. He sauntered up like the bad guy in a western. "Well, afternoon there, Johnny Smith!" he exclaimed. "How's it hanging?"

"I ain't seen you in a long time, Lether. I thought they ran your ass out of here."

Lether smiled as if he'd just heard his praises sung. "They tried, my friend, they tried. But you can't keep a good man down."

Ray pretended he didn't see Leroy there. "Listen, Johnny, we need to ask you a favor," he said.

"Oh, no, you don't."

"Me and Lether want to get in on a little card game down in Verona. I don't need to borrow a dime. Just the keys to your truck, for two or three hours. That's all. You can use the Plymouth."

"Ray, I thought you had a job."

"Just the keys. Three hours. I swear."

Leroy spoke up. "Daddy, I want to go with you."

"Sorry, son, this game's for grown folks."

"This your boy?" Lether grinned. "Looks just like you, Ray. Skinny as hell. How old are you, boy?"

He reached out to ruffle Leroy's hair. Leroy ducked.

Ray said, "Come on, Johnny. . . ."

Johnny fished in his pants for the keys. "If you wreck it, I'll kill you," he said.

"Don't worry." Ray snatched the key ring and backed away. "Y'all keep playing. We heard you down there. It sounds good."

Lether Gable followed him to the truck. They roared off in a cloud of blue smoke.

Leroy said, "Johnny, who was that man?"

"Nobody." Johnny picked up his guitar. He strummed one chord and stopped. "Don't tell your mama," he said.

〰️

Ray came back sober that evening, without Lether Gable. Johnny glanced in the bed of the truck and asked how they'd managed to pick up so much straw and mud at a poker game.

Ray said, "Sorry, boss. I gave those old Russell boys a ride home, and you know what a hell of a mess they are."

Leroy listened from inside Johnny's house, where he was supposed to be peeing.

"Leroy's in yonder," said Johnny. "We been playing awhile. He's a quick study."

"That's good."

Leroy loved to hear people talking about him.

"I was wondering, though," his uncle went on. "He don't seem to hang around any boys his own age, you know? 'Member when I was his age, our place was always crawling with kids."

"That's how Agnes wants it," Ray said. "She's particular about him."

"Yeah, but what do you think?" Johnny said. "He's so tight with her—you not afraid he'll turn out sissy, or something?"

"Ever since she lost the one, she's always been particular about Leroy," said Ray.

Leroy came out of hiding. "Hey, Daddy."

"Hey what?"

"Johnny taught me three songs. Wanna hear?"

"Naw, son, I got a headache right now. Run play for your mama. Tell her I'll be along directly." He took a swig from a Pabst. "Well, go on, what you looking at?"

"Nothing." Leroy grabbed his guitar and took off. "See you later, Johnny."

He ran home. He knew Ray would have wound up in some kind of trouble if Johnny hadn't been there, but he managed to keep his mouth shut about it.

He mulled over what Johnny said. It was true that Leroy didn't have many friends. But did that mean he would turn out like poor Bucky Bryant, who had to wear a dress around the house because his mama had always wanted a girl?

Mama's boy. Leroy was always accusing himself.

He loved his mama better than anybody. What was *wrong* with that?

The next week Johnny and Travis packed the pickup truck and took off for Memphis.

Ray jingled silver in his pockets. He bought Agnes a new print housedress, the first store-bought dress she'd had since Leroy was a baby.

Leroy played his guitar. He switched off the rest of his life. All that summer, unless he was walking around, sleeping, eating, or listening to the new radio—another surprise from Ray—Leroy was strumming a chord, bending an ear down to listen, crooning along—soft, so no one could hear. The minor chords sounded low-down, or eerie, or blue. The major chords all had a ring of hope.

He slung the guitar on his shoulder and carried it everywhere. Before long it had authentic scratches and pick marks of its own. He busted the D string and had to get by on five strings until he'd saved up to replace it. He played himself to sleep, night after night, stretched on his bed with the Sound Star on his stomach.

His fingers toughened up. He still had to keep his mind four beats ahead of his fingers, so he'd be ready for the next chord change. Then one morning he was staring off into nowhere, strumming "Carry Me Back to the Mountains," when he looked down to discover his left hand finding the chords on its own.

Old Jessie startled them all at the Sunday dinner table with the news that Mr. Kittrell, one of his Saturday-night drinking buddies, had offered him a job as second foreman on a federal dam project in Tunica County.

Everyone laughed and kept eating.

Jessie put down his fork. "Why do you laugh?"

"Oh come on, Daddy," Ray said, "you're too old to go off and do that kind of work."

"I'm not as old as you think," said Jessie, who never allowed anyone to celebrate his birthday. "How old do you think I am?"

"Sixty-five," Ray said.

"Wrong again. I'm fifty-two. I was born eighteen and ninety-six."

"Oh go on, you were not," Ray said. "Why, you're—you got to be ten years older than Mama, anyway. Isn't he, Mama."

"Ask him," Dodger said.

"I'm three years younger than her," Jessie said. "I can't help it if I look old. Maybe you-all made me look old. Maybe," he went on, his voice tightening, "maybe I'd have told you how old I was, if you'd ever asked me. Seems to me a lot of things get took for granted around here."

"Listen, Daddy—"

"By the way," he said, "I taken that job. I'm leaving as soon as I'm done with dinner."

"You're—what?" Agnes said. "Mr. Jessie. What in the world?"

Dodger looked up from her plate. "Well he may be going off somewhere, but I just started a new puzzle."

Dodger and Granddaddy went back to eating and said nothing more about it. Everyone else looked amazed.

After dessert Dodger carried the dishes to the kitchen. Jessie disappeared into his room, came out with his leather satchel, told them good-bye, and drove off in his truck.

In a month a letter arrived with a money order for forty dollars. The job was going fine, he said. The dam would take two years to build. Dodger was welcome to join him when she finished her puzzle.

She worked on one scene of the Black Forest all that autumn and straight through Christmas. Leroy suspected she was taking out sections she'd already put in, to make it last longer.

Once she realized Jessie was really gone, though, Dodger came out of her room. She swept the yard, went to church, walked over to North Green Street in the afternoons to cook up a pot of Brunswick stew for when Ray and Leroy and Agnes got home. She was more like Leroy remembered her from long ago, before she disappeared into her shawl. He missed Granddaddy, but he was glad to have Dodger back.

He was thirteen now, an important seventh grader, walking past puny old East Tupelo Consolidated on his way to Milam Junior High, where the water fountains and desks and urinals were all grown-up-size. He thought of himself as a loner, like Tom Mix. He stayed away from most people, especially girls. Girls giggled and acted superior and got better marks because the teachers liked them.

He kept a furtive eye on the pretty ones, though, especially on Mary Edna Meecham, a walnut-haired eighth grader with a dazzling smile and breasts that seemed to grow a little larger every day. When he finally whipped up the nerve to say hey to her in the hall, she turned up her nose and walked by.

Leroy's best friend that year was a redheaded boy named Jackie Bolton, who came up the first week of school and said he'd heard Leroy sing at the fair. Jackie knew a lot about music. His older brother was Tupelo's own famous country and western singer, Tupelo Joe Bolton, star of the "Hillbilly Radio Jamboree" Saturday mornings on WELO. Tupelo Joe sang through his nose, but he was popular. He had a smooth radio presence, and he twanged his guitar in a way that was lively and sad.

Leroy started tagging along on Saturdays to watch Tupelo Joe do his show. The WELO studio was tucked into Mobile Alley just across from the house where the Kirbys had lived the year before; Leroy had spent hours on that stoop gazing at the call letters on the plain brick building, but he'd never worked up the nerve to go in.

Inside was smaller but more wonderful than he had imagined. The air smelled purified. Every sound was deadened by carpets on the floors and walls. The rooms were jammed with black machines, dials, turntables, lights, microphones wrapped in gauze, cords, toppling stacks of phonograph records.

Leroy stood in a corner and watched everything with wide eyes. When the red light bulb flashed on, that meant, stand still don't breathe every whisper of sound in this room is going out over the airwaves to the people of the world.

Tupelo Joe sat on a folding chair, wailing and picking. He dedicated each of his songs to a former girlfriend; in all the times Leroy saw him do the show, he never mentioned the same girl twice. "I'm sending this one out to sweet little blond-headed Bessie Hamer in Butler, Alabama," he'd say. "Bessie honey, I miss you, and I'm coming back to see you just as soon as I can." Then he'd swing into "Wabash Cannon Ball" or "Mule Skinner Blues" or "In the Pines" or Leroy's particular favorite, "The Wreck of the Old 97."

Between songs Joe would pick up an index card from the stack on the table and read an advertisement for one of his sponsors: Ida's Pawn & Loan, Buddy Broad's Sinclair Station, Laufer Mortuary Chapel, the Tupelo Frosty Freeze.

In real life he was plain Joe Bolton, a skinny crew cut boy from East Tupelo, reading words from an index card. But the microphone worked magic for him. On the radio he became Tupelo Joe, folksy, handsome, and charming—a star!

This was a lesson to Leroy. *You can be somebody else.*

His father came into his room, way deep in the night. He shook Leroy awake and then stood with his mouth open, as if the news were too hard to say.

He lowered himself to a chair. He was still handsome, though every one of his failures had etched another line in his face. Leroy couldn't hate him now, not with those bruised eyes and his Adam's apple bobbing.

"We leaving right now?" Leroy said.

"Got to."

"Don't worry, Daddy. We'll be all right."

"Thank you, sport." Ray moved to the door, rubbing his arms. "It's chilly out. Don't pack your warm jacket."

"Honey," Agnes called, "can you find room for that box of quart jars? I just bought 'em, and you know how much those things cost."

"We'll see," said Ray. "It's pretty tight already."

"Leroy, take Doll's quilts off my bed and spread 'em out on the front seat. Then help your daddy. I know I ought to leave these dishes in the sink, but I just can't do it."

Leroy helped his father load the car in the dark. The trunk of the battered old Plymouth swallowed box after box, but when it was full, the pile still took up half the front hall. "We'll have to tie the rest on top," Ray said.

With fifty feet of white rope, they got everything on without waking up the neighbors.

Agnes came through the house, snapping off lights. When she caught her first glimpse of the car, she put her hands to her mouth. "My Lord. We look like Okies."

The Plymouth resembled an overloaded produce truck, with boxes and lamps and chairs and Leroy's pine baby cradle instead of tomato crates strapped to the top and sides.

Ray said, "You better take one last good look around in there."

"I did," she said. "That's everything."

"Well then." Ray pressed his hands together. "Let's get the hell out of here."

Everyone squeezed in through the driver's door. Leroy found a niche for the Sound Star in back, among his mother's winter clothes.

Ray started the engine. Agnes turned to poke in the backseat.

"Come on, you guys," said Leroy, between them. "Where are we going?"

"You'll find out when we get there," his father said.

Their headlights swung across houses and fences. There was no land-lord waiting at the end of the driveway. Of course, it wasn't every middle of the night they had to pack all their things and move to a new house, but this wasn't the first time either.

"Your mama's quitting her job and I'm done with mine," Ray said. "That man didn't like me, and I didn't like him."

"But I thought—"

"We'll explain later," said Agnes.

They glided down Holcomb Street. The new frame houses slum-bered. The only signs of the tornado were pine trees snapped off ten feet above the ground.

Ray turned onto the road out of town. He tested the pedal with his foot to see how much acceleration it would give him under this heavy load—enough to keep going, but not much more.

"We'll come back and visit," said Ray. "It's not like we're leaving forever."

Leroy had never heard his father sound so gentle.

"They won't have us back here," Agnes said. "Running off this way, not telling a soul—what will Dodger say?"

"We'll call her. We'll come back for her."

"Mrs. Crawley is gonna be fit to be tied. And oh, Dot . . . I didn't say good-bye to a soul."

"Better that way," Ray said. "A fresh start."

"Well I don't feel the least bit fresh," Agnes said, ending the con-versation.

They passed the Old Saltillo Road, which led up the hill to the house where Leroy was born. They flashed by so fast it might have been any street in the world. The streetlights had all been shot out, but Leroy filled in what his eyes couldn't see: the railroad tracks; the grassy bank where he had chased his mother; his granddaddy's house; the pecan orchard marching away down the hill. The land sloped from East Tupelo down to the tracks, then up again to Main Street, the courthouse, the empty-faced stores.

Already there were lights at the back of the Frosty Freeze, where they'd be making coffee for the six o'clock shift change at the shirt factory.

Every street triggered some story or memory, but Leroy was thinking, Where are we going? How far before we're there?

He'd never been any farther than Oxford, where he'd gone once to help his daddy pick up a truckload of green tomatoes. Life outside Tupelo was a dream.

He took a hard look at Milam Junior High sliding by. In a couple of hours the kids would wander into homeroom, the teacher would call down the roll, and when she reached "Kirby . . . Leroy Kirby?" no one would say, "Here."

Ray turned onto a road that dead-ended at U.S. Highway 78. He shifted out of gear and set the foot brake.

Straight ahead was a hint of the sun behind the horizon, waiting to rise.

Ray said, "Agnes, honey, I would say now is the time for one of your lucky guesses. Now this road ends up in two places. We can turn right and go to Birmingham. There's coal mines down there, and the steel mills, and jobs. I talked to a man who lives down there. He says there's good money."

"I don't know a soul," Agnes said.

"Or else we can turn left and go to Memphis. I know what it's like. It's hard to find a job and a place we can afford to stay."

"Johnny's up there," said Agnes. "And Travis. Maybe we could stay with them till we get on our feet."

"You know they ain't rolling in dough."

Leroy spoke up. "I think we ought to go to Memphis," he said, "since Johnny's up there."

"I reckon that settles it then." Ray flipped on the blinker and turned left on the highway.

They passed the blank side of the Welcome to Tupelo sign. "Don't look back," Ray said, "no telling what you'll turn into."

The sun punched a hole in the clouds.

Leroy hung his head out the window. Memphis! It sounded electric. The big time. The river a mile wide and wider. A whole lot of people going somewhere fast.

15

*T*he Plymouth trundled north and west, through miles of kudzu and cotton fields. As the sun rose, the land stretched out and began to lose its shadows and hills. The roadside was vivid with golden ragweed.

They passed through Belden and Sherman and Blue Springs and Enterprise, towns in the doldrums of morning. After a stop for doughnuts in New Albany, they crossed the iron bridge of the Hatchie River. Ray suggested they sing a song to get their juices going. Agnes said he was welcome to go right ahead.

He started in on "Zip-A-Dee-Doo-Dah" in his lusty out-of-tune voice. Leroy joined in. They were just into the chorus when Ray glanced in the outside mirror and said, "Oh shit, looka here," and pulled to the side of the road.

"What is it, Daddy?" Leroy couldn't see anything for all the stuff tied on the trunk.

Ray closed his eyes. His face scrunched up as if all his teeth hurt. "It's a God damned policeman."

"Honey?" Agnes reached across Leroy to touch his arm. "You were probably going too fast, that's all. Just be nice to him."

"Look, if anything happens," Ray said in a rush, "you get hold of Johnny. He'll come down and take care of everything."

"Ray, what is the matter with you? You're about to come out of your skin!"

His face flushed. He opened the door, set his feet on the ground. "Just remember what I said." He stood up. "Morning, Officer."

"Morning," came a voice, not unpleasant. "Mind stepping back here a minute?"

Their conversation dwindled away behind the car. Craning out, Leroy saw the hood of a white sedan with a red light on top.

"Come away from that window," said Agnes.

"You think Daddy's going to jail?"

"Don't be ridiculous."

But he knew by the way she snapped at him that she didn't think it was ridiculous. She sat looking straight ahead, as if that would take care of everything.

The car bounced on its springs. Ray stuck his head in the window. "Honey, this nice officer spotted some of our stuff about to fall off," he said. "He's helping me tie it back on."

Relief sweetened the air.

"Can I get out and watch?" Leroy said.

"You sit there," Agnes said. "You'll get in the way."

They listened to the shoving and readjusting in back. After a time Ray reappeared with a plump young policeman, who fingered his cap and leaned down to the window.

"Howdy, ma'am," he said, "I's tellin' your husband here, saw y'all coming along under all this stuff and I noticed one of your lamp cords out draggin' the ground—just a-spittin' up sparks on the pavement, wonder it didn't start a fire."

"It was thoughtful of you to tell us," said Agnes.

"Well, me and your husband here, I think we pretty well got it straightened out now. It's all in the way you balance your load, like I's tellin' him."

Ray grinned and nodded. He pumped the policeman's hand, backing around the car. "We can't thank you enough," he said, getting in.

The cop was still talking as they pulled away. "You-all take care now, and be sure to . . ." His last words were lost.

Within a hundred yards they passed a sign that announced the town of Myrtle. "They sure love to talk here in Myrtle," Ray said, checking the mirror. "Nope. He's going the other way. Bye-bye." He tooted his horn.

Agnes said nothing. Leroy wondered if her blue mood was returning.

Overhead, a great flight of blackbirds headed south in a single stream that undulated for miles. A lumber truck roared by at a wind-whipping speed. "That old boy better look out," said Ray. "If that cop don't throw him in jail, he'll talk him to death." He grinned and looked to see why Agnes wasn't grinning. "Honey, what's wrong."

"You lied to me, that's what," she said.

His foot touched the brake. "What the hell is that supposed to mean?"

"Let's see, what was it?" she said. "If anything happened, I was supposed to call Johnny and let him take care of it. Ray, you thought that man was going to arrest you back there, now don't lie to me."

"Oh, good gravy," he said, "is that all?"

"When he let you go, you looked so relieved I thought you were going to kiss him. Now you tell me what you did."

"I—I was sure he'd give us some kind of ticket. I couldn't have paid it, could you? He'd put us in jail." His laugh sounded shrill.

Agnes folded her arms and stared out the window. "You might as well just stop the car."

"I ain't stopping the car," Ray said, speeding up, his voice rising a note. "I'll turn around and go back to Tupelo and settle the whole thing, if you want. But I ain't stopping the car."

"Settle what whole thing?" said Agnes.

"Do you want to know?" Ray's eyes switched from the road to her face. They barreled through Potts Camp at fifty miles an hour; Leroy feared for their lives.

His father was shouting, "Shut up a minute! Just shut up!"

"And give you time to come up with some other fast story? No thank you."

The tires shrilled around a curve. "Daddy, slow down," Leroy cried.

"Don't tell me how to drive," he said.

". . . try to get us killed," Agnes cried, "not enough you come up with some wild story about how we got to leave 'cause you lost your job and somebody's coming to take the car."

"Well it's true," Ray said. "Every word of it. And if we hadn't got out of Tupelo when we did, we'd be in some real trouble now, Miss Know-It-All." Ray glanced at the speedometer. His eyes widened. He eased off the gas. "What the hell," he said. "Look. Lester Tines has been wanting me gone for six months. I been doing extra work on the side."

"What kind of work?" Agnes closed her eyes as if she didn't want to know, now that she had asked.

"A little livestock deal," he said. "Me and Lether."

She took a breath. "Go on."

"Lether heard this fellow bragging on his hogs, said he had one prize hog worth over three hundred dollars. Him and me, we sort of . . . borrowed that hog."

"You stole it," said Agnes.

"I didn't Lether did. I drove the truck."

"And you sold it."

"You're damn right we did. We didn't get three hundred dollars, but we did all right. I didn't hear you complaining about that new dress."

"Well, I'll know not to wear it, now I know it was paid for with yours and Lether Gable's filthy stolen money," she spat.

Leroy wrapped his arms over his head. He wanted out of the car.

"The man had three dozen hogs," Ray was saying. "He didn't need that particular one."

"Oh give it up, Ray."

"Lether got his stupid butt arrested last night," Ray said. "That's his third felony. They'll put him away. For all I know he's already confessed to the hog and give 'em my name and listed down every chicken we ever boosted between us."

136

This notion hung in the air for a moment, like smoke.

"Oh, Ray." Agnes shuddered. "They *ought* to put you in jail, I swear. What kind of a lesson is that for Leroy?"

"What's the big deal? We're okay." Ray waved at the sign flashing by: WELCOME TO BYHALIA. "We're almost to Tennessee now. They ain't gonna come across a state line for something like that."

"A hog," she said in a wondering voice.

"How much did you get for it, Daddy?" said Leroy.

Agnes said, "See there? What did I tell you?"

Flashing past Byhalia, they started down a long, gradual rise.

"Listen, son," Ray said, patting Leroy's knee, "if you do something, try and get away with it clean."

Agnes drew herself up in a line. "Like you got away clean to Parchman? Or has that just gone completely out of your brain? I thought that was one lesson you'd never forget, Ray Kirby, but I see I was wrong. You never learned it in the first place."

"Oh boo-hoo," he taunted, "poor sufferin' Agnes."

"Well I'm not going to sit here and congratulate you for thieving and bragging about it, if that's what you think. I've had enough of you for one day."

"Son, we sold it for a hundred dollars and split it between us," Ray said.

Just then there came a hard grinding sound as if the top of the car were torn away, whump! whump! whump! and the whole roofload of cargo sailed off in one sweep while the things on the sides bumped and fell off or dragged down the pavement the whole distance it took Ray to scream to a stop.

A grave quiet descended, broken only by the idling engine, hearts pounding, Ray's feeble voice: "Everybody okay?"

Agnes turned with a tight smile. "I've never been better," she said.

Ray snorted. He started to laugh, but cleared his throat and pulled off to the shoulder.

Leroy got out after him. Trucks and automobiles whizzed by swerving, honking. The wreckage was strewn two hundred yards up the highway: a mess of shattered dishes, Ball jars, lamps, clothing, pots and pans, pillows spewing feathers, pieces of Doll's rocking chair and the hall table, the pine cradle busted to splinters.

Ray danced in and out of traffic, slinging the bigger things into the weeds, shouting, "Stay out of the road!" A trucker honked and drove through the rubble without slowing down.

Leroy gathered up all the clothes he could find. He gave thanks that his Sound Star and the radio were safe in the Plymouth's backseat, and Granddaddy's silver dollar in his pocket.

Ray came up with an armload of broken things. "It's just more than I know what to do," he said. "Everything was fine till that . . . damn cop made me change it around," Ray said.

Leroy shrugged. Anything he said would be wrong.

"You know," Ray went on, "I keep thinking: Now *this* is as bad as it can get. And then it gets worse. What do you think?"

"I don't know," Leroy said. "What are we gonna do with all this stuff? It's broken."

"It sure the hell is. Let me talk to your mother." He set his load down on the ground and went to Agnes's window. Leroy was too far away to hear what they said.

It wasn't much. Ray straightened and came back.

"She don't seem too concerned about sorting it all out right now," he reported. "If it's broke, I don't reckon we need it. Let's just take this stuff and get out of here."

They straggled down the road, gathering things. Leroy was wondering what force might have sent everything flying off the car. Maybe he did it himself, with his mind. It sure put a stop to the fighting.

Agnes got out and stood with her arms folded while Ray crammed everything into the backseat. He held the guitar out by its neck. "Here, son, you'll have to hold this in your lap."

"Okay."

"I suppose that's Doll's china down there busted to pieces," said Agnes.

"No, hers is in back. That's those old plates, and the glasses and the crib and I don't know what all. We picked up what was left in one piece."

"It's a wonder you didn't get run over, both of you." Agnes shook her head. "I saw you dodging those cars."

"We still got a ways to go," Ray reminded her.

"We do," Agnes said, "and it was you in such a hurry that blew everything off the car, so don't you say one word to me."

138

Leroy wedged the Sound Star between his legs, resting the neck on his shoulder. Nothing he said would make anybody feel better. Agnes piled all the clothes at their feet and sat looking straight ahead.

They drove and drove. Once in a while a billboard held out a promise—PEABODY HOTEL, MEMPHIS' FINEST!—but the sun was well into afternoon now, and Memphis seemed to be nine hundred miles from Tupelo. The land was wide, brown, rolling out in stretches of woods. A red barn with SEE ROCK CITY on the roof. Lost stretches where kudzu had laid claim to everything. A peaceful creek running along the highway. A town named Olive Branch. Leroy dozed for a while, his head on his mother's shoulder.

He woke up when Ray announced the Tennessee line. They thumped onto better, blacker pavement, past a profusion of firecracker stands.

" 'The Volunteer State,' " Agnes read. "I guess we ought to get out and kiss the ground."

"Should have spit before we left Mississippi," said Ray.

"Hey Mama, have I ever been to Tennessee before?"

"No, this is your first time."

"Look. We're getting closer." Ray pointed to the biggest Peabody billboard yet, a painting of the swanky lobby and a Philip Morris midget calling, "Memphis' Finest!"

"Dot told me about that place," said Agnes. "They have ducks that come down every morning and walk across a red velvet carpet and swim in a thing in the lobby."

"I'd sure hate to see that dry-cleaning bill," said Ray.

Bait shops and gasoline stations were coming in now: Brown's Mid-South Chevrolet and the Sunbeam Bakery and the South Memphis Race Track—HI-SPEED ACTION EVRY SAT. NITE! They bumped over railroad tracks.

"Where's the river?" said Leroy.

"Oh, this isn't Memphis yet," his father said. "This is still the out-skirts."

The road widened. There were body shops and junkyards and bar-becue stands and used-car lots, a stoplight every two or three blocks, and millions of cars. Drivers waved their fists and sped around the creeping Plymouth.

Leroy tingled with excitement. He kept watching for a Welcome to Memphis sign, but then he decided Memphis was such a big city that if you didn't know you were here, a sign wouldn't help you.

The road looped around itself and came out on a high bluff overlooking the biggest river in the world.

Ray pulled to the shoulder. They got out and sat on the hood of the car and looked at the river. Nobody said a word.

The river was a colossal brown curve between high bluffs on this side and the tabletop land stretching west. The broad water did not reflect light.

On the east bank was the great city. Stone wharves sloped down to the water; barges and tugboats and riverboats crowded up to the wharves. Toy trucks moved across a distant bridge, bound for the great flat sweep of Arkansas.

Ray hooked his heels in the bumper. "Agnes, if I bought us a night at the Peabody, you think you could start acting civil to me?"

"I don't know. I prob'ly couldn't sleep for thinking how much it cost."

"Come on, Satnin, say yes," Leroy said.

She put her chin in her hand. "Tell you, Ray, I been forgiving you for so long. . . . I think you're just going to have to live this one down."

"Well, all right," he said. "I reckon it's cheaper that way."

"Don't count on it," said Agnes.

They got back in the car and drove around until they found a café. They ordered fried chicken and chicken-fried steak and a cheeseburger with fries for Leroy. Everything was greasy. Against the keen edge of their hunger it all tasted wonderful.

Ray went to call Johnny and Travis, but they'd gone off to the movies. "The man said the place is full up anyway," he related, "and they don't take kids."

Agnes frowned. "What about that rooming house where you stayed?"

"I tried them. Same story. No kids." He waved a scrap of paper. "But he gave me another address."

Memphis did not feel so friendly now that it was getting dark. Ray cruised up and down every street on the north side of town, searching for Poplar Avenue. If he hesitated more than an instant after a stoplight turned green, there was somebody right there to honk at him.

Leroy cried, "There it is, Daddy, Poplar!"

"Sharp eyes." Ray swung the Plymouth into the street and nosed along, reading the numbers aloud. "Here we go. Five-seven-two." He parked and went in.

The big old lopsided house loomed close to the street. Even in the dark Leroy could see the paint peeling. Lights shone in all the windows.

Ray came back to report that the room was cheap and the mattress looked all right. "There's a cot for Leroy," he said.

"After today I could sleep on a bed of nails," said Agnes.

Soon they were tucked into a small damp room behind the stairs. Ray said, "Sleep tight and don't let the bedbugs bite."

"Don't say that, I think I see one," Agnes murmured.

She drifted off first, snoring in her light, rackety way, and then Ray joined in, puffing and blowing.

Leroy lay on his iron cot, trying to fit their noises into some kind of rhythm. It was like trying to sleep with two clocks ticking. As soon as he had his own breathing aligned with his mother's regular sounds, Ray's ragged snore would break in and wake him up all over again. Once he might have crawled in with them; now he was too big.

He got up, dressed himself. He couldn't run all the way back to Tupelo, but he didn't have to lie turning and tossing on this hard cot.

He groped down the hallway, out the front door. The moon was hidden in clouds.

He shut himself in the car. Wrapping up in a blanket from the backseat, he drew the Sound Star onto his lap.

His life up to now, all his cousins and friends, all the familiar places of Tupelo—they counted for nothing. His guitar and his mother were his only friends. It made him lonesome to think how fragile his whole life had been. It was too easy, just hop in the car and drive away from it all.

He strummed an A minor, the saddest chord of all.

He played along on that awhile, switching to a D minor and back again, humming a mournful blues line. *Well, I feel so bad, I ain't never felt this bad before....*

As hard as he tried, though, he couldn't work up a good head of sadness. He was restless, the excitement of a new place. Daylight would uncover a brand-new town full of people who didn't know him yet. He could start his life over, just like his daddy.

He changed to a G major chord and tried the new Red Fairlie song.

> *Well I stand on a mountain, and I see the horizon*
> *And I hear the Lord a-calling me away*
> *Well I'm too close to heaven, miles over Jordan*
> *But I'll come to my home in the valley someday*

"Home in the Valley" was a serene spiritual in slow waltz time. It told of a journey filled with sorrow and tribulation, which ends in a beautiful place. It was a song about going to heaven, but when Leroy sang it, Memphis was the green and lovely valley, and he was the traveler who'd just made it home.

Memphis
1948-1954

16

~~~~~~~~~~~~~~~~~~~~~~~~~~~~~~~~~~

*O*n Friday, strutting the halls of Milam Junior High, Leroy had been a big deal.

On Monday morning he was nobody, cowering behind his daddy on the sidewalk in front of Humes High. Humes was too big for a school. You could fit seven or eight Milam Junior Highs inside it. The grounds took up two city blocks. The building looked like a prison with windows, a massive brick face crowned with turrets—lookout towers for guards?—and notches in the roofline, like gun emplacements. A stream of big-city kids chattered and laughed and flowed through the tall doors.

"I'm sorry, Daddy. I can't go here."

"What's wrong?" Ray turned in surprise. "It's just like Milam, only bigger."

"That's what I mean. It's too big."

"What, are you chicken?"

"No!" Leroy swallowed. "It's just—maybe we should come back tomorrow."

Ray grinned. "Aw, you'll be fine. These kids are no different from back home. You got to go up and introduce yourself, though. You can't go hanging back or you'll never get anywhere." A bell rang. Ray started up the steps. "Come on, son."

Leroy stayed where he was. There was no question about it. He could not go to this school. All the boys had on blue jeans and plaid or striped shirts. He was the only one whose mother had made him wear black Sunday shoes, a necktie, corduroys, and suspenders that pulled his pants halfway up his chest.

From the top of the steps his father said, "I'm not gonna stand here all day."

Leroy trudged up. The kids flooded through the doors. They all knew and liked each other and laughed and greeted each other.

The moment Leroy stepped inside, he became invisible.

One minute he was following his father through the door. The next minute he was nowhere at all. People brushed his arm or bumped into him, and he didn't feel a thing. Their glances went through him and out the other side.

He passed through a milky glass door marked OFFICE. His father was talking to a lady with cat-eye glasses. Now and then she glanced over to the spot where Leroy would be standing, if he were not invisible.

He stood in one spot. The river of students parted around him, even though they could not see him.

His father motioned off down the hall, saying something about where he was supposed to go. Then he smiled and clapped Leroy's shoulder and disappeared through the doors.

Leroy floated down a dark hallway lined with lockers. No one detected his presence. He turned toward the bright end of an intersecting hall and followed it to a flight of stairs, down, to another door. EXIT.

He stepped out. The door slammed behind him.

He scuffed along an endless brick wall, rounding the corner to the vast green football field. There were tall bleachers on two sides, grids of electric lights for night games, and forty or fifty boys in short pants performing jumping jacks to the chrp! chrp! chrp! of the gym teacher's whistle.

Leroy knew he could walk to the middle of the field, make faces, jump up and down—and still no one would see him.

He wondered if he could find the rooming house again, whether his mother would be able to see him if he did. He wanted to find her and stay near her until this weird feeling passed.

He set out walking, keeping to the side streets, zigzagging through backyards to throw pursuers off his trail.

He recognized the Esso station at the end of the block, darted across four lanes of traffic, and found to his relief that the next street over was Poplar.

He'd spent only one night in the sagging white rooming house, but from the corner it looked like sweet home. Skinny old Mr. Clifton was sweeping the front porch. He had cast a skeptical glance at Leroy the night before. Now he set his broom against the wall. "We don't want any noisy chillun in this house."

"Yes sir." Leroy tried to sidestep him.

"I don't give more than one warning," Mr. Clifton said.

"Yes sir." Leroy banged through the screen.

"And don't slam that door!"

Leroy hated Mr. Clifton, along with everything about Memphis. He had loved his first sight of the river, but now, when he thought back, even that seemed as huge and unfriendly as everything else. His hopeful mood of last night was gone. He wanted to go back to Tupelo.

It was all his father's fault. Stealing a pig—that was a Ray Kirby kind of crime. Leroy hadn't done anything wrong. Why should he have to pay?

He flung open the door to their room. Agnes dropped the wire brush she was using on the floor. "Goodness, you startled me! Y'all back so soon?"

"It's just me," Leroy said. "I don't know where Daddy is."

"Well, what on earth?" She craned past him, down the hall. "Shut that door. I don't want that woman to see what I'm doing. She went on and on about how much she cleans, but I swear"—her voice dropped to a whisper—"this floor is filthy."

"That old man is mean, too." Leroy hopscotched across the dry patches and climbed onto the bed.

"Well?" She scoured a brown spot shaped like Florida. "I am waiting to hear from you, Leroy."

"I can't go to that school, Mama," he said quietly. "I—I just can't. It's too big. I went in there and—nobody could see me."

"So what did you do?"

He shrugged. "I came home."

"Leroy, how do you expect them to see you if you're not there? Did you tell them you were leaving?"

"No, I—I wanted to. But I didn't. The next thing I knew I was here."

"Well, the next thing you know, you're going right down there again." Dropping the brush in the bucket, she got up on one knee. "Here, I've done my back again. Come help me up."

He obeyed. "Mama, don't make me go down there. You haven't seen that place. It's huge. It's—they—they wouldn't look at me!" Tears sprang up, as if his eyes didn't realize he was too old to cry.

Agnes hugged him and laughed. "Oh, I love you, sweetie," she said. "I'm so glad you came back instead of running off someplace. But you can't stay home from school. You got to have something smart to say when you grow up." She held him at arm's length. "Look at you. You're almost fourteen. You can stand up to anybody. What's wrong?"

He knew she wouldn't believe the truth, but he tried it anyway. "I'm invisible down there, okay? They can't see me. I don't know why, they just can't."

"You didn't give 'em a chance," she said. "I bet there's all kind of nice boys and girls down there."

"They all wear blue jeans and, you know, good stuff. I look like a—like a hillbilly."

"You do not, you look nice," she said, undoing her apron. "Take off your tie and put on your jeans, then, if that's what you want to do. Hurry up. They'll wonder what happened to you."

"Will you walk back down there with me?"

"Let me put on my hat," she said.

Leroy changed into his comfortable blue shirt and jeans. Agnes checked her hat in the mirror. They set out down the sidewalk.

"It's not so bad around here in the daylight," she said.

"I wish we were back home," said Leroy.

"Well, if wishes were horses, we'd all ride."

They walked down a street of tidy houses and turned the corner to the Humes High football field.

"It seems a lot closer when you're walking with me," said Leroy.

Agnes had to turn her head to take in the whole school. "I see what you mean. It is big."

He tried one last time. "Please, Mama . . ."

"You hold up your chin and come on."

He took a long breath and followed her up the steps.

When he passed through the doors, he vanished.

Agnes hugged him good-bye. Her arms passed through him. The cat-eyed lady came to take hold of his invisible hand and guide him to a large room full of kids who did not see him. He found a desk by the window, in back.

The teacher wrote numbers on the blackboard for an hour. A bell rang. Leroy ducked out the door.

He went to his next class and the class after that. He ate lunch at the only empty table in the cafeteria.

No one saw him all day. This was the longest day of his life.

Between fifth and sixth periods he wandered into a bathroom where some older boys were smoking cigarettes. He locked himself in a stall, sat down on the toilet. He could wait here for the day to run out.

A teacher came to chase out the smokers. He passed Leroy's stall without seeing his feet.

Leroy sat in the liquid quiet, resting one elbow on the toilet-paper holder. He could run away, run back to Tupelo.

Hide somewhere. Live in the woods.

But that was nine million miles from here. He would miss his mother too much. A few years from now, maybe, he'd be ready to try life on his own. But not in the woods. And not yet.

He had to stay here and go to school as an invisible boy.

He came out of the stall into the cigarette haze. He was alone with the mirror.

He went close.

Maybe the mirror couldn't see him either.

He went closer. "Anybody home?" He knocked with his knuckles. His nose touched the glass.

You're never alone.

Leroy said, "I thought maybe you stayed back at home."

You can't get rid of me.

"I wish I could find somebody to beat up," said Leroy.

It would have to be somebody little.

"I—I could take off my clothes and run around and see if anybody would notice me then."

That's an idea.

"It's all Daddy's fault."

He took you away from where you were happy. Don't you wish he'd gotten arrested and gone back to Parchman and left you and Mama alone?

"I could kill myself and they would be sorry," said Leroy. "I'm invisible here."

No, you're not. I see you. You see me. That's enough.

17

*A*t school Leroy was invisible. At home he was not allowed to play his guitar for fear Mr. Clifton might put them out of their miserable room. He longed for Tupelo. He blamed his father for everything.

He learned all the sad songs about home from the hillbilly radio stations and sang them endlessly to himself: "Little Cabin on the Hill" and "Carry Me Back to the Mountains" and "Sweet Old House of My Heart."

Some afternoons he carried the Sound Star to a tiny overgrown park at the end of Poplar Avenue, where he would strum and sing in the company of high weeds and buzzing insects, feeling as melancholy as somebody with a lifetime of troubles behind him. When he looked back, Tupelo seemed a grand place to live: buddies at school; big Sunday dinners; familiar trails through the woods.

Leroy glowed when his uncle Johnny congratulated him on his guitar playing, but then Johnny picked up his Gibson and whipped through "Mountain Dew" so quick and lively it made Leroy ashamed of his piddling few songs.

Ray got a job sweeping floors at Precision Tool Company. Agnes ran a sewing machine for a little company called Fashion Curtain, on the days when she felt up to it; she'd been down in her back since they came to Memphis. She blamed it on the Cliftons' cheap mattress, but that didn't explain her dark moods or her pale skin or why she was getting so thick around the middle. When she wasn't at work, she spent most of her time sleeping or eating sweets.

One morning Leroy came in to find her weeping into the pillow and eating Tom's Pecan Sandies from the bag. There were crumbs in the sheets. He went to her, hugged her, tried to make her stop crying, but she couldn't tell him what was wrong.

He fled the room. He never could stand to see her cry.

⌇⌇

A lady came to Poplar Avenue to decide whether the Kirbys were poor enough to qualify for a government apartment. Agnes left off spraying Flit for a week so the cockroaches would grow bold and come out in the open while the lady was there. The lady clucked her tongue and poked around, asking nosy questions. She peeped into a closet; a roach ran over her foot; she squealed and jumped straight off the floor.

About that time Mrs. Beavers in the next room threw open her window and shrieked, "Get out of here, you goddamn son of a bitch!" at a tomcat that was chasing her precious Susie.

A week later the Kirbys moved to their new apartment in Lauderdale Court, a government project. The place had a white-tiled bathroom with hot and cold water and an actual telephone on the kitchen wall.

Agnes sat down that night and wrote a letter to Harry S Truman. "We have never lived in a nicer place thanks to you," she read aloud. "I will always vote a Democrat. Yours truly, Agnes Kirby."

152

"That's fine," Ray said, "but why don't you just pick up the telephone and call him?"

Agnes licked the stamp. "And waste our good money? No thank you."

———〜〜〜———

Leroy kept having the same nightmare. Men without faces jostled him into the heat of their mob, hurling insults and threats and accusations, pushing him along. They seized him by the shoulders, poked him, shouted his name.

Some nights he woke up struggling with the sheet twisted around his throat, spiraling down him, binding his feet, the mattress soaked with his terrified sweat.

One night in this dream he managed to break free of the mob and run away fast through a thick greenish fog. He sensed a wall looming before him, felt down to a door, slipped outside, slammed the door quick—and the bang! woke him up.

He blinked. He was on the front stoop of Apartment 328, locked out and shivering in the deepest part of the night, wearing only his white underpants.

He hopped up and down behind the scrawny bushes, trying to think what to do.

Cupping one hand in front of him, he stole down the side of the building. His mother had taken to locking the windows at night, since Memphis was the kind of place where they would murder you in your sleep. He checked every window. Tonight she had not missed a one.

He went to the back door and began beating with the side of his fist. He pounded a long time until the kitchen light blinked on and his father appeared, bleary-eyed, wild-haired. "What in the hell," he said as he unlatched the door.

Leroy slipped in. "I had that bad dream again. I don't know how I got outside."

Ray yawned, shook his head. "Boy, you are peculiar," he said, shuffling away. "Go back to bed."

———〜〜〜———

Dodger called one Sunday morning to say she was at the Greyhound station, would somebody please come get her? Ray and Leroy drove down in the Plymouth. Dodger looked like a frail old country woman with that blue-checked bonnet hiding her hair. She had dragged her big suitcase out to the curb and was sitting on it, waiting for them.

"It's good to see you, Mama." Ray lifted her bag to the trunk. "Agnes is tickled to death. She's been pining for home folks."

Dodger climbed into the car. "I thought those brothers of hers were up here."

"Well, you know ol' Johnny. He's pretty much off to himself. And Travis is sportin' around all the time."

Dodger turned in the seat. "I declare, Leroy, you look like a different person. Tall as your daddy. You need to wash that face, though, and you won't get so many pimples."

Leroy shrank down in back. From the looks of that suitcase Dodger wasn't here for a weekend visit, and Leroy knew she wouldn't be the one sleeping on the floor. This notion threw him into a foul mood as they pulled off down Front Street.

"This city is too big," said Dodger. "I don't see how you stand it up here."

"You get used to it," Ray said. "Now tell me what happened. I didn't get all that on the phone."

"He came back to Tupelo," said Dodger. "He finished building his dam. Said he'd got used to having a place to himself. So here I am."

"He said that? Oh, I'm not believing it."

"You can believe it. You know I've never been one to stay where I'm not wanted." Dodger took off her bonnet. "Leroy, I been waiting all the way up here to hear one of your songs."

"I don't know any," Leroy said, in his mood.

Ray said, "Did you even talk to him and ask him what the hell, or did you just pick up and leave?"

"I can do what I want to do," said Dodger. "I don't have to ask anybody's permission."

Ray said, "Oh well, listen. We got plenty of room. There's a nice twin bed for you to sleep on till we get you a bed of your own."

"That's great," said Leroy, "I guess I get the floor."

"Don't pay any attention to him," said Ray. "He's been walking around with a big chip on his shoulder ever since we got up here." He glanced a warning in the rearview mirror.

154

"Growing pains," Dodger said. "How old are you, boy?"

"Five." Leroy folded his arms.

"That sounds about right," said his father, firing another warning look. "He's fifteen now and acting his age. But he's going to a big school, and we've got a fine place, Mama. You'll like it."

"I'll have to," she said. "I don't have anyplace else in the world."

Leroy said, "Since everybody's moving, maybe I oughta just go down and live with Granddaddy."

His father loomed in the mirror. "Young man, do you want me to stop this car?"

"Sure," Leroy said. "Go ahead and stop it. I don't care. I can walk."

"Well I will," Ray said, but that threat had lost its value. Leroy had learned he could get away with just about any smartass thing he said to his father. He had come to believe he was smarter than Ray, and he tried to demonstrate this a couple of times every day. Ray would ignore him or mutter something in kind. Either way, Leroy won.

He wasn't his parents' sweet-natured boy anymore. He was sick of playing that part. In the past months all sorts of unnerving changes had swept over him. He was growing so fast his bones ached. His arms and legs stuck out of clothes that had fit him a month before. His voice cracked and broke when he sang; words came out squeaking or not at all. He couldn't sleep. He couldn't get enough to eat. His stomach jittered as if someone had set up a card game inside him.

He was nasty to his parents all the time, and his nastiness wasn't the only new source of pleasure. A mess of dark hairs had sprung up in unlikely places. Leroy lay in the bathtub by the hour, playing with these fine, curly hairs.

It was while playing that way, rotating the spigot with his toe every few minutes to reheat the water, that he discovered a new and powerful thing to do.

When he shut his eyes and rubbed himself with his hand, he grew hard, and waves of a delicious sensation rolled up and down him.

It was all he wanted to do since the first night he did it and kept doing it while the waves swelled up wilder and wilder and suddenly burst in a frenzy of colors and sparks. He felt a raw burn at the back of his throat. Sticky white stuff shot out on his belly.

He shuddered. He thought he had done something terrible to himself.

He waited ten minutes. He didn't die. He tried it again. The same awful, spectacular result. The waves of fire spread through him, rippling, igniting.

It felt too good to quit. He didn't care if it killed him.

It gave him a whole new perspective. He stashed a roll of toilet paper under the blankets in the cedar chest, tearing off a few sheets each night to catch his mess. He tried to blank out his mind while he was doing it, to concentrate on forcing the explosion and making it faster and better.

He tried to keep still, but the bedsprings creaked and a little whimper escaped his lips every time.

Sometimes while he was doing it, his mind tried to wander back to that faraway day under his parents' window—but it was wrong to think about them that way.

It was the biggest thing in the world when it got hard that way, red angry and aching.

Leroy knew he couldn't be the only one in the world who'd discovered this secret. You'd think the Triplett boys would have mentioned it. Maybe they knew something he didn't. Maybe it could make your hair fall out or damage you in such a way that you could never pee again.

Still. There was no way to stop. It was like having a candy jar tied to your leg; how could you keep your hand out of it?

In the front seat Ray was consoling Dodger; Dodger was letting herself be consoled. In back, Leroy was feeling himself with his thumb through his pants pocket. He knew he should be glad to see Dodger, but all he could think about was not being able to lie on his bed at night and do that thing.

"Here we are," Ray announced.

"Oh you're right, Ray, it is nice. It's just real nice." Dodger creaked out of the car.

Leroy carried her suitcase in front of him, across the yard to the front stoop. "Hey Mama," he called through the screen, "Dodger's here and I'm going up the street to play."

"Okay, sweetie," she called from the kitchen.

He flashed past his father and Dodger, ran to the end of the block (all the time feeling the tenderness rubbing, the rubbing) and into the vacant empty lot, waist-high in weeds, hidden away behind the factory build-

156

ing. This was his secret place to do what he could not stop himself from doing. He couldn't do this the rest of his life, but right now it was the only thing.

He stretched flat on his back with the grass tickling his earlobes. His right hand found its way down his pants. He closed his eyes and grabbed himself, squeezing.

His mind started wandering, circling, lower and lower. The sun was hot on his eyelids. He brushed an ant from his cheek. He pictured the little girls on the jungle gym at East Tupelo Consolidated School. He used to stand up under there watching for a flash of underpants. He thought about that colored girl, Sally, and then she wasn't Sally anymore, she was Dolores Roselle, the most beautiful girl at Humes High. She was lifting her sweater so Leroy could see under there. She reached out to touch him. . . .

Leroy felt a roar and a hammering blood-pounding drumroll and boom! it went boom! off the image of boom! Dolores Roselle!

It was over.

His whole body glittered inside. The insects throbbed in the same rhythm as his blood. He smelled the sweet grass and his sweat.

He rubbed his hand on his belly and then on the grass. He fixed the front of his pants and sat up.

It was stronger than any feeling he'd ever known. The world glowed in startling color. Leroy couldn't understand why everyone in the world didn't lie around doing it all the time.

When it was over, he felt a little silly.

He stood and brushed himself off, tasting this morning's toothpaste on his lips.

Dolores Roselle.

He had seen her dozens of times in school; she had never seen him. He sat near her in the cafeteria and stared without fear of discovery. Long, glossy black hair swung away from her face, which was flawless and oval and pale. Her white fuzzy sweaters accented her breasts. She always looked a little distant, as if she were listening to some voice in her head—maybe Leroy's voice whispering, look at me, Dolores. . . .

She was a beautiful creature. Also she was a senior, two years older than Leroy, as unreachable as the stars in the night sky. If ever she did turn around and speak to him, he would certainly faint.

Rudolph Valentino would know what to do. He would lean across that cafeteria table and sweep her away with a violent kiss. But that was beyond Leroy's power. He contented himself with watching her, dreaming of her, smelling her when she walked by holding her schoolbooks against her breasts.

18

*L*eroy wrote her name again and again in the margins of his spiral notebook. He penciled fat hearts with arrows through them. Her name had a wonderful ring— Do-lo-res!—a name you might call from a mountain to hear the echo.

His feelings went much deeper than his crush on Mary Edna Meecham in seventh grade. This was real love. Leroy read *Romeo and Juliet* for sophomore English; the last part, where Romeo kissed her and fell on his knife—that was wild, that was what love felt like, that was something Leroy could picture himself doing for Dolores Roselle.

Walking by, she left him breathless. When he closed his eyes, he saw her face, the image that lingers after you've stared too long at the sun. He wanted to hurry up and grow up and marry her. He wanted to kiss the tip of her nose. He wanted to nuzzle up in one of those sweaters.

She must know she was torturing him. She must enjoy it. Why else would she make herself so beautiful every day if not to drive him out of his mind?

He was tired of longing in secret. Tonight, at the Harvest Moon Festival at Humes High, he was determined to ask her to dance.

He would do it. He would. He had sworn it.

Hello, Dolores, would you like to dance? Hey there, Dolores. Hi, Dolores. Hey, baby, wanna dance? Oh hi, Dolores, uhm, would you like to—*no*.

What's the worst she can say? *No.* A harmless word. Just go up to her knowing she will say *no.* Then it can't hurt you.

He stared into his closet. No wonder she never noticed him; his clothes were invisible, too. He had dark trousers and sensible corduroys, blue jeans, white shirts, and a couple of jerky button-collar plaids that Agnes had found at a fire sale. She wanted him to look nice, but she didn't notice what other kids wore; anyway, Leroy outgrew clothes as fast as she could scrape up the money to buy them. He had been thinking he ought to get a job so he could walk downtown and buy some sharp clothes.

Meanwhile, he would go to the dance in gray slacks, a white shirt, and the wide, flashy polka-dot necktie he'd borrowed from Johnny.

Dolores couldn't help seeing that tie. It was cool. Big jazzy pink dots on a tulip-yellow background. Tony Curtis would wear such a tie.

Leroy tied it, whistling "Dancing in the Dark." Tonight's the night, Dolores, look out.

He had never danced with a girl—never danced at all, for that matter, except swaying alone to a nice song on the radio—but he felt sure he could figure out what to do by the time he worked up the nerve to ask her.

His mother rattled dishes in the kitchen. Dodger was listening to her favorite radio preacher cranked up to a full shout, raving on about E-*zeek*-yul this and E-*zeek*-yul that and all heeeed the word of the Lord!

160

Leroy drew a wet comb through his crew cut. He didn't have enough hair to slick back; with longer hair and fewer pimples, he would like his looks better. He was shaving every other day now and letting his sideburns grow down his face. He tried on three or four expressions: Valentino, Marlon Brando, a sensitive sad-boy pout, a big shiny white smile. "Hey, handsome," he said.

The mirror admired him in silence.

He went to the kitchen.

"Oh don't you look nice," Agnes said, "except for that tie. I could see that tie with my eyes closed."

"It's Johnny's," Leroy said. "You really hate it?"

"I do."

Dodger turned down the volume on the preacher. "It looks like something off a clown."

"I think it's cool," Leroy said. (Tony Curtis said "cool" a lot in his movies.)

Agnes folded the dish towel. "Want me to walk with you?"

"That's all right, Mama, I'll go by myself."

"What time is it over?"

"Nine, I think."

"Well you don't need to be walking the streets at that hour. One of us will come get you. Be out front at nine sharp and look for the car."

Leroy said good-bye and set out walking. He couldn't wait for his sixteenth birthday, when he would take his rightful place behind the wheel.

He was already a good driver; more than once he'd driven Johnny's pickup down the back streets of South Memphis, but that was his and Johnny's secret.

Leroy was counting on driving to save him. Of course, he still meant to become a movie star, but in the meantime, he had to get through Humes and learn something useful, like how to drive a big truck. Then everybody better look out. He wouldn't be in any one place long. He would sweep Dolores Roselle off her feet and carry her away in his big diesel cab.

But first he would ask her to dance. He *would*. . . .

A full moon rose from the end of Poplar Avenue. Leaves scudded down the sidewalks. Halloween was a week off, but Leroy tasted it in the air. He walked the quiet streets, speculating on his lonesome time in Memphis.

Two years now, and still he had no friends at all. Once or twice he'd left off being invisible long enough to strike up a conversation with someone in class, but he ran out of things to say. No one ever turned around to strike up a conversation with *him*.

He still mourned for Tupelo. He seemed to remember that he was the most popular boy in town, renowned for his singing, admired by everybody—until he came to Memphis and vanished.

Tonight all that would change. He would dance with Dolores Roselle. The world would notice him. Everyone would see how beautiful the two of them looked together and be struck dead with envy.

His heart bounded when he turned the last corner. The Humes gymnasium was lit up; a crowd of girls in frilly dresses surged at the doors. Leroy straightened his tie, put on his Tony Curtis swagger, and stepped out of the darkness.

The Spirit Club had beautified the gym with orange crepe paper, cutout pumpkins and witch's hats, dancing grinning skeletons, black cats, a great big fat harvest moon made of papier-mâché. Under the scoreboard the Fred Lunsford Trio wheezed a fox-trot. Most of the boys had gathered on one side of the gym, the girls on the other. Hardly anybody danced except a few pairs of girls.

One authentic couple twirled away at the center of the floor. He was a football star named Morris Weed, and she was the head cheerleader, Mary Ann Brown. They were King and Queen of the Junior Class; from the way they danced, Leroy could see they loved being the only couple out there.

He sipped strawberry punch and studied the way Morris Weed held her. He imitated that position with his hands. Maybe if they played a slow song . . .

The old, tired men worked their instruments like machines in a factory, pumping out one dull tune after another—polkas, fox-trots, ancient Andrews Sisters and Dorsey and Glenn Miller tunes, all to the same monotonous, underheated beat.

Steady couples moved out on the floor. Some of the unattached boys began to make tentative forays in among the girls.

Leroy stood against the wall, searching the crowd. Dolores was late.

She was sick. She wasn't coming because she'd had a premonition that Leroy would ask her to dance.

But then she was there—slender, elegant, a lovely doll standing off to one side of a group of actual girls. She wore a simple white dress with a lace collar. Her luxurious dark hair was gathered at her neck with a white seashell clasp. She was delicious. Leroy felt a stirring.

Other girls crowded around her, laughing; none of them was nearly as beautiful as Dolores. That made her even more beautiful.

Leroy heard a whistling in his ears that had nothing to do with the Fred Lunsford Trio. The room got darker, or warmer.

Go ask her. Go do it. You can do it. You can.

He tore himself away from the wall, a movie monster awakening, drawn irresistibly through the multitude of kids dancing to "Chattanooga Shoe Shine Boy." He passed among them, unseen, heading straight for Dolores.

Somehow the air around her turned him aside. He wound up five feet behind her, off to the left.

He inspected the line of her neck, the glint of gold necklace, her delicate ear.

Her girlfriend whispered to her. Dolores laughed and swung around, still laughing. For an instant her gaze touched on Leroy.

Then a handsome tall boy—a basketball player—came to ask her to dance. Dolores performed a little curtsy. The boy swept her away.

In truth it didn't look that hard—you just stepped along sideways to the beat, more or less—but Leroy's fragile confidence had a crack in it. He didn't know how to dance. He was only beginning to consider the kind of humiliation that might come from dancing when you didn't know how.

The song ended. The boy returned Dolores to her girlfriends. Leroy edged closer, into her field of vision.

She turned. She really saw him this time. She looked into his eyes for a long moment, then turned back to her friends.

Had he seen a hint there? An invitation?

The trio thumped out "Tennessee Waltz." Another senior came up to dance Dolores away. Everyone wanted to dance with her. Everyone could see how beautiful she was. Leroy would have to be bold.

He practiced a dozen opening lines. For the moment he was happy just to stand this close to her until the next good-looking boy came to dance her away.

He felt his courage seeping back.

He was so close he could smell her perfume.

Suddenly she turned to him and said, "What do you think you're doing?"

She might as well have slapped his face. He swallowed and tried to think what to say.

"Every time I turn around, there you are," she said. "What is it with you?"

He had not yet spoken a word and she hated him, truly.

Her brown eyes shone. She was beautiful. "Do you want to dance?" she said. "Is that it? Come on, then, let's dance." She put out her hand like a mother helping a baby learn to walk.

Leroy obeyed. His fingers were numb. His whole body was numb, starting with his brain, which was working frantically to understand what had just happened.

He watched the news travel—a whisper, a glance, furtive laughter circling the gymnasium. Dolores had made sure her girlfriends heard every word.

She lifted his right hand and placed the left one against her side. "I guess I've got to teach you how to dance, too."

The band played "I Can Dream, Can't I" like a funeral march. The lights sputtered and fumed.

"Come on. Don't just stand there." She tapped the side of his foot with her toe, to get it moving.

Leroy bobbed his head and followed after her, burning utterly. He thought of poor Rocky Paul at the Mississippi-Alabama Dairy Fair.

"Where did you get that weird tie?" She seemed hard and cold, not beautiful. He longed for the song to end. He was such a fool! His hands sweated against her. He managed to keep up somehow. She glowed with pleasure at his embarrassment.

She had changed him. Forever. Never trust a girl. Just get out of here.

"Watch your foot," she said.

"Look," he said, finding his voice, "you don't want to dance, and neither do I."

Dolores waved over his shoulder. "Everybody was betting I wouldn't dance with you if you ever quit lurking back there and asked me."

Leroy felt sick to his stomach. How could he ever have imagined himself in love with Dolores? Why did she have to be cruel? He felt like an idiot child. He wanted to cry or throw up. He wanted to get out of there. He wanted his mother.

Morris Weed glided past with his cheerleader. "Hey, Dolores, who's the new Mr. Right?"

"Shut up, Morris," she said sweetly, and then, to Leroy: "Now, do you think you can find some girl your own age?"

Anger shot up inside him, as hot and wet as his infatuation had been a few minutes before.

He dropped her hand. "Listen, baby." He forced a hard smile. "You're not as wonderful as you think."

With that smile as his shield, he backed away. He abandoned her at the center of the dance floor.

Oh, yes, he was visible now. He walked naked through a valley of eyes laughing, mocking him. The music was horribly wrong. His only idea was to get out of there. He tucked his head and dived toward a line of girls; they parted to let him through, like girls playing red rover in kindergarten. A strand of drooping crepe paper snagged his arm. He snatched free, stumbled to the door.

Stunning darkness outside. He leaned over, hands on knees, heaving for breath. He hawked and spit, a sour taste on his tongue; he was about to puke right here on the steps of Humes High.

Don't do it. Those people watching. You showed her. You showed her.

He walked into the darkness, under the flagpole. A breeze came along to cool his face. The nausea faded. A dead feeling came in to replace it.

He did not love her now. There was no love inside him at all. It was vaporized in an instant by that look in her eyes.

He thought: You can't love somebody who hates you.

In the time it took to play "I Can Dream, Can't I," the invisible boy had become the laughingstock of Humes High.

He sat down on the curb and waited, forever and ever. Boys and girls streamed in and out of the dance, sneaking out for a quick smoke with the glowing cherry concealed in the palm of a hand, a stroll with someone beautiful in the dark. Everyone was in love for one night.

Leroy sat in one place, burning with anger.

At last the green Plymouth pulled into the parking lot.

He climbed in.

"Hey, sweetie, how was your dance?" Agnes wasn't accustomed to driving yet; she gripped as if the wheel might come off in her hands. "Did you have a nice time? I saw some of those girls coming out. They looked so pretty in their little dresses—"

"I don't want to talk about it," said Leroy.

Agnes steered to the street. "What's the matter?"

"It was the worst night of my whole life," Leroy said, and to his astonishment, he burst into tears.

This shocked him as much as anything he'd ever done. He was helpless to stop.

He slumped in the seat, his face in his hands.

His mother pulled over. "You just go on and cry now, if you need to. What's the matter, tell Satnin what's wrong. Did somebody hurt you? Did they hurt my baby?"

"Oh, Mama," he cried, and knowing she loved him just made it hurt more. No one else would ever love him as much. Her love was a big looming mountain that kept him away from the rest of the world. He let it all out, let it out. He told her the whole thing, how much he loved Dolores, how she plunged in the knife and twisted it, oh and the shame, the bright public shame.

His mother said, "It's all right, baby, I still love you. She was wrong to do you that way."

Somehow, after a minute or two, Leroy found a way to stop crying. He blew his nose. "She—she hates me," he choked. "She hates me."

"Oh honey she can't hate you, she doesn't even know you. I know it seems like the end of the world . . . but you're still so young! You'll find somebody else, I promise. Everybody does. It just doesn't always happen the first time."

"It won't ever happen to me," he said.

"You'll change your mind."

He pulled away. "I want to go home."

His mother stared at him a long moment. Now her eyes were shining. She started the car.

They drove a few blocks in silence.

Finally Leroy said, "Don't tell anybody, okay?"

"It's our secret."

"Thanks, Mama." He stared out the window. He loved her more than ever. He didn't need a girl who could use his own love as a knife, to cut him. He didn't need anybody as long as he had his mother. How many times would he have to learn that lesson?

19

*L*eroy stayed in his room. No one could hurt him in his room. He had the radio.

White folks were not supposed to listen to WDIA, the Mother Station of the Negroes. Leroy discovered the station by accident when he slipped off a weak gospel signal and found himself in a torrent of chatter from a mile-a-minute wild colored man called Howlin' Wolf.

"Blessin' all the slick-back babes and their cool-cattin' beaus, we spinning a hot one this evening for Miss Doretha Watley from a most faithful secret admirer," the Wolf said in a guttery voice, and then:

"Whoo, chillun! Hold on to who you hold on to, 'cause this is one sho-fo-real song! Call it Mr. Sam Davis, call it the 'Got No Home Blues'!"

Leroy bent over the Sound Star and whanged along. Sam Davis played the guitar with the side of his hand and began to wail:

> *I ain't got no home, baby*
> *Since you left and said good-bye*
> *Said I ain't got no no no no no home, bay-beh!*
> *Not since you went and said good-bye. . . .*

The radio was a cream colored Philco with a cigarette burn in the top. A whole new exotic world poured out through that little round speaker. Leroy couldn't get enough of it.

"Leroy," his mother called, "get up from there and come take out this garbage."

"Not now, Mama, I'm practicing."

Three chords would take you through every song on the Mother Station, but the changes these colored folks worked on those chords! They moaned and shouted; they sang about real pain and leaving and good-bye and gone. John Lee Hooker and Lightnin' Hopkins! Tiny Bradshaw! Big Bill Broonzy! The songs shared a smoky-barroom feeling, but each singer had his own rhythm, his own kind of sound.

> *Get off your high horse, baby*
> *And come on back to town. . . .*

Leroy sang the words as he figured them out. The Five Keys! The Dominoes! The Diamonds! The Clovers! "Hmmmmm, babes and babies, don't that just set yo legbone to shakin!" the Wolf cried.

Leroy got off the bed to play harder. Jimmy McCracklin! Wynonie ("Mr. Blues") Harris! Riley B. King, the Beale Street Blues Boy himself, the smoothest blues guitarist on the planet Earth, and the host of "Sepia Swing Time." "Sixty Minute Man." "Rocket 88." Joe Turner's "Chains of Love." Pee Wee Crayton! Big Boy Crudup! The bump and the shuffle, the slow low-down blues.

These colored men must know they were a bad influence on boys like

Leroy. They sang songs that might be dirty or might just be funny but were probably both. They knew the songs were loaded with sin; that's why they sang with such joyful enthusiasm. They said "rockin" when they meant "fuckin."

> *Come on and rock me Angelina*
> *Rock yo daddy all night long*

Lips touched the microphone. Voices sweated and wailed. People in the background coughed and dropped things.

"Leroy," Agnes called, "come to supper!"

"Not now, Mama!"

An irresistible beat started rackety-tacking along, and a joyous song came swinging out to banish all the sadness and meanness in Memphis to some other town down the road.

Have you heard the news? Mr. Blues shouted. *There's good rockin' tonight....*

Leroy jumped up off the bed, shaking and beating his guitar in time. Electricity shot down his legs, popped his fingers.

He danced over in front of the mirror. He was getting better-looking every day. For weeks he had avoided Ray's efforts to get him to a barbershop; his hair was nice and long, and his sideburns were looking very cool.

He put down the guitar. He poured a puddle of Vitalis in his palm and rubbed it all over his head. He combed and arranged his hair until the comb tracks stood out.

It was the same dirty blond as his father's hair. He wished it were wavy and blue-black, like Superman's, to set off his bedroom eyes. He practiced his insolent look: a curl of the lip, a rebellious half snarl.

He skipped supper and set out walking for the glow of downtown, trying to decide whether to be Tony Curtis or Marlon Brando for the evening.

It was Saturday night. Everyone in Memphis who owned or could borrow a car was out in it, driving around. The streets echoed with traffic and radios and front-porch conversations and kids pretending not to hear their mothers calling them to dinner. Half the radios in town were tuned to Arthur Godfrey, and half to the Mother Station.

Marlon Brando swaggered past the Peabody Hotel, through the electric daylight of Main Street and under the grand blinking marquee of the Loew's State Theater, announcing MARTIN LEWIS LAFF A MINUTE "AT WAR WITH THE ARMY" PLUS CARTOON SHORTS NEWS.

The Loew's giant arched entrance opened into a gallery of white columns and red carpets and velvet ropes. Brando approached the ticket booth, which resembled a giant gold jukebox. "One, please," he mumbled, putting down quarters.

The woman in the booth left off plaiting her hair to tear off a ticket. In the corner of the glass was a hand-lettered sign: HELP WANTED.

Well. Now. A job at the movies. That was an idea.

He pointed to the sign. "Who do I talk to about that?"

The ticket lady looked him over. "The manager, Mr. Faubus," she said. "In the projection room, upstairs."

Marlon Brando strode up the wide, curving staircase.

When he came back down fifteen minutes later, he was Leroy Kirby, movie usher, carrying an official usher's uniform on a hanger—black satin-striped pants, a gold braided vest, a red monkey jacket and cap. The short, bug-eyed Mr. Faubus had hired him on the spot. His head whirled. He would start tomorrow! A job at the movies! Twelve seventy-five a week! Oh, life was just fine.

He calmed down enough to remember that he'd already paid to see the picture. He entered the cavernous darkness of the theater and took a seat near the back.

Dean Martin was propped on a sofa in his fake army uniform with a drink in his hand and a lazy, arrogant look on his face—flashing eyes, that superior smirk. He was cool, cool, and Leroy was cool in the dark, breathing Dean's charm and his own hair oil and the rich smell of red velvet. Leroy was Dean Martin now, in his head. He was forty feet tall.

～～

Leroy saw *At War with the Army* sixty-three times. He stood at the head of the main aisle in his monkey suit, wielding his Sculpto flashlight, directing kids to the bathroom and helping cranky old ladies find seats.

The insane giggle of Jerry Lewis haunted his waking hours. At night he dreamed of Dean Martin singing "You and Your Beautiful Eyes" to

Miss Peavey, his algebra teacher. But it was the short subject, *Glacier Fishing,* that nearly drove him insane. Eskimos huddled around a hole. They speared a fish. They brought the fish up on the ice. They clubbed the fish to kill it. Leroy watched the same poor fish take it in the head three times a night, every night for five weeks. After a while he began to feel like that fish.

On the magic appointed afternoon Agnes drove him to the Highway Patrol station for his driver's license examination.

Leroy ran over the *Rules of the Road.* The little pamphlet was dog-eared from weeks of study. Leroy meant to pass this test. Once he had his license, he'd be able to drive around looking at life, checking out all the possibilities.

"If you studied half this hard for school, you'd have a perfect report card," his mother said.

"I can't flunk this test." He shook his head. "A girl at school flunked twice, and she has to wait six months before she can take it again."

"Six months isn't that long," Agnes said. "Sounds like she needed the practice."

The Highway Patrol station squatted beside the Nashville highway. Agnes pulled into a parking lot painted over with curves and arrows and stripes and squeezed the Plymouth into a tiny space.

Inside was a long line of kids waiting; Leroy remembered his first day of school, when the kids looked just this scared.

Agnes stood off with the other proud mothers and fathers.

Leroy whizzed through the written test. The questions came straight from the pamphlet. The test lady checked his score—92 of 100. He was halfway to freedom.

A tall, beak-nosed man came up and introduced himself as Weems. He was some sort of gym teacher, to judge from his skull-baring crew cut and his abrupt demeanor; he didn't say much except to direct Leroy behind the wheel of a Chevrolet sedan. "Start the car and drive out of the lot. Turn left."

The Chevrolet's brakes were grabbier than those on the Plymouth. Leroy screeched to a couple of abrupt halts before he learned how to apply subtle pressure.

Mr. Weems made a note in his ring binder. "Drive three blocks and turn right."

"This is a cool car," said Leroy. "Our car's a lot older."

"Pay attention to the road," said Mr. Weems.

Leroy flipped on the blinker and made a flawless right turn onto Davis Street.

"Now drive five blocks and turn left."

Driving was Leroy's best talent, after singing. He had no doubt he would be an excellent truck driver when he got his chance. He got to feeling so proud of his driving that he rolled right through a four-way stop at Ames Avenue without slowing down.

Mr. Weems said, "That looked like a stop sign to me."

"Yes sir, I think it was," said Leroy. What else could he say? He was guilty, guilty. He drove on, doing his best with the unfamiliar controls, sinking into the mortification of having blown the test outright.

"You always drive through a four-way stop without slowing down?" said Mr. Weems. "Turn left."

"No sir," he said. "I reckon I'm kind of nervous." He performed the turn with agonizing care. Blood throbbed in his temples.

"I make you nervous?" Weems barked.

"Yes sir, a little." They were almost back to the Highway Patrol station, which was just as well—no use going on with this.

"Hell, that's what everybody says. That's why I got out of the army," Weems said in a milder voice, almost to himself. "The recruits were all scared to death of me. I never did anything to 'em. I liked 'em. I don't know what it is. I guess I just look that way to people."

Leroy said, "Maybe you ought to let your hair grow out a little."

Mr. Weems smiled, made a mark in his book. "Hate to wind up as shaggy as you," he said. "Now turn into the lot and parallel park in that space over there."

Agnes watched anxiously from the sidewalk as Leroy maneuvered the car to a standstill, six inches from the curb.

Mr. Weems said, "You know, I have to fail you for a moving violation during the course of the test."

Leroy stared at his knees. "Yes, sir."

"I don't like to do it. I think you're a good driver. You practice and come back in two weeks and try it again."

"Yes sir," said Leroy. How could he face his mother?

Mr. Weems handed over a little green slip of paper. "You give that to the lady at the license desk next time you come, and you can skip the written part," he said. "Don't worry about it, son, lots of folks mess up the first time."

Leroy had only a few seconds to decide what to do. If his mother found out he had flunked this test, no telling when she'd let him try again.

He thanked Mr. Weems, walked to the Plymouth, waving the green paper, and climbed in. "I got it!" he declared.

"Oh honey, that's wonderful!"

"It was close, though." He stuffed the paper down in his pocket and laid his arm around her shoulder. "That man wasn't as mean as he looked."

That evening they all piled into the car with Leroy at the wheel. He drove down Winchester Avenue, steering with intense concentration along back streets to the river, the old cotton wharves. If a policeman stopped him without a license, he'd be sent off to the state pen.

He would sneak off somehow and take the test again, and nobody would ever have to know.

Dodger complimented his driving. Agnes said, "My baby's growing up."

They stopped at Murphy's Dairy Dream to celebrate. Ray ordered banana splits all around. Everything was happy until Ray started in on Leroy's hair, how dirty and shabby it looked.

Leroy threw his banana split in the garbage, went out to the Plymouth, and sulked.

The next day was Saturday. He took all the money he'd saved in his Folger's can and asked his mother for the car keys.

"Where are you going?" Agnes said.

"I don't know," he lied. "I just want to drive around by myself awhile. See what it feels like. I'll be careful."

"I know you will." She gave him the keys.

He climbed into the Plymouth, started the engine. The steering wheel tingled his hands.

Taking a deep breath, he inched away from the Lauderdale Court. When he turned onto Jackson Street, he laid into the gas pedal and felt

174

the engine, a kick in the pants. He sailed past Humes High. This old car had life, once you quit treating it like a little old lady and put down your foot.

He zoomed up to a stoplight, slipped out of gear, and sat grinning at his luck: To be alive and sixteen and behind the wheel!

He traveled a roundabout way downtown. He parked out of sight of his immediate destination, the Mary Jane Beauty Salon.

He had cased the place for weeks and never spotted anyone he knew coming or going.

With his hands in his pockets, he sauntered down the sidewalk as if he might walk on by. At the last instant he ducked in the door.

A bell tinkled. The smell of hair chemicals stung his eyes. A young woman with tight blond curls peered up from a manicure table. "Well, hello."

"Hi," said Leroy. "I, uh, I want to get a haircut."

She smiled a bright lipstick smile. "Sweetie, this is a beauty parlor," she said. "You want Mr. Beebe's barbershop across the street."

"No ma'am," said Leroy. "I want you to do mine."

The woman whose nails were soaking said, "Go on, Deedee, do his hair," and laughed.

The manicurist looked him over. "Sure I will," she said. "Have a seat over there and I'll get Lorraine to wash you."

The salon was a quiet place, soft beige and warm. Four middle-aged women were in various stages of beautification: one with her head in a sink, where a colored woman scrubbed vigorously; two under gray dryer hoods; another wincing as a beautician installed pin curls.

Leroy took the folded-up magazine page from his hip pocket and smoothed out the creases. Tony Curtis grinned up, impossibly cool. That was the hair Leroy wanted. A pompadour, full and tall on the top, finished like steel on the sides, tapered to a DA at the neck—a duck's ass, an honest-to-God pointed tail. This haircut would make him the envy of Humes.

Lorraine, the shampoo girl, steered him to a sink with a smoothed-out hollow for his head and fastened a long bib around him. "Boy, what you doing in a lady parlor?" she said.

Leroy waved the picture.

Lorraine studied it a moment. "Hm. Well if that's what you want, Deedee can do it. You got enough hair."

She adjusted the water to a milky temperature and set to work with a wonderful energy. Her strong fingers caressed and dug into his scalp, scrubbing, tussling each hair at its root; the warm water streamed over. Leroy was glad for the long bib since the pleasure of her touch was making him hard in his pants.

Too soon, she was done. She sat him up, rubbed his head with a towel. "Good hair," she said.

The blond girl, Deedee, beckoned from a chair at the front. All the customers glanced up from their magazines to get a look at Leroy going by. No doubt one of them was the mother of somebody at Humes; Leroy would become notorious for all the wrong reasons.

But it was too late now. He lowered himself to a pneumatic chair and showed Deedee the picture of Tony Curtis.

Swiveling him to face the mirror, she grabbed up a hank of his hair. "That's what you want?"

"Sure."

"Keep the sideburns, too?" They reached to his earlobes.

"Yep."

"All right, then." She reached for a pair of scissors, tilted his head, started snipping around his collar. She trimmed and shaped the back, rolling the long swatches of hair around pink curlers. "This is what gives it the body so it can stand up like that."

Leroy watched gobs of hair falling onto his knees. Now and again he glanced at the mirror, trying to satisfy himself that the ridiculous spectacle of his head wadded in curlers would not turn him into something even more ridiculous.

... Why did they call it a *permanent* wave?

Deedee handed him a magazine and told him to quit worrying. She poured a cold, strong-smelling potion over the curlers, stretched a perforated shower cap over the whole mess, and positioned Leroy under a roaring steel dryer.

For forty-five minutes he baked in the chemical stink, deafened by the dryer motor, his hair singeing at the roots. He inspected the delicate drawings of ladies' underwear in *Woman's Day*. He began to consider what might happen if all his hair fell out.

The dryer shut off, leaving a thunderous silence. Leroy yawned, blinking tears. A poisonous sweat trickled down his brow. Deedee led him back to the chair, wiped his face with a towel. The cap came off, and the curlers, one at a time; the fronds of his hair had baked into coils.

What have I done. "Oh, it looks awful curly...."

"No, you sit back. Wait'll we wash it and brush it out."

Lorraine repeated her magic at the shampoo sink, and then Deedee took up scissors and comb and a brush.

She snipped and tucked, rubbing in lots of Brylcreem, brushing, combing. Sure enough the curls relaxed into a soft flowing wave. She held up a mirror, angled so Leroy could see the back.

His hair was now full and wavy and smooth. A dramatic line swooped over his head to a V at his collar, sharp and shiny as a Cadillac's fin.

Deedee was an artist. "God, it looks great," he stammered.

She beamed. "I think so too. It looks just like the picture."

Oh cool. He was Tony Marlon Leroy tough guy, JD, DA, a cool rockin' cat. He snarled for the mirror. Deedee laughed.

When she swept off the bib, shaking hair to the floor, Leroy saw that his plaid shirt and tan slacks were all wrong with his hair. He looked like Andy Hardy with a pompadour.

"That's three-fifty," said Deedee, "and you're supposed to give me a tip if you like how I did."

"How much?"

"Make it four dollars."

Leroy held out five. "You—really—I mean, I love it."

"Thanks, hon. And listen," she said, "that Brylcreem is not gonna shine it up the way you want. You get you some pomade."

"What's that?"

"They sell it at the Woolsworth. It comes in this little pink can, see? It's what the colored folks use. Gives you that shine."

Ignoring the smirks of the ladies, Leroy put on his jacket and turned up the collar. He went out to the Plymouth and sat for a while, contemplating his hair in the rearview mirror.

It rose in front to a lofty height. The oil darkened it and made the sides gleam.

There was no turning back from this hair. Deedee had told him the wave would be in there for weeks.

Leroy had new hair and the car keys and money. Now he needed clothes.

He knew where to go. Howlin' Wolf recommended the place every night around midnight: "Check out Irving Brothers, the pride of Beale Street, these brothers are a friend to you, brother, stop on in and give 'em your business. Dandy duds for the cool blue man inside of you."

Leroy drove over the hill on Beale. This was a street for fancied-up colored folks at night, but in the daytime it belonged to poor people of both races. Thin winter light bleached the sidewalk. Pool halls and seedy lounges stood open, nobody inside. A withered old man leaned in a doorway, sheltering a beer bottle against his chest. Three boys chased each other around a broken-down car.

The Irving Brothers' store was set in a block of old falling-in places: a pawnshop, a smoke shop, a shoe repair shop, a juke joint, then the Irvings' shiny plate glass and wide-open doors. Leroy parked carefully at the curb.

A balding white man in white shirt and tie lounged out front, talking in business off the street. "Hey, brother," he said as Leroy approached, "slick hair, my friend. Come on in and let us fix you up."

Leroy grinned. "I've got money today."

"Well that's what we like to hear, you just step right on in, let Myron take care of you—Myron? Young fellow's got money, and he wants you to make him look sharp."

Myron was a copy of his brother: squat, balding, with eager eyes behind rimless glasses. "Come on in here, my friend! Haven't I seen you before? What can we do for you today?"

"I need some clothes," Leroy said. "I listen to y'all's ads all the time on WDIA."

"Well that's fine there, son, that's fine—looking for anything in particular?"

Leroy gazed out over racks of brilliant clothing. This was where colored people came to buy their Saturday-night outfits, and famous hillbilly singers their spangly shirts. "I don't know," he said, "it all looks pretty good. Why don't you let me look around."

"You go right ahead," Myron said. He stood watching Leroy flip through the shirts. They were all loud, these shirts: some purple, some yellow, some with crazy paisley patterns, or Hawaiian, or gray with red and white cowboy trim. "You like that?" Myron kept saying. "You like that?"

The Irving Brothers had unusual taste. There were shirts with sequins, leather trim, rabbit-fur collars. Leroy loved them all.

He loitered for a long time at the leather jackets, but he'd have to spend a lot more time ushering movies before he could afford one of those.

He unearthed a pair of amazing balloon-legged pants, shiny black material with stark yellow lightning bolts zagging from the hip to the ankle—a blaze of electricity down both legs. The tag said eighteen dollars.

The pants would look cool with the black slinky pullover shirt, woven with threads of what Myron said was Dutch gold. "Guaranteed not to rust," he said, "your wife can just throw it in with the rest of the wash."

Your wife! Leroy liked that. He felt like a big deal, picking through the clothes under Myron's watchful eye.

With a hot pink shirt, the lightning trousers, and a skinny yellow necktie added in, the bill came to forty-three dollars. That was two weeks of standing in the dark at the Loew's, but if everything fit, it was worth every minute. Leroy went to the tiny booth and changed in a hurry, taking care not to disturb his hair.

He stepped out from behind the curtain.

Myron whistled. "Would you look at that! Now *there* goes a man who believes in looking good."

Leroy found his way to the triple mirror.

What he saw stunned him.

The first thing was his hair. That was truly successful hair.

The slinky black shirt clung to his chest. The narrow-hipped pants flared out in the leg like something from a Valentino movie, with that flash of yellow electricity zagging up the legs.

He draped the yellow tie around his neck.

"Cool," he said.

"Cool? I'll say it's cool!" Myron exclaimed. "Ike! Come here! Take a look at this man!"

He was right. Leroy was beautiful. The hair made him older and sleek, and these clothes—yeah, cat, these were the clothes of a visible man.

He would look even better with his guitar.

Ike whistled, exactly as Myron had done. "Would you look at that," he said.

Myron spoke up: "You want me to wrap up your other stuff and you wear these home?"

"Sure, why not," Leroy said. "Let me get my money out of my pants."

He pulled himself away from the dazzling mirror and felt in his old limp pants pocket for his remaining bills.

"All right now," Myron was saying, "what else can we get you? Some socks? How about that green shirt you liked?"

Leroy handed over the money. "No, that's all for right now. Don't worry. I'll come back."

He took his change and his bag of old clothes and floated out into the light of Beale Street. He walked on new feet, with new hair and threads of gold on his skin. He walked like a star.

20

Agnes looked up from a big bowl of popcorn. Her eyes opened wide. "What have you done to your hair?"

Leroy brushed past her, down the hall to his room.

"Honey, come here, let me see!"

He stopped in the doorway and turned. Oh, the look on her face! She stared first at his hair, then his clothes, with mingled amusement and shock—as if she'd come around a sideshow curtain at the fair to encounter something truly unforgettable.

"Leroy," she said, "who did this to you?"

"A lady downtown."

"What lady?" She moved toward him.

"At a beauty parlor," he said. "Don't touch it! Do you like it?"

"Well it looks like somebody pumped air up in it, that's all," she said. "You go wash that mess out of your hair."

"I can't. It's a permanent wave."

"Good Lord." Agnes came closer. "That's exactly what it is. You've got so much shiny on there I couldn't tell. Son, what on earth gave you such an idea?"

"Aw come on, it looks great," he said, backing into his room, flopping out on the bed. "It makes me look cool, that's all." He picked up his guitar with one hand and laid it across his ribs.

She leaned on the door. The look on her face made him suddenly nervous; did he really look that bizarre?

"Did you spend all your money on this?" she said.

He strummed an E chord. "I've still got five dollars."

"How much did she charge you?"

"Three-fifty. And I gave her a tip."

"That's not bad. . . ." Agnes shook her head, to keep herself from saying something nice about his hair. "I never saw britches like that in my life," she said instead. "Where do you plan to wear those things?"

"Oh, you know. Around. To school."

"You don't mean it. You can't go looking like that."

"Watch me." Leroy found a G seventh chord: *Weeelll, I gave you all my money. . . .*

"You know what your daddy is going to say."

"Yeah, yeah." He dismissed that with a wave of his hand. "He doesn't care how I look."

"He will, once he gets a look at you," she said.

Leroy propped the guitar against the bed and looked her in the eye. "I tell you one thing, Mama," he said, "by this time tomorrow, there's not gonna be anybody at that dumb school that doesn't know who I am. I'm sick of being ignored."

"Honey, who ignores you?"

Leroy sighed. That was such a big question. "Oh, everybody. I've been invisible since the day I walked in there."

"Well, I reckon they'll pay attention to you now," she said. "I just hate to think what kind."

Leroy stood up, suddenly restless. He was a good ten inches taller than his mother. Was it his imagination, or was she also shrinking? Even the apartment seemed to be dwindling, tightening in. There was barely enough air to breathe.

Agnes shook her head and went to the kitchen.

Leroy switched on the radio. The Clovers were into "Good Lovin'," that nice high-tenor boy out front singing in hops and starts, a saucy guitar line cutting a counterpoint, rinky-tink barroom piano and the other boys doing wah-wah-wah-wah in flawless syncopation. When they hollered, *You got me tossin' in my sleep!* Leroy picked up his guitar and swung over in front of the mirror.

Oh cool. Amazing New Leroy. Dutch gold sparkled in his shirt. Bolts of lightning streaked down his legs. His hair rose to gleaming new heights.

The pompadour felt like a stiff and unnatural helmet, hovering inches from his skull. When he patted the sides, he might have been touching someone else's hair. His scalp still tingled from the chemical.

But it made him look downright heroic. He never wanted to look any other way.

He put down the guitar and took off his clothes, hanging the shirt and pants meticulously. He struck another pose in his underwear: head thrown back, a laconic, lazy, indifferent look.

He wasn't Charles Atlas, but he was getting to be one good-looking cat.

He heard his mother rattling cups in the kitchen. Time to put on the smelly usher's uniform, time for Richard Widmark and Jack Palance in *Halls of Montezuma,* now in its third endless week. Leroy had been so proud of the usher's uniform just a few months before; now that the novelty of the job had worn off, it seemed faintly ridiculous. No matter how often Agnes washed it, the uniform stank of popcorn and cigarette smoke.

He buttoned the vest, touched his hair one last time.

Ray had returned from Sparky's pool hall to sit in his undershirt and drink a beer. He glanced up from the sports page when Leroy came in. "You got a haircut," he said.

"Yep." Leroy braced himself.

Ray took a swig. "Looks better," he said, and went back to the paper. Leroy grinned. "Mama, I'm gone," he called.

He drove the Plymouth downtown. He had never imagined he could get sick of movies—but the same movie, night after night! He could recite whole scenes of *Halls of Montezuma* from memory. His shoes stuck to the floor. He couldn't stay awake in school. Mr. Faubus turned out to be a mean little man who tried to gyp him out of his pay, and Shirley, the popcorn girl, bossed him around as if she owned the place.

On this night Leroy slipped past her and took his place collecting tickets beside the velvet rope. The people streaming in to see *Halls of Montezuma* didn't even glance at his hair.

In the dark he concentrated on Richard Widmark's glossy, smooth-sculpted waves—never out of place, even under enemy fire.

By the time he got home that night, he had worked up his courage again. His new clothes made a wild-looking dummy-Leroy on the hanger. He knew he was about to take a dangerous step. His stomach fluttered. But he couldn't go to school looking half remarkable. He had to do this thing all the way. He had to wear the lightning bolt pants.

~~~

He woke early to get into the bathroom first. After a pee and a shower, he fixed the side of his hair where the pillow had flattened it out.

In his room he flipped on the radio, pulled on the prickly new clothes. The Mother Station was playing morning music, Nat Cole's new hit "Too Young." Great rushing waves of strings, and then Nat's pearly voice swam in on the receding tide. *They tried to tell us....* He pronounced the words so exactly you could hear his tongue click. Every note was round, complete.

Leroy swayed to the music, looking himself over in the mirror. He was not Mr. Smooth Nat "King" Cole, but he was an animal in a brand-new skin. A cool rockin' cat, as Rufus Thomas would say.

He grabbed an apple and hurried out the door without saying good morning to anyone.

The morning was breezy, warm blue. He took the shortcut across the grounds of St. Joseph's Hospital, up a long alley to Looney Avenue, east through yards and empty lots to the houses facing Humes High.

For a time he stood in a shadow, surveying the schoolyard. There were plenty of kids milling around the steps, chattering, kicking at odd tufts of grass that had managed to grow in the crannies.

Leroy wondered what kind of sensation he was about to create. Or whether anyone would even notice him.

His hair was shiny and sleek as the hood of a car. His clothes were Superman's clothes, invulnerable.

He straightened and walked out of hiding.

Heads turned.

Leroy was conscious that he was two people: the bold kid strutting across Manassas Street, daring a car to hit him, and the timid soul scanning the crowd for the first hint of ridicule.

The first group to see him was the brainy bunch that kept to itself near the flagpole. One girl said, "Look!" and the others turned.

Leroy felt eyes turn on him—heat rays. The world seemed to take a breath. Birds held off flying. The sun came to a stop.

He kept up a Rufus Thomas chant at the back of his mind: You look good, boy, keep walking boy, hey, ain't you cool. You're so much cooler than anyone here. They ain't never seen anything cool as you.

The news of him jumped from one group to the next.

Leroy fixed his gaze on the top of the steps and kept walking. He heard his name in whispers, but he just kept walking.

"Oh, man. Oh, man!" cried one of the earnest student council types gathered on the steps. He clutched at his heart and play-fainted into the arms of a buddy. The girls laughed.

Leroy assumed a haughty smile—oh, you kids—and stepped to one side.

A crowd of football players and their cheerleader admirers held court on the concrete pedestal to the right of the main entrance. Leroy was almost to the edge of their turf. He steeled himself.

"Hey, you!" one of the players called. "Hey! Lightnin' legs! Talkin' to you!"

Leroy remembered the first time he climbed these steps, cowering behind his daddy. Be brave, boy. You so cool you got ice down your back. These kids don't know what to make out of you.

He started up the steps.

"Look at his hair!" the same loudmouth crowed. "Look guys, there's a new girl in town!"

That brought a round of beefy laughter from the pedestal. The football guys were the last gauntlet Leroy would have to run. They were shuffling into position to block his way and hand him a very hard time.

At the other door the band girls were inspecting him with much giggling and pointing.

He made a move in their direction, outflanking the football players. "Morning, girls," he said.

"Mornin', big boy," said a Mae West imitator among them.

The other girls screamed with laughter and parted to let him through. Red rover . . .

He put his head down and went straight for the door, shielded from the hulking he-men by a gaggle of flute players.

He stepped inside.

The bell clamored overhead.

Safe! He had done it! He dropped into that crowd of students like a rock into a pond, and the ripples of his appearance were still widening. Every last boy and girl in the schoolyard had seen him and known who he was.

Instead of slinking around the halls unseen, Leroy loitered at his locker and made sure everyone got a good look. Each change of classes brought a new wave of attention, a hall crammed with kids noticing him for the first time.

Morris Weed, the star quarterback, passed by flashing a malicious smile. "Hey there, sissy boy," he said.

Leroy just smiled, but every student in that stretch of the hallway heard the remark.

By the time he came into the cafeteria for lunch, the tone of the attention had darkened.

"Woo-woo!" rose a cry from the football table. "Come sit over here, sweetie pie!"

Leroy held tight to his tray and kept walking.

"I need someone to loooove," came another jeer. Some boys made kissy sounds with their lips.

Leroy talked himself through. They're jealous. Just keep walking.

He headed for the empty table in back by the door.

Something caught his foot. The tray flew from his hand, strewing

186

spaghetti and mashed potatoes all over Leroy, the floor. He went sprawling. The girls at the next table squealed and jumped from their chairs.

He rolled over, and there was Chip McCormick, a big, ugly, block-headed boy—the same one who'd called him "lightning legs" on the steps this morning—offering his hammy hand. "Lose your lunch?"

Leroy pulled himself up on a chair. His head was reeling. This was a disaster. Honor demanded that he had to fight the bully. This wasn't written down anywhere, but Leroy knew it was so. He could feel it in the air.

He hadn't ever fought anyone. McCormick looked to be as strong as three of him.

"You wanna do something about it?" Leroy said miserably.

"I'll see you at the practice field after school," McCormick said, turning back to his snickering friends.

Leroy squatted and began to mop up the mess with a stack of napkins. None of the bobby-soxers said a word. The lunchroom hummed, a different sound from the earlier, interested buzz. Now there was an edge of impending disgrace.

He threw the remains of his lunch in the trash barrel and made the long walk across the cafeteria, down the hall, to the bathroom. He stood at the sink, trembling, dabbing tomato sauce from his wonderful shirt.

Of course, he would not fight the bully. They'd all seen him knocked on his face. That was the worst. What difference did honor make when the guy who dishonored you was a big, stupid bum? A little dishonor was better than a broken nose.

Besides. Wasn't Leroy twice as notorious now?

After lunch the clock slowed until it was barely moving. Leroy walked alone through crowded halls. He heard whispers as he passed—"sss, sissy boy." Did they all take their cues from Morris Weed? Didn't one of them have a mind of his own?

At the sixth-period bell a girl named Alice Jarvis stopped him. "Dreamy hair," she said, smacking gum. "Where'dja get it done?"

"Aw, I don't know." He kicked his toe into his other heel. The pleasures of fame were beginning to rub a raw place on him.

"The whole school's talking about it." Alice was horsey, with braces, one of those hopeless gossipy girls who would die of joy if anyone ever gossiped about them.

"That a fact?" Leroy said. "What's the school got to say?"

Some of Alice's girlfriends came up to urge her silently on. "We heard you had it done in a beauty parlor," Alice said.

"I don't know how you could have heard that," Leroy said, slamming his locker. "I wouldn't think they'd let you inside one."

"Well! Thank you very much!" she sputtered. Her friends glared. None of them was pretty either, so they all stuck up for her. They flocked around her, hurried her off.

Leroy was proud of himself. His skin was getting thicker. Nobody said being cool was easy.

He had almost survived the day. He would slip out that side door and be gone. He was headed to do just that when a big hand came out of a doorway and seized him by the shoulder.

"Hey, wait a minute!"

Big, rough guys surrounded him, dragged him through the door to the locker room, past the steaming showers, into the toilet.

There was big, blockheaded McCormick, with most of the Humes High defensive line behind him. There was the quarterback, Morris Weed, lurking in the shower door. There was a boy Leroy didn't know, holding him fast by the neck, one hand clamped in his armpit.

Football players. This was their secret domain. The smell of sweat socks and disinfectant. The urinals on the wall looked ominous, the looming lockers. . . . Leroy was no ninety-eight-pound weakling, but if all these guys together meant to beat him up—well, they could do it.

They could mess up his face for good. His heart thudded against his chest. His chant turned into a kind of prayer: Save me oh save me be cool now, be cool.

"Come on, guys," he said. His voice came out higher than he intended, almost a squeak.

The boys laughed.

Their hands on him.

"Look at his hair," said McCormick. "Maybe we ought to cut his hair."

Morris Weed made a kissing sound. Someone said, "Get him, boys." McCormick helped the other boy lift Leroy. They jammed his face against the tile wall. He heard water dripping, feet shuffling, someone rooting in a locker for scissors.

He spoke to the wall. "The whole school saw what you did in the cafeteria."

"Yeah? So what?"

"If you mess with me, they'll know it was you."

Chip laughed.

The door squealed, swung in. Everyone jumped with a guilty reflex, then relaxed. It was another football player. Leroy recognized him: Bubba Hayes, a big, brawny guy who sat two rows ahead of him in Mr. Turner's history class. Bubba Hayes wasn't as big as Chip McCormick, but he looked harder and stronger. "Hey guys," he said, "what's going on."

"Come on, Bubba, we're playing beauty parlor," said Chip.

Leroy managed to turn his head, to send a simple message with his eyes: Help. Please.

A pair of scissors snipped the air near his ear.

"What are you doing to him?" Bubba said.

"He needs a haircut. We're gonna take care of it."

"No you're not, now come on," Bubba said, folding his arms. "It's six against one. That ain't fair."

"Aw get out of here, Bubba," said one of the boys.

Bubba uncrossed his arms. "Leave him alone." Bubba could never have taken these boys on by himself, but his opinion seemed to matter to them. The scissors disappeared. McCormick's buddies slipped off to the showers.

Morris Weed said, "Hey, how's it going, Bubba," and wandered whistling to his locker, as if he'd had nothing to do with anything.

"If a fellow wants to look like that, it's his problem," said Bubba. "It ain't no business of yours."

McCormick shook Leroy by the collar and turned him loose. "It is if I have to look at him," he growled.

"Don't look at him then."

McCormick saw that his support had disappeared. He shot a murderous glance at Leroy, said, "You stay out of my way," and went off to cause trouble for somebody else.

Leroy felt the fingers on his neck, a ghost pain. The Lysol in the air smelled like fear. Bubba regarded him with a sympathetic puzzlement.

Leroy swallowed. "God," he said. "Thanks, man. You saved my life." He leaned on the sink. The cold water startled his fingers. You're okay now. Be cool.

He ran his comb under the water and with a shaky hand began to fix his hair in front where they'd messed with it.

Bubba said, "Mighty particular about your hair."

"You saw what they were gonna do."

"Aaaah." Bubba waved his hand. He was almost exactly the opposite of Leroy: big and powerful, built like a wall. His face was peaceable, his black hair cropped almost to nothing. He looked too strong to have run into much trouble from anybody. "Those dumb bastards have been cruising after you all day," he said. "I saw 'em drag you in here."

Leroy tucked his comb in his pocket. "I don't know what to say. If you hadn't come in—" His knees felt shaky. He sat on a bench. "Your name's Bubba Hayes, isn't it. I know you from history."

"That's right. And you're Kirby."

"Yeah. Listen, I'll try to pay you back some time. I don't know how." Leroy put out his hand. They shook.

"Tell me something, Kirby. Where the hell did you come up with those britches?"

"Irving Brothers," said Leroy. "This place down on Beale."

"I know where it is. Listen, son, if you gonna come to school looking like that, I ain't gonna be able to keep those boys off you."

"I don't care about them," Leroy said, struggling to sound tough. "I can look out for myself."

"Yeah, I could see that." Bubba went to his locker, pulled the shirt over his head. His chest was one big emphatic set of muscles. Leroy had never seen a chest like that outside the bodybuilding ads at the back of DC Comics.

Bubba said, "You ought to show those guys you ain't like they think." He pulled on a tattered practice jersey and stooped to lace his cleated shoes. "Maybe you ought to come out for the team. Are you quick? Can you run? Catch a ball?"

Leroy felt his nerve returning. "I'm pretty quick," he said, "but those guys would kill me!"

"That may be the only way to keep 'em from it," said Bubba. "Once you're on the team, they won't give you trouble. They'll be too busy worrying about the guys on the other team." He beamed as if he'd just solved Leroy's every problem.

Leroy had to admit it would be nice to wear the white jersey with red numbers, and walk around on cleats, and have girls admire him. But he was doubtful. He could still hear those scissors snipping the air.

"Hey, thanks." Leroy stood up. "You helped me out."

The big hand came down and clapped his shoulder. "Try to stay out of trouble, okay?"

"Okay."

Bubba checked both ways outside the door, waved the all-clear, and trotted off toward the practice field.

School was over, the long hallways empty. Leroy wandered out and down the high wall on the Manassas Street side of the school. He peered through a hole in the fence-eating vines. The team was running laps.

All the humiliations of the day built up into a dark cloud, hovering over him. His mood grew more furious every step of the way home. They had laughed at him! They had ganged up on him! This wasn't the way he had imagined his first day as a star.

He slammed the front door so hard that Dodger yelped and jumped back from her puzzle. He went to his room, threw himself on the bed, buried his head under the pillow. It didn't matter if he ruined his hair. He needed to cry.

He tried. He lay there and waited and tried, but the tears would not come. He was famous, all right, and now he could not even cry.

After a while he dragged himself over to the mirror. That wasn't a boy staring back, and it wasn't a man. It was some kind of changeling thing caught between changes, lonesome brown eyes, a big Adam's apple, fantastic smooth hair.

Leroy leaned close. "Say something." His breath made a fog around the image of his lips.

The mirror was silent.

"Are you there?"

No answer.

Leroy patted the glass with his fingers. "Come on. Talk to me." He pressed his nose to the glass, trying to see through the dark holes of his eyes to whoever was living inside him. "Don't leave me here by myself!"

But the boy in the mirror was gone.

21

He wore the lightning bolt pants. He wore the purple sweater with the shiny blue dice appliqués. He wore the chrome yellow socks, the peg-legged fake satin trousers, the oversize black gabardine jacket, the skinny, sparkly tie, the western shirt, and all his other purchases from the Irving Brothers' stunning assortment.

He spent all his movie theater earnings at the Irvings' store. They gave him a standing 20 percent off their already low, low prices.

The shocked expressions in the halls at school lasted only a few days, but the taunts of "sissy" began to wear on him.

Leroy decided to take Bubba Hayes's advice. One afternoon in September, in full view of Chip McCormick and the rest of his tormentors, he walked up to Coach Barnes and stuck out his hand. "Hi, Coach, my name's Kirby," he said. "I want to go out for the team."

He was wearing his latest Irving purchase, a bright pink bowling shirt with a flamingo on the breast pocket and the blue jeans he had convinced his mother to dye black.

The coach said, "You want to be a cheerleader?"

A couple of players got a laugh out of that.

"Nosir, I want to play football," said Leroy.

"What position you play?"

"I can run with the ball," Leroy said because it sounded like something he could do.

"Well you sure as heck can't run in that getup." Coach Barnes had a hooked nose and a snarl that came naturally to his face. "You get Jimbo to find you some warm-ups, and we'll take a look at you."

On his way to the locker room Leroy passed Bubba Hayes, who grinned and put up his thumb.

Leroy changed into sweatpants and a smelly shirt the manager dug up from the back of a bin and trotted back out to the field. The coach held a stopwatch while he ran a sixty-yard dash. Next came a maze of car tires arranged on the ground so as to trip you when you ran through them. Leroy went dancing through lickety-split.

"Go out long," said the coach.

Leroy caught the pass. When he came back, the coach said, "You're pretty quick. You need to learn about the game. Not sure you'll get to play, but we'll try you on third string. See what you can do at the corner."

"Hey Coach, that's great," Leroy said. He was amazed. It was so easy. He didn't ask what the corner was. He figured Bubba would explain.

It worried him a little to see how hard those boys slammed into each other—this was just practice!—but maybe it didn't hurt as much as it looked.

The players filed by for the showers, sweating and huffing.

Bubba Hayes smacked Leroy's hand when he heard the big news. "I told you!" he cheered. "About time we had a sharp dresser on this team!"

"It was all your idea," Leroy was saying when he heard an insinuating voice behind him.

"Hey, Bubba, when'd you start bringing your girlfriend to practice?" It was Chip McCormick, with two of his chums.

"Fellows, you know Leroy Kirby," said Bubba. "Coach just put him on the team."

"Oh, yeah?" said McCormick. "What as, the water girl?"

"I'm playing the corner," Leroy announced.

One of McCormick's buddies stuck out a hand. "I'm Tiger Cunningham," he said. "Welcome to the team."

McCormick snorted and walked off without another word.

<hr>

Bubba Hayes took Leroy on as his personal crusade. His goal was to make Leroy actually good enough to play in one game before the season was over. This mattered a lot to Bubba, even though Leroy was happy enough on the sidelines. Some part of him knew he would never be a football killer.

He hated any part of the game that involved getting hit. He was afraid for his face. He hated when someone caught him off guard, crunching his bones all together and slamming him hard to the ground.

He liked the bench. Nice and warm and safe. A good view of the cheerleaders' short pleated skirts when they flounced up, revealing white underpants.

Bubba spent hours teaching Leroy the rules and strategy of the game. He drew complicated charts with X's and O's and arrows going all different ways. Leroy enjoyed Bubba's company and tried his best to be interested, but he wasn't convinced he needed to know that much about football. The only time he got to play was in practice scrimmage. His whole job was to line up, wait for the snap, then keep the guy in front of him busy until the quarterback got rid of the ball. Who needed a chart for that?

The way Bubba fretted and studied over those X's and O's, you'd think he was trying to learn Chinese.

Sometimes, after practice, Leroy brought out his guitar in the locker room. He sang songs with racy lyrics off the Mother Station: "Honeysuckle Rose" and "Mister Night-Time" and "Wild, Wild Young Men."

The boys gathered around to listen. They started calling him Frankie, after Sinatra.

The miracle Bubba had predicted came to pass. No one called Leroy a sissy anymore. The whole school saw him in his jersey with the rest of the team on Friday nights, and sissies do not play football.

Even Chip McCormick fell into a grudging silence. Leroy figured that was as good as you could do with a bully.

He spent two hours after school, four days a week, trying not to get mashed at football practice. After a quick shower he put on his usher's uniform and carried his clothes in a brown paper bag (his "Alabama suitcase," Agnes called it) to the Manassas Street bus stop, where he hopped the number three downtown, arriving at the Loew's State just in time to take tickets for the early show. He stood with his flashlight at the head of the aisle until midnight, then went home for sandwiches, some quiet piddling with his guitar, a few hours' sleep—and the whole thing started over.

To make up for Friday nights off at the games, he was working Sunday matinees and evening shows, too. He had no time at all for homework. His grades slid to C's and D's. He didn't care; he never planned to be Einstein.

Once a month he returned to the Mary Jane Beauty Parlor to have his pompadour revived. Deedee was trying to talk him into dyeing his hair black, to set off his eyes. He'd played with that idea on his own for a while, but he wasn't ready. He didn't even know any *girls* who dyed their hair.

He contented himself with the perfect DA, combed and polished with Robinson's Brite-Shine pomade.

He spent money as fast as he made it. He was always planning to put some aside for a down payment on a car, but then he'd stop by the Irvings' and see some wild trousers, a purple turtleneck, a jazzy new tie. In two minutes he'd blow a week's pay.

At least he wasn't wasting his precious time and money on a girl. Lots of guys did nothing but moon over some girl in a nice sweater. Leroy was more ambitious than that. He wanted every kind of success the world could offer. He wanted the girls to come after him.

The riot in his blood had quieted some.

He was scrubbing his hair in the locker-room shower one Thursday after practice when he found himself staring down at Donald Douglas's thing. It was so much bigger than his own. Lord, it hung down Donald's leg like a big old pink snake. Leroy blinked. He got soap in his eyes. He didn't know what to think.

He turned the other way to check out Buford Meaders's thing. It was not as big as Douglas's, but it was at least five inches long, hanging there.

Leroy sensed his own thing drawing up from its usual finger length.

Buford and Donald were talking about Renee Blanchard, whose reputation had been in shambles since she dropped out of school and word got around that she was pg.

Donald Douglas said, "I never did anything to her but I let her do it to me a few times."

"Yeah, my brother said she did it to him, too," said Buford, scrubbing his armpit.

"Man, I don't know." Donald shook his head in the spray. "Most girls don't even want to *know* about it, but I guess she just likes it."

Buford said, "I wonder who it was."

"Well, it sure as hell wasn't me." Donald turned off the water.

Facing the lockers, Leroy toweled himself and wriggled into his Jockey shorts. Great big old Tiger Cunningham came in, sweating, out of breath.

Tiger shrugged his pads to the floor. He stripped off his practice sweats, bent over, snapped off his jockstrap.

Leroy was so glad to see that puny baby thumb poking out down there that he felt like giving Tiger Cunningham a big hug.

His own thing was big enough to do what he needed. It was not small enough to be mortified about, at least. Poor Tiger.

Leroy knew that when he got to work, he would sneak in the upstairs bathroom at the Loew's and take care of himself. He would sink into the flawless imaginary girl he carried around in his head: a jewel-like brunette with brown eyes, his own eyes. She no longer much resembled Dolores Roselle. Her lips were sweet. Her trusting smile told Leroy she would always love him. He conjured her breast under his free hand, and she carried him off to that hot explosion every time.

~~~

On the Thursday before the South Side game Leroy was dreaming about that girl—really asleep and dreaming—when he tumbled and fell and awoke to discover he'd fallen out of his chair in Tightass Turner's

196

history class, with Turner standing over him and the classroom convulsed in laughter.

The teacher said, "Am I interrupting your beauty sleep?"

"Oh, no sir." Scrambling up, Leroy knocked the books off his desk, setting off more hilarity in the room.

"Good move, Frankie!" crowed Bubba Hayes, two seats ahead.

Leroy slipped into the desk, desperate that nobody see the hard thing in his pants. Or maybe they'd seen it already, and that's why they were laughing.

He grinned, blushing. "Sorry, Mr. Turner."

"Third time is the charm, Kirby. I can't teach history to a narcoleptic. You go down to Mr. Sumner's office and wait for me there."

Leroy gathered his books and slouched up the aisle. The room hummed. This wasn't like grade school; at Humes being sent to the principal's office only enhanced your reputation.

He went to the high-ceilinged room where the principal's secretary received wrongdoers. "Hey, Miss Hammonds, Mr. Turner told me to come here and wait for him."

Miss Hammonds was a bespectacled youngish woman who harbored a secret admiration for Leroy; she always had a big smile for him when he got in trouble. "Okay, Leroy, what was it this time?"

"I fell asleep again," he said. "I can't help it."

"What's the matter with you? That's how many times now? What do you do with yourself at night?" She motioned him to a chair. "You can tell me."

"It's not all my fault," he said, leaning against the doorjamb. "Did you ever listen to Mr. Turner for about five minutes?"

Just then Turner arrived in a splutter, demanding to see the principal. Apparently the cutting up had gone on after Leroy left the room.

Action must be taken, the teacher said, blah-blah, he would no longer tolerate this behavior, blah-blah, parents must be consulted, and on like that.

Mr. Sumner was a fairly relaxed principal, but after such a scene he had to do something. He had Miss Hammonds bring Leroy's file, then picked up his telephone and began dialing a number.

Leroy watched with increasing alarm. "Listen, Mr. Sumner, I said I won't do it again. I don't see why you have to—"

The principal cut him off. "Yes, hello? Hello there, Miz Kirby? Good morning, this is J. D. Sumner down at Humes High? How you this morning? No, no, ma'am, nothing wrong. Everything's fine. Sorry to trouble you, but it seems Leroy has fallen asleep in his history class again, and we need to do something about it."

Leroy cringed, picturing the look on her face. He heard her squawk in the mouthpiece, way over there.

"Yes, ma'am, I know. Yes, ma'am. Uh-huh. Well, I'll tell you, we're going to send him on home to you now. It's a one-day suspension. Yes, ma'am. You-all work it out. Uh-huh. Bye now."

He replaced the receiver. "Nice lady, your mother," he said. "It's a shame I had to call her. You go on home now."

"Yes sir."

"Will that take care of it, Mr. Turner?"

"Yes, thank you," he said, and huffed out.

Leroy took one step out into the autumn sunshine and felt happy. It was a beautiful day to get thrown out of school.

He set out walking for home, juking along in the bright sun, stepping to the beat of a song he'd heard the night before on the Mother Station. What was it? . . . *hound dawg,* said the chorus, *ain't nothin' but a hound dawg.*

It was that wild-sounding Big Mama Thornton, barking and howling all through the thing. Big Mama sang the way Mammy talked in *Gone With the Wind.* When she got to howling and knocking around with a tambourine, it sounded downright uncivilized. Leroy knew he could play that song. Easy. Three chords. But he would have to hear it again for the words.

Agnes was waiting for him on the front stoop. She stood up, shaking her head in a pantomime of disappointment.

"Leroy," she said. "Leroy."

"Oh come on, Mama," he said. "It's nothing. I didn't do anything wrong."

"That man said you fell asleep again," said Agnes. "I've already called your daddy. I want you to go down there and tell that Mr. Faubus you're quitting."

"Aw now, Mama." He had expected something like this. Agnes had never liked having him working all hours, instead of home with her where he belonged. "I'm not crazy about the late nights either. But I can't quit."

"I'm not going to stand here and talk about it," Agnes said. "We're doing a lot better since your daddy started at the paint company. Dodger's got some money from your granddaddy, and she's helping out. You're trying to do too many things."

"But I need my own money!"

"Honey, I know that. I know how much you like buying all your little shirts and all. I've talked to your daddy. You quit that job, and we can give you ten dollars a week spending money."

"You—really? Oh, man." It was Leroy's turn to shake his head in disbelief. It wasn't as much as he made at the Loew's, but it was free money, and it was ten dollars more than they'd ever offered him in his life. "You really mean it? Oh, Mama, that's great!"

"Well, you're such a sweet boy," she said, with a tired smile.

"Ten dollars a week! How did you ever talk Daddy into that?"

"He doesn't always get his way, any more than you," she said. "Now you've made me late for work. You go down there and tell that man what I said. The idea! Falling out of your chair—like you weren't raised any better!"

Leroy leaned down, kissed her. "Satnin, I love you," he said.

She pushed him away. "Go on."

Mr. Faubus wasn't sorry to hear the news, since according to him, Leroy was lazy and had been about to get fired anyway.

That hurt Leroy's pride. He'd never been late once in nearly a year and had worked like a slave all that time, raking popcorn from under the seats.

Somehow he managed to hold his tongue. He would need his job back if Ray's newfound generosity suddenly gave out.

He sauntered onto the sidewalk. He'd never thought quitting would make him so happy.

He had a whole open day in front of him now and then the big game with South Side. There was the Mother Station and the Sound Star and no school, nothing else to do. Life was too sweet.

～～～

The lights of South Side Stadium lit everything an unnatural blue. The two bands blatted away at each other with fight songs. Cheerleaders leaped and hollered. The man in the black and white shirt tossed the coin, which twinkled and fell to the grass. Humes won the toss.

Leroy paraded along the bench, clapping his hands, yelling, "Get 'em! Let's go!" with the trainers and the other boys of the second and third strings.

The hot crosstown rivalry had filled the stands. Leroy scanned the passing crowd for pretty faces; he was becoming an expert at playing the bench.

Humes got off to a thundering start. Morris Weed threw two touchdowns in the first quarter. On a field goal attempt Bubba Hayes went roaring through the line and threw all his weight on the poor South Side kicker, who lay doubled up on the ground for a long time, then hobbled off on the arms of his coaches and did not return.

In a show of appeasement Coach Barnes pulled Bubba from the line, but everyone clapped his shoulder pads and congratulated him.

The Humes fans went out of control. They'd come to witness their team's annual trampling under the feet of the bigger, meaner South Side boys. Suddenly Humes had a whip in its hand and was flogging South Side up and down the field.

"It's one hell of a game, ain't it?" Bubba shouted. "We're stomping their ass!"

"We sure are!"

"Listen—" Bubba dropped his voice. "I got a feeling tonight's your big chance. I already said something to Coach. If we stay this far in front, he's *got* to put you in."

Leroy's heart started pounding. "You think so?"

"It's a massacre!" Bubba cried. "You better get ready."

"I don't know," said Leroy. Those South Siders looked big, and they hit mighty hard. With eleven boys on each side of the field, a massacre could turn either way.

"Come on, Frankie. You can't pussy out. Think how hard we worked, man! When he points at you, you better go, or I'm coming to beat the hell out of you." Bubba broke out in a grin. "Damn. You don't want to put on your helmet, that's all. Afraid you'll mess up your hair."

Leroy grinned back. "I reckon you're right," he said, patting his temple.

Coach Barnes blew his whistle and waved the second-string cornerback, Davy Lee Williams, out of the game.

He turned and pointed his finger at Leroy.

200

Leroy pulled on his helmet. He took a deep breath and trotted out for the mud-stained huddle.

He heard his name, far away on the public-address system. The crowd roared. Were they roaring for him? His clean uniform made him stand out. He wished his folks were here to see this.

He ran into the line. The other boys' faces shone with happy exhaustion and sweat. Morris Weed's unbeatable smile gleamed through his faceguard. "Hey, we must have this thing won. Look what Coach is sending in."

Leroy was trying to remember what he was supposed to do when the ball was snapped. Morris Weed called a screen pass to Donald Douglas. On cue, they all clapped their hands, shouted "hunh!" and turned to face the defenders.

Leroy weighed 143 pounds. The boy opposite him weighed 190, 200. He was built like a wall.

Leroy thought: Okay, Leroy. This is it for you. If you don't hit this guy, you're queer.

"You're the one they call Frankie, ain't you," said the South Side boy.

Leroy knew from Bubba's instructions that this was an effort to mess with his mind. "You better watch out," he growled, imitating Bubba. "I'm lookin' straight at you."

The referee whistled. At the snap Leroy lowered his shoulder and closed his eyes and ran hard for the big boy's midsection.

He ran into a wall in the dark.

He knocked the wall back a good three feet through the force of the hit.

Weed got the pass away, but Douglas couldn't hold on. Second down, ten.

Leroy loped back to the huddle. At least he had not humiliated himself on the first play. The crowd seemed a million miles away, on the other side of all that green grass.

He stuck his head in the circle of boys.

"Great catch, Douglas," Morris Weed was saying. "Let's try it again. Dub, you go wide to the right." The huddle broke. "Hunh!"

Once again the big South Sider snarled at Leroy: "Come on. Come get me."

Weed shouted, "Two! Twenty-three!" and the snap went off.

Leroy shut his eyes, doubled his speed. He slammed into the bigger boy and knocked him clean off his feet.

He stood over his victim, breathing hard. "Keep running your mouth," he said. "See what it gets you."

He felt strong. He was capable of killing after all. This wasn't X's and O's. This was a guy who would drag your nose down through the dirt if you didn't smash into him first.

Leroy strutted back to the huddle.

Morris Weed said, "Nice block, Frankie. Let's see what you can do with a pass. Get around your man and go out ten yards, then hook right. I'll throw it to you."

Oh God. Leroy was not a receiver. This was a Morris Weed trick, had to be.

But he had no choice. The quarterback called the plays.

Clap. "Hunh!" He took his place in line.

The ball went off. Leroy feinted left, then right, dived under the South Sider's arm, and found himself in the open. He ran all alone for the twenty-yard line. If he caught the ball, there was clear air to the end zone. If he caught the ball.

He turned. He couldn't find Morris Weed in the chaos of grappling players.

But then he saw the ball pop up; he thought it was fumbled. No! It was a high, lofting pass spiraling down toward him.

A hand reached up from nowhere and tipped the ball—it tumbled end over end for the grass—

Leroy lunged through the air.

The ball struck his arm. He juggled it, tip! tip! his feet flying up in the air; then he got his hands on it, clutched it to his chest—

He was flat on his back. Light bulbs flashed in his eyes. A siren wailed in his head.

The coach and the manager were bending over him with anxious faces.

"I'm okay," Leroy said, "what—what happened?" He could see blurry images of Morris Weed and the others peering at him. From their faces he knew his landing must have been spectacular.

"You came down on your head!" said Coach Barnes. "Think you can get up?"

"Sure," he said, and made a move to do that, but his knees wobbled and failed. They grabbed his arms and helped him off the field to a resounding cheer from the whole stadium.

"Coach, did I catch it?"

"Dadgum right you did," Barnes said, steering him to the bench. "Held on to it and got the first down, too. Lucky you didn't break your neck."

"Let me play," Leroy said. "I was doing all right."

"Yeah, and you got your bell rung, too," said the coach. "You sit here. We'll finish this up."

Leroy watched through a wall of shimmering glass as the Humes boys scored ten more points in the glorious closing minutes. The final gun cracked. Humes fans swarmed the field. The score would look great in tomorrow's *Commercial Appeal:* HUMES 31, SOUTH SIDE 3.

Leroy moved in a daze. He had made a first down. He had this shaky headache to remember it by. The showers resounded with the hoarse cries of the victors.

Bubba pounded his back and said he'd made the best damn catch of the game. Even Morris Weed stopped over to see if he'd gotten his head screwed back on.

"I'm okay," Leroy said. "Thanks for throwing to me."

"It's too bad you had to go out of the game," said Weed. "The next pass would have been *really* hard to catch." He swaggered off, snapping the air with his towel.

The Sunday newspaper mentioned Leroy's big play: "Humes's fourth-quarter drive was kept alive by cornerback L. Kirby's acrobatic catch of a Weed toss, resulting in a first down and a trip to the sidelines for the shaken junior."

Agnes went crazy when she read that. " 'Shaken'!" She rattled the paper at him. "Leroy! You didn't say you were *shaken!* Does this mean they had to *carry* you out of the game?"

"I was fine," he said. "I tried to get Coach to let me stay in, but—"

"I don't want to hear anymore," said Agnes. "You're quitting the team."

"Aw good grief, Mama, anytime I do anything these days, you want me to quit. I'm fine. Look at me. This is how I looked." He wobbled across the room, imitating a drunkard's walk.

"Would you stop? You might have wound up in a wheelchair."

"Your mother is right." Dodger looked up from her puzzle of Buckingham Palace. "Edna Wallace's grandson broke his neck jumping into shallow water, and now they have to feed him with a spoon."

"Y'all worry too much." Leroy picked up his guitar. "I wasn't even supposed to catch that ball, but I did." He strummed a chord, sang a line: *Hear that lonesome whistle blowin'. . . .*

At practice the following Monday Coach Barnes called Leroy out of line. He loped over, expecting a word of praise for his head-standing catch. Instead, the coach said, "You're off the team."

"What—wait a minute! What do you mean?"

"Your father called me," said Barnes. "Said your mother's worried after what happened at the game. I can't let you play without their permission."

Leroy sputtered and protested and vowed to come back in the morning with a signed permission, but the coach wouldn't even let him dress out for practice.

He went home. Agnes and Ray were off at work. Dodger made a great show of surprise at what had happened.

Leroy carried his guitar outside, to the porch. He got to playing that hound dog song, slow and mournful. Sometimes it seemed his mother would suffocate him. At other times it was his love for her that threatened to choke off his air.

If things went like normal when she got home, he would rail at her, probably even provoke her to tears. Then he'd have to back off and give in and agree not to play football. It would be his decision—the same way Charlie McCarthy decides to open his mouth when Edgar Bergen pulls the string.

In two days Agnes had maneuvered Leroy out of his job and off the team. If she had her way, he would never leave home. He would stay on the front porch all day and play songs for her.

He couldn't do that.

He had his own plans. He'd gotten all the benefits of the team anyway: his name in the paper; an end to the teasing at school. Wasn't that the same as victory?

When Agnes got home from work, Leroy could tell by her nervous smile that she was expecting a big argument.

He just smiled back. "I heard you talked to Coach Barnes."

"I don't want to hear a thing about it," she said. "You could have broken your neck."

"You treat me like I'm a kid," he said.

Agnes said, "Well, at least you're alive and you can walk, so be grateful."

He left it at that.

The next morning he told Bubba Hayes the news. "Oh, man," Bubba said, "you were just getting started!"—but Leroy said he had other things on his mind.

Every day his future became a little clearer to him. The real talent inside him had nothing to do with football. His future was music. He knew it. He'd seen it work magic on people. Even his teammates thought he sounded good, in the locker room.

Now he had nothing but time to play music.

He got serious with the radio. He listened to gospel choirs rollicking like Brother Love's congregation, and hillbillies singing through their noses on Uncle Richard's WMPS country hour, big stars like Roy Acuff and Bob Wills and Hank Williams, Sinatra's butter-smooth croon, lazy, sexy Dean Martin—and, of course, the Mother Station.

He took fifteen dollars from his savings to Horace's Pawnshop and bought a secondhand RCA phonograph, an old beat-up portable with a heavy Bakelite tone arm. He began spending his extra money at Poplar Tunes, the record shop just the other side of the Lauderdale Court.

He bought singles: "Reconsider Baby," "Rag Mop" by old Doc Sausage, Big Boy Crudup's hot, wailing "My Baby Left Me," Ruth Brown and Big Mama Thornton and the Diamonds' song Hot Rod Hurlburt loved so well, the Clovers and the Chords and Nat "King" Cole's "Mona Lisa," Bill Monroe's "I Hear a Sweet Voice Calling." He listened to the records thirty, forty, eighty times—miming the singing styles, learning the words, changing the tunes all around.

LaVern Baker had a new song, a silly thing called "Tweedlee Dee" with a hook that got into Leroy's brain and stayed there, scatting around inside him, for days. The words were nonsense syllables, mostly. The slangy, offhand rhythm made you think of a sugared-up woman flouncing down a street. Leroy went around popping his fingers and tweedlee-deeing for days.

When he spotted a notice on the Humes bulletin board announcing the talent show in December, he knew the song that might win it.

He sneaked into the music room to hand in his entry when no other kids were around. He spent a week pondering what to wear. It had to be cool. This was his big chance at Humes. He didn't want to wear the wrong clothes and get tripped up by some sophomore version of Tupelo's little Miss Mary Lynn Bradley.

He practiced "Tweedlee Dee" until Dodger begged him to stop. It amazed him to find that he only got better, the more he played it; he found new curlicues in the beat and syncopated some of the lines LaVern Baker sang straight. He worked the whole thing up before his bedroom mirror, to see how he would look to the audience.

He kept one eyebrow up and sang with a sardonic grin on his face—his new snarl, somewhere between Marlon Brando and Coach Barnes.

After he had sung those nonsense syllables enough times, Leroy began to hear a secret meaning behind them. The song was a come-on, an invitation. "Tweedlee dee" stood for something you couldn't sing on the radio.

He sneaked his costume out of the house in a gym bag and changed in the locker room at school. With the Irving Brothers' help, he became cool beyond cool: a pink and black rayon V-neck shirt with chevrons on the elbows; a white scarf at his throat; black peg-legged jeans; pointy shoes. He squeezed an inch of Maybelline Mystic Brown eyeliner on his finger and rubbed it over his eyelids, to bring out his eyes.

"Good luck," he said to the mirror.

No answer.

He came out into the hall. The kids pouring in for assembly peered down the hall as if the talent show contestants were creatures from another world, huddling in their spangly costumes and stiff, unnatural hairstyles. Leroy slouched against a wall, holding on to the Sound Star, trying to look bored.

He surveyed the field of contestants. He knew he was better than any of them.

He had done this before, so he knew what to do. He had the song, the costume, the hair, the guitar, the voice, the talent—and the need to win.

206

He was the fifteenth of nineteen acts on the bill. He went off by himself down the hall to strum a soft tune, while the others performed. He wasn't competing against them. They were wasting their time. He would concentrate and go out and do it just the way he had practiced at home, and he would win.

Someone called his name. He said, "I'm here," and went calmly among the piano players and flutists to the dark side of the stage. The previous performer, a magician, was picking up white feathers from the floor.

Mrs. Thomas, the music teacher, walked into the spotlight: "Our next act is one of Humes's lesser-known singing talents, Leroy Kirby. Let's hear it for Leroy."

Light applause, a few jeers from the football section. Leroy carried his Sound Star out to the giant beam of light. When the girls got a look at his costume, they started up clapping again and whistling.

Someone in front hollered, "Sing it, Frankie!"

Leroy blinked, raised the microphone stand. "Uhm, thank you Mrs. Thomas, boys and grills." Some of the footballers haw-hawed. Leroy's voice echoed back from all around. "Like to do a little song for you, one you may not have heard, it's called 'Tweedlee Dee,' and now I'm gonna stop talking and sing it."

Leroy started strumming that loose, jangly beat, a hop-skip-and-jump kind of rhythm that made you want to get up and strut off somewhere, feeling proud of yourself.

He raised up that eyebrow and swung his hips in time, just rolling in time with the beat. He looked for smiles on their faces, and there they were, yes, shining, yes, smiling up at him, we like it, sing it some more, don't stop, go!

He did it exactly the way he had practiced. He did not miss a lick. On the high notes, he closed his eyes and made as if to swoon, staggering back a few steps—then recovering, grinning at himself. *Jiminy Cricket, Jiminy Jack, you make my heart go clickety-clack.* . . .

They loved it—the same kids who'd harassed or ignored him all these years. Why had he waited so long to do this? He felt more comfortable on this stage than he ever had on the football field or walking down the hall. Music was his power.

He flailed away at the Sound Star. He shook his leg, beating hard on the break—the girls squealed, down in front.

Too soon the song was over. The whole school applauded. They clapped loud and kept clapping.

Leroy ran off.

Mrs. Thomas beamed at him with her arms out. "Honey, where have you been? I didn't know you could sing like that!"

He couldn't stop grinning. He stood around backstage, soaking up congratulations and stares of envy from the other contestants. They knew he had won.

He waited patiently. When the last act was over, Mrs. Thomas called him to center stage for the blue ribbon and the ten-dollar first prize.

Leroy grinned and bowed, waving the bill in the air. Take that, Mary Lynn Bradley, wherever you are.

He played an encore. "Old Blue." They loved it.

He took a long way home that afternoon, wandering downtown to stare at the Gibson guitars in the Memphis Music Company window. He was all the way visible now—but his life hadn't changed. He didn't have a Gibson, or a car, or the money to buy either one. He hadn't bothered to go back for his driving test since he never got to use the car anyway.

He ambled out Union Street with the Sound Star over his shoulder. A convertible roared by, trailing a radio song in the air.

Leroy noticed an interesting neon sign on an unremarkable brick building. MID-SOUTH RECORDING SERVICE.

The light changed. He jogged across the street. On the door was a painted red rooster crowing, with a painted yellow sun rising behind it. He leaned to read the notice in the window:

WE RECORD ANYTHING—ANYWHERE—ANYTIME
A complete service
to fill every recording need.
Combining the newest and best equipment
with the latest and finest
SONOCOUSTIC STUDIOS!

The place was no wider than the shoe shop next door or the café on the other side. It hardly looked large enough to contain something as imposing as a Sonocoustic Studio.

There might be someone in there making music—and someone recording it, through a process that was an utter mystery to Leroy. But no sound escaped. The place was sealed tight. A brown curtain concealed whatever was going on behind the plate glass.

Leroy tried the door. Locked. He saw a little card in the door:—BUS. HOURS NOON–5—and a phone number, which he jotted on his ten-dollar bill and tucked in the back of his wallet.

Anything . . . anywhere . . . anytime.

Every recording need.

The neon sign hummed as if flies were trapped inside it.

Leroy put his hands in his pockets and headed for home.

22

*L*eroy lay on the floor with his head on the purple fringed pillow, listening to the Mother Station. Hot Rod Hurlburt was so crazy for the Diamonds' new song, "A Beggar for Your Kisses," that he played it three times in a row. It started off with a vibraphone riff. An oddly girlish-sounding male singer laid down a slithery melody line; then his three harmony boys came pouring in, smooth as melted silver, dripping down the song. *Can't you spare a little love for me?*

"Mama, come scratch my back," Leroy said.

Agnes sat in her armchair, shelling field peas in a skillet on her lap. "You silly," she said.

"No I mean it. Come scratch my back like you used to." It was one of his favorite memories: going to sleep with her fingers grazing his back through the pajama top. This song made him sad with its halting heartbeat shuffle and those harmonious wailers, that tremulous voice out front. For some reason it put him in mind of old times.

He pulled himself up to the sofa, stretched on his side. "Come on. . . ."

"Aw, all right." Agnes set the skillet on the floor and came to sit beside him, on the edge of the cushion. They barely fit together on the sofa anymore. She began skimming his back with just the tips of her fingers—a soft tickle. That was just what he wanted.

She turned him so his head rested in her lap. "What's the matter, baby? You feeling lonesome?"

"That song," Leroy said. Gooseflesh spread down him from the points of her nails.

"They sure do play it enough," she said. "You'd think they'd play something else once in a while."

"That's Hot Rod," said Leroy. "When he likes something, he plays it till he wears out the grooves." He stretched his arm, his hand, his fingers. "Mama, you reckon they'll ever play me on the radio?"

"Sure they will, honey, if that's what you want them to do."

"It's not that easy."

"Anything's easy if you put your mind to it," said Agnes. Her nails traced overlapping circles down his shoulder blades, the ticklish hollow in the small of his back.

Leroy shivered. "I've got to make a record first."

"Well then, make one. You know how much I love to hear you sing. You sound better than most of that stuff you listen to."

Leroy wondered if he'd ever find anyone who could scratch his back like his mother. That was a real talent, the way she applied just enough pressure to be felt, to suggest a deeper pressure.

Leroy crooned along with the melody line. The Diamonds' vibraphone sounded like a hollow bell inside his chest.

"There something I want to tell you," Agnes said. Her fingers wandered up and down, more slowly now, in straight lines.

"Don't stop," said Leroy.

"We got a letter from the housing authority," said Agnes. "They say we're making too much money to live here. They're evicting us."

Leroy closed his eyes. Not now. Not again. When things were finally going along right. "They can't do that," he said.

"I think they can. My four dollars a week from St. Joseph's has pushed us up over the line." Agnes had taken to working Saturdays as a nurse's aide at the hulking pile of hospital just north of the Lauderdale Court. "Can you believe it? Too much money. Us." She patted his shirt, a signal that her hand was tired. "We're just too rich to live here."

Leroy rolled over, sat up. "Mama, you can quit your job."

"It's too late. They've served notice. We have to get out. I hope you didn't have any big plans for Wednesday. We need you to stay home from school."

"Where's Daddy? What does he say about this?"

Agnes threw him a look. "Where do you think he is?"

The silence between them was the answer. When Ray wasn't off packing cans of house paint into cartons at United Paint Company, he could always be found at Sparky's pool hall.

Agnes's hand rested. The spell was broken.

Leroy fixed his shirt, wandered to the screen door, peered out into the dusk. "We've been moving ever since I can remember. You got any idea where we'll go?"

"There's always someplace," she said.

"Mama, I'll go bring Daddy back. We'll figure a way out of this."

"No you don't, now. He's already tried. I'm going downtown to talk to them. He's got enough on his mind."

"What? What has he got to worry about besides his next beer?"

"You hush your smart mouth."

"Well, it's true," he said.

"When I think of the sacrifices that man has made for you . . ."

"Yeah, right. Name one." Leroy kicked the door with his toe. "I'll tell you one thing. You guys can leave if you want, but I'm staying in Memphis."

"Well honey, who said anything about leaving? We just have to move, that's all. Your daddy always finds us some place. Don't worry. Come lay down. I'll scratch your back some more." She looked at him with hopeful eyes.

212

Hot Rod Hurlburt said, "Chillun, I just cain't get enough of this tune," and started the Diamonds over one more time. Leroy felt bluer than ever.

He went back to the couch. That song was just what he needed, and his mother's touch.

23

*L*eroy came through the door in a hurry. "Hey folks—" He was halfway across the room when he noticed Ray and Agnes nuzzled up together on the sofa. "Good grief," he said. "What are you doing?"

His father stayed where he was. "What does it look like we're doing? I'm checking your mother for fleas."

Agnes snorted.

Ray said, "There's one," and kissed at a spot on her neck, and they broke up laughing.

Leroy shook his head. "Y'all are crazy. Mama, what's to eat?"

Agnes said, "I'm going to cook those turnip greens for supper."

"I don't have time for that." Leroy unbuttoned his shirt, heading for his room. "There's a big sing downtown tonight. I'll grab some hamburgers or something."

"Leroy," his mother said through the curtain, "you just went out Wednesday night. You don't need to go out again."

"This is a good one," he said, pulling on his sharp new green and black shirt. "It's colored tonight."

He heard his father say, "Aw, let him go."

Leroy wondered if all that kissy stuff was going to lead to something else once he left the house. He couldn't believe his parents were really still doing anything. Look how old they were! In April Agnes would turn *forty!*

He put on the black slacks with the satin leg stripe, tied the pink necktie, slipped on the shiny gray sport coat with the wide, wide shoulders. He paused to check his hair in the mirror over the sink.

Sometimes he missed the silvery voice in the mirror, but he supposed it was something he had outgrown. He had to rely on his own advice these days.

When he came out, Agnes and Ray were still snuggled on the couch. "Don't wait up," he said. "It won't be over till late."

Agnes said, "Are you really going down there to listen to those colored people?"

"Sure I am," Leroy said. "Y'all look pretty cozy anyway. You don't want me hanging around. Daddy, where's the keys?"

"Sorry, son, you can't have it. I'm meetin' some boys at Sparky's later on."

Agnes glanced over with a look that said: Oh, you are?

"Aw come on, Daddy. It won't hurt you to walk. It ain't but two blocks."

Agnes pulled away from Ray and tried to struggle up from the sofa, but her back and the weight she'd put on made it difficult. "Here, son, give me a kiss before you go," she said.

He helped her to her feet. "Tell him to let me have the car."

"It ain't your mama's car," Ray said. "If you want to borrow it, you ask me."

"Well then, come on, Daddy, please?"

"Not a chance. You're young. You can walk."

Leroy slammed out the door.

This big rambly apartment house would never be home. It was a place for Leroy to sleep and shower and change clothes and grab something to eat—sometimes—on his way somewhere else.

These days he did pretty much what he wanted, no matter what his folks said about it. He was a big-deal senior at Humes, with nothing but time on his hands. They didn't know what all he did.

He spent plenty of time at the mirror, playing with his hair, imagining himself as a movie star. His olive skin and dark-lidded eyes, his heavy bottom lip—his whole face had the cast of a Latin lover, a romantic type like Dean Martin, or Lanza. This is how he began to style himself.

In the afternoons he carried his guitar to a grassy bluff overlooking the river from the end of Carnahan Street, a secret place where he sat for hours, singing "That's Amore" and "When My Blue Moon Turns to Gold" and "Harbor Lights" to the muddy water and barges sliding under the bridge.

Late at night he would loiter in the doorways of the blues joints and the Palace Theater on Beale Street, hearing the music leak out—hot licks and shuffling heat, live applause.

Sometimes, as now, he would wander out Union Avenue for a look at the curtained window of the Mid-South Recording Service.

He'd found out a few things about the place. A young white man named Dan Tobias was actually cutting records in that little storefront—demonstration records of Beale Street musicians for colored labels in Chicago and Los Angeles. Tobias called his operation Rocking Records.

Leroy wanted to rock.

Standing on the sidewalk, he tried to convince himself to open that door and walk through.

He could imagine himself as a star—oh, he'd buy his mama so many fine things—but he couldn't imagine how to make his hand open that door.

It was one thing to stand up in front of the kids at Humes. The thought of singing for a professional record producer sent a cold rush down his spine.

216

Maybe he should call first.

In his head he heard Lowell Fulson begging "Reconsider Baby." He snapped his fingers in time and moved off down the sidewalk.

At the corner of November and Union he saw a small crowd gathered in front of the window at Goldsmith's Department Store.

He stopped humming and went closer.

The people gazed at the window, transfixed. Nobody said anything.

A sign said A WINDOW ON THE FUTURE—AT GOLDSMITH'S TODAY!

The television stood alone on a circle of black velvet: a dark oak cabinet with a glowing oval porthole in the front.

Leroy had heard about television for years, but this was the first set he had seen in real life.

It flickered, pouring eerie white light from its window. There was the floating image of a man. He wore a bow tie and plaid jacket. His face was interrupted by a black bar that kept rolling down from the top of the screen. Now and then a storm of white dots would blow through the picture. The plate-glass window kept the sound in.

"It's like the radio," a man said.

"Except you can see him," said the lady next to Leroy.

"How much does it cost?"

"Somebody said six hundred dollars."

Everyone said "Ohhh."

The bow tie man spoke to a pretty woman in a pleated dress. The picture changed to a big shiny Buick, then to a woman holding a pack of Chesterfield Kings. Magic! The crowd made little noises of pleasure.

Leroy watched their faces. He was thinking how good he would look on television. He'd love to see that magic screen from the inside. To have his face broadcast through the air, to materialize in somebody's living room or the window of Goldsmith's!

He could get famous that way.

"It's kind of hard to take your eyes off it," said the lady beside him.

Leroy said, "Yes ma'am."

She glanced over. "You look like you ought to be on there with them," she said, "all dressed up that way."

People turned to look at Leroy's clothes and then his hair.

Leroy grinned. "I'm not on there yet, but I will be," he said. "Keep an eye out for me."

He winked at the lady and struck off down the street with the stares of the crowd to keep him company.

The television thrilled him. A window on the future. He had seen a vision of himself on there, singing his latest hit record.

Nobody ever got famous by sitting around waiting for something to happen.

He had to try. He was good.

The gospel was already filling the rafters of Ellis Auditorium, but Leroy had to find a phone and *make the call*. The whole thing came down to one phone call, the nerve required to make it.

A pay phone, by the door of Berman's Drugs.

Leroy crossed the street. He took the creased bill with the phone number from his wallet, lifted the receiver.

"Operator . . ."

"Kokomo three-five-seven-one-four," he said.

"Five cents, please."

He dropped in a coin. Three rings, then: "Mid-South Recording Service, Claudia Cash."

Instantly Leroy forgot what he had planned to say.

"Mid-South Recording Service. Can I help you?"

"Hi, yes ma'am. Uhm—" Don't give your name! "Listen, I saw that sign that says you-all do recordings."

"That's right," she said.

"Well . . . how much does it cost?"

He heard the impatient click of her tongue. "We do all kinds of recordings," she said. "Maybe you could be a little more specific."

"Like, if I wanted to come in and do a couple of songs," he said. "How much would that cost?"

"For two songs we've got a flat rate, three ninety-five. That pays for the studio time, the mixdown, and one ten-inch acetate. Extra pressings are two dollars each." She rattled this off as if she'd done it a dozen times a day her whole life. "Hello?" she said.

"Yes ma'am, I'm here," said Leroy.

"Is there anything else?"

"Well . . . am I supposed to set up a time, or do I just show up when I'm ready?"

218

"If you're only doing two songs, any day between noon and five will be fine, except Sunday," she said. "Just come on in."

"Thank you," he said, "I sure will. Thanks a lot."

He put down the receiver. Four dollars was nothing. He could have done this a long time ago. Now he needed two songs—an A side, a B side—and practice, practice.

24

Leroy liked all kinds of music—the wild thumping late nights on the Mother Station, and the Moonglows, and Kitty Wells, Dean Martin, Jerry Vale, Roger Williams's swirly piano. The Orioles' stupendous harmony on "Crying in the Chapel." Plain blues from Mississippi, Perry Como and Tony Bennett, Hank Snow on the "Grand Ole Opry," tight-faced old Bill Monroe fiddling his way into a delirium. Leroy even liked the nasal hillbilly woman who sang during Bill Monroe's breaks.

But he liked his own voice best on the sweet songs, the sad ones, the love songs and ballads—especially those with a story, a twist in the words. It seemed to him he had just the right kind of voice to make people cry. He'd never forgotten the way "Old Blue" worked on the crowd at the Dairy Fair, back in Tupelo.

At last he settled on two songs for a demonstration record. "That's When You Know It's Over," one of Dodger's favorite weepers, featured a talking part in the middle, and "My Happiness" was a simple, sorrowful tune that had been a big hit for the Pied Pipers. Leroy worked and worked on these songs at his bluff by the river. They weren't right yet. They were getting closer.

Agnes got to where she couldn't stand the roaches and the noise through the walls at Cypress Avenue. Ray set out to find another place. A week later they moved to the bottom of a two-story apartment house on Alabama Street, just down from the Lauderdale Court.

They surely knew how to move. Agnes and Dodger stood back and gave instructions. Leroy and Ray hauled boxes and ignored them.

Along about April the teachers quit trying to get anything useful out of the seniors. Leroy discovered ways to skip whole afternoons. *Study hall* was a very loose term. Other seniors went off in their parents' cars on wild adventures involving French kissing and Arkansas beer. Leroy carried the Sound Star to the river bluff, to practice his songs.

All the cool seniors swore they wouldn't be caught dead at graduation, but when Leroy alluded to this at the supper table, his mother and Dodger whipped out their brooms and flew around the ceiling. "Why, you're the first one in this family to ever finish!" Agnes cried. "You may not care about it, but you're going. No backtalk."

"Your mama and daddy have sweated and prayed for this day," Dodger said. "I can't figure young people. What else have you got to do that's so important?"

"Okay, okay!" Leroy held up his hands.

On the morning of his graduation he went to the West Tennessee Employment Office for a test required of all seniors, to help guide them toward suitable careers. He sat in a classroom with a bunch of unfamiliar kids. A stern-faced Mrs. Davis doled out test booklets. "I hope you all brought pencils," she said through her nose. "The first group took my pencils home with them."

Leroy looked over the first page of the "General Aptitude Test Battery."

> Q. Which of these activities would you consider to be the most "fun" way to spend leisure time?
>   A. Working on an automobile engine
>   B. Planting a vegetable garden
>   C. Reading a mystery novel
>   D. Baking a layer cake

Well now, what kind of test was this? Four possible answers, and not a right one. Were they looking for opinions? Obviously B and D were answers for girls, and the mystery novel sounded brainy but unrealistic. Leroy picked A and went on to the next item.

> Q. When you have conversations with groups of friends, would you say you:
>   A. Generally lead the conversation
>   B. Wait until I have something interesting to say
>   C. Don't speak unless spoken to
>   D. Try to give everyone a turn at speaking

Oh, that one was loaded like a gun. If you said A, you were a domineering bully. B meant you were insecure and softheaded. Only a wallflower moron would choose C, so of course, they intended for you to choose D. But D was the dumbest of all! If you give everyone a turn at speaking, what does that make you?

Leroy chose A, even though he rarely had a conversation with anybody these days except his mother. He would rather sound like a domineering bully than the chairman of some committee.

He worked down the test in this fashion, making the choices that fit his image of himself—tough getting tougher, smarter than most people, too smart to make the sentimental, easy choices. Whenever he hit one of those loaded questions, he picked the most disagreeable answer, as a kind of protest.

Two hours flew by. Mrs. Davis came around to collect the booklets.

"Wait here until I call your name," she said, "and a counselor will evaluate your results with you."

Leroy stretched his arms, popped his shoulders. The test hadn't been bad at all once he figured out the thinking behind it. If all tests were that easy, he might consider going to college.

"Kirby," Mrs. Davis called. "Leroy Kirby."

He raised his hand.

"You go with Miss Waverly here."

Leroy was happy to. Miss Waverly had high, firm breasts pointing plainly through her thin cotton blouse. Her glossy red hair was gathered in a bun with a tortoise clip. In her hands she held Leroy's booklet and a cardboard sheet punched with holes.

He followed her down a hallway to a windowless office with two chairs, a telephone on a small table.

"Have a seat, Mr. Kirby," she said.

Leroy sat. "Did I pass?"

"You don't pass or fail this kind of test. We're trying to determine the kind of career you're best suited for, and then we'll try to place you. Okay?" She placed the cardboard grid over his booklet and began making little red marks off to one side. "Hmm." She bit the end of her pencil.

"Something wrong?"

"Oh, no. I'm just evaluating. I can tell you like to do a lot of work with your hands," she said.

She paged through the booklet, making red marks and little comments about his nature. Her eyes kept switching from his face to the page. The longer they talked, the more she seemed to linger on his face.

"These answers show you like to think for yourself," she was saying. "You're not just one of the crowd. You're not afraid to step out and try new things. Different things."

"Thank you, ma'am," Leroy said.

"Let me see your hands," said Miss Waverly.

"Ma'am?"

"Your hands," she said. "I need to confirm some of these findings."

Leroy felt his collar tightening, or maybe it was just warm in here. Was she telling his fortune, or giving him more than the usual evaluation?

"It's all right, I'm not going to bite you." She took his hand, turned it over. "Thank you."

"You're welcome," he said, taking it back.

Now that he had a good long look, it seemed that her breasts were displayed in the most conspicuous way. If she ever had a notion to shake herself out of that blouse, Miss Waverly would be a ravishing sex goddess on the order of Rita Hayworth.

This idea nearly scared him to death.

"Now, as I told you," Miss Waverly said, "there are no right and wrong answers on this test. Your answers show that you're a levelheaded young man, with the ability to carry out a responsible job. I find that you're especially well suited for a career as a machinist, electrician, or metalworker. Those are all highly skilled occupations."

"Machinist," said Leroy.

"Working with tools and dies," she said.

"I know, I—I've got a couple of uncles who work at Precision Tool," he said.

Her eyes lingered. "See? It must run in your family." She turned to a card file on her desk. "I'll set you up an appointment with Crown Electric. They've got an opening that I think you'll just fit."

"I don't know . . . how much does it pay?"

"We'll find out," she said, reaching for the telephone.

Was that—did she mean for her skirt to ride up on her thigh that way? Was this a dream? Leroy could see the top line of her stockings, the pelvis-shaped clasp with the little white button that hooked to her underthings.

He stared at the floor while Miss Waverly spoke to someone at Crown Electric. "I'll send him over at three o'clock," she said, "and I don't want you to worry when you see how he looks. He's a nice young man, and I'm sure he'll do a fine job for you. Yes sir, thank you, too." She hung up. "Here's their address. Be on time. If he likes you, you'll start right away. He pays one-fifty an hour."

"Listen," said Leroy. "What you said. Is there something wrong with the way I look?" This red and white zigzag print shirt with black jeans was one of his more conventional combinations. Of course, his hair was flamboyantly long, and the sideburns . . .

Miss Waverly was looking him over. All over.

"As a matter of fact," she said, "I think you look really good."

224

That remark dangled in midair for a long moment.

Leroy spoke softly. "Uh, well, in that case . . . do you think you'd ever . . . like to go to a movie or something?"

Her eyes were explicit. "I can't," she said. "I'm engaged."

"Oh," he said. "I just thought—"

"I know what you thought," she said. "I thought of it first." She stared at him, unblinking. "Shut the door."

"What?"

"Shut the door."

Leroy was afraid to move.

Miss Waverly rose from her chair, kicked the door shut, turned the lock. He smelled her vanilla perfume. Her skirt swirled at her knees when she turned. She pressed against the door. "Do you know how old I am?"

"No ma'am."

"I'm thirty-two. Does that seem old to you?"

"No—no ma'am." He crossed his legs.

Oh she was overheated, for sure; what else could those eyes be telling him, and that provocative smile? "I'll bet the girls at school never let you get past first base, do they?" she said. "They've all got their eyes on somebody older. They don't know what they're missing. The best boys are *exactly your age.*" She thumped his chest with her finger.

Leroy could not believe it. He had never been this close to any woman except his mother. Miss Waverly's legs pressed against his knee. The office was so small. Her legs were hot. She was the answer to every boy's prayer.

His whole body trembled with fear and excitement. "Won't somebody come in?" he croaked.

"No." Her hand raised the skirt. She caught the slip with her finger.

Leroy's hand followed it up, up the soft, hot, smooth leg, and there they were: white silky underpants. He clutched with his hand. Instantly he was hard in his pants. He uncrossed his legs and sat up.

"Have you ever done this before?" said Miss Waverly.

"Yes," Leroy said, "I mean—no." He swallowed.

She laughed, a tinkly sound. How could she laugh at a time like this? Leroy's blood was just about to pound out of his veins. "It's got to be one or the other," she teased. "Don't worry. I'll show you how."

He tasted his fear in the back of his throat. She drew him up beside her. His finger traced the elastic of her underpants. She undid his shirt buttons and touched his nipple with her fingernail. "Ooh, such a pretty boy," she said. "You're so soft. I want you to do it to me."

Oh! She was shocking! To talk that way— Leroy was hot now, confused and completely erect. He wasn't soft. He was ready to do what she wanted. He wanted it, too. But he was afraid. Her hands were all over his chest, the front of his pants. She was fumbling with his belt, the buttons on his fly. She squeezed his hardness with her hand.

He did not breathe or make a sound. He heard people walking up and down the hallway just outside the door. What if they— Maybe he ought to kiss her. He moved to do that.

"No, stop," she said, "don't." She seized his hand as if it were a stupid thing that needed a lesson, and guided it back to herself. Her nostrils flared. Her shining eyes stared at him, an encouraging smile. Leroy had the feeling she was looking straight through him to the other side.

She seized him through his Jockeys and squeezed—oh! Too hard! He winced.

"Sorry—" She leaned to touch his neck with her tongue. With her free hand she yanked her underpants to her knees. "Come on," she whispered. "Do it to me."

Leroy tried to think of her name. Miss—something. What was it! Miss Peavey? No. Algebra teacher. Miss Waverly. Right. Wait till I tell—Bubba about this! Jesus Christ he will never believe it. Oh! God! You only hear about things—like this. Never believe it not really not in real life.

Miss Waverly hiked her skirt over her hips and sat back against the edge of the table. "Now. Come on." She reached into his underwear, brought him out. There was her tangle, her— She made a little hop against the table. The phone went crashhhrrrring! to the floor. Leroy lunged forward one step and slid into an infinite softness, a wetness enfolding him down there.

Now he had. More of an idea. What to do. He grabbed her hips. He started humping. That was the word! Hump! That's just what it was! He was doing it! He was inside! He dared to look. Her eyes were closed, her tongue clamped between her lips and her face all scrunched, jolting up and down "ooh ooh ooh." Leroy said shhhh in her ear and kept driving. He felt a white surge beginning to rise from the very deepest

226

part of him. He gripped with his hands. She pinched him so hard he almost cried out. He bit his tongue. It was so fast and burning up, burning. Oh come on. Ride the pony. That's right. Come on. Was she saying these things? In his head.

He heard footsteps approaching the door . . . right outside, standing there just at the instant the volcano blew.

Her body absorbed the whole force of his explosion. Leroy did not make a sound. His ears rang. White stars whizzed through his eyes.

The footsteps went away.

He was buzzing all over, every muscle.

"Mmm," she said, "don't—don't—stay there—" She pushed against him one final time. The heat, the most luxurious waves of heat rolled through him.

They opened their eyes at the same time. He started to speak, but she put her fingers to his lips and slid free of him. She said, "Hurry, pull up your pants."

Leroy bent over. Change spilled from his pockets all over the floor. He gathered it up, crammed and zipped and buttoned himself. Miss Waverly pulled up her underpants, snapped the elastic with her thumbs.

"That was—that was *wild*." His breathless whisper.

She knelt for her tortoiseshell clip, which had fallen to the floor. With one hand she gathered her hair and began to refashion her prim little bun. "You know something?" she said, a tight voice. "You're much too good-looking for your own good. I believe I lost my head for a minute."

"That's okay." His voice was just a husk. "Can we . . . can we do that again sometime?"

"Oh my God," she said, and now the fear was in her eyes. "Oh. No. We can't." She took two steps back from him, stumbled into a chair. "You can't tell a soul about this, now, you promise. I can't see you again. I'm engaged. If he— Never mind. Just get out of here." She stooped to retrieve the telephone.

"Aw come on," Leroy said. "What's wrong? A minute ago you were—"

"Quiet," she said, low and fierce. Her nipples still hard in her blouse. "Do you want me to lose my job? Now you listen. You go keep that appointment. But I don't want to see you around here again. Don't you dare call me or come here."

"Whatever you say." Leroy ran his fingers through his hair. "Don't worry, I won't tell."

He opened the door. Nobody in the hall.

She pushed him out with her glare.

He sauntered down the long hallway, into the late-morning sun. Millions of birds chirruping. He could not believe what had happened to him. Only her smell on his fingertips convinced him that he had done it, really and truly. It was not a waking wet dream. She jumped on him, and he did it, beginning to end. She pounded the virginity out of him.

Surely everybody could see that he was transformed. His whole body sang with the birds, every nerve twitching, feeling the touch of his powerful blood, to the beat of Miss Waverly, Waverly, Wave.

She took one look at him and wanted him. They did it standing up. They did not even take off their clothes. Already it was becoming part of history in Leroy's mind.

Oh it was better than anyone could ever say. Fast and furtive and so much better than the thing with his hand, although he had the urge to run home and do that thing, right this minute, with the force of her hips still impressing his flesh.

~~~~

He brought the radio into the bathroom and took an extralong bath that afternoon, in honor of his miraculous morning. He scrubbed himself in places he'd never considered before. He sang along with LaVern Baker on "Soul on Fire," an irresistible song that started out small and sweet and ended with a note of bitter irony. LaVern toyed with the song, flashing the rough edge of her voice. *But now you set my soul on fi-hi-ah—*

Leroy ran the long-handled brush down his back and splashed soap from his eyes. Late sunlight slanted in through the blinds, illuminating the tiles in the bathroom. The bathwater shattered the light into rainbows. Leroy remembered Dorothy in *The Wizard of Oz* when she stepped through a door and suddenly her drab world glowed in brilliant Technicolor. He had walked around in color all day.

Agnes knocked on the door and said hurry up. He pulled the drain plug with his toe.

He kept searching the mirror for some sign, some mark, but he looked the same. Agnes hadn't seemed to notice any difference; when he

228

came in with the news that he'd landed a truck-driving job at Crown Electric, she glanced up to say it was fine with her until he could get something better, then went back to her bowl of Planter's cocktail peanuts.

Leroy dried his back with a towel.

He wanted to climb on the roof and shout, "Look at me! It happened to me this very day! I am not a virgin!"

Thank you, Miss Waverly! Thank you! Thank you.

"Leroy? Are you ever coming out, son? We don't want to be late."

"Right now, Mama." Wrapped in a towel, he opened the door. "I just got to put on some clothes."

"Well, honey, it's nearly six-thirty." Agnes wore the new green and white sleeveless shift she'd ordered from the J. C. Penney catalog. She'd put on her best nylon stockings, ivory Sunday shoes with heels, even a white hat and gloves.

"You look nice, Mama." Leroy made a move to kiss her.

"Quit, you're wet!" She pushed him away. "You're dripping all over the floor."

Leroy tiptoed to his dresser. "You look just as good as the picture in the catalog," he said.

"It was a good buy." She turned this way and that, showing off the dress. "I was afraid it wouldn't fit."

With all the weight she'd put on, and her tired, shadowed eyes, Agnes was not so pretty these days, but tonight she had tried extrahard—ruby lipstick, eyebrow pencil—in honor of Leroy. She was growing older. He was not her baby now, no matter how much she might want him to be. He had done what you do to become a man. There was no undoing it. No way to explain. If she couldn't see it in his eyes, he would not be the one to tell her.

"Now I'm going out front to wait with your daddy," she said. "You come on. He's got a present for you."

Leroy dropped the towel. He was kind of nice-looking, naked. He wiggled, checking it out.

He wondered what the present might be: work shoes; a savings bond; a Goldsmith's gift certificate for a new Sunday suit.

He took his time choosing his clothes, even though the gray silky graduation robe covered all of him except his shirt collar.

The mortarboard smushed his hair any way he tried to wear it. He

229

grinned at the mirror. "You devil," he said, and then, in a whisper: "Oh. Do it to me."

Leroy ran up the hall.

"Shut the door, son," Ray called from the street. He was leaning against an old car at the curb, talking to Agnes and Dodger and some neighbors.

Leroy trotted over.

"Whoa, here comes Mr. Big Shot Diploma," said the neighbor man.

"Hey Mr. Hastings," said Leroy. "Hey Miz Hastings."

"Get his picture, Agnes," Mrs. Hastings said. "Doesn't he look happy." The Hastingses offered their congratulations. Leroy shrugged and stammered. Agnes snapped away with a borrowed Kodak.

Then Ray said, "Son, your mother thought we ought to get you something for graduating. So we got you this." He patted the hood.

At first Leroy didn't understand.

"The car," said Ray. "Happy graduation."

"Quick, make his picture!" cried Mrs. Hastings. "Look at his face!"

"I just took the last one," Agnes said.

The car was an ancient Lincoln, a coupe. Once it had been green, but now it was mottled and rotted-looking, like an upended stump in the woods. It was a 1942 Zephyr, a real heap, one running board missing, the backseat ripped out entirely. It was the most beautiful car Leroy had ever seen.

He threw his arms around his mother, dragged his father in, hugged them both. "I can't believe it!"

Ray came up with a key. "It's all yours," he said, beaming. "A workingman's got to be able to get to work. Your mama told me you finally went out and got an honest job."

"You folks . . . you're the greatest. I, really. I don't know what to say."

"Oh, I knew you'd like it, honey," said Agnes. "I'm just worried about you driving too fast, and you know there's all kinds of crazy drivers out there that kill innocent people."

"You mind what your mama says," Dodger put in.

"I'll be careful." Leroy kicked a tire. A car of his own!

"Well, we got to go eat our supper," said Mrs. Hastings as they drifted away. "You-all make a fine-looking family."

Ray said, "If we don't go now, we'll be late."

"Hey, let's all ride in it!" Leroy danced around to the driver's side. "Come on, Mama, jump in!"

"There's not room for four people in there," said Agnes.

"Well, let Daddy take Dodger, and you ride with me! I'll ride you down there in style."

Ray and Agnes traded a look: Why not? Dodger followed Ray to the Plymouth.

Leroy slid under the wheel. He loved the dusty smell, the scratchy pedals under his soles. His car. His own car! Freedom! Wheels! The white stripe in the wide-open road!

His mother got in beside him. The old car didn't look like much, and it didn't have a radio, but the engine started with a healthy rumble. Leroy pumped the pedal and ran his hands over the wheel. "Listen to that," he marveled. "Mama, I never expected such a great present in my life."

"Well, we've always tried to do for you when we could." Agnes gazed out the window. "Your daddy thought you should buy it out of your first paycheck, but I said you didn't need such a big burden, starting out."

Leroy trailed the Plymouth onto Poplar Avenue. He couldn't wait to be alone with this car, to find out what it would do. "How much did it cost?"

"Where's your manners? That's rude."

"Come on," he said.

"I'm not going to tell you," she said. "Fifty dollars."

Leroy whistled. "He got a good deal."

They rode most of the way downtown before Agnes spoke again. "Leroy, you might as well go ahead and tell me."

"What, Mama?"

"Whatever it is. You've been acting peculiar all day. What is that look on your face?"

"Good grief," he stammered, "I'm happy, okay? I'm—I'm about to graduate, and I just got this great present. . . ."

"There's no use lying to me," she said. "Something is going on in that head of yours. Have you been drinking?"

"No!"

"Because if you have, you better go on and tell me. I don't like you keeping these secrets from me."

"I don't have any secrets," Leroy lied. He wondered if she could see his red face in the dim light from the dashboard. "Well, I don't! Stop looking at me like that!" He laughed to cover his nerves.

"I know you, Leroy. Something has happened to you."

"I'm just so glad to be getting out of that damn school—"

"Watch your mouth!"

"Well, I am, and that's all." Leroy turned left on Main Street. He was glad for the first glimpse of Ellis Auditorium. He circled for a place to park.

"As soon as this is over," Agnes said, "I want you to come straight home with us. I've fixed a special dinner."

Leroy pulled into a space. "Sorry, Mama. The guys are getting together tonight." He switched off the engine. "You can save mine in the oven. I'll eat when I get home."

She bit her lip. Suddenly she looked ready to cry.

"Come on, Satnin," he pleaded. "Don't make me feel bad. Everybody in the *world* goes out on graduation night."

"Well if everybody jumped off a cliff, would you do that, too?"

"I might," Leroy said. "If I wanted to."

Her eyes shone. "I made your favorite pork chops."

He opened the door, put his foot on the ground. "I said I'm sorry. But I'm going out."

He came around the car. Agnes made a point of refusing his help. She drew herself out of the car, straightened her hat, set out three steps ahead of him.

They met up with Dodger and Ray at the door. "I've got to go line up," Leroy said. "Where are y'all sitting? I'll find you when it's over."

"Somewhere without any steps to get to it," said Dodger.

Agnes gazed into the distance.

"You stay down front," said Ray. "We'll find you."

Leroy kissed Dodger. Agnes turned away.

He went around the side of the building. The members of his class were robed, capped, lined up in the parking lot. Leroy found his place in line between Roscoe Keeney and Janey Sue Kittrell.

They went in single file, in the halt step they had rehearsed on Monday. Mrs. Roberts struggled with "Pomp and Circumstance" at the piano. The auditorium was jammed with mothers and fathers and

232

grandparents, brothers and sisters and teachers and friends. The class of 1953 filed into rows of folding chairs.

Leroy sat in back between Roscoe and Janey Sue. After the invocation the school chorus bleated a song called "That One Great Step Before Us," then Mr. Sumner got up and made a little talk about honor and responsibility and Life, and then the smart kids received honors for academic achievement.

Leroy buried his hands in his gown, closed his eyes. The robe felt like silk. He thought about Miss Waverly licking his neck.

Someone poked him. Diploma time. Mr. Sumner was calling their names.

The first dozen seniors tiptoed across the stage, shook the principal's hand, and skittered off with their diplomas. Then a boy named Royce Bentson got a big laugh by strutting and waving his mortarboard over his head like a trophy. That started the smartasses in class to competing displays of humor as they crossed the stage. The principal and the teachers looked irritated, but all the kids and even some parents were laughing.

When Sumner said, "Leroy Kirby," Leroy sprang up the steps, strode across the stage, shook the hand, took the diploma, swept off his cap, and made a deep bow. He held it long enough to hear the laughter start up; then he slapped the mortarboard on his head and ambled from the stage.

He hadn't planned it. But when he saw those boys grabbing the spotlight, he couldn't resist taking his share. The other kids grinned and prodded him.

At the end of the ceremony they threw their caps in the air and cheered. Leroy joined in. In truth he didn't have much feeling about graduating, one way or the other. Once he'd made a name for himself, Humes meant nothing to him. A piece of nice paper in a red Leatherette folder. He was glad to get out of there and get on with his life. That was enough.

Some of the girls actually clutched each other and sobbed. Bubba Hayes sought Leroy out through the crowd. "Hey, buddy, you ready to go? We got Davy Lee's jalopy, and Sammy's bringing the stuff. It's wild times tonight!"

From one corner of his eye, Leroy saw his family making down the aisle toward him.

"Listen, Bubba," he said, "maybe I can meet up with you later. My folks are kind of giving a party at home. I got to go for a while anyway."

"Sure, Frankie, whatever you say," said Bubba, but his eyes said it all: Mama's boy. The same unspoken taunt that had haunted Leroy from his first day in school to his last.

"Sorry, Bubba."

"I don't know where we'll be," Bubba said, "but stop out at the Gridiron. We'll have to get some cheeseburgs before we're through. We'll tell the gals where we're headed."

"Sure. Listen, you guys have fun." Leroy hated missing this chance. It was practically the duty of a senior to go wild on graduation night. Hadn't he just lived through the most exciting graduation day in history? If only they knew!

But he saw his mother heading for him with her chin up and that proud, determined smile on her face, and he did not have the strength to refuse her.

25

*L*eroy carried the Sound Star with him in the cab of the Crown Electric truck. Often he had an hour to kill between runs, and he'd park the truck in some quiet alley where no one could hear him practicing.

His job was delivering switches and condensers and rolls of wire to electricians all over town. It was a fine way to make forty-one fifty a week—on his own, cruising Memphis all day, searching out addresses in the industrial parts of town. He had wanted to be a truck driver since he was a little boy. So what if it was just an old Ford pick-'em-up and he never got to stray very far beyond the city limits? He was breathing real air, not cooped up in some stupid school. He had plenty of time with the Sound Star.

This was a slow, hot afternoon, growing hotter. The sun whitened the sky. Nobody worried much about electricity in such heat. Leroy sat in the Ford behind Crump Stadium, under great shady oak trees, drinking his third Coca-Cola of the day. The bugs sang a hymn to the heat. He sang along, strumming the chords to "My Happiness."

Some days his voice sounded tinny or hollow. Some days it would break. Today, for some reason, he sounded better than ever. *Evening shadows make me blue. . . .*

Thwang, thwangg! That was it! Enough! He knew that song backward and upside down.

There would come a day when he would quit practicing and go ahead and do the thing.

Why was he so shy about it? Did he think his fantasies of stardom might wither and die the minute he stood up to a real microphone? Was he afraid someone would laugh or say the wrong thing?

He had been restless since the morning of Miss Waverly. The world offered a whole host of tantalizing secrets; he was ready to start finding them out. For the moment he was happy enough to drive the Crown truck. But he always knew he was driving toward a brighter light, just over the horizon.

His voice sounded good today.

At this moment he was parked within ten blocks of the Mid-South Recording Service. This was fate.

He drained the Coke, rubbed his thumb on the mouth of the bottle.

He had money in his pocket, an hour before his next run.

He scratched off in the parking lot gravel. His work shirt was dirty, his hair all over the place—but then he wasn't auditioning for Cecil B. De Mille. He was paying these people to make a record, something they did every day.

He parked across Union Street from the studio.

No excuses. Go to it. Do it. You can.

You are Amazing New Leroy.

Holding the old trusty Sound Star by its neck, he got out of the truck. He wished his mother were here to hold his hand.

He carried the Sound Star across the street, put his hand on the doorknob, pushed in.

It was just as hot inside. A large electric fan turned its face side to side, moving the hot air around. Leroy had expected a big room with recording equipment and photos of singing stars on the walls. This looked like an insurance office—two desks piled with papers, filing cabinets standing open. But also there were reels of recording tape with their tongues hanging out and four guitars propped on a sofa. This must be the place.

"Anybody home?"

The studio must be past the large curtained windows. That door was closed. A hand-lettered sign said SHHHH. A red light glowed on the wall. Leroy sat down to wait.

He peered at the papers on the desk—mostly invoices and bills, but there was one letter with a large official-looking seal that looked interesting, even from a distance.

He inched closer. A quartet called The Rhythmaires had been requested by the governor of Tennessee for a performance at his Labor Day picnic, and since Mr. Dan Tobias held an exclusive contract with the group, it was necessary that his permission—

The door swung in. "Oh! You startled me," said the woman behind it, who was carrying a box of rolled-up electrical cords. "How long have you been here?"

Leroy moved away from the desk. "Just a minute or two. I saw the red light, so I waited."

"Oh, that," she said, "that stays on all the time. It hasn't worked right in years. What can I do for you?" She was striking, maybe forty, small-boned and slim, with a boyish Debbie Reynolds haircut. She placed the box on the desk. Her eyebrows rose to say, "Well?"

"Uhm." Where to start? "I want to make a record."

"What kind of a record?" she said.

"Two songs. They're both pretty short."

"Just you by yourself?"

"Yes ma'am. And my guitar."

"Do you already know about our rates?"

"I called awhile back." Leroy fingered his lip. "I think I'm ready, I—I'm not sure."

She was having a good look at him—the opposite of the Miss Waverly kind of look. "That's quite a haircut," she said.

"Thank you, ma'am," said Leroy. "I usually dress better than this, but I was at work."

"Those sideburns," she said.

"Yes ma'am."

"Please stop calling me ma'am. My name's Claudia Cash. And yours is?"

"Leroy," he said, "Leroy Kirby."

"What kind of songs do you sing, Leroy?"

"I sing all kinds," he said.

"Who do you sound like?"

He thought about that a minute. "Well. I don't guess I sound like anybody."

Her smile flickered. "Let's go back and see what we can do. I hope you've rehearsed. Thirty minutes means you've got time for two songs. One take on each song." She slid on a pair of cat-eyed glasses like those worn by sophisticated girls in the movies. Leroy liked her right away.

He followed her into the studio, a tall, narrow room with perforated acoustical tile on the ceiling and walls. Two upright pianos were shoved against the rear wall, under an elevated plate-glass window that stretched the width of the room. Three steps led up to the control room.

Miss Cash pointed out a microphone: a trapezoid of wire mesh hanging from a boom, one of many microphones jumbled in with speakers and chairs and wooden stools and music stands and guitars in open cases. Some band might have just put down these instruments and slipped out the back.

"Do you want me to stand up?" said Leroy.

"Whichever way you're more comfortable." Miss Cash adjusted the mike. "But you have to pick one spot and stand still."

"This is my first time for this," he said. "I'm kind of nervous."

"There's nothing to it. I'll get you to sing a little so I can get a level. Then when you're ready, you tell me, I'll point, and you start. Just open your mouth and sing."

"Will you be in there?" He indicated the control room.

She nodded. "I can hear everything you say, but you can't hear me. Got it?"

238

"Yes ma'am—yeah, okay. I think so." Leroy strummed with his fingers. The Sound Star was as much in tune as it ever would be.

Miss Cash went up behind the glass. Leroy was overcome with wonder at what he was about to do. It was going too fast. He wanted to remember every moment. He stood in a pool of white light. There was no air in the studio, only heat and absolute, close-in dead silence.

He listened. He snapped his fingers. The sound was dead. No echo. Wing-shaped panels of dotted tile dipped down at angles from the ceiling. Maybe that was the Sonocoustic part.

The studio seemed three hundred yards long, the petite Miss Cash floating behind glass at the far other end, fiddling at a control panel that was hidden from where Leroy stood.

He picked out the G chord and settled in to play the first verse of his song. The room swallowed the sound, no reflection at all.

Miss Cash moved her hand in a circle that meant keep playing. He played. She pointed to her mouth. He started in singing: *When your sweetheart tells you she's busy tonight....*

Her hand circled faster, keep singing. Her other hand fiddled on the panel before her. She was all-powerful in the glass room, hovering over everything.

The beginnings of sweat trickled down Leroy's face, but inside he was calm. He was in the right place. All of his life had brought him to this microphone. All he had to do was stand in this spot and sing.

"I think I'm ready," he said.

She held her finger to her lips—shh—then nodded and pointed go.

He played four opening bars, then sang in his smoothest starting-out voice the first part of the line, *When your sweetheart,* and the melody soared way high on sweet*heeeeaaaart, tells you she's busy tonight, we-ell, that's when you know it's over....*

It was a soap opera song, a favorite of Dodger's. It told of two lovers and a best friend. When the best friend gets too friendly with the girl, it all goes to pieces. There was a quiet part in the middle where Leroy spoke the verse aloud; it was a little corny but nice. Simple chords, not too many words, and the melody swooped up and down, allowing Leroy to show off the high and low ends of his voice.

He tried to sound tender. He wanted girls to fall in love with his voice. He wanted them to squeal, the way they did for Frankie Sinatra on the old live recordings.

By the time he reached the last verse, he was hamming it up, holding on to the notes, loading on the emotion.

> *When all her hellos*
> *Start to sound like good-byes*
> *We-heh-hell, that's when you know it's over*

Buhm, buhm, buhm, buhm. Thrinnggg!

Leroy grinned. Victory!

Miss Cash smiled and nodded and flipped switches. No time to think. Time to sing again. Leroy found his spot on the floor. She pointed to him.

This was "My Happiness." He sang this one soft and romantic, acting the part of a failed, heartsick lover. *Evening shadows make me blue....*

In the chorus he glanced up to see Claudia Cash bustling about the control room. He wondered if the machine had messed up, but she didn't make any signal, so he kept on to the end.

She ducked around the door and came to the top of the steps with a delighted smile. "That was very, very nice," she said. "You're good."

Leroy felt himself glowing like the red light on the wall. He *was* good. He knew it. She said it. He couldn't quit grinning. "Well thank you," he spluttered, "could you hear me in there?"

"Loud and clear. You know, you have a good voice for a ballad."

He nearly split open with joy.

"Come on in now and let's hear the playback," she said.

"Wait! You mean—that's all? But ... I kind of messed up that second one. I was hoping I could do it over."

"Don't be silly," said Miss Cash. "We get people in here, a lot of people think they can sing. But I really liked you just then. With the right kind of material, I think you might get someone to listen to you."

Leroy unslung the guitar and tiptoed up the steps after her, into a breathtaking wall of cold air. "Air conditioning!" he said. "Y'all have everything."

"It's for the equipment. Shut that door." Miss Cash stepped to the console. She knew just which buttons to press among all the buttons and switches and dials and lights and cords everywhere. She transferred a tape from the reel-to-reel recorder to a large, complicated record-cutting machine and set it to spinning.

240

The Sound Star made a lonesome twang. The sound came at Leroy from six speakers overhead. His voice sounded nasal and thin, awful country. Almost hillbilly. *When awwwlll her helloos start to soooound like good-byes....* He winced. "Is that how I sound?"

"Oh go on, you know it's good," she said, pulling the cat glasses to the end of her nose. "You were right. You don't sound like anybody."

Leroy thought he sounded puny and country and ragged, like an underage Hank Williams. At least he would know to sing deeper next time, not so much through his nose. He wished he could do it over.

Claudia Cash tapped her fingers on the console in time to his clumsy guitar. He began to relax. The talking part was nice and dramatic and sad. Once he got over the strange sensation of hearing his voice, he decided it was not all that terrible. He really sang those last verses. He jumped on top of them and rode them right down to the end.

He stared at the floor between songs, a long silence.

The Sound Star started up again, and then the hillbilly boy was back, singing "My Happiness." Leroy sat on the edge of the table. The dread had faded away, and now a thrill was spreading through him, like warm new blood. That was his voice, that was Leroy Kirby singing all by himself on a record, folks! Step right up! Listen! The lady says he has a good voice for a ballad!

"How much singing have you done?" said Miss Cash.

"A lot," he said, "I don't know. Since I was little."

"I mean, have you ever performed?"

Play it cool, now. Don't look too eager. "No, ma'am, not really. School, and stuff. But I'd like to, sometime."

The song ambled on. "I got part of this down on tape," she said. "Maybe I'll play it for Dan when he comes in. Why don't you give me a number in case we want to reach you."

Leroy thought fast. There was no phone at Alabama Street because of an old unpaid bill from Lauderdale Court.

"Our telephone's out of order," he said. "I'll give you our neighbors'. They can find me." He searched the phone book for Hastings on Alabama Street, scratched his address and their number on the index card. His hand was shaking so he could hardly hold the pen.

From the mouth of the record-cutting machine Claudia Cash brought forth a ten-inch circle of black flexible plastic, threaded with grooves like any phonograph record. She slid it into a white envelope.

"Now, don't get too excited," she said. "I don't think Dan has anything for you now. Maybe sometime, if we get the right song. You owe me three ninety-five."

"Oh. Right." Leroy fumbled in his pocket. Four crumpled ones. She gave him a nickel in change. "Miss Cash," he said.

"Yes."

"Just . . . I guess you tell everybody they're good."

"I meant what I said." She showed him what she had written on the card: LEROY KIRBY—GOOD BALLAD SINGER—HOLD. "This will go right in my file," she said. "Don't worry. We'll call you sometime."

She handed over the envelope. Leroy took it with both hands, stammered more thanks, and walked into the blinding white heat of noon. He carried his record to the truck, baking in the high sun.

He had found magic in that darkened room—the enchanted circle under the microphone, the machine cutting records with its mouth, inscribing his voice as a groove on black acetate. He felt at home in that room. He wanted to spend time there.

He climbed into the truck. The gearshift seared his hand. That felt like real life. He wrapped his shirttail around it, glanced at his watch—one-thirty. Three circuit breakers had been due thirty minutes ago at Mr. Mallory's across town.

He made a wide, screeching U-turn and put down the pedal.

He got there in no time, but the delivery took longer than he expected. He came out to find his record melted into an exact impression of the top of his toolbox.

26

*L*eroy gathered every-
one in the front room to announce that he'd made a record, the lady
really liked his singing. "She went on and on about it," he said. "She
might be calling any time."

"Oh honey, that's just real nice," said Agnes. "Play it for us! Where
is it?"

"Well I—I left it in the truck, and it kind of, melted," he explained.

"Oh, no!"

Dodger said, "A waste of good money."

"If it's okay with everybody," said Ray, "I'm going down to Sparky's."

Leroy went to his room and settled in to wait. He believed in Claudia Cash. He prayed she would call. It was only a matter of waiting, of figuring out how to pass the days until Mr. Hastings appeared to say, "Leroy? A phone call for you." Right now, in his mind, Leroy could see Mr. Hastings at the front door, speaking those very words.

He pestered his father to pay off the old bill so they could get a new phone number. Ray said they were better off without the thing ringing its head off all the time.

All day long Leroy drove the truck for Crown. He figured out that electricians make all the money and eat steak and drive the fast cars. Not delivery boys.

The old Zephyr was his freedom. He drove out the highway to the Gridiron to eat double cheeseburgers with Bubba Hayes and some of the Humes football boys. They liked to get fresh with the Gridiron's colored waitresses, who were guaranteed to laugh their heads off no matter what you said.

Now and then he would cruise past the front door of the West Tennessee Employment Office, searching the faces going in and out, but he never caught another glimpse of Miss Waverly. (What would he say if he saw her? Hey, baby, let's do it again?) He drove to the Rainbow Rollerdome to watch girls skating, to Fairground Park to ride the roller coaster and the Dodgem bumper cars.

He loved the Dodgem cars so much he could ride them ten times in a row. He loved the bone-jarring collisions and the sparks flying from the metal strip as it scraped the electrified ceiling.

Wandering home, he would drive past the Mid-South Recording Service. Sometimes musicians were lounging on the sidewalk out front, smoking cigarettes, taking a break. They worked late. Leroy drove slowly by, burning with envy. What kinds of wonderful sounds were they making in there?

Most nights he sat home in his room, working up new songs for when Claudia Cash would call. He could not make her call any sooner by thinking about it. He tried to think about other things. That didn't work, so he waited, and practiced, and bought more singles at Poplar Tunes, and learned new songs.

He bought a Big Joe Turner song, "Honey Hush," and "Smoke Gets in Your Eyes," the Hilltoppers' "P.S. I Love You," Ruth Brown's "Mama He Treats Your Daughter Mean," Joni James's heartbreaker "I'll Never Stand in Your Way," some new Ray Charles, and "Hey Hey Little Girl," "Casual Love Affair," Hank Snow's "I'm Gonna Bid My Blues Goodbye."

He thought he might go crazy from the waiting. Had Claudia Cash led him on? He remembered her last words exactly: "Don't worry. We'll call you sometime." *Sometime?* When was that?

He folded his hands behind his head. Why would she say those things unless she meant them? The Mother Station crooned "In My Solitude," poor, melancholy Billie Holiday.

Leroy could not stand it. The waiting. The clock seemed to slow down every time he glanced at it.

He decided he could not wait anymore. He would go back to the studio, pay his four dollars, and make another record.

On a cold, rainy Thursday, the week after New Year's, he carried the Sound Star through that door a second time.

This time he had dressed with some flash—an egg yellow shirt with black polka dots, his lightning bolt trousers, his black rain slicker. Claudia Cash recognized him right off. "Sideburns! What are you doing here?"

"Thought I'd give it another shot," said Leroy.

"I'm glad you came by. Dan's here. Come in and meet him."

Leroy rejoiced at his timing. He followed her under the glowing red light into the studio.

A young man in white shirt and plaid necktie looked up from the floor, where he had laid open the wiry innards of a loudspeaker. He had merry eyes, a wiseacre grin. His hair was swept back on his head—not quite Leroy's pompadour, but a cool look nonetheless. A Camel dangled from the side of his mouth, shedding ashes.

"Dan, this is that kid I was telling you about," said Claudia Cash. "Remember? The ballad singer. I'm sorry, I've forgotten your name."

"Leroy," he said, "Leroy Kirby."

"Dan Tobias." He stuck out his hand. "How you getting along."

They shook hands. "I've heard a lot about you," said Leroy. "I know all kind of stuff you've done. The Rhythmaires and Little Jimmy Sutcliffe and B. B. King, and Howlin' Wolf, and—and Hot Shot Love. . . ."

245

Dan took a drag, dropped the butt on the floor. "That's pretty good, son," he said. "You studied up."

"No, sir," said Leroy, "I just listen to WDIA a lot."

"Every day now it's some white boy that wants to be a colored singer," said Dan. "What can I do for you?"

"I made a record before—you know, the four-dollar deal. I want to make another one."

"Fine. Claudia, you want to handle this?"

"Why don't you come in and give him a listen?" said Claudia. "He's pretty good."

"Okay, okay," said Dan. "Let's go."

That made Leroy nervous all over again. Suddenly there was a big rush for him to begin. Claudia Cash placed him under a different microphone, closer to the control-room window, then went to join Dan behind the glass. Dan pointed a finger.

Leroy started in singing "Casual Love Affair."

When he did this song at home, he sounded loose and lazy as Dean Martin, but today he couldn't seem to relax—not with the famous Dan Tobias gazing down cold as glass, his arms folded: Okay, prove it to me.

Leroy rushed the guitar break, came in late on the second chorus, straggled to the finish.

Dan did not look impressed.

Leroy took a deep breath. Keep it simple and sweet. One more song. Just sing for the man. "I'll Never Stand in Your Way" was a country lament, nothing complicated: four chords, three verses, one chorus. Leroy sang from the low end of his voice, to keep from sounding squirrelly.

In the middle of the song Tobias turned away to strike up a conversation with Claudia Cash.

Leroy closed his eyes and finished with a flourish, holding the last high note three measures extra, to show them he would not be ignored.

He opened his eyes. Dan stared, holding his chin in his hand. Claudia Cash came to the door. "He wants you to do that one again," she said.

"Okay," said Leroy. Again!

"And don't hold that last note so long."

Leroy rubbed the floor with his toe. "Sure, whatever you say. Sorry."

He waited in the warm light, swaddled in comfortable silence. She returned to the control room. He toyed with his E string, searching for the pitch. He felt calm. You're good. He wants you to sing it again. You don't have to knock him down with it.

He sang it as simple and plain as he knew. His version was closer to Ernie Lee's than Joni James's. It was a man's song. The man loves the girl long after she's quit loving him. Now she loves somebody else. He loves her so much he's willing to let her go. He tried to pack all of those feelings into one song.

When he finished, Tobias waved him into the control room. "Boy, you're not bad," he said. "Let me tell you what I hear. A good voice, a little thin, good range. Not much on that git box. I don't think you know what you want to sound like yet. I sure as hell don't think you're Mario Lanza. Tell you what I need. I need something new. I've heard both those songs sung just as well by the folks that recorded 'em. What have you got to show me that's new?"

"I can sing anything," Leroy said.

"Yeah, well, I hadn't got time to waste on just anything," Dan said. "Claudia will give you your acetate. We got your telephone, right? If I find something I think you can sing, I'll call you. Okay?"

"Okay," Leroy said. His heart slid three notches down his ribs. *We'll call you sometime. . . .*

"Take care of yourself," Dan said. He went back up front, to his loudspeaker.

Claudia moved to the hulking record-cutting lathe. "If he didn't like you, he wouldn't have had you sing it twice."

"I don't know." Leroy sighed. "He wasn't all that excited."

"It takes a lot to get Dan excited. You go home and keep practicing. I'm going to keep my eye out for a song for you. I promise we'll call."

Leroy pulled out four dollars. "I sure hope you will."

She gave him the white envelope with his record. "Now go on. We'll see you soon."

Leroy collected the Sound Star. Dan glanced up as he went by: "Good luck to you, now."

Leroy wanted to tell him how much he longed to sing, to learn, find a band, be a star. But he just said, "See you later," and went to the truck.

He drove straight home, ate a bacon sandwich, wrote down the things they said:

1. Dont hold last note too long.

2. Good range & voice. (Thin)

3. Need something NEW

4. Claudia will look for song—call

He tacked the page on the wall above his bed. He lived by the words.

His agony was solitary. He felt a real chance that Dan Tobias might call him this time, and he didn't want to jinx it by telling anyone.

He waited until everyone was out of the house, then plugged in the record player and gave his acetate a spin.

The Sound Star sounded ragged, out of tune. He had rushed through "Casual Love Affair" as if he were in some big hurry to get it over with and go home. Then he had dragged the Joni James thing, twang-twang-twang-thud. The record was terrible. The tape recorder was merciless. Leroy heard the nasal, unsteady truth. He needed practice, and practice, and practice.

After just a few spins he hid the acetate in his underwear drawer. He put on Hank Snow's "A Fool Such As I," with that great lilting opening: *Pardon me if I'm sentimental....*

That was a real professional there. Leroy snapped his fingers and sang along. He wondered if he would ever be that good.

He installed a radio in the old Zephyr. He had found a new secret place in the wilderness ten miles south of town. Someone had hacked out a two-lane track that bumped and doglegged through the woods for miles, finally breaking out to a raised clearing, the highest place for miles around, with a sweeping view of the great muddy water and Arkansas stretching flat into infinity. Leroy reclined on the hood of his car with the door ajar, radio tuned to the Mother Station, Sound Star on his belly, bare feet on warm metal.

He welcomed the summer that way. He turned brown. He learned a thousand new songs.

The sun fell in the trees. Leroy started the car and bounced along the rutted track. The Zephyr's feeble headlights swung onto the pavement of the highway.

He drove into town, to the Gridiron. Bubba Hayes was there with Davy Lee Williams and a couple of bleached-blond trashy-looking girls. Leroy ordered four cheeseburgers well done, with fries, and pulled a chair to their booth.

"We ran into these girls downtown," Bubba said. "I don't remember their names. Girls, this is Frankie." The girls giggled and said they were Betty Ann and Charlene. Leroy said he was Leroy, not Frankie. They said ooh, his hair was too much.

He ate the first two cheeseburgers in six bites. He enjoyed listening to the girls' chatter; they seemed oblivious of the fact that Bubba and Davy Lee were aching to do it to them. Betty Ann, the girl with Bubba, was pinkly attractive, but Davy Lee's choice ... Leroy was glad he was not that desperate. He had the memory of Miss Waverly to make him warm.

"I worked up a new song, Bubba," he said. "It's that Gisele MacKenzie, the song is called 'Since You're Gone.' You know it?"

"Ooh! Are you a singer?" said Charlene, snaking her arm around Davy Lee. "Sing something!"

"You hear from anybody yet?" Bubba said.

"Not a word." Leroy sipped his Coke. "I haven't been home. Maybe they tried to call today."

"I'm tellin' you, Frankie, puttin' your eggs in one basket," said Bubba. "Why don't you try playing for some of these clubs? I bet there's five places around here that would have you."

"It doesn't do any good unless you have a record." Leroy bit into his fourth cheeseburger. "Those places don't pay. I'd be wasting my time. You got to have something to sell."

The girls were bored by this conversation. "Let's go to the party," said Betty Ann.

Davy Lee said, "Come go with us, Frankie," but Leroy said he had work to do.

"Work? On a Friday night? Are you crazy?"

"Maybe so," Leroy said.

He paid the bill, said good-bye, drove on home.

Dodger was sitting up late working her puzzle, a gauzy scene of a little girl running through spring flowers.

Leroy threw his jacket over a chair. "Anybody try to find me today?"

"Not a soul," she said. "Sit down and help me find these edge pieces."

"I'm kind of tired, Dodger. I think I'll go take a bath, maybe play my guitar."

Dodger held a piece to the light. "Leroy, your mama had a bad day," she said. "I think it's the change, myself, but she won't hear a word about it."

"Where is she?"

"In her room."

"What's the change?" he said, not really wanting to know.

"It's what happens when a woman gets older and starts to dry up," Dodger said. "Your mama won't believe she's old enough to have it. But Mynelle Riley's daughter had it when she was thirty-two."

Leroy said, "What does it do?"

"Oh, you know how she cries over every little thing, all these sick headaches, and she says she can't ever get warm. That's just how it is. I have told her but she will not listen to me."

"Well I wondered." Leroy spotted the three missing pieces of the edge and arranged them near the gap so she would find them herself. "Daddy said something to her the other night, I forget what it was. Nothing, really. She started crying, just like that."

"The only thing to do for it is take long walks," said Dodger. "I heard that from a friend of mine in Birmingham. It worked wonders for her. She told me too late to do me any good."

"I can't imagine Mama going for a walk," Leroy said.

"Well it wouldn't kill her. But she won't listen to me."

"You need the bathroom?" Leroy picked up his jacket. "I might be in there awhile."

That night he lay in bed thinking about his mother. For some reason Dodger's revelation shocked him. Maybe he had still been holding on to the notion that she might have another baby someday, a little sister for him. He remembered hiding under a window when he glimpsed his parents doing the thing. For months after that he had waited for a baby to come.

Now Agnes was drying up. It was sad. He wondered whether she and Ray were still doing it, whether this meant they had to stop. If it worked that way, Leroy thought, he had better hurry up and do it as much as he could.

The next morning he rolled out and wandered into the hall, yawning, in his Jockey shorts.

250

There was Mr. Hastings, hand cupped at his eyes, peering through the screen. "Leroy," he said, "there's a call for you at my house."

The world stopped.

Leroy cried, "I'm coming!" and ran to his room, jumped into his blue jeans, ran up the hill past Mr. Hastings, across the yard. Mrs. Hastings held the door for him. He searched desperately for the phone; she pointed it out, on the coffee table. He snatched it up. "Hello!"

"Hello, is this Leroy?"

"Yes!"

"Hi, this is Claudia Cash. At Rocking Records, remember?"

"Sure! Yes!" Leroy thought he might leap right out of his skin.

"Dan Tobias asked me to call. We've got a song here he wants you to try out for him if you're free today."

"A song? Great! Oh that's great! Listen, I'm coming right over!" He shouted, "Good-bye!" at the receiver and hung up. "Oh thank you, Miz Hastings—I'll see you—" He slipped past her and ran across the yard yelling, "Mama! Daddy!"

Agnes came out of their room with a look of alarm. "Honey, what is it?"

"They called me! They want me to go down and sing! I've got to go now! Where's Daddy?"

"Here I am," he said, stepping in from the kitchen. "What's all the commotion?"

"Oh Daddy—it's the studio! Dan Tobias! He's got a song he wants me to sing! Oh man, isn't that the greatest thing you ever heard in your *life*?"

"How much will it cost you?" said Ray.

"If he likes me enough, he'll pay *me*! I didn't tell you, but I went back down there. He liked me. I *knew* he'd call. I *knew* it!"

Agnes said, "Well you can't go down there barefoot."

Leroy laughed and said no, he couldn't; he embraced her, swung her around in a little dance, and ran in. He banged on the bathroom door until Dodger tottered out, clutching her bathrobe together.

"Sorry, Dodger," he said, "it's an emergency."

He doused his face, fixed his hair. He put on his cowboy boots, his imitation lizard belt. He charged out of the house and all the way to the car before he remembered the Sound Star. He had to come back.

"Slow down," said his father. "You're about to wet yourself."

Leroy grabbed the guitar by the neck. "This is a big deal, Daddy," he said. "Wish me luck."

Ray smiled. "Good luck, son. You go knock 'em dead."

Leroy ran to the Zephyr. All he needed was the microphone and a little time. He could do the rest by himself.

27

*C*laudia Cash looked up, amazed. "I just hung up the phone from talking to you!"

Leroy shut the door, breathing hard. "I got here as—fast as I—could."

She smiled. "Have you been sitting by that telephone since the last time you were here?"

"Yes ma'am," he said. "I—I knew you'd call."

"Stop with that 'ma'am' business. From now on it's Claudia. I hope we'll be seeing a lot of you around here. Dan's inside. You can go on in."

"Listen—thanks. I really mean it. For—for getting him to call me."

"Oh don't be silly, it was his idea." She carried her mug to the hot plate. "Want some coffee? No? There's Cokes in the Frigidaire in the control room. Honor system. They're a dime. Well, go on, what are you waiting for?" She shooed him under the shining red light.

"Hey there, Leroy," Dan called. He was up in the rafters on a ladder, stringing wire. "Glad you could come."

"I think he ran all the way," said Claudia.

Leroy just grinned.

Dan climbed down from the ladder, clapped his shoulder. "Kiddo, I liked what I heard the last time," he said. "I got a song in from Nashville, a colored boy made a demo. It's a big song, I think, gonna be a big song for somebody, I don't know." Dan's eyebrows jumped up and down as he talked. His whole body popped with energy. "I like the way he does it on the demo. I'd go on and release that, but I been calling all over the goddamn state of Tennessee trying to find the boy that sung it, and nobody knows. I want you to sing it just like he did. Come on in here. I'll let you hear it."

They went into the cool humming air of the control room. Dan placed an unlabeled disc on a turntable. "It's called 'Without You,' " he said. "Now listen." He set the turntable turning and lowered the needle.

From the speakers above came a plaintive guitar line, a phantom pale voice wailing out loneliness. It was a my-baby-left-me song—slow and low, kind of stealthy, a mood like "Stormy Weather."

Leroy concentrated on the words. He had most of it down by the time the record was over.

"Whaddya think?" Dan said.

Leroy said, "I think I can sing it."

"Yeah, but can you sing it like that?"

"Well . . . I don't know," said Leroy. "I guess we'll have to see."

Dan handed over a sheet of paper with the words and chords charted out. Leroy wandered into the studio, resting his arm on his guitar, studying the page.

In a minute or two he had roughed out the chords. The job now was figuring out how to sing it.

The key was too high; he shifted down. He was glad when Dan came out to scuttle up the ladder again since it gave him a few minutes to get his anxiety under control and work with the song.

254

After a while Dan said, "That ain't sounding too bad."

"What are you putting up there?" Leroy said.

"It's a monitor so you'll be able to hear me from in yonder, when I tell you to start over. Like the voice of God."

Leroy smiled. "I was just getting good at figuring out Claudia's hand signals."

Dan climbed down. "Let's see how you sound from in there. Remember how that fellow sang it. Need to hear it again?"

"I don't think so," said Leroy. "I think I got it."

But of course, he didn't have it. How could he? He'd only just learned it a minute ago.

Dan went behind the glass. His voice crackled through the speaker. "You hear me in there?"

"Yessir, just fine," Leroy said. "It works good."

"Okay now, I'm gonna roll some tape. Anytime you are ready . . . set . . . go."

Tapping his foot in an easy rhythm, Leroy set in to play.

He hadn't gone two bars when Dan said, "No, huh-uh, let's stop. This is a lonesome song, buddy. Slow it down. Tape's rolling. Start again, whenever you're ready." Strange to see Dan's mouth moving behind the glass while his voice came from the speaker overhead.

This time Leroy started off more slowly. He managed to get through most of the first verse before Dan broke in to say, "Check your E string."

Leroy tuned it and started again. Dan let him go almost the distance, then: "Whoa, huh-uh, that's not it. I want to hear some more feeling in there. Don't try to sound pretty. Just sing it, you know, like you mean it. Let's go again from the top."

Welcome to the business of music. Stop, start, do it again, and again, and again. . . . The song's words began bouncing around like marbles in Leroy's head. He wanted Dan to like him and make him a star. He sang until his shirt was stuck to his back.

He mopped his face with a handkerchief and sang it again.

Dan brought him into the control room to hear the playback. Leroy liked the way his voice was enhanced and magnified by the echo Dan dialed in at the controls. But the song was going nowhere. He could hear the problem. It was not a bad imitation of the black man's singing, but it was an imitation, no real spirit at all. The beat wasn't steady. The song was flat—no fizz. Leroy sounded like what he was, a kid fumbling around with a song he didn't know how to sing.

Dan seemed to have infinite patience and time and recording tape. Leroy sang "Without You" ten times, a dozen. Each version seemed more dismal than the last. He didn't know what was wrong.

He asked to hear the demo again, listened to it three times with his eyes fixed on the ceiling, then went out and tried to capture that ghostly sound. Nothing worked.

Finally Dan said, "Wait there a minute."

Leroy's heart quickened.

He just couldn't do it. He could not sing this song. Now Dan would send him packing, and Leroy would drive a Crown Electric truck for the rest of his life.

Dan flipped off the lights in the control room and came to sit beside him on a piano bench. "I tell you, son, this just ain't getting it."

"I know," Leroy said. "Maybe if I had some time to practice. I like the song, it's just ... I guess I can't sing like that guy."

"Well now let's cut the crap," Dan said. "What can you sing?"

His voice was not unkind, but neither was he smiling.

"Sir? You mean—"

"I mean, what kind of song can you sing? You told me you could sing anything. So I give you a perfectly good song, and maybe it's not your kind of thing, okay. Why don't you show me what is your kind of thing?"

"Well, sure. You want me to—"

"Just do it. Sing. Whatever you want."

Nobody had ever talked to Leroy like that, but then nobody had ever taken the time to really listen to his music either. He picked up the Sound Star. He had spent two thousand days and nights with his guitar, practicing for this chance, and he wasn't going to scaredy-cat out of it now.

He started with "Swing Low, Sweet Chariot." That was easy enough. Then "Home in the Valley" and a faster-moving tune from his gospel nights—"Take the Name of Jesus with You"—then some of his romantic Hit Parade stuff, Perry Como, Sinatra, "Hello Young Lovers" and "Always" and "When You're in Love."

Dan lit each new Camel off the one before. He sat with one shoe up on the piano bench beside him.

256

Leroy sang "Goin' Home Blues" and "Good Rockin' Tonight," "Finger Poppin' Time," Big Mama Thornton's ol' "Hound Dog." He sweated and played and enjoyed the profound way Dan listened, with his big ear tilted just so.

Leroy's fingers were raw, but he didn't give out. He sang, and Dan listened, for most of two hours. Claudia Cash wandered in and out. Leroy sang "Blue Moon of Kentucky," "Harbor Lights," "When It Rains, It Really Pours." He sang "A Beggar for Your Kisses," "Money Honey," "Soul on Fire," Leon Payne's old hit "I Love You Because," "Crying in the Chapel."

With every song his voice got stronger. He really tried showing off, showing everything he could do. Dan sat quietly, urging him on. Leroy remembered the words to songs he'd played only once or twice. He played slow ones and fast ones and snatches of things. He sang more like Dean Martin than Dean Martin, and for a minute he sounded as blind as Ray Charles.

Dan said, "Hell, son, you sold me. I think you got something. Don't know what it is, but we'll find it. Now we need a pop song, and we gotta find somebody to play behind you. Whyn't you go get a Coke and let me make some calls."

Leroy wrapped his raw fingers in Kleenex. His right shoulder and elbow were numb. But he was shining inside. He had reached in and brought forth all kinds of music. He showed Dan he wasn't just another white boy who thought it was cool to sing colored songs. He sang the words, what they meant.

He had earned this Coca-Cola. He drank it all down without stopping and let out a tremendous belch.

Dan came back. "I want to get you together with this fellow Tommy Hannah. Bailer Street, here's the address. I just talked to him. He's a good picker. He and these boys have a little band, the Cadillac Cowboys. You call him. I think you-all might play some together sometime, next week or so. Then we'll set you up a time to come back in."

"You want us to work on that song?" Leroy said.

"Which one?"

" 'Without You.' "

"Naw, I think that one's pretty much a dead dog, don't you? Why don't you boys see what else you come up with?"

It was fitting together, piece by piece, like one of Dodger's puzzles.

Leroy saw the possibilities. Dan liked him enough to want him back. Next time there would be a band.

━━∿∿━━

He didn't want the Cadillac Cowboys to think he was some rube from the hills. He put on one of his best Irving Brothers numbers—the pink zigzag shirt, pink pants with a white stripe down the leg, pink jacket, white bucks—and set out with his guitar for Bailer Street, in a tattered section of South Memphis near the paint factory where his father worked. Hank Williams yipped and yodeled "Kaw-Liga" on the radio.

The summer was hotter than anyone could believe. Sometime in late June the temperature had crawled up over one hundred degrees and stayed there; by the Fourth of July a cool breeze was a faded memory. The air was heavy and full of the steaming river. Everyone moved slowly and talked about the heat.

Number 209 Bailer was a shabby one-story building, and 209-A was a tiny apartment attached to the back. A young man appeared at the door in a white undershirt and blue jeans. He was six or seven years older than Leroy, and nearly as skinny. He had red hair, jug ears, a wide, skeptical grin—a friendly Howdy Doody kind of face. "What's up," he said, squinting into the glare.

"Hey there. I'm Leroy. I think Dan Tobias told you I was coming by."

"Yeah, right, come on in there, Slick, how's it going." He held the door open. "I'm Tommy Hannah."

"Leroy Kirby."

Tommy's handshake was strong. That must be his guitar-picking hand. "Look at you," he said. "I don't see how you can wear all that stuff in this goddamn heat."

"It doesn't get to me," said Leroy. "I don't know why."

A beagle dog came up yapping. Tommy hollered, "Gawn!" The dog slunk off to the back room. The floor was strewn with newspapers and magazines, empty cat food and Chicken of the Sea cans.

"Folks dying in this heat and you got on pink clothes," said Tommy. "Dan told me about you."

"Yeah? What did he say?"

"He said we should play some. Find out what you can do."

"That sounds all right to me." Leroy had discovered that music people always started off this way, trying to sound tougher than you. Once you showed them you knew something, they turned out all right. "I appreciate you taking the time out," he said. "Dan told me you guys are busy. I see your name all over town."

Tommy reached for the phone. "Jack lives right up the block. Hang on—yo there, Jackie! Hey. Listen, that guy Dan sent is here. Leroy. Yeah. Uh-huh. Okay, we'll see what we can get going, and you come when you can." He hung up. "Jack Brown. He plays bass. He'll be down after while; it's his sister's birthday party."

"That's nice," said Leroy.

"Yeah," said Tommy, "real damn sweet." For the first time he noticed the Sound Star. "That your box?"

"Yeah."

"Baby's got a few miles on her, ain't she?" Tommy reached around for his own guitar. It was an authentic Gibson, a newer and showier model than Uncle Johnny's, with mother-of-pearl frets and a band of silver sparkles around the sound hole. No wonder Tommy had to live in such a cheap place. He was holding a fortune in his hands. Leroy had held one just like it in Memphis Music downtown. The man said, "Three hundred dollars," and Leroy handed it back.

"That's a fine guitar," he said.

Tommy placed long, slender fingers against the frets. "My wife's in yonder taking a nap." He grinned. "This here's my *woman*." He lit into "Wabash Cannonball," playing fast, no wasted motion. The train was speeding down on him, and he outran it with his fingers. Leroy tried to keep up awhile, dropped behind and then out. This was Tommy's way of showing right off how good he was, and Leroy was impressed. He said, "Go, cat! Get it!"

Tommy lit up with a big goofy grin. He was just as grateful for praise as anybody. He wangled and doodled and raced the train down to the final four bars and slammed through the end.

"Man, you're hot!" Leroy cried. "That's some wild picking! What else can you play?"

"I can play 'em all," Tommy said. "What kind of stuff do you do?"

"I'm the same. Pretty much anything." Leroy took off his jacket and dug in his pocket for a pick. "I don't know if I can keep up with you playing. But I can sing."

They started racing each other through the lickety-split songs—"Tennessee Stud" and "Santa Fe Trail," some old Bob Wills and some new Hank Snow, Marty Robbins, Eddy Arnold. Then Leroy slowed down to show off a little himself. He sang "Cold, Cold Icy Fingers," "Have You Heard," and "I Don't Hurt Anymore." Tommy strummed background chords in slow time, but Leroy could tell he'd rather be rocketing down a fast song with his fingers flying.

Jack Brown wandered in. He was about Tommy's age, twenty-seven or so, jolly-looking, with curly red hair, reddish five o'clock stubble, a big light-up sunshiny grin. He leaned against the doorjamb awhile, listening. He made a crack about Leroy's pink clothes, said he had to get back to his sister's party, and drifted out.

Leroy kept beating his guitar and singing. He sang most of the songs he had sung for Dan Tobias. He was thrilled to stand back and really sing, with Tommy's magic fingers to support him on the guitar. When he concentrated on his singing, he could make his voice do tricks—hops and unusual skips, little hiccups he'd learned off the Mother Station, six-note jumps, a nice rounded-off Jimmie Rodgers yodel.

They got to clowning around on old Bad Boy Roberts's signature song, "You Better Look Out for Me."

Well I'm a bad boy, baby
I'm no good for you
I don't care a-what your mama says
But your daddy says we're through

Tommy played it double time while Leroy hipped and scatted and shouted it out. They broke down, howling with laughter.

"Whoo, shit," Tommy said as they wiped away tears. "I reckon we ought to quit this mess-around and get down to some serious music."

Leroy agreed. They spent the next while working up "Harbor Lights" and "I Love You Because," a pair of romantic ballads they picked as their best shots at a record for Dan. Leroy sang in the style of a high-tenor Dean Martin, lazy trying to sound sincere. Tommy came up with a dreamy, lazy sound—a trickle of counterpoint to Leroy's sleepy rendering of the melodies. It was different all right. It might not have been any good.

"Maybe we got something," Tommy said. "I'll talk to Dan. See what he'll do for us."

Leroy stretched up from the sofa, cracking his knuckles. "I tell you, man, this is fun. You don't know how much fun this is."

"Yeah, we don't sound too terrible. Who knows? Maybe Dan'll like it."

As Leroy left, he saw Tommy reaching for the telephone.

～～～

All evening Leroy sat with his guitar on the front stoop, where he could hear the Hastingses' telephone if it should ring. The next day was Sunday. He sat on the stoop all morning, flipping through the Sunday *Commercial Appeal.* The heat wave was killing old people in stuffy rooms on the south side of Memphis. There was a big deal going on over a place called Formosa that appeared to be near China. Ike and Mamie were off on their summer vacation.

The phone rang next door. Leroy forced himself to keep his eyes on the paper.

But then Mrs. Hastings came to the door and said, "Leroy? Telephone for you."

He shot to his feet.

It was Claudia Cash. "Can you be down at the studio Monday night at eight? Dan wants to hear an audition."

"Sure. Of course. Eight o'clock."

Another audition? Leroy had already sung his heart out for them. He was running out of songs. He must have sung fifty songs, in all.

But still. This was how you get to the big time. When the red lights all turn green, you go.

"Oh, and Leroy?"

"Yes ma'am."

"Dan likes to work late, so be ready."

～～～

Leroy arrived thirty minutes early. He might have expected that Claudia Cash in her crisp cotton dress was the only person in Memphis who wouldn't look slain by the heat.

261

She explained that the Mid-South Recording Service was just a sideline to Dan's real ambition, the Rocking Records label. All those four-dollar vanity recordings and weddings and sales talks paid for Dan's after-hour sessions with musicians. He was looking for a hit. He'd had a couple of near misses, including a colored singer named Lee Allen Harper, who left Rocking Records for Chess in Chicago and went on to become mildly famous. But Dan hadn't been able to put the right singer with the right song.

"What kind of sound does he want?" Leroy said.

"I'm not sure he knows," said Claudia, "but he always liked the Negro singers best."

Leroy shook his head. "So do I. I don't know what it is. I wish sometimes I was part colored so I'd have some of it."

Claudia looked around as if someone might be listening. "Oh, don't wish such a thing."

Already Leroy was sweating his new black shirt, which he'd purchased in honor of his first-ever professional recording session.

Tommy and Jack arrived together at eight, grappling a huge beat-up string bass and three guitar cases through the narrow door. "Hey there, Mr. Pink," said Jack. "Lookin' kind of ordinary tonight, ain't you?"

Leroy ignored the crack. He needed everybody to like him, in order for this evening to succeed.

He had a plan.

His last time in front of this microphone, Leroy had spent two hours trying to sing like somebody else.

Tonight, if he saw a way to grab the chance, he would stand up and sing in his own voice. He would use the others to get something powerful out of himself. Dan Tobias was a pro, Tommy and Jack did this all the time. But only Leroy knew what was surging inside him, trying to get out.

He had to sing, so people would listen to him. All he'd ever wanted in life was love and attention. As he grew up and saw his classmates at Humes headed for boring, ordinary lives, Leroy had come to realize that would never be enough for him. He wanted to be famous. He wanted bigger love, more attention. His singing might not be good enough to make him famous, but it was his best chance, his only chance.

He would never be a background singer. He had left his invisible cloak at Humes High. He had to stand up and sing, up in front of a band, to find out how good he might be. He might get famous. He knew now that he needed more than a microphone; he needed these guys to help him find his voice.

Dan Tobias came in with a little sack leaking coffee from one corner. "Leroy, how you gettin' along?"

"Just fine," he said. "I'm just fine."

Dan took out two paper cups, drank the first one off, and poured the other into a mug. "You ready to sing?"

"Yes sir."

"How'd it go with Tommy and Jack?"

"It was great. Me and Tommy played a long time. Jack came by for a little while. They're in yonder, getting ready."

"Tommy said he didn't think you had too much experience, but you got a good voice," Dan said. "I told him I thought the same thing."

"Yes sir." It embarrassed and thrilled Leroy to hear their opinion of him, blunt as it was.

"You hadn't done too much singing in public, have you, son?"

"Nosir. I—I sing a lot by myself."

Dan lit a Camel. "How'd you like playing with those boys?"

Leroy considered a moment. "Tell you, I think it was about the most fun I ever had. That Tommy . . . he's something. He really knows how to play."

"Well, we're not here to hear Tommy," said Dan. "He's had his turn. We're here to hear you. You ready? Let's go."

Leroy followed him under the red light, saying a prayer in his head: Make me a star.

Tommy and Jack took a long time fussing with their instruments. When Leroy picked up his own guitar to tune it, they wrinkled their noses as if the Sound Star carried a guitar blight.

"I don't think you need to play that just yet," said Tommy. "Whyn't you let Jack and me play, and you concentrate on your singing. That's the hard part."

"Fine with me," Leroy said, and it was, for now. These boys knew how to play.

Tommy slung the beautiful Gibson around his neck and lit into "Cannonball," as a warm-up. Jack Brown handled the ungainly string bass like a giant violin, twirling it into place, his strong fingers dancing, making a bottom for the sound: thoom, thoom, thoom.

They stopped to retune. Leroy wandered to one of the upright pianos and began picking out the melody to "Onward Christian Soldiers," the way he used to do during pancake suppers at the Priceville Assembly of God. The cool touch of the keys sent a wave of happiness through him. He was back in the studio, where he belonged.

"Okay boys, let's do it," came Dan's electrified voice. "What you got for me?"

Tommy leaned to the nearest microphone. "We worked on 'Harbor Lights' and that Leon Payne thing."

"All right, I'm not gonna roll for a while." Dan folded his arms and propped his feet on the control panel. "Let's hear what you got."

Tommy said, "Why don't we start with 'I Love You Because.' Leroy, you gonna whistle the introduction like you did Saturday?"

"Let's see if my whistler's working."

Leroy counted off the song. Leon Payne had done fine with this tune, and Eddie Fisher had a hit with it, too. Maybe it would be good luck for Leroy. Girls loved it. It was a romantic guy listing all the reasons he loves the girl, because she understands him and she never doubts him, but, most of all, *because you're you.*

Tommy brought a shimmery Hawaiian sound from his guitar, while Jack thumbed a slow, gentle beat. Leroy tried to sing it like every heartthrob singer he'd ever heard. He spoke the talking part from his heart.

I love you because—because my heart ... is lighter....

They played it five or six times, and Leroy improved his performance a little each time. Tommy and Jack were figuring out their parts as they went along, so he saw no reason not to try for something different, a new phrase or a better way of pronouncing the words.

"I don't know about this one," Dan said, "but I'll turn on the machine and get something down anyway."

Leroy whistled the little introduction, a pure Bob Wills trick. It set the right mood for the song—corny and sincere.

When the take was over, Dan said, "Let's go for two."

Leroy changed it around some. Tommy kept right up and improvised over his changes.

"Take three."

Four, five, six, seven. They played it and milked it and switched it around. They undid the things they had done to it. Dan would not be satisfied. Leroy hadn't realized the process of recording required so many stops and starts, so much blank tape.

They moved on to "Harbor Lights." Tommy plucked his guitar in a dawdling Hawaiian style, making frilly little chords. Leroy crooned the way he'd rehearsed it.

"It's not a bad song" was the best Dan would say. "Let's take a break." He came out to adjust the microphones while Leroy went for Cokes from the refrigerator.

The control-room air conditioner pumped out a river of cool. Leroy stood in front of the vents, holding the cold bottles in his hands, his energy seeping back. He had to get something going in there. Dan's boundless patience was bound to run out sometime, and Tommy and Jack looked bored out of their skulls.

"Leave that door open a minute," Dan said, coming into the control room. "Let some air in there. It's hotter'n hell."

Leroy carried the Cokes to the boys. Jack drank his straight down.

Tommy placed the bottle against his neck. "Glamour and glory," he said.

"You got it." Jack groaned. "The musician's life."

Leroy picked up the Sound Star. "Hey Tommy, you remember what we were doing the other day—"

And he whanged off into that old Bad Boy Roberts song "You Better Look Out for Me," an infectious, quick-tempered tune about a dangerous guy who's messing with a nice girl, and she knows he's bad news, and still she doesn't care.

He sang it in a falsetto, hopping and jumping around, cutting up, laughing.

Tommy put down his Coke, picked up his Gibson, and set up a swift, happy beat—rack tacka rack tacka rack tacka.

Jack got a big goofy grin on his face. He levered himself up under his bass and began plucking out the rhythm, clowning, slapping the soundboard in syncopation.

Tommy played an opposing lick to Leroy's rhythm. Leroy hollered the song.

Well I'm a bad boy, baby
I'm no good for you
I don't care a-what your mama says
But your daddy says we're through

Jack popped the strings. Tommy's grin was all over his face—
Dan burst through the door. "What is *that?*"

Leroy and Tommy broke up laughing. Jack said, "That's wild, ain't it, Dan?"

"Sorry, Dan," said Tommy, "we're just messing around."

"Well you may be messing around," Dan said, "but you better remember what it was you were doing. I'm going in there and get the damn thing on tape while you can still do it."

"What do you mean?" said Jack. "Jeez, Dan, we were only playing."

"Hell, I know you were! That sounded different! You were *playing.*" Dan's eyes were on fire. "Go back and find you a place to start it. You slap that box like you did, Jack, and Leroy, I want you to sing just that way. Don't slow down. That was good! I mean it! Let's go!" He headed for the control room, slamming the door behind him.

Leroy looked at Tommy and Jack. Tommy and Jack looked at him. It was joking-around music, but Dan wasn't joking. He liked it.

"Will wonders never cease." Tommy lifted his Wurlitzer electric guitar from its case.

They moved back into position. Leroy kept the Sound Star around his neck; after all, it was his guitar that had started the song. He said, "You guys got any idea how to start the thing?"

"I think it should just start," said Tommy. "I'll play a lead line, and, Jack, you play this." He demonstrated a simple one-two beat for the bass, a straight country rhythm for Leroy. Then he embroidered the thing with fancy licks on his electric guitar. But what made the song fly was the excitement of that bouncing speeded-up beat, rack tacka rack tacka. . . .

I'm bad news
Well I'm bad news
I'm bad news baby, can't you see?
You better look out-a for me

266

By the third take Leroy had loosened up. Dan said they were getting close to something. "Keep going," he said, "make it pop. Tommy, don't overdo it. Keep it simple. And quick."

Lightning started jumping.

Leroy sang high and straight, the way he would sing at his secret place by the river, for his own pleasure. He didn't care if he sounded hillbilly or not; he wanted to make the song pop, like Dan said. He jumped and wiggled to get his juices going, but also he had to strum the right chords and keep his mouth a constant distance from the microphone.

> *I heard what your daddy told you*
> *That don't make it so*
> *You can stick by your mama's side*
> *Or let me kiss you nice and slow*
> *Well I'm bad news. . . .*

Dan got more excited with every attempt. The fifth and sixth takes were better, cleaner, the rough edges smoothing out.

After the seventh, he called them in to hear the playback. "It's almost there," he kept saying, "almost there."

It was nearly midnight. Claudia brought a sack of small square Krystal burgers. Tommy took three; Leroy and Jack ate nine each. Leroy was filled with music, the thrill of the song running all through him. He had to find ways to make it better.

"Boys, we just got to play it faster," he said, chewing. "I hear it in my head and it's *fast*."

"You're right," Tommy said. "If I come in quick on that first thing . . ."

They went out and did another take, faster. Dan clapped his hands. "Hey, that's good! Yeah, man! Yeah!"

"One more time," Leroy said.

Jack's hand skedaddled down the neck. "I don't know," he said, "we got it right. Maybe we should go on to something else before we get worse."

"I messed up," said Leroy. "Come on, boys. We can get it. One more time."

"One more time," Dan said.

Leroy counted off.

He had a strong idea of the song. He knew how to sing its hidden meanings. He was the bad boy. The girl was Miss Waverly with softer edges, Dolores Roselle with love in her eyes.

> *I'm bad news baby, can't you see?*
> *You better look out-a for me*

Leroy found a new way to sing on that take, number nine. He saw the whole song stretching out in front of him, he knew how to sing it, and then he let go of himself—shook his leg, flailed around, churned up the air—and the act of jumping around gave his voice a hot spark.

Tommy slid in with the simplest, most understated guitar line, buoying him along. Leroy sang a *dee, dah, dee-dee* scat in the second guitar break. Jack rapped and patted and thumped in perfect sympathy, like a whole rhythm section.

Dan's hand hit the monitor switch. "Hoo, dog! You done it that time, boys! That's it! I'm coming out!"

Leroy turned all sparkly inside. He knew he had just done something no one had ever done.

Dan Tobias urged him on to it, Tommy and Jack conspired in it . . . but Leroy was the one who had changed. Suddenly, on that last take, he let go. He opened his mouth and jumped around and sang it, and it came out just wild.

Dan kept saying it was a hit, a hit, bound to be a hit. He gathered them in the control room. They prodded each other and joked about how they would spend their first million dollars.

Dan threaded the tape, started it running. The Sound Star's twang fell right in with Jack's enthusiastic bass line—rack tacka tack tacka. Tommy's electric guitar came cruising in, sleek and elegant as a new car.

Leroy's voice ranged way up above it. That big electronic echo made his voice sound twice as big. He loved his voice. There was love and lust and rebellion in there. The guitar solo skittered along. The song was over almost before it began.

"Let's hear it again," Leroy said.

"Yeah, man!" Dan rewound the tape. No one said another word. Leroy wondered if they were thinking what he was thinking: Is it really that good?

268

They listened again. They stared at the floor, holding in their smiles.

This funny old song wasn't funny anymore. It was new. It was cool. Leroy didn't hear anything wrong with it. When it was over, he wanted to hear it again, but he didn't say so. His face was red. He did not want anyone to know how good he thought it was.

Dan said, "The third time's the charm," and rewound the tape.

Leroy's hands trembled: Too many Coca-Colas? He clasped them behind him.

The song ran by, quick as a flash.

Dan said, "Boys, it's a hit. It's brand-new. It's just exactly what I been waiting for. Thank you Jesus. Now we got to find a B side, and I mean tonight."

Tommy and Jack grinned so wide that Leroy knew Dan had never said anything like *that* before.

They clapped each other's shoulders and pushed back into the studio, giddy with praise and the thrill of doing something right from beginning to end. Leroy took up his Sound Star in a euphoric heat. Already he felt closer to Tommy and Jack than he'd ever been to any friend, except maybe Bubba Hayes. These fellows connected through their music. Their best talking was done with their instruments. They took pride in playing like nobody else. At first they had reflected Leroy's excitement; now they were excited themselves.

They ran through half a dozen songs, searching for one they could speed up to match the pace of "You Better Look Out for Me." Dan smoked Camels. Claudia made another pot of coffee and announced that they'd have to fend for themselves, she was going home to sleep.

Leroy felt like singing all night. He picked up that old Bill Monroe chestnut, "Blue Moon of Kentucky." He swung the song, syncopating it, clowning around to see if he could get another rise out of the boys.

Sure enough Tommy reached for his Gibson and jumped on the beat, and Jack Brown caught it, too, and Dan said, "That's it! That's it! Go, now!" and hurried for the control room.

He spoke through the monitor. "Tommy, you play the acoustic. Jack, set this one out one time. Leroy, you sing."

They made the first take at a nice, easy stride, just feeling out the song. Tommy strummed the Gibson while Leroy searched for places to do his vocal hops and skips and exaggerations. Dan seemed to like these tricks, so Leroy gave him plenty. *Blue moon of-a Kentucky, a-keep on shinin'....*

Dan came out beaming. "Hey, that's fine. Hell, that's different. That's a pop song there, nearly 'bout!"

They all laughed.

"Okay now. Leroy on acoustic, Tommy on electric, and, Jack, you play this time. I want you to do it twice as fast."

Leroy said yeah! and Tommy said yeah!

Jack said, "Bill Monroe would roll over in his grave,"

"He ain't dead," said Tommy.

Leroy grinned. "Let's kill him."

Dan said, "Tommy, keep it simple."

Leroy moved back to the microphone. "I don't know what we're gonna do with old Carl Perkins over there," he said with a grin.

They lit in at a blistering pace, fast as Tommy playing "Wabash Cannonball."

By take six Leroy was pulling out his tricks at the very start of the song, chanting *Blue moon* a couple of times and then hip-hopping down the line

> *Blue moon, keep on-a shining bright*
> *You gonna bring-a me back-a my baby tonight*

and prancing through the song. It was hammy and wild. That old sweet "Blue Moon of Kentucky" lumbered down a long runway, and took off, and flew.

Leroy jumped around, shaking his leg the way he had to make the girls squeal at the Humes talent show. He let the music out through his body. He had to move around to give his voice that wild, abandoned sound. He couldn't do it standing still. He didn't know why.

Dan loved it. He ran the playback of the seventh take over and over, until Jack said, "Stop. Dan. Hey, it's two o'clock in the morning."

Leroy would have been happy to sit in the chilly control room listening to his songs until the sun came up. But Dan said they'd all done a good night's work. "I can get somebody to play this," he said. "I know I can."

He cut a copy of the acetate for each of them. "You listen in the morning and see what you think," he said. "See if I'm crazy. See if it's still any good."

Leroy said good night and stepped out to the sidewalk. The muggy air made him exhausted, all at once. His hair was down in his eyes. His new shirt clung to his back from the sweat. His hand ached. In the morning he would get up and drive the truck for Crown.

He crawled into his car.

As he drove, a smile grew on his face, a weary smile just for himself. He had won the talent show, he had gotten Dan Tobias to listen to him, and now he had made a hit. The record in that white envelope was a hit. He knew it.

He knew what to do. He went in and did it. His power frightened and thrilled him. He could do anything. He only had to believe.

28

On Saturday morning Leroy went to the pay phone at Maxie's Market and dialed the studio number.

Dan said he'd already given a demo to Uncle Richard, the nighttime country deejay on WMPS. "He likes 'Blue Moon of Kentucky,' and he's gonna play it on his show tonight."

Leroy smacked the wall with his hand. "Oh, you're kidding! Dan, that's great!"

"And get this. I just took one to Dewey Phillips down at WHBQ, you know that show 'Red Hot and Blue'? He flipped, son. He loved 'em both but especially 'Better Look Out for Me.' He's got Tennessee Ern on the show tonight, but he swears he'll play both sides sometime after nine-thirty."

"Oh man, it's so quick! What did you *say* to those guys?"

"I didn't say anything. I just played the record."

"That's ... it's—!"

"Yeah, I know. Now I'm taking one over to Sleepy-Eyed John. You be sure to turn on your radio tonight."

"Oh, don't worry." Leroy couldn't believe how fast things were happening. Every hour brought another piece of good news.

Dan said, "Call me tomorrow," and clicked off.

Leroy stood holding the phone. The lady at Maxie's cash register came all the way out the door to investigate the excitement. Leroy gave her a big mysterious wink and walked away on a cushion of air.

He floated straight home. Ray snored on the couch. Dodger hunkered over her puzzle. Agnes was on her knees, leaning into the oven; her free hand dipped a brush into a bucket of soapy water.

Leroy went to his room for the white envelope.

"Hey Mama, come in here a minute."

"I'm busy." She sounded far away.

"This is important. I mean it. Daddy, wake up."

"Don't bother your daddy," said Dodger, "let him have his nap."

"Daddy, come on." Leroy punched a finger into Ray's ribs.

"Huh? What? What's wrong?" Ray blinked and sat up, confused. "What's the matter?"

"Wake up a minute," said Leroy. "I've got a surprise."

Agnes appeared, her hair bound in a rag, a sooty smear down her cheek. The oven-cleaning powder had made her eyes water. "Honey, I'm right in the middle of this."

"This'll only take a second," said Leroy. He went to the phonograph, put the acetate over the spindle, and lowered the tone arm.

The rack-tacka rhythm hopped out into the room, then Leroy's voice. He stood back to watch. For the first verse of "You Better Look Out for Me," they looked as if they didn't know why they were being forced to listen to this rowdy music.

Leroy couldn't stand the suspense. "That's me," he blurted. "That's me singing."

Agnes's eyes widened. "Oh, you're joking. It is not."

"That doesn't sound a thing like you," said Dodger.

Ray blew a sigh. "I was trying to sleep. . . ."

Leroy stood back and grinned and felt hugely proud.

He flipped the acetate to play "Blue Moon of Kentucky." Dodger patted her foot. She said she liked this one better since she knew the song already.

When it was over, Agnes cried, "Leroy, that's wonderful! I can't believe that is you!"

He could hardly believe it himself. The songs still sounded cool, in broad daylight.

He put his arm around her. "Guess what," he said. "They're going to play it tonight on the radio. Uncle Richard on WMPS and 'Red Hot and Blue' on HBQ—maybe even Sleepy-Eyed John."

"Oh Leroy," she said, "that's just—it's wonderful, son! I'm so proud of you. Ray, isn't that wonderful?"

"Yeah it is." Ray yawned, swung his feet back onto the couch. "They gonna pay you for that?"

"Well no, Daddy, but they might make a record out of it and then try to sell it."

Ray said, "That's about what I thought."

"If you want my opinion," said Dodger, "folks are gonna like that 'Blue Moon' song better than that bad news one. People don't like to hear about bad news."

"I don't know," Leroy said. Had he made a mistake, bringing his big euphoric balloon in here to be punctured? What if Dan Tobias and the deejays were wrong? What if everyone hated the record—both sides?

"Honey, run down to Maxie's," said Agnes, "call Johnny and Travis, tell them to come for dinner and stay to hear your song on the radio."

"We can't afford to be feeding your kinfolks," Ray said behind closed eyes. "They ought to be feeding us."

Agnes rolled her eyes. "This is a special occasion," she said. "Go on, son, and do what I tell you. I've got a whole fryer and I'll make potato salad. There's plenty for everybody."

"Do you really like it, Mama?" Leroy said. "Tell the truth. Do you think folks will like it?"

"I didn't say anything," Dodger protested. "All I said was I liked one song better than the other."

"It sure is hard to get a nap around here," said Ray.

"Well Ray, there's a perfectly good bed in yonder that you can go get in." Agnes knelt before the oven. "Can you imagine? Our boy on the *radio*. I wish I could tell everybody in Tupelo. Honey, play it again. I didn't really hear it the first time."

Leroy lifted the tone arm and started "You Better Look Out for Me." Ray pretended to snore.

The afternoon was too long. Leroy had too much time to think about it, to play the acetate until it began to sound foolish and hollow and show-offish. The holes in his confidence began to widen.

Get out of the house.

He went down to Crown Electric. It was a slow Saturday; Joey Weaver had finished all the deliveries early, and Leroy wasn't needed.

Find something to do.

He drove out of town, to his meadow above the river. He sat on the hood of his car, trying to relax. The buzzing insects made him more nervous.

Think about something else.

He lifted the Sound Star and started to play "Harbor Lights." He didn't enjoy it. His heart wasn't there. He couldn't sit still. He kept hearing his record again in his mind.

He shut his eyes and held himself still while he tried to count to sixty.

At forty-eight he couldn't stand it. He got back in the car, drove to town, to the Gridiron. Five well-done double cheeseburgers calmed him down some, and Patti Page singing "Doggie in the Window" on the jukebox. At least Leroy's record was better than that, any day of the year.

When he got back in the car, Bill Haley was chomping through "Shake, Rattle and Roll," as smooth a lift job as Leroy had heard yet. Haley had picked up Joe Turner's arrangement, his beat, his whole sound, and moved it to white radio. He was selling a billion records. Leroy hoped he could do the same thing for Bad Boy Roberts.

He got home just as Johnny pulled up in his pickup. "What about that big news, boy! that's fine!"

"Thanks, Johnny." He left his guitar in the Zephyr and followed Johnny to the house.

"What's the matter, Leroy? You don't look too happy."

"I don't know. Kind of nervous, I guess."

"Well forget about that. Come on in here and play me your record!" The way Johnny said it, *record* rhymed with *nekkid*.

The house was stifling, an overwhelming smell of grease from the kitchen. That meant Agnes was frying chicken. She hated to be bothered in the middle of that.

Dodger got up from her puzzle to receive Johnny's hug. Johnny turned to Leroy. "Okay Mr. Sound Star, let's hear it."

"Now tell me what you think, Johnny." Leroy swallowed, lowered the tone arm.

He couldn't bear to watch Johnny listening. He pretended he was interested in something going on outside the window.

He turned to see a big smile on Johnny's face. "That's good, Lee! I mean it. Got some real spunk to it there. Hell! Who's those other boys playing with you?"

"Tommy Hannah and Jack Brown," said Leroy. "They're part of the Cadillac Cowboys. Here, we did a flip side." He put the needle on "Blue Moon of Kentucky."

Johnny listened, patting his knee in time. "Real damn good, Leroy. I mean it. That's fine." He shook his head. "And they're playing you on the radio. Hell, boy, you've done more in a week than me and all my years of pickin' put together. I'm proud of you."

This praise should have sent Leroy soaring, but right now he was feeling earthbound and a little queasy. All day he had swallowed great swells of excitement and fear. Now his nerves and the fried-chicken smell were beginning to make everything turn inside him.

Ray arrived with Travis and his rambunctious beagle dog. Leroy used the distraction to slip away to the bathroom. His face felt clammy. He got down on his knees in front of the toilet.

He spit, but nothing happened.

After a minute or two he knew he wasn't really going to puke. It was all the excitement, attention, anticipation, fear, and desire sloshing together inside him, a bad soup. He had to get out of this house. He couldn't stand to hear his song with everybody watching.

He sat on the toilet lid until his stomach calmed down. He couldn't fall apart now, not when everything was just starting to get good. He had to be the coolest boy on the block. He splashed his face with water and crept to the kitchen. "Mama, I don't feel so good."

"What's the matter, baby? You're all flushed. Come here!" She pressed her hand to his head. "Are you taking a fever?"

"No, I'm not sick. It's just—I can't stay here. It's making me too nervous with everybody around."

"Your songs are good. What are you nervous about?"

"I don't know. I—I can't explain it, I can't stop thinking about it. I just gotta get out of here. I'm going down to the Loew's. Maybe that'll take my mind off it."

She frowned. "Now, Leroy—"

"Don't *mess* with me, Mama. I'm going!"

He had never spoken that sharply to her.

"I'm sorry," he went on, in the face of her speechless surprise, "you just got to understand. I need to be by myself. I love you for getting Johnny and Travis over here to celebrate, but you'll have to save me a drumstick. I'll be home later." He kissed her, patted her shoulder, slipped out the back.

He felt better at once. The sun hovered low in the west, adding heat to the heat that was already there. He got in the Zephyr and drove straight for the coolest place in Memphis, the newly air-conditioned Loew's.

Cigarette-smoking penguins on the doors said, "Come In—It's KOOL Inside!" The theater was jammed with people who had come to see the Red Skelton diamond heist comedy and the Gene Autry-Slim Pickens western and to sit in the dark, enjoying the oceans of chilled air pumped out by the mighty refrigerators.

Leroy found a seat in the third row, between a fat man and a little girl. The fat man thought everything Red Skelton did was hilarious. The little girl kept peering around Leroy to watch the man bellow and laugh.

Leroy didn't really notice the movie. A lot of car chase scenes and Red Skelton making funny faces. He imagined how many people in Memphis were cruising around in their cars right now, or at home with their radios on.

The machine-cool air smelled like the control room at Rocking Records, and that made him think of his record, and the radio stations where actual disc jockeys would be placing it over a spindle, and the tall towers waiting to send his voice through the air. . . .

He was glad he wasn't at home thinking these things, with everybody looking at him.

He squeezed past the fat man, up the aisle. Some people were watching the movie with their eyes closed, smiling in the cool.

The new usher, a spindly kid with pimples, flashed his light on Leroy's fine white-tipped shoes as he passed.

He bought a tub of buttered popcorn, two boxes of Milk Duds, a grape Nehi. The new popcorn girl gave him a flirtatious smile with his change, but Leroy was too distracted to flirt back.

He carried his snacks down the aisle. This time he took a seat in the very first row. The Skelton picture was over; Slim Pickens's grizzled face filled the screen. Slim gol-darned and fumed and threw his hat on the ground, acting the sidekick fool. Gene Autry smiled at his antics. Gene's teeth sparkled. He rode a fine horse in fancy harness.

Leroy worked his jaw on a Milk Dud. He thought of Dan Tobias and Tommy and Jack and Claudia Cash, all in separate places, tuning their radio dials. He thought: Well, if nothing else happens, at least they played your songs once on the radio.

He heard someone say, "Leroy?"

He turned.

In the reflected light from the screen he saw his mother walking slowly down the aisle, searching every row. "Leroy?"

He stood up. "Mama?"

"Shh," said a woman behind him.

Leroy went to the aisle. "Mama?"

Her hands flew up. "There you are!"

"Mama, what's wrong?"

"Shhhhh!"

"Oh shoosh yourself, you fresh thing," Agnes snapped. "Come on, Leroy, let's get out of here."

That brought a bigger chuckle from the people around than anything in the movie.

Leroy followed her up the aisle to the lobby. "Mama, what's wrong?"

"Oh, honey, it's happened. It's a miracle. They just called from the radio. They want you down there! They already played your songs a bunch of times. Folks are calling and sending in wires—oh come on, we've got to hurry! They're going to put you on the radio!"

The popcorn girl stared. Leroy stared. "Mama. You're kidding."

"I'm not. Now come on."

He followed her out, trying to make sense of what she had said. This had to be some giant joke, something Johnny and Travis dreamed up to get him to come back to the party.

"I've got my car," he said.

"Then I'll ride with you. We have to go *now*."

They got into the Zephyr. Leroy started the engine.

"Quick," she said, "turn on the radio."

"Which station?"

"That red, white, and blue thing," she said. "Oh come on!"

He found it way up the dial—the hurried, slurred voice of Dewey Phillips, WHBQ's nighttime deejay and fast-talking commercial announcer. "Now you get you a mess of wild chickens, cut off their heads, watch 'em running around—and tell 'em you heard it from Phillips on 'Red—Hot—and *Blue*'! Coming to you live from the Hotel Chiska—on the magazine floor! Now we gone play that song everybody been callin' about—here it is, hot from Mr. Dan Tobias at Rocking Records here in Memphis!" And then, his stopwatch ticking, Dewey played "You Better Look Out for Me."

He kept his microphone live on the air, humming along here and there, saying, "Yep! Get it, boy," after the guitar break, chuckling out loud as if he loved the song so much he couldn't stay quiet.

> *I'm bad news baby, can't you see*
> *You better look out-a for me*

Leroy put the pedal down. His dreams were toppling over, bam-bam-bam, ducks in a shooting gallery.

"Mama, where are we going?" he said.

"The Chiska Hotel."

"I can't believe it," he murmured.

"Me neither. Your daddy's so happy—oh, and Johnny is just beside himself."

At the last bars of "You Better Look Out for Me," Dewey Phillips crowed, "Look out for you, all right, look out for me, too—you asked for it folks—here it is, turn it over—we'll play the other side again! Ladies and germs, Bill Mun-roe as performed by Lee-roy Kirby." And then it was "Blue Moon of Kentucky."

Leroy gripped the steering wheel. "I can't believe it."

Agnes said, "It is a miracle."

Dewey came on: "Yeah yeah yeah, boys and ladies, it's sizzlin' hot—and you heard it here first, call it 'Red—Hot—and *Blue*'! We're trying to get the cat down here right now, so hang on now hang on!" His voice dissolved in a commercial for San Ann gasoline.

Leroy scratched to a stop. The Chiska was a large old brick building that had seen its better days too long ago for anyone to remember.

"I'll stay here," Agnes said. "Leave your key, so I can listen to you."

"Oh Mama, come on up."

"You don't need me. I'll just set here and listen. You mind your manners with that man. He sounds peculiar to me."

"Well, okay. Wish me luck anyway."

"Good luck, honey." She kissed her fingers, touched his cheek.

Leroy woke the ancient bellman to ask directions, then ran the steps two at a time, to a door labeled "WHBQ—Memphis Music!"

A dark-haired young woman glanced up when he came in.

"I'm here to see Dewey Phillips," he said.

"Sorry, he's on the air. You'll have to wait."

On the wall monitor Leroy heard himself singing "You Better Look Out for Me."

He pointed to the speaker. "No, see—that's me. That's my song. He called for me. He wanted me to come down and be on the radio."

"Oh! Well! Well of course! Come in!" She fluttered up from her chair. "You're Leroy? My goodness, that's a popular song. I've taken forty-nine calls since Dewey started playing it." The phone rang. "Fifty." Flashing a dazzling smile at Leroy, she picked up the receiver. "WHBQ Memphis Music! Uh-huh? Yes, thank you, we like it, too. No, his name's Leroy Kirby. No, I don't know that. I just work at the station. O—o—okay now, good-bye." She hung up. "The fellow just came from the Western Union with telegrams. I haven't seen anything—"

The phone rang again.

"Excuse me," she said. "You just be real quiet and go through that door there. Wave to Dewey before you go in—he's on the air. WHBQ Memphis Music! Yes. 'Blue Moon of Kentucky'? Well he's already played it seven times, ma'am, I'm not sure if he'll be able to—"

Leroy shut the door quickly to protect the velvety silence inside. He walked a long carpeted hall to a glassed-off room where a man hunched over a microphone, muttering to himself, spinning records with each hand.

Leroy caught his eye.

The man waved him in, swung around in his chair. "Well hello there, young fellow," he said. "You must be Leroy."

"Yes sir, I am," said Leroy. He didn't see a red light anywhere.

"Sit down, son, sit down! Let me shake your hand! That's quite a record you made—got the phones hopping—folks from here to Little Rock sending in wires—man, you have caused quite a stir!"

"Well that's—really something," said Leroy. "Thank you, sir."

Dewey Phillips had a wide-open face, bushy eyebrows, a gnawed-on bottom lip that suggested he was wound up inside like a clock spring. Leroy had listened to his show for years. Dewey's trademark was talking so fast you could barely understand him. He set the needle on the first groove of "You Better Look Out for Me."

"Sit down now, son, I'm gonna interview you."

"I've never been interviewed before," said Leroy. "I don't know much about it."

"Just don't say nothing dirty. Now tell me—you from Memphis, right?"

Tommy's guitar twanged in the background. "Yes sir. I'm from Tupelo Missippi, originally."

"That's fine. Who's your folks?"

"Uhm, my daddy's Ray Kirby, and my mama's name is Agnes."

"What school'd you go to, Leroy?"

"Humes."

"That's Humes High School right here in Memphis, right?" Dewey said.

"Yes sir."

"When'd you finish at Humes?"

"Just this year."

"How long you and your band been together, Leroy?"

"Wellsir, not long. A couple weeks or so."

"A couple weeks! Now that's something. You all got any plans for performing anywhere around?"

"No sir, but I sure would like to if we get the chance."

"Let me read you some of these telegrams, Leroy. Here's one says, 'You Better Look Out For Me Is Something To Look Out For All Right Stop Who Is This Leroy? Love Angela.' Ain't that a fine pack of crackers?"

"Well yessir, that's—kind of wild," Leroy said. "This is all just real hard to believe."

"Here's one: 'Leroy I Love You Will You Marry Me Betty Ann.' You might want to get that gal's number, ha-ha-ha. Here's another one: 'Fine New Singer on Your Show' from Shiloh, Tennessee. Thank you, Shiloh."

"Well that was sure nice of folks to go to all that trouble," said Leroy. "Can they hear you as far away as Shiloh?"

"You bet. Okay now, who are the boys playin' with you?"

"Tommy Hannah on guitar, and Jack Brown on the string bass."

"That's Leroy Kirby on the Rocking Records label, right? Plan to make another record?"

"If Dan'll let me," said Leroy.

"Hahaha! I bet he will after this. Thank you, Leroy, glad you came down."

Dewey sat back in his chair, lit a cigarette, started a jingle for Luzianne coffee. "Thanks a lot, son, I think you really got something there," he said, waving at the turntable.

Leroy said, "Aren't you gonna interview me?"

"I just did," said Dewey Phillips. "The mike was open."

"It was—what? Oh—oh, no! I hope I didn't say anything wrong." He hadn't had any warning! He'd just opened his mouth and said anything that came out!

"You did fine," said Phillips. "You know, a lot of these folks calling in think you're colored, the sound of your voice. That's why I wanted you down here, to tell 'em you went to Humes, so they'd know you was white."

"They did?" Leroy said. "Well, why would they—"

"It's kinda hard to tell from the record," said Dewey. "And with a name like Leroy . . . Listen, kid, I got to get on with it—but I wanna tell you I never had a record pop the way yours did tonight. You take care. I'll be talking to Dan. And you better believe I'll be playing this tune."

"Hey thanks, Mr. Phillips, that's great."

282

"You want these telegrams? Might as well take 'em. Stop by tomorrow and see if there's more."

Leroy gathered the stack of yellow sheets and floated along the corridor, through the receptionist's office, down the stairs to the car.

His mother's eyes were shining with tears, her hands clasped together and pressed to her mouth.

Leroy climbed in. "Mama, I swear I didn't know that was going out over the radio," he said. "I don't remember a word I said."

"Oh Leroy, I am so proud," she said. "Just so proud."

"Get a load of these." He dumped the pages on the seat. "All these people sent wires."

Agnes gazed out the window. "When you were little, you sang at the fair that time . . . I told your daddy you had a special talent. I wanted to take you to Hollywood or somewhere so you'd have a chance to sing for people."

"Mama—"

"Hush, honey, you wait. He thought I was crazy. He said it was just the way every mother felt about her own child. But I knew it was more than that. I knew. I felt it. I told you."

"I remember," he said.

"And now you've gone and done it," said Agnes. "And your daddy was right, too. We didn't have to go to Hollywood. You were gonna do it all the time. You always knew you were special."

"I know, Mama."

"You got everything your poor brother had saved up inside of him." She shook her head. "I always had a feeling."

"I know." Leroy started the car. "I had it, too."

29

$\mathcal{D}$an Tobias dropped
by the Kirbys' apartment Sunday morning with the news that seven
Memphis disc jockeys had called for a demo of "You Better Look Out
for Me." Claudia was rushing all over town, delivering copies.

"Man oh man." Leroy sank to a chair.

Agnes offered Dan a doughnut from the Piggly Wiggly box. "It's all
so exciting," she said.

"The deejays keep playing one side; then they flip it over and play the
other side," Dan went on. "They're all getting calls. The country guys
especially like 'Blue Moon of Kentucky.'"

"Is it really a hit, Dan?" said Leroy. "I mean, is this what it's like when you get a hit?"

"I don't know, I never had one," said Dan, "but I think we got to sell some records first. I could sell five thousand today if I had 'em. We got the pressing plant working overtime, but the first batch won't be ready for a week. It's happening too quick."

Agnes poured more coffee in his cup. "Don't you think folks will wait a week if it's something they like?"

"I don't know, Miz Kirby, in this business things happen fast. You can move five thousand records in an hour, if you're hot."

Leroy paced in front of the window. "You think I'm hot?"

"I'd say you are," said Dan, his face lighting up. "You come on back down to the studio tomorrow night. I got the boys coming at seven. We'll see what else we can do."

Tommy and Jack and Dan were all waiting when Leroy arrived at the studio Monday after work. He strode in with a big fat we've-got-a-hit grin on his face.

"Hey, Slick," Tommy said. "What do you think?"

"Way to go, boys." Leroy shook hands all around. They grinned at each other. "We struck gold."

Tommy said, "Looks like there may be some money out of this thing, Dan. I talked to the boys last night, and we went on and drew up a contract." He produced four long sheets and a ballpoint pen.

"Here we go," Dan said, "hadn't even pressed the damn record yet and here you come makin' contracts."

"Better safe than sorry," said Tommy. "I already heard from Sleepy Eyed John and a couple of others that want to get a piece of Leroy. I'll be the manager. That way when they ask him if he's got a manager, he can say yes. It's his show, so he gets half of everything. Jack and me split the other half. Leroy? That still okay by you?"

"Like I said last night, I'm just glad to be playing with you boys." Leroy was dying to get started. He would have signed anything. Lightning was striking *now;* the whole thing might be a pleasant memory by this time next week. He had to hurry up and make another hit, while he still remembered how he'd done it.

"Long as you boys are happy," said Dan, scanning down the page, "it looks all right to me."

Tommy handed Leroy a pen, indicating a dotted line.

Leroy signed "John Leroy Kirby." He handed over the pen in a fog of joy. He was honest to God a professional musician now.

The other boys signed, and then Dan said, "Y'all all have day jobs, don't you?"

"I'm ready to quit anytime," Leroy said, and the others said yeah, they were, too.

"Well you can't quit yet. We hadn't even got a record to sell. But I want you down here every night and working."

"Fine with me," Leroy said.

"Me too," said Jack. "Tommy?"

"I reckon I can talk to my wife. . . ."

"Thataboy." Dan hooked his thumbs in his belt. "We got to make sure this thing ain't a fluke. Get this one out and another one quick as we can. I'm working on finding some bookings."

They went in. They picked up their instruments.

Now that Leroy knew he was good, he had no fear at all in the studio. Dan and Tommy and Jack were old friends already. The fun started early and went on till late. He was learning how to sing with a band— timing and offbeats and downbeats and drum breaks. The guys showed him how to build a song by complicating it, trading off the melody between the singer and the band.

He showed them he could keep up with any fast beat they might devise. He lit up their eyes with his own vocal tricks. They loved when he hip-hopped down a line, *buh-buh-b-baaaaby!* cutting up, scatting that cool syncopation, throwing the song off its rhythm foundations.

For three nights Dan stayed right beside them in the studio— listening, advising, joking, clapping, finger snapping, or drumming along on a guitar case. He never turned on his tape machine. He said, "Leroy, you can't sit back and half sing that song, now. We're all on to you. You're *good,* son. You got to sing out, every time. Give it all you got."

"Man, I'm trying," said Leroy.

"Try harder."

On Tuesday night they set out to conquer Mr. Blues Davis's "Rockin' Saturday Night," one of the down-and-dirty Mother Station tunes Leroy had loved first. Where Mr. Blues played it loose and cool, though, he shouted and hollered and caterwauled: "Weeeelllll . . ."

He's holding his baby tonight, he's a tough guy, he's heard about all the big doings in town, cat they're rockin' all over—he bopped and jumped under the boom mike—

Hey come on it's a rockin' Saturday night
Hey hey a-come on, we're all-a rockin' Saturday night

Dan said, "Yeah, that's good, that's gettin' there. But it ain't there yet. Let's tighten it up."

They shouldered the tempo up, just a little.

My baby's got a new pair of dancin' shoes
Tonight ain't nobody singin' the blues

The song came together all at once, one take.

"That's it!" Dan cried. "Got it! Got it!"

Suddenly Leroy knew something no one else seemed to know: He could bring a song to life by playing it fast, to that rocking-blues beat, and jumping around while he sang it. He had only to find songs that fit his new style. The world was full of songs.

He brought in singles from his own stack at home. Dan pulled out sheaves of sheet music. They rehearsed every night after work and all through the weekend.

Tommy was the manager on paper, but Leroy led the sessions—picking the songs, counting off, stopping when something messed up. He set the tempo and key according to what he could sing. He was the singer, and they were his band.

At the Sunday-night session Dan opened a box and handed around a stack of 45 rpm records, ripe with a new-plastic smell. "Congratulations, boys," he said. "They can't take these away from you."

Leroy held the disc with two fingers in the center hole. He examined the bold Rocking Records label and the prim lettering:

"YOU BETTER LOOK OUT FOR ME"
(Reginald Arthur Roberts)
LEROY KIRBY
and the
BLUE RHYTHM BOYS

That made him laugh. "Blue Rhythm Boys! Dan, where'd you come up with that?"

"Well I had to put something. I was standing there and the man was waiting."

"I like it," said Leroy.

"Well that's good," said Dan, " 'cause that's what they're going to call you on opening night."

Jack Brown laughed. "What do you mean?"

"I mean, Leroy Kirby and the Blue Rhythm Boys are on the bill with Slim Whitman at the Overton Park band shell, a week from this Friday night. What the hell do you think about that?"

"Dan!"

"God *damn!* Really?"

"Slim Whitman!"

Leroy grinned, smacked his hands together. Jack and Tommy whooped and pounded each other like a football team after a touchdown.

"I didn't call them; they called me," Dan said. "It's this damn record. I never seen anything like it. I had two calls this morning from Texas!"

"Texas!" Leroy sat back on the table and started the record spinning around his index finger. "Dan, when are we gonna make another one?"

"When you guys quit messing around and come up with something for the flip side of 'Rockin' Saturday Night.' "

"Okay, boys," said Leroy, lifting the Sound Star, "boss man says back to work."

~~~~~

Leroy drove home Tuesday on his lunch break to show Agnes the advertisement on the movie page of the *Press-Scimitar*.

IN PERSON! THE SENSATIONAL RADIO-RECORDING
STAR SLIM WHITMAN—DIRECT FROM THE
LOUISIANA HAYRIDE!

Slim's smiling face, pencil-thin mustache, and cowboy neckerchief were imposed on a whirling musical staff. Quarter notes danced alongside him.

COME HEAR SLIM SING: INDIAN LOVE CALL, KEEP
IT A SECRET, ROSEMARIE, SECRET LOVE.

In small print to one side was a list of special added attractions.

BILLY WALKER
"THANK YOU FOR CALLING"

NEW MEMPHIS STAR
LEROY KIRBY
"YOU BETTER LOOK OUT FOR ME"

CURLY HARRIS
SONNY HARVILLE

ONE BIG SHOW
FRIDAY NITE 8 P.M.

"Honey, I'm so excited I can't hardly sit down," Agnes said. "Look, they even spelled your name right!"

"I know," said Leroy. " 'New Memphis Star.' " He was glad to see his mother so thrilled; the excitement had brought her back from one of her dark spells.

She used her egg money to have a telephone installed, so she could call all her friends and relations back in Tupelo with the news.

Ray said, "We'll be in hock to the telephone company before Leroy ever earns the first nickel off his record."

"I don't care," said Agnes. "Slim Whitman is a big, big star, and Leroy is third on the bill with Slim Whitman, and I used my own money so I guess you'll just have to live with it."

"You tell him, Mama," said Leroy.

With some fast convincing, Leroy got Tommy and Jack to the Irving Brothers on Thursday. They came out in matching western shirts with black curlicue edgings on the collar and chest. For himself he selected baggy linen trousers, a crimson necktie on a white shirt, his old faithful black gabardine jacket—plenty of room to move, and you couldn't beat those wide shoulders. White socks. Black loafers.

He spent two hours Friday afternoon at the Mary Jane Beauty Parlor. The girls were beside themselves with excitement about his big hit. Deedee sculpted his hair free of charge. She said she was coming to Overton Park that night to watch him perform. "Don't forget to blow me a kiss," she teased as he left.

When he looked in the mirror at home, he hated his hair. It was puffed up too high on top. Deedee had done it the same way since the first time Leroy went in with his picture of Tony Curtis. It was too stiff. He wanted to look cool—not as if he'd spent all afternoon getting ready to look cool.

He spent the next hour washing out Deedee's work, styling it over, oiling it down with Robinson's Brite-Shine to make it gleam under the lights.

He reached under the sink for his latest discovery, Max Factor Blue Mystery eye shadow. It brought out his eyes more dramatically than Maybelline Mystic Brown, and it went better with his hair. Bedroom-eyes-in-a-tube. He daubed the stuff along each eyelid, blending it with his thumb.

He stepped into the hall. Agnes and Dodger were making a big racket up front, cooking food for all the people who might stop by tonight before and after the show.

Leroy slipped to the living room, intending to sneak out the door without any big inspection. Agnes headed him off. "Where are you going?"

"It's time for me to be getting on down there."

"Honey, look here at me. What is that on your eyes."

He turned to face her. "Nothing. Just a little makeup. It was—it was Dan's idea."

"Well I never," she said.

"Show business, Mama."

"You taking your car?"

"Yes ma'am."

"We'll all be down as soon as everybody gets here," said Agnes. "Hardy and them should have been here an hour ago. Now you behave yourself and do good. We'll all keep our fingers crossed."

"It's liable to be a big crowd," he said. "I hope I don't get nervous."

"You won't. You've done this lots of times now."

290

"Yeah, but this is the big time. I'll see you tonight." He kissed her and carried the Sound Star to the Zephyr.

He drove away from the curb and down the street. He reached to switch on the radio.

"You Better Look Out for Me" came out of the speaker.

His song. Playing now. On the radio in his car.

Leroy pulled the car to the shoulder, to listen.

His song, on the Mother Station.

When the song was over, Hot Rod Hurlburt came on. "In case you been in a cave all this week, that was Memphis's own Leroy Kirby with 'You Better Look Out for Me' on the Rocking Record label. They tell me the cat is white, but ain't nobody hold that against him. That is one cool tune. . . ."

Leroy couldn't see. Something in his eye. He must be crying.

He switched off the engine. He leaned his head on the steering wheel and let the tears run. He was the luckiest boy in the world. He didn't deserve it. He thought unspeakable thoughts and committed unthinkable acts. Sometimes he hated the people he loved.

In the face of all that, surely this kind of luck woul come back to haunt him.

Traffic rushed by.

Why was he being so hard on himself? *Crybaby. Mama's boy.* Wiping his eyes, he managed to smear Blue Mystery all over his face. Now he looked like some kind of movie vampire.

He rummaged in the glove box for tissues and began repairing his eyes in the rearview mirror.

Tonight was his big night. No reason to cry.

But that was his *song.* They played his song on the Mother Station.

God, he was so lucky. That's all it was. Dumb luck. It could dry up any minute.

He wanted to be famous. He wanted it real bad.

He took the tube of makeup from his pocket and squeezed out an inch on his finger.

~~~~~

An hour later he was leaning against the hood of Tommy's Chevrolet, admiring Slim Whitman's glittery red and black cowboy getup, the white silk bandanna at his neck. Slim's band was late. Slim was fuming, pacing a circle in the dirt lot behind the Overton Park band shell.

His resplendent costume made Leroy's dark baggy suit look like something you might wear to a Mormon church, but he wasn't worried. He was cool. It was more daring to dress in black. His doubts had dried up when he stepped from the car and saw the big crowd streaming into the amphitheater. This was bigger than any crowd ever. He felt giddy and a little reckless. Ray and Agnes stopped by with Dodger, Travis, Johnny, Hardy and Irene, Mr. and Mrs. Hastings, a couple of Ray's buddies from the pool hall. The ladies fussed and fluttered and cooed around Leroy. The men made cracks about Slim Whitman's outfit. At last Leroy got them all hugged and headed off for their seats.

Slim Whitman stopped pacing. He turned on the nearest person, who happened to be Leroy. "Damn it, where can I find a telephone around here?"

"Well damn it, Slim, I don't know," Leroy said, "but I'll be glad to help you look for one."

Slim ignored the mild laughter from the stagehands. "Sorry kid, just my band's late and I can't go on by myself. I need to make a call."

"Don't worry, there's four or five acts on before you," said Leroy. "Tommy? You know where's a phone?"

"Never mind," said Slim, "here they come." A long wood-sided station wagon pulled up. Slim yanked a door open. His sheepish band members piled out, ducking his insults.

Leroy promised himself he wouldn't go around acting that way when he got famous.

Curly Harris wound up his act, and Sonny Harville set to yearnin' and burnin' through his. Leroy and the boys gathered at the tailgate to tune up. Tommy poked Leroy's shoulder. "You nervous?"

"It's funny, I—I oughta be, but I'm not," he said. "I feel good. That's a big crowd out there."

He wandered to the rim of stage left for a closer look. In the stage light he could see hundreds of people on long benches, the shadows of hundreds more in the standing-room darkness beyond. There were dozens of teenage kids loitering in the aisles, paying no attention to Sonny Harville's old-fashioned twanging.

Hang on, kids, Leroy thought—I'll give you something to listen to, here in a minute.

Then it struck him.

Maybe that's why they were hanging around.

Maybe waiting for him.

Name in the paper. The song everywhere. It was just possible. He rushed back to tell Tommy and Jack.

He kept his voice low, since Slim was dressing down his tardy musicians nearby. "Now you know they didn't come to hear *him*. You reckon they came to hear us?"

"It could be," said Jack. "My sister and her girlfriends are all here tonight." He rolled his eyes at Leroy. "Emma says you're the most."

"The most what?" said Leroy.

"The most likely to screw up tonight, if you don't look out," Tommy said. "Come on, boys, I don't think poor ol' Sonny's gonna get much call for an encore. We better get on up there."

Leroy checked his hair one last time in the Zephyr's outside mirror. He looked good. All those people waiting for him. The biggest crowd of his life. He was ready. He had spent some of his happiest moments dreaming himself in front of a crowd, with the spotlights shining on him. He sprang up the stairs.

Sleepy-Eyed John Lepley went to the microphones at the front of the stage. That looked to be about a mile from where Leroy stood. The great white curve of the band shell stretched overhead, opening out onto tiers of brilliant lights and the endless crowd.

"Thank you, thank you, Sonny Harville," said Sleepy-Eyed John. "That was some fine playing, I'm sure you'll agree. Now, folks, we have a special added surprise for you tonight, a young man a lot of you've been hearing about. He and his friends put together a little record that seems like it's going all the way to the top. We're proud to have them play it for us tonight in their first live appearance anywhere, ladies and gentlemen, please welcome, Memphis's own—Leroy Kirby and the Blue Rhythm Boys!"

The applause was a little louder than it had been for the first two acts. Leroy trotted onstage with a salute and a big white smile.

Tommy and Jack arranged themselves at separate mikes on either side and two paces behind him.

Leroy shook the announcer's hand, grabbed the microphone stand, and looked out over the vast sea of faces spreading up into darkness. His mama and daddy were somewhere out there. Who knows? Maybe Miss Waverly. Maybe Dolores Roselle.

"Thank you, Mr. Lepley, thank you everybody." The band shell projected his voice; he could whisper to someone in the farthest row. "We'd like to play a song for you that we got out now on the Rocking Records label. It's called 'You Better Look Out for Me.'"

He tapped his foot and counted off: "Three four!"

Tommy and Jack slid right into their nimble groove, and Leroy forgot all about everything. He let go, the way he had learned. He banged his guitar like a bucket and jumped around and shook his leg and sang high, wild, and fast. He would wake up these kids. He would get something going.

> *I heard what your daddy told you*
> *That don't make it so*
> *You can stick by your mama's side*
> *Or let me kiss you nice and slow*

He was sick of hearing music played too slow, and he was betting they were sick of it, too. All they wanted was somebody to do something different and fast.

He kept his eyes up in the lights and sang and hopped and wiggled his foot out in front of him. Then he planted the foot and let the rest of his body wiggle around it.

He heard something in back of the amplified sound, some kind of metallic screeching ... a bug in the PA system? He ignored it. He bopped and jived to the end of the song.

A big cheer rose up, and the screeching grew louder. Leroy turned to Tommy with the question in his eyes, but Tommy just grinned and mouthed the words *blue moon.*

"Thank you very much, everbody," Leroy said to the mike. "Now we'd like to do another song, a Bill Monroe song, 'Blue Moon of Kentucky,' and we hope you enjoy it."

He swung the song off with the chant "Blue moon," and he laid out the syncopation of that opening run with the rhythm of his body, shaking his hips—his own kind of dancing, the way he moved all alone

294

in his room whenever Big Mama Thornton came on the radio. He skittered back to the microphone in time for the first verse.

Tommy and Jack hammered the song out even faster than on the record. Leroy let his leg go, a wild thing, shaking. *Well it was on a moonlit night....*

The high-pitched screeling got louder and louder, a saw biting into sheet metal. When the song was over, Leroy bowed and started off the stage with one hand over his ear. "What is that noise?"

"It's you!" Tommy cried, pounding his back. "It's the girls! The way you were shaking your leg! They're yelling for you!"

"What—what do you mean?"

"Don't you hear 'em? It was the way you were jumping around! It's the girls! We got to go out there and do some more!"

Leroy saw them, dozens of girls surging close to the stage with their hands stretched out, squealing for him.

He grinned and waved. A cloud of keening arose.

"Go on, boys," shouted Sleepy-Eyed John through the din, "go give 'em a couple more. They love it."

They huddled for a moment, then strode back out into the lights.

Leroy bent the microphone stand almost to the floor, like Valentino in a tango, and cried, *Weeelllll, hey come on—it's a hot rockin' Saturday night!* and the girls just went wild. The cold-metal screeching started up again, raising the hairs on his neck, sending a shiver down the length of him. That only made them scream louder. It was as if he'd pressed his finger on some button inside these girls' heads that brought them, shrieking, to life.

It was the way he moved. He set out to do it some more. He put on his best Brando snarl, shook his hair in his eyes, flailed his leg all over the place. Tommy and Jack encouraged him: "Go man, go! Yeah!" He didn't really try to play his guitar but made a great show of swinging his free hand around in a circle, in time.

The last song was Joe Turner's "Shake, Rattle and Roll." *Get out in that kitchen and rattle those pots and pans!* Leroy tore down the house. This was tough stuff, get out there and get to cooking, baby, you have mixed up with one hungry man. The amphitheater rang with the squealing of girls.

Leroy cried, "Thank you very much! And good night!" and ran off.

He stopped halfway down the stairs. Slim Whitman blocked his way.

"Now how am I supposed to follow that?" Slim said, flinging out his arm to indicate the horde of girls pressed against the near side of the stage, squealing.

"Aw come on, Slim," said Leroy, "we just got 'em warmed up for you."

"What's your name, kid?"

"Leroy Kirby. This is Tommy Hannah, and Jack Brown."

"That's the goddamnedest display I've ever seen," said Slim. "Who's your manager?"

"I am." Tommy stuck out his chest.

"Well I hope you know that kind of thing don't happen every day in this business." Slim stepped aside and slapped Leroy on the shoulder. "You ever want to try out for the 'Hayride,' you give me a call."

"Well hey that's great, that's terrific, Slim, you mean it?"

"Now get out of here and let me try and pick up the pieces." Slim stepped around him, to the stage.

Leroy followed the boys. He could hear the excitement still rolling out behind him, in the crowd.

Jack fished under the seat of his pickup and came out with a pint of whiskey. He took a swallow and offered it to Leroy.

"No thanks," he said, "I don't think I will. I feel just as fine as I ever want to feel. Cats, we killed 'em."

"We knocked 'em dead," Jack agreed.

"Leroy, you got to remember how you was shaking that leg." Tommy grinned all the way to his ears. "You got to hold on to that."

The Big Time
1954-1958

30

*L*eroy made his first appearance after Overton Park at the Bon Air Club, a honky-tonk on Summer Avenue. He wore his black hoodlum suit, jazzed up with a pink shirt. He felt hot and handsome and wild out in front of the band—Tommy and Jack and a drummer, a rhythm guitarist, the skinny boy, Luke, whaling away on piano. The crowds were small the first few nights, but they made a big noise anyway.

By the second week the Bon Air's regular beer drinkers were outnumbered two to one by the girls coming in to see Leroy.

He never entered the club before showtime; he thought audiences liked a little mystery from their performers. They didn't want to see you until you were ready to do something. He hung around in the parking lot with Tommy and Jack and the other players, tuning and laughing and working up hot licks.

Then he led the charge through the door, shouldering a path through the crowd, a look of serious business on his face.

He jumped onstage with a grin for the girls who squealed. Every time he got up to sing, there were a few more of these girls who loved him. He recognized some of them from two nights ago—the walnut-haired girl in the pink sweater, her chubby blond friend . . . his fans.

"Thank you, ladies," he said, "thank you, friends, welcome to the Bon Air, I'm Leroy Kirby, and these are the Blue Rhythm Boys. Like to play you our latest Rocking Records escape—uh, release, it's called 'Blue Moon of Kentucky,' we hope you like it." He nodded, and Tommy swung in, and they were off running on their B-side hit.

Tommy picked out an ever more intricate lead line, wangledy dangling and twisting around while Jack thumped along and Leroy wailed, *moonlit night, stars shinin'.* . . . Oh, it was good. It was good.

Leroy played a forty-five-minute set—fifteen songs fast. He sang "I Love You Because" to the waitresses. He winked and flirted with the girls. He juked across the tiny stage, squinting into the pink spotlight, singing "You Better Look Out for Me" and "Rag Mop" and "Hurtin' Time" and "Shake, Rattle and Roll."

There was never enough applause for the work he put in. Some of the people in back kept talking over his singing. One day he would make them all shut up and listen to him.

As he came off the stage, Mr. Sweeney waved him over. "Call for you. Long distance."

Leroy went to the phone, mopping his brow with a handful of cocktail napkins. "Hello?"

"Is this Leroy Kirby?"

"Yes it is."

"This is Everett Dawes, son, I'm a booking agent with the WSM 'Grand Ole Opry,' how you doing tonight. Listen, caught your act at Overton Park with Slim Whitman. We thought maybe you'd come to Nashville to appear on the 'Opry.'"

Leroy's mouth dropped open. The Opry! The holy temple of country music! He covered the mouthpiece. "The Opry!" he said through his teeth.

Tommy and Jack exploded in shouts and hurrahs and went off to the bar, leaving Leroy to sputter his gratitude into the phone.

Ten days later he was in the backseat of Dan's Ford Fairlane, headed for Nashville and the biggest big time of them all. The Opry! Martha White Flour! Goo Goo Clusters! Hank Williams! Minnie Pearl! Leroy Kirby!

Dan and Claudia sat in front, like somebody's parents. Jack and Tommy followed with the instruments in Tommy's Chevrolet.

On the radio station out of Lawrenceburg, the Crew Cuts were singing "Oop Shoop." It was lively enough; it sounded like everything else; the words didn't mean anything. It was a hit, but Leroy suspected the Crew Cuts would always be four faceless white harmony guys. Nobody ever became a real star by blending into something that smooth.

The white radio needed a touch of wildness. At least that's what Leroy meant to bring it tonight. He and Tommy and Jack had worked up two hot new songs at their sporty new rocketing beat, "Rockin' Saturday Night" and "If I Ever Hear Your Name Again." These were quicker and harder than the usual "Opry" songs, and Leroy was counting on the difference to set off a spark.

The "Grand Ole Opry" was the starting place for anybody who ever made it in the world of country music. Ernest Tubb, Bill Monroe, Kitty Wells—all the great stars had done time on the show. The whole South listened on Saturday night. If Leroy could score a hit his first time on the "Opry," no telling where it would end. Lightning might strike. They might offer him a regular spot. Then he could kiss Crown Electric good-bye. He might wind up bigger than Hank Snow.

He gazed out the window, drinking in new scenery—rocky hills and broken valleys of cedar trees. The houses huddled next to the hills. There were barns and little farms, immaculate yards with old ladies in them.

He wondered how far his music would take him. He wanted to see the whole world—New York, Hollywood, Florida, East Tennessee. . . . He wanted to hear cheering in every one of those places.

Claudia said, "This is pretty country in here."

Leroy stretched his legs on the seat. "I's just thinking . . . the last time I rode this far was the first time Mama and Daddy and I came to Memphis."

"Well, I think you better get used to riding." Dan tossed his cigarette out the window. "Soon as we make another record or two, I'm putting you boys on the road. You won't be home any longer than it takes you to change your underwear."

"Suits me," said Leroy. "I don't change 'em unless Mama makes me anyway."

Dan snickered. Claudia said, "I talked to your mother yesterday. She sounds just so pleased about everything."

"Yeah, they're pretty worked up," Leroy said. "She doesn't know what to think. Daddy keeps asking if I'm ever going to see any money out of all this."

Dan's eyebrows went up in the rearview mirror. "Your daddy's a smart man," he said. "Just do good. The money will take care of itself."

"Look look look, y'all!" Claudia waggled her hand out the window at a sign:

WELCOME TO NASHVILLE
Home of the
WORLD FAMOUS
WSM "GRAND OLE OPRY"

Tommy roared around, honking, weaving all over the road, while Jack hung his head out and hollered, "Hoooeeee!"

They came over a rise. The city spread out before them on green hills, a steep-sided river winding through. Where Memphis seemed to roast in the sun, Nashville glittered. On the highest hill were tall buildings and the Capitol dome. A cluster of radio towers rose from a ridge just north of downtown.

WSM's mighty transmitter must be the tallest one there in the center, tethered with miles of shining cable. Tonight Leroy's voice would soar to the top, out through the air to millions of people. Not hundreds, not thousands. Real millions.

He rolled down his window to hear the traffic. They drove past stately homes on wide lawns, a clutch of stores, some kind of college, and

302

then into sight of a sweeping green park, a sandy brown classical temple with huge columns marching down every side.

"Would you look at that," Leroy breathed.

"That's the Parthenon," Dan said. "It's an exact copy of the one in Europe. The same exact size."

"What's it for?"

"I'm not sure. Some kind of world's fair, I think."

Leroy felt a twinge of disappointment. "I thought it might be the Opry."

"Not yet."

Tommy pulled alongside at the stoplight, racing his engine. "Hot dog, we made it! Which way to the Opry?"

"Hey, don't I know you?" Leroy taunted. "Ain't you Carl Perkins?"

Dan said, "Follow me." He steered through heavy traffic along a row of motor hotels, across a railyard, into downtown Nashville. Hank Snow sang "I Don't Hurt Anymore" on WSM. Leroy gaped at everything.

"See all those honky-tonks down the hill?" Dan pointed through the windshield. "That's where the stars go to drink while the show's on. There's many a picker got discovered playing in one of those dives."

They turned up a sloping street. In the next block Dan pulled over. "This is it."

Leroy hung his head out the window. The old red-brick barn of a building was about the size of Ellis Auditorium back home. "This is the Opry?"

"You got it." Dan opened his door. "What's the matter?"

Leroy climbed out. "You mean this is what I've been dreaming about all these years?"

Dan laughed at the look on his face.

Tommy came up strutting. "We made it! The by-God Grand Ole Opry!"

Jack said, "I can't believe we're here."

"Somehow I pictured it bigger," said Leroy. "I guess it grows in your mind when you hear it on the radio."

They locked up the instruments and found the main door with a large sign, RYMAN AUDITORIUM, and a smaller sign, WSM GRAND OLE OPRY 8 P.M.

The Opry was old, all right, but Leroy didn't see a thing grand about it. Inside, the hall was like a basketball gymnasium with pews. Four men were setting up folding chairs near the front. The stage, hung with fake farm scenery and Prince Albert chewing tobacco signs, was half the size of the band shell at Overton Park.

Dan went to find out what was what. Leroy wandered the auditorium, inspecting the stage from every angle, fighting off disappointment. The grand aura of the "Opry" was an illusion, transmitted by that radio tower he'd seen on the way into town. It was much grander when you couldn't see it.

Dan came back trailing a red-faced, big-bellied man who wore a string tie with a silver rattlesnake clip. "Leroy, this is Mr. Lou Penney. He's in charge of the show. This is Leroy Kirby."

Leroy grinned and said hello and stuck out his hand, but the man just looked at him. "You the truck driver, huh?"

"Well, yessir, I drive a truck on my job. We're sure happy you asked us on the show. I been listening to—"

"Where's your band?"

"There." Leroy pointed to Tommy and Jack, surveying the place from the head of the aisle.

Lou Penney frowned. "Where's the rest?"

"Well that's all of us," Leroy said. "Guitar and a bass, and I sing."

"Wait wait wait just a minute," said Penney, backing up a step. "Now damn it, Tobias, don't start messing with me! Where's the rest of the band? The contract calls for the same instruments as the record. What are you trying to pull?"

"Hold on there, my friend." Dan's voice was cool; Leroy saw the flash in his eyes. "Nobody's pulling anything. These are the boys on that record, and I know because I produced it. Now they're here to play. You just tell 'em what to do, and they'll do it."

"All right, but you oughta know I don't like surprises," said Penney.

"I can see that," Dan said.

The big man harrumphed and glanced at his clipboard. "They're set for Hank Snow's part of the show."

Leroy's heart took a bound.

"I want 'em backstage at eight-forty, ready to go," Penney went on. "You got two songs. Give me the names." He poised his pen.

Leroy said, " 'If I Ever Hear Your Name Again,' and the second one is 'Rockin' Saturday Night.' "

304

"Wait, wait a minute. That ain't your record."

"Well, no sir. We worked up a couple of new songs for tonight."

"Not on my show you ain't," he growled. "Now the contract called for the songs on the record, am I right? So that's the ones you're going to do. What's the names?"

Leroy looked to Dan for help. Dan shrugged. It was obvious this man held all the strings. Leroy wanted to say, "Go to hell, you old fathead," but he meekly said, " 'You Better Look Out for Me' and 'Blue Moon of Kentucky.' "

Mr. Penney wrote that down and trundled away.

"Whoa, that guy looks like a load of laughs," Tommy said, coming up. "What'd we miss?"

"We have to play the first record," said Leroy. "I don't think he likes us."

"He hadn't even heard us yet," said Jack.

"I know."

"Aw don't get too concerned," Dan put in. "He's a famous old tightass. But you got to get past him to get on the show. Just play what he told you to play."

He herded them outside, down an alley of honky-tonk lounges and pool halls and pawnshops, out onto the boulevard. They settled in a greasy diner for coffee and cheeseburgers, distracted conversation. Dan picked up the check.

When they came out, the alley was filling with "Opry" fans; Leroy could tell by their Sunday hats and Kodaks. Some of them gawked at the tall buildings as if this were their first time in a city.

He remembered that feeling. He was having a twinge of it himself.

He wriggled into his stage clothes in the backseat of the Chevrolet, while Tommy stood watch. Leroy had spent all his Bon Air earnings on tonight's outfit: a red-stitched western shirt with crisp pleats and imitation pearl buttons, a string tie, a white sport coat, black cowboy jeans, fake lizard boots. Tommy and Jack wore their Irving Brothers cowboy shirts.

Leroy climbed out. "You guys look great."

The street in front of Ryman was clogged with shiny cars and taxicabs honking, like a Hollywood premiere. Leroy led the way to the stage door. They waited while a doorman checked a troupe of square dancers off his list, one at a time.

Backstage they made their way through electronic equipment and men with headsets, bustling stagehands, performers in sequined costumes. Leroy didn't recognize anybody right off, but he'd probably know people once he heard them.

Lou Penney told him to wait over *there* and pointed out a spot against a wall.

Dan said, "Well boys, we're gonna go find our seats. Good luck."

"I know you'll be wonderful," said Claudia, giving them each a quick hug. "I'll be cheering for you."

Leroy and the boys stood around for a long time. The other performers seemed to know exactly what they were doing. Out of nervousness, Leroy started noodling on his guitar. A stagehand came and told him to hush, didn't he know they were on the air?

It was hard to tell from where he was standing. He could barely hear an announcer's voice between strains of music—the familiar jingle, "Go get a Goo Goo—it's goooood."

A quartet of girl singers huddled a few feet away. In back, the square dancers paced through their do-si-dos in slow time.

A short, impeccable man with sharp features and receding black hair stepped from the hallway behind the dancers. It was Hank Snow, in the flesh. His magnificent suit of clothes was the color of buttermilk. In the fanciest western style, his clothes seemed to be pointing to him; stitched leather arrows and darts swam all over the jacket.

He said something to a stagehand, who turned and pointed to Leroy.

Hank Snow came over. He was no taller than Agnes. "How do you do," he said.

"Fine, Mr. Snow, I'm sure proud to meet you. We heard your record on the way into town."

"I'm going to introduce you," said Hank Snow. "What's your name?"

"Leroy Kirby."

"No, I see that here," said Snow. "I mean what name do you sing under."

"That's it, sir. Leroy Kirby. This is Tommy and Jack. The Blue Rhythm Boys."

"Leroy ... Leroy. It doesn't sound right. You ought to look into changing that. You need something the people can remember."

"Well thank you, sir." Leroy grinned. "Maybe I should change it to Hank Snow."

306

Snow cut his eyes over. "That's taken," he said. He glanced at his watch, a chunky golden diamond-encrusted affair. "I'm on as soon as Buck does the Martha White spot. You be ready and get out there when I call you, no fooling around."

"Yes sir," said Leroy.

Hank Snow went to the curtain to await his cue.

Jack said, "I can't believe you said that to him."

Leroy shook his head. "Man, that is one beautiful suit. And did you get a load of that watch?" Leroy promised himself he would own a watch like that one day.

"Look here, fellows," Tommy said under his breath. "Minnie Pearl." The famous comedienne glided up in her granny dress and that notorious hat with the $1.98 price tag dangling from the brim. On the radio she made herself sound like the countriest hick in the world, but in person she appeared dignified, not at all homely.

She glanced over at Leroy with a little smile. "Hidy boys, how y'all getting along?"

"Fine," they choroused.

"First time on the 'Opry'?"

"Yes ma'am," said Leroy.

"They treating you right?"

"Yes ma'am, so far."

"Well give 'em time, give 'em time," she said, and stepped forward to speak to Hank Snow. Hank turned with a big, shiny smile, put his arm around her shoulder. They chatted, watching the stage.

The announcer beckoned Hank to the microphone.

Leroy edged up beside the curtain. The audience sat very straight in the pews, paying close attention, as if Hank were reading the received word of the Holy Ghost instead of an advertisement for Kellogg's Corn Flakes. "The best to you each morning," he said. "Minnie? What about that? Ladies and gentlemen, Minnie Pearl."

"Howwwww-*dee*!" Minnie clumped onstage in her oversize brogan shoes. They loved her. Applause drummed like rain on a roof.

"Well I tell you Hank, I always eat Kellogg's Corn Flakes in the morning," she said, turning this way and that with her hands on her hips, "and sometimes I use 'em for a beauty treatment."

"A *beauty* treatment?" Hank marveled, winking at the audience. "You use Kellogg's Corn Flakes as a beauty treatment?"

Minnie leaned to the mike. "That's right. I mash 'em up and put 'em all over my face every morning. Do you think it's working?"

"Well—ho-ho-ho," said Hank Snow. "Ladies and gentlemen, Minnie Pearl." He put out his hand and waved for the applause to begin.

Minnie looked at him oddly—he must have dropped his line—but then she recovered, howwwdeeeed, did a bowlegged curtsy, and went off to the wing.

Hank Snow squinted at the card in his hands. "Ladies and gentlemen, got a young man for you, his very first time on the 'Opry,' he's going to play for us his new release from Rocking Records, won't you please give a warm 'Grand Ole Opry' welcome to Leroy . . . Kirby, and the Blue Rhythm Boys. Boys? Where are you? Here they come." Hank clapped the card between his hands.

Leroy trotted into the lights.

Nobody screamed. Nobody was about to make a loud noise in this temple of music.

A cardboard collar was attached to the microphone stand, WSM GRAND OLE OPRY spelled out sideways. That would prevent Leroy from grabbing the stand or swinging it around. He would have to stand still.

He tried not to think about all the people listening through this microphone.

"Good evening friends," he said, to his amplified echo, "like to say we're honored to be here tonight, want to play for you our new record we have out now; it's called 'You Better Look Out for Me.' Ready, boys?" He counted off.

The fast beat came naturally to them now. Leroy stood still, jigging his right leg out in front of him. The toe of one boot connected him to the floor, to the wildness he needed to sing the song right. A tingle shot down his leg. *I don't care a-what your mama says, a-but your daddy says we're through.* . . .

The people clapped to show they knew the song was over; then they stopped clapping. No one squealed.

Leroy cleared his throat and looked around. The boys wore uncomfortable smiles. "Thankyouvermuch," he said. "Now we'd like to play a song by the great Bill Monroe, we hope you like it—here we go—one, two, three. . . ."

He kicked off "Blue Moon of Kentucky" in high gear. If he couldn't reach the dead people here in Ryman Auditorium, he could sing it for somebody he'd never even seen, some lonely old lady in a shack on a hill. He took that old song, turned and twisted it, speeded it up. He hit the high notes on *briiiiight* and *niiiiight* with an effortless yearning that must have reached through that microphone, over the miles.

The applause was polite but unexcited. Leroy hoped it sounded louder on the radio, for his mother's sake.

He grabbed one end of Jack's bass to help hustle it off. Tommy made a circle with his thumb and forefinger: okay.

There was Mr. Penney chewing on a cigar. "Well, I hope you're done with that," he said.

"Sir?" Leroy blinked.

"Let me tell you something, son. If I'd listened to that record, you wouldn't be here. This is the 'Grand Ole Opry.' We don't do that kind of nigger music."

"I don't—"

"That's right you don't, and you won't, and you ain't, not again on this show," said Lou Penney. "Let me give you a piece of advice. You go back to driving a truck."

Leroy felt a fire in his face, in his hand. His fingers closed in a fist. His hand was seized with the desire to haul off and slug this pompous man in his big rolling belly. He saw the same desire in the faces of Tommy and Jack. It would be useless. If the man said they had flopped, they had flopped.

Leroy said, "Thanks a lot. Let's get out of here, boys."

"Yeah, you do that," said Penney, "and tell Dan Tobias I'll send him the check, which is the most generous thing I ever done in my life." He nodded *so there* and lumbered away.

The boys stared after. Leroy felt a great rift opening inside him.

Dan and Claudia came up, all smiles and hurrahs. "Oh, you were wonderful!" Claudia cried.

"The man hated it." His voice sounded funny. "He *hated* it. He said it was nigger music, it was— He said I ought to go back to driving a truck." He bit his lip. He did not want to burst into tears in front of his friends.

There was someone else watching—a performer in a fancy wine-colored cowboy suit, edging closer.

"I heard what Lou Penney told you," he said, and Leroy recognized instantly his round Texas twang: Ernest Tubb, "Opry" star, owner of the world-famous Ernest Tubb Record Store and host of the "Midnight Jamboree," which followed the "Opry" broadcast on WSM. Ernest Tubb was skinny, but he had a prosperous look about him; his suit glittered with rhinestones. "Let me tell you, son. I watched you. You did a fine job."

Leroy said, "Well sir, thank you, but Mr. Penney didn't care for us much. And neither did they." He waved his hand at the audience.

"Sometimes they just don't know." Ernest Tubb clapped Leroy's shoulder. "The next time you're coming to Nashville, you call me ahead of time. We'll have you on the 'Jamboree.' " He nodded to the others, said, "Good luck," and went off to his dressing room.

Leroy knew he should have thanked him, but his manners had been swept away in a tidal wave of disappointment. The backstage buzz went on as if nothing had happened to him. Penney's words were burning holes in his brain.

"Hey now, that ain't so bad, is it, coming from Ernest Tubb?" Dan asked. "Don't let that other bastard get you down."

Leroy barely heard him.

"Listen to Dan," Claudia said. "Maybe the 'Grand Ole Opry' 's just not ready for you."

"No," Leroy said, "he was right. I'm the one who's not ready. I was lousy. Did you see how the people just sat there? Just—let's get out of here."

"Claudia, make sure we sent Ernest Tubb some copies of the record when we get back."

"Got it."

"Leroy, wait for us—"

Leroy pushed past them all, past the man at the stage door, onto the sidewalk, clearing a path through the crowd with the neck of his Sound Star. He wanted to mow them all down.

A black cloud came down from the sky and fell over him. He had ruined his chance. He would never be invited back in a million years. He had counted his chickens and killed them. Make a record, get a hit, land a spot on the "Opry," take over the world—it just doesn't happen that way!

Maybe Lou Penney was right. There was no shame in driving a truck. At least you don't live and die for somebody's opinion of you. You drive the truck and deliver supplies, and as long as the electricians are happy, you get paid every Friday. You never get stabbed in the heart.

Dan unlocked the car, keeping a respectful distance.

He and Claudia spoke in hushed tones. Leroy watched the lights of the city sliding by. He would go back to Memphis, go to work Monday morning, quit living in this fantasy.

On the outskirts of Nashville he said, "If you stop, I'd like to get out of these clothes."

Dan flipped on the blinker. "Listen, son, we've sold nine thousand records in three weeks. I've never had a record move so fast. So what if one guy didn't like you?"

Leroy didn't answer.

Tommy's Chevrolet trailed them into an island of light, an Esso station.

Leroy took the sack with his everyday clothes around to the men's room. He shot the bolt on the door. He whipped off the tie and shirt, shucked off the pants, stuffed it all in the sack, and stood looking at himself, mostly naked, in the dirty mirror.

His skin was pale green in the fluorescent light. He drew a length of toilet paper from the roll and began to wipe the shadow from his eyes.

The mirror said, Look at you standing there shaking. Put on your clothes.

Leroy gaped.

Don't worry, the mirror said. I never left you. I've been here the whole time.

"You—you never said anything." Leroy held the white knit shirt in front of him. He felt naked. The silvery voice shocked him, after years of silence and his own grinning face in the mirror.

You didn't need me until now.

"I don't need anybody," said Leroy. "I'm going home."

You can't give up. You're better than anyone knows. You can be a big star. But you have to work hard and keep going, keep going.

Leroy wriggled into the shirt and stooped to pull on his khakis. He hadn't outgrown the voice after all. Maybe he was crazy.

"I'm not going to stand here and talk to a—talk to a mirror," he said.

Keep going. The big stuff is just about to happen. You can buy Mama everything she ever wanted.

Leroy put his foot on the toilet to tie his shoelace. "I have been fooling myself," he said. "It's over. Three months. It lasted three months."

You're good. You're better than anybody. They don't deserve you.

Leroy wrenched the door open.

Tommy was waiting. "Damn, boy, you had to *go,* didn't you?"

"Sorry. . . ."

The others were buying Cokes and Paydays. Leroy put his head down and got in the car with Claudia.

"Leroy, listen to me," she said. "You've been so lucky so far, and so much has happened already . . . but it's nothing compared to what's going to happen to you. I want you to think about that."

Leroy clutched his knees to keep his hands from shaking. He had to get a grip on himself. It was bad enough with his nerves flying out of him like bats from a cave; now he was hearing that voice in his head again. His mind playing a trick. Saying the words he wanted to hear.

"Listen, I—I'm sorry," he said to Claudia in the vibrating silence. "I guess I'll just have to keep playing till we find somebody that likes us better than that fat old man."

"Now you're talking," she said.

Dan climbed in. "What's that?"

"Leroy just said he's gonna keep playing till he finds somebody that likes him."

"Well damn right he is," Dan said, revving the engine. "Hell, son, we're just getting started."

They headed off. Leroy sat in back with his guitar, staring into the dark.

They were almost to Memphis when he realized he'd left the sack with his stage clothes on the floor of the Esso men's room, two hundred miles back.

He didn't tell anyone.

31

Leroy sat on the front steps way past midnight, playing his guitar and watching the great silver settling moon. He was trying to pick out "Make Yourself Comfortable," a sultry Sarah Vaughan number that was hot stuff this week on the Mother Station. Leroy admired Sarah's big, brassy horn of a voice, but he couldn't find the chords or the jazzy tempo. The Sound Star was accustomed to straight four/four time.

He heard a noise behind him. He turned.

Agnes yawned in the door. "What time is it, honey?"

"I don't know," he said, "it's late. Go on back to bed."

"What are you doing up?"

"Couldn't sleep," he said.

"It's cold out here. Come in the house." Her hair was all frazzle. Her cheek bore the imprint of pillowcase wrinkles. She clasped her chenille robe at her throat. "I'll make us something hot to drink."

He propped the guitar against the porch wall. He'd send her off to bed and come outside again.

"You want me to make some hot chocolate? Doesn't that sound good?"

"Sure, Mama." He followed her to the kitchen.

She poured milk in a saucepan, lit the burner. "We don't have any marshmallows," she said, stirring a paste of cocoa and sugar and water. "I can't keep them in the house. I always wind up eating the whole bag."

"It's okay," Leroy said. "You look tired. Why don't you let me do this and you go on back to bed."

"It's two o'clock in the morning, of course I look tired," she said. "Everybody's always telling me how tired I look. It makes me tired to hear it. Here, stir this." She handed him the spoon.

Leroy set to stirring. "Satnin, we need to talk."

"What about?"

"The 'Hayride.' We promised Mr. Buncombe we'd let him know tomorrow. Dan thinks we ought to sign."

"Well you already know what I think about it." She drizzled chocolate into the steamy milk. "You'll do what you want anyway. I don't know why you even ask me."

"I wanted to talk to you first." He had to be careful. He didn't want to bring on one of her grieving spells.

In the first rush of his success Agnes had been all excited for him, but that had faded as the truth began to sink in. Leroy was gone all the time. He was farther away from her every day.

"It's so far down there," she said. "Do you plan to drive down and back every weekend?"

"Scotty's got a good car," Leroy said. "We can do it."

"Well, as long as you keep your job, I think you should sing all you can," said Agnes. "You know I'm happy about everything that's happened."

"Yeah you say that, but you're not gonna like it when I'm gone to Shreveport every Saturday night for a year and off playing somewhere the rest of the time. You won't ever see me."

"I don't anyway," Agnes said. "How many nights have you been home since you went to Nashville? Two? Three?"

"Oh, what do you mean. I'm here every night."

"I mean *home,* sweetie. Not coming in the middle of the night just to sleep and get up and run off again."

"The 'Hayride' is two hundred stations, Mama. That's millions of people." He took a sip of the sweet hot concoction. "I got a hundred fifty-two dollars from Dan yesterday. Advance money on the records he's sold. It's still selling. The next one's ready to go. And now with this 'Hayride' thing—I'm thinking about quitting the job at Crown. I want to try to do the music all the time."

Agnes averted her eyes. "Well now, honey, you like driving your truck, and Mr. Teague has been so nice to you," she said, stirring two big spoons of sugar into her chocolate. "Why can't you just do both things awhile, till you're sure you've got enough money?"

"I've got a hundred and fifty-two dollars," he said. "I can't keep singing at night and give Mr. Teague a good day's work. We'll make as much at the 'Hayride' as I make at Crown. And besides, Dan says once you're a regular on the 'Hayride,' you can set your own price."

"Dan says, Dan says. I wish Dan was paying you steady money like Mr. Teague. Then you'd know to believe him."

"That's not how it works, Mama. You know that. Dan's taking a gamble on me. Now I got to make up my mind whether I'm gonna gamble on myself."

"It sounds like you've already made up your mind."

"Well, I—I guess I have," he admitted. "I'm talking to Mr. Teague tomorrow."

"Talk to him then." Agnes hugged her own arms. "I think sometimes you get a little too excited about the things Dan says, and maybe you just ought to wait and see, that's all. I don't want you to get hurt."

He sat up. "How could I get hurt?"

"You were hurt when you came back from Nashville."

Oh, she knew where to slip in the knife.

"Look, Mama," he said, "the 'Hayride' may not be the 'Opry,' but we've got a real hit. Number three on the chart in New Orleans, and—and Dallas, and—don't you see? People like me all over."

"They like you right here," Agnes said. "I don't know why you couldn't be happy staying here and playing in all these places in town. You know it's hard for me to sleep when I don't know where you are."

Leroy said, "I think this is something I just got to do."

She placed her cup on the saucer. Her face was old and sad in this light. "I just never thought you would go off and leave me for good."

He flopped over, facedown. "I'm not. I'll still be here whenever I'm not someplace else. And soon as I save up some money, I'm gonna get us a house, Mama, a real house."

"You and your big talk." Her mouth made a straight line.

"I mean it. You start looking for the house you want. Dan says I'm gonna make a whole lot of money, Mama. You watch me."

"I don't care about that."

"I'll be on the road all the time," he said. "I may have to work years and years before I make a name for myself. But I've got to try this thing."

"Why?" she said. "I don't understand, honey. Why is it so important to you?"

"Because I'm good at it, Mama." There. That was enough. If you found one thing you were good at, you should do it and do it the best you can. Not everybody is blessed with even one thing. "I want to be a big star," he went on. "There's nothing else I want. You used to want it, too. You used to think it was great."

"Honey, I need you." There it was, the sound he dreaded most, that edge of alarm in her voice. "I need you to talk to," she pleaded. "I don't know what I'd do—oh, don't go off and leave me."

"That's not fair." He got up. He felt blood rising in his face. "Do you think I'm going to get famous hanging around the house? Think the 'Louisiana Hayride' 's going to move to Memphis just to suit you?" He towered over her. "It's all out there, Mama—everything, the whole world, don't you see? If I want it, I'm going to have to go get it. That's the way it works. You know that."

She shook her head. "I don't have to like it."

Leroy smacked the wall in frustration. "I'm only doing it for you," he said, his voice thickening. "To make you proud."

"Hush, you'll wake everybody." She stood up, waved her hand at him, dismissing him. "You do what you have to, honey. Don't do anything because of me." She shuffled away down the hall.

"Good night," he called. She didn't answer.

He went out. The moon emerged from a cloud and filled the porch with frozen light.

Leroy picked up the Sound Star and played the Orioles' "Crying in the Chapel," a holy, hushed kind of song. The peaceable melody soothed out his jangled feelings.

He had to sign. Anybody would sign. He had a taste of applause, and he wanted more. He couldn't get enough.

The road was unrolling in front of him. He had to go. It would never make his mother happy, but it would not kill her.

32

*L*eroy took a turn at the wheel while Tommy cradled the Gibson in his lap, running wild on a blues line from Lonnie Johnson.

They were headed south from Big Sandy, Texas, where they'd just finished playing five songs on a flatbed truck for the grand opening of Byrum's Drugs, to the crossroads town of Palestine for a quick set at a place called Eddy's Sho-Boat Lounge, then the sprint to Shreveport and their nine-thirty spot on the "Hayride." Jack was wedged in the backseat, between his bass and the suitcases.

Leroy put down the pedal. *Weeeeeelllll, I feel so bad,* he sang over Tommy's lead line. *I ain't never felt this bad before . . . yeaaaaaahhh, I feel so bad, never ever never felt so bad, bad, bad before . . . if I ever feel this bad again, you go ahead and put me under the floor, whoa yeah mama. . . .*

"Beautiful," said Jack. "Howlin' Dog."

"Aw go on, let's hear the one you wrote then," Leroy said.

"Did you write that," Jack said, "or did it just come to you in a dream?"

Leroy grinned in the rearview. "Your sister whispered it in her sleep last night."

"Yeah yeah," said Jack. "Shut up and drive."

"Fellas, we got to quit playing these chickenshit drugstore things." Tommy's fingers diddled the blues while he talked. "What did we get for that? Ten bucks apiece? It ain't worth it."

"Listen, it's good practice," Leroy said. "By the time we got done they were all hollering, not just the girls. In a durn *parking* lot."

"But there weren't thirty people there," Tommy said. "We'll do anything for ten bucks, you know? Like some cheap little old gal."

Leroy kept his foot on the gas as they flashed through St. Clair City, which didn't even qualify as a town. "Look, man," he said, "as long as Dan's selling the records and the crowds keep getting bigger."

"That's what I'm saying," said Tommy. "The big towns is where the people are. I don't know why we waste our time on some stupid drugstore in Nowhere, Texas."

"When we signed with Roger, we told him we'd take anything he could get us," said Leroy. "Remember?"

"And that's what he gets us. Anything."

Leroy thought, Well, you had your hot turn as manager, but he didn't say it. They'd all had great hopes when Dan put together a management deal with Roger Pate, a Memphis promoter who was supposed to have important national connections. So far, though, Roger's bookings had tended toward grand openings and flatbed trucks in parking lots.

"What's the matter, Tommy?" said Jack. "Your butt tired of riding?"

"You got that right. My butt wants to go home to my wife."

"Well okay now, we're starting to get the truth." Jack reached over the seat to pat his shoulder. "I'm tellin' you, son, you should have gone for that redhead last night when we told you. She was ready to dance."

"Yeah boy," Leroy said. "She had eyes that were looking at you."

"Y'all thought every girl in there was ready to dance." Tommy smiled. "Tell you the truth, I was kind of ashamed to be there with you."

"Yeah, right," said Jack. "You looked about as ashamed as my grandmaw in church."

"I tell you boys, I sure didn't mind that brunette," said Leroy, remembering how close they had danced in the light of the jukebox. She had stood off to one side of the stage while he performed, not squealing like the other girls—just watching him, smiling a dreamy smile. After the show he asked her to dance. In the misty blue light they moved slowly to Nat "King" Cole, "A Blossom Fell." He kissed her. Then it was time to go.

Leroy had discovered that very few girls were as easy as Miss Waverly. None, in fact. Not even these girls with big crushes on him. They fended him off, even as they adored him. He'd thought his encounter with Miss Waverly was just his first taste of a world full of beautiful sex-hungry women, but he'd never found anyone like her. He didn't have time.

There was something wildly unfair about it. The girls came to his shows and squealed when he shook his leg. They loved him. They cried out for him.

It excited him, too. Their eyes on him felt like hands. He loved making them squeal. Onstage he had learned the secret to making girls feel sexy: You had to think sexy thoughts and let the music come out of your body, just move to the beat. . . .

But then the show was over. Sign a few autographs. Sweet-talk a girl or two. Pack the instruments in the car. Roar into the night.

For the first time Leroy was out from under his mother's eye, and he was moving too fast to do anything about it.

"Either you boys happen to catch her name?" he said.

"Who?"

"The brunette. Last night."

"I don't think I ever heard it," said Jack. "Probably Flossie. Or Jezebel. Something like that."

"Come on, man, she wasn't that way. She was in love with me, that's all."

"Oh, a blind girl," Jack said, laughing. "Scuse me, I didn't notice her dog."

Tommy said, "Y'all hear something under the hood?"

They all hushed a minute, to listen.

"I guess it's nothing."

"Don't scare me like that." Leroy resumed his speed. "Ol' man Buncombe would skin us alive if we missed a show."

"Don't drive so fast then, if you don't want to bust another hose."

"Lay off, Tommy," said Leroy. "I'll buy you a new car the minute I'm rich."

Leroy spotted the distant glow of Palestine. The man in Gladewater had said Eddy's Sho-Boat was right on the way into town, can't miss it, and sure enough Leroy spotted the electric sign:

E DY S SHO BO T LO NGE

Eddy's was a joint, but it was not jumping. One strand of Christmas lights framed the door. In the parking lot were three pickup trucks and a motorcycle.

Tommy said, "How much did you say we were getting for this?"

"A hundred bucks."

"Not in a hundred years," said Tommy. "Take a look at this dump."

Leroy said, "I wonder if Roger told us the wrong night? This is Saturday, right?"

"Right. I saw it in the paper this morning."

They piled out and went in. Eddy's Sho-Boat looked even less glamorous on the inside: no jukebox; one pinball machine; a few tables and chairs; a radio playing a Kitty Wells tear-jerking tune. The place had once been fitted with curving banquettes, to judge from the outlines on the floor. Four large men hunkered over their beers at the bar. A raven-haired fortyish bartendress glanced up from painting her nails.

"Excuse me, ma'am," said Leroy. "We thought we were supposed to play here tonight. Looks like we made a mistake."

She said, "What you mean, play?"

"I'm Leroy Kirby and these are the Blue Rhythm Boys. We had a deal to come here and play music."

"Oh Lord. That Eddy . . . I don't know when he'll be back. Can I get you boys a cold one?"

"Hell, why not?" Tommy slumped to a barstool.

Leroy said, "Tommy, call Roger."

"You call him this time. I want a beer."

"Course, I wouldn't mind a little music," said the bar lady, sliding a mug under the tap. "Liven things up around here."

Leroy went to find the phone. The corridor in back reeked of smoke and old beer—but then Leroy's whole life smelled like that these days.

He ought to feel better than ever. "Rockin' Saturday Night" had climbed past "You Better Look Out for Me" on the charts, and "You're Breaking My Heart" was moving up fast—with a bullet, as they said in the *Billboard*.

Dan said Leroy's new cover of Arthur Bailey's "Let's Play" was a surefire smash.

But Tommy was right: Leroy had played too many two-bit engagements lately to feel like he was going much of anywhere. And now he'd traveled 160 miles out of his way to perform for an audience of four bored-looking middle-aged men.

Roger Pate boomed over the wire: "Yes operator, I'll take it. Leroy, how you?"

"Not so good, Roger. We're in Palestine, right where you told us to be, and there's nobody here and the lady doesn't know anything."

"Wait a minute, wait a minute." Leroy heard rustling papers, and then Roger said, "Okay now, you're where? You're supposed to be opening the Rexall in Big Sandy."

"We already did that. And then you said six o'clock at this place. Eddy's Sho-Boat. It's a hole, by the way."

"Eddy's. Right. Six o'clock, what it says here. Hey, buddy, I don't know. The problem must be on that end."

"I tell you, Roger, it's an awful long way to come down here for nothing."

"I appreciate that, Leroy, I sure do. Listen, I'm working on something right now that's big news. I can't tell you yet, but it's big."

Leroy had heard that song before. "Okay, Roger, but in the meantime we're here, and what do you want us to do?"

"Well, find this guy Eddy, and see what the hell. I didn't book you in there, Leroy. It came through that fellow in Gladewater. Douglass. Maybe you should give him a call."

"We're nearly out of money," said Leroy.

"What's that? Listen, I'm going to have to go, son. I'll wire you some to that place y'all stay in Bossier City. How much you need to get by?"

"Our bill's up to fifty-seven dollars at the motel."

"I'll wire you sixty," said Roger. "You boys call me tomorrow. All right? See you now."

"Yeah." Leroy stared at the receiver a long moment, slammed it on the hook.

He took a deep breath. He couldn't afford to get discouraged in front of Jack and Tommy. He was the singer, and they were his band. It was his job to keep everybody's head up.

He went to the front. The boys were playing pinball.

"Roger says it isn't his fault," Leroy reported. "He's sending us enough for the Al-Ida. Unless y'all really love this place for some reason, I say let's hit the road."

"Let us finish this game." Jack slammed his hand on the glass; the silver ball slipped down the hole. "It'd be a shame to come all this way and waste a dime."

Leroy ordered a Coke and stood around watching them play. The front door swung open. A tall, rangy white-haired man came in, followed by a bony old Texan, who ambled across the room on a cane and tossed his Stetson on the bar. "Gimme an ice tea, Lorene."

The bartendress said something and pointed to Leroy.

The old man swung around for a look.

He was *old*. A thatch of pewter-colored hair crowned his large, ruined head. His hand trembled reaching for the glass, and a dribble of tea escaped the corner of his mouth. "Howdy do there, young man," he quavered. "Lorene says you got some bitness with me."

"Sir, my name's Leroy Kirby. A fellow by the name of Douglass had us booked to play our music here tonight, or at least we thought we did."

"Y'all the Blue Rhythm Boys?"

"Yes sir, we are." Leroy's heart lifted.

"Well I been waiting for you," he said. "We all been waiting, ain't we, Lorene?"

"I don't know what you're talking about," she said with a warning look in her eyes. "Is this one of your—aww, Eddy...."

Eddy cackled as if she'd told a joke. "Old friend of mine called me from up'm Tennessee, said he had some Blue Rhythm Boys that wanted to come play, so I told him to send 'em on down. Where's your geetars, boys?"

"Out in the car," said Tommy.

"Well go get 'em! Let's hear you! We hadn't had music in here since—hell, I guess it was nineteen and forty-six."

Leroy smiled. "You mean . . . you want us to play for just you?"

"Eddy, what have you gone and done?" said Lorene. "Now you realize these boys are gonna wanna get paid?"

"Yeah," said Tommy and Jack.

Eddy said, "They'll get paid." He turned to Leroy. "Lorene thinks I'm soft in the head on account of my leg. A mad dog tuck it off at the knee. This here is wood." He knocked, to prove it.

"Boys, I'm sorry you come all this way." Lorene tapped the side of her head. "Eddy gets these ideas sometimes. He can't afford to pay you."

"The hell I can't," Eddy said, fumbling in his pants pocket. "One hundred dollars." He came out with a wad of new bills.

"What'd you do, rob the bank?" Lorene said. "Put that money away."

"Listen, you heard the man," said Tommy. "We had a deal."

"A deal." Eddy clapped the money in Leroy's hand and folded his arms in triumph. "Now let's hear you. My ears is lonesome for some music."

"C'mon, fellas, don't do this," said Lorene. "You don't understand. Eddy can't spare that money."

"Hush, Lorene." Eddy smacked the floor with his cane. "You're turning into a lizard again. Lorene turns into a lizard about this time every evening."

Either the old man was crazy or this was some kind of weird private joke. Leroy couldn't decide. "As long as you're paying," he said, "I reckon we can give you a show. Come on, boys, let's go get our stuff."

Leroy managed to hold in his laughter all the way to the car, but then Tommy and Jack broke down. They whooped until they cried.

"I ain't . . . never played for a lizard before," Leroy sputtered, and that set them off again.

When they managed to quit laughing, they carried their instruments into the bar.

The beer drinkers turned around on their barstools to listen. Lorene sat down beside Eddy, patting his elbow in time to the beat.

Leroy sang the same set he'd performed at the Big Sandy Rexall:
"You Better Look Out for Me" and "Blue Moon of Kentucky," "Rockin'
Saturday Night," "Let's Play," and the B side of the latest single, a
scalding quick-boogie rendition of "Milkcow Blues." He didn't bother
moving around. He just sang all the words, hit the notes, and savored
the look on Eddy's face.

The old man listened with dancing eyes, sucking his tea through a
paper straw. He cried, "Ho!" and clapped hard at the finish of each
number. He even shamed the men at the bar into clapping a little; the
tall white-haired man stood up and tipped his gray fedora to the boys.

"Yessirree!" Eddy waved his cane at a roomful of invisible people.
"There it is! You got 'em all up and dancing, now! That's a hum-
dinger!"

"Thank you, Mr. Eddy," said Leroy. "Uhm—listen, that's about all
the songs we got. I guess we better be gettin' on." He bit his lip. He saw
the boys getting ready to laugh again, but there was something unbearably sad about this old man with his wooden leg and his rheumy eyes.

"Thank you, boys," said Lorene. "That sounded real fine. We sure
did enjoy it."

"So did we," said Leroy. He reached in his pocket for the sheaf of
tens, peeled off two to pay for the gas, and handed the rest back to Eddy.
"That man Douglass told you wrong," he said. "We only get twenty
dollars for a private party."

Tommy's jaw dropped. Jack rolled his eyes.

Leroy ignored them. Okay, so they were nearly busted. He didn't
care. Sooner or later they'd get some more money, and then the boys
would realize this was the right thing to do. For now they had quit
laughing.

"Mighty fine." Eddy folded the money away and saluted Leroy with
his cane.

Lorene mouthed the words *thank you* behind his back.

"You take care, Mr. Eddy," said Leroy. "We'll be seeing you around."
He went smiling into the night.

Jack was disgusted. "Don't you think you should have divvied up that
money before you gave away our share?"

"Aw come on, Jack, that poor old man ain't toting but about half a
load," Leroy said. "We couldn't just steal his money from him."

"Who said anything about stealing? We did what he hired us to do. I don't get it, Leroy. That pomade must have gone to your brain."

"He liked us." Leroy got in the passenger side. "You heard what he said. His ears were lonesome."

Jack stuffed the bass in back, slammed the door. "My share comes to seventeen dollars."

Leroy knew Jack was as quick to get angry as he was to make a joke; usually his temper blew over in a minute or two.

Tommy slid behind the wheel.

Leroy handed over the remaining twenty. "That's for gas to get us to Bossier City and home," he said. "I hadn't got the rest, Jack, but I'll pay you as soon as I get it."

"I hate to say it, Lee, but Jack's right," Tommy put in. "I understand why you did what you did, but we ain't exactly rich enough to be playing for charity yet."

Jack said, "Hell, we *are* a charity."

"I'll pay your share too, Tommy. I'll pay you both. It'll be worth it. I was glad to play for that man." Leroy watched the lights of the Sho-Boat receding in the rear window. He would not let them ruin this moment. For the first time he knew how it felt to make someone's life better.

Tommy and Jack stayed miffed all the way to the Louisiana line. They refused to sing along on "The Ballad of Davy Crockett," which usually got them going anytime. They sat silent while the Clovers sang "Blue Velvet." Somethin' Smith and the Redheads came on. Leroy turned it up: *it's a siiin to tell a lie....*

Then the Grambling colored station played that really wild "Tutti Frutti" by the new falsetto singer Little Richard: *a wop bop-a-loo bop—a-lop bam boom!* It wasn't a song. It was some kind of explosion. That boy had a shout that could kill you if you needed killing or wake you up if you were already dead.

Jack drummed his fingers on the seat. Tommy reached for his guitar and showed how he'd do it: a straight lickety rhythm line.

Leroy grinned. "We gotta work that one up." He glanced at his watch. "Thirty-five minutes," he said. "Cuttin' it close tonight. Here comes Shreveport."

"Eighth wonder of the world." Jack stretched and sat up. "My God, it is beautiful here. It just stops my heart."

They passed through a strip of gas stations and low-rent motels on Shreveport's west side. The boys stayed across the river in Bossier City, which was also a homely town but had the advantage of Barksdale Air Force Base and the pool halls, strip joints, and honky-tonks clustered near its gates.

Tonight the streets of Shreveport teemed with hot rods and sedans jammed with teenagers, circling the blocks near the Shreveport Municipal Auditorium, parking two deep at the curbs.

"Hot rockin' Saturday night," Leroy said.

"I wish they'd get out of my way." Tommy swung off Linwood Avenue, down the ramp to the loading dock.

They worked fast. Tommy went to park the car while Leroy and Jack manhandled the bass and guitars through the double doors.

Leroy propped his poor old Sound Star gently against a wall. It was earning more scratches every day. The strap held on for dear life. Every time he tuned it, he was afraid the neck might crack.

He stuck his head around the curtain for a peek at Tillman Franks winding up his set with an energetic "Foggy Mountain Breakdown." The houselights at the Hayride always stayed up; Leroy could see every face in the hall. The place was packed to the rafters with country people, young couples with children—and teenagers by the hundreds.

A bunch of girls near the front spotted Leroy peering out. Their mouths made big Os; they pointed and squealed and ran toward the stage.

He grinned and stepped back from the curtain. "Looks like we got a whole squadron out there tonight."

Jack looked up from replacing the D string on his bass. "You mean, the girls?"

"There's a mess of 'em. Come have a look."

"I'm busy with this," said Jack. "I'll see 'em when we get out there."

Leroy spotted Dub Winston, the thin-lipped "Hayride" emcee, picking his way toward them through a group of pickers. "Hey, Mr. Winston, got a big crowd tonight."

"Have you talked to Roy?"

"No sir, not yet. We just got here. Listen, you won't believe this show we just played down in Palestine—"

"Never mind that." There was an excited edge to Winston's amiable radio voice. "One of those songs last week really did the trick, Leroy. We had five hundred phone calls for tickets this afternoon. There are kids out there who drove from Dallas to see you. We've already turned two hundred and fifty away at the door. I hope you're ready to put on a show."

"Are you serious, man?" Jack came to attention. "All those cars out there for us?"

Leroy flushed. "A sellout. . . ."

"You've never seen a happier man than Roy Buncombe," said Dub. "The last time the 'Hayride' sold out was Hank Williams. That's almost five years ago."

"Good Lord," said Leroy. "Hank Williams. Look, here comes Tommy. Tell him."

Dub repeated his news. Tommy lit up like a thousand-watt bulb. "That's crazy, man. Let's go do it!" He grabbed his guitar.

Tillman Franks came off. Dub Winston went to the microphone. Leroy huddled with the boys near the curtain ropes. They played a little "Swing Low, Sweet Chariot" to get the blood pumping.

Dub read down his list of advertisements, then beckoned to the boys: "Now let's get him out here, the young man you've been waiting for— please welcome to the stage the Bad Boy from Memphis, ladies and gentlemen—Leroy Kirby!"

The girls squealed. Leroy trotted out into the blaze of light, waving his hand over his head. The girls squealed louder. He grinned and waved, waiting for the noise to subside. He hadn't done anything yet.

Tommy and Jack moved into position behind him, identical grins on their faces; how else could they answer such a storm of greeting? This was a long way from Eddy's Sho-Boat.

Dub Winston jumped in at the first lull. "Well good evening there, Leroy, how you getting along?"

Leroy leaned to the mike. "Just fine, Mr. Winston, you doing all right?" His first words provoked a cloud of sighs.

"Any better they'd have to shoot me," said Winston. "You boys all ready for a big week of personal appearances in Texas?"

"Yes sir, we are."

"Ye-ahhh," the announcer went on, "we're going to be down there with all these fine 'Hayride' people, appearing in Galveston Monday,

Bryan Tuesday, Odessa Wednesday, Houston Thursday, and Gonzales Texas on Friday. Going to give all the folks a big time."

Leroy straightened the strap on his shoulder. "You gonna be with us, Mr. Winston?"

"Yessir, I am. I pure-D am."

"That's tough—I mean, that's good," Leroy said, earning scattered laughs from the crowd. The last traces of his stage fright had dried up somewhere in West Texas, weeks ago. He loved making wisecracks with all the people to laugh at him.

He put on his biggest, friendliest smile. "Thank you, friends, glad to be here again tonight, we'd like to do a little song for you now, it's about—it's about—well, it's about two minutes long, and it goes something like this. . . ."

> *Wo*
> *Baby baby baby buh-buh-bay-beh!*
> *Baby baby b-b-b-b-b-buh-bay-beh!*
> *Hmmmmm, baby!*
> *Tired of workin'*
> *Come on baby let's play*

The arena erupted in squealing. Leroy abandoned himself. He bent the microphone stand to the floor, shook the hair down in his eyes, and started juking. This song made him wild. He wailed it and hollered and clowned with the stutter on *b-b-baby,* flung himself to one knee, beating hard on the Sound Star.

A string busted twannk! and nearly popped him in the eye. He jumped up and bounded around the stage, crouching down while Tommy twangled the lightning-fast break, hollering, "Go!" at Jack slapping the bass. They made as much racket as any three boys, ever.

> *I'm not a rag doll baby*
> *I'm a man for sho*
> *If you won't play with me little girl*
> *You won't a-be a-playin' around no more*

That line always chilled him. The song sounded carefree, but it carried that deadly undertone: Play with me, baby, or live to regret it.

The threat was reckless, exciting. Leroy sharpened it and drove it home.

Girls left their seats and streamed down the aisles toward him. They took their cues from each other; their squeals arose and fluttered and changed course in unison.

He slammed home the last line: *come on a-baby let's play....*

Tommy hit the open seventh chord and held it.

A great commotion went up.

Leroy took a deep bow. He spotted Mr. Buncombe, the producer, waving and smiling from the wing, looking happy indeed.

Leroy stripped off the broken string. He would keep playing with five; nobody could hear him anyway. "Thank you, friends...." His words echoed back with the yelps of the most zealous girls. They filled the first ten rows at stage left—his fans! They wore braces and gawky glasses and pink skirts with white blouses. They jumped up and down to get his attention.

He shot one of his heavy-lidded seduction looks over that way. One girl went cross-eyed and fell over backward into the arms of her friends.

He hadn't meant to do that. He walked to the edge of the stage with the microphone, peering down. "She all right?"

The other girls waved yes and squealed because he was speaking to them.

"Too much excitement, I guess," he said. "Thankyouvermuch, friends, we'd like to do for you now a song we hadn't done on the 'Hayride' before, mostly because we just learned it a week or so ago. We hope you like it."

And that was how he launched into "Maybellene," Chuck Berry's new song about a girl who's done started back doing the things she used to do. There were so many words in the middle of it that Leroy's tongue could barely keep up, but the song kept circling back to the uncomplicated wail at the heart of it: *Why can't you be true?* Tommy and Jack found a syncopated groove that scratched like shovels on rocks—a hard sound to go with Chuck Berry's hard opinion of Maybellene.

It wasn't a song the girls knew, so the screams were not as well timed. The one who had fainted came back to life. She stood watching Leroy with a dazed expression.

Dub Winston came to read a spot for Southern Pride doughnuts; then he said, "Leroy, got a two-minute version of 'You Better Look Out for Me' you can play for us?"

"Uh, yessir, we do." Leroy counted it off. He could sing this song in his sleep. He and the boys had nearly outgrown it—their sound was getting harder and faster all the time—but the people loved a song they already knew. Leroy tightened it up and sang it with a new irony, to the girl who done him wrong. That's all right, girl. Stick by your mama's side. You will pay for your stuck-up ways in the end.

He was playing a dangerous game, teasing these girls with these songs. The air crackled. He was no longer a nice boy who sang in a pretty voice. He was bad news in a pink suit and white bucks, prowling the stage with his guitar, shaking his hips.

He had never felt so much excitement coming in through the lights. They were nice girls. They wanted Leroy to show them how to be bad. He brought a chorus of squeals with one flick of his finger. The girls liked to squeal, as much as they liked what they were squealing at. It excited them to go to pieces that way, in front of their friends.

"Thank you, thank you, friends, we'll see you next week!" Leroy cried. "Good night!" He waved his hand over his head and strode off in a storm of cheers.

~~~~

The thrill of the crowd carried him across the Red River. Three carloads of girls swung in behind Scotty's Chevrolet and trailed the boys all the way to the Al-Ida, honking and weaving and hanging out the windows.

Leroy was relieved to see the No Vacancy sign in the motel office. If those girls landed here for the night, he wouldn't get a lick of sleep.

He went to flirt with them and sign autographs—to keep them distracted while Tommy and Jack unloaded the instruments into their rooms.

The girls were all from the same school in the East Texas town of Tyler. For three weeks in a row they had borrowed their daddies' cars and driven eighty miles to see Leroy. They told him this with lots of giggles and bashful introductions and tooting on car horns. Mr. Labreaux, the round-shouldered Cajun motel manager, came out to hush them up.

They were just kids, not a kissable one in the bunch. Leroy gave each of them a smile and a nice word and an autograph; then he sent them away.

"Leroy, got a wire for sixty dollas this afternoon," Labreaux said, when the last car had gone. "You want, I could put it against your bill."

"Yessir, that's what it's for." After all the high-minded pleasure he'd felt at giving back old Eddy's money, Leroy wished he had the cash in his pocket right now. He was down to eleven dollars and change, and tonight's rave-up at the Hayride just begged for a celebration.

He said good-night to Labreaux, stuck his hands in his pockets, wandered down the row of rooms. The door to 29 stood open. Tommy had flopped out on one bed, Jack on the other.

"You boys look settled in," said Leroy. "Not ready to call it a night, are you?"

"Hell no." Tommy rolled over on his back. "Just catching my breath. I don't see how you stay so damn lively."

"Man, I got fired up out there tonight." Leroy went through the connecting door to Room 28, shedding his jacket and shirt, stepping out of his pants. "Did you see that one faint? All I did was look at her."

"It gets wilder and wilder." Jack pulled in his feet and sat up. "I don't know what it is, Lee. What you do to these girls. If we could bottle that and sell it . . ."

"What do you think we're doing?" Leroy hung his pink suit with care. He'd been wearing it every night this week.

"I mean, you're okay, I guess," said Jack, "but you ain't *that* good-looking."

Leroy grinned. "You just got to see it through their eyes." He held his shirt up in front of him and performed a little harem dance. "It's natural sex appeal, Jackie, either you're born with it or you're not. Just I happen to be born with it."

"Put some clothes on," said Tommy. "The door's standing wide open."

"Come on, girls!" Leroy waggled his fanny at the door. "Come and get it!"

Jack hooted.

Tommy rolled over and kicked the door shut. He inspected them with a look of extreme gravity. "Boys," he said, "I think we need to get drunk."

They said yeah! and got dressed and slammed out of the room.

Highway 80 in Bossier City was a glittering strip of sin, twenty times brighter than the midway at the Mississippi-Alabama Dairy Fair. It seemed to have sprung from the minds of the airmen at Barksdale; the neon signs said LIQUOR and GIRLS and TATTOO and GIRLS and OPEN ALL NITE. Blinking lights stretched into the distance. Leroy had seen the crowds of flyboys staggering between bars, tripping over their shoelaces, roaring songs with filthy lyrics.

He liked to hit the bars after a show, to blow off steam and flirt with girls. He was a little shy about taking more than one or two drinks. He'd tasted somebody's whiskey once in a while, but never beyond that first giddy tingle. He was afraid of becoming unhinged. He remembered Granddaddy cutting up with his buddies on Saturday night. He never wanted to look helpless and silly like that.

But tonight he had soaked up all the wildness of the girls in the crowd. Excitement was building inside him like steam under pressure. He needed some kind of relief.

They walked across the Al-Ida parking lot to a dive called Big Louie's.

Leroy explained to Louie how he'd just made a thousand girls swoon, and Louie said, "Your first beer's on the house then. I am honored you have picked my place to get started."

The beer tasted sweet. Leroy drank it right down and let out a belch. He hardly felt different at all; maybe his head was a little bigger.

Those girls tonight—they loved him before he sang a note. They loved him for the sound of his voice on the radio, his picture in the newspaper. He was the hottest thing for three states around.

He didn't know what kind of miracle it would take to kick him up into the really big time, but he thought he had glimpsed the first stirrings tonight.

There were no girls in Louie's. After the first beer they moved on. Leroy used the same line in the next three joints and earned three free rounds.

Plenty of signs said GIRLS, but the only girls seemed to be the strippers or painted-up party girls cruising for airmen with cash.

Leroy concentrated on not letting the alcohol go to his head. He wasn't too worried after his fourth beer. Now that he was really drinking it, beer tasted like some kind of harmless soda pop for grown-ups. He noticed that he was feeling happier and happier. As long as he could restrict his drunkenness to this streak of cool happiness, he would be fine.

If anything, the beer was helping him think and speak more clearly than ever. He told a string of knock-knock jokes that had Tommy and Jack on the floor. Then he started in telling the one about two guys who stow away on a ship with a gorilla monkey and ten gallons of gasoline, but while he was trying to remember the punch line, Tommy drained off his glass and said it was time to move on.

Outside, Tommy said, "Wait up, guys. Take a look what Oscar Moore gave me backstage at the Hayride tonight." From his pack of Camels Tommy withdrew an odd, skinny, hand-twisted cigarette. "It's smoke weed," he said.

"What is it?" said Jack.

"You smoke it and it makes you high. All the colored boys use it before they play dates."

Oh, Leroy had heard all about marijuana; he'd even sniffed out the telltale sweet-pungent aroma in a couple of colored clubs down around Mobile, after Tommy taught him to recognize it. Here it was, right in front of him. The idea of actually smoking it was dark and dangerous and alluring. . . . You're not a mama's boy. You're not afraid. You're hot stuff. You can try something wild and new. It won't kill you. It's your life. Go ahead.

Tommy struck a match.

Jack peered into the corners of the parking lot as if J. Edgar Hoover might jump out and grab him. "That stuff's illegal," he said.

"Yeah, so is most kinds of fucking if you go back and look it up," said Tommy. "They make everything illegal if it's too much fun." He struck a match to the cigarette, took a long, noisy puff from one end, and held the smoke in his lungs. In a funny, tight voice he said, "You got to hold it in to make it work. Oscar showed me."

He offered it over to Leroy.

Leroy took it. He turned it this way and that, inspecting the glowing ember. Go ahead. Try it. Why not? Tonight is a night for new things.

He was not accustomed to breaking the law. A thrill spread through him. Dope fiend! Lawbreaker! He grinned and took his first tentative sip of the smoke. "I hope it don't make me too crazy," he said, exhaling. It tasted like pinecones. . . .

"Take more of it," Tommy said. "Hold it in."

"Boys, hurry up and let's get out of here," Jack said. "I don't want to go to jail, for God's sake."

Leroy took in a big, healthy lungful. The smoke filled his chest. He felt it expanding. He'd never even tried a real cigarette before. He coughed and hacked and coughed and had to bend over to spit. White stars danced in his eyes.

"Whoa, that looks like fun," Jack said.

"You got to go easy." Tommy demonstrated. His eyes shone. "You feel anything?"

Leroy took a medium-size puff. He held the smoke in this time, even blew it out through his nose like Tommy. "I'm not sure," he said. "A little dizzy." He couldn't imagine how he could feel any better than he already felt on that stage tonight, those girls out there screaming for him.

They smoked the cigarette to its nub. Jack took one puff before it went out.

Leroy had never noticed until this moment that he and Tommy were the exact same height. He remarked on it to Tommy, who said, "Leroy, I believe you are high. You just told me the same thing a minute ago."

That struck Leroy as funny, and Jack joined in laughing. . . . They were all howling when they stepped through the door of the Golden Derrick.

This place was the liveliest yet—a big crowd of pilots and truckers and cowboys and pickers and fast girls and even some regular girls, some with dates, some without. Several couples were two-stepping on a little dance floor near the bar. Leroy liked the warm glow and the smoky noise and the song on the jukebox: *Your cheatin' heart will make you weep.* . . .

"This is more like it," he said, rubbing his hands together. He waded through the boisterous crowd, skirting the dancers to the one open spot at the bar.

The tall-haired blond waitress wore a dress six inches too short for her age.

Leroy said, "Howdy, ma'am."

She turned an appreciative eye on him. "Well, hello to you, you tall drink of water. I know you. You're that singer. I've seen you in here before."

"That's me," he said. "How about some beers? Me and my friends here just knocked out a whole mess of girls across the river."

"Well they ought to give you the prize," she said. "Shirley, take a look who this is. That singer you were talking about. It's him."

Then four or five women were gathered at Leroy's elbow, chattering, taking him in. They'd all heard him on the "Hayride." They'd seen his picture in the *Shreveport Journal.* The waitresses made most of the fuss, but there were also two classy-looking younger girls watching from the end of the bar.

When Leroy spotted them, they glanced away and smiled at each other.

The one holding the cigarette looked sophisticated. Leroy liked the other one. Sweet face. Little dark-haired doll with big eyes.

Jack slipped his arm around to grab his mug and whispered, "Here we go, take a look at those two."

"I'm looking as hard as I can," Leroy said without moving his lips.

Jack said, "Who goes first, me or you?"

"*They* looked at *us.*" Leroy slouched against the bar. "Just ignore 'em. They won't be able to stand it."

The waitresses dispersed. Tommy was shooting pool with a tattooed man.

The pretty brunette left her perch on the barstool and steered her friend through the dancers toward Leroy.

Jack said, "Two at ten o'clock, coming in low."

"Hello, ladies," said Leroy. "I s'pose you're wondering what a couple nice guys like us are doing in a—in a place like this."

The brunette moved between Leroy and the bar, fishing behind him for a match or something. The movement brought her close, and it wasn't an accident.

"I'm not wondering," she said with a little smile, handing Leroy his beer. "You're Leroy, aren't you?"

"Well now, that's right, I am," he said, leaning over her, "and that means you got to tell me who you are."

"My name is Betty," she said. "You're famous. I've heard you on the radio. The 'Hayride.'"

"Right again," he said. "You know, you're a pretty good guesser." He took another long swig. He didn't remember the floor in the Derrick sloping down at one end, and also he'd never noticed the hundreds of out-of-state license plates nailed to the walls. In fact, he'd never really noticed anything the way he was seeing it now. The beers and the smoke weed gave everything a pearly glow.

His stomach felt a little peculiar at the moment, swashing around like an unsettled ocean, but the happiness, the warmth of his love for all things, was spreading down to the ends of his toes.

Betty winked at him. Instantly he felt his love for all things narrow itself down to a bright, narrow beam of desire, aimed at this girl.

She had a shy, crinkly smile, big, bashful eyes, a dainty lace-trimmed blouse, a little mole at the edge of her mouth, lips like red.... He wanted to kiss her.

"You boys are drunk," said her friend. She was pretty enough, a bit freckled and snooty-looking.

"We're not drunk," Leroy said, slamming his hand on the bar so the glasses jumped. "We're *going* to get drunk. We set *out* to get drunk. But not yet."

Betty kept that smile on her face. "Are you rich?"

"I ain't yet," Leroy said, "but I'm going to be." He grinned. He could have this girl. He knew it from the way her liquid eyes looked into him. It made a thrill in the back of his throat, down his spine, down into right where he lived.

She was saying something about his singing. She liked it; he could tell by the look on her face, but he couldn't quite make out her words.

He had to get all his thoughts back together and concentrate. He drank most of his beer.

They talked about nothing for a while, blah-blah. "Listen, baby," Leroy said, looming close, "tell me, am I as beautiful as you think I am?"

"Yes," she murmured, gazing into his eyes. "I think you're real nice. Are you going steady with anybody?"

"Not—not really." The barstool seemed to want to slide out from under him. Leroy stood on his own feet. "Least, I don't think so." The air in the Golden Derrick was stifling. He wondered if it was time to move on to the next place. "I was just thinking...."

"Drink up," said Betty, and he did. Suddenly she was so close he smelled her perfume and felt his stomach churning, and he wasn't sure

337

it was such a good idea, whether it was the beer or maybe something he ate, maybe not eating, or some kind of tilting of the earth, but it didn't seem like a good idea to stand there and let this awful feeling just sweep over him, so Leroy shook the girl off his arm and set off stumbling for the door and made it out into the cool, clear air, to a car, the front seat of a car, sprawled out on the seat. Everything went dark.

33

*L*eroy was caught in an angry crowd that was trying to drag him down off the stage and rip off his clothes. He seized the mike stand and waved it to keep them at bay. Bells rang. Drums pounded. Hands came to strangle him from behind—

It was the top sheet, twisted around his throat. He was awake now, naked and sweating, in his room at the Al-Ida Motel. Someone pounding hard on the door. His mouth tasted like a dirty rag.

He freed himself from the noose. "Who is it?" he croaked.

"Get up, son, got a trunk call from Memphis, and the man ain't gone

339

hang up till he talk to you." That was Labreaux, the Al-Ida manager.

"Just a minute." Leroy could not believe how awful he felt. Poisoned. Aching all over. A film on his eyes; he rubbed with his hand.

Wild wild young men like to have a good time.... How did he get here? Tommy and Jack must have brought him. Clothes, covers strewn everywhere. A wild night—when did he—? He couldn't remember anything.

Oh. God. It was terrible not to remember. He heard his mother: That's what you get. How much had he drunk? Four or five beers, maybe—not enough to knock him out and give him this cratered-out, smoking-rubble headache.... Was it that funny cigarette? It made him feel so spacious, so warm and alive, but now he was a walking dead thing.

He pulled on jeans, opened the door, and blocked the blinding sun with his hand.

Labreaux said, "It's that Mr. Pate. He called four times in an hour. I *tol'* him you boys come in late."

Leroy squinted. "Oh—okay, hang on a minute, let me get my shoes."

"Come on, the man calling long distance."

Leroy followed, barefoot and shirtless, to the motel office. He lifted the receiver. "Roger?"

"Leroy, where the hell have you been? I've been trying to reach you all morning! Damn it, when I've got important news, I need to know where you are!" Roger went off in a noisy fit of indignation. Leroy held the phone away from his ear until the squawking died down.

He said, "Roger, I was asleep." More squawking. He said, "Roger, I'm right here. You don't have to yell."

"The man's waiting now, Leroy! Right across the street!"

"Who did you say it was?"

"Damn it, boy, wake up and listen to me! It's only Sam Sanders, who's only managing the biggest act in all of country music, so if you've got a brain in your head, you'll go wash your face and get over to that coffee shop before he gives up and goes home."

"Sanders? You mean, Sam Sanders, as in Billy Ray Jordan?"

"You bet your ass," said Roger Pate. "I told you I was working on something big. He caught your act last night, and he's there now, across the highway from you. Waiting on you."

Leroy squinted through the blinds. "Lucy's Coffee Shop?"

340

"That's the one. Why didn't you pick up my message last night? Now get over there. Call me the minute you're done."

Leroy spotted a long black Cadillac among the pickups and Fords in front of Lucy's. He thanked Labreaux and ran to his room. He was wide-awake now. Sam Sanders was waiting.

Leroy knew enough about the music business to know that when somebody as big as Sam Sanders comes to see you, he's not bringing bad news.

He splashed his face in the sink, slicked his hair back, pulled on a white shirt, black pants, a tan jacket. He caught a glimpse of his puffy red eyes in the mirror. He looked as if he'd been asleep for a week.

He rummaged in his suitcase for the slick aviator glasses he'd picked up in New Orleans. They were cool Ray-Bans with inky black lenses. Nobody could tell a thing.

He hurried outside, across the highway.

Lucy's Coffee Shop was still crowded; it must not have been too long past the breakfast hour. Leroy spotted a tall man sitting alone in the last booth.

He had suave, wavy white hair, a big hawk's nose, an elegant gray linen suit, and five enormous jeweled rings on his fingers. Tortoiseshell glasses, too large for his face. A fat cigar clamped in his teeth, unlit. A gray felt fedora parked by his elbow, with a black feather in the brim. He looked tall and important, sitting alone.

Leroy kept his sunglasses on. He went to the booth and sat down. "Morning," he said, "hope you hadn't been waiting too long."

Sam Sanders said, "You're Leroy."

"Yes sir, I am."

"Take off those glasses so I can see your eyes."

Leroy did as he said. The glare made him wince. A waitress arrived to pour coffee.

"You out carousing last night?" said Sanders.

Leroy nodded, grateful for his first sip of coffee. "I don't do it too much, but we sure enough did it last night."

"You know you kept me waiting forty-five minutes."

Leroy stiffened. "Well I'm sorry, Mr. Sanders, but I never heard a thing about it till five minutes ago when they came to get me out of bed."

Sanders waved his hand. "You call me Sam," he said. "I don't let

341

nobody call me Sam. There's only one other person I let call me Sam, and that's Billy Ray Jordan."

"Well . . . thank you, sir." Leroy felt the ground shifting; the tall man had turned friendly, in one stroke.

"Lemme get to the point," Sanders said. "I been keeping an eye on you. Saw you play twice yesterday."

"Twice?"

"I was at the Hayride, and before that down in Palestine. At the Sho-Boat. Eddy's an old friend of mine."

Leroy stared. His mind went reeling back to that honky-tonk road-house, fitting the pieces together. "You—he's—wait a minute, I know you. You came in right before he did. And you sat at the bar with those other guys."

"That's right," said Sanders. "I didn't introduce myself. I know a lot about you, son, but I'm still checking you out. I wanted to see how you'd act in a pinch. I got Eddy to pretend like he was the one paying to hear you. He bet me you'd take the money and get in your car and keep going. He lost his bet."

Leroy stared. "You mean—the money came from you?"

"I needed to find out what kind of fellow you were," Sanders said, with a smile.

Leroy shook his head. "That's a pretty fancy way to go about it."

"Most singers I know wouldn't have played a full set for an empty house," said Sam Sanders. "And I don't know *nobody* who would give the man his money back. I like you, son. I only do business with people I like."

Leroy felt his heart skip a beat. Everybody knew that Sam Sanders's promotional skills had taken Billy Ray Jordan to the very top. "The Kentucky Crooner," they called him. "You—you want to do business with me?"

"After what I saw last night, I do. I think you're gonna make more money than anybody I ever saw. And I'm gonna help you to do it."

If Leroy hadn't felt so terrible, he might think he was still dreaming—these promises of fame and fortune from a man he'd never met! His temples were pounding, and here was the famous Sam Sanders holding out a golden treasure in his hands.

Careful now. Don't seem too eager. Play it cool.

342

Leroy said, "Well, sir, that's something."

"What I'm about to tell you is between you and me," Sanders said. "You can't tell a soul, or I'll come after you and kill you. You understand?"

"Yes sir," Leroy said.

"I don't have but one client at the time," said Sam Sanders. "Billy Ray Jordan is my client right now. One year from now you'll be my client. I'm gonna be your manager. I'm gonna take over your life and run it for you. You've got the talent. I'll show you what to do with it. I'll make you the biggest goddamn star in the world."

Leroy grinned. Those were his own words to himself. "Do I get to say anything about it?"

"All you have to say is yes," said Sanders.

"But I've already got a manager. Roger Pate. You talked to him."

"I'll buy your contract when the time comes." The tall man waved his cigar; details were hazy, indefinite things, like smoke. "Nothing will happen right away. I want you to tell everybody I wasn't all that interested in you. We'll book you into some shows—start you out with Billy Ray in Texas this weekend. Let me worry about Roger Pate."

"But we've signed for two years with Rocking Records," Leroy protested. It struck him that Sanders had planned every word of this conversation before he ever sat down in this booth.

"I'll take care of that, too," said Sanders, waving the girl over with coffee. "Bring this young man some breakfast," he told her. "He looks hungry. Go ahead, it's on me."

Leroy ordered six eggs over easy, three patty sausages, three sides of bacon, grits, biscuits, a large glass of milk, and a cinnamon roll. Sanders did not blink.

"Healthy appetite, that's good," he said. "Listen, son. I know what it feels like when you're up there singing and those girls are screaming at you."

Leroy said, "How do you know?"

"It feels like they're touching you. You can feel every one of them reaching out to touch you with their eyes. Sometimes you can't sleep at night for thinking about 'em all looking."

Leroy dug his fork into a pool of grits. "It feels pretty good, all right," he said. "There's no secret about that."

"You want to live in a big house. You want to drive a fine car, like my car." Sanders stuck his thumb over his shoulder at his Cadillac. "You want to do right by your folks. I know all about it, Leroy. I can help you."

"How?"

"Son, this business is feelings. Just feelings. That's all it is." Sanders leaned forward in the booth. "I got a feeling about you. I tell a few people, the word spreads ... before you know it, every little girl in America's got another kind of feeling about you. You got this sexy thing, and the girls seem to like it. I can see the whole thing."

"What about Tommy and Jack?" Leroy said, chewing bacon.

"Who's that?"

"My band."

"You keep on playing with them awhile," Sanders said. "Don't tell 'em anything. You're going to need a better band behind you, but I'll take care of that when the time comes."

Don't worry, leave it to me, it's all been decided. "Now wait a minute," Leroy said. "Those are my friends."

"A year from now you'll have more friends than you need."

"Hey now, listen, Mr. Sanders—"

"It's Sam."

"Yeah well, everything is sounding pretty good until you get to this part where you're going to handle my friends. Now, Dan Tobias has been pretty durn good to me, and Tommy, and Jack—we're a team. None of this would have happened if we hadn't started playing together."

Sanders smiled, a kind, motherly smile. "Son, I admire your loyalty. But you're the one getting those girls all excited. You're the star. Not them."

"They're good," Leroy said. "If you want me, you got to take them."

"Waaaal, I'm not gonna push that. You'll change your mind." Sanders slid his plate of toast across the table. "Go on. Have mine."

"I'm not leaving Dan," Leroy said, reaching for the jelly.

"You need a bigger label than whatever it is Rocking Records," Sanders said mildly. "You need somebody national that can sell your records everywhere. Columbia. RCA. You may be a big deal down here, but up above the Mason-Dixon line they never heard of you."

"They will," said Leroy.

Sam Sanders leaned forward, biting hard on his cigar. "Not as long as you're stuck in the small time, kid. I been there. I know. Now what do you say?" He checked his watch. "My time's almost up."

"I can't give you an answer," said Leroy. "I'd have to talk to my folks before I even thought about it. They'd have to sign. I'm not twenty-one yet."

"I know all about them," said Sanders. "Your father's Ray, works at United Paint Company. Your mother does some work as a nurse's aide, right? Agnes." He folded his arms. "I understand they're fine Christian people. Wanna meet them as soon as the time is right. I know we'll all get along."

Leroy mopped toast in the egg juice. "You sure got it all figured out."

Sanders balled up his napkin. His rings sparkled. His long car gleamed through the window behind him. "Just waiting for you to say yes," he said.

He was the real thing, the picture Leroy held in his mind of a successful man.

How did he know so much? Leroy had the stuff, okay, yes, he was ready—hadn't he been secretly praying to be discovered by someone like Sam Sanders?

"If I did something like that," he said, "how much percentage would you want?"

"A straight twenty-five."

"I don't know. It's a lot to think about," Leroy said. "I'll talk to my folks.... How do I get in touch with you?"

"You don't need to. Your itinerary's been canceled. You're joining the Billy Ray Jordan tour Thursday in Laredo. You've got the big spot right before intermission."

Leroy was impressed. "Really?"

"Really."

"Roger knows about this?"

"We settled it last night. He'll give you the dates." Sanders pointed to Leroy's plate. "Go ahead. Finish up."

Leroy picked up his fork. The food was easing the jackhammer in his head. "Tommy and Jack, too?"

"All of you. And we'll see if we can't get you with a drummer."

"How much are you paying?"

"Six hundred a week," said Sanders.

The figure did a dance in Leroy's head.

"That's nothing," Sanders was saying. "Soon as I get you out of this 'Hayride' thing—"

The numbers stopped dancing. "Get us *out* of it? We were lucky to get on in the first place."

"Son." Sam Sanders looked amused. "You got to quit thinking small. You think small, you stay small. You want to stay small?"

"No sir."

"Then think big. And leave the rest up to me." He unfolded himself from the booth, towering over Leroy.

This man rolled in like some panzer tank, blowing holes in everything in sight. You couldn't argue with him; he'd have your argument planned out before you did.

"I sure thank you." Leroy swung his feet out of the booth. "I'll think about everything you said. And we'll be proud to play with Mr. Jordan."

"I ain't worried." Sanders put on his hat. "Long as you don't go carousing yourself to death, you and me are gonna make a good team."

Leroy trailed him to the cash register. Sanders unfurled a ten-dollar bill and told the girl to keep the change. They stepped into the warm morning sun.

Leroy said, "You act like I said yes, before you even asked me."

The tall man squinted his face up into a smile. "Waaal, you didn't say no. I figure that's about the same thing."

"We'll see," Leroy said. That was Agnes's favorite answer when she didn't have an answer.

They shook hands. Sanders reached out and tucked something in Leroy's jacket pocket. "That's for you," he said, squeezing behind the wheel of his Cadillac. The electric window glided down.

Leroy reached in and drew out a tight little green-paper triangle. He unfolded it. Two fifty-dollar bills.

"You know," he said, "this won't make any difference on what I decide."

"Yeah I know," Sanders said. "It's the money from Eddy's. You played a full set. You oughta get paid."

"Thanks." Leroy crumpled the bills in his hand.

346

Sanders switched to a pair of enormous sunglasses, with rhinestones set in the temples. "I don't guess you would know this," he said, "but I never waited forty-five minutes for Billy Ray Jordan." He waved and was gone in a cloud of brown dust.

Leroy stood by the highway, watching him go.

He wished he had a big, long Cadillac to take him away. The lounges and liquor stores of Bossier City swam before his eyes, unbearably tawdry and sad in the morning light. Sam Sanders knew exactly which buttons to push. He had money and fame and promotion and connections; he knew Leroy wanted all of those things. The biggest God damn star in the world. Did he say that to all the singers?

It had taken all of Leroy's self-control to keep from saying yes, please yes make me a star make me rich beyond my wildest dreams why not? yes! let's get going now! but a cautious voice spoke up with *maybe*. He didn't trust anybody all the way, except perhaps his mother.

Still: Sam Sanders. Six hundred is nothing. Every little girl in America. Biggest God damn star. One hundred dollars cash money.

That was just the tune Leroy wanted to hear. He tucked the bills in the back of his wallet.

He walked across the road to the Al-Ida office, where Mr. Labreaux was watching church on television.

Leroy picked up the phone and dialed O.

Roger Pate answered on the second ring and accepted the charges. "Yeah, what happened?"

"Well, I don't know if he was too impressed." Leroy squeezed the lie out between his teeth. "He's booking some dates for us, but other than that he didn't have much to say."

"You didn't say something to make him mad, did you?"

"No, Roger, do you think I'm stupid? It was all right. Now, he said you got a new schedule for us. . . ."

Roger spelled out the new dates and times. Leroy scribbled them on the back of an Al-Ida envelope.

Roger's voice held a note of suspicion. "You sure that's all he said?"

"He gave us a good spot on the show. Listen, Roger, I'll call you tomorrow. I need a bath something fierce. And a nap."

"You take care of yourself," Roger said. "Don't mess up your voice."

As soon as he hung up, Leroy's headache came back into bloom. He wandered down the doors. Room 29 sounded quiet inside.

Leroy fished out the key to 28. After a long, hot shower he flopped across the bed, still damp, and fell sound asleep.

Hours later Tommy woke him, tugging on one foot. "Come on, man, it's two o'clock. Time to get up. We're starving to death."

Leroy had slept hard, no dreams at all. He pulled on his clothes and his Ray-Bans and followed the boys across the highway to Lucy's. He was hungry again. He ordered a ham sandwich and a cheeseburger and a side of bacon and a Coke and french fries.

When the boys were well into their plates, Leroy announced that he'd met with none other than Sam Sanders, famous manager of Billy Ray Jordan, this very morning in this very booth, while they were sleeping.

Tommy slapped the table. The silverware jumped. "Goddamn, he's the big time."

"He came to hear us last night." Leroy skipped the part about the secret audition at Eddy's. He didn't want to lie to his closest friends in the world, but he couldn't tell them everything. He had given his word to Sanders. "He liked us. He's booked us starting Thursday with the Billy Ray Jordan tour. He's worked it out with Roger. Get this. Six hundred a week."

Jack whistled.

Tommy said, "Sam Sanders drove all the way over here by himself to tell you that? I don't believe it. Man, he's bigger than Colonel Tom Parker."

"I think he wanted to get a look at me," said Leroy. "I looked like hell. He said how much he liked you two. Said you were some of the best pickers he'd ever heard."

"You could have come woke me up for that," said Tommy. "I'd have wanted to meet him."

"You will. I think he travels with the tour. He said I needed a lot of work." Leroy curled a whole strip of bacon into his mouth. "I talked to Roger. He's excited about it. I don't know if it'll come to much, but it beats the hell out of Eddy's Sho-Boat, don't you think?"

His lies were falling like cinders, burning him. Already in his mind he was figuring how he would break it to them—Sam said he needed better players.

Tommy said, "You seem mighty perky today, considering last night."

"Man, I don't know what happened." Leroy pressed fingers to his temples. "I tell you this much. That's the last time drinking for me. I don't know if it was that or"—he dropped his voice—"or that stuff we smoked. But I don't remember a thing."

Tommy said, "You'll get over it."

"You didn't seem to mind that gal much," said Jack. "I guess the rest of the night made up for it, huh?"

"That . . . what? What do you mean?"

"Well, I don't know her name. Christ, don't you remember?"

"I'll let you in on a secret," said Leroy. "I know I walked out of the Derrick and got in some car. But that's the last thing I know. I don't remember you guys bringing me home."

"Wasn't she still there this morning?" said Tommy.

"Who? There . . . I don't get it."

"What a waste." Jack shook his head sadly. "He doesn't remember. Boy, that was her car you fell into. Convertible. A Plymouth, I think it was. We didn't bring you home, Leroy. She did."

Leroy's eyes widened. "Who are you talking about?"

"What was her name, Tommy? Come on and help me," said Jack. "Denise. Something like that. Boy, you were more messed up than you looked. I didn't think you had that much."

"I didn't. For some reason it knocked me out like a hammer. You mean that—the pretty one, the brunette?"

"That's the one."

"Betty."

"See there, it's coming back to him."

"She brought me back to the motel?"

"Well hell yes, Leroy, I wish you'd been alive to see it. You took out of that place like your toes were on fire. Little Betty went after you. Last we saw she was driving off with the two of you all wrapped up together."

"We were?" Leroy felt the flush in his face. This was a new kind of humiliation, to do something like that and not remember. He swore it, a pledge: No more alcohol. Never again. That other stuff— well, that was an interesting feeling, all that room in his head. Maybe Tommy could find him some more of that stuff. "So what did you guys do?"

"We shot some pool. I couldn't make an inch with her friend. Miss

Redheaded Tease. We gave up and came back. When we saw that convertible parked out front, we just knew you'd hit the jackpot."

"Maybe he did," said Tommy. "Only thing is, he'll never know, 'cause he don't remember." He snickered. Jack joined in.

Leroy didn't hear them. He was trying to sift through last night. He remembered every moment in the Derrick. He felt fine, clearheaded and expansive and strong, until that pretty little girl came over to stand beside him. That's when the floor started tilting, the circle of his vision tightening in.

He checked himself with his hands. He didn't feel any different. It worried him not to remember.

34

*L*eroy had just finished a remote broadcast of the "Hayride" from the Heart O'Texas Coliseum. He and the boys were fifteen miles east of Waco, rolling along in high spirits, when something terrible happened under the hood of Tommy's Bel Air. Ten seconds of metal clang-banging and they knew it was fatal. Tommy kept it going for another mile, but a rise in the roadway slowed them to an irreversible stop.

They abandoned the car, flagged a ride back to Waco. The next morning they pooled their Billy Ray Jordan money and bought two cars off the same OK lot: a fat gold 1952 Oldsmobile for Leroy and another '54 Chevrolet like the one that had died, out of remorse for the names they had called it.

Leroy was all over the map. He played five or six nights a week, sometimes two or three shows a night, sometimes in two or three places. He lived on burgers and chocolate shakes and pure energy from the audience, the good times with Tommy and Jack, throngs of excited girls at every show, endless highway miles, rolls of new cash.

He zoomed across flat Arkansas toward Memphis, with the wheel in his fist and the ivory-plastic bit of a panatela slim cigar in his teeth. (He didn't smoke them, but he liked the way he looked holding one.) He found the Mother Station on the radio: Bo Diddley raving off on that song with his name. It was a scratchety unforgettable guitar riff, one cry of "Hey, Bo Diddley" repeated; it was, in fact, one long advertisement for Bo Diddley. Leroy thought maybe he should do a song called "Leroy Kirby."

He had tried to write a couple of songs. He couldn't do it. His good parts were all lifted from other songs, and the rest was plain bad.

The river slid under. Jack and Tommy peeled away at the Memphis end of the bridge, headed for the south side, and home.

Leroy waved out the window. He had a stop to make first. He drove the big Oldsmobile up Beale Street, swung the car onto the sidewalk, and switched it off. Little pops and grunts went on under the hood, the big engine settling in.

Ike Irving was in place on the sidewalk in front of his store, scanning for customers. He brightened when Leroy stepped from the wide car. "Would you look at this? Mr. Singing Sensation!"

"Howdy, Ike," said Leroy, "how's business?"

"It just got a lot better," said Ike. "I see it's treating you good. We been reading the paper. Hey Myron! Take a look! Mr. Singing Sensation!"

"Knock it off, Ike." Leroy sidled inside. "You'll give me the big head."

Myron Irving abandoned a customer and came with his arms out, as if to a long-lost son. "Leroy Kirby!" he said. "How did those turquoise trousers do last time? Did those fit all right?" He beamed, clapping Leroy on both shoulders. "We're so proud, all we read in the papers.

Look here, we got a whole lot of brand-new stock for you. Come right this way."

He motioned for Ike to wait on the man he'd deserted and steered Leroy past the racks of cheap stuff to the sparkly-silky things on the platform in back. "We hear your records all the time," he said. "We make people stop and listen, and we tell them we know you."

"Well that's fine, Myron. I try to send you boys all the business I can."

"And so polite. You don't mind if we drop your name?"

"Course not," said Leroy. "Just give me a deal."

"You know you always have your extra twenty percent with us." Myron bustled around with his arms full of shirts, matching ties, a new group of slick jackets. . . . Leroy tried on most of it and bought everything he liked. He liked a lot. The bill came to $317.

He pulled out his roll and paid cash.

Myron's eyes widened. "We'll fix up those hems and get it all over to you in the morning," he said, counting out change.

"Wait," Leroy said, "we've got a new address." He pulled out the slip of paper with his mother's loopy handwriting: 1414 Getwell Road. "Send the stuff here," he said.

"Moving up in the world, huh?" Myron peered over his half glasses. "Getwell Road?"

"Yeah, they just moved. I haven't even been there yet. I'm on my way."

"Here." Myron reached into the stack. "Put on your nice new shirt for your mother. She'll want to see you looking good."

Leroy slipped off the T-shirt and pulled the slinky midnight blue tunic over his head. He studied his reflection in the triple mirror. He looked like Dean Martin dressed for lounging around the cabana. "Thanks, Myron. It's good. You're right, she hasn't seen me in a while."

Myron and Ike followed him outside to shake his hand again, to thank him again for his business.

Leroy's heart sang all the way down Beale Street. It was the same comfortable Memphis; only Leroy was new. He was almost rich. He was very happy. He had a big car.

He turned south on Lamar Avenue, away from downtown and Humes High and the Lauderdale Court and his old slummy life.

He'd made good on his promise to Agnes. He wired home a hundred dollars at a time, then two hundred. Their first step away from Alabama Street was the house on Getwell Road, at the western edge of the suburb where some of the finest people in Memphis lived. Leroy had ordered up a real moving van, the day before Easter.

Light traffic on Central Avenue—nobody hurried in this neighborhood. Everyone was polite at the four-way stops, waving "no, go ahead, after you." The houses were neat, painted white, some with brick facings and two-car garages. Around each house was a patch of green lawn. There were bikes on the lawns, kids on bikes patrolling the side streets and dead-end circles.

Leroy drove at a crawl, searching for house numbers. At last he spied the old shabby Plymouth parked beside a neat white house, number 1414: black shutters, brick face, a lawn, cedar trees, a driveway leading to a one-car garage.

Leroy would do something about the Plymouth soon as his next batch of money came in.

Nothing wrong with the house, though. It was all lit up and warm-looking, the nicest place they'd ever lived. He hit the horn bop bop bop bop and pulled in the drive.

He heard Agnes before he switched off the engine: "Oh look, he's here! Woo-hoo, Leroy!" She waved coming onto the carport. "And he's got a new car! Ray! Come out here, come see!" She opened her arms and let Leroy walk to her. "Honey, welcome home!"

"Hey Satnin, I'm here." He bent down to receive her hug.

"Oh it's so good to see you, looky here, Ray, here he is, here's our boy! Is that a new shirt, too? You look thin, honey, have you been eating? What have you done with yourself? Well come in, come in, you haven't even been to our new house."

She was heavier than ever. There were dark circles under her eyes, and her skin was too pale. Leroy hadn't seen her so worked up since the night she came to fetch him out of the movies. He said, "I've got some things—"

Ray stepped out into the yellow light from the bug bulb. He wore a cardigan sweater and khaki slacks, like a Sears, Roebuck advertisement for Father's Day. He was still plain old craggy-faced Ray, but the new clothes were an improvement. He opened his arms. "Welcome home, son."

Leroy had found the way to get them up out of their chairs when he came home. Rent a nice house, send hundreds of dollars—they're guaranteed glad to see you. Even Dodger was crowding up to hug him around the waist.

Money gets their attention. You buy things for people who love you; they love you more. What's a better use for money?

Maybe that was cold, but there were colder things: that drafty old apartment on Alabama Street in February, for one. This house, now, was built to keep out the winter. It sat snugly on its concrete slab. It had an electric furnace and electric burners in the stove. Agnes showed off the washing machine and the brand-new Hotpoint icebox, the slick new linoleum floor.

"And in here is the dining room," she said, leading the way. "Won't it be nice when we get us a table in here, and some chairs? Dodger says we can bring her armoire and set it right there."

"It'll be real nice," Dodger said.

Everybody waited for Leroy's reaction.

He smiled. "Which one is my room?" He strode down the hall. He liked the low ceilings in here; his hair brushed the Sheetrock.

"First door on the right," Agnes said.

"Well, you gave me the smallest one! Look at all my stuff!"

"Honey, I haven't had time to go through it. We just got here."

"Reckon I've got a bed in there somewhere?" Leroy flung his arm around his mother's shoulder. "Come show me the rest."

"See, Dodger's got her own room now, and here's the linen closet, and down here is ours." In its fine new setting the old furniture showed its scuffs and worn places.

"Everything looks real fine, Mama." He patted her shoulder. "You're right. This is a lot nicer house."

"You like it?" said Ray. "Gettin' uptown now, ain't we?"

The four of them made quite a crowd in the little hallway. Leroy wondered if he should tell them it was all right to go sit in their chairs. He knew that was Dodger's place at the card table with her puzzle, and Ray's in front of the brand-new RCA television set, and Agnes's old overstuffed rocker drawn up with an eye to the kitchen in case something boiled over. They'd lived in so many places that this familiar arrangement was all it took to make the house feel like home.

"Hey I mean it, it's swell," Leroy said. "Plenty of room. Mama, you like the yard?"

"Well, I feel just like a queen," said Agnes. "Sometimes I go out with my magazine and I just set up there, pretty as you please. You ought to see our new lawn chairs."

Leroy said, "Let's go get some steaks and have us a cookout."

"We've got hamburgers. Ray, go see about your fire," she said. "Leroy, you're not done yet." She pointed out a large cardboard carton in the corner, overflowing with letters. "The man from the post office brought those."

He picked an envelope from the top, addressed to

Leroy
Memphis, Tennessee

He slid his thumb along the seal and shook out a pink letter scented with stinky teen perfume. In the corner of the envelope was a tiny school photo of a girl smiling with her mouth closed, hiding her braces.

Dear Leroy,

How are ya! I am fine! My name is Tammy Stephens, age 14. I am in 9th grade at Clinton H.S. (Miss.) I have loved ya so much ever since I heard "You Better Look Out For Me" the first time. I have all your records so far! Do ya have a girlfriend? My friend Shirley said she saw where you did but I didn't believe her. Tiger Beat it says you are looking for "the right kind of girl." I think I am the 1 4 U. . . .

Leroy smiled. "Did you read any of these?"

"Just a couple," said Agnes. "Where they get their ideas, I don't know."

"They all get an allowance," he said, waving Tommy's photo. "They spend their allowance on records. Sam says I'm gonna have to hire somebody to write 'em all back."

"Honey, there's something else. It came for you yesterday."

She led him to the tiny living room. Propped on pillows on the sofa

356

was a magnificent guitar, a decorated rosewood Gibson with LEROY KIRBY inlaid along the neck in mother-of-pearl.

It took his breath. "Mama," he said. "Where on earth—"

"A man brought it on a truck," she said. "It was wrapped in brown paper. This came with it." She held out an ivory-colored envelope.

Inside Leroy found four one-hundred-dollar bills—Agnes's turn to gasp—and a typewritten note:

> To help with your music, a new guitar
> —An Admirer

"Let me see, honey." Agnes reached for the note. "Who is this?"

"His name is Sam Sanders," said Leroy. "He's a promoter. Not just any . . . he's Billy Ray Jordan's promoter."

"Well Leroy, does he just send you presents and money like this for nothing?"

Leroy said, "He wants me to quit Roger and sign with him. God amighty, this is one beautiful guitar." He cradled it under his arm. It sat on his knee with a perfectly balanced weight. He hadn't realized how much he wanted it; but here it was, and he did. The Mighty Sam Sanders pushing buttons on every side. "He wants to meet you," said Leroy.

"I don't know who all you run around with these days," she said, stepping close. "Oh, I missed you, baby. It's so good to have you home." She embraced him again.

He sat her down and told her all the latest news: how many thousands of records, the *Billboard* review that called him a "potent new chanter"—whatever that was—the names and details of all the motels and restaurants and towns and shows he could remember.

His mother was happier than she seemed on the telephone. The new house had lifted her spirits.

He told her about the girl in Knoxville who fainted dead away when he walked into the hotel lobby. "Oh my stars," Agnes said, alarmed. Then he told how he'd knelt to see about her, the girl's eyes had fluttered open, and she'd murmured, "If you want to make me feel better, you could kiss me."

Agnes laughed. "Well, did you kiss her?"

He grinned. "You bet I did. Got her back on her feet in two seconds."

The next morning Leroy took the Oldsmobile and the four hundred dollars to McWhirter's used-car lot on Union and drove out in a cloud white 1951 Cadillac Eldorado.

He felt like some kind of prince. The windows moved up and down at the touch of a finger. He had driven this car in his dreams, waking and sleeping. He deserved this car. Money in his pocket, more on the way. His career was taking off like a big white jet airplane. In the Cadillac he glided soundlessly along the back streets, past his old haunts and addresses.

Agnes marveled over the car—"but, honey," she said, "you come home with a new one every day!" She got in on the passenger side; Ray climbed in back with Dodger. They waved to the neighbors and purred off.

Leroy drove to Murphy's Dairy Dream and ordered banana splits all around.

A group of teenage girls surrounded the car, squealing for autographs. Leroy got out. He was almost used to this now, but it was the first time for Ray and Agnes and Dodger.

They sat thunderstruck while he went through his movie star routine. "Where you girls from?" he said, leaning on the hood.

"Ooh, I'm from West Memphis, Leroy, I just love your records," said the cherry blonde in the poodle skirt. "I think you're the most."

"They sure grow you gals pretty over there," he said with a grin. The girl said ooh! and melted into the arms of her friends.

"Where you from, honey?" he said to a sweet-faced freckled girl with big round spectacles.

"I live right near your house, Leroy. Forty-three fifteen East Lake Drive. My big sister knew you at Humes. Janey Sue Kittrell."

"She wasn't half as good-lookin' as you," Leroy said. "What's the matter with your friend back there? Is she shy?"

The dark-haired girl in the curvy pink sweater peered over a shoulder. "I'm—I'm from North Carolina," she stammered. "I'm just here for a visit."

"Well that's okay, darlin'," said Leroy. "You oughta stick around awhile. We need more girls like you in Memphis." He scratched "Yours, Leroy" on the napkin and handed it back. The girl lit up as if he'd asked her out on a date.

The cherry blonde said, "Are those your parents? Ooh, I want their autographs, too!" The other girls giggled and handed pens and paper through the open windows.

Ray got right in the spirit of it, flirting back at them, inscribing "Ray Kirby, Leroys Dad" on their napkins and ring binder notebooks. Agnes smiled and added her name beneath his.

Dodger blushed and said she wouldn't have anything to do with such foolishness; why would anyone want her name on a paper? Leroy could tell that secretly she was as tickled as any of them.

35

*L*eroy stripped to his Jockey shorts and sat on his bed, softly strumming the new Gibson. It was the finest guitar anyone ever owned. No one else would ever play it; it said so in mother-of-pearl, right there on the neck. He pressed his fingers ever so slightly. The strings laid against the frets without the least tension. He moved his thumb. A flawless round tone came out.

Ray appeared in the door. "Hey, son."

"Daddy, how you doing."

"I'm all right, little tired. You practicing, huh?"

360

"Breaking in this guitar. I tell you, all of a sudden I'm a whole lot better picker than I was."

"Seem to me you were doing all right before."

"I sure put a lot of miles on the old Sound Star," said Leroy. "Think I'll leave it here when I go. It's about to come apart."

Ray lowered himself into the only chair not heaped with Leroy's clothes. "When you taking off, son?"

"Crack of dawn. We got to be to Jacksonville tomorrow evening. We're playing the Gator Bowl."

"Ain't that something?" Ray shook his head in wonder. "The Gator Bowl. Is it just you boys?"

"No, it's hooked in with the Billy Ray Jordan Jamboree," said Leroy. "There's thirty-one acts. We don't all play the same towns. Between Roger and Mr. Sanders, they got us running every which a way."

Ray said, "Son, I think we ought to talk for a minute."

Leroy sat back. What now? He never had heart-to-heart talks with his daddy. Surely Ray didn't need more money. Leroy was already sending half of everything he made. Some kind of lecture, probably, something about honor and duty, leading around to more money. "What you want to talk about?"

"Son, you're doing so good, and we're proud of you," Ray said all at once. "I hadn't told you that, but there it is. Now I said it."

"Thanks, Daddy." That couldn't be all.

"All that time you spent messing with your guitar . . . I'll be the first to admit it, I always thought you was wasting your time. I never in a million years thought it would turn out like this."

"Well, it ain't over yet, Daddy. I'm just getting started."

"Yeah, but look how far you've come already. And all the fine things—I hope you not stretching yourself too thin, trying to do for your mama and me, and your Caddy and all."

"I'm getting along," said Leroy. "There's enough to go around. Things looking better all the time."

"A lot of boys wouldn't do for their folks," Ray went on, "and I just want you to know I'm grateful."

Leroy squirmed. He loved making them proud, giving them things. But it made him a little uncomfortable for his daddy to go on about how proud he was. Something about it seemed the wrong way around.

"Son, seeing those girls, the way they flock around you ..." Ray swallowed, a weak smile. "Mighty pretty, some of 'em. I can't say I'd mind it so much."

"No sir, I watched you." Leroy stretched back on the bed. "You didn't mind it at all."

Ray said, "I expect it's like that for you now, most anywhere you go."

"More and more," said Leroy. "They go crazy at the shows, Daddy. You oughta see. Listen, while I'm thinking—I got tickets for you and Mama to come hear us in Little Rock, first of August. Sam will be there. He really wants to meet you."

Ray cut his eyes to the Gibson. "Yeah, I want to meet him, too, any man that's got money like that to throw around."

"Not throwing it around, Daddy. He's investing it."

"Well, I reckon." Ray scratched his head. "Son, you and me, you know, we never talk too much, you're gone so much. But I got to thinking—all those letters coming in, all them gals hitting on you, maybe there's some things we ought to go over."

Leroy couldn't contain his smile. "I think you're about three years too late on this speech, Daddy."

"What do you mean?"

"Aw, come on, I'm twenty, remember? I already know about—you know, sex and everything."

Ray said, "Everything?"

Leroy laughed out loud. "There's been one or two along the way that's given me trouble, but mostly it's a lot of lookin' and not touchin', if you know what I mean."

Ray reddened, glaring at the floor. "Now you know it's a man's part, to ... well, a man owes it to himself and to, you know, the girl, to have some kind of protection—just in case. Not that I'm saying you ought to be—" He caught sight of Leroy's face. "Hell, I'm not telling you anything, am I?"

"Nosir," said Leroy. "But it's nice of you to try."

"Sit there grinning at me like I'm some idiot. But I'm telling you, there's all kind of gals out there, and just because they talk sweet don't mean they all are. There's bound to be one or two agunnin' for you."

Leroy wished he could tell his father about Miss Waverly and the couple of near misses since, but anything he said was liable to get back to his mother. He didn't want her thinking he'd betrayed her. It wasn't a betrayal, exactly, but anyway, he couldn't trust his old man with the truth, and that was too bad.

He said, "Five o'clock comes early, Daddy."

Ray put his hands on his knees and stood up. He appeared glad it was over. "Good night, son. Take care of yourself."

"Good night." Leroy reached for the guitar.

He listened to the old man's footsteps treading down the thin carpet in the hall. After all these years Ray was reaching out and Leroy was the one pulling back. But it only made sense, Ray's sudden concern. Hadn't he always carried a healthy respect for the man with the money, whoever it was?

Leroy decided he liked it. More power. He was like a father to his own daddy now.

He glanced at the mirror.

The mirror said, You were bound to win. You got all the luck that was supposed to be his, and more besides.

Leroy dropped his eyes. He was ashamed of himself, twenty years old and still playing this game with the silvery voice. "I don't want to talk," he said.

Just listen. You can own the whole world. Trust Sam and work hard, work harder, keep going. Keep those checks and letters coming in.

"What if it all falls apart? What if they forget about me?"

They won't. Nobody could forget you. I'm watching out for you. I'm making sure.

36

*L*ong before dawn Leroy came out to the carport with his costumes and his guitar. "Morning, boys," he said. "Sure is early out here."

Jack and Tommy were busy inspecting the new Cadillac in the headlights of the Chevrolet. "You did it," breathed Tommy. "You went on and did it. It's fine, man. It's . . . Jesus, it's beautiful."

Jack ran his hand down the tailfin. "I want it. I can't stand it. It's not fair."

"You really like it?" Leroy opened the door. Their envy made him feel shiny inside. He said, "I traded the Olds and four hundred bucks for it."

"You did all right." Tommy stroked the hood. "Where you coming by all this new money, Lee? You holding out on us?"

"Right, sure," said Leroy. "Listen, we got a long way to go. One of you cats want to ride with me?"

"I will," said Jack, climbing in. "Man, I do hate your guts."

Tommy followed with the instruments in the Chevrolet.

Leroy's Cadillac swallowed the miles. Everything about this car was oversize, like his ambition. He never wanted to drive a car smaller than this. He and Jack sang along with the McGuire Sisters on "Something's Gotta Give."

They drove straight through the morning. Jack curled up in back and slept all the way to Georgia. Leroy entertained himself with the powerful radio, the rich red bounce of the seat, the purr of the gigantic V-8, the wide wheel in his hands. Flashing through these tiny South Alabama towns in a white Cadillac, he was a bolt of white lightning, automatic big news. Heads turned. Girls recognized him and honked and weaved all over the road.

He heard breathless announcements on stations in Dothan and Crestview and all the way down the panhandle—"Big show tonight, everybody's in a state of Lee-roy-citement! Stay tuned as the big Leroy ticket giveaway continues right here on the Voice of Milton. Meantime, here's his latest on the Rocking label, looks like another big hit, kids and kiddies, John Leroy Kirby with his new song, 'Let's Play.' "

Come on now
A-let me show you how
It's the difference 'tween night and day—
Baby let's play!

Leroy felt a million feet tall every time he heard one of his songs. He had seven songs now on three *Billboard* charts. He soared through the hot afternoon, savoring the music and his stardom and the stream of velvety cool air from the dash.

Jack woke up when the Tallahassee station played "Rockin' Saturday Night," and then, just as they reached the outskirts of Jacksonville, the

365

latest single—"Black Train," a hot lick lifted from an old Carter Family blues by way of Little Junior Parker and the Memphis producer Sam Phillips. Leroy thought it was the best record yet. Jack rapped the beat with his fingers on the dashboard.

The song had a hopped-up racy hillbilly feeling with a dark undercurrent, a clackety-clack like a train.... Leroy's voice went high and wavery, like the whistle. He carried the melody all over the place; he even yodeled a little at the very end and broke off the note in midair.

"Man, that sounds good on the radio," Jack said.

"It's really wild, that last verse," said Leroy. "Sounds like I was really mad at somebody, you know? Let's play it tonight."

Leroy was the headliner now, although the show was still called the Billy Ray Jordan Jamboree. (Billy Ray got a cut of the gate; he'd been happy enough to give up the big spot before intermission.) The Jamboree started in midafternoon with pickers and jugglers and hillbilly yodelers, progressing through small acts to the better-known names, Faron Young, Martha Carson, Jimmie Rodgers Show, and then at sunset—Leroy!

He couldn't wait. He felt juicy, knowing all those new girls were out there fixing themselves up for him. He counted on the girls to work him up to a fever. That was the way he had learned to outdo himself, night after night.

He tried to stay quiet and peaceful, inside himself, on the afternoon of a big show. It was hard to wait.

In his mind he was already onstage making the moves that would drive them crazy. He bent the microphone stand like a lover in a tango. He fell to one knee, stretching his hand toward them; they went crazy when he shook his leg or went into one of his spastic knee-jerking fits.

It drove them even crazier when he stood very still for most of a song, made them wait for it, beg for it; then he'd let himself be seized by one line and set in to flailing, possessed. That did it. That made them wild.

Give less. It makes them want more. Leroy didn't like to plan his moves too much—better to let it happen in the thrill of the moment.

He drove across a high bridge, up a wide boulevard. The Gator Bowl was a great man-made basin reclining in the bend of the river. On the edge of the vast parking lot, Leroy slowed to a stop. There were racks of floodlights on tall poles, thousands of cars in the lot.

366

Even from this distance he could see banners and painted legends on some of the cars:

LEROY OR BUST
LEROY I LUV YOU 4-EVER
LEROY'S MY BOY!!!

"Look what's waiting for us," he breathed.

"It's an army," said Jack.

There were hundreds, thousands of girls milling among the cars, wandering in and out through the stadium gates. They ignored the Jamboree, already in progress. They paraded around in a carnival of anticipation.

Leroy said, "Wall-to-wall."

Tommy pulled up. "Man, you have drawn 'em like flies!"

Jack said, "You know, we could drive over there and wade in and just take our pick."

"Plenty of time for that later." Leroy gazed over the wavering asphalt. This show would be different. He smelled something new in the air. Thousands of girls, now, not hundreds but thousands waiting just for him. He could hear their shrieks and giggles above the amplified twanging from the stadium.

This was power. This was his music, spread out over the radio, into the lives of these girls. He had touched every one of them some way. Maybe they just liked his picture in the paper; maybe they loved him enough to write one of those pink perfumed letters in the cardboard cartons at home. Maybe they dreamed about him every night.

Jack was right: They were an army. Leroy's army. They would buy his records until the day he stopped making records—if only he could keep touching them that particular way.

He got back in the Caddy. Tommy led the way around the stadium to the south entrance, where a policeman recognized Leroy and waved them on through. Stagehands came to hustle the gear through a concrete tunnel, into the Gator Bowl.

Leroy took his time in the dressing room, perfecting his hair, putting on his black linen slacks, the crisp white shirt with snap collar, the skinny silk tie, the gorgeous new cream yellow double-breasted jacket.

Tommy and Jack wandered in.

"Hey boys," he said, "come help me break in my new guitar."

Tommy's eyes widened. "Where'd you get that?"

"The folks. Early Christmas," he lied. "They were embarrassed how the old one looked."

They spent the next hour playing around, just the three of them ripping through songs and collapsing in laughter. It was good to be out of the car and making music just for themselves in a place where they could hear each other. Other performers stuck in their heads to wave hello, but no one interrupted the music.

The boys wandered off to find Cokes. Leroy went to the practice piano. He was learning to pick out the chords of old gospel songs. He would never be Ray Charles, but he sure loved the feel of the keys. He sang "Swing Low" to himself.

A man from the *Jacksonville Sun* arrived to take his picture—ten flashes, fifteen, twenty. Leroy posed with his guitar, with Tommy and Jack, with the mayor of Jacksonville. . . .

Two terrified fourteen-year-old girls crept in to present a certificate from the local chapter of the Leroy Kirby Fan Club.

Leroy said, "I'm sure lucky to have such good-looking fans down here." The girls blushed, giggled, and fled.

He was learning the ropes. He had only to say one thing to each person, and everyone went away satisfied.

A delegation from WFLO radio arrived with a plaque: WELCOME— LEROY KIRBY—JACKSONVILLE 1955. A reporter from the *Jacksonville News* appeared at his elbow. "Tell me—Leroy—how does it really feel to be famous?"

"Well sir," he said, "when I get famous, I'll let you know."

"Did you know there are some girls who camped out all night to be first in line for your show?" the man said.

"No sir, I sure didn't."

"What do you think about that?"

"Well sir, I hope they get in," Leroy said, to much laughter.

Somebody called, "That's enough, thank you all, let's clear out now and let 'em get ready"—Sam Sanders, looming tall in his fedora with the black feather in the band.

"Good to see you fellows," he said, rubbing his palms together as the room cleared. "Lord, I do love a sellout."

"Guys, you know Sam Sanders," said Leroy.

368

"How y'all doing?" Sam stayed where he was in the door. "You mind if I get a word with Leroy before the show?"

Tommy looked at Leroy.

Leroy shrugged.

Tommy said, "Sure, whatever you say. Come on, Jack, let's go tune up."

"Sure," said Jack, "we'll tune up." They walked out, aglow with suspicions.

"Sam, I have to live with those guys all the time," Leroy said.

"Never mind that. Have you thought about what I said? Did you talk to your folks?"

"Listen, it was your idea not to tell Tommy and Jack what was going on," Leroy protested. "If they didn't know something was up, they do now."

"Waaaal, I've been doing some talking for you," Sam said. "When I get the kind of money I'm hearing, those boys and Dan Tobias are gonna be happy to let you go. We'll put 'em all on easy street. And then it's our turn."

"What are you going to tell Billy Ray?"

"Let me worry about it," said Sanders. "He's a pussy. Does this mean you sayin' yes to me?"

Leroy thought a minute before he spoke. "I think Mama and Daddy will come to Little Rock," he said. "You talk to them; then we'll see."

We'll see. The nonanswer answer again.

Leroy knew that the minute he signed Sam's paper, other people would start to get hurt.

"That's fine, that's fine son, good work," Sam said. "Don't say another word. Here you go." He slipped one of his green cash triangles into Leroy's shirt pocket. "We're right on track. I'll take it from here. You just drive the gals crazy tonight."

"Listen, Sam—thanks for the guitar."

"It's nothing," Sam said. "It's a gift."

Leroy opened the door. Tommy and Jack stood waiting.

Tommy said, "Leroy, we thought we were all in this business together, so we don't care for all this big mystery behind closed doors, if you know what I mean."

"Come on in, guys." Leroy backed into the room. "Sam, I think the guys have a point."

"Sure they do," said Sam. "Come in, boys, come in. Shut the door there, Leroy. Now let's see. These boys are saying you all have a three-way deal, and they don't like being left out of the discussion. But see, my point is, these boys had better learn to appreciate what they got."

Leroy gasped. "Sam!"

"And they better get down on their knees and start praying it lasts." He pulled a cigar from his shirt pocket and stuck it in his mouth.

Tommy and Jack were speechless.

This man was a bulldozer. There was not a polite or subtle bone in him; but he knew what he wanted, and Leroy was beginning to think he just might get it.

He felt helpless, the way he felt when his mother told him what to do.

Tommy said, "Leroy, is he speaking for you?"

"No, Tommy." Leroy flopped on a chair. "He's speaking for him. He wants me to sign a deal with him, and I haven't made up my mind."

"Gee, thanks for telling us," said Jack.

"Look, guys, there's a lot going on." Leroy picked up his guitar. "For one thing, we've got a show to do."

Jack said, "Maybe you've got a show. . . ."

Tommy laid a hand on his arm. "Come on, Jack. It's our show, too."

Sam said, "We'll talk about it after the show."

Leroy opened the door to a crest of applause from the stadium, the last of the Wilburn Brothers and the first squeals from the girls who knew which act would come next.

Another crowd formed around Leroy in the little courtyard between the tunnel and the stage: a man from WROR asking questions, three or four photographers flashing their flashers, the local promoter, his wife, their twelve-year-old daughter with three thunderstruck friends, on and on.

Leroy switched on the polite automatic man. He smiled and signed and nodded and posed and said sir and ma'am.

Tommy and Jack stood to one side, tuning up.

Leroy knew that some vital thread had snapped in that dressing room, but he had not been the one to break it. He couldn't help what Sam Sanders said.

He would gladly play music with Tommy and Jack every night for the rest of his life if it worked out that way. If it didn't, it would not be his fault. He had to put his career in the hands of somebody who knew what to do with it.

"Excuse me, folks," he said to the assembly, "it's time for us to go to work. Boys?"

Jack nodded. Tommy's smile was grim.

Leroy slung his guitar around his neck. He took a deep breath. He liked to charge onto the stage and seize control from the very first instant.

He ran from the darkness backstage into the center of a whirlwind of bright flashing lights, a frenzied howling like wolves.

The sound knocked him off-balance. A shrieking to set hair on end, his own hair prickling up. A great flood of hot light, center stage. A microphone.

If there were eighteen thousand people in that great arc of faces, twelve thousand of them must have been teenage girls, screaming their heads off.

They were not squealing now. This was screaming, an edge of frantic delirium.

Jack lit up with his big goofy smile, backing up a step, staggered by the wall of noise. Tommy grinned all the way to the edge of his face. The backstage friction vaporized in that first atomic moment.

Leroy grabbed the microphone. "Hello friends," he said. He could not hear himself—like shouting into a ninety-mile-an-hour wind. He motioned for the sound men to turn up the monitors.

They fiddled and adjusted. He tried again, "Thank you, friends," but there weren't enough amps in Florida to drown out this racket.

He grinned at the boys and started tapping his foot, and a scream went up OOOOOHHHH like a car going over the top of a roller coaster. The uproar lightened enough so he could hear a moment of Tommy's guitar, and then Leroy was off and running on "You Better Look Out for Me."

It didn't really matter how he sounded since no one could hear him; but there were thirty-six thousand eyes on him, and he could sure give them something to see. No holding back, no teasing—not tonight! Not if they would scream like that for him!

I don't care a-what your mama says—

He didn't stand still a second. He would give them wild Leroy on every song.

He juked and bounded around, doing that seesaw thing with his arm, his leg tucked up, that drove them to jumping up and down, grabbing the air with their hands.

He dropped to one knee and leaped up and kept going. He couldn't hear himself. The girls near the stage reached out, screaming and crying and begging for him. He sneered. They loved it. They screamed in pain.

He slammed into "Let's Play." *Buh-buh-buh-b-b-b-bay-buhh!* The volume of the screaming never lessened, wave after wave of hysteria sweeping in like the winds of a storm. This was a new order of madness. Leroy controlled it with his little finger.

> *Come on now*
> *A-let me show you how*
> *It's the difference 'tween night and day—*
> *Bay!beh let's play!*

If he told them all to throw money at him, they would do it, and he would be killed by the shower of coins.

At last they had to stop screaming to breathe. Leroy hurried in with his little speech: "Thankyouvermuch, like to say we're glad to be here in Jacksonville, glad to see all you folks, thanks for coming down—now we'd like to do a new song for you—" The rest of his sentence was lost in the rising tide of screams.

The song was "Black Train," but the girls didn't know; all they knew was the fast-moving moments caused Leroy to leap and thrash about, and that made them scream.

Leroy teased them right to the edge of something perilous. He slowed it down, wiggled his leg, and brought the song around to its hot final chorus just to get them all going again. *I never met a girl who could move me like you do. . . .*

He was alive like nobody else in the world. He had them all hot and bothered and out of control wanting him, right there in front of their mamas and daddies and preachers and the Jacksonville cops. They were a sea of open mouths and love-crazed eyes and lust and longing and fear.

Leroy moved to make them think he wanted them: one of them, all

372

of them. He bumped out his hip. He shook his leg as if it was on fire. He brought down a deluge of screams.

He kicked off into "Rockin' Saturday Night," then "Lawdy Miss Clawdy," "Maybellene," "Hurtin' Time": *Well, I can feel it in-a my heart, ever since-a we broke apart—it's hurtin' time....* He couldn't hear more than a phrase now and then.

He didn't want to stop. He loved every one of these girls. He took a deep bow, turned halfway, bowed again, leaned to the microphone. "All right girls, good night!" he said, waving, starting off. "I'll see you all backstage!"

That was the wrong thing to say.

Somehow, in that great vale of noise, the girls heard him say it.

They took him at his word.

Nine of them jumped onstage and scrambled toward Leroy with their hands out, screaming.

A flood of girls poured up onto the stage behind them.

Leroy froze.

The first twenty rows of the Gator Bowl exploded in a mad rush of girls, hell-bent on getting at him.

Tommy and Jack scattered, wild-eyed.

An open corridor stood between Leroy and the dressing-room tunnel. He lobbed his guitar to a stagehand and bolted for cover.

The swarm came after.

One girl got a hand on him. Three girls blocked his way. He was trapped. He thought they might kill him. They were screeching now, screaming his name. A great surge of girls pushed in behind them, swirling around, yanking his hair.

Someone snatched off his necktie. Then the handkerchief. The jacket. Hands on him. An elbow jabbed. "Hey, stop! Hey that hurts!"

He smelled perfume and toothpaste and sweat. He tried lunging through—come on, red rover, come over, get out of my way!—but they screamed and pulled his hair, ripped at his shirt. He lost one of his shoes. Good God: fingers fumbling at his belt. If he didn't get away now, they would strip him naked, and then what?

"Sorry, girls," he yelled, throwing up his arm in a football block, closing his eyes, lunging forward, knocking the hell out of two of them. They toppled to the pavement. Someone grabbed the back of his shirt.

"Let me go!" He shoved hard. The shirt ripped down the back. Girls screamed in his ear.

He hurdled the fallen ones. He ran for his life.

The mob came howling after. He shoved a photographer out of his dressing-room door, jumped in, slammed the door, shot the bolt.

Pounding, screaming on the other side.

If they came through that door, he was gone. He looked wildly around for some way to prevent it.

He seized two metal chairs, propped them against the door. The riot grew louder, the banging and shouting.

He dragged a table from the opposite wall to reinforce his barricade. Hoarse male voices mixed in with the girls—the police?

He leaned against the table, gasping for air. His shirt, his new jacket in tatters. Blood from a cut on the chin. His watch was gone, and both shoes, his heart thudding. Beyond the door was bedlam.

He wanted to be a big star, the biggest goddamn star in the world, but he never imagined they would rip him apart. What kind of insanity had he started?

He shook his leg. He sang. He cut up and acted the fool. He sang racy songs and wiggled his pelvis.

The magic had always been brewing, steaming inside him, just waiting for the right set of girls to come along and explode. He was the same boy, but now the world had gone crazy around him.

A smile started down in the pit of Leroy's fear and grew, spreading out on his face.

This was not a usual night in Jacksonville, Florida.

Suddenly the pounding and screaming sounded like music to him. A riot of girls—think of the newspaper headlines! Billy Ray Jordan was probably eating his ruffled shirt right about . . . now.

Follow that, Billy Ray, old boy, Leroy thought. Follow *that*.

A cop hollered for Leroy to sit tight while they secured the area. In a minute or two the hubbub began to subside.

He pulled the furniture back to its former arrangement.

He opened the door an inch. In the corridor were ten or twelve cops, looking confused.

"Hey fellas," he said, "is it safe?"

A sergeant spoke up. "Mr. Kirby, we're going to escort you to your vehicle now. We've pretty well got it secured back there now. It was pretty hairy for a minute."

"Listen, I'm sorry to cause you all this trouble," said Leroy. "I've never seen 'em do that way before."

More cops filed into the corridor, followed by Tommy and Jack.

Leroy greeted them: "Looks like we started a riot."

Jack laughed, amazed. "My God, Lee, what happened? A pack of cats get you?"

"My new jacket . . ." He held up the tattered cream yellow remains. He was glad to see his Gibson clutched firmly in Tommy's hand. "Guess I shouldn't have opened my big mouth, huh, boys?"

A phalanx of cops led them through the belly of the stadium, outside, past a wall of chain link. Across the parking lot Leroy saw a horde of girls hemmed in by a line of cops.

He stepped around a corner to his car.

His new Cadillac. Ruined. The antenna and hood ornament snapped off. Lipstick smeared on the windshield, LEROY I LOVE YOU YRS FOREVER DOT. A web of scratches all over. Cupid hearts carved in the paint with keys and fingernail files. LK + ASL. DEBBIE LOU, SUSIE, YVONNE, MARY LYNN, ALICE, SALLY, BETTY.

These were his fans. They loved him. They wanted to make sure he knew.

Everyone was watching his face.

He grinned. He didn't want anyone to know how fast his heart was beating. "It's okay," he said, sliding behind the wheel. "It just means they like me."

37

*L*eroy drove the muti-
lated Cadillac straight to Memphis, to the old neighborhood, to Bubba
Hayes's run-down rented house on Georgia Street. He blew the horn.
Bubba lumbered across the yard, big and beer-bellied, cheerful as ever.

"Hey Frankie," he called, "I just got through reading about you!
Sounds like you had a hell of a time down in Florida."

Leroy stretched out of the car. Joints popped all the way down his
back. "Take a look at my car," he said.

"Yeah, I see. Man, they got to it, didn't they? Whoo! How you doin'?" Bubba slapped his shoulder and squatted to inspect the legends scratched in the paint. "I think you need a paint job."

"I think I need more than that," said Leroy.

"Aw, I'm crying for you, Frankie, I am," Bubba said. "Look at this! 'I love you Leroy, Wanda Faye.' 'Be mine.' 'Yours forever.' Here's a damn phone number!" He traced a message with his finger. "You ever, like, get to *meet* any of these girls?"

"I met up with about three hundred of 'em, night before last at the Gator Bowl," Leroy said. "They nearly tore me to pieces."

"Come in the house, son, I was just gonna open a beer," said Bubba.

"Just don't tell me how lucky I am," Leroy said. "I'm so sick of hearing it I could puke."

"Listen, I'm sorry." Bubba headed for the door. "That's some dangerous females, to get after your *car*."

Leroy trailed him inside. If he didn't have his music, he'd probably be living just like this: dirty underwear on the floor; a TV set flickering a boxing match; empty beer bottles everywhere; tacked-up bed sheets for curtains. It felt strange, after the unreal nights on the road, stepping into somebody's normal, everyday life.

He cleared shirts from a chair and sat down. "Bubba, you still work the same place?"

"Yeah, you'd think a high school education would be good for something better than the loading dock, but they need big guys. I'm big. I get paid." Bubba settled on the sagging couch, popped the cap off a Schlitz. "You want one?"

"No, thanks, not right now." Leroy had practiced his side of this conversation all the way from Jacksonville. "You like it down there?"

"One seventy-five an hour." Bubba took a long swig. "I could be happier. Why? You got a job?"

"I just might," Leroy said. "This thing in Jacksonville—man, it got to me. There were plenty of cops down there, but nobody was ready for what happened. I got scared. I'm not ashamed to tell you. I did. Those girls took over. I mean, they went out of control. They tore off my clothes, and they cut me here, see? I got bruises all over. I had to knock a couple of 'em down to keep from getting trampled to death. It's a wonder somebody didn't get hurt and throw my ass in jail or something."

"Yeah I see what you mean," Bubba said. "I guess it sounds a lot better when it's not happening to you."

"And it's not just the girls," Leroy said. "All of a sudden there's these jealous boyfriend types that want to take a swing at me."

Bubba grinned. "Man, I'm sorry." He held up his hands. "I know I promised. But this is just about the *nicest* problem I ever heard."

"Well, okay, now, you said it, that's once," Leroy said. "You want to find out for yourself? I need somebody to go around with me, keep those girls from killing me. You're big, and you're smart. And you're just about the oldest friend I got. I want you to do it. It'll be like the football team all over again."

Bubba sat forward. "You want me to keep a bunch of little girls off you? You mean, like a bodyguard?"

"Whatever you want to call it. You can check out the places, you know, work it out with the cops where I'm supposed to go. Besides keeping 'em off me."

"This is a paying job, right?"

"The minute you say yes, I'll talk to Sam Sanders," Leroy said. "I know we can do better than one seventy-five an hour. Come on, Bubba, I need you."

"I don't know," Bubba said. "You're gone off all the time. I got a girl or two myself around here, you know. What are they gonna do with themselves while I'm gone?"

"Well, I don't know about them," Leroy said, "but if you come out with us, you can have just as many crazy little girls as you want. You'll see."

"I think you just sold me, Frankie." Bubba's grin showed a happy gap in the middle. "When do I start?"

"Next show is Friday in Monroe, then back here, then I think it's Texas," said Leroy. "You can ride with me. Oh, listen, by the way. It's no big deal, but . . . it's not Frankie anymore. Just Leroy. Or Lee. I don't care."

Bubba's grin faded. "Sure, Leroy. Whatever you say."

Leroy stood up. "I'll call you tonight when I talk to Sam. And listen, Bubba. Thanks. You won't be sorry. We're gonna have a big time."

Leroy and Bubba were stretched on red sofas in the Razorback Suite of the Star-Lite Motor Lodge, ogling a naked picture of Marilyn Monroe in the new magazine *Playboy,* when Agnes and Ray walked in without knocking. Leroy jumped up, stashing the magazine under the couch. "Hey, Daddy, hey, Mama, we been looking for you all afternoon!"

He hugged them and made a big fuss. Bubba stood to one side, grinning.

"Your father wouldn't go more than forty-five miles an hour in the new car," Agnes said, taking off her hat. "I told him it would take us forever, and it did. Hello, Bubba. It's nice to see you."

"Hello, Miz Kirby," he said.

"It's so sweet of you to look out for Leroy like this," she said. "It helps me sleep better at night."

"Thank you, ma'am. . . ."

Leroy thought: She looks as if she hasn't slept in weeks. He glanced through the door. "Hey hey, check out that car! Hey, Daddy, that's slick." It was a real house on wheels, a pink and black '54 Ford with big curvy chrome bumpers.

"I can't get used to that big of a car," Ray said. "You know I drove that Plymouth so long."

The money had come from Sam Sanders for the sole purpose of bringing Agnes and Ray to Arkansas in style. He had mounted this visit like a military operation. "I want to make damn sure they like me," he said. He quizzed Leroy at length about Agnes's favorite colors and foods and radio stars, then fussed over every detail himself. He had some plan, some ace in the hole he was keeping a secret.

"Well, you picked out the car, Ray," Agnes was saying. "I can't believe you're afraid to drive it."

"Guess I'm gonna leave you-all to catch up." Bubba hastened for the door. "I got to find this deputy chief guy and see about those barricades."

Leroy followed him to the door. "Come get me in an hour," he muttered. "I may need rescuing."

"You got it, boss." Bubba headed off to his car.

Sam had embellished the Razorback Suite with floral arrangements, candy, a bottle of real champagne in a chrome ice bucket. Agnes stood with hands on her hips, looking around. "Would you look at all this."

"It's from Sam." Leroy lugged the suitcases over the threshold. "He's really excited to meet you."

"It looks like a circus in here," Agnes said, but she couldn't resist the open bowl of chocolate-covered cherries. "You know these are my favorite. And white roses ..."

"I know. He asked me what you'd like."

Ray tested the bed, stretched out. "This is right fancy, son. How much you reckon this costs for a night?"

The pink telephone rang. Leroy answered.

It was Sam in his command post, two doors away. "Okay for me to come over?"

"Sure," said Leroy, "come on."

Before Ray got up off the bed, the big man was in the room, shaking hands, saying, "Hello, God bless you, ma'am," to Agnes, and, "How are you, Mr. Kirby, good to finally meet," chatting and waving his hands with an animation Leroy had never seen.

His cigar stayed in his shirt pocket. For half an hour he perched on a tiny pink chair with a heart-shaped back, passing the time of day. He played it folksy and warm. You could see the showman's charm oozing out of him: a silk tongue, a smooth line. He asked about the drive up, the weather in Memphis. Not a word about business. He gave them special passes for their front-row seats at tonight's show, and oh by the way, he'd like to spend a few minutes with them on Sunday—he had worked up a special surprise. But that wasn't all: He had hired a car to take them to Little Rock's fanciest steakhouse for dinner tonight, while Leroy went to warm up for the show.

Agnes said, "That's real nice of you, Mr. Sanders," but her mouth made a skeptical line. She had not fallen yet.

〜〜〜

Bubba drove the repainted Cadillac. Leroy sat in back so he could lie down on the seat when the time came. Tommy and Jack and the drummer would travel to the Arkansas Coliseum in a separate car; nobody tried to get at them.

"Okay now," Bubba said, "let me give you the setup. It's a big indoor hall, seats I'd say about twenty thousand. We've got fifty Little Rock cops and a dozen deputy sheriffs, plus about twenty volunteers. They'll

380

be the ones in red hats. We're bringing you in through a tunnel. We'll drive right straight under so you'll never see anybody. The whole lower level is supposed to be secured."

Leroy fingered his shoelace. "How many are you putting in front of the stage?"

"Five," Bubba said. "We've got Jimmy and Kyle, and me, and two other guys that are supposed to meet me. I think we got this one nailed."

"Tell you, Bubba, it sure sounds like you do." Leroy had known Bubba would be the man for this job. One month, and he sounded like a Secret Service agent.

"You just gotta work it out ahead of time," he was saying. "There's nothing to it, really. That deputy chief did most of the work." He squared his shoulders and peered ahead through the windshield. "Ah-oh. Here we go. It's night-night time, Leroy." He checked the locks on the doors.

Ahead, in the bluish arc-vapor glow, a big crowd of girls surrounded the mouth of the sloping tunnel, which was guarded by ranks of police. "See you in a minute," Leroy said. He stretched on his back, pulled the white cotton blanket over his head. He felt a little silly.

He could hear the excited female babble through the window when Bubba rolled it down. "Hey, I'm Bubba Hayes, I think we're expected."

"Yes, sir, we'll try to clear you a path," said a reedy voice. "Okay, you girls need to move away, now, move back from the barriers, please! Please move away from the barriers and let this car through!"

Leroy smiled to himself. This is all for you, boy, this is all just for you.

He could tell by the sound that the car was surrounded; he could feel them peering in through the windows, through the blanket, X-ray eyes. Just as Bubba started to accelerate, a girl shrieked, "He's in there! He's in the back!" and a chorus of wild screams arose.

Girls surrounded the car, pounding on the windows. Leroy jerked the blanket from his face and sat up. Faces pressed to the glass, girls crying, pounding.

"Go, man, go!"

Bubba hit the pedal and roared into the tunnel, but the police line at the mouth had been breached. A wave of girls poured down the ramp, in pursuit.

"Jesus Christ!" Bubba glanced over his shoulder. "Jesus Christ!"

"We're okay," Leroy said, "we're okay—"

But then they reached the foot of the ramp, and there was nowhere to go. The horde swallowed them up, climbing on the hood, screaming and pounding. "Leroy! Leroy!"

"Stay in the car!" Bubba was shouting. "Let's just stay in the car until those guys get down here!"

Leroy knew the glass would give way any second. What do you want, girls? You want to tear me apart? Right now he should be in his dressing room singing a hymn, finding that quiet spot.

"We've gotta make a run for it!" he cried. "They're tearing up the car!"

Bubba looked around wildly. He was a good bodyguard, but he couldn't stop a hurricane. "Okay," he said. "Okay." He wriggled into the backseat, got on his knees by the door. "Okay, I'm gonna open it, and I'm going out, and you're going out right behind me," he said. "Don't stop. Don't close the door. Just go. Follow me. Okay—one, two, three—"

He kicked the door open, hurtled himself into the crowd. Leroy scrambled out hard on his heels. A great shrill cry burst from the girls. The sight of Leroy stepping out into their chaos stunned them just enough to give Bubba an opening.

Leroy stuck close. Bubba hunched over in his best fullback posture and opened a path through the wildness. They slammed through the door, through a line of struggling cops, and then they were around a corner and safe, in an empty hallway.

They bent over, breathing hard. "Jesus," said Bubba. "Now I can— now I can see what you mean. They're crazy! They're out of their minds! Look at your shirt!"

The left sleeve was ripped off and hanging. Part of the collar had come loose. Leroy grinned. "It's an old one of Daddy's. Tommy and Jack are bringing my costume with them. I told you, Bubba. I figured this thing out at the Gator Bowl."

"They can try to claw your eyes out, but you can't even hit 'em, you know?" Bubba said. "Jesus!" He ran off to help the cops save the Cadillac from the keys and lipstick.

Leroy straightened. The uproar echoed down the hall.

Sam Sanders came toward him with a big grin and a stack of eight-by-ten Leroy photos on his arm. "Hello, son!" he said. "Get your folks settled in all right?"

"Yeah, I did, but those girls just about settled me, just now." He held up the torn sleeve.

"Lots of 'em back there?" Sam looked pleased.

"Bubba's helping the cops get 'em off the car."

"Well, hang on a minute," Sam said, striding off for the ramp, "don't run 'em out yet! They'll want to buy pictures!"

Leroy found his dressing room. The local promoter had sent in a big spray of roses, an ice tub full of Cokes, a tray of cold cuts and cheese and sliced pickles.

Leroy made a big double-decker sandwich and carried it to the piano. He ate while he picked out the chords to "Home in the Valley." He considered how strange it was to spend half your life in the company of a hysterical mob, and the other half alone. There must be some kind of life in between.

He put on the hot pink shirt with pearl buttons, the pink black-cuffed trousers, the black gabardine jacket, white tie, white bucks, white belt. He wanted to look sharp. His mother hadn't seen him perform since the band shell at Overton Park.

Tommy and Jack came in slicked up and ready, along with D. D. Crosby, the new drummer. D.D. was a quiet, amiable fellow from Covington, Tennessee; he had strong shoulders and mild opinions. He laid down an unstoppable backbeat. He never even seemed to notice the hysteria onstage. He just banged away on his drums and looked happy to be there, wherever he was.

He fiddled with his drum set while the boys tuned up, ran through snatches of songs, wandered to stage right to await the introduction.

The announcer said, "Here he is, boys and girls, the one you've been waiting for—" and the screaming began.

Leroy ran into the light. He spotted Ray and Agnes in the first row, far left, behind a row of policemen.

He waved and made a special bow.

Then he grabbed the microphone and hollered *train traiiiiiiin* ... and forgot everything but the music.

He jittered and bumped, got them wild from the first. With the big Peavey monitors blaring in his face, he could actually hear Jack's bass and Tommy's guitar. Best of all, he could hear D.D. hammering hard on the skins; he couldn't lose the beat now, in all the commotion.

He banged into "Rockin' Saturday Night." He could see his mother over there, but he couldn't imagine what she might be thinking.

Well rock rock rock in the mornin'

"Tutti Frutti" and "Maybellene." No slow songs. Only short, hot, fast rocking songs. "If I Ever Hear Your Name." Keep them screaming the whole time. "You Better Look Out for Me" double time.

He let go with his leg and went skittering downstage.

The girls howled, broke from their seats, and surged into the open space between the stage and the first row. They clawed at the policemen and Bubba Hayes and other men trying to move them back.

Keep them screaming. That's what they want. "Leroy! Leroy!" Slam bam thank you girls, and good night!

He stood in the wing, breathing hard, waiting to go back on for the encore. He looked over to the first row, far left.

His mother was crying. His father's arm around her shoulder.

He ran on. Standard encore, two songs fast: "Hurtin' Time," "Shake, Rattle and Roll."

He ran off, handed the guitar to Bubba, shucked his sweaty coat. "Come on, let's go!" Bubba hustled him fast down the passageway to the ramp.

The Cadillac was pointed out, door open, motor running, guarded by a ring of police. Bubba jumped in the driver's seat, Leroy beside him. They roared up the tunnel and onto the street before the girls inside had a chance to stop screaming.

When they were clear of the coliseum, Leroy said "Bubba, Mama was crying."

"Oh, you know mothers," Bubba said. "Don't worry about it. Probably it just gets her to see how they carry on over you. My mother would tear out her hair."

"Sam's got somebody to get them to the motel, doesn't he?"

"You know he does."

"I hope she's okay. . . ."

Agnes and Ray arrived at the Star-Lite moments after Leroy and

Bubba. She was red-eyed, but she hugged him. "Honey, I'm so proud," she said. "I'm just so proud. I—I had no idea you could affect people that way."

"Thanks, Mama," he said, glowing inside.

Ray smiled and nodded and smiled.

"It's a wonderful gift," Agnes went on. "It tore my heart to see those girls, the way those girls looked at you! Leroy! Oh, it just tore my heart."

Ray popped the cork on the champagne. "Look here, folks, this wine comes from France. Now that's class. That's the best kind there is."

"Ray, how would you know," said Agnes.

"I'm not as dumb as you think, Miss High Hat."

"Well, I'm glad to hear that," she said. "That gives me comfort."

Leroy switched on the television. Ray poured the sparkly wine into three Dixie cups. They climbed onto the bed, propped themselves up with pillows. Leroy proposed a toast to the future. They dozed off watching cowboys shoot each other.

〜〜〜

The next morning Sam invited them all to his room for coffee and cinnamon rolls. When they'd eaten everything in sight, he sat back in his chair, his eyes aglitter. "Leroy, you and I need to go over a few things. Miz Kirby, I have a surprise for you. . . . Now, I don't expect you to take just my word on the fact that I'm an honest man, and I plan to do right by your boy. I talked to Leroy, trying to see if there was any friends of mine you'd especially like to meet, and he said there was."

Sam ambled to the connecting door and swept it open to reveal a small, wiry middle-aged man in a beautiful white cowboy hat, which he swept off his head and held over his heart. "Good morning," he said, stepping in. "Are you Agnes?"

Her mouth dropped open. "Good Lord," she cried, "Ray, look! Whitey Ford!"

The famous radio comedian took her hand and kissed it, as if that were the most natural thing in the world.

Agnes had always thrilled to his voice on the radio. She said he sounded like a real man and he had such a nice sense of humor, like Will Rogers, only southern.

"Sam has told me a lot about you, ma'am," he said. "I'm always proud to meet a good fan of mine, especially when she turns out to be so good-looking—how 'bout you, Leroy?"

"I'm the same way, Mr. Ford. Nice to see you again."

Agnes stared at her hand where he'd kissed it.

Ray shifted from one foot to the other, gawking at the famous man. Whitey Ford stuck out his hand and said, "You must be the father of this firecracker here. Mr. Kirby? Whitey Ford."

"Good to meet you, sir," Ray said. "Wife and I've listened to your carryin's-on a long time. She won't tell you, but you are her very favorite one on the radio. You surely are."

Sam was watching Agnes's face. "Leroy, why don't we run along and let everybody get to know each other." He led Leroy into the hall and shut the door softly behind them. "Bingo." His tiny eyes glittered behind the large tortoiseshell glasses. "I think we got her, boy, what you think?"

Leroy said, "She looked surprised. I don't know."

He followed Sam to the motel restaurant. They drank coffee for more than an hour while Whitey Ford explained to Agnes and Ray what a fine Christian, upstanding, God-fearing man Sam Sanders was, how much good he could do for their boy's career.

Sam had coached him well. They came out all smiles, like old bridge partners. Ray clapped Whitey on the shoulder. Agnes was laughing. She looked younger around the eyes. Leroy thought: Now she is falling.

Whitey Ford kissed her hand again and departed.

Sam herded them into the suite. He took the big chair himself.

"Like I was telling Whitey," Ray said, "I think you run a pretty smooth operation, Mr. Sanders."

"Why, thank you, Ray. I'm sure happy it worked out we all had a chance to get acquainted."

"Whitey seems to think you're a mighty fine man."

"Ray, hush now, you've done enough talking for a while." Agnes placed her purse on her knees. "Let's hear what Mr. Sanders here wants to tell us."

"Ma'am, I like the way you get down to business." Sam stretched his arthritic leg. "I have a management contract down in my room. I'd like for you-all to sign it. The contract says Leroy will do two hundred and forty performances for me at two hundred dollars a show for one year.

386

I take a straight twenty-five percent off the top. It's fair to everybody. If the money gets better, which I have a feeling it will, the boy stands to make a real good piece for himself." He spread his hands. "That's as plain as I can be."

No one said anything.

Leroy rolled over on the bed. "Well, Mama, what do you say?"

"I want to go home and think about it awhile," she said. "I can't think here with the roses and all the candy and—and Whitey Ford . . . I just don't know. There's something I don't like."

Sam said, "What don't you like, Miz Kirby?"

She looked him dead in the eye. "I'm not sure I like you, Mr. Sanders."

That sat him back in his chair.

Ray covered his face with one hand.

"I don't mean to be rude," she said, "but it strikes me funny that you'd go to all this much trouble to convince us to sign this piece of paper, when you say it's in our best interest anyway."

Leroy's heart dropped a beat. He admired his mother's courage in the face of Sam's all-out assault.

Instantly Sam recovered himself. "Ma'am, I know your boy is special to you. I've never met a young man in this business that's as close to his folks as Leroy is to you all. Reason I'm going to all this trouble is he's gonna make a big success of himself and I want to be there to help. Now I know we can't have a legal contract unless you all sign, but I also know that if you don't sign, we can wait till his birthday in January and do it without you."

"Don't you threaten me," Agnes said.

Ray said, "Aw, now, nobody's threatening anybody, sweetie!"

"Stay out of this, Ray!"

"Mama, don't get upset."

"Miz Kirby—"

Agnes stood up, eyes flashing. "I'm not signing anything," she said. "Ray, I'm going home. Pack our things and let's go. I will wait in the car."

"Mama . . ."

"Leroy, I don't want to talk about it right now. We'll be home tonight. You call me then." She closed her purse with a *snap!* "Mr.

Sanders, I suppose I ought to thank you for all you've done for Leroy. I expect you'll get your way before this is over. But that doesn't mean I have to approve it. His father can sign for us both. I won't do it. Ray, give me the keys."

"Sweetie, don't you think you're being a little bit—"

"Ray! Give me—the *keys!*"

He obeyed. She marched from the room.

Sanders got out of his chair. "My mistake. I'll go out right this minute and apologize."

"I don't think you better," said Leroy. "She's really mad." He moved to help his father with the bags. No use trying to tell her a thing. He knew that tone of voice.

Sam said, "Ray, let's hold on here a minute and think about this. She's right, you know, what she said. You can sign by yourself and it's one hundred percent legal. Why don't I run get that contract?"

"I don't know." Ray hefted a suitcase. "Maybe we ought to hold off. We'll see what she says when I get her home. Pleasure to meet you, Mr. Sanders. Really is. You been real neighborly."

They shook hands.

"Leroy, come out and kiss your mother good-bye," said Ray.

"I'll be right back. . . ." Leroy carried the bags to the steaming trunk of the Ford.

Agnes sat in the passenger side with her arms folded. Leroy leaned in to receive her kiss on the cheek. "Bye, Mama. Y'all be careful driving."

"Bye, sweetie. Don't you worry about a thing. It's just me. I had one of my feelings. I'm a silly old fool."

"No, you're not." Leroy straightened. "I'll call you tonight."

He waved at the big gleaming car creeping out of the lot. No wonder Ray drove it so timidly; it was twice the size of the old car. It swallowed them up.

Leroy went back inside. Sam puffed on his cigar. On the table by his elbow was a long typed document. A fountain pen lay open on top, its nib pointed at the dotted line.

Leroy thought: If you don't sign this, he will know you are truly your mama's boy.

He picked up the pen, scanned down the sheet to check one number— "25%"—and signed his name: John Leroy Kirby. "You know, Sam, I'll tell you the problem," he said. "The problem is, you and Mama think almost exactly alike. She saw you coming a mile away."

"She surely did." Sanders blew the ink dry, tucked the contract in his pocket, and smiled. "I'll send this to your father tomorrow. He'll sign it, won't he?"

"You might put in a little something extra for him," said Leroy. "She'll give him hell about it."

~~~~~

In Fort Smith the next night, when Tommy and Jack and D.D. came to the dressing room to tune up, Leroy told them he'd signed with Sam.

"You're all in, if you want to be, at least for a year," he said. "Sam's selling my recording contract with Dan anytime now, and we don't know what the new folks will do. He's going to try and take me national."

Tommy set his guitar down. "Go on."

"Well, that's about the size of it," Leroy said.

"What happens to Dan?"

"Dan's out. He'll get paid."

After a moment Jack said, "Congratulations," and put out his hand. Leroy shook. D. D. Crosby stepped forward. After their handshake Tommy had no choice.

From that moment Leroy was the boss.

He slapped Tommy's shoulder. "If we play our cards right, we can all make a lot of money in a hurry."

Tommy said, "I'll take what I can get, buddy boy. I was beginning to think you were gonna cut us out all the way."

"Hell, I need you guys." Leroy put on his guitar. "Come on. Let's go drive 'em up the wall."

38

~~~~~~~~~~~~~~~~~~~~~~~~

*L*eroy's hand sweated against the telephone. He had dreaded this conversation for weeks. He said, "You sure you're not mad?"

Dan Tobias said, "Don't worry about it, Leroy, thirty-five thousand dollars will buy a whole lot of recording tape."

"Well, you sound mad," said Leroy.

"Hell no," Dan said, "business is business. I don't think you need what I can give you anymore, kid. You're going all the way to the top. I plan to keep on with these guys starting out."

"Listen, Dan, I wish everything could just stay like it is." Leroy cradled the phone on his shoulder. "If it wasn't for you I'd be driving a truck."

"Son, do appreciate you taking the time to call before this thing hits the papers," Dan said, in a hurry. "You stop by when you're in town. I know Claudia'll want to see you. Gotta go now, okay?"

He was steamed. Leroy could tell. "Wait, Dan, hold on. Listen. We go way back. You don't have to pretend with me. Tell me what's on your mind."

"Aw, now, I don't think you want to know," Dan said. "Let's just leave it like it is, you know? No hard feelings."

"Let me at least try to explain."

"You don't have to. This ain't the first time it's happened. I know the whole song, my friend. RCA's the big time. Greener pastures. National distribution. You got to look out for your wallet."

"It's not just the money." Leroy twisted the telephone cord into knots. "The main thing is Roger Pate doesn't have the clout to get me anywhere. Sam Sanders does. If I want him to manage me, I have to take his advice."

"Sure you do," Dan said.

"And he says we have to go for a national contract. He says the time's now while the lightning is striking."

"He's right." Dan's voice was cold. "Listen, son, gotta go. Claudia's out for a week, got me running sideways here."

"Don't hang up while you're still mad," Leroy said. "You're my friend, and I want to keep it that way."

"That's great. Leroy, let me give you one piece of advice: Don't ever put too much expectation into any one person, you hear? You're always bound to wind up disappointed. Okay? Good-bye."

Dan hung up.

Leroy stared at the phone in his hand.

You'd think he had committed some terrible betrayal instead of doing what any smart person would have done, saying yes to a big fat RCA Victor recording contract.

"Good-bye, Dan," he said aloud, to himself. "Bye, Claudia." He could only imagine what she'd have to say about it. Claudia was loyal to Dan Tobias for life, and she'd never have a kind word for anyone who wasn't.

Of course, it was a betrayal. Why else had Leroy dreaded it so?

It was too easy. Cut your friends out of the picture, snip snip.

At least Dan didn't try to talk him out of it. No one could deny the sweetness of Sam Sanders's latest deal making, and Dan didn't try. Through a series of confrontations and maneuvers Leroy hadn't been able to follow, Sam had swapped the remaining months of the "Louisiana Hayride" contract for one big benefit show. Then he had jacked the price of Leroy's recording contract to sensational heights, with Mercury, Columbia, and Atlantic Records all jumping into the bidding. RCA Victor finally snapped for a cool green forty grand—thirty-five to Dan Tobias, five thousand in cash to Leroy as a bonus for signing.

He woke up one morning, and there it was, beaming down on him: the big big time.

He bought another Cadillac. Pink.

Three days before his twenty-first birthday, he drove it to Nashville for his first session at RCA. There hadn't been any public announcements, so he didn't need Bubba's protection for this trip. He kept the speedometer needle under sixty. His life was going so fine it would be just like God to step in and even things out with a wreck.

The radio brought the latest Ray Charles song fading in through the static—"A Fool for You," Ray's great churchly voice and his rhythmic piano, now asking a question, now tinkling a necklace of bones. A mournful horn section slogging along. Ray sang it cool at first; then he got hotter, hot as fire, a burned soul moaning in a great empty echoing church. *Reach over and feel the pillow-ohh, mm-hmmm, where y'baby used to lay. . . .* You could hear every scratch in his voice, every cigarette and lonely blind night of his life. He wailed without shame for his baby.

Some songs were born for the car radio. Ray Charles leaped from the speaker and spread his misery all over the Cadillac's shiny red leather upholstery. That great echo made him sound ten times as holy. Leroy felt lonesome and joyful and angry, at once.

Soon enough another song came on, but "A Fool for You" echoed in his head all the way to Nashville. If he could pack that much emotion into one song . . .

He drove past Ryman Auditorium. He smiled and kept driving.

RCA had rented studio space on the third floor of the Methodist Television, Radio, and Film Commission building. Leroy spotted the sign on the door: Nipper the Dog staring into his famous gramophone.

392

The secretaries in the front office stopped typing when he walked in. He started to introduce himself, but they swarmed around chattering, touching him, drinking him in.

The prettiest one was a long-limbed, wise-eyed brunette named Sheila. Leroy liked the way she stood back while the other girls fussed and flattered and posed for each others' Kodaks.

With a warm smile she drew him out of the stir he'd created, past the barnlike studio, down a hallway.

"You enjoy that, don't you?" she said. "Everyone grabbing at you all the time."

"I don't know." Leroy grinned. "Depends on who's doing the grabbing."

Steve Sholes got up with his hand out, booming hello and welcome. Now that RCA had landed Leroy in its net, Sholes was more jovial than ever. He rattled off the latest chart positions and press coverage and RCA's corporate pleasure at Leroy's impending debut on Jimmy and Tommy Dorsey's "Stage Show."

"You've never seen how we can move a record with a kick from coast-to-coast TV," Sholes said. "Now all we need is a record to move."

Leroy put a panatela slim between his teeth and scanned the session sheet. Tommy, Jack, and D.D. were there. That was good; Sholes liked what he heard on the master tapes he'd bought from Rocking Records.

The famous Chet Atkins would sit in on lead guitar, the famous Floyd Cramer on piano. The Speer Family was on call as backup singers, and also a quartet of Nashville studio singers, who were billing themselves as the Leroyals for the session.

"Mr. Sholes, I don't see how we can go wrong with all these fine people," said Leroy.

"I don't think we can. How much rehearsal time do you think you'll need?"

"Wellsir, I never have done much in the way of rehearsing. We just get in there with some songs and mess around till we get something we like. Sometimes it takes us all night."

Sholes said he had songwriters all over the place writing songs just for Leroy. "Connie Askey and Jimmy Langtree sent me one I want you to hear." He placed a demo on the turntable. "Tell me what you think."

The song lasted about a minute. A man shouted a blues lament, a plain imitation of Leroy's style. His baby has run off with another man. He is drowning in loneliness. So blue. A hot, sudden song of lost love and maybe death.

> *I walked a lonely highway*
> *A thousand miles for you*
> *But baby all the time I thought that you were lonely too*
> *Don't leave me this way, baby*
> *Don't leave me this blue*
> *You're breaking my heart*
> *You're breaking my heart—*
> *In two*

Leroy asked to hear it again.

The second time he knew just how it should sound. A higher key, so the first line rips open the silence—and faster, a heavy, sweaty Ray Charles echo on his voice, as much echo as the engineers could conjure up.

> *Well there's nothin' wrong with dying*
> *A lot of people do*
> *I know there's no more heartache in the place they take you to*
> *Don't leave me this waaaaay, baby....*

"Hey, that's *great*," he said. "Did they really write that for me?"

"It's got the word *blue* in it, doesn't it? Think you can sing it?"

"I can't wait, man. It's like the blues, you know, but it rocks! Is that all there is to it? It's pretty short."

"Four verses, but you can sing a verse twice," said Sholes.

They spent the afternoon sifting dozens of songs, sketching a rough outline for the session. Leroy signed a few papers, posed for photos beside a plaster Nipper. Sholes gave him a quick tour and sent him back to the front office. "See you tomorrow," he said, "and keep thinking 'number one hit.'"

Dark-haired Sheila was waiting for him at the water cooler. "How was your meeting?"

"I can't wait to get started," he said. "Everybody's real friendly here."

She held out a tiny paper cup of water. "Want a drink?"

"Uh, no, thanks, never touch the stuff."

"We don't keep anything stronger around here," she said. "You crazy musicians would never get any work done."

Leroy propped his hand on the wall and gave her one of his patented soulful looks. "I'm not like that."

"Really? What are you like?"

"I live with my folks," he said, "and I spend a lot of time working and driving. You want to have supper tonight?"

"I probably will," she said. "I usually do."

Leroy liked the way her eyes poked fun at him. "Well in that case," he said, "you want to have supper with me?"

"I don't know. What are we having?"

"Cheeseburgers?"

"Famous singing star, I think I'd expect something a little fancier than that."

"Oh well, maybe next time . . ." He turned, pretending to go.

"Wait, don't give up so soon," she said. "There's a place out near Vanderbilt where they serve Italian food."

"What's that, like pizza?"

"Spaghetti," she said.

"Oh. Well, I guess I could eat that."

"If you're sure it won't kill you." She smiled. "I'm working late. Pick me up out front at seven?"

"Sure thing." He strolled on out, acknowledging the smiles and waves of the front-office girls. They'd probably be shocked to know that Leroy the famous girl killer had just set up his very first date.

The teen magazines had him dating half the girls in America and planning to marry about one out of three. Why hadn't he tried this in high school, like everyone else?

He checked into a TraveLodge near Union Station and took a long, lazy shower, wasting all the hot water in Nashville. He scrubbed his teeth, toweled his hair, applied layers of pomade to darken it and make it shine. Sheila wasn't one of his starry-eyed teenage fans. He wanted to impress her. He rubbed Mennen under his arms, on his chest and neck. He pulled on his swell tan corduroys, the alpaca sweater that was his Christmas present from Ray and Agnes.

When he pulled up to the curb, she was waiting, fresh and smiling.

She may have been working late, but somehow she'd managed to change from her office girl getup to a full-skirted pale yellow dress.

Leroy climbed out to open the door for her—proper dating behavior, he supposed.

"This car sure is pink," she said.

"Yeah, I wanted it pink."

"I want you to know the girls at work hate me forever, starting this minute." She settled into the seat. "But I don't care. I'm going to have fun tonight."

"I noticed you didn't seem too impressed." He started the big V-8. "Which way am I going?"

"Turn right. Impressed about what?"

"Well, usually these days when I meet a girl," he said, "she either wants an autograph or some piece of my clothes."

"That must be awful for you." Her eyes mocked him. "Now right again, and keep going until I tell you."

"Don't get me wrong, I ain't complaining," he said. "It just makes it kind of hard to have a conversation when they're fainting on you."

"I promise not to faint." She struck a match to a cigarette. "Want one?"

"No thanks, I got this." He bit down on the ivory tip of his cigar. He felt very grown-up, driving this attractive young woman to her favorite restaurant. Italian food was supposed to be romantic. He wondered if Sheila was in the mood for some kissing.

Mama Luisa's was a tiny place with red and white tablecloths and candles in wine bottles. The headwaiter greeted them with an accent and menus written in Italian. Sheila ordered the something-something with something sauce; it rolled right off her tongue.

Leroy said, "I'll take spaghetti."

He kept glancing across the table, thinking how pretty Sheila was, how he'd like to marry a girl like that someday—a girl who could make him look better just by sitting across a table from him.

The spaghetti was wonderful. Sheila told him all about the studio, the tangled love lives of the front-office girls. Leroy spun out a little fantasy: He was just another guy, working a job, married to this swell girl, watching Lucy and Ricky on TV. . . .

A middle-aged woman appeared from nowhere. "I'm so sorry to bother you," she said, "but my daughter Elizabeth is such a big fan of yours, I wondered if you would . . ." She held out a creased piece of paper and a ballpoint pen. "It's for her birthday. I want you to write something kind of lovey-dovey . . . you know, kind of a joke."

Sheila smiled at Leroy's embarrassment. "Go ahead," she said. "I'll tell you what to put. 'To Elizabeth' . . ."

Leroy wrote "To Elizabeth." "Okay, what else?"

" 'I will always love you. Forever, Leroy.' "

Leroy grinned and wrote it just like that.

The woman thanked him lavishly and disappeared.

Sheila said, "You were sweet to her. I'm so glad you're not like some of these famous people. I heard James Dean liked to scare old ladies by pretending he was going to run them down with his car."

"He was great," Leroy said. "I love it in *Rebel Without a Cause* where they pull out the knives; you never know who's gonna get it, and then wham! Ugh!" He faked being stabbed in the gut.

Sheila folded her napkin. "Some people think he's a bad influence."

"So am I," said Leroy. "I reckon that's why I like him."

She reached across to squeeze his hand. "You're a terrible influence on me, I know that," she whispered.

"Oh, yeah?" He could feel it: the rising—his hopes and the heat in the restaurant, rising together. This was his best chance in a long time. He was famous, good-looking, about to be rich, and all on his own in Nashville. He barely knew Sheila, but she was a wonderful girl. "I'm glad we ran into each other."

"Well, I have a confession to make," she said. "I was lying in wait for you at the water fountain." She wore the laziest smile; maybe it was the effect of two glasses of wine, or maybe Leroy's warm feelings were working their way over to her.

He paid the bill. They held hands, walking to the car. He wondered if he should make his move right here in the Cadillac on this darkened side street. He couldn't ask a nice girl to go to a motel.

But Sheila said, "Where are you staying?" so maybe she was not too nice for that after all.

"Some motel on the main drag. I forget what it's called; you know, they all start to run together after a while." He swallowed hard. "Do you want to go there?"

"I don't know." She stared ahead through the windshield. "I'm sure it would be a mistake, and we would be sorry."

"Maybe not." Leroy started the engine. "Maybe we would be glad."

She didn't give any directions. Leroy found his way back to the TraveLodge by instinct. He didn't know anywhere else to go. He parked in back.

"You're awful cute," she said in a small voice. "I bet you do this six nights a week."

"You'd be surprised. Hardly ever." He didn't know if it was smart to admit that, but there it was, the truth. "I don't really have time to meet anybody. We're always moving too fast." He touched her arm. "I think you're nice, too. Want to come up and see the room?"

"Maybe for a little while. I can't stay."

He went around to open her door. When she stood up, he kissed her. She tasted like cigarettes and wine. He kissed her again. He liked kissing her there among the cars in the parking lot.

"Mm, you lied," she said, drawing back. "You've had plenty of practice."

"No, it's just natural talent." He led the way upstairs, digging for the key. He wished it were a better room. The green curtains smelled funny, and there was nowhere to sit but one spindly chair and the bed.

He wasn't sure how to proceed. His only experience was Miss Waverly and some slow dances in roadhouses that never amounted to anything. The big roaring subject was filling the room, but neither of them had acknowledged it yet. He supposed it was up to him to go first.

He went to the bed. "Come here," he said, patting the mattress. "It's okay."

She did.

He put his arm around her.

"You're nicer than I thought, Leroy. I thought you were supposed to be such a bad boy."

"I am," he said, kissing her. He felt tension that hadn't been there before. Maybe the wine was wearing off. He should do something to help her relax. He remembered what Tommy told him about smoke weed, the sexy effect it had on women. "Let me ask you something," he said. "Did you ever, like, smoke any, uhm, marijuana?"

Her eyes widened. "Gosh, no, Leroy, do you do that? I've never even seen any."

"There's this guy that gives it to me," he said. "All the colored musicians use it. I've got some if you want to try it."

She shook her head. "I—I think I'd be afraid. I might go out of my head. Wasn't that what got Robert Mitchum in all that trouble?"

Leroy cleared his throat. "Maybe I should turn off that lamp. It's kind of bright."

She said, "That's a good idea."

He snapped it off. A faint radiance of streetlights leaked in around the curtain, with the traffic noise. He would have to proceed just as he was, with only his lips to show him the way.

Sheila put her arms around him. Everywhere she touched him, he tingled. He kissed her.

"Oh, you are a bad boy," she said.

"You taste good." Leroy's tongue toyed with hers. His fingers began to explore the buttons of her dress. In the dark she could be anyone. She was warm. She kissed him, stretched against him. They kissed and kissed.

"Do you have a boyfriend?" he said, coming up for air.

"Shh . . ." She pulled him down.

The dress worked down around her shoulders. He nuzzled in at her throat, making little licks down the plane of her shoulder, and lower, and then his chin was grazing her breast; he kissed it.

"Oh Leroy," she said. "Oh, me."

And her sigh was a signal that he could do more, that she wanted out of the dress. He helped her. A flash of white underpants in the dark. That made him hard.

She said, "Take your clothes off. I want to see you."

He didn't make a sound. He liked hearing her whimper when he touched her. He was no longer feeling the great breathless throb that had rushed over him when he realized what was going to happen. He was clear in his mind; he wanted to remember every moment of this.

He yanked his shirt over his head, wriggled out of his pants.

"Take off your little underwear," she said with a giggle.

He stood up on the bed, towering over her. He pulled his Jockey shorts down and off. "Tarzan, lord of the jungle," he said, thumping his chest.

He fell on her, laughing. She was so warm and smooth in his arms, so willing and warm flowing around him like a skin that had been invented for him.

He tugged at her underpants and thought about Miss Waverly and a redhead in the audience in Port Arthur, Texas, and girls everywhere. Now he was doing it. Look at him. This was nicer than any of those times.

Her knees came apart. She pushed against him. She laughed and rolled over. Her hair swung down in his face.

He took time. When he discovered something she liked, he did it that way again and again. She wrapped her long legs all around him. She swallowed him up.

Then he got serious and started to work on it, working and working and moving ahead to a light he saw shining just ahead of him, waiting to burst in a million bright stars. She was crying his name. The light came to shine. He smelled her. Her name was Sheila. He was in Nashville. The walls blew out of the room.

He lay panting, still there, still inside. He loved her. At that moment he loved her. The only two people in the world were right here, joined together forever.

He kissed her. She made that soft musical sigh. "Oh, you're a dream," she said, "this is a dream."

"No, baby, this is real life." He wished he could lie here forever, twitching and glowing.

But Sheila grew restless after a minute. "Let me up. I've got to go."

"Stay here. I'll take you home in the morning."

"Oh no sir, Mr. Kirby. I may be this kind of girl, but I'm not *that* kind of girl. My roommate would be scandalized."

"You're nice, Sheila." He tightened his grip. "Just about the nicest girl ever."

"Let me up. I want a cigarette."

He rolled over, flat on the sheet with his butt in the air. Two minutes before, he had been a hot golden place, and here he was naked and alone on the bed.

He snapped on the lamp.

Sheila came back from the bathroom with a towel around her and a lit cigarette in her hand.

"Take the towel off," Leroy said. "It's my turn to look at you."

She drew it tighter around her. "Why?"

"I don't get much chance to look at a girl as pretty as you with no clothes on. That's all."

"I think you better call a taxi," she said.

400

"I won't let you go." He smiled. "No chance. Sorry. You're trapped. I just met you." He wriggled forward on the cool sheet. "Come on back to bed, Sheila. I want to do that again."

"I can't."

"Why?"

"I'm afraid of you, Leroy." Her eyes were cool, almost clinical. "You just needed somebody tonight. I was ready and willing. That's all. Now I'll fall in love with you, and you'll go off to some other town."

"I'll be back," he said. "I'm always coming in and out of Nashville."

"That's good." She stubbed out her cigarette.

Leroy jumped from the bed, snatched the towel away. Sheila squealed. He snapped it in the air, crack! and flung it away. "Now you can't leave!" he crowed. "Now you're as nekkid as me!" He flung his arms around her. They toppled to the disheveled bed. She giggled and pretended to resist.

"Oh yeah? You wanna play rough?" He made a Jimmy Cagney grimace, pinning her arms back. "Don't fight me, baby." He planted a kiss on her lovely creamy throat. "Don't fight me. I'm dangerous when I don't get my way." He kissed the velvet skin in the cleft of her breasts.

"No!" She giggled, tossing her head side to side. "Oh please no, no, you brute!"

He kissed her stomach. He put the point of his tongue in her navel, and that drove her nuts.

He did it some more.

"I warned you," he growled, scratching her with the day's beard on his cheek.

"Come here, you devil." She drew him up by the shoulders. He loved the way her body melted into his; they'd been designed to fit together.

She forgot about leaving. She did a thing with her hand. He kissed her, again and again. They rolled all over the bed, kissing and tasting, murmuring encouragement to each other.

Leroy raised up on one knee to go at it, really go at it; she liked him growling, holding her in place with his hands.

It lasted a long time. Leroy studied her face. The passion made her even more beautiful. She clenched her jaw and winced as if the pleasure were causing her pain.

Oh, the feelings were so close together.

They were alone. The world stopped at the walls of this room. There was only this time and a bed and two bodies; Leroy had never had someone to fondle and tickle and stroke and squeeze and kiss and lick and nibble and press down against with all his strength, oh and she didn't break. Sheila was soft everywhere, and strong underneath, strong enough to flip him on his back and hold him there while she did what she wanted to do.

He wanted it, too.

They reached that sweet hot place in a moment of wild crying out.

She collapsed on his chest. They lay together a long time, taking in air and the smell of each other.

He was shaken and shivered and bent to the very last muscle, and wrung out, and spread out to dry.

"Oh Leroy," she said, "you're gonna spoil me."

"You need spoiling." He yawned, tickling her arm with his fingers.

"I tell you what," she said.

"What?"

"If you promise you won't tell anybody—"

"I won't tell."

Her eyes flashed. "I think I'd like to try a little of that—of that stuff."

He grinned. "Sure you do," he said. "You'll like it. I promise." He scooted out of bed for his shaving kit, the crumpled Chesterfield packet with the skinny cigarettes tucked inside. After scouting the drawers for matches, he lit one up and settled, cross-legged and naked, on the bed. "My friend Tommy says it makes you feel sexy," he said. "I hadn't smoked it enough to know. But I like it. It makes me feel kind of smiley inside."

Sheila was used to cigarette smoke, so she was able to hold it in without coughing. Leroy showed her how; he felt like an evil opium dealer corrupting this lovely girl with soft white breasts that trembled when she laughed.

She kept saying the weed wasn't doing anything to her, but then she got started giggling and biting his ear with her tongue and cooing.

Leroy's head expanded. He felt empty and cool and endless.

He floated off in a wonderful dream, a warm girl in his bed, doing unimaginable things to his soft, hard, helpless body.

Think of all the nights he'd missed, being a good boy. There was no future in that.

39

$\mathcal{L}$eroy got on the elevator with a bunch of Methodist youths headed up for the broadcast of "The Methodist Youth Hour." They wore crew cuts, sport coats, and neckties. They looked at Leroy with his fancy guitar and cowboy boots, his tight pink pants and lightning bolt shirt. They drew back as if they'd stepped into the elevator with the devil.

"Don't be scared," Leroy said. "It ain't catching."

The youths got off in a scramble on the second floor.

Leroy rode up to three. RCA's front office was empty; they'd all gone home at five o'clock. He stopped at Sheila's desk to leave a note: "To Sheila. I will always love you. Forever, J. L. K."

He heard the sound of a guitar floating down the hall, as sharp and distinctive as a voice. It was Chet Atkins, doing little frog-handed runs and trills, showing off.

Leroy bought a Coca-Cola and tipped it back.

Sheila came out of the ladies' room. The sight of Leroy made her catch her breath and raise her hand to her mouth. "Oh, you startled me. I thought I'd be gone by the time you got here."

He stood there grinning. He couldn't think what to say. "I left you a note," he said finally, tilting his head in that direction.

Sheila was blushing, just as she had blushed when Leroy kissed her in his car in front of her apartment house, early this morning. She glanced both ways to see if anyone was listening. "I told the girls we didn't get along and you dropped me off early," she said. "I don't want them to know."

"Don't worry," said Leroy. "Our secret." He looked down to hide his own embarrassment. "You like my new boots?"

"They're beautiful," Sheila said, "and your pants are as pink as your car. You look great."

"Gotta make this record, so I figured I should look sporty. You want to go get some cheeseburgers when we're done?"

"No, I can't." She glanced at the floor. "We can't go out anymore, Leroy. I'm sorry. It's my fault."

"What's wrong?"

"Nothing, it was—it was, oh, it was nice. Remember when I said you'd spoil me? What I meant was, you'd ruin me. You would."

"I didn't ask if you wanted to get married and have kids," he said. "Just—I wanted to see you again."

"No, I don't think so," she said, turning away. "You're sweet. But I just know I'd get hurt."

He dropped his voice to a murmur. "I wouldn't hurt you, Sheila," he said. "Did that hurt you last night?"

Her eyes brimmed. "Don't do this," she said. "Go make your record. I have to go." She grabbed her coat from a chair and hurried up the hall, swirling it around her shoulders.

Leroy thought: Well, good-bye. Thank you ma'am.

He drank the rest of his Coke, remembering her sweet smile when she woke up on the pillow beside him.

He wandered into the studio.

Chet Atkins kept on with the tune he was playing. "You know this one?"

" 'I Really Don't Want to Know,' that's Eddy Arnold," said Leroy.

"That's right. You as good as Eddy Arnold?"

Leroy grinned. "I hope I get as rich as Eddy Arnold."

Chet Atkins smiled. "You'll be all right."

The high ceiling was festooned with black fabric baffles. Leroy picked his way through the jumble of mikes and chairs and black boxes to the door of the control room. Two engineers looked up from the panel.

"I sure hope you guys can make a lot of echo with all this gear," he said.

The one in the sweatshirt said, "There's a stairwell back yonder that makes one hell of an echo chamber."

"Well, set me up a mike back there, would you? I'm doing one song that needs one hell of an echo."

"You got it."

Sam Sanders arrived with his assistant, Tim Drexel, then Tommy and Jack and D.D.—everybody was friends now.

Leroy went back to Steve Sholes's office. He didn't want the producer to think he was pushy, his first time out. "Hey, Mr. Sholes, I hope you don't mind," he said, "I told 'em to set me up a mike back yonder on the stairs. I keep hearing a big echo on that song 'You're Breaking My Heart.' "

"You like that?" said Sholes.

"Man, I can't get it out of my mind," he said. "I hear it just the way it ought to sound."

"Come on in and let's give it a shot." Sholes led the way into the large open room. "Everybody here? Like to welcome all y'all to RCA, specially those who're with us for the first time, Leroy, good to have you. Let's get on and make some big music."

Sanders and Drexel took chairs at the back of the control room, out of the way.

Leroy loosened up with "Home in the Valley" at the piano while everyone found his place and tuned his instrument and did what he had to do. The room was full of talented musicians, so Leroy could concentrate on his singing. All week he had aimed himself at this session—extra sleep, good eating—and then last night Sheila had taken him to a new kind of thrill. . . .

He felt hot and ready.

First they glided into "I Got a Woman," a Ray Charles song with a party beat set against a great gospel melody line. Chet and Floyd Cramer caught on at once, filling out the sound that Leroy and Tommy and Jack and D.D. had hammered out all those nights on the road.

"Leroy, I tell you, that's all right," Sholes said on the PA, "but let's see if you can't soften it up a little. I don't mean sing it softer. But sweeter. Not so much like she's your *womun,* you know? She's your little old gal. Your sweetie."

Leroy grinned. "I don't know, Steve, the song ain't called 'I Got a Sweetie.' "

"Well, try it that way, and let's see."

Leroy lightened it up for him, softened the edges, and the song fell together just right, four quick takes. *I got a woman way over town—she's a-good to me . . . wo, yeah!*

They took a break. Steve played the demo of "You're Breaking My Heart."

"There ain't a thing sweet about this one," said Leroy.

"You go on back in your stairwell," Steve said. "Let's try it a time or two, see what we've got."

The stair landing was behind the band and off to one side; Leroy had a good angle to watch D.D.'s arm for the downbeat. He checked out the echo: "Well, I walked a—weeeeeeell—I walked a lonely—" The sound man was right; this was better than any control panel echo. Like shouting into a hollow barrel three stories high.

Leroy hummed a bit, "testing, testing, well, I walked a lonely highway—Mr. Sholes, how's that sound in there?—a thousand miles for you, a million miles for you—you like million better than thousand there? A million miles for you . . . man, this sounds great back here."

Sholes said, "Hold on a minute. We got some fixing to do."

Leroy studied the sheet in his hand. He felt odd standing apart from the band, but maybe that was right for a song about a lonely highway.

"Okay, whenever you're ready," said Sholes.

406

Chet and Tommy squared off with electric guitars, playing counter-point to Leroy's bluesy warming-up crooning of the song. D.D. punctuated the downbeats with sharp hits on the drums. Jack thumbed a cool beat down the spine of his bass—so cool that Steve Sholes came out to move him closer to the mike.

"Jack, that's great," he said. "Now we gotta make it simple, fellows. There's two things in this song: Leroy, and Jack's bass line. D.D., you sit this one out. Everybody sit out the first verse but Jack. Then, Floyd, you come in with just that rinky-tink thing, just a little—ya-na-na, ya-na-na—and you guitar boys, you just hit the accents." Sholes stood around, showing them just how he wanted it, stripping the song to its bones. "Leroy, now give us some more," he said. "Don't hold back. Shout it out."

This song didn't need a beginning. The songwriters had packed a sad story into just a few words. Leroy hollered into the silence, *Well I walked a lonely highway*

The boys came back with duh-dunh!

A million miles for you

Duh-dunh!

Leroy came right down on it. *But, baby, all the time I thought that you were lonely, too. . . .* The guitars spread out and went for separate walks down the same cool street, ending up back in the same place.

Tommy and Chet worked out a guitar break, jangling notes against each other while Floyd Cramer made bright little splashes of sound at the top of the keyboard. It all came back together at the end with Jack's descending run and the final suspended twang-twannnng!

"That's good," said Sholes. "That is good. Let's try it again."

On every take Leroy reached inside himself for a more desperate feeling. He thought about a lonely man standing by the highway, waiting for the girl who will never come.

This song was a whole new style, all by itself. Leroy squeezed the last trace of hillbilly from his voice. He remembered Ray Charles crying alone in his personal darkness, just Ray and his piano shouting and wailing the way you weren't supposed to wail on records—only in church or late at night into your pillow. . . . *don't leave me this-a way, a-bay*-beh! *Don't leave me this a-blue....* Leroy wasn't blind, and he wasn't black, so maybe he didn't have any right to shout the blues; but he stood on that landing and shouted anyway. ... *you're breaking my heart in two!*

At the end of the song he was down on one knee, out of breath, the microphone jammed against his lips.

He recovered himself and went back in the studio. Everybody was grinning at him.

Chet Atkins said, "That's a hit."

"Man, alive!" said Steve Sholes, behind the glass. "Leroy, you shot out the lights! Come in here and listen to this!"

Sam just smiled.

"Boy got a little worked up on that one, didn't you, Lee?" Tommy pointed. "Turn around."

"What?" He turned to look down his back. The seam of his pink pants was split all the way, the white of his Jockey shorts peeping through.

"There he goes showing his ass again," Jack said. "Look behind you, Leroy, there's my suitcase. Grab a pair of my jeans."

Everyone laughed and made lurid remarks while Leroy performed a quick change.

Then they went back in and made two more hits.

40

―――――――

 *T*he Cadillac limousine
shot from the tunnel onto one of the suspension bridges Leroy had seen
from the air. His heart went faster. All the tall buildings in the world
were lined up in his left-hand window, a wall of brick and steel blocking
one whole side of the sky.

Oh, if Agnes could see him: *Boy's in high cotton now....*

The limousine rolled down the river on an elevated highway and
plunged off into the skyscraper district, where the buildings crowded
out the weak winter sun.

The driver raced through crowded streets, bounding over ruts, speeding up whenever a pedestrian dared to cross his path. Taxicabs honked and swerved past in breathtaking near-collisions. Leroy held on to the seat with both hands. He'd never seen anyone drive like this. He loved it. He feared for his life.

The driver screeched to a stop. "Dis is it." Leroy shook his hand, thanked him, gave him a five-dollar bill.

A man in a red uniform opened the door. "Welcome to the Warwick, Mr. Kirby."

The trip from the curb to the room involved five men in red uniforms, three front-desk ladies, and the hotel manager. They ushered Leroy to the Staffordshire Suite with a great deal of fanfare, considering it was no bigger than two connected rooms at the Al-Ida Motel.

The minute he was alone and opened the suitcase to hang up his clothes, the telephone rang.

"They get you settled in, son?" Sam Sanders, of course. Sam was everywhere, like radio waves. He seemed to know Leroy's every move at the moment it was made.

"Hey, Sam. That was mighty fine, flying on that plane. I want to do some more of that."

"You will, son. Now I've just been talking to Drexel. Got your new schedule when you want to take a look."

"I thought I'd get a shower first maybe."

"Fine, I'll send it down with a bellhop. When you're done, come up here, and we'll go find something to eat. I'm in eighteen-oh-eight. We got a six o'clock with the *Herald Tribune*."

Leroy said "okay" and "mm-hmm" and wrote it down. He had imagined himself on his own, his first night in the big city, but no chance of that; when Sam had promised to take over his life, he meant what he said.

This life was one endless whirling tornado of concerts and recording dates and photo sessions and interviews and hotel rooms, sanitized for Leroy's protection. He could not slow down. In advance of "You're Breaking My Heart," RCA had reissued all the old singles from Rocking Records; they were hits all over again. Leroy's live appearances sold out hours after they were announced.

He was afraid that if he stopped to wonder *why*—*why* is this happening to *me?*—the whole circus might fold up its tents and load up the

410

train and roll out of town in the middle of the night, while he wasn't looking.

Why *not* him? Good things happen to people who want it bad enough. Leroy was good-looking and talented. He tried to be good. He wanted it bad. He worked hard. He deserved it. He'd spent his whole life being poor, poor, poor, his family always one step ahead of the landlord, always wanting things they couldn't afford. He wanted to pile up a big pile of money and climb up to the top, and sit there, and laugh at the world.

He didn't have time anymore to think about what he would do onstage. He just got up there and let the songs and the moves come rocking out of him. Life onstage seemed more real than the crowded blur of highways and dressing rooms and coffee shops, between times, when Sam was in charge. Under the spotlights Leroy controlled everything.

The screaming hit him every time like a bolt of the strongest hot coffee. It got his heart pumping, woke up his head, set him jittering in ways he could not control.

He wondered how it would be to perform in this big, cold city, where the girls didn't know him yet.

Sam got impatient and came to get him. They walked down the block to a delicatessen.

The waiters were rude. Leroy didn't recognize anything on the menu except sandwiches. He ordered a foot-long submarine and a Coke and ate in a hurry like everyone else in the place. Nobody recognized him. "Did you ever see so many yellow taxis in your life?" he said, gazing out to the street. "I bet you could make good money with a car dealership up here. These folks need cars."

"After the *Herald Tribune* it's a guy from the RCA office," Sam was saying, "and three phoners in my room with those Florida stations, and then we go to the Plaza to meet the Dorseys."

"Uh-huh . . ."

"Leroy, would you pay attention?"

He rolled his eyes. "Okay, Mom."

. "You want to make a good impression on these Dorseys," Sam said. "If they go for you, I think I can get 'em to spring for more dates. They need something. Perry Como is wiping them out."

Tommy and Jimmy Dorsey had been hauled back from radio heaven to compete with Perry Como's variety show on NBC-TV, but the famous big-band brothers weren't making much headway. Everybody knew "Stage Show" was a second-string imitation of Ed Sullivan's "Toast of the Town." That's how Sam had been able to snare Leroy a chance on the show when the other New York producers said he was nothing but a southern flash in the pan. And that is why Leroy was wearing his pin-striped suit and his most eager smile when the Dorseys walked into the dark, swanky Oak Room.

The Dorseys were living legends, but they looked like a pair of old bean farmers who'd been talked out of their overalls and into tuxedos. You would never guess girls had once swooned for them. Tommy Dorsey's left hand was shaking so badly he had to hold it still with his right. He said, "Scotch." His brother said, "The same for me." Sam ordered bourbon. Leroy had a Coke.

"Leroy, I've heard a lot about you," said Jimmy Dorsey.

"Well, sir, there's a lot going around," Leroy said. "I'm sure proud you'd have us on your show. I watch you all the time. I hadn't ever done any television, except just some things around Memphis."

Tommy Dorsey took his drink from the waiter's hand and brought it straight to his lips. By the time he set the glass down, his hand had quit shaking.

Leroy asked the waiter for a straw for his Coke. You would think he'd ordered a dead animal from the way the man turned up his nose and stalked off.

Jimmy Dorsey smiled. "Now, Leroy," he said, "there's three things you need to know about television. The first is, it's live. Don't say anything you don't want your aunt Edith to hear. If something goes wrong, keep going."

"I'm used to that," Leroy said. "Last week in Miami three girls got up on the stage with us. I just kept singing while the cops chased 'em around."

"Well, our audiences are pretty well behaved," said Jimmy. "One thing you will see, though, is that time goes by a lot faster on live TV. Our show is twenty-three minutes, not counting commercials. That means you have to stick to the times we give you in rehearsal. No stretching. And the most important thing: If you're not on your mark and ready to go when that little red light on the camera goes on, we've got dead air."

412

"Don't worry," said Leroy, "I'll probably be three hours early. I'm excited."

Jimmy said, "So are we."

Tommy coughed, drained his glass, rattled the ice, and said, "Jimmy." It was the first thing he'd said since "Scotch." He stood slowly, balancing with both hands on the table.

Leroy thought: I hope I don't look that old when I'm old. Maybe that's what life on the road does to you if you don't stop in time.

He had imagined the four of them sitting around swapping show business stories, but Tommy Dorsey had on his overcoat and was making a dead line for the door.

Jimmy stood up. "Just look straight into the camera. That's all there is to it. See you tomorrow." He grabbed his coat and went after his brother.

Sam said, "Sit down a minute, son. There's a lady from the *Daily News* coming by. I promised her thirty minutes."

"Come on, Sam, it's after ten! I've smiled so much today my face is about to crack."

"Thirty minutes, that's all," Sam said. "I promise. It's a big paper, son, we can't afford to make 'em mad."

It was past midnight by the time Leroy was alone in his room, munching a room service cheeseburger. Pat Boone's wholesome, cheery face filled the TV screen; the sound was off so Leroy could bear to be in the same room with Pat Boone. The hissing radiator was working overtime. Leroy opened a window.

Cold air and the racket of horns and sirens floated in. Snow drifted down past the streetlights. From the seventeenth floor the avenue looked like a model, with model cars jamming the lanes.

There were lights in a million windows: warm lights and the cool blue flickering lights of TVs. Just three years before, Leroy had seen his first television set in the window at Goldsmith's. Now the whole country gathered around the small screen at night, and in the morning they talked about Lucy and Ricky and Ethel and Fred and George and Gracie and Sid Caesar and Imogene Coca and Pat Boone and Steve Allen and Ed Sullivan.

Tomorrow night some of them would talk about Leroy.

He felt so small in the face of this monumental city. Lately he had slipped into thinking of himself as some kind of big deal—hard not to think that way, with the screaming and camera-flashing and crowds and cops—but here he was, invisible again, an unknown in television land, starting from zero.

You could add up all the people who'd ever seen Leroy, add them in with all the people in New York City, and you still wouldn't begin to reach the millions who would see him on "Stage Show" tomorrow night.

All his past performances counted for nothing. He had brought himself up to another starting line. Once again it was all up to him. He had to focus everything he had learned all those hot, sweaty nights on the road and cool it down enough for the TV cameras. He wanted to set off a spark, not frighten people out of their living rooms.

He rolled over, reached for the phone.

The froggy ring of the Memphis telephone system made him homesick. Agnes picked up on the third ring.

"Leroy?" Her voice was asleep.

"Hey, Mama. Sorry to wake you. I just needed to talk a minute."

"What time is it, honey?" He pictured her snapping on the light, carrying the phone to her green upholstered chair, settling in. He could hear Ray snoring.

"Midnight your time," he said. "Guess what? I met Jimmy and Tommy Dorsey tonight."

"Oh, that's wonderful, Leroy," she said, coming awake. "Were they nice?"

"Aw, they were all right," he said. "That Tommy looks bad. I think he likes to drink."

"I can't wait to tell your aunt Irene," said Agnes. "She always thought he was the greatest thing since sliced bread." She yawned. "Are you in your hotel?"

"Yeah. It's snowing. I wish you could see it."

"Oh, I couldn't stand it," she said. "You know I never liked the cold." She hesitated. "Leroy, something is wrong."

"Nah, not really . . . guess I'm a little nervous about tomorrow night." He drew his knees to his chest. "It's such a big deal, Satnin. I don't ever get scared onstage anymore, but Sam keeps going on and on about this show, how important it is, and—I don't know. It's kind of scary. What if I blow it?"

"Well, honey, you can always come home if you want," she said. "You don't have to do it if it makes you too nervous."

"Thanks, Mama." He smiled to himself. That was her favorite advice: Come home, honey, let Mama take care of you. It made him feel better, just hearing it. "I oughta let you go back to sleep," he said.

"I'm awake now. Tell me about that Tommy Dorsey."

He told her everything he could remember, the Dorseys and the Plaza Hotel and the horse-drawn carriages in Central Park, the traffic, the shining skyscrapers, the scorched-chestnut smell of the air.

He told her he loved her, and Agnes said, "I love you too, sweetie. I know you'll do fine. Just pretend you're singing your songs to me."

"Good night, Mama. Sleep tight."

"Good night, Leroy. I love you."

He hung up, rolled over, switched off the light. His love for her had not faded, not even a little. He felt so close to her, even though he was far away. On the phone he could pour out everything, without seeing her face. She was always glad to hear from him.

But he was still alone.

He fished around in his shaving kit for the bottle of sleeping pills Dr. Davis had given him. He couldn't lie awake tossing all night before his national TV debut. The dark circles would show under his eyes.

He swallowed two pills, with a glass of milk from the little refrigerator.

He fetched a marijuana cigarette from the pack he kept tucked in the toe of his loafer. His colored friend Jackson in Memphis provided a steady supply and never asked Leroy for any money. "Glad to help out a friend," he said.

The weed helped Leroy relax. It was better than sleeping pills. Lately the weed and the pills together had been making for a lovely serenity late at night, in his room, after the daily uproar. The lights of the skyline pulsed and glittered, like stars. Leroy fell asleep in the chair.

While he slept, the snow kept falling, frosting the tops of the cars, the outcroppings and ledges of buildings, the sidewalks, the streets—flakes big as silver dollars falling and rounding off rough edges, whitening, smoothing, drifting over cars and mailboxes.

Leroy awoke to a brilliant blue sky and a silence so profound that he thought maybe he wasn't in New York after all.

Somehow he had gotten himself from the chair to the bed. He crept back to the window. The avenue was white, nearly empty of people or cars. The great stone buildings marched away in a perfect man-made cliff, receding forever. Everything was silent and white. Leroy imagined he owned the whole city. . . .

The phone jangled.

"Take a look out your window," Sam said.

"I'm looking right now. You don't reckon they'd call off the show, do you?"

"Hell no, the show must go on, that's the first rule," Sam said. "You ready? The gal from *TV Guide* is waiting downstairs. She must have come over on a dogsled."

"Give me fifteen minutes."

A quick shower was Leroy's last moment alone the whole day. He met a thousand questions with a smile and a sincere half answer, posing and greeting and cooperating as hard as he could. He hid the nervous part of himself. A smooth, grinning stranger stood in his place, doing all the talking.

Tommy and D.D. and Jack arrived five hours late, with harrowing tales of their slip-sliding taxi ride from the airport.

"Folks up here drive crazy, don't they?" said Leroy. "It's like the demolition derby."

Jack said, "I can't wait to get back where it's warm."

Leroy was glad they were there, to take his mind off the hulking cameras waiting in Studio 50. Tommy broke out the guitars, and they set in to playing Big Mama Thornton's old "Hound Dog," and the room felt as much like home as any dressing room in the world.

The script girl appeared in the door. "Ten minutes . . ."

Tommy and Jack wandered out to tune up. It was time for Leroy to climb back inside his own skin and take over. It was up to him to find the reason for all this fuss. It was nobody else's job. The automatic man couldn't do it.

Two makeup ladies appeared with palettes and brushes and hand mirrors. They primped and admired Leroy's hair, which he had darkened one Miss Clairol shade at a time until at last it was blue-black and shiny as Superman's hair.

He said, "Hold that mirror still a minute, honey." He grinned, checking his teeth.

A knock on the door.

"It's open. . . ."

Sam stuck in his head. "Everything okay?"

"Come on in." Leroy wrinkled his nose at the dusting of face powder.

"How you feeling, boy?" Sam came over to inspect him. "This is the big one now. Coast-to-coast live. You all right?"

"Durn, Sam, you sound more nervous than me," Leroy said. "I did most of my worrying last night."

"You want more spray on that hair?" the makeup lady said.

"No, ma'am, that's enough." He patted the stiff sides. "It would take a big wind to do damage to this." He shrugged out of the smock. The wardrobe lady had helped him select the big-shouldered charcoal gray suit, the black shirt, the white tie. To absorb the hot lights, she said. So his face would stand out.

"You look sharp," Sam said. "Knock 'em dead."

"I'm ready. Let's do it."

Studio 50 was a chaos of people running with clipboards or some piece of lighting or sound equipment in their hands, everybody yelling, in a desperate hurry. The banks of klieg lights were hot enough to cast the black shadows that made for a sharp image on home televisions. The stage manager called out the time every thirty seconds.

Sam went off to find a good seat in the control room. The musicians of the Dorsey orchestra climbed onto their gliding rider. Three stagehands made ready to roll them out onto the stage as the curtain came back.

Leroy was surprised at the cheap scenery that had appeared since the rehearsal—gaudy glitter-painted backdrops and drapings of tinsely fishnet with plastic ornaments. But when he peered over a technician's shoulder at a tiny monitor, he saw that the lights and the camera transformed the stage into an elegant setting in crisp black and white.

"Live from Broadway in New York City, the entertainment capital of the world," the announcer proclaimed, "it's Jimmy and Tommy Dorsey's 'Stage Show'!" The orchestra rolled out onstage, sounding its blitzkrieg fanfare. The audience applauded on cue.

The cameramen hunched on the backs of the hulking cameras; stagehands trundled them into position. That glass rectangle on front, with the flaps unfolded around it—that was the eye, the open hole to the nation. Leroy concentrated his attention on that. The red light would wink when it was looking at him.

The Dorseys spoke to camera one in convivial tones, then led the orchestra into a swing number. The June Taylor Dancers dipped and swirled, leading into a commercial for Kellogg's Rice Krispies.

Jimmy Dorsey worked up a stiff smile to introduce the first guest, Sarah Vaughan.

Sarah Vaughan was as fine-looking as Leroy had imagined from her voice. On the song "Moanin' Low," when she dropped into her low register, she would have made a French horn proud. Leroy had tried to sing along with her records from time to time, but her rhythm was just too eccentric for him. He stood to one side of the curtain, tapping his toe.

An assistant producer came to hustle him to a masking tape X on the floor. At his cue he was supposed to walk downstage in a spotlight to his second X, under the microphone boom.

Some girls in the audience spotted him and squealed. A stagehand gestured wildly to make them stop—Sarah Vaughan was right at the moody part of her song.

Leroy was sorry, but he would have to blow Sarah right off the television screen in a minute. He would sing a song for those impatient girls in the crowd, for girls everywhere propped on their elbows on the floor, bored silly by the Dorseys and begging their parents to switch over to Perry Como.

Camera three approached him. Three attendants crept along behind it, cautiously draping cables as if one hasty move might provoke the one-eyed monster to turn and devour them.

Leroy stood rooted to his X. He applauded with everyone else when Sarah Vaughan finished her song and bowed off. The lights dimmed for a Purina Dog Chow commercial.

Stagehands swarmed everywhere, fixing, adjusting. The makeup ladies came to dab powder on Leroy's brow.

"Okay, boys," he said, "let's jump on the downbeat. And don't forget a big smile for the folks back home."

Tommy grinned, fiddling with his E string.

"Thirty seconds to air," called the stage manager.

Bill Randle, the Cleveland disc jockey, took his place before camera two. "Okay, quiet, girls," he said. Tommy Dorsey appeared from no-where to stand in front of camera one. He nodded to Leroy.

"Fifteen seconds!"

Leroy straightened his tie.

The stage darkened. The Dorseys had decided to present Leroy against a black background, outlined in spotlights.

"... four, three, two ..."

The stage manager pointed his finger at Tommy Dorsey.

Camera one winked on.

The orchestra blatted the fanfare.

Tommy said, "Ladies and gentlemen, I'd like to give you one of radio's best-known disc jockeys, Bill Randle."

A red light on camera two. Bill Randle said, "Ladies and gentlemen, we'd like to introduce you to a young fellow who, like many performers, has just seemed to come up out of nowhere to be overnight a very big star. Tonight we think he's going to make television history. We want you to have a chance to meet him now—Leroy Kirby—here he is!"

A shaft of white light shot down. Girls squealed. Leroy walked in the light to the center of the stage.

He did not waste an instant. He raised his hand in a little half wave for his mother and brought it down on his guitar.

Get out in that kitchen and rattle those pots and pans!

The boys jumped down hard on the beat. The lights came up: instant sunrise. Leroy forgot Sarah Vaughan and sang to the vacant glass eye. It was right in his face, closer than anyone ever came while he sang.

He did every one of his tricks without skittering out of camera range. He threw back his head, shook his hair, sneered at the camera. He moved easily behind his guitar, taking care not to stray from his X.

He looked deep into the glass eye. Down deep in the layers of curved, coated glass, he saw a reflection of his mother in her chair in the living room in Memphis.

The spotlights turned Leroy into electricity, blazing an image that traveled through the cables in the stagehands' fingers to the glassed-in control room, along lines through the walls to the basement, to be transmitted on thicker cables to TV stations all over the country, where

419

the signal was scrambled and sent up tall towers, spreading out through the air on invisible waves, captured by millions of home antennas, drawn into Zeniths and Admirals and Motorolas, into the living rooms of everyone in America who was not watching Perry Como or the ABC Saturday-night movie or out on a date at the drive-in, or too poor to own a TV.

The new RCA set at 1414 Getwell Road provided a sharp, unwavering picture. Agnes sat back in her rocker with tears in her eyes. "Did you see that? He waved to me."

All the people in her living room raised a cheer for Leroy, knocking them dead in New York.

Leroy had made Ray and Agnes the talk of Memphis. People came from the newspaper to take their picture and ask questions about every little thing. When Agnes saw her picture in the paper she wanted to die, she was so fat. She hadn't let it worry her one bit until those cameras started snapping, snapping. She asked Dr. Davis for some diet pills and they made her nervous but so far she had lost eight pounds. When the telephone rang she nearly leaped out of her skin grabbing it. "Leroy?"

"Hi, Mama. Did you see us?"

"Oh honey, you were so good!"

The others raised another cheer. Agnes reeled off the list of who all was there: Dodger, of course, and Johnny and Travis, Mrs. Chester and the Hastingses from Lauderdale Court, some of Ray's pool hall buddies. . . .

"Mama, I can't talk long." Leroy was standing in the producer's office backstage at Studio 50, surrounded by a noisy mob and two assistant producers waiting to take him to the after-show party. Agnes sounded so far away.

"Listen," he said, "they've already invited me back for five more appearances. How about that? Now you tell everybody howdy, and I'll call you tomorrow night. Satnin—I love you."

"I saw you wave to me, sweetie," she said. "I love you so much. You come on home soon."

"Thanks, Mama. Take care. Good-bye."

It thrilled him to imagine them all gathered around the set, watching him, cheering his mother, talking him up. This was his reward. Those were the people he wanted to impress.

He had also managed to impress a lot of people he didn't know. The next week "Stage Show" received 78 letters in praise of Sarah Vaughan, and 158,000 fan letters for Leroy.

He was a hit.

He posed for publicity shots beside the huge sacks of mail. People stopped him for autographs on the streets of New York. There were girls everywhere, mobbing the hotel, the CBS building, the delicatessen.

At the RCA studios on East Twenty-fourth Street, Leroy worked with Tommy and Jack and some session men from 11:00 A.M. until midnight. He laid down six songs in a row, bam bam bam bam bam BAM! "Blue," "Tutti Frutti," "Hurtin' Time," "I'm Not As Bad As They Say," "Don't Stop Falling in Love with Me," "I've Never Been Lonely Like This." Six hits! No waiting! His touch was golden.

Before his third TV appearance Leroy got into a wrangle with Tommy Dorsey, who insisted that the whole orchestra play backup on the unveiling of "You're Breaking My Heart." Of course, Dorsey won, but what he got was the most pitifully ragged out-of-time mess ever heard on live television. Just as Leroy couldn't begin to sing like Sarah Vaughan, the orchestra couldn't get the hang of Leroy's dropped beats and tight, high-strung rhythm.

He just sang his part and hung on, a goofy smile on his face, while the orchestra struggled and flumped to the end.

Tommy Dorsey surrendered. The next week Leroy sang the song with Jack's big bass thoom-thooming down the spine of it, Tommy cutting in with little jolts of electric guitar—just like the record.

> *Don't leave me this-a way, a-baybeh!*
> *Don't a-leave me this-a blue*
> *You're breaking my heart*
> *You're breaking my heart*
> *In two. . . .*

Leroy knew it would create a sensation, and it did.

He sat beside his phone at the Warwick. Whenever it rang, it was Sam with another piece of good news. Three hundred thousand fan letters in four days. A radio station in Cleveland playing "You're Breaking My Heart" nonstop for forty-eight hours. Girls rioting at a record store in Rahway, New Jersey, on the rumor that Leroy would appear.

"Jesus, Sam," he said, stretching out on the bed with the phone on his chest. "I don't know about this. It's kind of getting out of hand, don't you think?"

"That's just what we want," Sam said. "Just hold on. There's more."

"I don't know what else it could be," Leroy said.

"Well, son, what I'm holding in my hand right here is the brand-new *Billboard,* hot off the press."

"Don't tell me," said Leroy.

"You got it!"

"Yeow!" Leroy kicked his feet in the air. "Number one!"

"Get this," said Sam. "Number one on the pop chart. Number one on the race chart. Number one on the country chart. You got 'em all, boy. All three. Nobody's ever done that."

Sam stayed in his Warwick suite, fielding telephone calls, smiling wider and wider. What he wanted was a call from Ed Sullivan. He wanted Hollywood. And he wanted a whole lot of money.

Leroy grinned all day long just for himself. Everybody in the country knew his name. They were all out there hearing his record. He was climbing up to a place where they could never forget him.

Maybe getting to the top was a fluke. Staying there would be harder. Everyone would try to knock him off. He would have to do it all on his own.

By the time of Leroy's final appearance the young screaming army had taken over Studio 50. "Stage Show" was a den of howling, interrupted at times by commercials. Leroy bopped in the spotlight. He beat his guitar and trusted the microphones to carry some music out, along with the hysteria.

The next morning a man called from the Ed Sullivan show. Sam informed him that Leroy's price was five thousand dollars.

Ed Sullivan wrote in his "Talk of the Town" column that Leroy Kirby was overrated and overexposed and would never appear on his show.

When Leroy read that, he smiled, folded the newspaper, and dialed up Sam. "If he thinks five thousand dollars is too much," he said, "wait till he sees what it's going to cost him next time."

Sam laughed. "Son, you're beginning to sound like me."

Leroy knew he had more than a few trump cards up his sleeve. The first one arrived bright and early Monday, the new *Life* magazine with a big photo spread: "Leroy the Wild Boy—A Howling Hillbilly Success."

Milton Berle called, and Steve Allen.

Sam said yes to them both, at five thousand a shot. "Sullivan will come around," he said. "A matter of time. I don't care for that mess in the *Post* this morning, though. You see that?"

"I just woke up," Leroy said.

"Hang on, I'll read it to you." Leroy heard rustling papers. Then Sam said, "Here it is, page nine. 'Kirby Concert Canceled. The commissioner of police in Birmingham, Alabama, told the Associated Press today he has personally ordered the cancellation of singer Leroy Kirby's scheduled March 15 performance in Birmingham.' "

"What? Sam, what is that all about?"

"Let me read it. Hmm, let me—here, here we go. ' "This music promotes immoral behavior in young people," the commissioner said. "We do not want any nigger music in the white community and that is just what this so-called Leroy Kirby is promoting." ' What you think about that, son?"

" 'So-called Leroy Kirby,' " Leroy mused. "I wonder what he means by that? That's my name."

"I wouldn't give the man too much credit," said Sanders. "Shame to lose that date, though. I guess we'll play Bessemer or somewhere."

Suddenly Sam's calls were bringing troubling news along with all the good stuff. A Georgia radio station banned "You're Breaking My Heart" because it was "un-Christian." The police chief in Newark, New Jersey, canceled a big stadium show, citing reports of riots in Rahway and Jacksonville and other cities. "We will not allow riots in Newark," he said.

A newspaper columnist in South Carolina wrote that Leroy was a corrupting influence on youth, and his records should be burned.

"I bet you his daughter likes me," Leroy told Sam. "That's why he wrote that. I bet she plays my records all day long."

"It ain't hurting your bank account any," said Sam.

Tommy and Jack kept one set of instruments in New York for "Stage Show." On Saturdays Bubba Hayes would drive the other set to the site of the Sunday concert. Leroy and the boys would fly to meet him as soon as the broadcast was over. They flew on one airplane after the other, all over the country now, not just the South.

Billy Ray Jordan was out of the picture. Leroy toured the country headlining the Leroy Kirby Jamboree, a Sam Sanders creation featuring comics and jugglers and dog acts and hillbilly quartets and an Irish tenor, with the last spot reserved for Leroy.

He felt sorry for the performers who went on before him, but the buildup made sure the girls were in the proper frenzy by the time he came on.

He kept track of the cities by particular girls. He'd pick them out from the stage while he was singing, and Bubba Hayes would fetch them backstage during the encore. Norfolk was Mary Ann with long blond hair, Tulsa was Louise, the half-Indian girl with blue eyes, and La Crosse, Wisconsin, was beautiful redheaded Linda, who took Leroy to her small, chilly apartment and did things to his body he had never even heard about.

Every time he found himself in bed with a girl, he sent a silent thanks to Sheila in Nashville. She'd shown him how easy it was. All he had to do was ask.

Most nights he played cards with Bubba Hayes or hung out with Tommy and Jack and D.D. in his hotel room, working up new songs. He couldn't go out. His fans seemed to have some advanced form of radar, like bats; they detected his presence and swarmed around him, squeaking. Bubba was there to protect him, but after a few weeks of being squealed at and batted and clawed every time they set foot out the door, Leroy decided it was easier just to stay in.

On the morning of the last "Stage Show" Sam telephoned with big news in his voice. "Come up to the room," he said. "You got to hear this in person."

Ed Sullivan, at last?

Leroy didn't wait for the elevator. He sprinted up two flights of stairs, down the hall to Sam's room, and burst through the door. "What is it?"

"Sit down."

"Oh, come on, Sam!"

Sam chewed his cigar. "It's Hal Wallis."

"I don't know who that is. . . ."

"He's a movie producer. Paramount Pictures. He saw last week's show. He wants you in Hollywood a week from Friday for a screen test." A smile spread across Sam's face.

"Oh you're kidding. Tell me you're not kidding." Leroy sank to a chair. The movies! "Oh Sam, you don't know! All my life I wanted to hear you say that! A screen test!" He stopped. "What's a screen test?"

"They film you doing a couple of scenes," said Sam. "Long as you don't fall down or pick your nose, they'll probably sign you."

Hollywood, Leroy thought. Rudolph Valentino. Tony Curtis. Marlon Brando. James Dean.

Leroy Kirby.

The movies.

He got out of the chair. He took a deep breath. He paced a circle on the rug. "Oh, Jesus," he said.

A movie star was a real star. Every inch of Leroy, every smile and smoldering look would be blown up to superhuman scale and captured forever. Strangers would sit in the dark and watch Leroy and dream, as he had dreamed in his usher's uniform at the Loew's State Theater. The movies!

"It all fits in with the Berle show," Sam was saying. "But the Steve Allen people are acting funny all of a sudden. They're antsy about all the publicity, the sex thing."

Leroy wasn't listening. His eyes were filling with tears. The biggest, finest, most unreachable dream of his life had just come true, and here was Sam rattling on about Steve Allen.

Leroy stood abruptly. "Sam, I've got to get out of here a minute. I just—it's too much. I need to go think for a while."

Ignoring the look of surprise, he hurried out of the room.

He needed outside air. He needed room for his joy to spread out and inflate into something the size of the giant Popeye in the Macy's Thanksgiving parade.

He stopped on the fourteenth floor to pick up a warm jacket and his new Humphrey Bogart fedora.

The movies!

The elevator doors slid open at the lobby. Twenty girls ran toward him, squealing.

Oh God. He'd forgotten. He held up his hands. "Okay, girls, please—okay!"

They babbled and swarmed and withdrew Leroy from the elevator, thrusting pieces of paper and pencils at him, asking four questions at once, squealing and hugging each other in their excitement. He didn't try to escape, and they didn't try to tear him apart; he signed and grinned and answered and made creeping progress toward the front door. "Don't you ladies ever get any sleep?" he said.

"Not while you're up, Leroy."

"Okay, okay," he said. "Y'all in the back don't push. I'll sign one for everybody."

"Leroy, where'dja get the dreamy jacket?"

"Leroy—"

"Leroy, I love you."

"Thanks, honey," he said. "I love you too."

The girls all went ooohhh. The one he'd spoken to tottered back on high heels, in a daze.

When he reached the door, he held up his hand. They fell quiet. "Big news tonight, girls," he said. "I just heard. I'm going to Hollywood. I'm gonna be in the movies."

They squealed and congratulated him. He let some of them kiss him. When he'd had enough, he turned to open the door and saw two hundred more girls waiting across the street, behind a police line.

The crowd in the lobby was made up of those who'd managed to slip through. The hotel manager was noisily trying to round them up.

The last thing Leroy wanted was to go back up to his room and celebrate this unbelievable news by himself. But there were too many girls.

He made his way back through the lobby, signing and grinning the same way he'd come, and slipped into an elevator.

He got off two floors below his own floor, to throw them off the track. He climbed the stairs, locked himself into the Staffordshire Suite.

The movies!

He switched off the television. TV seemed tawdry and silly and cheap, compared with the glamorous Technicolor vision that was forming in his mind.

Leroy couldn't stand being alone in this room with this news.

It wouldn't be fair to get Bubba up at this hour.

He picked up the telephone. Agnes answered on the second ring. "Leroy?"

He smiled, settling in on the bed. "Hey Mama, guess what? I'm going to be in the movies!"

"Oh, Leroy," she said. "What next?"

41

$\mathcal{B}$efore he ever saw his first movie camera, Leroy spent a long morning with a battalion of Paramount hairdressers and makeup artists and wardrobe people. He expected some glamorous result from all the fuss, but he came out looking pretty much like himself, in a plain blue work shirt and jeans. All his pimples had been erased.

"You'll want to have those teeth capped," one makeup man told him.

The sound stage was vast, the film cameras with their bulky sound-muffling devices even more imposing than the ones for TV. It was thrilling to see how these people made magic out of colored lights and fake buildings and painted backdrops.

Twenty crew members hustled around setting up. An instrumental track of Leroy singing "Blue" echoed through the giant space. Friendly hands guided him to a chalk mark on the floor.

He was supposed to stand on that spot and strum his guitar and sing "Blue" to the taped accompaniment. He ran through it twice with the lights in his eyes and those cameras looming. He shouted along with himself:

> *Well it's one time baby—a maybe so*
> *Two-time woman get on out the door*
> *You make me*
> *Blue blue*
> *Blue hoo-hoo, a-baby!*
> *Blue blue*
> *Woo-hoo-hoo!*

Hal Wallis, the tanned, soft-spoken producer, kept reminding Leroy to stay on his mark.

He tried it again. It didn't feel natural.

"I'm trying, Mr. Wallis," he said, "but I—I can't help it. I got to *move*. I can't stand still. I got to move around when I sing."

"You've already done the song," Wallis said. "It doesn't matter how you sound. This is a lip sync. The camera loses your face when you go off the mark. Let's try it without the guitar."

By the seventh take Leroy had relaxed in the face of the cameras and was singing naturally, snapping his fingers, moving just enough to tele-graph the beat without straying out of range.

> *I love you like a train*
> *You driving me insane*
> *You make me blue oo-hoo-hoo!*

Hal Wallis said, "Great, kid, fabulous!" and handed him a black folder with gold stamping on the cover: *The Rainmaker*. "This is a script for a movie we're planning," he said. "Fred Farmer here is one of our best character men. He'll walk you through your scene. Fred, Leroy Kirby."

They shook hands. Leroy recognized him from an old Gene Autry western; he'd played the crusty landowner who gets gunned down at his daughter's wedding. Farmer was all business, like everyone else at this place. In five minutes he taught Leroy his lines, how to stand, how to move.

The lines didn't make much sense because they came from the middle of the story, but Leroy did his best at acting out the emotions as Farmer explained them. The scene involved a lot of different feelings. Leroy was supposed to start off swaggering angry, railing at the old man about all the injustices in the world, then indignant, remorseful, pleading. . . .

Hal Wallis said, "Leroy, you're being too nice. You have to make us believe you're really angry at him! Yell! Push him around a little!"

Fred Farmer nodded. "He's right. Ham it up."

Leroy swaggered and strutted and blustered and begged and pretended to weep. Fred Farmer reacted. The cameras crept forward and back.

"Not bad," said Wallis. "Let's try it again."

The first beads of sweat appeared on Leroy's forehead; two makeup girls ran in with powder puffs.

The crew lolled about, chatting, paying no attention at all to Leroy or his acting.

Wallis shouted, "Quiet on the set! We're rolling! . . . Speed! Aaaaaand action!"

Leroy stomped up to Fred Farmer, stuck his finger hard in his chest, and let fly with a string of abuse. Farmer looked startled—just the way the script said—and sputtered his comeback lines.

Leroy seized his shoulders, shook him hard, trying to make him understand. Real tears welled in his eyes.

This time there was a murmur from the crew.

"Cut it, print it," Hal Wallis called. "Thank you, people. Thanks, Leroy. That's what I needed to know. David, I want that film in my office."

"Is that it?" Leroy wiped his eyes on his sleeve. "Shoot, I was just getting started."

Wallis smiled, clapped his shoulder. "I'll talk to Sam."

Leroy went to his room at the Beverly Wilshire Hotel and stretched out on the huge bed. He waited. Everywhere he went these days telephones were ringing, but the phone in his room sat silent for one whole day.

At nine o'clock that evening it rang. "Waaaal, we've got us an offer," said Sam, crackly and far away in New York. "Wallis loved the test. Paramount wants you for three features. A hundred thousand for the first one, a hundred fifty for the second, and two hundred for the third. Plus a percentage of the gross if they make back their cost."

Leroy opened his mouth to say "wow, Jesus Christ, Sam," or something like that. But no sound came out.

"Boy, you still there? Hello?"

"I'm—I—" His head was spinning. "Oh. Can you say that again?"

Sam repeated it. "That adds up to four hundred fifty thousand dollars, less my commission," he said. "That ain't peanuts."

Leroy couldn't begin to get his mind around such a number. Sam was waiting for him to say something. "I don't know what to—god*damn*, Sam, I can't believe it."

"Believe it." Sam chortled. "Never made an easier deal in my life. Listen, I need to call him back. What you want me to tell him?"

"What do you mean? Tell him yes!" Leroy cried.

"That's what I thought you'd say. Talk to you later."

Leroy hung up the phone. He stood up from the bed. He went to the mirror over the dresser.

"You're rich," he said. "You are rich."

Big fat deal, said the mirror. So what.

"I've never even *known* anybody rich."

What will you do with all that? Burn holes in your pocket? Spend it all in one place? Put it in your shoe? Give it all to the poor?

"Rich, rich, rich," Leroy said. He liked how it sounded. He scouted the desk drawer for a pen and the fancy Beverly Wilshire stationery. He started a list of things to buy.

42

*L*eroy didn't like bumpety rides in small planes, but there was no other way to get from Los Angeles to Tucson to Dallas to Tulsa to Memphis, and then on to Nashville in time for his recording session. One stroke of Sam's pencil these days meant a thousand-mile trip, no complaining allowed.

Rain lashed the windscreen. The charter pilot, Del Freeman, hummed a little tune under his breath, easing the plane through pockets of unsettled air. Jack Brown sat beside him, keeping his eye on the gauges; Jack didn't care for flying in any kind of plane, especially these six-seater jobs. Tommy, Bubba, and D.D. snoozed in back, oblivious.

Leroy was wide wide-awake. He'd swiped some of his mother's diet pills to keep him alert on these long hauls. The pills did the trick, but also they dried out his mouth and made him jumpy. Whenever the plane shuddered through a rain cloud or the pitch of the engine changed, something clenched inside him.

"What was that?" he said.

"That was nothing," said Del Freeman. "Sometimes a little drop of water or something gets in the fuel line."

"I wish to hell we were home," Jack said. "Can't you get us up over this mess?"

"We'll punch through anytime now. Set back and relax. We're making good time with this tailwind." The plane lurched. "Whoopsy-daisy, hold on there." Freeman eased back the throttle. The nose tilted up.

Leroy gripped the armrest. This airplane was a small thing in a big wind. He decided to think about tomorrow's session. He dug around in his shoulder pack for the song sheet, but he couldn't keep his eyes focused on the page.

"Del, if we don't quit this bouncing around, I'm gonna pee in my pants," he said.

Jack muttered agreement.

"It's sure not keeping your buddies awake," Del said.

At that moment the right engine made a sputtering cough, like old Granddaddy clearing his chest in the morning.

Leroy froze.

"Holy shit!" Jack cried.

Bubba Hayes yelled, "Mother!"

D.D. and Tommy came bolt upright in their seats. "Huh! What!"

The engine died.

The plane banked over sideways.

"Aw *come* on," Del Freeman shouted, wrestling the wheel, kicking the rudder pedal. His disgusted tone gave Leroy a flicker of hope. He didn't sound like a man who was ready to die.

But they might. They might die. They might fall through the night and splatter all over Texas in pieces, as Agnes had feared and predicted. Leroy bit down on his knuckle. *Mama* . . . This was the answer to all his good luck—his life smashed to bits, just when the good part was starting. Mama, I'm sorry, I tried to be good. . . .

Now Bubba's face was in his hands, Jack yelping and Del Freeman roaring, "Shut up, damn it, shut the hell up!" The Cessna staggered, the propeller fluttering, kicking. Del stared at his gauges.

Shouldn't somebody be screaming, "Mayday," into the radio?

Leroy heard himself say, "Do something, Del," in a calm voice he did not recognize.

The altimeter needle quivered and began to sweep around in a downward circle. Jack's eyes fixed on this spectacle. His yelps stuck in his throat.

Tommy mumbled a prayer. "The Lord is my shepherd," he said, "is my shepherd, the Lord is my shepherd—"

"Come on, Del," said Leroy.

Now he knew he would be awake and clearheaded to witness the end of his life. He had always wondered how it would come. He tried to remember the last thing he said to his mother.

The right engine coughed a few times—hack! hack! ptrrrrrrr, and came back to life.

The force jolted Leroy hard against his seat belt. Pencils and paper clips drifted up, weightless.

"Come on, come on, baby," Del said through clenched teeth.

The Cessna pitched headlong through a wave of rain and came out on the other side intact and moving, both engines howling, climbing away from the dark yawning—darkness and rain and maybe the earth. Leroy would never know how close they came.

D.D. was the first to catch his breath. "Mother of God ..."

Del shook his head. "Here we go," he said, "we're okay."

Leroy's nerves shot off like a string of firecrackers. His whole body was shaking. He put his hand on his leg and discovered that he had peed all over himself.

"Put us down, Del," he said. "Put us down on the ground."

Both engines roared as if they could run all the way to China without stopping.

Leroy said, "Fellas, I believe I have done pissed myself," and Tommy said yeah, he had, too, and they shared a nervous laugh over that. Bubba edged to his side of the seat.

Del switched on his radio. "Texarkana center, Alpha Delta Bravo one-four-one-niner," he said, "wondering if you could give me a vector to the nearest airport."

"Roger, Alpha Delta Bravo, Texarkana center—you got a problem up there?"

"No, no problem, just need a vector to the nearest airport, if I could."

The radio voice reeled off some numbers. Somehow Del found a hole in the clouds. A string of blue lights glowed in the black earth like luminous jewels.

Leroy was still shaking when he stepped down to the wonderful mud of the airstrip at Mount Pleasant, Texas.

Del Freeman said, "A little water in the fuel line. No big deal. Soon's we flush it out and fill her up again, we're ready to go."

"Oh no, Del." The diet pill had nothing to do with the way Leroy was trembling. "That's it for me. I'm down for one night, and I'm staying down." He turned. "You cats can do what you want. I'm gonna find me a car and put on dry britches and get the hell out of here."

And the boys said damn straight, so long, Del, take it easy.

The man who brought the rental car from Texarkana must have called the newspapers the minute they dropped him off because the *Commercial Appeal* had the story on front stoops all over Memphis by the time the boys drove into town the next morning: KIRBY OK IN AIR INCIDENT. Leroy had called Agnes at midnight to say he'd be late, but he hadn't said why. He came through the door to find her yelling and waving the paper in his face.

"I told you," she wailed, "I knew this would happen! I told you, I told you."

"Okay, Satnin, it's all right, it happened and it's over now. I'm okay. See? Look." He held out his steady hands. "I'm all right."

"Right here. Look what it says. 'Narrowly averted.' Leroy, you nearly got killed! Why didn't you tell me last night?"

"I thought you might get upset," he said.

"Upset? Up*set!*"

"Pretty dumb of me, huh."

She smacked him with the newspaper. "Don't you smart-mouth me, young man, you're not too big yet for a whipping."

He had to laugh. "Oh Mama, I am so."

She threw her hands up and burst into tears.

Oh God. It killed him to see her cry.

He hugged her. She wouldn't stop crying.

"Stop, Satnin, please stop." He could not stand it. He had to do something. "Listen to me, listen, hush now. I'll call Sam. I'll tell him— no more planes. That's all. We'll take trains, and we'll drive, or—or—I don't know. It's not worth it to see you torn up this way."

She fumbled for a Kleenex. "Do you mean it?"

"I swear to God. I'll call him right now."

"Don't swear."

He paced the kitchen. "You just—Mama, you can't get like this, it's not good for you."

"I just love you so much, Leroy . . . oh, and I had that feeling, I've been waiting and waiting for something awful, I told you, and now it's gone and happened." She had twisted the Kleenex into a rope.

"I'll call him right now." Leroy picked up the phone. "What's wrong with you? Did you take one of those pills already this morning?"

"I have to. I can't stand being fat. You look so nice now, and look at me."

"No, no, you look great, you look thin," said Leroy. "I think you've lost some more."

"Oh, I'm so hungry," she said, and she was off crying again.

Leroy made the call. Sam said, "No sense tempting fate. You tell her I said not to worry. I know how scared she must be. We'll get you a bus to run around in. I'm glad you're okay."

Leroy told her what he'd said; the news settled her down some. He went to his room, stretched out, closed his eyes, but his brave face had crumbled. His hands were trembling again—the diet pill and the fear and the driving all night and his mother's hysteria. He had to get out, get his mind clear.

He put on his cowboy boots, stuck his checkbook in his fringed leather jacket, and drove downtown. At Foler's Jewelry he bought himself a ring with fourteen diamonds arranged in a lucky horseshoe. At Southern Motors on Union he bought a brand-new white Eldorado to go with his Sedan de Ville, and a Lincoln Continental Mark IV to go with his Cadillacs.

He picked out a pink Coupe de Ville for Agnes and told the ecstatic salesman to take it right over to her. She didn't drive anymore, but he knew she would love admiring it in the driveway.

For a week Leroy wrote big checks all over town. Every purchase brought him a surge of joy that lasted for hours. He bought Ray a Ford pickup, Johnny a new Gibson, Dodger a huge stack of jigsaw puzzles and a red silk Japanese kimono; she laughed and put that in a drawer.

He bought a Harley-Davidson and a motorcycle cap like Brando's in *The Wild One,* and then a Messerschmitt three-wheeler—a bad-looking futuristic vehicle like nothing ever seen on the streets of Memphis. He bought a pink Princess telephone, a gold neck chain, and three pairs of alligator boots. He rode his Harley down to Beale Street and told the Irving Brothers to send over one of everything in his size. Myron Irving was impressed.

The Oldsmobile dealer especially was impressed when Leroy walked in and wrote a check for four blue Olds 98s: one each for Bubba, Tommy, D.D., and Jack.

On Friday, he made a down payment on a beautiful ranch-style house on Audubon Drive, the nicest street in the nice neighborhood beyond Getwell Road.

He was Santa Claus every day. He spent as much as he wanted to spend. Every day there was more in the bank.

43

~~~~~~~~~~~~~~~~

*H*e stayed close to the ground. He had to move fast to be everywhere at once.

He had never imagined there were so many girls in the world. They surged from all directions. Every last one of them was a hot young budding thing, jumping with hormones and energy, going wild at every twitch of his randy left leg. They spent their whole allowance on his records. They came out in swelling thousands to his shows. They formed I Love You Leroy fan clubs.

He wasn't quite sure what he'd started, but each day he repeated a prayer: Don't let it end.

He and the boys had worked up two great new songs: a cool Otis Blackwell cruise-o-matic powerglide called "Don't Say No" and a version of Big Mama Thornton's "You Ain't Never Been Good" sped up and played hard, hard, hard. He began using "You Ain't Never Been So Good" for his big finale at the shows; he slowed it down at the end and shouted the chorus in slow time, humping across the stage on his toes, waggling his knees.

> You ain't—a-nev—er been a goood-uh baby!
> Not once in your life
> You ain't—a nev—er been a good-uh baybeh!
> Not a minute of your life
> Weell you ain't never home Sunday
> And you ain't no preacher's wife

When he did that in San Diego, they had to call out the Shore Patrol to get the girls back in their seats.

When he did it on the Milton Berle show, newspaper columnists raised alarms about the "Leroy Kirby controversy." Preachers began flocking to their pulpits to preach against him.

Suddenly he was making ten thousand dollars a week and all the polite people were turning against him.

The rumors came flooding in through Sam's pipelines: Leroy had killed a man, done time in jail, smoked marijuana, fathered three illegitimate children, and taken a shot at his mother with a pistol.

Sam arranged an appearance on "Hy Gardner Calling," in which Leroy denied everything as politely as he could. He smoked a weed in the car on the way to the television studio—his little joke on the polite world. Agnes said he was wonderful, he seemed just as nice and sweet and relaxed, but the interview didn't stop the ominous buzz in the press.

Leroy was disgusted when a Birmingham radio announcer started a movement to burn his records, and the archbishop of New York said good Catholic girls should not listen to obscene and vulgar rock and roll music.

Girls everywhere regarded such opinions and the police lines as minor obstacles to their holy mission: to get closer to Leroy. Bubba Hayes hovered in the wings during every show, to haul away the ones who managed to scramble onstage. In Des Moines and Wichita Falls and Tallahassee, Leroy had to stop the show and talk the girls back to their seats before the cops would let him continue.

Sam chuckled and waded into the mobs with an eight-by-ten glossy of Leroy stuck behind the feather in his hatband and stacks of them in his arms to sell.

Leroy shook his leg even harder. He wiggled and thrust out his hip. He wanted to show all those pious fools this was a free country. If any one of them could get on a stage and shake his leg and bring home ten thousand dollars a week, he would surely do it. If a girl wanted to scream and cry and spend all her money on his records, she was free to do that, too. It was nobody's business. It was between Leroy and the girls.

<hr />

"Stage Show" had convinced Steve Allen that Leroy was just the thing to help him beat Ed Sullivan in the Trendex ratings. But as the buzz grew louder, and the date of his appearance drew nearer, Allen's producers began to get anxious. They did not want to win the eight o'clock Sunday time slot at the risk of bringing down righteous condemnation upon themselves. By the time Leroy got to New York for the rehearsal, the producers were all in a tizzy. Phone calls flew between NBC and Sam Sanders's suite at the Warwick.

Finally Steve Allen proposed to defuse the whole controversy with a joke. He would dress Leroy in white tie and tails, introduce him to the accompaniment of lush strings, and play off the bad boy angle for every laugh he could get.

"We'll show 'em another side of you," Allen told Leroy, waggling his eyebrows. "Nobody realizes you've got a sense of humor."

"I don't know," Leroy said. He walked through the rehearsal being nice to everyone and laughing along with the jokes, but he wasn't sure it was funny. The monkey suit was only the first humiliation. They had him singing "Blue" to a basset hound; Allen made a cute reference to Leroy's legendary childhood performance of "Old Blue." They had Leroy playing a cowpoke named Tumbleweed Kirby in a comedy skit. They intended to make him ridiculous and harmless.

When Sam Sanders came to his dressing room, Leroy said, "Sam, I'm not so sure this is such a good idea."

Sam said, "I think you best just go along with it now. I don't think it can hurt anything. It might even help."

"Well, the girls ain't gonna like it," Leroy said.

"Son, I believe you could get up there in a burlap sack and sing 'Mary Had a Little Lamb' and the girls would still scream their heads off. You don't need to worry about that."

Leroy strapped himself into the dress tails. The white bow tie pinched his neck. The coattails brushed the backs of his knees. He went on and did the whole thing just the way they wanted. He cupped the dog's face in one hand and held the microphone in the other.

> *You driving me insane*
> *You make me blue blue oo-hoo-hoo!*

Sam was right. The girls screamed just as loud, and the rest of the audience roared at the spectacle of the corrupter of American youth looking as wholesome and ridiculous as anybody on television.

But Leroy was right, too. It was the wrong kind of ridiculous. When he opened his mouth, he still talked like a boy from Tupelo. Singing his red-hot song to that mournful-eyed basset hound felt like the most miserable thing he'd ever done in his life.

Bubba Hayes and the boys gave him hell about it. Twenty thousand girls wrote letters of protest. A television critic in New York announced that Leroy had been "devitalized," whatever that was.

He made a vow, like Scarlett O'Hara holding up that radish in her hand: As God is my witness, I'll never wear another tuxedo.

On Monday Trendex reported that "The Steve Allen Show" had whipped "The Ed Sullivan Show" by four points.

On Monday afternoon Ed Sullivan telephoned Sam Sanders.

Leroy heard the start of the conversation from the other end of Sam's suite at the Warwick. For an hour Sam and Ed Sullivan went at each other like fighting dogs, while Leroy spun the new singles he'd bought downtown: the Platters' "Only You," Eddy Arnold's "Cattle Call," "I Got a New Car," "Life Is but a Dream." He was digging these harmony things, now, especially since the Leroyals had come on board at the RCA sessions. With enough smooth bop-bopping and wah-wah-wah-oooing, you could turn any song into a big fancy rolling machine, with fins and chrome bumpers.

He heard Sam say, "Listen, Sullivan, you could have had him for five thousand bucks. Now you're gonna pay and you know it, so you might as well quit with this bullshit and let's set some dates."

It was quiet for a long moment after that, and then Sam said, "Fine, that's just fine, and I promise you, you won't be sorry. I'll call your people tomorrow."

Leroy squeezed his hands between his knees. Exultation spread out inside him.

Sam said, "Leroy, you want to step in here?"

The room was a haze of blue smoke. There were four cigar stubs in the ashtray beside Sam, and a notepad with numbers scratched all over. "Done," he said. "Three appearances. September nine, October twenty-eight, January the sixth. You're the headliner."

Leroy swallowed and tried to sound nonchalant. "How much?"

"Fifty thousand." Sam cracked a smile. "Only the biggest deal in the history of TV."

Leroy said, "I guess we got some good out of that monkey suit anyway." Ed Sullivan! Three shows! Fifty grand! Famous forever!

"Bingo. That Sullivan's one tough son of a bitch, but he's smart enough to recognize lightning when it's striking."

The glory of that moment carried Leroy downtown for his recording session. The boys had grown almost jaded at the daily parade of big news, but Ed Sullivan was big enough to make their jaws drop.

Tommy said, "Damn!" and D.D. said, "Man!" and Jack said, "Awright, boys, a*wright*!" They slapped Leroy on the back.

He didn't need to warm up. He was Red-Hot. He was Leroy the Wild Boy. He was back in the studio now, his territory, in his own clothes: jeans and a nifty dotted-rayon shirt. No tuxedos and no basset hounds. He was in charge. He didn't have to be nice. He could go just as wild as he pleased.

He knew who was buying his records. The girls didn't want him nice. They wanted him wild. Maybe Steve Allen knew more about television, maybe those critics knew more about broadcast standards and the preachers knew more about the Word of God, but Leroy knew better than anybody in the world what those girls wanted.

He had seen them in the audience, night after night, tears streaming down their faces. He had listened to their excited jabber, whenever they got him cornered. They liked the fast ones, the wild ones, the ones that made him move and swing his hips and act out the feelings their daddies didn't even know they had. He felt waves of pure longing coming up from them.

He knew what they wanted most: a boy, just one boy, a perfect date for the perfect prom, a dark-haired stranger who would come into their ugly fifteen-year-old lives and take them away.

Leroy had wanted a girl like that, too; he had never stopped being the shy tenth grader lurking at the back of the dance. He remembered the timid, gawky girls who had lurked back there with him. The unpopular girls. Now they were out there in millions. Leroy was their tall dark stranger. He was singing for them.

Onstage he tried one trick, then another, feeling them, finding the moves that got to them: Hey girls, you like when I do it that way? Okay then, let's do it some more.

In the studio he knew enough to have three microphones mounted on booms over the spot where he would sing, so he could move around and let the music take over his body. The magic always came out when he was moving.

He started with "You Ain't Never Been Good." The boys caught his mood and heated it up. They played faster and faster. D.D. ripped out machine-gun bursts on the snare. Tommy plucked out a lead line you could reach out and touch with your fingers.

It was better than old times: faster, wilder. The Leroyals crooned a slightly sour chord in the background, like an old hound dog moaning, and back of it all was Jack's solid bass line.

Leroy let out everything he'd been holding back onstage for fear of inciting a riot. He jumped and shouted the song the way he'd shouted his lines at Fred Farmer on the movie set—with every kind of turned-loose, rebellious, go-to-hell inflection he could muster.

The song was a tell-off, a novelty tune, but Tommy's notes jangled and clashed and Leroy hollered with so much passion that he turned it into a cry of burned love. You wouldn't get this worked up about somebody unless she was driving you mad.

Weelll don't be crying at me, baby
The cryin's all mine!

Leroy heard a missed beat, a squashed guitar run. "I think I was a little off on that one," he said. "Can we try it again?"

It took fourteen takes before he sang it wild enough to suit himself and everybody drilled the song at the same time.

He grinned, hearing the playback. "There's your hit, Steve."

After that, "Don't Say No" was easy, an effortless melody line syncopated against the rhythm, with plenty of room for hiccups and embellishments. D.D. laid Leroy's guitar case across his lap and struck it with mallets. The Leroyals worked out a light, swinging "bop . . . bop . . . bop-bop" to accent the high points of the beat.

Leroy climbed on as if the song were his Harley. He cruised along, revving his voice, holding back now—teasing, teasing.

> *Weeeell, baby did I kiss you right?*
> *Mess your pretty hair*
> *Did you feel a tingle running through you everywhere?*
> *Don't say no*
> *I don't want to go*

He burned with a new determined fire.

Maybe it was the news from Ed Sullivan, or maybe his flirtation with respectability on Steve Allen had settled something in his mind. He knew he couldn't sit back and sing as well as last time and be satisfied. He had to do better. He had to keep topping himself from this moment on into the future.

He could do it. He was young, rich, good-looking, and famous. There were plenty of songs with "blue" in the title and songwriters turning out more every day.

The session went on past midnight. Sholes cut a lacquer on the spot. Leroy carried it in the taxicab to Grand Central Station. He looked at it on the seat beside him in the train all the way from New York to Tennessee.

He convinced the engineer to slow the train on the outskirts of Memphis, at a clearing half a mile from Audubon Drive. He hopped down with the record in his hand.

"Don't Say No" on one side. "You Ain't Never Been Good" on the other. It was a perfect record. Perfect. Leroy had no doubt his next one would be even better. His life was lined up in a beautiful formation, the way some stars in the night sky just happen to arrange themselves into a dipper or a bear.

He strode across the field toward the grove of trees surrounding the fine homes of Audubon Drive. He thought of all the times his family had moved, usually in a hurry and usually to someplace worse. At last he had bought his mother the kind of house she deserved.

Audubon was a wide, curving street with no traffic. The houses were brick ranchers, the lawns carefully tended; the neighbor men were bankers and lawyers and doctors and insurance men. Agnes said they were mostly too busy tending their lawns to be neighborly; but there was a nice couple, the Busbees, across the street, and anyway, she loved how her Tupelo friends envied her when they drove up for a visit.

The house fitted right in with the other houses. It wasn't as showy as Leroy would have liked. You'd never notice anything about it except the profusion of Cadillacs in the driveway. He patted the hood of the pink one and went through the carport door.

Ray sat at the kitchen table. His face was shut tight. He was holding something awful inside.

"Hey, Daddy," said Leroy, "what's wrong?"

"Son, sit down."

Leroy stayed where he was in the door. "What is it?"

His father did not answer.

A bolt of terror struck him. His mother was dead.

Oh, no. Oh no.

He tasted dust in his mouth.

His father stared at him.

"Daddy. Say something. Where's Mama."

"In yonder in her room," he said. He shook his head and blew out a heavy sigh. "I don't know what to say, Leroy. I just don't know what to say."

"Well for God's sake, what's wrong? What's the matter?"

"I think her heart is broken," said Ray. "I think you have gone and broken her heart. She's locked herself in there."

In the flood of relief Leroy heard those words as good news. She was always locking herself in her room. Whatever Leroy had done, he could undo it, and she would be all right again.

He slumped into a chair, flopping the envelope with his record on the kitchen table.

Ray reached behind him for another envelope and tossed it to him. "Catch."

Leroy caught it, and took the letter out, and read it.

He read it again.

He folded it, put it back in the envelope.

"It's not true," he said. "It's a lie. Did Mama see this?"

"She opened it," Ray said. "It came registered mail, and she opened it. I came home last night, and she'd locked herself in. Oh hell, Leroy, it's a mess."

"Well Daddy, what did you tell her? You don't believe this stuff, do you? They've got the wrong guy." His mind searched frantically backward. "They're just trying to get something from me."

"I tried to tell you," said Ray. "You laughed in my face. But I tried."

Leroy rolled his eyes to the ceiling. He got up from the table and walked down the hall to her door. He rapped with his knuckle. "Mama, it's me. I'm home, now. Open up."

There was no answer. He rattled the knob and went back to the kitchen. He took out the letter and smoothed it on the table and read it again.

44

He read the name over and over. *Elizabeth*. He didn't know any Elizabeth. Liz. Liza. Beth. Betsy. Betty . . . *Betty!* Leroy remembered. The fox-eyed brunette who came after him that night in Bossier City, the Golden Derrick. He'd never even known her last name. Betty Simpkins. She had spun out her web and sat waiting and glittering at the center, waiting for Leroy to stumble in. And he had. He had stumbled right in.

Oh, she had him. He knew it. She must have been pregnant already when she laid the trap. She made sure there were witnesses. Maybe put something in his beer so he would pass out, so he wouldn't remember.

He might have done it to her. He couldn't swear that he hadn't. He didn't remember.

The lawyer's letter said they had evidence. Some sort of love note from Leroy to Betty. He couldn't imagine what that was—and then he remembered.

The night he met Sheila in Nashville. A woman appeared from nowhere during dinner. She wanted an autograph, something mushy for her daughter, or niece. . . . Sheila teased him into writing it.

What did he write? "I love you forever." Something like that.

And the name was Elizabeth.

She must have sent her mother all the way to Tennessee to procure that note. They waited until the child was born, waited until Leroy was good and famous, and then they pounced. They were a shrewd pair of spiders, and they'd laid hold of a big, fat, juicy, stupid insect.

Of course, there was always the possibility she was telling the truth and that little scrunched-up baby in the photograph . . . Leroy decided not to think about that.

He tried his mother's door again. Still locked. He pounded with the flat of his hand.

She said, "Go away."

"Satnin, open the door. It's all a mistake. I can explain it. Come on now."

"Go away."

He scuffed down the hall to his room with the flowered wallpaper and the pink telephone and the big round mirror on the wall.

He phoned Sam, who went off in a spluttering panic and said, "Just sit tight, I'm on the next plane to Memphis, don't do anything until I get there." He never even asked if it was true.

Leroy stared at his face in the mirror.

You don't look like a daddy.

"It's a lie," Leroy whispered. "It's a trap."

Are you sure? How do you know? You don't even remember. You were drunk that night. And that weed from Tommy.

"It's blackmail. She set me up." Leroy shuddered. "They could ruin everything."

A boy. A little towheaded boy baby. Your boy.

"That's it for me," Leroy said. "I'll never touch another girl."

Yeah. Right. You love it too much.

"Leroy, you on the phone?" It was Ray, just outside the door.

"Yeah, just a minute—" He grabbed the receiver, "and so anyway, that's all I know right now, I've got to go. I'll talk to you later. Good-bye," and hung up with a clatter.

Ray came in with that long, solemn face.

"Daddy, if you came in to say 'I told you so' some more, you can save it." Leroy stretched back on the bed.

"No, son, I just—I thought you might want to talk about it."

"Sam will be here this afternoon. He'll take care of it. They're trying to blackmail me."

He told what he remembered of that night in Bossier City.

"Well you can't let them get away with it," Ray said. "You've got to stand up and tell the truth."

"What good would that do? The papers are already saying I'm a bad influence. Can you picture something like this? It wouldn't matter what the truth was. Ed Sullivan would drop me like a rock."

"What do you mean, Ed Sullivan?"

"I didn't get a chance to tell you. He's signed me for three shows."

"Well, that's—that's wonderful, son." Ray's eyes gleamed like pennies.

"Yeah, it's great." Leroy shook his head. "And now this."

"How much are you getting for that?"

"Fifty."

Ray whistled. "That's—Jesus Lord. Fifty thousand?"

"You got it."

"I think maybe you're right," Ray said, "you could probably pay this gal a little something and the whole thing would just blow over and nobody the wiser."

"Sam will know what to do," Leroy said. "What are we gonna do about Mama?"

A shadow of pain crossed Ray's face. "She won't listen to me. She gets off on these jags and sometimes I think I'm gonna have to call somebody to come get her. I don't know if it's these pills she's taking or—"

"It's me," said Leroy. "It's my fault. It's all happening too fast, and I'm not around to see about her. This won't be the last time for stuff like this, Daddy. I've had too much luck, too fast. They'll all be trying to knock me down."

"I know that, son."

"But Mama can't go and have a nervous breakdown every time," Leroy said.

Ray stood up. "Let's go see if we can't get her out."

They went to the door and started knocking. Leroy hollered that they would keep knocking until she opened up, and after five minutes of hammering the door latch clicked open.

Leroy was shocked when he saw her. She must have been crying all night. Her eyes were red; her face was puffy. She had gained back the weight she had lost with the pills, and more besides. She wore a ratty old chenille bathrobe with her hair flying everywhere. The darkened bedroom was strewn with covers and candy boxes and a half-empty bottle of Smith's brandy on her dressing table. Leroy smelled it on her breath.

"Mama, Lord, you've been drinking." He brushed past her to pull up the blinds. "I didn't know you even drank."

"I have it sometimes when I get too nervous," she said. "It helps me to calm down."

"Mama, this letter you opened is trash." He pulled it from his pocket. "It's a lie. You ought to ask me about something like that before you go get yourself all messed up this way."

Ray went to make coffee. Leroy sat Agnes down on her bed and told her a cleaned-up version of the truth. A girl had set out to blackmail him. . . .

She stared out the window, her face lined with sorrow and confusion. "But you must have sweet-talked her, Leroy. Or led her on some way."

"Mama, she came up to me. I never did anything but say hello to her. I swear."

Ray came in with a mug of coffee. "Here, sweetheart, this'll make you feel better."

She took a sip. "I don't know," she said. "I don't know how you expect me to stand it. The phone never quits ringing, and there's always somebody out in the yard, trying to see in the window, and—and I try so hard to look pretty, you know, honey, I really do, but then something like this comes along, and it just makes me want to . . . I don't know."

Leroy couldn't tell whether she was talking to him or to Ray. She was gazing off somewhere behind them both.

450

"A baby," she said, in a smaller voice. "Did you see what they named him? David Robert. That's a nice name."

Leroy glanced to his father. No help there. "I told you, Mama, I had nothing to do with that girl. Or her baby."

"I wonder what he looks like," said Agnes.

Ray said, "I can't stand any more of this. Son, you see if you can deal with her." He stalked from the room.

"No, I'm serious." Agnes brightened. "Maybe he looks like you, Leroy. Maybe he does. Maybe that's where she got the idea, poor girl. She probably saw a resemblance—"

"Poor girl? Mama, she's trying to steal money from me! She's trying to ruin me!" He waved the letter.

"But you said you don't remember. So maybe it's possible—"

"No it's *not* possible!" He checked himself: Don't shout at her. "Don't you see? I'm famous. Everybody wants a piece. This is a mess of lies, and she knows it. She's betting we'll pay her money to shut her up anyway."

"I understand that, honey. I'm not a child. All I'm saying, if you would just listen to me . . ."

"Go ahead."

Agnes said, "Maybe we could go get that baby."

Oh God. Leroy was trying to deal with a blackmailer, and here was his mother deep into losing her mind. "Oh, Mama. Don't be ridiculous."

"I mean it." Her eyes were alive. She sat up in her chair. "She says she can't support him! We have plenty of money, Leroy—more than we'll ever need, long as we live. And I could look after him. You know I always wanted another baby, but it never seemed to be the right time. . . ."

"Mama, you're forty-four years old," Leroy said. "You don't want a baby. I don't know what's got into you."

"Stop saying that!" she flared. "Your father says that ten times a day, 'I don't know what's got into you.' Nothing's got into me. It's you. It's all of you. You're out running all over the country singing on TV and God knows what else, your father's out drinking, and what am I supposed to do besides set here and try not to eat and watch Dodger work her damn puzzle!"

"I'm sorry," he said. "You could come with me sometime."

"I don't want to come with you, Leroy! I need somebody here!"

"Well, you don't need a baby," he said. "Good Lord."

"You don't know what I need," she said. "That girl can't afford to raise him. We can. And you know that if we did that for her, she would be glad to forget all about this lawyer and everything."

"Mama. Now calm down. Now listen to me. Sam's coming. He'll work it all out. We're not getting any baby."

"You just don't want it," she spat. "It's yours, but you want to get rid of it. That's all you want."

"You're crazy," he said.

Agnes rose from her chair and seized the mug and flung it against the opposite wall. Coffee spewed all over.

"I am not crazy," she said. Her eyes were wild.

Leroy blew out a long, heavy sigh. "Whatever you want to call it. I'm going out for a ride."

He stood up and walked out of the house. He could hear Agnes calling him. He kept walking.

The cluster of young girls at the end of the driveway squealed when he appeared. Any other day he would have swaggered over to flirt and sign their autograph books, but he slung his leg over the Harley, jumped with all his weight on the kick starter, and roared out of the drive without even a smile.

He zoomed from the neighborhood, bouncing the growl of his engine off the polite fronts of the houses.

He raced south out of town, down Highway 51, catching bugs in his teeth. Ten miles below Memphis the hills opened out to the immense flatness of the Mississippi Delta.

Leroy fishtailed off the highway onto a farm road that ran straight as a pencil to the west, toward the river. His hand urged the bike to full speed.

Birds skittered up from the bushes as if they'd been shot. A steady, uneasy thudding at the back of his heart. His second time through that letter, Leroy thought he had glimpsed the spectacular crash of his career. *Don't let it end.*

He thought back to Sheila, to the redheaded girl in La Crosse, to other girls he had touched. What was to keep them all from hiring lawyers and sending extortion letters? From now on Leroy would have to watch his step, guard his tongue, suspect *everybody*.

Girls are not safe for you now. You're not like anybody else. You can kiss them, tease them, lead them on all you like, but you better not touch one unless you mean to marry her. And right now, with Betty's treachery whirling around him, Leroy could not imagine a girl he might want to marry.

Think what Sheila in Nashville could do if she got the idea: Yes, sir, he drugged me with narcotics, yes, sir, and then he seduced me....

He hung on with his knees as the big bike rattled and banged over ruts in the path. He tore into a broad clearing, a river bluff, slicing a wide doughnut in the soft loam with his rear wheel. He juiced the engine, rhoom-rhoom, then cut it. Blue jays set up alarms in the trees.

Leroy was killing his mother. His success was tearing her apart, piece by piece. In that horrible moment when he thought she was dead, a black shroud of guilt had fallen down over him. He had accepted the blame in two seconds.

How could he stop it?

He loved her. She was getting older and stranger every day. He couldn't stop time or even slow it down.

He couldn't give up his career and come home and take care of her. He was just getting started. He had to ride this remarkable wave. To see how famous and rich he could get. He wanted it for her and for himself. He wanted to make good music for years and years. He wanted to star in thrilling, romantic movies and wear the coolest clothes in the world. He wanted the girls never to stop screaming.

The rumble of an approaching automobile ... Leroy trundled the Harley into a stand of weeds, out of sight.

A boy and girl were in front, the windows open, her bare tanned foot hanging out of the passenger window. Two teenagers on a lunch break, sneaking out to the woods for—what else?

On their car radio Leroy heard himself singing his new ballad, "I'm Not As Bad As They Say," released just this week.

They kissed right there in broad daylight with the whole Mississippi River looking on, Leroy crooning encouragement on the radio, Leroy watching from the weeds.

Oh no, boys and girls. That can get you in trouble.

When they were all wrapped up in each other, he kick-started the Harley and blasted into the clearing. Their heads bobbed up, smacking the roof. He cut a tight circle around the car to make sure they got a good look at him, then wrenched the throttle wide open and shot out of there, laughing.

〜〜〜

Leroy watched from behind the living-room curtain. Sam Sanders lingered at the end of the driveway, peddling his eight-by-ten glossies to the girls.

Leroy met him at the carport door. "Am I glad to see you."

"Let me have that letter." Sam pushed past him and strode to the kitchen table. He sat down and drew the letter from its envelope.

Ray came in, saying, "Howdy, Sam, good to see you, Sam," in his unctuous fashion. Sam ignored him.

Agnes was sleeping. She had become so hysterical that Ray had called Dr. Davis to come with a shot.

Sam read the letter three times.

Leroy tried to explain his idea of what had happened. Sam wasn't interested. "Doesn't matter," he said. "If you met this girl, you're good as gone," he said. "We got to kill this right now and forever. You hear me? Kill it. Nip it off in the bud. Is there someplace in this house where I can use the phone?"

Leroy ushered him to his own bedroom. Sam glanced around at the flowered wallpaper and stuffed animals, and said, "Leave me alone, son."

Leroy went to stare at Ray across the kitchen table.

Fifteen minutes later Sam came out. "I'm flying to Dallas this afternoon. I'll meet with this lawyer. He's bringing all his notes, all copies of the letter, everything. I'm taking five thousand dollars and a paper for him to sign."

"What do I have to do?" Leroy said.

"You already done it," said Sanders. "My advice to you is forget the whole thing. After tonight it never happened. You got a show to do. You keep your mind on that. And I don't want you ever breathing a word of this to anybody, you hear? Ray? That goes for you and Miz Kirby."

Ray scratched his neck. "I understand."

"Wait a minute," Leroy said. "Five thousand dollars? That's it? How do we know that girl won't try to pull the same thing again?"

"They'll sign a piece of paper," said Sanders. "You just leave it to me.

One more thing. I can't help what's gone on in the past, but Leroy, my friend, starting right now, you better stay clean as a Goddamned whistle. One sniff of real trouble around you, and those Hollywood boys will blackball you so fast you won't even believe it."

"Don't worry," said Leroy. "I already thought about that." He would swear off the marijuana—imagine that particular headline: NARC KING KIRBY GETS 5 YEARS.

From now on only prescriptions from a real doctor, nice and legal and clean.

And no more girls on the road.

Five thousand dollars. It seemed so easy. Leroy had almost forgotten when five thousand dollars seemed like all the money in the world.

45

*T*here was nothing in
California Agnes wanted. She hadn't lost anything out there. Oh maybe
she'd daydreamed about going, a long time ago, when she was young
and had silly ideas. Now she knew there was nothing but trouble in the
world outside her own room.

In her room nobody bothered her. She had candy stashed all over, in
the lingerie drawer, in hatboxes, in the trunk at the foot of her bed. She
had her *Reader's Digest*s and her Agatha Christies, her bottle of Smith's
brandy in the top dresser drawer.

Agnes had decided she wouldn't get fatter if she took the diet pills and ate nothing but candy. She would have been perfectly happy to stay in bed forever, living off Agatha Christies and Whitman's Samplers, but nobody would leave her alone. Ray came in and out all the time to say, "I don't know what's got into you." Once she thought: *You're* what got into me, but she bit her tongue.

Agatha Christie's characters treated each other with exquisite courtesy, just the kind of consideration that was missing from Agnes's life. Dodger kept nagging her to get up and go for a walk, a long walk was just the thing, no matter how many times Agnes said no, thank you, she didn't feel like a walk. She thought it was hypocritical of Dodger to go on like that when she hadn't been fifty feet from her jigsaw puzzle in years. There was nothing wrong with Agnes except sometimes she cried and had ideas other people thought were peculiar.

Leroy was the only person she wanted to see. He called almost every night, but she knew he told her only the nice parts.

When he came home, his mind was always somewhere else, on some song or recording session, some girl he wasn't telling her about. Probably he had an entire secret life that would shock her to death if she ever found out. All those girls clawing at him. That Betty in Bossier City was the tip of the iceberg.

As far as anyone knew, Agnes had given up the idea of that baby, but sometimes she heard it crying in her dream. Its cries were broken by a tiny, hesitant cough, as if it were taking down with a cold. In her dream Agnes wandered around a huge rambling stone-floored mansion with no lights, trying to find the baby by following the sound of its cough. She knew it would look just like Leroy if she could find it. She would know how to hush its crying.

Leroy looked worried, these days, when he saw her. He must be ashamed, the famous singing star on his way to becoming a movie star, to have such a fat, unsightly mother. Agnes hated the mirror. She wished Leroy could have seen her when she was young and pretty.

He was so full of spirit, so cool and unflappable at the center of all the commotion. Nothing bothered him. Agnes was amazed to find she had raised a boy who could stand on a stage with thirty thousand girls screaming at him and still remember to call his mother when he got home.

All his life he loved being the center of attention, and now he was getting it all.

She had always known something big would happen to him. She had seen it at the Ouija board. She had done everything in her power to make it come true. But her sweet, bashful boy was a figment of her memory. He was gone, like the baby in her dream.

She might have done something to stop it, instead of buying that accursed guitar, leaving him alone in his room for months with that and the radio and his record player. Now it was too late. He had emerged from that room like a butterfly from its own little silk pouch—Leroy the world-famous star, spreading his flamboyant wings.

Now he had this idea that Agnes would go with him to California, thousands and thousands of miles away, while he started work on his movie.

He only wanted to keep an eye on her. He thought if he took her to California and fussed over her, it would make up for all her pain.

She couldn't tell him what was wrong. She didn't know. It had started about the time they came to Memphis, and it got worse with each year that passed.

It was a black, yawning emptiness, an unspeakable fear. She knew it had something to do with Leroy, but she wouldn't let herself turn around and see what it was. To keep her mind away from it, Agnes ate chocolates and sipped brandy and imagined she was slim and beautiful, with photographers making her picture.

Leroy wheedled and pleaded and begged her to come to California. Now he proposed to take everybody: Agnes and Ray and Dodger and Bubba Hayes and Tommy and Jack and D.D. and Sam Sanders and all the assistants and secretaries. The movie studio had reserved an entire floor of a hotel called the Hollywood Knickerbocker. That brought a picture to Agnes's mind of a turquoise swimming pool, a perfect palm tree, a slice of green lawn in the sunshine.

She could always take her pills, her brandy, and her Agatha Christies. She could buy chocolates in California. She would be close to Leroy. She would see him every night. He wanted her there. He was not like other sons. He loved her more than most. She had raised him that way.

She gave in. It made Leroy so happy.

Sometimes she pictured Ray gone, Ray dead gone and buried and Agnes a widow, sorry to see him go but still able to continue her life. Not Leroy. She would die without him. His voice on the telephone was like air when she'd gone a whole day without breathing.

He reserved a Pullman sleeper car, so she would have plenty of room to stretch out. What a sweet boy. Of course, Agnes couldn't read or sleep on a train—it was too much distraction—but she lay for hours drowsing, hearing the click of the wheels, watching the country turn browner and drier. The last tree went by somewhere in Texas.

Ray played cards in the club car with some men from Memphis and left her alone.

Leroy spent most of his time with Bubba Hayes and the others. Now and then he came in to sit by her window and sing a song or two for her.

Agnes stayed in her little compartment so she wouldn't have to talk to Sam Sanders. That man treated her with such extravagant courtesy that it made her skin crawl; there was such a thing as *too* polite. . . .

They reached California on a cloudless blue morning. Palm trees marched along the tracks. It thrilled Agnes to see green again after all that dry brown. She thought maybe Leroy was right; this change of scene would do her good.

Bubba Hayes came to help her through the crowd at the station. He seemed like a nice boy although Agnes wasn't sure what kind of influence he was on Leroy. More than once, back home, she'd had to remind him to take his feet off her nice new furniture.

If only her old friend Dot Simmons could see her getting off the train in Hollywood, California, with reporters buzzing and cameras flashing and the horde of girls squealing, "Leroy! Leroy!"

The movie people sent three black limousines to carry them to the hotel. It was such a waste of good money that Agnes decided to sit back and just watch them do it. She couldn't wait to tell everybody back home.

In fact, she had imagined herself riding in a swanky car in Hollywood; she had bought a pair of cat-eyed sunglasses like the ones the movie stars were wearing these days, so Leroy would not be ashamed to be seen with her.

She put them on and smiled at his reaction.

"These are my Hollywood glasses," she said.

"They're cool," he said. "Where'd you get 'em?"

"At Goldsmith's when I bought that dress," she said. "Do I look like a movie star?"

He grinned. "Mama, I knew you'd like it out here."

46

*L*eroy informed Bubba Hayes of the new rules: "No girls backstage at all without a chaperon. And from now on you can't leave me alone with any girl we don't already know. I mean it, Bubba. Not ever. Not for any reason. Even if I get down on my hands and knees, now, and beg you, you gotta say no. That's the rule."

Bubba's quizzical smile. "What happened, Leroy? You afraid your mama's gonna find out you like girls?"

Leroy said, "She knows that already."

"What is it then? You get too friendly with somebody?"

"I didn't get as friendly as somebody says I did," Leroy said, remembering Sam's injunction of silence. "It was nothing, really. But it's your job to keep 'em away from me."

"What can I do?" Bubba put his feet on the table. "I run into girls all day long, you know? All they want is you. It's all I ever hear. Leroy this. Leroy that. I make up stuff to tell 'em, just so they'll talk to me."

"What kind of stuff?"

"I tell 'em you don't ever sleep with a gal unless your bodyguard goes first, to make sure it's okay." Bubba grinned, showing the gap in his teeth. "They love it. Sometimes they even buy it."

Leroy laughed. "It's a good thing you came on the road with me," he said, patting Bubba's shoulder. "Think how bored you'd be, sitting in Memphis right now."

"Maybe so." Bubba popped the cap off a bottle of Schlitz. "I wouldn't have nearly got killed in a plane crash or clawed to death by those little sharp fingernails. But I sure would be bored."

Leroy was happy in California; his mother seemed to perk up in the bright, clear air. She went for little walks on the hotel grounds, sat in the sun reading movie magazines, even came to visit the set on Leroy's third day of shooting. They tried to take her picture with Leroy and the starlet Debra Paget, but Agnes wouldn't allow it.

Hal Wallis had lent Leroy to Twentieth Century-Fox for a western called *The Carson Brothers*. Richard Egan was the star. Debra Paget, a lovely brunette, was Cindy, the love interest. Leroy played Egan's younger brother, Clint Carson, who gets killed at the end.

The Carson brothers were a gang of Rebel outlaws who robbed trains after the Civil War. But Leroy didn't need to know that to play his part in the movie. All he had to do was get up at five o'clock in the morning, step into the studio limousine, spend two hours in wardrobe and makeup and hair, climb on the cast bus for the ride to the movie ranch, stand where they told him to stand, wait endlessly, squint into the sun and the lights and reflectors, speak a few lines or jump on a horse or walk from one place to another, then do it again, and again, reverse angle, close-up, wide shot, now another one, just one more. . . .

It took so much longer than making a record. There were fifty people buzzing around. Leroy had to cool his heels for hours without moving or sweating or ruffling his hair, while somebody changed a light bulb.

He flirted with Debra Paget. He studied the lithe way Richard Egan moved when the camera was on him.

He liked these movie people. They were good-looking and friendly and not at all stuck up. They seemed to like him, too. Debra Paget flirted back, wrinkling her little debutante nose. Richard Egan said Leroy would do fine in the movies if he could learn to pronounce the *L* in *help*.

The studio dentist capped his teeth with a pearly white smile. The hairdressers dyed his hair even blacker. The eyebrow lady plucked and pulled. The skin lady smoothed out his complexion with a rotary brush mounted on a cable.

On the tenth day came his big dramatic moment, the death scene. Clint Carson had brought his fate on himself. His confused loyalties had led him to side with some bad men against his brother, Vince. In this scene he took a shot at Vince, intending to miss, but in horror he watched his brother tumble wounded to the ground. He realized all his mistakes at once. He was sprinting off down the hill to help Vince when one of the dirty bastards in the bushes took him down with one shot.

Leroy dropped to the ground.

Debra Paget came running up, crying, "Clint! Clint!"

Vince crawled over. He would survive his wound. But Leroy was done for. He felt the cold fake blood dripping down his chest.

Bob Webb, the director, called a halt while they moved the cameras into position for the three-shot. "Leroy, everybody, keep your places."

Debra cradled his head on her lap. "That was good," she said. "You're good at this, Lee. We've only been working ten days."

"You guys are good teachers," he said as the special effects man squeezed more blood from the tube. "Listen—I'm not sure how I'm supposed to die. I mean, do you just shut your eyes, or let your tongue hang out, or what?"

"It's easy," said Egan. "You know that moment right before you fall asleep, when everything in your face goes slack? It's just like that. Don't open your mouth too much."

"Leroy," said Debra, "are you going to that party at Ginger's Sunday?"

462

"I promised to take Mama to the La Brea tar pits," he said. "She's got her heart set on it."

"Okay, everybody," the director broke in, "now this is a big emotional scene, let's get into our frame of mind here. Leroy, you're sorry for what you did, and you're desperate; you want Vince to forgive you before you die. You don't want to worry Cindy, though, so you're keeping a stiff upper lip. When you say that last line, you really want to make her believe it. You ready?"

"Yes, sir." He grinned, snuggling into Debra's lap. "I believe I could lay right here forever, though, if you'd let me."

She swatted him. "Pay attention!"

"Come on now, kids," Webb said. "No giggling. This is a death scene."

"Okay. Here we go." Leroy cleared his throat. He tried to imagine the damp chill on his shirt was real blood.

"Rolling! . . . and . . . action!"

Vince forgave him. Cindy pulled him close. Leroy squinted up at her and said, "It's gonna be all right. Everything's gonna be all right." He closed his eyes, let his head fall to one side.

"Cut!" The camera moved back and then in again. "Leroy, your line again," called Bob Webb, the director. "We need to get some real feeling in there."

He tried again. "It's gonna . . . be all right. Everything's gonna be . . . all right."

Again. And again. Four times. Webb wasn't satisfied. "No, your dying is fine. It's before that. You don't look hurt. I want to see tears in your eyes."

Leroy remembered Fred Farmer's advice: "If you have to cry, think about the worst hurt you ever felt in your life."

He conjured up the time he came home from running away and thought his mother hadn't missed him.

His eyes filled with real tears.

"Okay, let's roll 'em now, and . . . action!"

He felt sodden, thudding pain from the hole in his chest. He peered up through tears to Cindy's beautiful face. "It's gonna be all right. Everything's gonna be all right." His eyes fluttered; he felt everything going dim—

463

"Cut! Print it! Kid, that's great. They'll be weeping in the aisles."

On the fourteenth day Webb announced that *The Carson Brothers* had been retitled *Tender* to take advantage of the new ballad Leroy had recorded for the sound track. The shooting schedule was bumped up four days, to rush the movie for a November release.

That meant there was no time for a cross-country train ride to New York for "The Ed Sullivan Show," and Leroy had sworn to his mother he wouldn't fly. "It's out of the question, Sam," he said. "I don't care. Nuh-uh. No. I don't care. I don't want to talk about it."

Sam spent a whole morning wrangling long-distance with the Sullivan people. At last he struck a compromise: a live coast-to-coast network hookup. Ed would introduce Leroy in New York; Leroy would sing on a studio stage in Los Angeles.

The upcoming appearance was already notorious with all the screeching in the newspapers. To capitalize on the wave of attention, the mighty publicity machines of RCA, Paramount, Fox, and CBS were cranking it out by the carload; every day Leroy sifted through another pack of lies and embellishments in a manila envelope marked "Publicity." The studio people were especially fond of the rags-to-riches angle; you'd think Leroy was born in a log cabin, grew up splitting fence rails, and was getting set to free the slaves any minute. But that was all part of the game. They had to make you more interesting than you really were.

Then Ed Sullivan messed up the whole thing by crashing his car in Connecticut, three weeks before the show. Leroy felt sick when he heard the news. Two broken ribs wouldn't kill the old crustacean, but he couldn't go on TV like that. For a week Leroy anxiously followed the gossip column rumors that Sullivan would postpone the start of his season.

At last a stand-in of suitable eminence was found, the great actor Charles Laughton, whom Leroy had admired ever since he saw him gnawing a huge drumstick in *The Private Life of Henry VIII* on the late late show.

Tommy and Jack and D.D. flew in from Memphis for rehearsals four days before the show. They played at night in the Knickerbocker ballroom when Leroy got back from the set. Leroy wanted every hot lick of these songs nailed down by the time that red light blinked on.

From the car he glimpsed palm trees and green lawns, but mostly

Hollywood looked like klieg lights and cameras and mikes and the eleventh floor of the Knickerbocker.

Leroy came straight awake at 5:00 A.M. on the big day. He had to get up in front of those cameras tonight and set a whole nation on fire. Brother, that took a leap.

CBS gave two hundred tickets to girls waiting outside the Los Angeles studio—guaranteed screamers for the audience. The producer said he cared as much about morals as anybody, but he wanted the country to get a good look at Leroy in front of some real fans.

That evening Leroy waited in a tiny anteroom with Tommy and the boys and the four Leroyals. They watched on a monitor as Charles Laughton lumbered like a battleship through the early stretches of the show, intoning the names of the guests in his magisterial voice: Dorothy Sarnoff, Eddie Fisher, the Germantown Jugglers....

An assistant producer came to lead Leroy to his camera position.

The girls in the studio screamed.

The voice of Charles Laughton rang from the monitors. "And now, live, via coast-to-coast linkup from Hollywood, California, a young man, please give your warmest welcome to—Elroy Kirby!"

Elroy? Did he say Elroy? The red light winked on. Leroy grinned. He said *Elroy!*

"Leroy! It's Leroy!" the girls shrieked in protest.

Leroy grunted and made a quizzical face, as if he hadn't heard quite right. He smiled. Never mind. They all know who you are. "Thank you Mr. Laughton, ladies and gentlemen," he said, and though he hadn't prepared a speech, it just rolled out of him. "I want to say this is probably the greatest honor I've ever had in my life ... it really makes you feel good, and we'd like to thank you from the bottom of our hearts. And now"—he backed away from the microphone—" 'Don't Say No.' "

The girls screamed. The boys cranked up the beat. Leroy climbed on and went for a ride. The girls yelped into their fists through the first part of the song, but then Leroy did his Jerry Lee Lewis thing, *HMMMmmmm,* rolling his eyes, and they exploded.

> *Don't say no*
> *I don't want to go*
> *The feeling for you baby*

465

The feeling starts to grow
Don't say no

He played straight through the camera, to the girls in family rooms everywhere.

The girls in the audience screamed.

"Thankyouvermuch," Leroy said, with an extra bow. "Thank you, ladies." That got a big laugh in the studio and raised a smile from Mom and Dad in the family room. "And now, friends," he said, "if I can, I'd like to introduce you to a new song. It's not like anything we've ever done. This happens to be the title song of our brand-new movie, and it's also my newest RCA record."

He ticked off the plugs Sam had requested: "Want to say the folks over at Twentieth Century-Fox have really been great, all the wonderful stars in our cast, our director, Mr. Bob Webb, Mr. Weisbart, the producer, Hal Wallis. . . . This is my very first picture, and they really hepped me along." Take that, Richard Egan. "And now, with the *help* of the very wonderful Leroyals . . . 'Tender.' "

He knew it was risky to sing this slow, easy ballad for the first time before a wild-headed collection of his fans; they might shriek and drown out the song, or worse, they might be bored. But Leroy had a hunch they wanted a softer side of him, and this was the song—simple as a nursery tune, a three-chord stroll on the instruments, straight humming from the Leroyals. He remembered the tricks he was learning on the set. He made puppy-dog eyes at the camera.

For the first time ever he put down the guitar and simply sang for the folks.

You're so tender
Holding me this way
So tender
Your smile, your arms, your kiss—
I'll always remember
The moments like this
So tender
Tender
Tender

In the family room the girls flung themselves down before the TV, propped their faces in their hands, sighed, and fell in love.

So many fans called CBS to complain about Charles Laughton's mistake that the producers made him correct himself after the commercial. "And now, ladies and gentlemen, once more we'll switch to Hollywood, for a chance to see and hear that young man again ... Mr. Lee-rrrroy Kirby! To Hollywood!"

Ripe screams in the studio. Leroy didn't say a word this time, just opened his mouth and shouted

> *Ready, cats? Time to go!*
> *I gotta find a gal I know! I'm rockin'*
> *Ready set roll I'm a-rockin'*
> *Rock a-rock a-rock I'm a-rockin'*
> *Roll my blues away....*

"Rockin' Roll" was his cue to the girls: *Go Wild Now.* They obliged him with rainstorms of screaming. He beat his guitar. A spasm took over his leg. He had calculated beforehand just how far he could stray from the red eye and still stay in camera range. He jumped all over the TV screen at home.

Behind him Tommy and Jack and D.D. played as hard as they could without breaking strings. The Leroyals were off the stage now; this song was for rockers only. Leroy made it up as he went along. He knew the song so well that every change was an improvement. At the line *My baby's sweet like a scuppernon'—Lord, she rocked me all night long* he crossed and uncrossed his eyes, provoking a freshet of shrieks.

He almost gave too much. At the end he found himself all out of breath with the director waving him toward the camera: Say something!

He grinned, sucking air through his teeth. The hot lights— "Thankyouvermuch," he said—oh! His lungs might burst! "Phew!" He made an exaggerated swipe at his brow, sneaking his other hand around to make sure his pants hadn't split on that final lunge for the floor.

The girls screamed as if their lives were ending.

"Uhm ... Mr. Sullivan, like to say I know somewhere ... out there you're looking in on the show tonight, and ... the boys and myself are looking forward to seeing you back on TV again. Hope you're feeling fine, we'll be seeing you October twenty-eighth in New York." His mind raced: Had he thanked everyone? Was it time now to knock them dead?

It was.

He struck the tough pose with the guitar—shoulder up, leg cocked at an angle. "Friends," he proclaimed, "as a great old philosopher once said . . ."

You ain't a-nev ah-been a-goooood, bay-behh!

Leroy gave the song its wildest performance right then. He was not that sweet good-looking boy who had them all sighing "ahhhh." He was a juvenile delinquent menace in a black suit, thrashing around the stage. There was no holding back. There would never be a bigger moment.

The whole family was gathered in the family room now. Dad muttered, "What on earth?" and Mom smiled in spite of herself, and the girls went crazy on the rug. . . .

Leroy snarled at the camera. He hoped Ed Sullivan's ribs were aching right now.

47

*L*eroy boarded the train through a flying wedge of Los Angeles policemen. Girls swarmed over Union Station, pushing, shouting his name. He was glad for all the cops. He tasted frenzy in the air, like that first wild time at the Gator Bowl. He tumbled through the door of the Pullman car and hollered for Bubba to quit shoving, he was okay.

The last car of the train had been roped off for his entourage. Agnes sat in a corner of the parlor, peering around the window shade at the mob.

"Mama, come away from that window," he warned. "They'll see you and come through that glass."

"Don't they have mamas and daddies?" she said. "How can anybody let young girls run around acting this way?"

"I don't know, but thank God they do," Leroy said. "Bubba, go get my suitcase and bring it back here."

Once they were out of the chaos and headed east, to the steady rhythm of the wheels, Bubba went off to the parlor for a serious game of poker with Ray, D.D., Tommy, Tim Drexel, and a bottle of Old Forester.

Leroy changed to a sweatshirt and comfortable jeans and stretched out on one of the fold-down beds. The train made good music on the rails. He slept all the way to New Mexico.

When he awoke, he wandered to the parlor to watch drowsily over the shoulders of the poker players. Jack Brown and Sam Sanders had joined the game. Tommy was the big winner so far, but Sam's little nest egg was growing.

The train lurched, toppling his neat stacks of chips.

Leroy wandered back to the sitting room. Agnes was eating chocolates from a wax-paper bag, staring at the blackness rushing by the window.

"Let me have one of those." Leroy took the bag and stashed it beside his leg.

His mother said nothing.

"Wasn't that a great party last night?" he tried.

"Those people are fake," she snapped. "Every one of them tries to be something they're not. I'm glad you're done with that movie. You ought not have anything more to do with any of them."

"Why Mama, they liked you! What happened? Did somebody say something to you?"

"Oh, no. They were all just as friendly as they could be. Just as put on. You'd think we were old bosom buddies, the way some of them painted-up women kept trying to hug my neck. I'll be glad to be home where people don't act like they're your best friend the first time they meet you." She folded her arms.

The train sped through a crossing ding ding ding diiiiiaang dang dang. . . .

Agnes had done so well in California. The sunshine had lightened the circles under her eyes. She hardly ever drank brandy. She'd made a big hit at the wrap party for *Tender*, telling the story of the time Leroy ran away. But now she was into her chocolates again, and that sad, distracted look was coming over her face.

Leroy said, "Well. Anyway. Debra thought you were nice. I thought you two had a good talk."

She reached around him for the wax-paper bag. "She wouldn't have a thing to do with you if she didn't know you were rich." She popped a chocolate-covered cherry in her mouth.

Leroy shook his head. "Never mind. Forget I mentioned it." Debra Paget was a sweet, lively girl. They'd shared plenty of laughs over the fake gossip column romance cooked up by Publicity, and Debra had taken special pains to dote on Agnes.

Agnes said, "I can't wait to tell all my friends what a bunch of put-ons you got mixed up with out there. And you acting like you were one of 'em, I saw you, don't think I didn't. I had my eye on you."

Leroy thought: She is trying to provoke you. She doesn't have any friends. You are her only friend.

"Now, Mama," he said. "Come on. It wasn't that bad. Anyway, we're going home now. You don't have to go back out there if you don't want to."

"Neither do you," she said, with that coy little smile that said you don't want to hear this, but I'm going to say it anyway. "Well you don't," she said. "You could do just as well staying in Memphis making your records. You don't need more money. You have plenty of money."

Leroy said, "I want to see how much more I can get."

"That's just greedy," she said.

"No it's not. I *like* it. I like *doing* it. It's easy. You only have to do one thing right, one little thing at a time. And they string it all together, and it looks like you did something great, and they pay you a zillion bucks."

"You act like money's the most important thing in the world." Agnes sniffed. "We never had any money, and we got by all right."

"No we didn't!" cried Leroy. Anger overwhelmed him. "We were always just about this far from being put out in the street, and you know it! Those days are over, Mama. Nobody's ever gonna make us move again."

"Lord," she said, "poor, poor. Did you ever miss a meal? Did you spend a single night in the cold? I think you are starting to believe all that garbage those people put out about you."

Leroy stood up. "Okay, that's it, that's enough, I love you, good night." He kissed her briskly, went to his compartment, pulled down the bed.

He had gone around this argument so many times that he had run out of answers. He lay in the dark, watching the moon in the dancing telegraph wires.

He had tapped a vein of secret electricity, a miracle current that flowed out to people through his songs, through the cameras, on invisible waves through the air. Agnes wanted him to flip off the switch and come home and sit with her in the dark.

Someday he would have to make the grown-up decision and hurt her feelings all the way, and start to live his own life.

But when? How could he ever do that? He loved her too much. Wasn't it better to go on being swallowed up by her love, her notions and moods and demands, than to strike out on his own and risk destroying her?

All that night he dreamed of flat green fields, tractors raising dust in the distance. He awoke to discover it was true; they were streaking across Arkansas, headed for home.

He returned to the sitting room. His mother was all by herself, as if she'd sat right there the whole night, staring out the same window.

"I'm hungry," she said without looking up.

"I'll get us some breakfast," Leroy said. "What happened to the card sharks?"

"They took each other's money and went to bed."

Leroy rang the porter and ordered up a big meal: brown sugar oatmeal with raisins, fried eggs and grits and crescent rolls and hash-browned potatoes served on gold-rimmed plates, on lacquered lap trays. The wide fields rolled by. School buses waited at the crossings. Dogs tried hilariously to race the train.

"Leroy, I've thought about this all night," said Agnes.

Oh no. Here we go. "Come on, Mama, let's don't start again. . . ."

Agnes said, "I want you to tell Sam Sanders you're not making any more movies. You're going to stay closer to home from now on."

"I can't do it, Mother."

That sat her back in her seat. "You never called me Mother before."

"It just came out that way," he said.

"Leroy, you've changed. You're not my same boy. You're just not. Oh, I haven't wanted to tell you, I've bit my tongue a many a time"—Leroy thought: Name once—"but I don't like what's happened to you. You're, you're bigheaded, and pushy, and smart-mouthed. Why, the way you boss poor Bubba around, you'd never know the two of you used to be friends. It's that Sam Sanders. You act just like him. Now I want you to stop all this foolishness and come home and act like a normal person."

"I'm not a normal person, Mama," he flared. "The whole damn world knows that by now." He said "damn" just to put an end to the conversation.

The fields opened up wider, wider. The cotton rows ran from the tracks clear out to infinity.

Bubba Hayes wandered in, rubbing sleep from his eyes. "Leroy, I hope you're happy. Sam took every last nickel I had."

"I didn't make you play," Leroy said. "Listen, Bubba, do I boss you around? Mama was just getting on me saying I boss you around too much."

"No, sir, Leroy." Bubba smiled sleepily.

"That's good. Now take these trays up to the porter for us." He waved his hand at the breakfast remains.

Bubba laughed, and Agnes said, "Oh Leroy, you're silly," but Leroy was not smiling.

"No I mean it, Bubba," he said. "Go ahead. Take 'em on up."

"Well, sure, Leroy," Bubba said, "if that's what you want." He looked at Leroy with a quizzical smile and bent to straighten the cups and saucers.

"See Mama, Bubba does what I tell him," said Leroy. "I'm the boss. I can't help it, and neither can he. That's just the way it worked out. We're still friends. Right, Bubba?"

"He's right, Miz Kirby," said Bubba, avoiding Leroy's gaze. "Leroy pays me good. He's the best boss I ever had." He disappeared with the trays.

Leroy smiled, turned to his mother. "See? You see that? Bubba Hayes used to be the biggest man on the football team. Now he works for me. We're still friends. We're just as good a friends as we ever were. Only now I'm the boss and he knows it. Sam Sanders works for me. And Sholes. And all those secretaries, and half the people at RCA. That's the part I like."

"You're not my boy," Agnes said. "You're somebody else. That was a cruel thing to do."

"You said it yourself one time, Mama. Everybody can't win."

The train left the ground and rose into the air, soaring over the levee, out onto the steel carriage of the bridge, over the wide brown Mississippi.

Leroy was thinking: a fast ride on the Harley, maybe a cheeseburger at the Gridiron, just get out of the house. . . .

The train crept up the riverbank into Memphis. As the gloom of the train shed descended, the porter came into the car, saying something about trouble ahead in the station.

Leroy parted the curtain an inch. He could see all the way down the platform to a seething crowd of girls, pinned back by police.

The moment the train stopped moving, the girls broke free and thundered down the platform.

"Get ready," said Leroy, "it's crazy out there."

The girls of Memphis had never gone crazy before.

They had no way of knowing which car he was on—or did they? Of course they did. They were girls. They *knew.* They swarmed down the length of the train and surrounded the last Pullman car—hundreds of them squealing, jumping in the air.

Bubba Hayes ran through with a wild look. "Stay here!"

Agnes said, "Leroy, what's happening?"

"Don't worry, Mama, there's plenty of cops. Let's just sit tight a minute and let them work it out."

Girls were leaping up, smacking the windows with flat-open hands.

"This is nuts," said Ray, rushing in. "They'll break that glass!"

A bullhorn squawked outside: "Will you please move away from the train now? Please move away! Everyone please move back from the train!"

The floor swayed. Were they rocking the train with their hands?

"Oh, I think I'm going to faint." Agnes slumped to her seat.

"Daddy, see about her." Leroy walked to the front of the car. Thank you, Memphis. Thank you, Ed Sullivan.

Bubba and D.D. were huddled with two flustered Memphis cops. "There's too many of 'em," one was saying. "Sergeant's afraid somebody's gonna get hurt!"

"Well good Lord," Leroy said, "Bubba, you go get the car and get it started. I know how to stop 'em." He seized the door handle, wrested it open.

The screams rushed in. The three nearest girls fainted. Other girls tripped over them in a stampede toward Leroy.

He hopped up to the conductor's platform so they could all get a good look and stop pushing from the back. He didn't want anybody trampled to death. He held up his hand: Stop.

They jumped up and down, squealing, "Leroy! Leroy!"

He saw a blue knot of policemen working toward him through the crowd. He clung to his handle, just above the heads of the girls. He didn't say anything. He just smiled and let them look at him, and the sight of him began to work its magic. They stopped screaming and gazed at him, some with tears in their eyes. That's all they wanted right now—a good, long look.

A gabble went up:

Leroy, will you please sign my

Oh Leroy, I

My favorite song is

I'm Betty Jean and we came all the way from

Oh Leroy

Just sign this one little

Will you sign this

Can I please get an autograph

Can I please take your

Leroy, I want to

Leroy, I

Please can I

Leroy

Leroy!

"We'll see you ladies tomorrow night at Overton Park," he called, and hopped down from his perch into the wedge of policemen. "Okay boys, get me out of here."

The cops pressed ahead hard enough to get moving without knocking anyone down. The mob began to shift down the platform, retreating and folding back upon itself. Cameras flashed. Men hurried with microphones. The squealing started up again. In the midst of that madness, three deep in policemen, Leroy walked alone. No one touched him.

Bubba waited behind the wheel of the Caddy with the door open. The huddle of cops spilled out onto the sidewalk. Leroy leaped in. Bubba stomped the pedal. They screeched away from the curb, trailing a few of the fleet-footed girls in their wake.

Leroy twisted in his seat to watch them pour, shrieking, into the street.

Bubba grinned. "Man, welcome home!"

Leroy switched on the radio. The WMPS announcer was breathless: ". . . has just departed Union Station, and now we can see his parents, Mr. and Mrs. Ray Kirby, making their way toward us down the platform. Let's see if we can get a word with—no, it looks like the police are escorting them past us. . . ."

Leroy twiddled the dial: "You Ain't Never Been Good" on WHBQ. "Don't Say No" on WJDL. "Let's Play" on WMPS.

Leroy was everywhere. Memphis was his.

"I thought the train schedule was supposed to be a big secret," he said. "Sam must have called everybody in town."

"Well, I didn't tell anybody," said Bubba. "Where we going anyway?"

"Take me home."

A carload of girls pulled up alongside the Caddy to wave and honk and shout at Leroy, and then another car, and another. It took all of Bubba's skill to avoid a collision. He gunned around them on the shoulder and put down the pedal.

"Hey, Bubba, listen, sorry for that business this morning," said Leroy. "I was just trying to make a point with Mama. She's all over me these days."

"Don't worry about it," Bubba said, but Leroy could tell he was still ticked about it. No problem. Drive downtown this afternoon and buy him something.

They flashed up Airways Boulevard, made a couple of evasive maneuvers through the Getwell subdivision, and pulled into more chaos on Audubon Drive: cars everywhere, double-parked or cruising; girls on the lawns; three cops directing traffic. The focus of the uproar was 1034 Audubon, the brick-faced house with the Cadillacs in the carport. Girls lounged all over the grass. Neighbors stood around in their yards, looking unhappy. A couple of them were arguing with a cop.

"Oh, turn around and take me somewhere else," Leroy said.

"Sure. Where you want to go?"

"Never mind. . . ." Leroy took a deep breath, opened the car door, and hit the street running, running across the yard, fumbling for the key. The girls spotted him and gave chase. He barely had time to get the carport door open, get inside, and bolt it shut before they were pounding, ringing the doorbell, crying his name.

Go away, he said to himself. This is my house. Go away.

Their shadows waved at the windows, on all four sides of the house. Leroy was under siege.

He heard Bubba shouting, "Let me in, Leroy, it's me," but he pretended he didn't hear. He moved from room to room, drawing the curtains. The doorbell rang and rang. Leroy muttered under his breath, his heart banging in his chest.

He went down the hall to his room, pulled the blinds, drew the curtains over the blinds. The darkness, the peaceful little flowers on the wallpaper made him feel safe.

The doorbell rang and rang. Go away. This is my room. Leroy stretched out on the twin bed nearest the wall and switched on the radio: wild Little Richard screaming "Rip It Up," a call to chaos if there ever was one, the perfect song for a time like this. *Have a ball toni-hi-hight!*

The telephone rang. Leroy hung up on whoever it was and left the receiver off the hook.

Dodger was down in Tupelo, seeing about Aunt Edith's sickly baby. Agnes and Ray had their own key. They'd be able to get in when they got home. Right now Leroy didn't care about anyone else.

What do you want? Everybody wanted a piece. Everybody was banging on his door, trying to get in. He was handing out pieces all over—on TV, in the studio, onstage, interviews and sessions and meetings. He left a piece of himself in each place, and still they wanted more!

He glanced to the mirror.

"I wish it would stop," he said. "Not for good. Just a little while. Give me a rest."

You've got them all running to you, the silver voice said. This is what you wanted. This is what you get. Do you want it to stop?

"No—I don't know," Leroy said. "Mama's right. It's all happening too fast."

It happens the way it happens. Quit if you want to. Retire. Sit back on your little pile of money and let the world hum on by. Is that what you want?

"I can't make up my mind."

What do you want? said the mirror. You can have anything. Just work hard and leave it to me.

Leroy blinked. "I want to be happy," he said.

The mirror-boy blinked. You're a star.

Leroy combed his hair and smiled. He was. It was true.

He heard his parents come in then, with Bubba. He put on his it-don't-worry-me look and went to meet them.

Agnes said, "Leroy, what do you mean locking Bubba out of the house?"

"Sorry Bubba, I thought you had a key," he said. "I had to pee something fierce."

"So do I," Ray said, making for the back.

"Well I just can't believe what has happened to our neighborhood." Agnes took off her coat. "Would you look out there? There's a hundred girls in my front yard. Bubba says some of 'em have put up a tent in the backyard."

"It's wild," said Bubba. "Leroy, this ain't like when we left, you know? It's Ed Sullivan. It's gotta be. This is insane. The cops said they can't keep 'em out of the neighborhood short of blocking the street, and the neighbors won't let 'em do that."

Leroy peered through the curtain at the girls. Police cars cruised back and forth, flashing the neighbors' houses with their red revolving lights. A man was snapping pictures for the newspaper. Six patrolmen directed a stream of cruising teenmobiles.

"Listen, Bubba," Leroy said, "what about if I went out and played 'em one song. Do you reckon they'd go away?"

"Well, it sure didn't hurt when you gave 'em a look at you back at the station," said Bubba. "They didn't go away, but least they quit trying to tump over the train."

478

Leroy lifted the Gibson from its case. "I don't guess it could hurt, huh. My hair look all right?"

"Sure, boss...."

Leroy stepped through the front door to a flurry of squeals. The girls rushed at him from the street; some of them sprinted off to fetch cameras.

Leroy held up his hands. "Whoa, slow down!"

Bubba stepped out the door and stood with his arms folded, looming large.

The girls came to within three feet of Leroy, squealing and snapping, but Bubba's stance made it clear they shouldn't come any closer.

"Leroy, sing us a song!"

" 'Love Me Blue'!"

" 'You Ain't Never Been Good'!"

"Oh, Leroy, come on baby let's play," a girl cried. They all squealed at that.

He grinned. "Hold on, hold on," he said. "Now just listen. You gals, I'm gonna sing you a song now, and then you're all gonna go on home and leave these poor folks alone." He waved to the neighbors. "All right? That's the deal. One song, and then you'll go home. Okay?"

They squealed oh yes yes please sing a song!

"Okay then...." Something easy, a lullaby to lull them into leaving. He stepped out on the grass, strumming. The girls fell back in a reverent semicircle; by instinct the ones in front dropped to their knees, so the girls behind them could see. The police lights flashed red in Leroy's eyes.

You're so tender
Holding me this way
So tender
Your smile, your arms, your kiss—
I'll always remember
The moments like this
So tender
Tender
Tender

Some of them were crying. Many looked as if they couldn't wait for him to finish so they could run tell their friends.

A beautiful dark-haired girl gazed at Leroy with a wordless smile. He singled her out for her eyes.

Then he recognized her.

She was Dolores Roselle.

She wore her hair pinned behind her, no makeup at all. She was perfect, fresh, alive, unspoiled.

Dolores Roselle on his lawn, among all his young fans, in a beautiful white dress she must have chosen just for him.

> *I'll always remember*
> *The times that we kissed—*
> *So tender. . . .*

Dolores was even more beautiful as a woman. It hardly seemed fair. She must have spent sleepless nights wanting him, gazing at his picture with those infinite brown eyes, hating herself for the way she had treated him so long ago, before he was famous and rich.

He finished the song. He smiled at the dizzy-eyed girls leaning against each other for support.

Dolores took two steps toward him.

What a moment! What a perfect ending to the story! After all these years Leroy was worthy of Dolores Roselle's attention! Call the newspapers! Snap a picture!

"All right, now ladies," he said, "you promised. No autographs, I'm leaving and I want you all to clear out. We'll see you down at Overton Park tomorrow night."

Dolores stayed where she was. The other girls melted back toward the street.

Bubba waited at the wheel of the pink Cadillac.

"Hello, Leroy," she said. "Do you remember me?"

"Oh yes. I sure do." He unslung his guitar.

"I saw you on 'Ed Sullivan,' " she said. "You were wonderful."

"Thank you."

"I've been thinking about you a lot," Dolores said. "I just wanted to tell you I was sorry we never really had a chance—you know, back at Humes."

Leroy was starting to enjoy this. Dolores must think she was the only girl on the planet. She must think he had pined for her all these years. "No, we never did," he said. Let her speak. She has worked up a speech.

"We all acted so silly back then," she said, "I was all caught up trying to be Miss Popularity. I remember I was awful to you one time. I've always felt bad about it."

"I'm glad to hear it," he said. Let her squirm.

"Have you hated me all this time?" Her eyes glimmered. "You act like you hate me."

Leroy felt his cold smile beginning to soften.

She was so lovely. How could he be cruel? Wasn't he miles past the pain she had given him?

No. He was not. He *had* pined for her all these years.

She hurt him so bad. He could not let himself be hurt that way again. He was famous now. He didn't need pain.

"That was a long time ago," he said, thinking: How could I ever hate you? I loved you! "We were just kids."

The girls, growing jealous, began to edge back across the grass toward them.

"I know I don't mean anything to you now," Dolores said, "but I see your face everywhere. I had to come find you, and tell you I was sorry."

"I'm glad you did," he said. "Really. I didn't mean to be mean. . . ."

"I don't want anything from you. I just thought . . . maybe we could be friends."

A frizzy-red-haired girl sidled up. "Leroy, can I have your autograph?"

Dolores backed away. "I won't bother you. I know you've got—" She waved her hand at the girls, closing in now like buzzards circling a kill.

"Can I call you?" he said. "I'll call you."

"Leroy, can I take your picture?"

He lost sight of Dolores among the barrettes and eager faces. He fended his way through to Bubba in the Cadillac.

He could have her if he wanted. He could have any girl in Memphis. They all wanted him. He remembered the poor little sensitive boy who would have died for one kind word from Dolores Roselle.

He was harder inside now. He let everybody else do the wanting. He let them want *him*.

"What was that all about?" Bubba steered around the blue barricade. "Don't I know her from somewhere?"

"Went to Humes." Leroy stuck a panatela slim between his teeth. "Her name is Dolores."

"Oh yeah, oh sure!" Bubba smiled. "Man, she turned out all right. Are you gonna go for some of that, or what?"

"I don't think so." Leroy checked his hair in the mirror. "I tell you what, Bubba. I feel like spending some money."

They headed downtown.

A crowd gathered out front while Leroy was in Foler's Jewelry and trailed him down the street to Goldsmith's.

Leroy spent a few minutes leafing through sport coats while Bubba and two security guards tried to keep the girls from knocking over the shoe displays.

Leroy paid cash for a nice cashmere blazer and a rich-looking white wool sweater, size XXL, while Bubba worked out an escape route through back elevators and an alley.

"I don't know, Bubba," Leroy said when they reached the car. "Maybe we can get Goldsmith's to open up after hours. I wanted to go by the Irvings', but I can't try on clothes with all these people looking at me."

He steered the Cadillac down Union Street, past the Rocking Records studio. Dan Tobias was probably in there mixing it up with some new singer, some nervous skinny kid dying to sing. Okay kid, what have you got to show me that's new?

"Bubba, look in the bag," Leroy said. "That sweater's for you."

Bubba fished it out. "Looka here, man, that's great. Look, it's my size and everything! You didn't have to do that."

"Well I wanted to," Leroy said. "After this morning."

"Forget it," said Bubba. "I already forgot it. Great sweater." He put it back in the bag.

"Tell you, Bubba, I thought Memphis was the one place on earth where folks would leave me alone. You want me to drop you somewhere, or you want to come home with me?"

Bubba threw his big, hammy arm over the seat. "There's a game on TV. I guess we can just stay in the house, huh?"

A car full of teenagers raced alongside, honking and waving. Leroy barely noticed. "I can't stay in the house for the rest of my life, Bubba," he said. "What am I gonna do?"

"I'll tell you, man, you may just have to stay in for a while." Bubba rolled down the window. "I'm just one guy, you know? I can't protect you. There's fifty of 'em gathered up any time you set foot outside. If you want to go out like this and let 'em run all over us, it's fine with me. You're paying the bills. But I think you gotta realize, friend. It *is* different now. It is. You can't run around like you used to."

"Why the hell not," said Leroy. "Why can't I do what I want?"

"You're the king, son." Bubba grinned. "That's what they call you now. Leroy the king. That's you. Now you did it, and nobody else did, so quit your bitching and start loving it. Jesus, how I would love it. I'd switch places in a minute. You want to? Come on."

Leroy had to smile. "The king," he said, "go on. Where'd you hear that?"

"The deejays," said Bubba. "You hadn't heard it?"

"The king." Leroy swung the de Ville around a corner. "I kind of like it."

"I thought you would."

Leroy touched the brake. Now there were eight police cars flashing lights on Audubon Drive, officers placing barricades at the intersections. The crowd of girls had swelled so that there was no room for the car to get through.

"Man alive," he said. "Reckon I shouldn't have sung 'em that song. Looks like every one of them ran home and brought back three or four friends."

"Okay, okay," said Bubba, "how we gonna get you in the house?"

"Hit and run," Leroy said. "Here I go." He flung open the door and set out flying across the yard, counting on speed and surprise to save him. He got inside the door and locked it before the herd made it around the side of the house.

The pounding, the squealing, the ringing doorbell.

Agnes looked up from her chair with tears in her eyes. "Oh honey, where have you been? You've got to do something! We're prisoners in our own house!"

"It's okay, Mama," he soothed, "I'm here now. Bubba's coming in. We'll watch some TV. Just ignore them. They'll see I'm not coming out, and they'll go away." A siren went blooowoop outside. "There's plenty of police," he said. "It's all right. Let me run in here a minute."

He went to the bathroom, undid the buttons on his fly. He heard something thumping at the window, drew the shade aside with his finger; three girls pressed to the glass and shrieked when they saw him.

He dropped the shade. He couldn't even pee in private.

It took a long time before he could forget about the noise they were making and start his stream. This was some kind of wonderful nightmare. The girls loved him. They were crawling out of everywhere, invading his life. They wouldn't leave him alone.

He walked into the living room to find Agnes eye to eye with three girls who had simply opened the front door and marched in.

"There he is! There he is!" they cried, rushing for Leroy. Bubba Hayes dashed in to grab them and hustle them back out the door. He wasn't too nice about it.

"Mama, I'm sorry," Leroy said.

She sank to a chair. "My stars. They just picked the lock and walked right on in."

"I'll figure out something," said Leroy. "Don't—Mama, don't. Don't cry, now, it's okay. I'll figure it out."

48

*E*arly on a September morning Leroy packed Agnes and Ray into the pink Sedan de Ville. They slipped out of the driveway without waking the girls in sleeping bags and pup tents on the lawn.

They turned south on Highway 78, for Tupelo. This was their first fresh air since California, their first time on this road since the day they came to Memphis.

"How many years ago?" Agnes rolled down the window to admit the cool breeze. "Could it just be eight years?"

"It's got to be longer than that," Ray said.

"No, that's about right." Leroy switched off the radio. "I think I was thirteen."

"Your daddy tied everything to the car," Agnes said.

Leroy was the first to laugh. "Yeah, he had it tied," he said, "and remember how that cop helped him tie it better?"

"Ah ha-ha—" Once Agnes got started laughing, she got so tickled the tears streamed down her cheeks and she couldn't stop.

Ray didn't look all that amused; Leroy remembered that his mother hadn't laughed very much when it happened.

"Oh the look on your face, Ray," she gasped, "oh I'll never forget it! And all because you and Lether had—had stolen a pig!"

Ray had to laugh then, because it was true and they were so far away now from those desperate days. "You know," he said, helping the conversation along, "I wonder what would have happened if we'd gone to Birmingham that day, instead of to Memphis. We almost did, you know."

"I'd hate to have to live it all over again to find out," said Agnes.

"That was a big day." Leroy drummed fingers on the wheel. "I remember every single inch of this road. I can show you right where the stuff came off the car."

"No thank you," Ray said, stretching out in back. "I thought we were done with all that, but it looks like we're moving again. Least we can afford a moving van these days."

"We're not going anywhere," Leroy said as they flashed through New Harmony. Every one of these towns stirred a memory. "We're staying right there on Audubon Drive."

"That Mr. James from the neighbor committee came over night before last," Ray said. "You know they've got up enough signatures to present that petition. They're taking it down to the city council on Tuesday. We have to do something."

Leroy said, "If those people don't like having a few girls around, why don't *they* move? We're not even done putting the pool in yet!"

Agnes said, "I think your father is right. We ought to find a house with a fence around it. Those neighbor women look down their noses every time I hang my wash out to dry. It's not as if I don't have a dryer. But sheets just don't smell the same if they don't hang out on the line."

Leroy slowed to let a Greyhound bus roar by. "Look, our house is bought and paid for," he said. "All the snotty lawyers on that street will still be making house payments twenty years from now. I say let *them* move, if they don't like it."

"Son, let's face it," said Ray. "That's supposed to be a quiet street, not a hangout for girls. You're a one-man disturbance of the peace."

"I'm so embarrassed," Agnes put in. "Those poor people, I'd be just as mad as they are, girls trampling all over the yard and no place to park in front of their own house. I won't even walk outside, I'm so afraid I might see one of them."

"If we get a place with a fence," Leroy said, "the girls will just climb over the fence."

"Not if you make it high enough," said Ray.

"We could come back to Tupelo," Leroy said. "I could buy the whole town and put a fence around that."

"Yeah you could," Ray said, "but then what would you have?"

Agnes put on her cat-eyed sunglasses. "Well all I know is I can't hold my head up on that street," she said. "I can't stand the thought of those people having meetings and setting around talking about us."

They were right, and Leroy knew it. He was too big for Audubon Drive. Maybe it wouldn't be so bad to have a place where he could step out his front door without a crowd there to gawk at him.

"Okay, Mama. I'll start looking when we get back. But I still don't think it's fair."

"No it's not fair," Agnes said. "I never had any idea you'd get so popular we'd get run out of our own house either."

Leroy drove on for an hour while she stared out the window, lost in her thoughts. The radio played "Tumbling Tumbleweeds."

The hills of Mississippi looked poorer and meaner now, the cows hungrier, the shacks faded and bleached out like bones.

Ray began snoring softly in the backseat.

Leroy was glad he had held off coming back until his fame was bigger than Tupelo. A day of pure, unfiltered hometown glory would taste sweet.

He glanced at the rearview. A police car was tailing him, right on his bumper. "Ah-oh." His foot touched the brake. The red light flashed and began to revolve.

Agnes looked back. "Oh, my stars. Were you speeding?"

"No." Leroy pulled to the shoulder. His heart went flump.

Leroy still did not have a driver's license.

He had meant to go back and take the test sometime; he had kept meaning to do it for years after that brush-cut army sergeant flunked him for running a four-way stop. The first year or two he didn't go because he was afraid his mother would find out he'd lied to her. Then it came to seem terribly illegal that he had been driving all that time without a license. He thought they might toss him in jail.

He was a good driver. He never got stopped.

After a few more years he had forgotten all about it.

Until this moment. Sweat broke out on his palms. A skinny cop strode up in the rearview mirror.

LEROY NABBED ON LICENSE CHARGE

He never even carried a wallet, just a wad of cash in a gold lightning bolt money clip. He wondered: How much does it cost to buy a Tupelo cop?

Agnes peered at him curiously.

The cop squinted down. "Leroy Kirby?"

"Yes sir, that's me."

"Well, welcome to Tupelo! We had a description on your car and they put me out to take you to your official escort."

"Well, gee, thanks, Officer, thanks a lot," Leroy said, "but I don't think we really need all of that." He let out a lungful of dread.

"Oh yessir, we surely do. They've got Main Street blocked off and there's buses parked all around down there, it's just a mess down there. You'd never get through on your own."

Leroy knew his homecoming appearance would be a big deal to the folks at the Mississippi-Alabama Dairy Fair, but he'd almost told Bubba Hayes to take the day off; he didn't expect any real hullabaloo. He hadn't considered the madness might have spread all the way to Tupelo.

Agnes leaned across him. "We're trying to get to my sister's house," she told the officer. "Irene and Hardy Kirby. It's on the Old Saltillo Road. She's waiting dinner on us."

Ray stirred in the backseat.

488

The cop said, "Ma'am, I believe that's scheduled for this afternoon. My instructions were to bring you straight on to City Hall, got the mayor and everybody down there waiting on you."

"Well, you're the law," Agnes said.

"I'll have the dispatcher call your sister and tell 'em you'll be delayed," said the officer.

"Can you do that? Oh, thank you." She settled happily into her seat. "Irene'll have a fit when she gets a call from the police!"

"I didn't know it would be like this," Leroy said, swinging in behind the officer's car.

The siren set up a wail. Ray came bolt upright. "What's that!"

"It's okay, Daddy, it's a police escort. Wake up now. The whole town has come out to see us."

Quickly the lead car was surrounded by six black-and-white Mississippi Highway Patrol cars, flashers on, sirens screaming, four motorcycle cops on blatting Harley cruisers.

Leroy was thinking: Make a note. Have Bubba call the license bureau. Tell them you lost your license. Let Bubba work out the confusion when they can't find the paperwork. Deny everything. You are a star.

Cars and pickup trucks jammed the streets leading downtown. The motorcade weaved around sawhorses and roadblocks.

"Look Mama, look at the picture show." The marquee said WELCOME HOME LEROY AGNES RAY KIRBY. Main Street was jammed with people, as for a parade. A blue-lettered banner stretched over the street: WELCOME LEROY TUPELO LOVES YOU. Katz Drugstore sported a *Tender* display in its window, and Mr. Bobo's hardware had a giant blue plywood phonograph record hanging from the sign out front.

The pink Cadillac glided through the crowd to the steps of Tupelo City Hall. Two ranks of patrolmen closed around it. Across the street on the steps of Belk's Department Store, the Tupelo High School marching band played a ragged arrangement of "Don't Say No."

Leroy stepped from the car. A big cheer rippled the crowd, and screams from a whole block of girls held back by a line of state troopers.

Leroy was swept through the crowd and right up to Mayor Ball, who beamed at him as if he were a welcome visitor from another planet. The mayor shook his hand, kissed Agnes on the cheek, pumped Ray's hand, shook Leroy's hand again. "We surely are proud of you, son," he kept saying, "we surely are."

Another herd of policemen brought in C. T. Just, the governor of Mississippi. Leroy shook the governor's soft, sweaty hand and turned to the crowd.

He looked for familiar faces, but it was as anonymous as any of his audiences. There were plenty of older folks mixed in with the girls. He was glad he'd had the Caddy washed and polished, with all those people standing around gaping at it. A sheriff's deputy had been posted on each bumper to prevent any damage.

One thing you could say for Tupelo: They had all the law and order in the world down here.

Someone produced a microphone. Governor Just read from a scroll: ". . . and the great state of Mississippi joins this proud community in proclaiming today, September twenty-sixth, 1956, Leroy Kirby Day, and welcoming home America's number one entertainer in the field of popular music, Tupelo's own native son, Lee-roooooooy Kirby!" The girls squealed and struggled against the police lines. Leroy waved the scroll over his head.

The mayor advanced with a three-foot-long key to the city, shaped like a guitar. His amplified voice echoed from the storefronts: "Ladies and gentlemen, this is a historic day for the city of Tupelo. . . ."

Leroy let his attention drift. Leroy Kirby Day. Who would ever have imagined? He had thrilled to Valentino in the picture show, just over there. He had spent long summer afternoons dawdling in and out of these stores, wishing he had a dime to buy something, anything.

Now his mother looked stunned behind her cat-eyed sunglasses with all of Tupelo in the street before her. His father nodded and grinned, shifting back and forth on his feet.

Now the THS band stood at rigid attention. The townspeople beamed up at him. Blue plastic streamers flapped above the packed street. A flight of crows winged over, paying no attention at all. Leroy was home. This was his day.

". . . behalf of all your old friends and neighbors, it gives me great pleasure to welcome you back to Tupelo and to present this key to our city."

Leroy stepped to the microphone. He held the key like a guitar, pretending to strum a few chords. "Thank you, Mr. Mayor, Governor, thank you, friends. Like to say it's wonderful to be back home. I can't tell you. . . . We hope to see everybody out at the fairgrounds, and we'll try to put on a good show for you."

Girls howled. Flashbulbs popped. Leroy grinned. Agnes took a step back at the onslaught.

The chief of the Highway Patrol came up to report that a group of girls had broken the lines and was making an end run through a back alley. "It's too risky for you to ride in the parade," he said. "We can't guarantee your protection."

The governor mulled it over a moment and decided to remove Leroy from the scene for his own safety.

"What parade?" Leroy said, waving to the girls as the governor hurried him to the Caddy. A state trooper had taken over the wheel. Leroy piled in back with the folks.

The motorcade wound up its sirens, matching the screams of the girls breaking through the blue line in twos and threes. Some of them got close enough to lay a hand on the car before they were dragged away, kicking and crying.

The insistent nudge of the lead black-and-white cleared a path. The line of cars swerved around sawhorses and shot onto a road leading out of town. The trooper explained that they would approach the "Hardy residence" from the east, to avoid the parade route.

The howling caravan crossed the highway and circled Tupelo on a farm road.

Ray said, "Son, I want you to know this is just about the greatest day of my life."

Leroy wasn't sure whether that was for his benefit or the state trooper's, but he said, "Thanks, Daddy. I'm glad you could be here to see it."

"I hope Wilbur Dees was out in that street," Ray said. "And Tyrell Banks, and old man Tines. . . . I hope they all saw that. Nobody down here ever thought I'd amount to a hill of damn beans."

The first time Leroy sang at the fair, he remembered, Ray was off looking for work. After all these years, Ray had found the perfect job: Father of Leroy. It paid him well, and it didn't require much work. He was good at it.

"It's not Ray Kirby Day, you know," Agnes said.

"I don't care, he's my boy and I can be as proud as I want. This town never did me no favors. Son, you go ahead and lord it over 'em."

The trooper smiled, with his eyes on the road. "I don't think they'll be interrupting your dinner," he said. "We've sealed off the whole neighborhood. Nobody gets in or out without going through the checkpoints."

The motorcade whizzed past a settlement of Negro houses; children ran to the road, waving. A huddle of great oaks shielded an empty space at the middle of a bean field, where the Greater Mount Zion A.M.E. Church was supposed to be. Fire or wind must have erased it.

Leroy was amazed at how measly and insubstantial everything looked. He remembered a great distance from Mount Zion to his granddaddy's place, but the trip took about three minutes.

The junction of the highway with the Old Saltillo Road was blocked by three sheriffs' cars and two men on foot checking IDs. The motorcade peeled away. The lead car and the pink Cadillac roared on through.

Another brace of cops stepped aside at the entrance to Hardy's driveway.

The yard was crowded with pickups and cars. Dodger had come down three days early with Uncle Johnny to help Irene get ready for the reunion. Hardy and Irene lived in Granddaddy's old house now; the last anyone had heard from the old man was a card in 1953 postmarked Midland, Texas.

The sirens brought them all to the porch—Kirbys and Smiths and friends of the family and old ladies and young girls and kids spilling down the steps.

Leroy said, "Mama, don't get too far from me, now. I don't know half these people."

"Neither do I," Agnes said, getting out. "I believe Irene has invited the entire town."

"I'll wait right here," said the trooper. "We leave for the fairgrounds at two-oh-five."

Leroy spied his aunts Irene and Christine huffing across the yard with their grandchildren, racing to see who would be the first to hug him. They cried, "Here he is, look! Mr. Movie Star! Oh, welcome home," and mobbed him like a crowd of fans, Irene pinching his cheek, Christine hugging his waist while the younger cousins and nieces yapped and pulled at him.

Leroy held up his hands in surrender. "Whoa, stand back! Don't handle the merchandise!"

Then Uncle Hardy was there to slap his shoulder, and Cousin Bobby and his new wife, and Travis, Annie Lois, Jake and Inez and Billy and Renee and their children and friends of their children, barking dogs, a gaggle of old ladies, Brother and Sister Wilson from the church. . . .

Agnes wept, hugging their necks. Ray beamed and shook every hand in sight.

Leroy let them touch him and poke and pat. The eyes of the old ladies lit up when their turn came to hug him. "Honey, I'm just an old woman," whispered hunchbacked Great-aunt Lucy, batting her eyes up at him, "but I do declare you're just about the cutest thing I ever seen."

Even Dodger stood in line, Dodger who lived with them on Audubon Drive and saw him all the time—even Dodger came out in her apron and got in line with the other ladies to receive a hug from the famous Leroy.

"Minnie, you must be so proud," they said, and, "Doesn't he look darling," and, "When are you going to get married, Lee?" and "Lord, I remember when you were just this high," and all the other embarrassing things they could think of.

Some of the older cousins and nephews skulked around in back, looking sick with envy.

Leroy was trapped. This wasn't a family reunion. This was Leroy Kirby Day. He didn't have Bubba Hayes to clear out a circle around him; anyway, these were his kinfolks, they knew him too well for that. It was his duty to let them fondle him just as much as they wanted. He'd made each of them famous within their own circle of friends; he had to give them something to tell when they got home.

He found himself standing on the front steps surrounded by twenty people waiting to hear what he would say next. Separate crowds had formed around Agnes and Ray and the pink Cadillac.

"Skeeter, how much money'd you make last week?" That was Hardy, grinning ear to ear.

"Aw I don't know, Uncle Hardy, about a million dollars I reckon," he said, laughing.

Inez said, "Did you like Ed Sullivan? Is he nice?"

"I hadn't got to meet him yet, Aunt Inez," he said. "He had a car wreck and missed my first time on the show, remember? I'll see him next month. I understand he's kind of hardheaded."

That was just the stuff they wanted: inside dope on famous people. He told about Tommy Dorsey's shaky hands, Steve Allen's wisecracks and backstage antics, the price tag on Minnie Pearl's hat, Richard Egan's fire red Jaguar, Debra Paget's kidney-shaped swimming pool, Milton Berle's big, bushy eyebrows. They ate it up.

"Leroy, tell about New York City!"

"Wait, wait," he said. "Come on, folks, this ain't a press conference. Hey Annie Lois, didn't I see somebody walk by with a plate of food awhile back?"

"You sure did, poor child," she said. "Sit right there. I'll make you a plate."

"No, I'll get it." Leroy got up, and his audience got up and decided they would go in and eat, too. Of course, they made him go first in line, then stood around to see what he put on his plate. He took a little of everything, so as not to hurt any feelings. When he spooned up a double helping of oyster dressing, he saw Aunt Inez light up in triumph.

"Here, Leroy," said Irene, bustling up, "try a piece of my sweet potato pie. You always used to like it."

He went to sit at the table, but everyone crowded around. He carried his plate to the porch. They followed him there. He went down into the yard and stood with the plate in his hand. The food was delicious, but he couldn't eat it because no one would give him a moment's peace.

He put down his plate. "Y'all excuse me just a minute. I'll be right back." He stuck his hands in his pockets and strode off down the hill toward the little house where he was born. They all stayed on the porch and watched him go. For once nobody tried to follow.

The back door hung on one hinge. Leroy set it off to the side and stepped in. The poor little place had been open to the weather for years; the wind had piled brittle leaves in the corners, and vines were reaching in through open windows, curling over the sills. No furniture. A yellowed wall calendar, Liberty National Life Insurance, 1936. The year after he was born.

There were only two rooms. A broken chair, a tumbled brick fire-

494

place. The whole house would fit inside the kitchen on Audubon Drive. The curtain between the rooms hung in rags.

Leroy never realized until this moment just how poor his parents had been. Through the years the Kirbys had always kept moving, and inch by inch, things had improved. It was a shock to come all the way back to the beginning. Imagine carrying on a whole life in these pitiful rooms!

This was the truth, the sagging ruined truth. The people from Publicity should come take a picture of this.

Leroy moved to different places around the floor, trying to feel out the spot where he took his first breath.

The house smelled like the damp woods.

Leroy smiled at himself, at his fortune. He ought to buy this house from whoever had let it run down. He ought to set it back on its foundations, put the door on, fix the fireplace. He didn't know what he would do with it, but this house belonged to him. He was born here. He couldn't just let it collapse.

This idea made him feel better. He went outside and back to the porch, where everyone was waiting to look at him some more.

Uncle Jake tried and tried to convince him to sing one of his songs for the kids, but Leroy had spent enough time on display. He was glad when the trooper signaled time to go. He made his way back inside for another round of hugs and kisses. He stepped out in time to hear Jake mutter, "And I reckon he don't sing unless you pay him."

Leroy wheeled. "What was that, Uncle Jake?"

"I didn't say nothing. Why, what did you think I said?"

Leroy knew everyone was watching for the first sign that he'd grown too big for his britches, and he wasn't about to give them the satisfaction. "Well, I thought you said you'd pay to hear me sing," he said, "but I already gave Aunt Irene enough tickets so everybody can go tonight for free."

They all cheered. Jake turned red. "Well, that's fine, Leroy, that really is," he sputtered, "real nice thing to do."

"Now I got a matinee show," Leroy said, starting down the steps. "Y'all don't let Jake eat all the pie. Save me a piece." He strode to the Cadillac and waved the trooper away from the car. "I'm driving myself."

"You're the boss," the man said.

Leroy started the car, put his hand out the window, waved, and honked the horn all the way out of the yard. He felt as if he'd escaped a new and ingeniously subtle form of torture.

Four Tupelo police cars picked him up at the roadblock. They set off at full cry for the fairgrounds.

Twenty-five thousand people jammed the arena for the afternoon show. Mayor Ball came out onstage to present Leroy with the key to the city all over again. The governor made a short talk.

The city fathers trundled Leroy's seventh-grade teacher, Mrs. Lathem, onstage to read a shaky little speech about what a well-behaved boy he had been. "And in conclusion," she quavered, "those of us who remember you fondly are especially pleased that you have set such a fine example for children just beginning their journey through the Tupelo Consolidated School District. Welcome home, Leroy Kirby, and God bless you."

Leroy leaned to the mike. "Thank you, Miz Lathem. . . ." He stared out across a sea of people who knew him.

These people didn't care about the hip shaking, the rumors, the bad boy image. All they knew was Leroy was the richest and most famous young man in America, and he came from Tupelo.

"You know, friends," he said, "I used to sneak over that fence out there sometimes, and they'd escort me out of the fairgrounds. But this is the first time I ever got escorted *in*."

That earned a big laugh.

When the stage had been cleared of all the respectable people, Leroy turned to the boys, put his hand in the air, and brought it down. *Well I walked a lonely highway—*

The girls screamed, pressing up to the stage.

—a million miles for you!

Cops flooded in from all sides, struggling to prevent a riot while Leroy did everything in his power to make it happen. You're Breaking My Heart. Rockin' Saturday Night. You Better Look Out for Me.

He sang and jittered and teased and got them all shrieking, the ones way in back by the exhibit halls, the ones in the front row, every one in between. Tender. I've Never Been Lonely Like This. Tupelo girls were

496

made of the same stuff as girls everywhere; they knew what to do. All he had to do was ignite the fire.

He roamed the stage. Don't Say No. He fell down on one knee. Let's Play. He picked out individual girls and pointed his finger and watched them keel over. Love Me Blue.

Four times a wave of girls rushed the stage, and four times the cops pushed them back.

A riotous close: *You ain't a-never been a-gooood, baby!*

He ran off to a thunderous roar.

Governor Just pulled him aside. "I've ordered up fifty National Guard for tonight's show," he said. "Better safe than sorry. That was pretty serious out there."

"Well thank you, Governor," said Leroy. "I don't know what makes them act like that."

"Yeah, I bet you don't," said the governor. "I saw you shaking your fanny up there."

Leroy grinned. "It ain't that, it's my leg. I don't know what it is. They just seem to like it."

The governor said, "Well, I know I wouldn't let my daughter come to watch you."

"Aw, you might try to stop her," said Leroy, "but I bet she'd find a way to sneak out and come anyway."

That brought a stricken smile to the governor's face. Leroy guessed he'd touched a nerve; one of those thousands of girls probably *was* the man's daughter, and he'd just realized it.

Before Leroy got a chance to do any more damage, Bubba appeared with more cops to lead him away. They passed behind the stage through a dark hallway, past the grandstand where he had stood long ago to watch the baby show. Men in uniform were posted every five feet to guard his path.

Exhibit Hall E had been cordoned off for him. Bubba ushered him to a cinder-block kitchen at one end, where he was to wait between shows.

"Okay, Leroy," said Bubba, "we got fifty-six people out there claiming to be close personal friends and relations of yours. How you want me to handle it?"

Leroy inspected the homely surroundings. "Bring 'em one at a time," he said, sprawling in a chair at one end of a long table.

Tommy and Jack and D.D. wandered in, doing their imitations of Governor Just: "Lee-roooooooy Kirby!" Leroy congratulated them on a hot set. "Now we got to stay hot for tonight, boys," he said. "No slacking off. These are the home folks. My whole family's gonna be here."

"Man, them cops was getting concerned during the last couple tunes," said Jack Brown.

Leroy told them the governor had called up the National Guard for tonight. They thought that was swell.

Bubba came in with the first visitor: Dot Simmons, Agnes's old friend from the shirt factory. She was thrilled when Leroy remembered her name and got up to kiss her cheek. "Oh, how is your sweet mama?" she said. "I've been meaning to call her for ages, but—I just know she's so busy, with all that's happened, and I didn't want her to think I was—anyway, I had to come see you. Oh! You were marvelous."

"I'm glad you could come," Leroy said. "I know Mama will want to see you. She's out at Hardy's. Why don't you go out there? Bubba, can you get Miz Simmons some kind of a pass to get up there to Hardy's?"

Bubba went to take care of it. Dot blew Leroy a kiss on her way out.

Next came his fifth-grade teacher, Mrs. Dempsey, all bright-eyed and fluttery, snapping his picture with a Polaroid camera. She still bubbled with enthusiasm, even though she was tiny and gray-haired now. "Leroy, honey, you don't know how proud we are!" she cried, waving the wet print in the air. "I've told so often about the time I brought you out here to sing that my Lakey says he can't stand to hear it! Oh, don't you look good!"

"Thank you, Miz Dempsey," he said. "That was the first time anybody ever asked me to sing in front of folks," he said. "Look what you started."

She blushed. "Don't say that. It was you who had all the talent! I'm just so pleased what you've done with it. You come across so politely on TV."

"Well, thank you, Miz Dempsey. I know my mama'll be glad when I tell her you said that."

"I won't keep you, there's others waiting—" She craned up to kiss his cheek. "You just stay sweet," she said. "Don't get the big head."

"Don't worry." He escorted her out. Mr. Jennings, who used to live two doors away on North Green Street, cried, "Ho! There he is!" and came in, trailed by Roland Purvis and his mother. Roland ran the auto parts store now. He said he could get Leroy any part he wanted at straight invoice. He slipped Leroy his business card as if it were worth big money.

Next came Mr. Cole, the old Lawhorn principal, and three of his daughters. Then Leroy's old pal Jackie Bolton, his wife, and two toddlers; Jackie brought the news that Tupelo Joe Bolton had given up singing and had gone off to do missionary work in Venezuela.

Mr. Bobo from the hardware. Emma Davis Foster, who still limped on the leg Elmer Russell broke playing dodgeball at East Tupelo Consolidated School. Two of the three Triplett boys, greasy and shiftless as ever. Four members of Leroy's Sunday school class at the Priceville Assembly of God.

One by one and in small groups, they came. Most of them started off with "I know you don't remember me," and sometimes they were right and went away disappointed.

They all knew *him*. They'd seen him on TV. They'd bragged to their friends about what close friends they were with the famous Leroy Kirby. But how could they expect him to recognize them? They weren't the same people. They'd grown up or grown old, widened out or turned gray, gotten married, had babies, lived their lives.

He was polite to them all. To the ones who asked for his phone number, he gave Sam's office line. He signed autographs, hugged necks, posed for snapshots.

Mary Edna Meecham, his seventh-grade crush, came in. She was fat with four kids and a dumb-looking husband; that gave Leroy a twinge of satisfaction.

When her time came to leave, Mary Edna burst into tears.

"What's wrong, honey?" he soothed, putting his arm around her plump shoulder. "Don't cry, Mary Edna. What's wrong?"

The husband stood glaring at Leroy with burning eyes. "I'll tell you what's wrong," he said. "Not a day goes by she don't tell me how you used to be sweet on her, how she oughter married you so she'd be rich today. I hope you're happy. I hate your damn guts."

"Shut up, Earl," Mary Edna blurted through her tears.

Bubba came to hurry them out.

"Well, admit it," Earl cried from the doorway, "you were sweet on her, weren't you! Admit it!"

Leroy scratched his head, leaned back in the chair. He couldn't help gloating a little. He popped open a Coca-Cola.

Bubba appeared in the door. "You probably want longer than three minutes with this one," he said. A classy-looking young woman came in—slender, willowy, her hair pulled back in a severely fashionable Grace Kelly style. She wore a tailored gray suit, a big diamond brooch on the lapel.

"Leroy." She put out her hand as if he might kiss it. "How are you."

"Fine," he said, smiling uncertainly, shaking her hand. "Nice to see you."

"You don't remember me, do you," she said.

"Sorry. I get to where I wouldn't know my own mother if she came backstage." He had never seen such an expensive-looking diamond within the borders of Mississippi. He couldn't take his eyes off it.

"Honey, I'm Mary Lynn Bradley," she said, sliding her other arm around his waist. "Or I was. I'm Mary Lynn Powderman now. The cottonseed oil Powdermans. Leroy, you and I were in the talent show out here together. Don't you remember? I won."

"Oh yes." He smiled. He hated her all over again. Her and her Powderman diamond. "You've grown up a lot."

"So have you," she said. "Listen, Leroy, I know this is just the rudest thing here at the last minute, but I didn't know how to reach you—it's just a few close friends, just my Ronnie and the bunch from the country club, at our place this evening. The old Davis mansion, you know it? Relaxed and informal, you won't have to lift a finger. Ronnie is making piña coladas." She smiled, just as pretty. How did a woman this sleek stay happy in a place like Tupelo? Diamonds, Leroy thought. Big, glittering diamonds. Mary Lynn Bradley had not done badly for herself.

"Gosh I'm sorry, Mary Lynn," he said, "I'd like to, but I've got another show and then we're heading back to Memphis."

"Oh no, I won't hear of it," she cried. "None of us ever get to see you!"

"Well, it's crazy these days, you know," he said. "Running sideways to keep from flying." He ushered her toward the door. He wished she

500

still wore her hair in ringlets so he could yank one. Wasn't it enough she had beaten him once? Did she have to come back to remind him, on Leroy Kirby Day of all days, sporting her diamond and her Grace Kelly hairdo? She was welcome to Tupelo. She could have it. Leroy had won first prize in the rest of the world. He had all the blue ribbons, back at his house in Memphis.

He was glad to see Bubba at the door. "Sorry," Bubba said with a big smile for Mary Lynn, "he's got one more waiting, then he's got to start warming up for the show."

"Sorry, Mary Lynn," Leroy said. "Thanks for coming."

"Bye, honey." She leaned to kiss his cheek, concealing any offense she might have taken. "You just keep making those hits!" She went off through the exhibit hall, her high heels clicking faster every step.

Leroy said, "Look at her. All she needs is a baton in her hand."

Bubba said, "Leroy, I don't know about this next guy."

Leroy glanced down the hall. "Yeah," he said, "I know him."

He was bigger and darker than life, worn down with age, shuffling on a cane, bent over, eroded. His hair was pure silver. In place of his fabulous robes he wore grimy dungarees and a tattered white T-shirt that revealed his belly in all its folds and rolls. He shuffled in, flip-flops scratching on the concrete floor.

"Kirby," he said.

Leroy said, "Brother Love, I didn't expect to see you here. How you getting along?"

The Brother positioned himself over a chair and settled down— slowly, slowly. "Not so good, Kirby, how long it been since I seen you?"

"A long time," said Leroy. "You gave me a ride."

"I sho did," Brother Love said. "I sholy did."

Leroy took the chair beside him. "So ... what are you doing these days?"

"Well I reckon you known I lost my church," the Brother went on. "Sister Arleta left the skillet on one night after the pancake supper. Place went up in ten minutes." He blew his nose in a rag. "I ain't got much place to stay these days. It look like you doing all right."

"Yes I am," Leroy said. No sense denying what everybody knew. "I'm just trying to keep my head down."

"I heard you singing," the Brother said, "heard you on the radio. I was mighty disappointed, Kirby, I got to speak the truth. I always thought you was cut out to sing the songs of the Lord."

"Well I do, Brother Love, all the time," Leroy said. "The boys and I have just been working on a new gospel song."

"That ain't what I heard," said the big man. "What was that mess? Something about a rag doll."

"That, um, that one's 'Let's Play,'" Leroy said, and he had to admit it sounded silly when you just said it out like that.

"That's the one," Brother Love said. "I don't know what to say about that."

"It's just a song," said Leroy. "You still singing these days?"

"Naw, I'm an old man now," Brother Love said, "and I was kinda thinking you might be able to spare a little something, maybe something to hep your old Brother."

So. The bottom line. Poor old guy. "How much do you need?" Leroy said.

"Ever how much you can spare," said the Brother. "It grieves me to come asking favors, you know, but like you say, I give you a ride one time, so I figured you might."

Leroy stood up, digging in his pocket. Money was the easiest kind of power. He had plenty of money and more every day. He could buy anything, even a man he once looked at with awe. He was beginning to enjoy it. He liked having people line up to see him. He wished he could buy every one of them a shiny new Cadillac. Maybe he would.

He brought out the clip and peeled off five twenties. "Listen, I think I know a place you could stay," he said. "It's down from my Uncle Hardy's. It needs some fixing up, but I bet we could find somebody to give you a hand with that."

He scratched Hardy's phone number on one of the bills and handed all five to Brother Love. "Here you go. See how this gets you along. You call him up. Or go by and see him. You know where it is."

The Brother folded the bills into a triangle. "I'm mighty grateful to you," he said. "I always thought you was a good boy. The Lord will bless you some way. I can see it all now. Just a big shining light up ahead for you, Kirby. A big shining light."

Leroy patted the old rounded shoulder. Brother Love scuffed away, flip-flop.

Leroy felt proud of himself. He would buy the old man a new chance and a chance for the little falling-in house. He'd write Hardy a check to buy it and fix it up; it would have to be a big check, so Hardy couldn't complain about having a colored man just down the hill.

Tommy and Jack jogged up, laughing, from the other end of the exhibition hall. "Come on, Leroy, you got to see this," Jack said. "Come on, it's okay, there's nobody down there. I mean, this you got to *see*."

"What? What is it? Listen, guys, I need to change to my—"

"No, you don't," Tommy said gravely. "You need to come with us."

Leroy smiled. "Look—okay, then, all right, quit pushing, I'm coming!" They pulled him along with big goofus grins, as if some incredible wonder of the world were waiting on the other side of that high partition.

And it was. The giant cow of the Seale-Lilly Dairy stood proudly on its trailer, watching out over a sea of exhibits and folding tables with its calm painted eye.

Leroy lit up inside. The cow was his old friend. He was amazed at how youthful it looked; its white patches had been whitened, and a recent coat of lacquer gleamed on its papier-mâché flanks. Now that he was grown, he could appreciate how much trouble someone had taken to build it.

Jack said, "Would you look at the tits on that thing?"

"You know, I'd like to buy it," said Leroy, "but I don't know where I'd put it."

They laughed some more and wandered back to tune up for the evening show.

Leroy thought about the cow for the rest of the night. He really could buy it if he wanted to. He was going to have to buy a bigger house anyway, with a yard, a high fence. He would have room for a giant cow.

But after he thought about it, he decided the cow looked happy enough on its pedestal, watching over the fair. It was better to leave it where it was. The Seale-Lilly people were taking good care of it. Probably there were little boys out there who would be heartbroken if it disappeared. There are some things you just shouldn't buy.

49

*G*irls sent letters vowing
to commit suicide if Leroy didn't phone them at once. Girls broke into
the house on Audubon Drive; they pried off the screens and pulled up
the windows and climbed in. Girls showed up from places like Australia
and Denmark with nothing but a sleeping bag and Leroy's address on
a scrap of paper.

Leroy phoned up Doris Lewis, the real estate agent who'd sold him
the house on Audubon. "Doris, we have to get out of here. Mama can't
stand this anymore. Now I want you to sell this thing. I want to buy

something not too far from town, with some land. Something I can put a fence around. And I want to move fast. This week."

"You just sit tight," Doris said, "I'll pick you up in fifteen minutes. I know just the place."

When her big black New Yorker stopped at his driveway, Leroy ran out through the swarm of girls and hopped in.

Doris said, "Leroy, my dear, let me tell you, you're doing the right thing. Look at this! I can just imagine what this is doing to the property values on this street."

They headed south, through the little town of Whitehaven, past the Gridiron—still serving double cheeseburgers, around the clock. Doris Lewis chattered about tax incentives and shielded investments. Leroy fingered his checkbook and hoped he wouldn't have to spend too much time with Doris Lewis before he found the right house.

They pulled up before a plain two-story farmhouse with a big white barn to the side. "Now," said Doris. "Isn't . . . that . . . lovely."

Three years ago Leroy would have been honored to visit somebody who lived in a house this fine. But it wasn't a movie star's house. "Nah," he said, "it's not big enough. I want a big house. You know. . . . like a mansion." If Mary Lynn Bradley could live in a mansion, by God he could have one, too. "You got anything like that?"

Doris peered at him a minute, turned the car around. "Bear with me, bear with me," she said. "I have got the perfect place. I mean, perfect."

They turned back past the Gridiron and drove a mile; then she pulled the Chrysler to the curb. "Now," she said, "is that big enough?"

"It's big all right." Leroy had admired this house many times, driving by on his way to eat cheeseburgers. It looked like Tara in *Gone With the Wind*—a big sandstone pile of a house, high on a hill among large old oak trees, with a white-columned portico, a driveway that swept up the rise in an elegant curve. There was only a low picket fence at the street, but plenty of room for the world's highest wall if that's what Leroy decided to build.

"It's cool," he said. "Is it really for sale?"

"I don't know what she's asking, but I know she'll let me show it to you," Doris said. "Let's ride on up there."

The lady of the house blushed and put her hands to her mouth at the sight of Leroy on her portico. "Well, of course, come in, come in, how do you do?" she trilled. "I just love your records! I believe I'm a bigger fan than my Cathy!"

She ushered them in. The house was called Hopeville, she explained, named after her grandmother, Hope. She pronounced it "Hope-ful." That pleased Leroy no end—the idea of a house with a name.

"There are twenty-three rooms and thirteen acres," Doris Lewis said, steering him into the long living room.

Leroy said, "I think it could use some bright colors in here, you know? I went to Red Skelton's house in Hollywood. You ought to see his place. Blue drapes and white leather furniture."

The owner lady said, "Well, we've wanted to paint for so long now. But the house is so big, and—well, frankly, it's expensive to keep it up." Her eyes flashed dollar signs. Leroy could see she was dying to sell.

"How much do you want for it?" he said.

Doris said, "Well now, Leroy, we're not even sure Mrs. Woodard is planning to sell the house."

Mrs. Woodard said, "One hundred thousand dollars."

Leroy said, "I'll take it."

"Wait now, wait!" Doris said. "You can't just buy a house like that!"

Leroy smiled, taking a peek at the kitchen. "Sure I can. Can't I, Miz Woodard?" He winked.

The owner lady blushed again. "Honey, you've got a deal."

"Write us up a contract, Doris." Leroy strode to the door. "I'll come back and take a real good look whenever Miz Woodard has a chance to move out."

"Oh, thank you, Leroy," Mrs. Woodard said, "you don't know what a thrill this is—"

He stepped onto his new portico. This was a place for a king, all right. A wide driveway with plenty of room for Cadillacs. A wide sidewalk out front for the fans to gather. A nice spot on the side for a swimming pool, all those acres in back for horses, and this green sloping lawn between Leroy and the girls. He would put up a wall, a guardhouse at the foot of the driveway, a set of gates. Round-the-clock guards and Gridiron cheeseburgers just up the road.

Leroy felt safe already. Hopeville would be home, forever and ever. He knew it. He loved it. Those big white columns would make his mother feel just like Scarlett O'Hara.

Sam fretted about Leroy's image, something he called overexposure. After the final appearance on "Sullivan," he said, no more TV for a while. "Why give it away free when we can make them pay for it?"

Leroy couldn't deny the logic of that.

"In the meantime," Sam said, "better ease up the wiggly stuff onstage a little bit."

In Jacksonville Leroy had no choice. The city fathers remembered his last concert there and the ensuing riot. They applied to a judge, who instructed the police to film the first of Leroy's three shows. The judge would watch the film, and if he determined that Leroy's act was vulgar, obscene, or likely to incite disorder, he promised he would not only shut down the show but also put Leroy in jail.

Sam said, "Son, if I was you, I would stand still out there tonight. You can sing, just don't move around. Publicity's one thing, but we don't want you to wind up in jail."

Leroy did as he was told. He trusted Sam now for everything: the money, the contracts, the deals, the promoters, the movie people, the merchandisers, the publishing companies, the local officials.

He ran out on the Gator Bowl stage, planted one foot on each side of the microphone stand, and jumped into "Rockin' Roll" as wild as you please. But he did not move. He let his little finger do all the wiggling for him. He sang standing still and let that finger just go wild. *My baby's sweet as a scuppernon'!*

It drove the girls mad.

They screamed at him to move, dance, do anything—just don't stand there! They tore at their hair and overran the police.

Leroy had to stop the show for five minutes until the cops got them back to their seats. It didn't matter what he did. They went wild. Standing still was just as dangerous as thrashing around. It was the girls. They brought their hysteria with them from home; they learned it from TV; they inspired it in each other. Leroy wasn't even doing anything to cause it anymore. The girls were running wild on their own power now, the volume of their own screams. They didn't even need to hear Leroy. They needed only to see him.

That night the judge looked at the film and issued a conditional permit for the second night's show—with a warning and the police cameras still in place.

The same thing happened again. Leroy stood still and wiggled his finger. The girls broke from their seats and ran for the stage. Leroy had to stop the show.

The judge canceled the third concert.

Leroy flew to New York. Sam was waiting in his suite at the Warwick. It seemed Ed Sullivan was happy enough with the ratings from the first two appearances, but all the rioting and court action were making him nervous.

Leroy listened on the extension phone in the bedroom while Ed and Sam thrashed it out.

"Listen, I'm not chickenshit Steve Allen," Ed Sullivan blared. "I don't give a damn if the pope himself comes out against your boy. But if a bunch of teenagers watch my show and make up their minds to go break a window in the corner drugstore, I'm gonna get blamed for it, and the FCC will have my ass. Now tell Leroy to clean up his act, or else. No more wiggling around on my show."

Sam reminded Ed that Leroy now had eight of the top ten records on the *Billboard* pop chart and that his first "Sullivan" appearance had received the highest Trendex rating of any television show in history.

Leroy softly hung up. Sam talked for a minute more and called him to the living room.

"He's going ahead with it," Sam said, "but he's telling his camera people to shoot you from the waist up only."

"From the—what do you mean?" Leroy couldn't believe it. "Sam, he's seen my act! I don't dance around naked. What's he complaining about?"

"He's not complaining," said Sam. "But it's his show. He's got the right to shoot it any way he wants."

Ed Sullivan called all the newspapers and made a big announcement: LEROY—FROM THE WAIST UP ONLY. The story went straight to the front page of every Sunday newspaper in America, the morning of the show.

In the studio Ed was all smiles and hello, how are you, son, good to have you back. He was stooped over with the start of a hump in his back and that long, unpretty face. He didn't mention anything about camera angles. He told a couple of lame jokes and that was that.

508

Leroy went off to the makeup department.

He realized Ed Sullivan wasn't a bit scared of riots or judges. He just wanted people to think he was, so more of them would tune in. It was Publicity.

The excitement backstage was like a gunpowder smell in the air. Everyone had heard about Sullivan's order; Leroy noticed people glancing at his crotch, the source of all the trouble. He thought about stuffing a big old sock in there, something to raise the short hairs on the back of Ed's neck.

But Sam said play this one nice and clean, and Leroy was going all the way with that suggestion. He had broken his vow against tuxedos when RCA presented him with a very cool and expensive tuxedo: glittering gold lamé, head to foot, with silky white lapels and cuffs, and gold sparkling boots. A king's tuxedo.

Leroy and the Leroyals had worked up a lovely version of "Home in the Valley," the world's most respectable spiritual, for the close of the show. And Leroy had learned in Jacksonville that he didn't have to move around to ignite the girls. He didn't even need a fast song. He could do it with his eyes, with his finger, his voice, his half snarl, half grin. Let them shoot him from the waist up, then, if that's what they wanted to do. The most dangerous part of him would still be right there on camera: his face.

He joined the boys backstage. Sam came up, grinning around his cigar. "Now he's worried people will tune in late," he said. "He's got you spread out all through the show. Three different spots. He's giving the whole show to you."

"You mean, to the top half of me," said Leroy. "From here to here. Boys, you ready?"

"And now—ladies and gennamen," Ed Sullivan said, "as I promised at the outset, we've got a really big show for you tonight—a really big shew. . . ." He grinned, waited for the laugh, and held his arm up in the air, stiffly waving, turning his whole body as he barked, "*Leroy Kirby!*"

Tommy and Jack followed Leroy into the light. The girls screamed. They grinned. They would only be surprised if nobody screamed.

The cameras moved close to his face. *I need you, a-baby—night and day!* Leroy cruised through the tune; it was built just for him, his new hit, "Help Me," a smooth rhythm bop from the Nashville song factory that was churning out hits faster than Leroy could get them on vinyl. Every record he made was a great big fat hit.

Leroy did his from-the-bottom-of-our-heart speech on the intro to "I'm Not As Bad As They Say." He thanked his fans and said, "Ladies, we sure are sorry we couldn't give every single one of you a brand-new Lincoln for Christmas, but the boys at the car lot wouldn't sell us that many."

That earned a huge laugh, changing to a storm of squeals when Leroy kicked off the song.

"I'm Not As Bad As They Say" was a skittery little hot country number, like something Leroy might have worked up for Dan Tobias at Rocking Records. He forgot the words to the second verse, but the Leroyals went waaaaah-doowah and Leroy mumbled through it, sneering as if he'd meant to do it just that way.

He found his place, *Well, I've got years of love saved-ah—up for you,* and the Leroyals kept the beat with *saaaaaved for you!* They crooned and snapped their fingers in such perfect time you'd think they were born to the same mother.

Leroy came off to find Ed Sullivan all lit up and glowing. Lincoln-Mercury was Ed Sullivan's major sponsor. Leroy had known that, of course; that was why he'd said Lincoln instead of Cadillac, which is what any girl in her right mind would rather have.

Ed Sullivan got all excited and told Leroy he would say a little something extra at the close of the show.

Leroy had waited until this moment to choose his last song for the night. He knew everyone in America was tuning in to see what he was doing so dirty that he couldn't be shown in a full-body shot.

He could sing one of the rowdy songs he'd borrowed from the wild colored singers—"Rockin' Roll" or "Rip It Up" or "Long Tall Sally." He stole without shame from Little Richard and Chuck Berry and all those boys; they had his kind of wildness in mind when they banged out a song. With one of those songs he could stir up the girls, get them shrieking and rioting all over America. Take that, Ed Sullivan! Okay, girls, here's your wild boy. They can't cut me off at the waist!

There was another choice.

He could sing a sweet song, a song for the ladies, a song to make the preachers happy, to make the columnists lay down their pens.

A song to make his mother proud.

Leroy loved to play wild boy for the girls, but he didn't want the mothers of America thinking their daughters weren't safe at his movies.

He changed to a dark blue double-breasted big-shouldered suit and checked his hair in the mirror.

Bubba cleared out a path from the dressing room, through the hubbub, to the curtain at stage left. Tommy and Jack and the Leroyals had worked up five or six songs for this moment. Leroy took a deep breath. "Okay, boys," he said. " 'Home in the Valley.' "

The lights went down. The Leroyals formed up in their own spotlight, to one side.

In all his time onstage Leroy had never sung a song just for his mother. She pretended to like his records, but he didn't sing her kind of music—the soft ones, old hymns, the tender, pretty tunes with a melody. Not these wild, crazy, shouting, jumping-around things that sold millions of records.

He pictured her watching the RCA set in the living room on Audubon Drive.

He had sung enough songs for the girls. Right now he would send one to her. Here you go, Mama. This is for you.

He stepped into the light. "Thankyouvermuch, friends," he said. "I'd like to thank Mr. Sullivan for being so nice to have us on, and all ... now I want to sing a song for somebody watching tonight. And I hope this'll tell her how much I love her."

Girls everywhere sighed. Tears welled in their eyes. Every one of them imagined Leroy was speaking to her.

Well I stand on a mountain, and I see the horizon
And I hear the Lord a-calling me away
Well I'm too close to heaven, miles over Jordan
But I'll come to my home in the valley someday

Leroy pretended he was alone with the Leroyals and a piano, making harmonies. He sang it just as pretty and peaceful, a stroll through the valley. He pictured his mother's smile.

I'll have to journey forever
But my home in the valley is waiting for me

The Leroyals ended on a dizzy high note, took their bows, and started from the stage. Sullivan waved Leroy over to the microphone.

"Leroy, ladies and gennamen," he said, "since Leroy will be heading out now to Hollywood for the start of his new picture, this will be the last time we'll see him for a while"—the girls groaned and cried no! no!—"but I wanted to say to Leroy and to the whole country that this is a real fine, upstanding young boy, and the guys in your band—we'd like to say that we've never had a nicer time on our show with a big-name entertainer than we've had with you, you're thoroughly okay, so now, let's have a big hand for . . . Leroy Kirby!" He lifted his arm in that stiff, body-twisting salute. The girls screamed.

Leroy grinned at the camera's eye.

The red light winked off.

That did it. The sweet song at the end and Ed's little speech would hush all the gossip. Mothers everywhere had been waiting to fall in love with Leroy, just like their daughters. Now they all had Ed Sullivan's permission.

50

*S*am Sanders was right.
Nice and clean. Big money. Leroy made fourteen gold records in a row.
He wore his solid gold tux. He ordered gold-plated fixtures for the
bathrooms at Hopeville.

The year 1957 was written in gold. For one whole glorious year Leroy
was the most successful entertainer in the world.

One out of every three records sold by RCA in 1957 was a Leroy
Kirby record. He played dozens of sold-out stadium extravaganzas. Sam
peddled licenses for Leroy Kirby dolls, guitars, shirts, hats, lamps, socks,
bubble gum cards, buttons, belts, hairbrushes, Leroy salt and pepper

shakers. . . . Leroy made a few pennies off each item sold, and the pennies were turning into one long, beautiful line of numbers at the First National Bank of Memphis.

Don't let it end.

On the day before the moving vans were to carry the Kirbys' furniture out to Hopeville, Leroy called a meeting with Sam and Bubba Hayes to tell them about his new way of doing business. "As of today," he said, "the fans are not running my life anymore. I am."

"That's fine." Sam shifted uncomfortably on his chair.

"From now on, unless I'm working," said Leroy, "I'll be out at the house with the folks. I don't know what's wrong with Mama. I need to be with her."

"What you do on your own time is your department," Sam said.

Leroy said, "I'll make that swing out west, then I want to lay off touring awhile."

"Fine by me," said Sam. "That's what I been talking about, overexposure. Is that everything?"

"Bubba," Leroy said.

"Yeah, Leroy." Bubba put his thumbs together.

"I want somebody in that guardhouse twenty-four hours and at least one other out on foot, walking the wall. I mean, I don't want to see *nobody* inside that wall."

"Gotcha, boss. This new setup is gonna make my job a lot easier."

Leroy drove out to Hopeville. The foundrymen were still touching up his new gates with black paint. Leroy had commissioned a portrait of himself and his guitar in wrought iron, eighth notes and quarter notes dancing all over.

He realized with a start that the ironworkers had fashioned two figures, one for each gate—twin Leroys holding twin guitars, facing off against each other. The figures wore some weird kind of flare-legged pants.

Leroy and his twin, together at last. . . . He shook off the spooky idea.

Anyone driving by would have no doubt who lived inside. The crossbars were made of tempered forty-gauge steel rods. Nobody could just come waltzing on in.

"Lookin' good, fellas," Leroy said, "but tell me the truth. Do you think that really looks like me?"

"Sure it does," said the beaming foundryman. "Stand up there beside of it."

Leroy did.

"Don't get paint on you, now." The man reached into his toolbox and came out with a Polaroid camera. "The guys at the shop, they made me promise," he said. "You mind?"

"Hell no," said Leroy, "you boys'll have to come over soon as we get settled in. I know we'll have a big housewarming party."

That was how Leroy envisioned the new, improved Hopeville—the world's finest party house. If he couldn't go out, he would stay in and have a big time. His plans went way beyond new paint and carpet and white leather furniture, and the kidney-shaped swimming pool.

He set off for a stroll up his very own drive. First he wanted to plant more trees everywhere. It had been so easy to buy the place; he was just now beginning to feel the connection, the power that came from owning your own chunk of earth, knowing you could plant trees and live in one place long enough to see them grow tall.

Maybe a recording studio in the side yard. A stable for horses. A garden, so Agnes could have her tomatoes and Dodger her okra and Ray his purple-hull peas. A great big carport in back, so you wouldn't clutter up this pretty front view of the house with a lot of Cadillacs.

The front door stood wide open, inviting him in. Workmen hurried in and out, bearing ladders and cans of paint. Leroy stepped over the threshold.

Mrs. Woodard wouldn't recognize the place, and probably she wouldn't like what Leroy had done to it; but he thought it was coming along just swell. It was just like Red Skelton's house. The walls and ceilings were painted a deep nighttime end-of-the-sky blue, all the moldings and baseboards gleamed white, and a plushy white carpet lay under the painters' tarpaulins.

A painter came up from the basement with a can of paint in each hand. "Hey, you're Leroy!" The guy was about seventeen, with paint-spattered white overalls and an Abe Lincoln beard on his chin.

Leroy patted his pocket for a pen. He gave autographs now by reflex.

The guy said, "Am I glad to see you. I think there's some mixup on this color for the rec room. Look at this stuff!" He pried off a lid, so

Leroy could see. The paint was red, Chinese red, jungle red—bright, cherry, hot, party, lip-smacking red.

"No, that's right," Leroy said. "If you can make it any redder, go ahead and do it."

The guy laughed. "You're the boss."

Leroy grinned and started up the stairs to check out his room.

〜〜

He owned seven cars and four motorcycles. Agnes said if show business failed him, he could open a used-car lot. He rarely had time to enjoy any of his vehicles, though, or the new house. He shuttled back and forth to Hollywood on the Southwest Crescent to wrap up postsync recording for *Thinking of You* and to start work on his new picture, *Prisonhouse Blues*.

He bought a white Eldorado convertible just for the West Coast. He stayed in whichever Beverly Hills hotel happened to have an entire floor vacant when he was in town.

If he went out, he was mobbed, so he stayed in. He and Bubba Hayes made friends with Nick Adams and all of Debra Paget's good-looking crowd, screenwriters, other young actors. They were movie people themselves, and they treated Leroy like anybody. The guys played records and talked about cars and flirted with the girls—and sometimes with other guys, something Leroy had heard of but didn't like to think about. The girls drank cocktails and danced on the coffee tables. The parties grew bigger and louder.

After the *Thinking of You* wrap party, the management of the Beverly Wilshire Hotel politely asked Leroy to find another hotel. The TV in the swimming pool was apparently the last straw.

He moved the party to a sprawling bungalow at the Beverly Sunset: five big rooms and a private pool. Every night there were dozens of people in and out; Leroy had no idea who most of them were. They dressed smartly, they had great suntans, they laughed a lot, they drank plenty of cocktails, they teased him constantly about his drawl, and they made him feel gorgeous and strong.

Natalie Wood appeared one night. She was even more beautiful than her movie image. Her eyes were green fire, like emeralds. She told Leroy a dirty joke about the French Foreign Legion and a camel named

Sarah, and her spectacular beauty made the punch line even more shocking.

Sometimes, late at night, when the girls had enough cocktails in them, things could turn naughty; that was what Leroy liked about the West. Natalie Wood and Debra Paget were nice girls, but some of these girls didn't think a thing about stripping down to bras and underpants and leaping into the swimming pool.

Where there were girls willing to do that, there were boys with bright eyes, wriggling out of their trousers. Then splashing and screams and games in the water.

Leroy watched, but he didn't join in. He was chilled by the idea of another letter like the one from Betty Simpkins's lawyer. He had kept to his oath: He couldn't touch a girl. He was just too famous. He would have to marry one first.

Usually he stayed right out in the open where everybody could see him. One night, when the sounds from the pool became less hilarious and more personal, he got up and went to the master suite to watch some TV.

NBC featured a drama about a young farm girl who moves to the big city and falls into a life of sin. Leroy switched over to Ed Wynn making goofy faces, then switched again to "What's My Line?"

He kicked off his shoes and settled back on the vast bed with a bowl of potato chips, wiggling his toes in the air. He was tired of the party. He had a five o'clock call. He could ask them all to go home—but hey, these were his friends, right? He was learning how to be a Hollywood playboy, right?

Right.

In the hall just outside his door two girls were giggling hysterically. It had nothing to do with him.

"Hey," he yelled, "could you please keep it down?"

Connie DaSilva stuck her head around the door. "Oh—*there* you are," she said. "Look, Mitzi, here's Leroy! Doll, we've been looking everywhere for you! Why don't you come out and play?"

Mitzi Meadows joined Connie in the doorway. Mitzi and Connie were friends of Nick Adams's. They were starlets who went everywhere together. From this distance, between Leroy's toes, they looked like twins—big teased-up blond hair, the same flawless nose, the same pouty

517

red mouth. They wore snug mohair sweaters and short skirts. They were fun girls who wanted to be Marilyn Monroe. Leroy thought their movie names were beautiful.

They spilled into the room, giddy from rum and pineapple drinks.

"Go on, girls," he said, "I'm watching TV."

"Oh, boo, that's no fun!" Connie said. "You should see what Jackie just did to your buddy—what's his name? The wavy hair?"

"I don't know," said Leroy. "Move, you're blocking the set."

"Jackie put the thing up on top of his head, you know, and he wasn't looking and she took it away and—whoop!" Connie exploded in laughter.

Mitzi advanced over the carpet toward the bed, stealthy as a cat. "Come on, Leroy, honey," she purred, "you can't leave! The party's no fun without you!" She sank to the rug at the foot of the bed, flopped her arm out, seized his big toe.

Connie went to shut the door.

"Go on, Mitzi," Leroy said, withdrawing his foot. "Go pick on somebody your own size."

"Darling, I'm not picking on you! Here. Take another yellow baby and wake up. Here." She stretched out her hand, with a pill in it.

Leroy palmed it into the little coin pocket of his jeans. No telling when he might want to wake up. These Hollywood folks had shown him you could feel any way you wanted to feel, as long as you had the right prescriptions.

Connie came back with bright eyes, the same eyes as the boys taking off their pants. She settled down on the fake leopard bedspread beside Mitzi.

Leroy sat up on the pillows to see over their hair. If he ignored them, maybe they would go away. Any man in the world would kill to have two beautiful babes in the same room, begging, but Leroy couldn't take the chance. It was okay for the girls to be here—it was better than that, it was sweaty and exciting—as long as he did not touch them.

"Leroy looks kinda lonely up there all by himself, doesn't he?" Mitzi rubbed her cheek on the satin bedspread. "Maybe he needs a little company." Her hand crept out.

He pulled in his foot. "Now, girls, I know what you're thinking, and I appreciate it, I really do, but I . . . it just ain't gonna happen."

"He knows what we're thinking," said Connie. "He knows what we're thinking, Mitzi."

"He's reading my mind." Mitzi kissed the air. "I can *feel* it." Her bosom heaved. "Oooh, stop that."

"Go put on some music," said Connie. "I feel like dancing."

"That's a good idea," Leroy said. "You girls go dance."

Mitzi went to the portable phonograph beside the TV and dropped the needle on Leroy's latest single. "Wanna beeeee yore baby doll," Mitzi mimicked, twirling, placing her hands so her sweater inched up from her waist, revealing a lovely band of tanned skin.

Leroy grinned, touched his toes together.

Connie jumped up and stripped off her sweater, shrieking. Mitzi shrieked and stripped hers off, too. The two of them wiggled and shimmied in their bras and tight skirts. "Don't wanna play with fire!" they shrilled. "Fire burns too hot!"

Leroy laughed. These Hollywood girls were always putting on little shows for him. He let them do all the work. All he had to do was lean back and watch. To them, he was sexy just lying there watching with a big fat grin on his face.

Mitzi edged up to the bed and kissed his big toe.

He said, "Quit," but he didn't mean it.

She started tickling the sole of his foot.

Meanwhile Connie was wriggling out of her skirt. Her low-cut push-up brassiere lifted her breasts like a pair of twin airplanes, straining to take off.

Leroy tucked his hands under his hips, so they would not be tempted. He would surely like to touch those breasts, to see if they were as bouncy and succulent as they appeared from across the room.

Now Mitzi had hold of his leg and was kissing her way up the inside of his knee.

There they were—oh—Connie's white silky panties. Look how the elastic molds itself to the curve of that sweet little . . . Leroy drew his knee up to hide his excitement.

"Get his other leg!" Mitzi squealed.

Then he saw who was on television between them.

He swallowed his grin. He bolted up on the bed. "Jesus Christ! Turn that down!"

"Oh, Leroy," said Connie, "don't be so boooring." She sashayed between him and the screen.

"I *mean* it!" He bounded over, grabbed the needle off the record with a skrtch!

That was his granddaddy, there on TV.

Honest to God. In his brown pin-striped tailor-made suit with the pearl buttons. Looking eighty years old. Grinning just as wide as his face would go, that was old Jessie Kirby himself, the mystery guest on "What's My Line?"

Leroy turned up the volume just in time to hear Dorothy Kilgallen say, "Let me see. Are you . . . a millionaire?"

Old Jessie cackled. "No ma'am," he said, "wish I was." The studio audience laughed.

Bill Cullen said, "Do you work in some field of the entertainment industry?"

"Wellsir, you might could say that . . . I used to do a little sangin' at fairs," said Jessie. "I'd say you're gettin' warm."

Connie bopped Leroy on the shoulder. "You're no *fun,*" she whined. "Why you wanna watch this dumb old TV show when you could be—"

"Quiet!" He turned it louder. "That's my granddaddy," he said. "Right there. That's him. I can't believe it."

Connie cupped her breasts in her hands and stared. "Oh, are you kidding? How cute! Look, Mitzi, isn't he cute? Doesn't he look like Leroy?"

The celebrity panel was trying to guess Jessie's claim to fame; if he stumped them, he would win a prize. Jayne Meadows finally caught on to the family resemblance, and her line of questioning began to zero in. "*I* know," she said at last. "You're Leroy Kirby's *father!*" She clapped her hands, delighted with herself.

"No ma'am," he said, but his face gave it away.

"Well then, you're . . . Leroy Kirby's *brother!*"

The old man grinned, showing his gold tooth. "No ma'am, I'm not."

Dorothy Kilgallen cried, "I know! I know! You're his *grandfather!*" and Jessie nodded yes, and the audience applauded.

Jessie was miffed about losing the prize, but he managed to work up his smile for the little interview. Garry Moore asked if music ran in the

Kirby family and when was the last time he spoke to Leroy—"just a while back," he said.

"Mr. Kirby, which song of Leroy's would you say is your favorite?"

"Aw, I don't know, I like purt much all of 'em," Jessie said. "I guess my favorite would have to be, what was it called, 'Bad Boy.'"

"Aw, that's sweet," said Connie.

Leroy pushed her away. "Put on your clothes." He blinked—something in his eye.

"What's wrong, doll?"

A wave of inexplicable sadness crashed over him. He turned away. "I haven't seen him in ten years," he said. "I reckon he's famous now, too."

Old Jessie went off to a crash of applause, a tinny mock "Blue" salute from the band.

Leroy picked up the telephone. "Get out of here, girls," he said. "This is a private call."

They went hmp!

He started dialing.

The girls picked up their clothes and huffed out with their noses in the air.

"Hello, Mama."

"Oh honey, what you doing," said Agnes, "I been so nervous all day."

"I'm sorry," he said. "Did you watch any TV tonight?"

"Well no, I was down on my hands and knees trying to get whatever that is off the floor in that kitchen," she said. "It's a big ugly spot shaped like a devil's head and it's about to drive me out of my mind."

"It's two o'clock in the morning your time," Leroy said.

"Well I couldn't sleep."

"Take a wild guess who showed up on 'What's My Line?' tonight," he said.

"Who?"

"Granddaddy."

There was a long silence. "You're joking."

"He was the mystery guest. They had to guess who he was. They guessed."

"Oh, Leroy, you can't be serious."

"I couldn't believe it either," Leroy told her. "He looks pretty old. He said he'd just seen us awhile back."

"Ten years is awhile, all right," Agnes said. "I can't believe he would—what are you doing, honey? What's all that ruckus I hear behind you?"

"It's a party," said Leroy. "I don't even know who invited these people. I'm going to try and get some sleep."

"Leroy, come home," she said. "It's not good for you out there. I need you here."

"What's the matter?"

"Oh, everything," she said. "I can't get this spot off the floor."

"Mama, don't worry about that." He cradled the phone on the pillow. "Let Annie do that. That's why we hired her."

"She doesn't clean well enough to suit me," Agnes said.

"Yeah well, anyway, listen. I got an early call. You try and get some sleep now, Mama. I love you."

"Come home," she said. Then her voice dropped to a plaintive whisper: "Leroy. Be careful. I had one of my bad dreams."

"Good night, Mama." He sighed. "I'll call you tomorrow."

51

*A*s soon as he wrapped the shooting of *Prisonhouse Blues,* Leroy headed for Memphis to put on the biggest Christmas in history. He ordered a twenty-five-foot Canadian blue spruce for Hopeville's front lawn, six hundred yards of blue lights to outline the driveway and house, three thousand dollars' worth of fireworks for a Christmas Eve pyrotechnic display. He contrived to buy three of the fat, pampered ducks from the fountain of the Peabody Hotel for the Christmas dinner table.

Bubba set up a secret after-hours Christmas shopping foray through all the downtown department stores. Leroy bought everything he thought might bring Agnes out of her latest funk: silky robes, slippers, earrings, bracelets, coats, purses, scarves, hats, gloves, crystal vases, landscape paintings, a new television, a new upholstered chair, a fancy Turkish ottoman for her sore feet. He spent buckets of money. Delivery trucks rumbled all day up the long, curving driveway to Hopeville.

He bought new Cadillacs for his daddy and Bubba and Sam and a jeep for his uncle Hardy, who had taken over as gatekeeper and official girl greeter in front of the house.

Six days before Christmas Leroy was stretched on his custom-made fifteen-foot white leather sofa, trying to figure out what to buy next, when Hardy came in breathless and excited to announce that a man from the Memphis draft board was at the front gate.

Leroy's blood froze in his veins. He swung his feet to the floor and sat up. "Who did you say?"

"It's that Chastain, the chairman," said Hardy. "He says he has to hand you something directly. What you want me to do?"

Leroy went to the picture window and peered down the lawn to the white Chevrolet at the gate.

He swallowed. "I guess you better let him come up."

Hardy hurried out.

This was some mistake. Leroy had played this draft board thing by the book. Everyone knew you could get out of a peacetime draft as long as you played it smooth and legal and eased the right money into the right hands.

Sam Sanders was supposed to have done all that.

Peering into the smoked glass mirror by the door, Leroy saw stark naked fear in his eyes.

They can't take you, the mirror said. This is a plot. They can't do this. Run. Hide.

Leroy thought: Maybe this was some kind of formality, they serve you with papers to let you know you've been exempted, or . . .

No. Jesus. A double cross.

Beyond his own reflection, his mother and Dodger sat in chairs on the pool terrace, soaking up the rare winter sunshine.

He could not be drafted. It was impossible. It would ruin his life.

Last January he'd taken a day off from the set of *Thinking of You* for his army physical. Sam assured him it was just for show; they had to make it look as if they were serious, right up until they granted his exemption. The doctors pronounced him 1-A, "available for service," and all year the fan magazines had been filled with anxious speculation on the future of Leroy's famous hair.

Leroy wouldn't let himself speculate. The moment he signed the registration papers, he pushed the glimmer of this nightmare to the back of his mind, like a dull headache. He trusted Sam, who said Don't think about it. You might make it come true.

Leroy could not imagine anyone taking him away from his new house, his fans, his mother, his money, his cars. Sam said Don't worry about it. Everything's worked out and paid for. Friends in high places.

Leroy stepped out to the veranda. A flock of blackbirds made a raucous chatter down the lawn. "Hey, Mr. Chastain. What brings you this morning?"

Dan Chastain was a tall, stoop-shouldered man with gentle eyes. "Hello, Leroy." He held out a folded white sheet. "This is your draft notice. I wanted to bring it out to you myself."

Oh.

God.

Help me.

Did the law require you to accept a draft notice, like a subpoena? Leroy didn't see any choice about it. His hand trembled when he took the sheet and unfolded it: "You are hereby directed by the Selective Service of the United States of America to report to 198 South Main Street, Room 215, Memphis, Tennessee, at 7:45 A.M. on January 20, 1958, to commence a period of compulsory service to your country."

"Mr. Chastain, I don't understand," he said. "We worked with you all along on this thing, didn't we? Didn't you promise us plenty of notice before anything like this would happen?"

Hardy hovered in the background, straining to overhear.

"Leroy, I'm sorry," said Chastain. "Much as I'd like to accommodate you, the board can't be seen to play favorites. We can't treat you different from anybody else."

"But I *am* different," Leroy said.

"I know," Chastain said. "You're in a special situation. But we can't treat you that way. I'm sorry. Your number came up. I did what I could. I let you know before the newspapers."

Leroy could not go to the army. It was just that simple.

He knew show business well enough to know you don't stop a career in its tracks for two years and expect to pick up where you left off.

This might be the very first moment of the beginning of the end. . . .

The idea terrified him.

This was a job for Sam. Arguing with Dan Chastain wouldn't help. Leroy thanked him for his trouble, wished him a merry Christmas, walked him to his car.

"Sorry," said Chastain, "I know it's not much of a Christmas present."

"It's not your fault." Leroy shook his hand and stood watching while the white Chevrolet retreated through the gates.

Hardy came to the top step. "Bad news," he said.

Leroy said "Hardy, now damn it, don't you breathe a word about this to Mama. I got to talk to Sam."

Without waiting for an answer, he hurried inside, up the stairs to his room.

Oh God a disaster. There had to be a way out. Sam would find it. He would pay somebody.

Leroy made the call.

Sam said, "Get in your car and get your butt up here now."

Leroy invented a story for Agnes about some legal papers that had to be signed and set out in his latest Eldorado for Madison, the suburb on the north side of Nashville where Sam lived.

He drove fast for four hours. His panic increased every mile.

He would do anything. Pay any amount.

The army would destroy his career. They would cut off his hair. They would take him away at the height of his fame.

Don't let it end. Don't let it end.

Sam would think of something. Fallen arches. Heart murmur. Family responsibilities.

Oh! God. Why? Weren't there millions of worthless, stupid boys in America walking around, breathing up good air, taking up space? Why not take one of them? Why take Leroy, in his very most prime? Wasn't he the richest twenty-one-year-old self-made man in America? Didn't he generate more cash this year than any other performer in the world?

Don't take it away.

If he was paranoid, he might think it was a plot—a handful of jealous old bastards sitting around the Selective Service office, smacking their chops at the prospect of taking the famous long-haired Bad Boy of Memphis down a notch or two or three: all the way down.

Oh, they wanted to cut off his hair!

Leroy was in a fog of desperation by the time he reached Sam's respectable ranch house. Sam's wife, Sally, took one look at his face and offered him a shot of whiskey.

He said, "No thank you, ma'am," and went straight to Sam's office, a small windowless room jammed with plaques and photos and stuffed replicas of Nipper the RCA dog.

"Come in, son," Sam said, "sit down. I'm working out some figures."

"I'll pay anything," Leroy said. "Tell me how much."

"Hold on, hold on." Sam knocked the largest Nipper off the green sofa with his foot. "Take a seat. You had a long drive."

Leroy flung himself down. "Sam, this is it. If you don't get me out of this, the whole game is over."

"Son, you're overexcited," said Sam, exactly as Agnes might have said it.

"You told me not to worry!" Leroy waved his hands. "You had it all worked out!"

Sam bit his cigar. "I thought I did. I paid some people a lot of money. Obviously I paid the wrong people." He swiveled his chair. "I didn't think it would happen so quick. It's a good thing we invested your money, you know, planned ahead. The next couple of years are gonna be tough."

"Don't *tell* me that!" Leroy smacked the desk with his hand. "They can't do this to me!"

"Hold on, son. They just did. The AP already has it on the wire. Two-year tour of duty, starting with basic at Fort Hood in Texas. The whole country knows. It's a done deal."

"My God." Leroy reached for the phone. "I've got to call Mama. She can't find out from the radio."

"Go in yonder in Sally's room, and use the extension. And settle down. I know this looks bad, but it ain't the end of the world."

"Not for you, maybe!" Leroy went in among the frilly bed ruffles and needlepoint pillows of Sally Sanders's bedroom. He dialed the private line at Hopeville. Annie picked up and went to fetch Miss Agnes from her room.

"Hey honey, where are you?"

"Hi Mama, I'm up here at Sam's," he said, struggling to sound casual. "Listen, there's some news you need to hear. I got my draft notice today. I been drafted."

A long silence on the other end, followed by her little sigh. "Oh Lord, the bad news always comes at Christmastime."

"Don't worry, it'll be all right. . . ."

"I knew it was going too good," Agnes said. "Something always has to happen."

"We're trying to figure out something," said Leroy.

"I'll tell you the truth, sweetie, I don't think I can take it this time. I just don't think I can take it."

"I'll be home late tonight," Leroy said. "Now you go tell Daddy, and you two watch TV or something. Don't think about it. We'll talk about it when I get home."

"Oh, but, honey, they can't take you away from me!"

He heard the hysterical note in her voice. "No, they can't, Mama. You take one of your Miltowns, now. I'll be home before you know it."

He soothed her until it was all right for him to hang up.

He wandered back to find Sam punching buttons on his adding machine.

"I'm telling you, Sam, she's not real well," he said. "She was just starting to get better. This will tear her apart, don't you understand? You have got to do something. They don't need me to go. There's no reason. They're just trying to use me as some kind of example."

"You got that right," said Sam. "I've done some figures. You want to know how bad they want you? To start with, if you don't work for two years, the government loses four hundred thousand dollars in income tax. You lose a million two hundred thousand—three pictures canceled, and all the recording, no telling what else kind of damage to your career. Paramount and RCA will each lose three times that much. And then there's the tax they would pay on top of that." He might have been reading from a grocery list.

"Well, Jesus, Sam! That's what I'm saying! We've got to stop it."

"Wake up, Leroy, you're dreaming." Sam clamped down on his cigar. "Now listen to me. This is page one news from here to Hollywood. You're drafted. That's it. They've got you. Nothing I can do. There's not a trick on earth that can get you out of it now."

"I bet I can think up a way...."

"Well, I wish you luck."

"You seem pretty relaxed about it," Leroy shot, "considering it was all your fancy arrangements that fell through."

"I may be relaxed, but that don't mean I'm happy," said Sam. "From my point of view, let me tell you, twenty-five percent of nothing is nothing."

"I won't go," Leroy said. "I just won't, that's all. I'll figure out something. Flat feet. I don't care. There's got to be some way. I could—I could go to college."

"Don't be an idiot." Sam hunched forward, jabbing the air with his finger. "Son, no matter how you look at it, you're not Joe Blow. You can't just go dodging the draft. Now there's two ways to look at this thing. One way is to somehow get out of it, and then everybody will know that's exactly what you did. You'll never be doodly-squat in this country again. You'll be Draft Dodger A Number One."

"Yeah well, that's what you say—"

"And the other way is to play along, play the perfect soldier boy all down the line, skip the million, let the can get empty, keep the fans hungry for two years, and then we'll put on the biggest goddamn comeback anybody ever saw. Now which do you think we ought to do?" He stretched his long legs so his heels balanced precariously on the desktop.

"Sam, they want to cut off my hair!"

"When you're a private citizen, you can grow your hair as long as you want." Sam waved the draft notice. "But they're damn sure gonna prove that Uncle Sam has the right to cut it off."

He was right. Leroy argued for an hour, but he knew he was trapped, sheared, nailed, and skinned.

He had believed in the ultimate power of money, and now it had failed him.

The government would prove to the youth of America that even Leroy Kirby must bow to the greater power.

Two years of his wonderful life wasted in some far-off miserable hole, peeling potatoes to show that he had as much respect for authority as the next guy. Two years in the role of Private Kirby, Good Sport. It sounded like a death sentence. Any other white boy in the world would be able to find a way out of this.

"Isn't there anything we can do?" Already he sounded miserable and whipped, even to himself.

"I'll work on getting some kind of deferment so you can go ahead and shoot this picture with Curtiz. Paramount's got three hundred fifty thousand in it already; Hal Wallis is hitting the roof about now. Even the army ought to be able to appreciate a number like three hundred fifty thousand."

Sam went on to sketch out some of his ideas. They would milk the induction for maximum publicity: a farewell tour; a final recording session; exclusive photo deals with the big magazines—the works. He said every cloud has its silver lining. Who knows? This might turn out for the best.

It was obvious Sam was not interested in a public brawl with the Selective Service. He was already thinking about how to keep Leroy's name alive while he was gone. "Maybe they'll let you make records on the weekend," he said.

In his darker moments that night, driving back to Memphis, Leroy imagined he saw the shadow of Sam's hand behind the whole thing. Sam seemed almost unrattled by the disaster, as if it meshed with one of his grand invisible schemes. Maybe he thought a tour in the army would be just the thing for Leroy's image. What better cure for "over-exposure" than two years of Private Second Class Leroy Kirby, U.S. Army?

If it was true—if Sam was working against him in secret—then Leroy had to fire him and find someone who would get him out of this mess.

But he couldn't conceive it. He felt disloyal even thinking such a thing. Sam Sanders had laid hands on his career and produced a flood of miracles. Who was Leroy to question his advice?

He glanced at the rearview mirror.

Run. Run to Mexico. Disappear. Get away from Sam. Don't let them cut your hair.

His eyes swerved back to oncoming headlights. Careful. Don't want to be a dead draftee.

Of course, if he died now, he would be the most famous suicide ever. DISTRAUGHT LEROY DIES IN HEAD-ON CRASH TO AVOID DRAFT.

He could fake it. Make it look like an accident.

He was deathly afraid of what the army would do to him, but he couldn't show it; everybody in the world was watching to see what he would do. He had believed in the power of fame, and now it had him trapped.

He was not quite twenty-three years old, and his best days were already over. He had been at the top of the hill for two years. That was more than he had any right to expect.

It looked like down from here, in every direction.

A glimmer of light—the first outskirts of Memphis.

He couldn't run.

He did not want to face the music.

But that is what he had to do.

Maybe there was a way to survive. Maybe if he worked very hard, kept his head down, kept his mother close by, he could get through this thing.

By the time he reached Hopeville, he had made up his mind that he had no choice. He saluted Hardy at the gate. He left the keys in the ignition, bounded up the front steps, and greeted everyone in the living room with a big movie star smile: "Well folks, it looks like I'm going to play GI Joe for a while."

His mother broke down in sobs against his shirt. Dodger hugged his waist. Ray said, "I'm proud of you, son."

Agnes reared up to say, "It's not fair! It's not fair! We can fight this! We can! We can write to the president!"

Leroy tried to talk sense to her, but suddenly Agnes shrieked that she couldn't stand hearing any more about it. She fled to her room and locked herself in.

Leroy dialed Dr. Davis. He came with a shot. Agnes unlocked the door to admit him.

When he emerged, Leroy pulled him aside. "Is she okay?"

"She's upset, but that's to be expected," said the doctor. "How about yourself? You seem pretty calm."

"I'm okay," Leroy said. "I tell you, though, Doc, I'm still having trouble getting enough sleep. That last prescription doesn't really do me much good. I was thinking maybe you had something else I could try."

"Well, matter of fact, I've been getting some samples of a new medication called Seconal," the doctor said. "Seems to be very effective for some of my patients. I can write you up a small dosage and see if that helps."

"Thanks, Doc. And listen—I'm going to need you to keep a close eye on Mama for me. I have a feeling this is going to be rough on her. I'm worried about her. I don't care what it costs, you just send me the bill."

"I'll do it, Leroy." Dr. Davis scribbled the prescription. "And you take care of yourself. I have a hunch the minute they get you out marching with the other boys, you won't have any more trouble sleeping."

Leroy worked up a smile and called Annie to bring the doctor's coat.

The rest of that night was quiet. Agnes slept.

The next day the crowd at the front gates had swelled to three hundred girls, drawn by excited radio reports of Leroy's draft notice. Some of them carried signs: DONT TAKE LEROY AWAY and LEROY DONT GO.

Leroy didn't go to the gate, but he allowed Hardy to escort a few reporters up to the carport behind the house. He told one patriotic lie after another. He said he'd been expecting the notice for several weeks. He was proud to have been called, to get a chance to do his duty. He was looking forward to making new friends in the army, seeing new places. He hoped they'd give him time to shoot his new picture before he left. Other than that, he wasn't looking for any special treatment. Yes, sir. No, sir. Yes, sir. Yes, sir. Thank you, sir. Merry Christmas, everybody.

The photographers asked him to pose in a set of army fatigues they had brought. He went along with it; he grinned and posed and grinned. He played it just the way they wanted.

When they had all gone, he grew restless.

He dialed up Bubba Hayes. "Hey, Bubba, guess what. I got drafted."

"I heard on the news."

"So, big deal. I want to forget all about it. You want to play some football?"

Bubba set about phoning the guys. Leroy called the principal at Humes High School and rented the stadium for the evening. He called

Mueller's Sporting Goods to order up twenty-two blue jerseys with pink numbers, helmets, cleats in assorted sizes, balls, whistles, tees. He called the Memphis Athletic Association for a referee. He arranged with Jerry's Hot Dogs to have a dog cart and soda wagon on the sidelines at 6:00 P.M. sharp.

As he leafed through the Yellow Pages, his eye fell on an ad for the Rainbow Rollerdome—a hangout from his Humes days, when he was too shy to skate with a girl. He phoned up the manager and rented the place for an after-game party.

All the stadium lights were turned on when he pulled into the familiar parking lot at Humes.

The teams consisted of some of Leroy's old teammates, some of Bubba's cousins and brothers-in-law. Leroy was the star quarterback for the home team. He threw three beautiful spiraling passes, and made a long touchdown run. The home team won, 34–20.

Even more friends and girlfriends of friends crowded into the Rollerdome for the all-night skate party. They played war and crack the whip like wild children. Leroy's date was Dolores Roselle.

Months after he had seen her on the lawn at Audubon Drive, Leroy worked up his nerve and invited her out to Hopeville for a movie party. They wound up sitting in a corner, cackling like old pals at each other's jokes, whispering sarcastic things about the movie and the other people in the room.

Dolores had a steady boyfriend, Dave, in the navy; although she teased Leroy without mercy, she put up with no romantic nonsense. They were friends now, just friends. She had turned out funny and whip-smart, not at all impressed by his publicity.

All the newspapers wanted to make it a big deal, high-school-sweethearts-reunite-before-soldier-boy-goes-off-to-war kind of thing, but it wasn't that way. Dolores kept Leroy up on all the latest Memphis gossip, what people were saying about him. At the parties she kept the other girls from clinging to him. He liked her for that.

Now they glided together on roller skates, under a revolving mirror ball.

Leroy had not been at all sure he could be friends with a girl who had broken his heart, but his own life was proof that anything was possible. Anything. If you want it, dream it; then go out and make it happen.

He didn't want to fall in love with her again.

"Lee, I can't believe they're actually going to make you go," she said, sidestepping through a turn as Jerry Lee Lewis shouted "High School Confidential" on the PA. "It's not like there's a war on or anything."

Speckles of light drifted across her lovely face. He wanted to kiss her, but it would be wrong. "Now you'll have two boyfriends off in the service," he said with a smile.

She spun away from him, executing a nifty little turn on one foot, sweeping her lithe tanned leg around in an arc. "You're not my boyfriend," she said. "You're just a guitar player with a big opinion of himself."

"And you're a big tease," Leroy said, skating fast to catch up. He caught her hand, twirled her around. She kept her footing and bumped him aside with her hip. He bumped back, harder; they skidded, laughing, to the floor.

"No fair!" she cried. "No fair! You cheat!"

"I'm a born cheater, baby." He scrambled to his feet.

The others were hooting at them. Leroy helped Dolores up. She smoothed her frilly green skirt with her hand. Her eyes flashed. "Kiss me, Leroy," she said. "Kiss me right now."

The mirror ball turned. The PA played the Drifters crooning some harmony thing. Leroy held his breath. He leaned over and kissed her. He kept his eyes open so he would believe it was finally happening. Her lips were like velvet. The kiss lasted only a moment; as she pulled away, he felt something inside him tear loose, some tight-knotted muscle ripping away from the bone.

"What has Dave got that I haven't got?" he murmured.

Dolores smiled, rolling slowly back from him. "Nothing," she said. "Nobody has more than you, Lee. But you don't want to get married, and Dave does."

"How do you know what I want?" Whoa, boy. Slow down. Without realizing it, he had walked himself right up to the edge of an awesome cliff.

"Well, do you?" She stopped, put her hands on her hips.

Leroy thought about it a minute. "No," he said. "Not yet. I've got too much going on."

"Well, see there?" Her eyes flashed. "Come on, let's go get a Coke."

And she skated off to the others.

Leroy skated a solitary circle, coming around to the same place again and again, crossing one foot over the other to keep himself on the same track.

Dolores went off the next day to meet Dave in Norfolk.

On Christmas night the portico of Hopeville was jammed with Leroy's friends and relations—Agnes, Ray, Dodger, Hardy, Irene, and ninety-three others. Leroy and Bubba lit the fuses for the fireworks extravaganza. The very stars seemed to burst overhead. A red chrysanthemum shell exploded too low and set fire to the grass in the yard, adding an edge of authentic danger to the spectacle. Leroy danced the fire out.

Agnes unwrapped her presents that night. She exclaimed over each one; but there was dread in her eyes, and most of her sentences trailed off in meaningless curves. She was grieving these days, and she couldn't tell anyone why.

As if the fireworks had punched some remarkable hole in the clouds, the sky opened up with big white fluffy flakes. By midnight Hopeville was blanketed in beautiful snow. It was the first white Christmas anyone could remember since the year Leroy was born, and Dodger said that one didn't count since it was mostly freezing rain.

52

Nick Adams and Natalie
Wood threw Leroy a farewell-to-Hollywood blowout in his bungalow at
the Beverly Palms. Early in the party someone slipped him three tiny red
pills. Leroy swallowed them without even asking what they were.

He didn't remember anything about that night. He had no idea how
the sofa caught fire. He told the manager it must have been an accident.

He boarded the Southwest Crescent at Union Station. Sam had sent
copies of his train schedule to disc jockeys in every town along the
Southern Pacific tracks from Los Angeles to Memphis. Huge crowds of

girls came out at all hours for one last look at Leroy before the army took him.

At every station he went to the platform and waved his farewell wave. Dozens swooned.

A sign in Sanderson, Texas, said LEROY COME BACK.

That made him feel terrible. He wasn't even gone yet.

Think how far gone he would be at the end of two years.

His wonderful dream was coming to an end. He felt terrible pangs of love and advance nostalgia for his fans. He prayed they would keep loving him, but he couldn't imagine any human beings more fickle than teenage girls. To a fifteen-year-old girl, two years is approximately the same as forever. Two years from now these girls might be showering their adulation on Bobby Darin or Frankie Avalon or one of the other imitation Leroys that had been springing up lately, like mushrooms.

These boys sang the cheapest made-in-Hollywood moon-and-June junk. They borrowed the Leroy hairstyle, the swagger, the romantic pout, the snarl, the whole hip-shaking thing. But hadn't he stolen all those things himself? What if the girls couldn't tell the difference between Leroy and, say, Fabian?

Oh. That would be a new kind of hell.

On his last evening as a free man Leroy took an amphetamine and opened Hopeville all night for a party. Everyone he ever knew in Memphis came to pay their respects. They drank beer and ate burgers from the grill tended by Ray near the swimming pool. They danced to Leroy's vast collection of 45 rpm singles. They made jokes about his poor endangered hair.

"Hope they give you a hat, Lee," Bubba Hayes said in the rec room downstairs. "You know them winds in Texas blow cold."

"Oh, go on, Bubba." Leroy took a bank shot and dropped the seven ball. "You sure are ugly tonight."

"Yeah, but tomorrow this time I'll still have hair on my head."

"I took an inch off the sideburns and trimmed it back at the neck," said Leroy. "You reckon that'll satisfy them?"

Nobody came up with an answer.

Agnes did not appear at the party. She had been weeping on and off for four days. Dr. Davis came every six hours to administer a sedative.

Ray got tired of smoke in his eyes and announced he was going to bed.

Leroy sat in a circle of old friends on the patio, smoking panatela slims, drinking Cokes, and talking, all night. Bubba was there, of course, and Davy Lee Williams, Nick Adams, Anita Wood, Davis Turner, Deedee and Lorraine from the beauty parlor, Billie Sampson, Tiger Cunningham, Roland Peters, Janey Sue Pringle, Joey Weaver.... Some of them got tipsy and laughed until they cried. They told stories of Leroy as if he were already gone. It was like attending his own funeral.

He saw gray sky in the trees behind the house and glanced at his watch. Five-thirty A.M. He wanted to beat the reporters to the draft board. He went upstairs to wash his face and fetch the lone pitiful suitcase.

He heard Ray and Agnes stirring. In the driveway Hardy was arranging the caravan of Cadillacs.

Everyone was going down to see him off: the whole family; the friends who had stayed up all night; the secretaries and the cooks and the housekeeper and the gardener. They all piled in cars and proceeded in a line to South Main Street and found bedlam at the draft board at fifteen minutes before six in the morning—fifty reporters and three dozen photographers jostling at the door, spilling out into the street.

At the center of the mob Sam Sanders clutched a cloud of red balloons inscribed "See Leroy in KING OF THE RING," a promotion for his new prizefighting movie. Sam never missed a chance.

Leroy stepped from the lead car into a blaze of floodlights and flash-bulbs. The snapping, buzzing horde surrounded him, pushing in close as any crowd of girls, snatching pictures the way the girls snatched his clothes, hurling questions at him: "How do you feel, Leroy?" "Any thoughts?" "Is Natalie Wood here with you?" "Tell us how you feel, Leroy." "Is this the end of your career?" "Why did you decide to wait for the draft instead of enlisting?" "Who's your girlfriend now, Leroy?" "Will you make records while you're in the service?" "Leroy, how do you feel?" "Leroy—"

He held up his hand like Charlton Heston getting ready to part the Red Sea. The buzz lightened out.

"I'm proud to be here this morning," he said. "And now if you'll let me, I'm going inside."

They resumed shoving and snapping. Leroy was propelled along

538

through their midst, up the sidewalk and into the office of the draft board.

Dan Chastain was there, looking pained, reporters crowding around, the draft board members in their Sunday suits, shaking Leroy's hand, cameras snapping, Wink Martindale broadcasting live, Sam Sanders shouting to the boys to stop pushing, they could have all the pictures they wanted. Leroy's family jammed in behind him and hugged him for the cameras.

Agnes wore her cat-eyed sunglasses; her eyes were red from all the hours of weeping. She was utterly opposed to the army's taking her Leroy. He was too nice; he would get in trouble; the army didn't know him; the other boys would harass him; he would get confused, he wouldn't eat right; he would be killed, she had seen it.

Leroy hugged her. He leaned to her ear. "Go on home, Satnin, this is too wild for you," he murmured. "I'll call you tomorrow. Be strong now, don't make me cry."

She leaned heavily against Ray as if she might collapse.

"Take her home, Daddy."

"I will, son. Be careful. We'll see you next week."

The crowd parted to let them through—distraught mother, comforted by proud father: the old, old picture of a boy going off to the army. Cameras clicked.

Leroy signed papers and signed some more papers and stood with nine other boys in a line. The others looked terrified; no one had told them the world would be coming to watch them enter the army. Leroy concentrated on appearing serious and purposeful for the photographers.

A sergeant led the recruits onto a bus and drove them off to the VA hospital for the physical. No one said a word—not Leroy, not the sergeant, not one of the boys. Three busloads of press buzzards trailed along behind.

The film cameramen had staked out prime positions in the hospital's emergency bay. Somehow Sam had managed to get there ahead of the convoy; he stood on a concrete pedestal, directing the herds of reporters.

Leroy let the other boys off the bus first. When he stepped down, the emergency bay lit up like high noon. He waved. The questions flew. He ducked his head and walked in.

Sam Sanders appeared to be running this show; he invited all the reporters right into the hospital, and no one made a peep. Where was the army?

The mob barged through the doors, up two flights of stairs, down a long hallway to the examining room.

A team of grinning doctors surrounded Leroy. The *Life* photographer had been granted the position nearest his elbow while they probed his eyes and ears and nose. A doctor asked him to strip to his shorts. He obeyed. He stood up on the scale. The cameras chattered.

There he was, in his underpants for all the world to see.

The doctors prodded and peered and poked; when they wanted to go lower, Sam ordered the cameramen out.

But that was just a three-minute respite, interrupted by the terrible indignity of a doctor and his rubber glove.

Leroy switched off the part of himself that threatened to die of embarrassment.

Everyone kept asking how he felt. He couldn't dare tell them the truth.

Sam was loving every minute. Leroy knew how a piece of meat on a hook must feel.

He put on his underpants, his clothes, and his earnest face and waded out into the mob of reporters and doctors. The doctors pronounced him 1-A once again. Sam tugged at his elbow. "Look here, everybody gather around. I've got a telegram I'd like to read."

The cameras whirred and made ratcheting sounds. Leroy squinted into the glare.

"Here's what it says, 'Dear Leroy, You have shown that you are an American citizen first, a true Tennessee volunteer, and a young man willing to serve his country when called upon to do so. Sincerely yours, the Honorable Frank Dillard, Governor of the State of Tennessee.' How about that?"

Some of the newsmen applauded. Several shouted for Sanders to read it again or give them a typed copy.

"No, now, I've got some more here that I want Leroy to read you. He hasn't even seen these yet." Sam brandished a sheaf of yellow Western Union forms.

Leroy pulled back. "No thanks, Sam, I think they want me to go."

"Come on, son, don't keep the boys waiting," Sam said. "We've got one here from the mayor of Memphis. Read this one." He pressed it into Leroy's hand.

"No." Leroy drew himself up. He had been pushed around since the early morning, and he was tired of it.

"Leroy, I need you to—"

"Listen!" he exploded. "It's *me* that's going in the army, *not* you! This is happening to me, *not* you! So just leave me alone!"

The reporters' mouths dropped open as wide as Sam's. The cameras whirred and flashed. Pencils nosed down onto notebooks. Everyone gaped as Leroy excused himself and followed the other boys onto the bus that would take them to Fort Chaffee.

His outburst didn't change anything. Carloads of girls and reporters trailed the bus across the river to the Coffee Cup in West Memphis, disrupting the dinner stop so that the recruits had to leave their plates and return to the bus. Sam was right in the middle, hovering, grinning, organizing.

When the bus pulled out again, Leroy made a little speech of apology to the other boys. They loosened up then and said it was okay, and man, how do you stand it anyway?

"I don't mind," he said, his standard line. "I guess I'll start worrying when they quit bothering me."

They started talking then—records, girls, cars. They found out Leroy wasn't some kind of monster. The green army bus led the string of chartered press Greyhounds across the dark flat breadth of Arkansas, almost to Texas.

The whole commotion started up again when the procession pulled into Fort Chaffee. Sam had smuggled a busload of fans onto the base to witness the arrival. The press boys thundered down from the buses to record the hysteria. Sam beamed and waved. Leroy was whisked past the screamers, into barracks guarded by MPs.

The sergeant assigned him a bunk. He took off his clothes and fell down face first. The babble outside fell away. He was happier for that long, narrow bed than any he could remember.

The carnival cranked up at first light. Sam, who had contrived to sleep somewhere on base for the night, appeared at the barracks to tell Leroy there were fifty-eight newsmen on hand to record his first army breakfast.

The other boys were in earshot, so Leroy kept his voice low. "Sam, I guess you didn't hear what I said yesterday. I bet you'll be reading it in the papers. You got to give me a little more room."

"One more day, Leroy, just one more day," Sam said. "Give me today, and you've got the next two years to play army boy. This is great stuff, son, they are eating it up. You just don't know how much good we're getting out of this."

Leroy shook his head in disgust. "Why don't you get yourself a hobby or something?"

Sam smiled. "You are my hobby."

〜〜〜

Breakfast was a nightmare. Whenever Leroy brought the fork near his mouth, the cameras exploded in clicking and flashing. He drew further and further into himself. His body was an empty shell. The cameras took thousands of pictures of the shell. The least movement or smile set off a whir of shutters, a fearsome sound like birds flying right for his face.

He was glad when they led him away for five hours of aptitude testing. Sitting in a school desk alongside the other boys, pencils scratching, was the longest quiet time he'd had since the morning Dan Chastain brought his draft notice.

About half the questions were easy; the rest was mostly math stuff and science, and Leroy took wild guesses on those. He sat for a long time doodling a lightning bolt in one corner of the page, remembering the last time he took an aptitude test; Miss Waverly gave him his scores. That was back when anyone who paid any attention to him was a wonderful surprise. Thank you, Miss Waverly.

The bullnecked sergeant glared at him.

Leroy lowered his head and hurried through the rest of the questions. He didn't care where the army put him. He just wanted to get it over with. Everything was out of his hands anyway; someone in Washington had already decided what would happen to him as soon as Sam was through.

The sergeant led them back to the cafeteria for lunch—more bedlam, more pictures, more shouting and shoving. Once again Leroy had to give up eating after three bites of mashed potatoes. It looked as if he might starve to death in the army. He knew what was coming next, and he tried to keep his mind off it. He joked with the reporters. They came back with pointed questions.

"Leroy, any truth to the rumor of a rift between you and Sam Sanders?"

Sam popped up from the crowd. "Leroy is like a son to me," he said. "We've never had a cross word between us."

"Say, Pop, can I borrow the car tonight?" Leroy said. That got a big laugh. "No, listen, fellows, what Sam says goes for me, too. You can't argue with success, if you know what I mean. He'll be keeping real busy trying to make sure you guys don't forget me."

Leroy had them turned up now; he was playing these press boys the way Jack Brown used to thump his big old bass fiddle.

"How do you feel about having your hair cut?"

"Can we change the subject?" he said. They laughed.

The long day had built to this moment. The camera boys were all drooling for it. The girls outside begged for a strand of it. The army had brought in a civilian barber especially to cut it.

Leroy had hoped to avoid it by his judicious snipping at home, with the mirror's help, but he saw that they would have their way.

Sam drew him away from the other recruits and led him down a long corridor, which the newsboys had staked out; every step of the way was recorded for history. Leroy tried to swallow his panic. This was a scene from *Prisonhouse Blues*. He marched down death row. The prisoners hollered and hooted and beat their tin cups on the bars. The lights of the cellblock were harsh, with a yellowish cast. Leroy could not remember his crime. The prison officials had given him a pair of white cotton pants, loose-fitting, a drawstring at the waist, an oversize white cotton shirt, and no shoes; they said shoes would burn. The warden held fast to his elbow. It was strange that they marched at the same pace; shouldn't he be resisting somehow, struggling against his chains, at least walking at a different stride from the man who was leading him to the chair? He was powerless. They had him. They walked him down the corridor and into the brilliant light, the smiling barber, the razor, the tooth missing from the barber's smile, and the chair.

In the movie he turned to the camera and began snapping his fingers and jerking around, singing the hit title song.

In real life he lowered himself to the chair.

The cameras closed in.

"Don't stand too close," Leroy said. "Give the man plenty of room."

Poking, snapping, they jostled themselves into a hundred clear lines of sight.

Leroy thought: A man has a right to die in private.

The barber shook out a white shroud around his neck, then pumped a foot pedal to bring him jolting up a quarter inch at a time.

"Just a little off the top and back," Leroy said.

The reporters laughed and wrote it down.

"In the army everybody gets the same haircut," said the barber. He flicked his thumb. The clipper came to life in his hand with an alarming buzz. He attached a set of white ivory-colored plastic horns to the vibrating comb and held it up. Strobe lights flashed.

Sam stood to one side with his cigar and a grin in his teeth.

"Go slow, now, go slow!" the photographers shouted.

The barber obliged them, laying his clipper against Leroy's right cheek. The humming warmth of it tickled. The man sheared a slow, firm path against the skull up his sideburn, up the side of his head.

The cameras fluttered.

The barber held the hair up on the horns of his clippers, and tossed it into the air with a comic flip of his wrist. The hair drifted gently, like feathers, down to the floor.

The reporters murmured and shifted. Two or three clapped their hands.

"Slower! Go slower!" cried the man from *Life*.

Leroy kept one expression frozen on his face: serious, straight ahead. I-don't-care. Leave-me-alone. He would not smile for this picture. This might be a joke to all of them, but this was his life. He felt the teeth running through his beautiful hair, and wherever it passed, a new patch was exposed to cool air. It took forever. The barber loved tossing that hair, even after it stopped earning a laugh.

The teeth went up the sides, up the back, and then over the top of his skull, leaving no more than an inch of bristle at any one place. Leroy's hair fell in clusters, shining with pomade; an army private had been assigned to sweep up the clippings and burn them at once, to keep them out of the hands of the souvenir hunters.

Sam said, "Look how much money they're throwing away. I could get a dollar for each one of those hairs."

"How you like it so far, Leroy?" a reporter called.

He knew his smile was weak. He had to say something funny. He couldn't think of a thing. "Hair today, gone tomorrow," he said.

A few snickers. The *Life* man moved in for a close-up.

The barber removed the shroud.

Leroy stood up. He saw his denuded skull in the mirror, through the jostling crowd. He was skinned like one of those Auschwitz survivors in the newsreels—grinning for the camera, even as he was dying inside.

53

His name was not dead. His records were hotter than ever. His latest single, "Kiss Me Now," sold a million copies the week it was released. *Prisonhouse Blues* came out to glowing reviews. The *New York Times* said, "Leroy Kirby can act!" and he did, all day long, every minute.

Sam granted Hasbro a license for a GI Leroy doll. Its skin was pale white. Its eyes were dead. It had a crew cut.

One week after Leroy arrived at Fort Hood, his father drove out to Texas in the Cadillac, with Dodger and Agnes and Uncle Johnny trailing in the red Lincoln. Leroy had rented a nice ranch house just like the one back on Audubon Drive, except that it was in the hot, dusty town of Killeen, not in Memphis.

Agnes hated Killeen at once. She hated Fort Hood even more; she refused to set foot on the base and didn't like Leroy bringing his army friends into the house. She blamed every man in uniform for doing this terrible thing to her and Leroy.

She was having trouble walking these days—sore joints—and her weight was a problem again. She stayed in the house and watched TV and helped Dodger work a jigsaw puzzle. She drank her brandy on the sly, but Leroy was on to her tricks. He watered it down in the bottle.

After the reporters went away, the army was easy—a lot easier, for instance, than high school. The guys never taunted Leroy. They began to ignore him. Some of them were friendly, but he always had the feeling they were taking notes on things he said, to tell the newspapers.

His days were all the same: Get up, shine shoes, drive to the base, run two miles, push-ups, jumping jacks, windmills, toe touches, breakfast, drill, classes, drill, lunch, KP, afternoon drill, and then out to the house for an evening of TV with the folks.

On the day "Dangerous Woman" hit number one on the *Billboard* pop chart, Leroy received his orders to Friedberg, West Germany, to serve out his tour with the Seventh Army.

He was watching Bill Haley and the Comets on the "Motorola Variety Hour" when the phone call came. He went out of his mind with rage.

"What's wrong with Bill Haley?" he shouted at the television. "Why don't they draft Bill Haley? The son of a bitch looks healthy to me."

"Leroy! Watch your mouth," Agnes scolded. "Look what they're teaching you out at that place!"

"Well it's true! What about Jerry Lee Lewis? Goddamn Fabian! Johnny Cash—aw, no, he's got a record. But the rest of 'em—look at him, prancing around, not a care in the world. It makes me sick."

"Well, I don't believe it," said Agnes. "They can't send you all the way over there. How do they expect me to travel that far?"

"August sixteenth," Leroy said. "That's six weeks from now."

Agnes struggled up from her chair. "I'm going to bed," she said. "I don't feel good."

"What's wrong, Mama?"

"I don't know. I just feel like I'm taking down with a cold or something."

He went over to feel her forehead. His hand didn't work the same magic that hers could. "You feel hot," he said. "You should go to the doctor tomorrow."

"I don't have a doctor down here."

"Well there's plenty of doctors in Temple, I told you," Ray put in. "It doesn't have to be your own doctor from Memphis, you know. A doctor's a doctor."

Leroy spoke to his sergeant and took off the next afternoon to drive them to Temple. They bickered all the way. Agnes cried a couple of times. She said she hurt all over. Her skin was an odd color—pale and yellowish, sickly. Dark circles under her eyes.

She didn't like the doctor. She said his hands were cold. She told him that, right to his face.

The doctor mumbled and apologized. He asked Leroy and Ray to leave the room.

When he came out, he said she was ill, but he didn't think she wanted treatment in Texas. "Take her home," he said. "She wants her own doctor. That's understandable."

"I can't go," Leroy said.

"Well I can," said Ray. "We'll go home on the train. Soon as she sees Dr. Davis, she'll be better." His eyes were alive with concern.

Leroy drove them to the station for the night train. "We're fine, we're fine," Ray kept saying. "We just need to breathe some home air."

Leroy said, "Mama, I'll call you tomorrow afternoon. You do what Dr. Davis tells you, now, promise?"

She looked at him a long moment. "I'll be all right."

He helped her aboard, settled her into the Pullman, and kissed her good-night.

He watched the train until it was gone.

He brooded until the phone call the next day.

Dr. Davis had diagnosed hepatitis and put Agnes straight into Methodist Hospital.

Leroy made eleven calls to Memphis and three to Madison from the pay phone outside his barracks. He dropped in handfuls of change.

Every succeeding call made him more anxious. No one was saying, It's nothing, don't worry, she's fine.

He asked his sergeant for leave. The request was denied.

On the second day Dr. Davis reported no improvement. "She doesn't seem to be responding to the medication," he said. "I think it might be a good time for you to come home."

That terrified Leroy. He pushed back his fear and explained his problem to the doctor, who promised to call the base commander on his behalf right away.

The doctor made the call, but his request was denied, too.

Before dawn on the third morning Leroy was at the pay phone beside the barracks, feeding in dimes. The hospital report was vague: temperature stable, white blood count falling, some fluid in her lungs. . . . His next call reached Sam, in bed with his first cup of coffee. "Listen, Sam, Mama's sick, and I'm going home to be with her. If you don't get me some leave by about ten o'clock this morning, I promise you, I'm taking off without it."

"Now, don't do anything hasty," Sam said.

"Three days I've been trying to get out of here," Leroy went on. He knew how anxious he must sound. "I want you to call those guys we paid all that money to, and you tell them to pull every string they got because otherwise you're going to have one client gone AWOL."

"I hear you, Leroy. I'll make some calls. You call me back in an hour."

Leroy ran to join his unit for the morning drill. Halfway through, the sergeant pulled him out of line with the news that he'd been granted a week's emergency leave.

"Thanks, Sergeant." Leroy ran all the way to the barracks, threw his duffel bag in the back of his red Lincoln, squalled off across the dusty parking lot.

He raced to the Waco airport and chartered a twin-engine Cessna, exactly like the one that nearly killed him that time with Del Freeman and the boys. He took a good long look at that plane before he climbed in. He did not want to break his vow to his mother, but it was for her sake, after all. Memphis was twenty hours by car, and each hour Ray's voice sounded tighter on the phone.

The weather was perfect for flying. The pilot kept quiet the whole way except to talk to his radio. Leroy stared down at the endless dust brown of West Texas, the black earth out near Dallas, the first piney woods, then the thicker forest, the green swath of Louisiana, the wide river marshes, the big river twisting under, tiny boats on the river, the houses, the town, three bridges in the bend. Five hours had passed when the plane touched down in Memphis.

A black limousine waited on the tarmac: Sam's advance work. Leroy thanked the pilot and ran for the car. For once there was no crowd to greet him. He sank into the rear seat. His hands were shaking, but otherwise he was under control.

The small crowd of girls in front of Methodist Hospital grew quiet when Leroy stepped from the limousine. They had come to see about his mother. That magnified his fear. Some crowd sense had told them to gather, something was about to happen. They were too polite to ask for his autograph.

He shied away through a side door. A young orderly steered him through wards, up stairways, and down a long corridor to her room.

A frilly blue bow hung on the door, as if she'd just given birth to a baby boy. Leroy pushed in.

She was asleep on her side, facing away. A tube ran into her arm.

Ray sat in a chair by the window. His eyes came up when Leroy opened the door. He held his finger to his lips. "She's sleeping. . . ."

Leroy nodded. He pointed his thumb at the bow. "What's this?"

"She saw one on a door down the way and she wanted it." Ray shrugged. "Let's go outside."

In the harsh fluorescent hallway Ray's face was a map of worried lines. He dug around in his shirt pocket and came out with a cigarette.

"Daddy, I didn't know you were smoking again."

"Not lately," said Ray, lighting up. "Not lately. She hates it."

"What does the doctor say?"

"Well her liver's inflamed, but now they decided it's not the hepatitis," he said. "Irregular heartbeat and some other stuff I didn't get. Rheuma something. Rheumatic something."

"What are they doing?"

"They give her some shots and that stuff in her arm," he said. "Nurse comes in every time she gets asleep good and wakes her up, taking her temperature. I don't care for this place. Never did. I think she'd be better off at home."

They went back in. Ray stretched out on the empty hospital bed. Leroy took the chair beside his mother. He bent over, kissed her brow. He felt embarrassed, seeing her helpless in her sleep; he ought to be pulling her toe to awaken her. She wouldn't want him staring.

Her skin had the same yellow cast. Delicate blue veins had come out in her arms. Her breathing was rattly, shallow. The room was a cold white cell, one lonely picture of an angel on the wall over each bed, tubes and trays and railings and sterile white air.

Leroy pulled the chair closer. He leaned over and laid his head alongside her arm. She sighed and pulled her hand up under her chin.

He dozed.

When he awoke, he was sprawled back in the chair, and a nurse was staring at her watch, holding his mother's wrist up between two fingers. "Hello there," she said. "I know you. I've seen your movies."

Leroy cleared his throat. "How's her pulse?"

"No change. I'm sorry, but visiting hours are over. You'll have to leave now. She'll sleep through the night."

"I want to stay here with her."

Ray rolled over on the other bed.

"I'm sorry, it's the policy," said the nurse. "She'll be fine. Doctor's coming at eleven-thirty."

Ray stood up. "Come on, son, let's go. We'll come back first thing in the morning."

Leroy stared at his mother. Oh, Mama, wake up and smile at me. Get up and put on your clothes and come home and be well, and I will never leave you again.

He walked with his father down the hall, down the stairs, through the hushed crowd, to the limousine.

He stared out at Memphis. Familiar sights slid by without registering in his brain. It was just a town, the same lights and gas stations as any other town at night. His mother was sick. The people were sleeping.

Maybe a good night's sleep would help him.

A new guard was on the gate at Hopeville. Leroy had to step all the way out of the car before he was admitted to his own home. Dodger waited on the front steps. "Come on inside, how is she, oh I'm so glad to see you, boy, so glad you're home."

Later Leroy took two Seconals. He passed in and out of a strange fitful sleep. He kept dreaming the telephone was ringing. He would sit up and grab it and shout, "Hello! What!" and no one was there. It was only a dream. He put his head under the pillow.

When morning came, Ray drove him to the hospital. More fans had gathered—sixty or seventy now. A hush fell when Leroy walked among them.

In the elevator Ray said, "Maybe she's better this morning."

Leroy rapped on the door, and pushed in. Agnes was awake, sitting up, the hospital bed tilted to an angle. Her eyes grew wide, and a dreamy smile came across her face, and then tears, she was smiling and crying, then crying, and Leroy was crying, too. He went to her, hugged her, buried his face in the infinite softness of her shoulder.

The nurse happened in and saw Agnes's tears. "I'm sorry," she said, "you'll have to leave if you're going to upset her."

"Shut up and get out of my room," Agnes hissed.

The shocked nurse left the little cup with the pills and hurried out.

"Oh honey," Agnes said, "I'm so glad to see you."

"How are you, Mama." He stroked her arm.

"Oh I tell you honey, it feels like they're sticking me with a hot needle, right here." She shifted against the mattress. "But it goes away after the shots. How did you ... did they turn you loose from the army?"

"Just for a little while," he said. "Just till you get better."

She squinted up at him. "You've lost weight," she said. "You're not eating."

"They're working me hard," he said.

She raised her hand and said, "I'm thirsty."

By the time he got back from the sink with the paper cup, she had nodded off.

She talked in her sleep. Leroy couldn't make it out, except she kept saying "Jessie, Jessie." It scared him to hear her that way. He was helpless. She was his mother. She was the one who knew what to do at times like this.

Ray lay on the other bed and watched TV with the sound off.

The day went on, a river of hours draining away into the white walls and floor. Leroy and Ray took turns phoning Dodger.

In the late afternoon Dr. Davis prescribed a glucose IV. He said Agnes was becoming dehydrated.

A newspaper photographer sneaked as far as the nurse's station before Bubba Hayes discovered him and tossed him out.

When night came, Agnes slept. Nothing changed. Leroy sent a steady beam of love pulsing over her way.

At midnight Ray told him to go get some sleep, he would stay the night. The nurse said hospital policy allowed the husband to stay. Leroy called for the car and went home in a daze.

He hated the idea that she might wake up and find him not there—but it exhausted him to sit in that chair, watching her sleep.

Dodger made grilled cheese sandwiches. They ate in the kitchen, standing up. Dodger said she had a feeling tomorrow would be better.

Leroy climbed the stairs and sank into his king-size white bed.

A dream of the telephone woke him up at three-twenty.

No one was there.

54

~~~~~~

Ray had committed a va-
riety of crimes in his life, and he was bound to commit more before he
was through, but he never hurt anybody. He could not stand to see
someone hurting. He'd always been that way, and if that made him less
of a man, well then, that was the price he paid for telling the truth about
himself. He didn't deserve this, his wife dying in a hospital bed and no
way for him to stop it. He was not ready for her to die. Something like
this shouldn't happen until you are ready.

She was killing herself from inside. Ray was nobody's M.D., but that was his opinion. She had made up her mind to die, and it was happening fast. Her skin was the color of the pale yellow dress she used to wear to church on summer mornings. When he leaned close to press the cool washcloth against her face, he smelled an odd sickly sweetness on her breath.

The doctor said it was her liver, maybe cirrhosis, and rheumatic fever, and her heart. . . . Her body was caving in, giving up, pulling the plugs. She had never been really sick before, except for the close call when Leroy and his brother were born. That was nothing like this. Every kind of sickness had taken her over at once.

Clear beads of glucose slid down the tube into her arm. Agnes rambled on. Ray caught a few words now and then—"give the baby what he wants," and later, "I don't want any candy," and, "if it's not too much trouble. . . ."

Ray never meant to have a wife; but then he had Agnes, and she turned out to be all he ever wanted. Sometimes he couldn't stand to be around her—like now, when she was dying—but that didn't mean he stopped loving her even for a second. Even when she turned fat, when her moods and dark spells made her hard to live with, he always loved her. And she always loved him. That was all you could ask.

Life without her would be harder, and cold.

She opened her eyes.

In that moment Ray knew she was there with him, in the room. She had come up for air. She looked straight into him, clear-eyed as the day they met.

"Hello, Ray."

"Hey, sweetheart."

"I don't know what is happening to me," she said.

"You're just sick, is all." He scraped his chair closer to the bed. "You're going to get better."

"I got a phone call from Doll," Agnes said.

Ray smiled, embarrassed for her. "That's nice. What did she say?"

"She told me to have a good time. She said I'd be seeing her soon."

He rubbed his fingers over her arm. The shots were making her delirious, but at least she wasn't hurting now. "You think you've had a good time, Agnes?"

"Not always," she said. "More than some people."

"Thatagirl," Ray said. "We did have some fun, didn't we. Back there in the middle of all that other."

"Where are the babies?" said Agnes. "Is Doll looking out after them?"

Ray touched her hair. "Shhh . . ." He was afraid all the talking would sap her strength. "They're fine. They're asleep. You need to get some rest, too."

She smiled and closed her eyes.

She died.

Just that fast.

55

eroy, this is your fa-
ther." A voice, far away. "Your mother is gone."

Leroy didn't believe he had heard correctly.

"Daddy? What? I didn't—"

"She's gone. It just—oh, son, oh, I don't know—" A muffled thud, the phone falling, then the sound of it being retrieved. "I'm sorry, son, come on down here, it just—oh, it just—it happened so fast."

Leroy put down the phone, and the great yawning black hole of hell opened up beneath him, and he fell, he fell down into darkness forever, a darkness with no sides or middle or end, a grave heavy lightless and lonely place.

<center>~~~~</center>

When he knew where he was, he was up in a fork of the great oak tree behind the carport at Hopeville, wearing only his Jockey shorts. It was not cold, but he was shivering. Dodger stood at the foot of the tree, begging him to come down and put on some clothes.

"I can't come down," he said. "I don't know how I got up here."

"Leroy, come on down, honey," Dodger said. "We'll put on some clothes and go see your mama. Come on now. Don't you want to go see her?"

"I don't know," he said.

This was not the first time Leroy was trapped outside in a dream in his underwear. He wondered if he was awake. The phone call was a dream. His face was wet. A bad dream. A voice was talking inside his head: It's okay now. Just climb down. You're okay. It was only a dream.

He could see into all the backyards of his neighbors, the polite ranch homes backing up to his wall. There were lights on in windows, but he couldn't tell whether the people were awake or they'd left the lights on all night.

"Leroy, do you want me to get Hardy to bring you a ladder?"

"No, that's all right. I'm coming down."

The bark scraped his thighs when he swung to the next lowest branch. He dangled a minute to gather courage, then dropped to the ground and tumbled over in the grass.

Dodger threw a blanket around him and hurried him in, marched him up the stairs to his room. "Now stop this foolishness and dress yourself and let's go."

Leroy obeyed. He concentrated on the buttons on his Hawaiian shirt. He put on some plain khaki slacks. He wanted to look nice for his mother.

He checked himself in the mirror. He could see right through the holes in his eyes to the blackness inside.

The mirror said: It was only a dream.

"Why is everyone acting so strange?" Leroy whispered.

They get carried away. They're worried about her. She's real sick.

"I don't want to go down there again," Leroy said.

Don't act like a baby. You're a grown man now, a soldier. Act like a soldier.

"Leroy!" Dodger called from the foot of the stairs. "Johnny's here. It's time."

The mirror said, Don't listen to what they tell you down there. They'll try to tell you one thing, but it is a lie. Don't listen to them.

Leroy tore himself away and went down the stairs to join Dodger and Johnny. Their faces were frozen. They all climbed in the black Coupe de Ville.

The streets were empty. Johnny drove without a word. Leroy switched on the radio. Dodger said, "Turn that thing off." He left it on. Nat "King" Cole was singing "You Made Me Love You" with a soft velvet intensity. Leroy never sang any song half as well. It comforted him to hear somebody so much better than he would ever be. Maybe he wouldn't have to try so hard, from now on. *I need your love, it's true. . . .*

He put on a stone face for the hospital crowd. Three nurses and the hospital chaplain met him at the door and guided him down the corridor.

He went into his mother's room.

She was asleep, on her back. Her face was peaceful. Someone had combed out her hair.

Ray wept and staggered toward Leroy with his arms out. Leroy stepped around him to the edge of the bed. He bent down to kiss her cool brow. "Don't cry, Daddy. Look here. She's fine. She's asleep. Her fever's gone."

Dodger shook her head and went out of the room.

"Look Daddy, look how sweet she is." He held her hand, stroked it. "Oh, she's cold. Her hand's cold. Bring another blanket."

His father stared as if Leroy had lost his mind.

"Leroy," he said.

"What's the matter?" Leroy closed his fingers over her wrist. If she would wake up now, maybe everybody would stop acting so strange. "Mama, wake up."

"Leroy, stop," said Ray.

"It's the shot, Daddy, they give her these shots, and it just knocks her out. I don't know why you're so upset." He saw Johnny hovering in the shadows. "Come here, Johnny, come see our baby. She's sleeping now. Doesn't she look sweet with her hair all combed?" He stroked her hair.

Ray said, "Johnny, maybe you better wait outside."

The door opened, and closed again.

Leroy climbed into bed with his mother. There was plenty of room. He snuggled down into the pillow, holding her hand. He wanted to make her warm. "Satnin's just sleeping," he said, but he could not account for the tears in his father's eyes. Maybe there were tears in his own eyes, too—he wasn't sure. The room was all blurry. Maybe it was time for them all to get some sleep.

"Come on, Daddy, there's room on the other side," Leroy said, patting the bed. "Come here where it's warm. We can all be together."

Ray stared. His face was a cartoon of sorrow.

"Don't be sad, Daddy. Come on in here with us."

Ray snapped off the overhead light and let down the railing on the opposite side of the bed. He sat on the edge.

They stayed together like that for a while.

56

They took her away on a gurney. It was then Leroy knew she was gone.

He started screaming, it isn't fair, Satnin, come back! and tore down the hall in pursuit.

Three orderlies wrestled him to the white floor, five feet from the elevator. The doors slid shut on his mother. He went out of his mind, but this time he could remember every detail—his father clinging to him, dragging him back to the room, saying, what will we do now, oh what will we do? Leroy knew he did not want to go back in that room.

He broke free and started out again down the long hallway but Ray cried No! the reporters, and came to embrace him, and left him crumpled against a wall in a stairwell while he went off to bring the Cadillac around.

Bubba Hayes forged a path through the crowd. Leroy covered his face with his hands. A flashbulb went pop!

Bubba rushed the girl who had taken the picture, snatched her camera, flung it to the pavement, and stomped it to bits with one big foot.

Leroy went home. He cried for days, all the time, through the night choking with his face in the pillow or walking through the house when he would see a slipper or a hairbrush or something he'd given her—oh, he would break down all over again into tiny dead pieces.

The army extended his leave.

He did not want them to bury her. He argued and argued with Ray, but finally they did it on the fourth day; they put her down in the ground in Meadow Glen Cemetery, all by herself in the dark.

He made sure she had the finest rosewood casket. Sam arranged for the Leroyals to sing "Home in the Valley" at the funeral. Leroy couldn't go. He stayed in his bedroom, weeping.

He ordered the biggest monument in the stonecutter's yard, a great big granite Jesus with upraised arms, standing before a great big marble cross, a pair of marble angels kneeling in prayer on each side. He selected a message from the stonecutter's leather-bound list of suggestions: "She was the sunshine of our home."

The earth was gone out from under him. He did not know how he could live without her. For two days he thought up ways to kill himself. He would put a bullet through his brain, but he hated the thought of blood everywhere; he would take pills, but that would ruin his reputation; he would hang himself, drown himself, run his car into a brick wall.

The last one seemed the best plan.

He smashed his Cadillac through the music gates without bothering to open them. He cruised the dark streets of Memphis for hours, until he spotted a suitably massive brick wall on the northeast side of the Peabody Hotel.

He sat two blocks away, idling his engine, eyeing that wall. Nice and clean. No survivors. He would have to get up a good fifty miles an hour to be sure. What a noise it would make.

He couldn't do it.

After a while he drove to the river bridge, thinking he might drive through the railing and end it with a long fall, a splash—but he could not do that either.

He drove back to the house. Careening in, he knocked the left gate off its hinge.

He stumbled into the house, up the stairs to her room.

He looked in the mirror.

The mirror said: Now make a new start of things. She's not gone. She's here with us. She wouldn't leave us. You brought her two angels. We're all here together. Nobody's gone anywhere.

"I don't want to go," Leroy said.

You should never have gone in the first place. You're not meant for the army. You don't have to fight anyone. You don't have to go.

"I have to," said Leroy. "Everybody is watching."

Just sit back and relax. Sam knows what to do. Let him handle everything. Do just what he says. You don't have to work hard. We'll take care of everything for you. It's easy—some movies, some songs. Let us handle it. We can do it. You don't have to do anything. You just have to trust us.

"I don't even know who you are," Leroy said.

Sure you do. Stop fighting yourself. We're all here. It's what you've wanted all along.

"I don't want anything. The only thing I wanted is gone."

No, it's not. There's money and girls and fast cars, and fortune and fame, and mansions and parties and movies and records and girls.

"I don't want any of that."

Sure you do. You want whatever you can get.

"I want my mother."

I'm right here, sweetie. You know I would never leave you. I'm right here with you.

Leroy closed his eyes.

He took a deep breath and smiled.

He leaned over the sink to wet his comb. His hair was growing back now; he could make a part, and the sides were coming along. They say hair and fingernails keep growing even after you die.

He brushed a piece of lint from his uniform cap and fastened the buttons of his coat. He could hear the rumble outside, the snapping and mutter. The crowd was waiting for him. The army had ceased to pretend Leroy was just another private; the brass and Sam Sanders had invited 250 members of the press to the Military Ocean Terminal in Brooklyn, New York, to witness his departure for Germany. They gave Leroy five minutes alone in this bathroom to prepare himself.

The mirror said: Go knock 'em dead.

Leroy flashed his movie star smile and pushed through the door. Photographers sprang up blazing around him. Reporters shouted. Sam cleared a path to the table, a forest of microphones.

Leroy stood in his uniform and let the light bounce off him. They could not hurt him now with their flashes.

Sam said, "Are there any questions?"

Leroy sat at the table and made a quizzical face at the bunched-up mikes.

A reporter in front said, "Leroy, do you feel that your fans have been pretty loyal to you since you've been in service?"

One voice inside him said: Don't answer that; they're all vultures; they can't wait to call you a has-been.

Another voice said: Mind your manners.

"Yes sir," said Leroy, "they certainly have."

A lady at the back: "Do you think you have a rougher time than most soldiers because you're famous?"

"No, ma'am. . . ."

Of course you do. No one is your friend. You can't breathe without someone watching how you do it. The other boys hate you in secret ways.

Now, don't be like that.

". . . everything was just straight down the middle," Leroy said. "I wasn't treated any better or worse than the other boys. That's the way I wanted it to be because I have to live with those guys."

"Would you say the other boys treat you rougher?"

You bet.

He should never have been in the army in the first place. They took him because he's successful. He's not cut out for hard physical work. He's always been tender.

"Uh, no sir, not at all," Leroy said. "I kind of kept waiting for that to happen, but when the boys saw me working alongside 'em on KP or marching with a pack on my back, they figured well, he's just like us. I got along fine with 'em. They're a good bunch of boys."

"Leroy," said the man from *Look,* "what's your definition of the ideal girl?"

Leroy grinned. The voice whispered in his ear. He knocked the ball out of the park. "Well, sir, I'd say she'd have to be female."

That got a huge laugh and ended the press conference. Leroy put his cap back on and followed the brass up the gangplank, onto the gigantic bulk of the USS *Randall.* He was relieved that no one had asked about his mother. That was one question he could not have batted away.

Three anxious radio reporters pursued him, trailing long microphone cords.

"Leroy! Two minutes! Can we have two minutes?"

Sam was right behind them. "Come down to the library, boys, you can speak to him there."

Leroy walked onto the ship thinking about that last question. Dolores Roselle had gone right ahead and married her navy boy, while Leroy was grieving—and who could blame her for that?

Maybe there was another girl, someone he didn't know, waiting for him on the other side of the ocean. She would have to be young, so young she could never have done anything yet. He could teach her everything. She would be beautiful. She would look like that girl in his dreams; she would look like Leroy: dark eyes, dark hair, an olive complexion, an insolent curl of the lip. He saw her perfectly in his mind.

In the ship's library a reporter leaned forward with a serious face. "Leroy, since this may be your last opportunity to say something to your fans, is there any particular message you want to pass on to them?"

Sam had planted the question, and Leroy reeled out his answer. "Well yessir," he said. "Let me say that I know I'm going away . . . I won't be seeing the girls for a while. I'll be out of their eyes, you know, but I hope I won't be out of their minds."

The reporters nodded encouragement. Leroy staggered on. "I'm really, uh, I'll be looking forward to the day when I can come back and sing a few songs again, you know, like I did, and . . ." He ran out of words.

Tell them you don't want to go.

Don't be silly. He can't embarrass us all right here in front of everybody.

The ship's whistle sounded a long, mournful blast.

The reporter said, "All I want to do is wish you a wonderful time in the army, and good luck, and I know I speak for the girls when I say come home soon."

"Well thank you, sir," Leroy said. "I'll sure try."

Sam said, "Thank you boys, that's it, we have to get off now or we'll all be on our way to Europe." He herded them out. At the door he turned back to Leroy. "I guess this is it for now, son. I'll call you Thursday night, your time. You take care of yourself over there. I got big plans for when you get back."

"I'm fine," Leroy said. "I'll be fine."

Sam winked and closed the door.

There were no mirrors in the ship's library. Leroy sat with the books and the voices in his head. He looked at his hands.

You both have such pretty hands.

Thank you, Mama. They come from you.

Tell her what you were thinking before, Leroy. About the girl.

She doesn't care about that.

Leroy doesn't have any secrets from me. He tells me everything. Sometimes he calls me at two or three o'clock in the morning just to tell me he loves me. You both are such good boys. I always knew you would turn out that way.

Leroy folded his hands and smiled to himself. He would never be lonely again.

About the Author

MARK CHILDRESS is the author of two critically acclaimed novels, *A World Made of Fire* and *V for Victor*. A native of Monroeville, Alabama, he now makes his home in San Francisco.